Will I Am

Henrik F. Christensen

RockBySea Books
Copenhagen

Will I Am

A Novel by Henrik Frans Christensen

2nd U. S. Edition
1st print
Published 2003 by

RockBySea Books
www.rockbysea-books.com
Guldberg Hus
Guldbergsgade 9
DK 2200 Copenhagen N
Denmark

Printed in the U. S. A.

ISBN 87-988692-1-3

1st *edition published initially in 2001*
to celebrate
The bicentennial of the inauguration of
Thomas Jefferson,
President of the United States of America,
Author of the American Declaration of Independence

and

the 225th anniversary of the
American Declaration of Independence

*This historical novel is based on a true story
about the lives of three American seamen,
William Watson,
John Brown
and
Amos Stevens,
from 1805 to 1812*

Preface

For the first-time reader of this book, it is recommended to ignore the references indicated in the text. You can always return to them if you want to go into detail with a topic.

Read the Scandinavian letters of *æ, ö, ø* and *å* as follows: æ = ae; ö and ø = oe; å = oh.

It has come to the author's attention that improbable many scenes and persons in this mostly authentic historical novel can be made the negative or fun objects of comparison to present time. This has never been the author's intention. The author, for example, generally has a positive view on all the European Royal Courts, the British Royal Navy and the British and Swedish Military of today. The book reflects no personal experience of the author.

This book cannot be recommended to touchy local as well as national patriots with no sense of humour.

For my good friends, the Englishmen, reading this book some times demands your well-known self-control. Recall you are reading a somehow fictive historical novel and we are living in a new time, where a once unemployed author now earns more than the Queen of England. Today we shall protect the thousands of year old cultural heritage that lay within the European Royal Courts.

As a Dane, I have just as much to thank the British for, as I have to thank the Americans for when it comes to liberating Denmark from occupation by the Nazi regime during WW II.

It ought to be noticed that the first edition of this book was finished on July 8, 2001, before the Sept. 11 tragic events in New York, the Pentagon Building in Washington D.C. and Pennsylvania. The basic story, dates and historic persons appearing in this second edition have not been changed compared to the first edition and the novel does not relate to these events at all.

The 7 years working title of this novel was *One Book*.

Maps

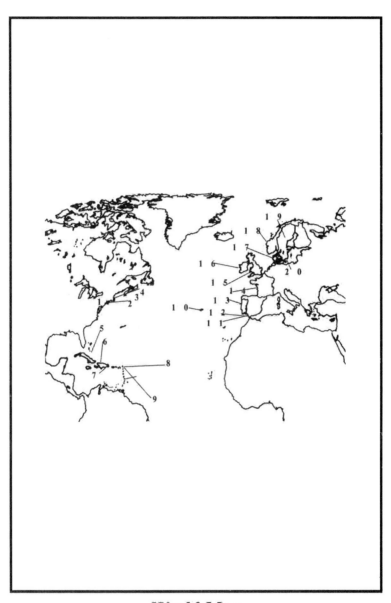

World Map

1 *Wilmington, DE.* **2** *New York, NY.* **3** *Boston, MA.* **4** *Salem, MA.*
5 *St. Luke's Islands (Bahamas).* **6** *Jamaica.* **7** *Kingston and Port
Royal.* **8** *St. Eustatia.* **9** *St. Thomas, St. Croix and St. John.* **10**
Azores. **11** *Bay of Trafalgar.* **12** *Cadiz.* **13** *Portugal.* **14** *France.*
15 *England.* **16** *Ireland.* **17** *Denmark.* **18** *Norway.* **19** *Sweden.*
20 *Hanö Island.*

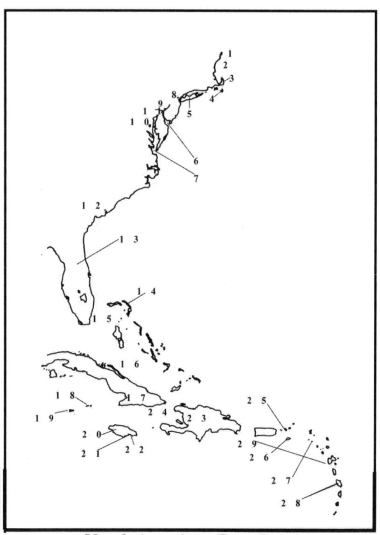

North American East Coast
and the West Indies

1 *Salem, MA.* 2 *Boston, MA.* 3 *Cape Cod.* 4 *Nantucket Island.*
5 *Long Island.* 6 *Delaware Bay.* 7 *Chesapeake Bay.* 8 *New York, NY.* 9 *Philadelphia, PA.* 10 *Washington D. C.* 11 *Wilmington, DE.* 12 *Charleston.* 13 *Spanish Florida.* 14 *St. Luke's Islands.* 15 *Straits of Florida.* 16 *Old St. Luke's Channel.* 17 *Cuba.* 18 *Cayman Island.* 19 *Grand Cayman.* 20 *Jamaica.* 21 *Kingston and Port Royal.* 23 *Haiti.* 24 *Wind Ward Channel.* 25 *St. Thomas.* 26 *St. Croix.* 27 *St. Eustatia.* 28 *Martinique.*

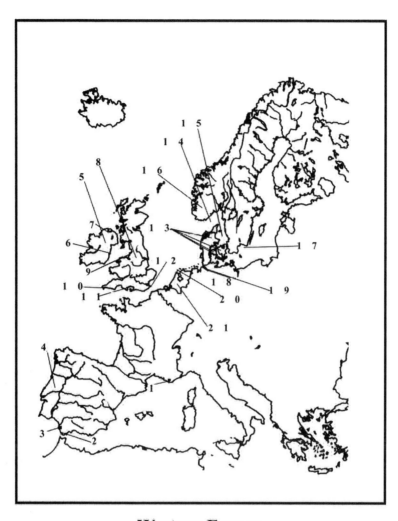

Western Europe

1 *Toulon, France.* 2 *Cadiz, Spain.* 3 *Bay of Trafalgar, Spain.* 4 *Portugal.* 5 *Ireland.* 6 *Dublin, Ireland.* 7 *Londonderry, Ireland.* 8 *England.* 9 *Liverpool, England.* 10 *Plymouth, England.* 11 *Portsmouth, England.* 12 *Sheernees, England.* 13 *Denmark (Jut land, Fun, Zealand + smaller islands.* 14 *Skagerak Sea.* 15 *Cattegat Sea.* 16 *Norway.* 17 *Hanö Island, Sweden.* 18 *Elbe River.* 19 *Hamburg and Altona.* 20 *Texel Island.* 21 *Holland.*

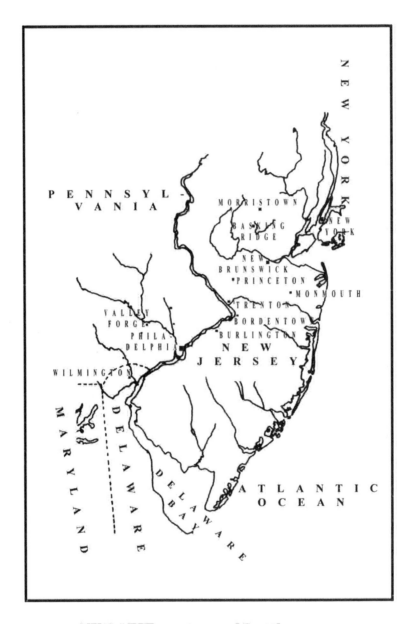

**1776-1777 routes and battle scenes
of the Revolutionary War**

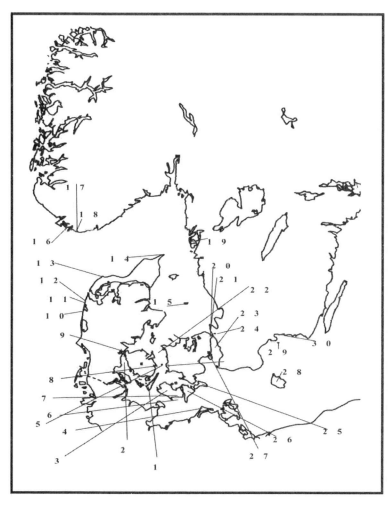

Scandinavia and the south of the Baltic Sea

1 *Langeland, Denmark.* 2 *Little Belt, Denmark.* 3 *Lolland, Den -mark.* 4 *Dars Head, Germany.* 5 *Sprogø Island.* 6 *Rødsand.* 7 *Nysted, Lolland.* 8 *Nyborg, Fyn.* 9 *Snoghøj, Jutland.* 10 *Fjand, Jutland.* 11 *Fjaltring, Jutland.* 12 *Bovbjerg, Jutland.* 13 *Hanstholm (The Holm), Jutland.* 14 *The Scaw, Jutland.* 15 *Island of Anholt.* 16 *Flekeö, Norway.* 17 *Norway.* 18 *Naze of Norway.* 19 *Lysekil, Sweden.* 20 *Elsingore, Denmark.* 21 *Kronborg Castle, Denmark.* 22 *Great Belt, Denmark.* 23 *Ear Sound.* 24 *Helsingborg, Sweden.* 25 *Møn Island, Denmark.* 26 *Falster, Denmark.* 27 *Copenhagen, Denmark.* 28 *Island of Bornholm.* 29 *Hanö Island, Sweden.*

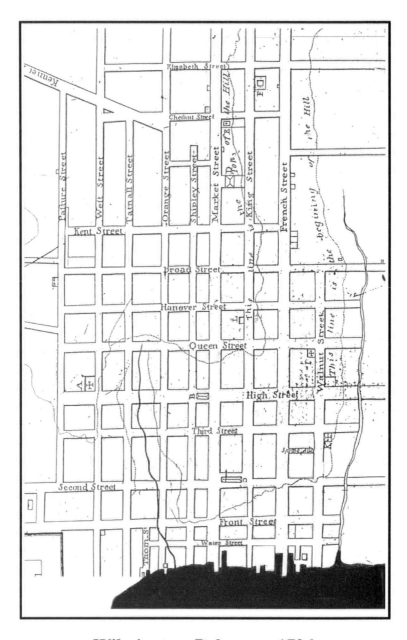

Wilmington, Delaware, 1796

1

A three-masted United States schooner[69,70] is cruising close to its maximum speed of six knots. The 15 wind-tight sails stand silent and fully stretched. The waves whisper and gurgle rhythmically as they break against the ship's portside bow. Cumulus clouds dash across the blue sky. In the shelter created on the deck by the cabin, the sun bakes the right sides of the faces of five browned, weather-beaten and serious-looking seamen. They are turned toward the ship's stern facing west, silently looking at the ever-diminishing port of Boston. The pale white, scrubbed deck planks, hairy from years of daily rough treatment with holystones, are sucking in the heat, and hence, warming the seamen's bottoms.

It is one of the last days in September in the year 1805.[69] The captain, two officers and the five seamen are on their way to Martinique, one of the most southeastern French islands in the West Indies, with a French-owned cargo that was loaded in the schooner's homeport of Boston.[200] The cargo is illegal supply for the French Army in the West Indies. One of the seamen is John Brown, a handsome young man, 5-feet tall and strong, with a boyish face, dark blue eyes and freckled cheeks, embraced by thick, curly blond hair.

John Brown was born at the east coast port city of Salem, 20 miles north of Boston, where he and his mother now live. He is 25 years of age. Most of his life has been spent at the harbor front in Salem or, as a boy, onboard coast-faring ships or occasionally, as now, ocean going vessels. He is an experienced seaman, and this experience has earned him much respect from his colleagues.[3]

England and France have been at war for more than two years, and the British Admiralty in London has blockaded the French fleet in the French ports. Admiral of the Blue Lord Nelson is onboard his flagship *H.M.S.Victory*, a 120-cannon first-class vessel, which can hold a maximum crew of 760 men.

The English ships arrived outside Toulon in the Mediterranean Sea in the summer of 1803, where they have waited ever since. The great, feared French Army commander Napoleon Bonaparte has successfully conquered parts of the European Continent and is now eager to send the

French Army across the English Channel to finish off England once and for all.

King George III of England and his Government at Whitehall know that it is the proper time to act. They are just as eager as Napoleon to meet the enemy. They want to meet in a final sea battle to eliminate the strength of the French Navy. They hope to fool the commanders of the French fleet by waiting for them come out from naval bases, and then quickly destroy them, thereby preventing the French army from crossing the English Channel to land troops on English soil.

Napoleon, a strategic genius, by pure intuition knows exactly what the Royal Navy wants to do. This constantly irritates the British Admiralty. Napoleon has ordered the Admiral of the Toulon fleet, Pierre Charles Villeneuve, to depart Toulon immediately and sail with his 11 ships of the line and seven frigates, not to the Channel, but to the West Indies. On the way, he is to meet the Spanish Fleet at Cadiz, adding nine ships to a combined fleet. Admiral Ganteaume of Brest is to sneak out his 22 ships of the line, too. Napoleon wants to fool the British into believing that the French fleet is crossing the Atlantic Ocean to attack some of the many British West Indian Islands.

The British fleet will of course be alerted, according to plan, and hurry to the British West Indian Islands to protect their possessions. Then the French Fleet can return to the Channel and send the French Army to England.

Napoleon laughed as he imagined the faces of the British First Lord and the rest of the members of the Admiralty when they finally learned about the fulfillment of a several hundred year French dream and British nightmare of landing French troops on British soil, while most of the Royal Navy ships is out for a "picnic" in the far away West Indies. Making such a brilliant military strategy was a very simple game and pure fun for the young genius Napoleon. A very easy game, and one he was even paid to play.

The more than 40 ships in the combined Spanish-French fleet will sail west across the Atlantic Ocean to meet at the French West Indian island of Martinique.[166]

The First Lord in the Admiralty in London did exactly as Napoleon expected. On June 4, 1805, now more than five months ago, Nelson's

Majestic war ships, "the grey geese," as he proudly called them, arrived in the clear waters of the Caribbean. At noon the British fleet is anchored off Bridgetown at Barbados, 100 miles from Martinique. It included His Majesty's Ship (*HMS*) *Defence*, a third class ship in the Royal Navy with 74 cannons and two decks.[166]

Although not part of this arriving fleet, another ship of the line, *HMS St. George III*, named after the present English King, a second-class vessel carrying 98 cannons and three decks, was also in the Caribbean Sea. *St. George* was anchored in Port Royal outside Kingston on the island of Jamaica, headquarters for the Royal Navy in the West Indies. *HMS St. George* departed later in the autumn to sail to the British North American station at Halifax to finally cross the Atlantic Ocean to return to England.[107]

Admiral Villeneuve, in his fleet anchored near Martinique, heard of the arrival of Nelson's fleet at Bridgetown and decided that the time had come to return to Europe and the English Channel. Nelson was firmly convinced that Villeneuve would return to Toulon in the Mediterranean Sea, and so he sent his fastest frigate, the *Curieux*, directly to London with a report on the ongoing chase. Captain Bettesworth of the *Curieux*, was given the shocking news by his lookout one morning, while they were in the middle of the Atlantic Ocean, that ahead of them, on a northeastern course, was a huge part of the French-Spanish Toulon-Cadiz fleet.

By pure luck, the fast British frigate had run into the French-Spanish fleet, which was *not* heading for the Mediterranean Sea but directly toward the English Channel! Captain Bettesworth reached England on July 8 with the news, which shocked the Admiralty as well.

That evening, the First Lord and British Admirals dashed about in the bedrooms of their London mansions in their white nightdresses and long nightcaps, like alarmed, rare albino cockerels, ranting and raving to their wives about their deep fear of Napoleon Bonaparte, Bony, whose fleet was quickly approaching the Channel, perhaps to come to the very heart of London to get them and ruin their careers.

When Villeneuve arrived in the English Channel, there was only a minor sea battle and twelve days later the French fleet decided to return to Cadiz. The French landing on British soil had failed for now.

The activities of Admiral Nelson and Admiral Villeneuve near Martinique and Barbados that summer had the British West Indian fleet and the British frigates patrolling in that region on alert. As a consequence, many frigates are determined to stop any military supplies from reaching the French West Indian Islands, to prevent them from being used to take over the British Colonies in the West Indies.

As John Brown inhales the fresh sea breeze hitting his face, he hasn't the faintest idea that the Royal Navy ships *HMS Victory*, *HMS St. George* and *HMS Defence*, which a few months ago had been around Martinique, now his own destination, will later play an important role in his own life. He is happy now, watching a dolphin playing off the Boston schooner's starboard side.

As Boston disappears on the horizon, silhouettes of houses, trees and church spires along the coast of Massachusetts fade in the sunset. The captain turns over command of the ship to John Brown, looks a final time at the horizon to be sure no ship in sight has a course toward them, and enters the galley for the night. Before he closes the door to the cabin, he asks Brown to change course from east to a steady southeastern course toward the lighthouse on Cape Cod, which will turn on its light soon.

In the twilight, they pass without noticing the community of whalers living in the small wooden houses on Nantucket Island. The ship moves south into the open Atlantic Ocean, losing sight of land for many days.

John Brown and the other seamen onboard the schooner know well that the West Indian Islands are dangerous to American seamen in these times of war. American seamen can be forced off their ships and into service in the Royal Navy, which is legally termed *impressment*. It has been this way for many years. It is a main topic of conversation when Americans, even strangers, meet in taverns along the harbor front in Boston, Salem or other east coast ports. On such occasions, people often talk about seamen from their own homeports who have been impressed or released lately from the Royal Navy ships.

But on this particular journey, the ship's owner and the crewmembers have no real idea how tense the situation has become in the West Indies, because of the recent visit by the European squadrons of the British and French-Spanish fleets.

As the Boston schooner continues south along the American east coast, it passes the latitude of the mouth of the Delaware Bay. John Brown looks for the 38-meter high, octagonal shaped stone tower of the lighthouse of Cape Henlopen, on the southern bank on the Bay entrance, but he can't see it. He is too far out on the open sea.

A gaff schooner with the name *Ino*, captained by John Goff, is at that moment sailing in Delaware Bay, traveling along the bay's south bank, inward bound. It is currently off the coast of Cedar Creek in Sussex County, the most southern county of the three counties that make up the State of Delaware. William Watson, an experienced 18-year-old seaman born in Delaware, is onboard, sitting in the cabin of the *Ino*.

The crew is returning from the harbor of New York, where it delivered a cargo of flaxseed. Watson is looking forward to seeing his new girlfriend, Mary Ann. He met her in Wilmington, where they both live, before sailing to New York.

William spots a copy of the Wilmington newspaper, *Mirror of the Times and General Advertiser*, dated March 15, 1803 [243] in a stack of old newspapers in a corner in the cabin. He often reads these old newspapers when he has time off work and is bored. William is a curious guy, and brightens when he sees a column on sea life in other countries located on page two.

He reads aloud to other seamen in the cabin, as he often does, since none of the others can read. *"Copenhagen, the capital of Denmark so often visited by our navigators and known to many in this town, is supposed to contain 80,000 inhabitants, and probably about one twenty-third of the entire population of the Kingdom. The provisions made for its seamen distinguish the nation, who is adapted not only to teach them their trade, but also to preserve their way of life on shore. Houses are erected for them in streets near the port, sufficient to provide shelter for 6,000 mariners and their families and the appropriate officers for such a situation."* William pauses to look at the faces of the others, who are eagerly listening, then continues. *"It is an acknowledged and easily proven fact that no nation has paid a greater attention–and with greater success-to the health of its mariners and the regulations made for them. The good order maintained might be an example to the entire world. The English provide for their fleet as well, but the Danes are happier with the good living conditions of their seamen."* [243]

William stops reading and shouts enthusiastically, 'Let's get our families, girlfriends and friends in Wilmington and go to Copenhagen. This seems to be a paradise on earth!"

The others laugh and nod their heads. One says, "Yes, William we should all do that some day." William replies, 'It is amazing how this country keeps on growing. Our former capital, Philadelphia, is so close by and it is already half the size of Copenhagen."

There is a strong easterly wind now and the *Ino* travels swiftly through the early hours of the afternoon. They pass the sandbanks of the Little Creek Landing in Kent County and soon reach the port of New Castle, which has given its name to the most northern county of the state, the same way the counties are placed in England.

Colonel Allen McLane, an old, longhaired Marshall for the District of Delaware and port collector for the port cities of Wilmington and New Castle, has an office and a revenue cutter here. The port collector and his staff use the cutter to inspect ships sailing on the Delaware River and Bay. The gaff schooner *Ino* now continues a bit further north to the outlet of the Christina River on the Delaware River's south bank.

The Christina River runs from the southeast through the entire Newcastle County before it reaches the Delaware River. From the river source in Maryland, the water flows slowly and silently downstream for six miles. Then the river takes 29 turns in only 10 miles, before running out into a wide flat delta at the outlet. The town of Christina Bridge sits where the river begins to make the turns, a perfect place for shipping out grain and flax seed to the larger cities downstream.

One and a half miles before the outlet, the water passes below the borough of Wilmington, located on a hill on the northern bank, overlooking the Delaware, Brandywine and Christina Rivers. The Brandywine River runs on the northern border of Wilmington to reach the Christina River, close to the Christina's outlet.

The gaff schooner *Ino* is destined for its home port, the borough of Wilmington, where its owner, merchant and wharf owner William Hemphill, captain John Goff, and the entire crew live.[2]

Before the *Ino* left for New York, Mary Ann and William stood on the quay in front of Hemphill's Wharf, in the end of King Street, to say goodbye. At the time, the *Ino* was loaded with barrels of flax seed and fine flour produced by the Brandywine Mills. Mary Ann tied a beautiful, colorful, red silk scarf around William's neck. She had bought the scarf in one of the expensive shops on Market Street, one of the broadest streets in Wilmington, running between the Brandywine and Christina Rivers. The store where Mary Ann bought the scarf was on the west side of Market Street close to the silverware shop Joseph Warner, Sr. once ran for the family. Joseph Warner, Sr. was the late father of William Watson's best friend Joseph Warner, Jr.

It was the kind of beautiful scarf any woman with fine taste in clothes could not ignore. It would be the first thing a girl in any foreign port will notice when seeing William, Mary Ann had thought when she bought it. Mary Ann had two purposes for giving William the silk scarf. The first was so that a girl in a foreign port, when seeing the scarf, would ask William where he got it. She expected William to answer that the scarf had been a gift from his girlfriend back home in Delaware. She expected this kind of answer would cool down any feelings of desire in these foreign girls, protecting her boyfriend William.

The second purpose for the scarf was to protect William against any danger that might show up out on the deep oceans. William himself was not too worried about it at all.

Mary Ann was not yet 15 years old, and she had been glad that William was taking only short trips along the coast of New Jersey to New York and back. Deep-sea trips to Europe normally kept many of the captain's and seamen's wives in Wilmington awake at night in their small apartments in the two and three-story red brick houses along Second, Front or Water Streets.

Many seamen, mariners, masters, captains and ships from Wilmington never returned from the sea, so the concerns of these women were not unfounded.

Ino runs up the Christina River outlet and sails the last one and one-half miles before it finally approaches the quay at the Hemphills Wharf on the west side of Kings Street. Mary Ann, together with a group of wives with their small children, already waits excitedly on the quay.

Large Wilmington merchants like William Hemphill, who frequently hire seamen like William Watson, often advertise in the local newspapers. These include the Democratic-Republican *American Watchman* and the Federalist *The Delaware Gazette* and *The Mirror of the Times and General Advertiser*, the newspaper William had been reading to the others onboard the *Ino*. William Hemphill normally advertises to buy flax seed in the harvest season from the New Castle County farmers, who will bring seed to the mills by carriage or in sloops sailing on the Christina River between Christina Bridge and Wilmington.

Ships like the *Ino* will later in the year take the flax seed out of the Delaware River, before ice sets in and makes it impossible. They go to large, ice-free ports like New York, where the barrels are reloaded on ocean-going ships, if they aren't already on one. These ships then stay in the harbor of New York or another ice-free harbor until early spring, when the price for the flax seed peaks in Dublin and Londonderry, Ireland, the flax seed's final destination. Then the ships sail together in large convoys for Ireland.

It is a long tradition among the children in Wilmington to gather on top of the hill near the Academy during the day to look out for ships. They can earn a good tip for identifying Wilmington ships approaching home when they are still out on the Delaware River. When one of the children knows for sure which ship is approaching, he or she eagerly runs down King Street to report to the men in the tavern 'Sign of the Ship," near Hemphill's Wharf on Water Street. When the ship actually arrives at t he quay in front of the tavern or near by, proving them right, the boy or girl gets the tip. The news then spreads to all corners of Wilmington to those with an interest in the ship or family onboard.

Mary Ann shares an apartment with her mother, in Water Street close to this tavern. Her father died some years ago. Since then, Mary Ann and her mother had become close friends. The mother had later found a good friend, who spends most of his off-work time with his friends in the tavern. He came to the apartment this day to bring Mary Ann the very good news about the arrival of the *Ino* and her boyfriend William.

Some of the young boys who spend their time running and playing along the quay on the north bank of the Christina River say that Mary Ann is Mary Ann Manuel and her mother is Jane Manuel, a nurse. Some of them believe Mary Ann's father was the late Captain Peter Manuel, who never returned when his ship went to sea more than two years ago.

But young boys have great imaginations and are known to tell stories from time to time.

William Watson is an orphan, and that is one of the reasons Mary Ann and William understand each other and get along so well. They both know from experience how dangerous, cruel and unjust this world can be when you are completely on your own. Ever since the first time they met, outside the Lower Market House on Second Street, the sense of loneliness they both felt for years, and which had been such an integrated part of their characters, has been replaced by continuous joyful thoughts of each other. These new and strong emotions comforted them both while they were separated when William was at sea or sailing in the Delaware River.

As always when his ship returns to Wilmington, Captain Goff allows the crew to spend five minutes greeting the people who have shown up on the quay to welcome the arriving crew. Then the captain orders the seamen back to work.

Mary Ann is four feet nine inches tall, almost as tall as William. William is an extremely strong young man, both mentally and physically. He has short, dark brown hair and green eyes. He jumps onto the quay even before the *Ino* has been properly moored and runs directly toward Mary Ann. She smiles and greets him with a joyful hello. Although she wants to, Mary Ann is determined not to let William kiss her right here in front of all these watching eyes. That would not be a decent thing for a couple that is not even engaged, to do.

Although moral standards are high among the inhabitants of Wilmington, they cannot deny that destiny can be harsh in a seaport. Many a wife has lost her husband, and some of them sons too, to the sea, without ever knowing the real fate of these loved ones.

Within the past thirteen years, yellow fever sent 30 percent of Wilmington's population to their graves, and traces of tragedy still remain from the Revolutionary War, with widows and crippled soldiers from the Delaware Regiments attached to the Continental Army. Therefore, untraditional alliances were often made between men and women in Wilmington, to support and help one another through difficult times.

Townspeople who knew the parents of William and Mary Ann and who had mourned with them are now delighted and approve of the growing love between them.

William and Mary Ann have a hard time hiding this love. William is completely fascinated with everything about Mary Ann. He absolutely adores her cute smile, her crystal clear eyes and her breathtaking kisses.

But standing next to her on the crowded quay, he realizes he will have to wait for a kiss today.

Being with Mary Ann is such a different and uplifting experience compared to the rough sea world where William normally spends most of his time. It is 5 p.m. and a darkening autumn evening as the two of them decide to meet later in the evening at her mother's apartment.

William returns to the *Ino* and begins to unload the cargo with the other seamen, and his concentration switches from Mary Ann to other familiar faces he now observes on the quay.

The Port collector, Allen McLane has walked out into the cold afternoon from his office in the four-story, red customhouse building on the northwestern corner of Front and French Street.[298] He has walked the short distance to the quay to check the *Ino's* papers and cargo manifests. He is assisted by two of his employees, who happen to be friends of William, John Freed, Jr. and William Windell.[12] Working in the Revenue Service under the American States Administration is a highly respected job in the borough and William's friends are very proud of the offices they hold.

The Main Custom Office in Delaware has recently moved from New Castle to Wilmington because of Wilmington's increase in size. In the last five years, more and more ships have been arriving in this port. The revenue cutter, however, stayed in New Castle, in the harbor on the banks of the Delaware River, where the main control and inspection of ships on the river will still take place. The treasury of the United States of America depends highly upon customs revenue collected at the east coast ports.

McLane normally receives instructions related to his duty as port collector directly from the Secretary of Treasury, Allen Gallatin. William often hears stories from John Freed, Jr. and William Windell about their boss McLane, and from them, William understands clearly that his friends are very proud of working with the old port collector.

They have reason to be. Colonel Allen McLane, with his long white hair, warm trusting eyes and winning smile, is a living legend[133, 161, 12] in Wilmington. Young and old alike Wilmington treat him with deep respect, with the exception of a few old hereditary enemies he has here, as would any living legend in such a small borough.

McLane has two sons, Allen and Louis, who are about the same age as William. The eldest son, Allen was born just a year after McLane's

10

return from the Continental Army and the Revolutionary War, after he and his wife Maria settled in the small village of Duck Creek Cross Roads in Kent County and he began work as a saddler. The town is named Smyrna today.[133] Later, the McLane family moved to Wilmington.

The present Secretary of Treasury, Allen Gallatin, and the Secretary of State, James Madison have the trust of their President Thomas Jefferson, now in his second term. Jefferson respects Gallatin deeply, and is well aware that foreign affairs and finance mingle closely in the American economy. Jefferson therefore knows that good port collectors like McLane are important at North America's many customhouses, and they are therefore strongly protected by the central government.

Like many seamen living and working out of port cities like Wilmington, Philadelphia, Baltimore and Boston William shares a small apartment with John Freed, Jr. so he can pay the rent and still have some money left over. The tiny apartment is on 33 E. Second Street[0], close to Lower Market House, the harbor front, and the Customhouse in Front Street, and not far from where John's family lives on 68 E. Second Street.[0]

Joseph Warner, William's best friend, is almost seven years older. Joseph Warner, who moved his silversmith business to Philadelphia[0] after his father's death to improve his business, is also on the quay this afternoon to greet William. His wife and their child accompany him. The three Warner's originally decided to come to Wilmington today to visit Joseph's elderly mother Mary and his half sister Ester Yarnall. They eagerly wave and smile at William, and he takes the time to wave back quickly before returning to the work he will have to finish before he can talk to them.

Damian Starr and Enoch Lang, two other good friends of both Mary Ann and William's [12], have also come today. Like William, Lang also has a new girlfriend, and when William now sees the two of them together for the first time, standing on the quay holding hands, it seems clear that Enoch is a much happier person now. It makes William happy to realize this. He gives each of them a firm look and nods his head at them. He looks forward to meeting them all in one of the taverns over a pint of beer soon. Now he concentrates on his work of unloading barrels.

As always when he returns after months at sea, William reflects on memories of this borough, where he grew up. He still has great interest in following the developments of the people and places from earlier on in his life. As a traveller and man who stays at sea for long periods, William finds it very important to update his knowledge with all kind of different information about the people and places he knows so well and who constitute fixed points in his life.

People who travel much have a much greater idea about the places and people they can't live without than do people who stay at home, mingling with the same individuals year after year. As William works, he thinks about the owners of the Wilmington wharves, built side by side along the Christina River.

The Wilmington wharves are located on the northern bank of the Christina River, most of them between two small runs, the Shipley and the Mulberry. From west to east, the streets run perpendicular to the riverbanks, Orange, Shipley, Market, King, French and Walnut Street. Parallel with the river are Water and Front Streets and then, up the hill: Second, Third, High, Queens, Hanover, Broad, Kent, Chestnut and Elisabeth Streets. West of Orange Street are Tatnall, West and Pasture Streets.

The first wharf to the east, between the two runs at the end of Market Street, is The Warner Wharf, which now belongs to John Warner, the big brother of William's best friend Joseph.

Between Market and King Street is a wharf belonging to Clark and Winzel. William does not know them and has never worked for them. Samuel Bush's wharf is on the east side of King Street opposite that of William Hemphill. Samuel Bush, 58 years old, was a pioneer among the Wilmington wharf-owners. He was the first to start a biweekly packet line between Wilmington and Philadelphia, 40 miles up the Delaware River. He began the line in 1774, shortly before the beginning of the Revolutionary War.

Before that, Wilmington merchants went to Philadelphia only once or twice a year to buy a huge stock of goods, which they would bring back to Wilmington in chartered ships.[161] Bush's plan proved a great success. His ship's frequent trips to Philadelphia were very convenient and inexpensive to the customer, and Bush soon had as much business as he could handle.[162] He named his first sloop after his dear wife, Ann, the year they married.

Ann was a special and independent woman. To get her hand, Samuel had to promise that he would never sail the deep sea again. After some consideration, Ann agreed that Samuel could start his biweekly ferry line to Philadelphia, but that there would be no more trips to the West Indies or other exotic and far away places. Such a strong attitude shown by a woman was quite unheard of in these days, and Ann was the subject of many loud dinner discussions in Wilmington homes.

Her birth name was Ann McKean, and her father was a wealthy Brandywine landowner.[161] Ann knew from experience how many widows of seamen, officers and captains now were forced to live quiet and lonely lives in small apartments in Wilmington, and since early childhood, she had been determined never to become one of them.

Ann did not like to spend time alone, especially at night. She needed people around her all the time to feel comfortable. Therefore it seemed natural for her to try and find a husband who was able to stay at home most of his time, especially on dark, cold and stormy winter evenings and nights, when strange noises from the dark outside the house terrified her.

It was hard for Samuel Bush to promise never to sail the deep sea again. He loved the sea as much as any seamen. Samuel's dear father, Charles Bush, a talented cabinet maker, wharf and ship owner, had successfully operated a line of sailing ships to the West Indies from what was now Samuel's own wharf.

The elder Bush imported such commodities as sugar, molasses and rum for the American markets. From many hours spent as a child around his father's wharf, Samuel had acquired a natural interest in ships, like most other boys living close to the harbor front. Samuel made his first trip to the West Indies when he was 16, a wonderful experience that left him with a permanent feeling of unbound freedom, convincing him that only the sea should be his future.

In the years to follow, Samuel made several other voyages on his father's ships on the Atlantic Ocean, mainly to and from the West Indies. Then his father promoted him to captain of one of the vessels.

Before Samuel promised Ann never to sail the deep sea again, he had been regarded as one of the most skilful navigators on the entire Delaware River. He fell in love with Ann at the age of 26 in 1773, and was lucky enough to have that love returned.[161] Samuel Bush gave his promise before getting married, and had kept it ever since.

After Samuel Bush's wharf is the wharf of Mr. Brown. William knew very little about him. The next wharf, on the west side of French Street, belongs to a highly respected Quaker and Brandywine mill owner, Mr.

Shallcroft. Next is another wharf belonging to Samuel Bush, one he bought from his main competitor, Foundrey, many years ago.

Finally, between French and Walnut Street, Joseph Tatnall, also a Quaker, Brandywine mill owner and prominent citizen, has his wharf and store. Tatnall and the other Quaker and Brandywine mill owners were some of the main suppliers of grain and flour to the Continental Army during the Revolutionary War, and Tatnall had developed a personal friendship with George Washington.

Rolling the barrels from the hull onto the quay is hard work and William has to take a break once in a while to catch his breath. He is strong as an ox, and only needs a few minutes rest before he is able to take up his work again.

William now recalls Thomas Mendenhall, another well-known wharf-owner in Wilmington who, like Samuel Bush, runs a packet line twice a week to Philadelphia with two sloops, *Farmer* and *Lydia*. Because both work around the port of Wilmington, William has talked to Mendenhall on several occasions and considers him a hero, though perhaps not on quite the same scale as Allen McLane.

"It surely feels good to be home again," William thinks, stopping his work and stretching as his eyes move slowly along the harbor front. He takes in the environment around the different wharves, almost inhaling the pretty sight of half-built ship skeletons erected outside some of the wooden wharf buildings. He looks across his right shoulder and sees in the distance the Customhouse with the flag of the United States of America, the Stars and Stripes, fluttering freely in the light eastern wind. This is his home, and although he does not know all the families here well, he is acquainted in one way or another with many of them.

Now William's mind fills with memories of his own family. There are five families in Wilmington that he may have belonged to, but only William knows the truth.

Most likely his parents were Mary and Thomas Watson, who previously lived in a house on the lot bordering that of Joseph and Mary Warner, the parents of William Watson's best friend, Joseph. The lot is west of Orange Street and between Second and Third Street. After Joseph Warner, Sr. died and Thomas Jefferson was elected president in 1800, they moved to a house on Jefferson Street in Georgetown in the District of Columbia.[0] Many of the 140 Congressmen and 34 Senators, who

14

worked on Capitol Hill, lived here among the 6000 that had settled in the little villages along the axis of Pennsylvania Avenue from the Eastern Branch to Georgetown.[182]

The butcher William Watson, who died during the Yellow Fever Epidemic from August to October 1798, together with 10 percent of Wilmington's population, could be the father. Joseph Warner; Sr. was Chief Burgess in Wilmington in that year of 1798. The butcher lived on French Street between Front and Second Streets, and was a friend of Joshua Wollaston, who, as tradition prescribed, gave a gift to the hospital when he visited it the day the butcher passed away, and who, like Joseph Warner, Sr. and Ester Yarnell's father, John Yarnall, was a Quaker and a member of the influential Quaker society, The Society of Friends, and the Society for the gradual Abolition of Slaves in Wilmington.[0] *In 1806, Joshua Wollaston and John Ferris, also a member of the Society of Friends in Wilmington and a good friend of Joseph Warner, Sr., were both members of the Brandywine Bridge commission.*

John Ferris, Joseph Warner, Sr., Thomas Mendenhall and others were the first directors of the Bank of Delaware, founded in 1795. John Ferris is also a tanner like the Starr family, to which William Watson's friend Damian Starr is related. He lives only a block from the Warner family. Tanners and butchers work closely together.

Other possibilities are a Thomas Watson, mortally wounded onboard the USS Delaware in 1799 in the West Indies, who came from Wilmington[0]*, and a Yeoman Thomas Watson, who at a time was selling land in Wilmington.*[0] *Finally, the carter Thomas Watson, selling land in Wilmington, could also be William Watson's father.*[0]

William stops unloading for a moment to catch his breath again. He smiles as his eyes travel along the harbor front. He has so many precious childhood memories connected to this borough, to every street corner, store and shop building. Strong memories of the countless times he and his playmates ran around on the quay in the harbor front or between the connected wooden wharf buildings, smelling so strongly of tar in the midday summer heat, when only young boys would be foolish enough to be outdoors.

William continues his work, recalling more families and individuals in Wilmington, especially those who have meant the most to him personally. He thinks of the family of his best friend, Joseph Warner. William has known the Warner family his entire life, and loved them all. Joseph's father, Joseph Warner, Sr., had told Jo seph and William about the Warner family as the three of them sat, one dark autumn evening, in front of the fireplace in the workshop at the back of the silverware shop in Market Street.

Joseph Warner, Sr. was an excellent storyteller and the two young friends sat glued to a stool, silently listening with half-open mouths. That evening was a few months before Joseph Warner, Sr. passed away. William still recalls most of the stories. The father Joseph had fallen in love with Mary Yarnall in 1774, the same year her husband John Yarnall had died. Joseph Warner, Sr. had been a bachelor and a young, promising silversmith at that time.

William Penn was the original owner of Pennsylvania under which the State of Delaware, or the Three Lower Counties as they were named then, belonged. He was an English Quaker and had a great influence on the people living under his jurisdiction. The church leaders, the top merchants, wharf and shop owners in Philadelphia used to be Quakers or Friends, hence, the city of Philadelphia was nicknamed 'The Quaker City." In these early times, the few Quakers in Wilmington went to Philadelphia for meetings in the Friends Meeting House there.

The Society of Friends in Wilmington finally raised enough money to build their own Friends Meeting House, on top of Quaker Hill on the northwestern corner of West and High Streets, just east of the Forest.

The Quakers and Friends are generally known to take good care of people, not only the members of their own society, but also lonely or sick people and those otherwise in need. Therefore, Quakers are highly respected in the local community.

John Ferris, another cabinet-maker, was known in the entire borough of Wilmington for taking time to visit sick people, speaking with them for long hours and praying with them for their recovery, or just sitting quietly beside their beds, if that was needed.

The bachelor Joseph Warner, Sr. showed up at almost every Society of Friends meeting and became a good friend of Mary and John Yarnall. He began to spend much time with them when he was not out with his best friend, another bachelor, silversmith and Friend, Jesse Zane.

When John Yarnall got sick several years later, Joseph Warner, Sr. found it only natural to visit now and then. Joseph Warner would sit at

Zane's bedside for hours, discussing matters of life and death or praying, in keeping with the Quaker tradition. John Yarnall highly appreciated these visits, which initiated Mary Yarnell's affection toward Joseph Warner, Sr. Soon after, John Yarnall died of a disease and was buried in the cemetery outside the Friends Meeting House on Quaker Hill. It was a beautiful ceremony and almost all the members in the Society of Friends, including Joseph Warner, Sr. and Jesse Zane, were present.

On Sunday a month later, Joseph Warner, Sr. and Mary Yarnall announced their engagement at the meeting in the Friends Meeting House. The wedding took place the following month. To this marriage with 31-year-old Joseph Warner, Sr. Mary Yarnall brought her daughter, Esther, and her son, John. They decided to let the children keep their last name to honor John Yarnall but John Yarnall, Jr. and Joseph Warner became such good friends, that John Yarnall, Jr. only accepted to be called by the name John Warner.

In 1775, Mary Warner gave birth to a son, named William Warner after Joseph Warner, Sr.'s own father. Joseph Warner, Sr.'s silversmith shop was located on the west side of Market Street between Second and Third. He owned the lot where his shop was built and the lot just west of it. In the early years, the shop was located a few houses from the Sign of the Ship inn, on the corner of Third and Market Streets, before the inn moved to the harbor front, a more profitable location.

John Marshall, a charismatic, fearless patriot, was its owner then. The inn was very popular and attracted guests from all over town. Joseph Warner secretly admired his conduct and names his own shop Sign of the Golden Can. 'Sign of …'' was a common way to begin th e name a shop in those early days, so this was not that original. A sign with the name of the shop, and a drawing of a golden can, was put up above the entrance to the shop. The drawing was to make it easy for people who did not know how to read to locate the shop, if they heard the name from others.

Mary worked many hours selling the silverware produced in the silversmith shop, and Joseph often praised her talents.

Joseph Warner, Sr. had become a silverware shop-owner before the Revolutionary War. William remembers that Joseph Warner considered those first three years the most peaceful period in the Warner family's life, except for a break-in at the Warner home on September 22, 1775. Several pieces of silverware were stolen, most of it was marked JW for

17

Joseph Warner. The break-in had caused great alarm in the small family, and Mary had been worried if this would be a frequent event, now they had bought a silverware shop. William Warner had just been born and Mary Warner was hysterical for several months after, because she hated having strangers near her newborn child.

The Warner family worked hard to live off the sale of the silverware that Joseph Warner produced in the workshop. Even with the help of John and the black slave Sine, whom Joseph shared with two Wilmington businessmen, James Bryan and Samuel Canby, Joseph Warner, Sr. soon found it necessary to extend the business to include a general assortment of ironmongery, furniture, paint, linseed, and lamp oil. John Ferris delivered some of the furniture the Warners began to sell.

To attract more customers, Joseph began advertising in the most-read paper in town. In these early days, it was *The Pennsylvania Gazette*. In his advertisement, Joseph Warner stated proudly that he would pay the highest price for old silver. Slowly but surely, Warner's industrious work had made him one of the most recognized silversmiths in the whole state of Delaware.

When the war broke out, although the Warner's were peaceful Quakers, they could not prevent the war from coming into their world. In the summer of 1777, a large Royal Navy fleet arrived at the entrance to the Delaware Bay, which caught the attention of the entire population on the Delaware-Maryland-Virginia Peninsula and led them to believe that the English fleet would go directly up the Delaware River to Philadelphia.

Instead, the Royal Navy's large fleet sailed up Chesapeake Bay and landed troops at the head of the Elk River opposite Wilmington on the peninsula. The troops marched over the peninsula, where the local people were shocked to see them approaching.

The Continental Army and the Royal Navy mariners and soldiers met just north of Wilmington and the Brandywine River in a battle that was later termed the Battle of the Brandywine. George Washington, Commander of the Continental Army, decided to place his local headquarters in Wilmington, just next to the Society of Friends Meeting House, of all places, east of the forest, on top of Quaker Hill.

In the summer and autumn of 1777, with British troops around Wilmington, Joseph Warner, Sr. was accused of treason for selling cattle to the British. Warner had his cattle inside a fence west of Pasture Street and close to Washington's Headquarters. The accusation infuriated Warner, a man of high integrity. The charges had to be dropped, because nothing could be proven, but Joseph Warner remained angry about it years later, whenever he thought of the episode or someone mentioned it to him.

Warner saw this as yet another cowardly attempt to compromise a distinguished member of the Quaker society. He wondered why anyone would come to the meetinghouse on Quaker Hill, this church hill, now local headquarters for the commander-in-chief, George Washington, who was trying to establish freedom for the Americans, and at a time where there was a general call for unity, to accuse him of treason. Warner would simply not accept old enemies using a temporary change in the local power structure, caused by a much larger crisis in the North American colonies, to attack him. He could not believe anyone should ever accuse a Warner of being unpatriotic. People who knew Joseph Warner, Sr. knew that he shared his father's strong intuition for revenge against his enemies, a power often found in those with high integrity. Those close to him didn't like it when Warner was angry, because they knew how persistent he could be in restoring justice in any matter, no matter how small. Thomas Mendenhall, for one, was simply scared of Joseph Warner, Sr.

William had a good working rhythm now and his thoughts shifted from the Warners to the Bush family. Samuel Bush had had two brothers, George and Lewis. Samuel Bush was a patriot who had helped the Continental Army by transporting weapons in his ships. His younger brother Lewis, a soldier in one of the Delaware Regiments in the Continental Army, had unfortunately been killed, singled out by the British in the Battle of the Brandywine, on September 11, 1777. The battle had taken place so close to the Brandywine River that the citizens of Wilmington could follow the battle from their rooftops. It had been hard for Charles Bush, and the eldest brother George, who was the Port Collector in Wilmington at that time, to learn that they had lost Lewis. Samuel Bush had been quite affected.

As he works, William recalls that George Bush held the position of Port Collector for the District of Delaware until President George Washington himself appointed McLane. Washington appointed McLane as one of his last Presidential Acts, in 1797. William remembers this clearly, because he had been 11 years old at the time.

William also recalled that in September 1777, when the Royal Marines and the British soldiers were rapidly approaching Wilmington and the Brandywine mills, one of the main grain and flour suppliers to the Continental Army during the war, George Washington personally ordered the Brandywine mill stones removed and hidden to prevent them from falling in the hands of the English enemy.

Mary Warner and the other young Quaker wives with small children had been nervous about the war coming so close to their homes. During the war, the peaceful Quaker men had held their regular meetings in the Friends Meeting House, next to Washington's headquarters on Quaker Hill. But that September, they discussed what could be done to secure their homes and property in case the British troops invaded Wilmington.

Responsible men and women from Wilmington had to react to this war quickly. Helping any sitting government was standard procedure for members of a Quaker Society, as evidenced by flour supplied to the Continental Army from the prominent Quaker Joseph Tatnall's own Brandywine Mill.

The patriot John Marshall was owner of the 'Sign of the Ship" inn a couple of houses from Joseph Warner's store on Market Street. One morning when Joseph Warner was standing outside his shop, he looked up Market Street and saw George Washington come out of the inn and walk up Third Street to his headquarters on Quaker Hill. Joseph Warner, Sr. had told that story to William and Joseph Warner, Jr. some years ago, and William had realized from the intonation in Joseph's voice that the older man had been quite impressed with George Washington.

William has forgotten what happened to the Warner family in the 1780s, but he assumes they have been working hard to build up their business according with the reputation the family had.

William remembers that his best friend, Joseph Warner, Jr. was born on April 20, 1780 in the middle of the struggle for American Independence. The other Warner children, Mary, Jesse and Hester, were also born in that decade, Mary on January 25, 1783, Jesse on December 30, 1785, and Hester on November 18, 1787, the same year as him. Jesse died at the age of eight, and Hester died at the age of 15 only three years ago. The death of these young children had, of course, been a dark time for the Warner family, but unfortunately was not that rare a phenomenon in Wilmington families in these years. Recalling the deaths of Jesse and Hester made William sad. But he only had to recall memories of the father Joseph Warner, Sr. to feel happy again.

Joseph Warner, Sr. had acted toward every living creature in the local community as if it was a special creation of God. His attitude made everyone near him respect him deeply. He was a man with a simple set of living rules, and he lived the words of God. The fact that he and his wife were influential members of the Society of Friends and he himself was a member of the Society for the Gradual abolition of Slaves also showed that action and words walked closely hand in hand. The most important values in the father Joseph's life and most of the other Wilmington Quakers lives were moral ones.

The *Ino*'s supercargo, the man responsible for all the cargo, suddenly interrupts William's thoughts, shouting loudly, 'Stop! Take a ten minute break, all of you." William pants heavily now and his body is very warm. The seamen will rest just as long as they still feel warm. When they start to feel the slightest cold and their shirts begin to feel wet, cold and glued to their bodies, they immediately take up work again.

None of the seamen feel the need to talk as they rest. They just sit silently along the bulwark, so William begins thinking about the different people he knows in the borough of Wilmington. He recalls the two eldest Warner brothers, John and William. His memories of them begin in 1793, 12 years ago. William Watson was six at the time, and Joseph Warner, Jr. 13.

John Warner had a good friend James Hemphill, son of the ship-owner William Hemphill, who owned the *Ino*. John and James were both born in 1774. As children, they played together often. In 1793, they had reached the age of 18, when their fathers allowed them to go on deep sea trips. John and James for some years sailed as experienced or 'able seamen" onboard William Hemphill's ships, sailing in the Delaware River or along the waters close to the US east coast.

In 1793, the two of them made their first voyage together as masters on one of the Hemphill's ocean-going ships sailing to the West Indies, to the French island of Martinique[161].

Wilmington merchants had traded in the West Indies as far back as anyone could remember. James Hemphill and John Warner were supposed to look after the cargo on the trip. When they finally arrived in the port of Fort-de-France in Martinique, the two of them were responsible for selling the cargo and negotiating with local merchants to buy proper articles to bring back home to sell in Wilmington.

William Hemphill instructed them carefully about the typical prices for different types of high-quality goods available on the island, in order to prepare them to make a good trade.

John's mother Mary did not like the idea of letting her eldest son go to the West Indies, when he first told her that he and James were going. When Hester then died shortly after John and James left for the West Indies, Mary was convinced she would never see her eldest son again. But both boys returned safe and sound and the whole trip actually was a great success.

James Hemphill had proved his worth and later was appointed captain on his father's ship *Sally*, which Halbert Watson now captains. On earlier trips with the *Sally*, with James as captain, the ship ran into a fearless privateer and on the way from Guadeloupe to Martinique, they ran into a hurricane that blew away the topmast and snapped three anchors.[161]

William remembered that his friend Joseph Warner was not very excited about listening to his brothers talk about their many sea adventures. Joseph mostly cared for a safe city life and the silverware business, and no one would get him out on the open sea. William found these sea adventures sweet fairytales that convinced him, that he, too, one day would become a seaman sailing the seven seas.

The single story James was able to talk about, that shocked and impressed William the most, dealt with James' first trip to Europe, when he once again had been entrusted to take care of the cargo. On that trip to Nantes and Paris in France, James had seen people been executed by the guillotine, and he had met the up-and-coming General Napoleon Bonaparte one evening at a Paris ball.[161]

Joseph Warner, Jr. did not like to listen to these strange, often macabre, situations James and John had been in while travelling abroad. Joseph Warner had always thought that the Frenchmen really lost their heads in that terrible French Revolution, so utterly different from the more civilized American one.

Because the American Constitution said that all men are created equal and because the Quaker societies in America, according to their traditions, always obey the laws given by any sitting government, the

Quakers had gradually come to the conclusion that it was wrong to hold slaves. As a consequence, the prominent members of the Society of Friends in Wilmington founded the Society for the Gradual Abolition of Slaves to help local slaves gain their freedom.

Two years later, in 1795, Joseph Warner, Sr. released the slave Sine, owned together with two other members of the abolition society, both from old families in Wilmington, James Bryan and Samuel Canby.[241] Sine's release was another sign that Joseph Warner, Sr. was a visionary and far-sighted man, one who took charge if needed. Joseph Warner, Sr. was always careful with his words, because of his own rule that action and talk always walk hand in hand in his life.

William could remember February 9, 1795, the proud moment when Samuel Canby, John Ferris and Joseph Warner, Sr. were rewarded for their many years of dedicated work to make the borough of Wilmington a better place to live. They were appointed members of the Board of the Directors of the first public bank established in Wilmington, the Bank of Delaware. Joseph Tatnall, the most prominent Quaker in Wilmington, was an obvious choice as the bank's first president. The merchants and wharf-owners William Hemphill, Ebenezer Macomb and Thomas Mendenhall were on the first Board of Directors, along with Joseph Warner's good friend Samuel Hollingsworth, another locally respected Quaker. Samuel Canby and Thomas Mendenhall were the only ones on the board who were not Quakers. Every one of these men had been chosen because of their personal high integrity and good character.

The building holding the Bank of Delaware was erected on the northwest corner of High Street and Market Street, just a few houses from Joseph Warner Sr.'s silverware shop. As expected, the Bank of Delaware turned out to be a moneymaker from the very beginning.

At this advanced point in his life Joseph Warner, Sr. was glad he had received so much recognition from the local community. He was not young anymore, and felt that now was a proper time to find out what his children wanted for their future lives and see if he, when writing his will, could fulfill the wishes of his sons and daughters. Joseph Warner, Sr. knew that from the time they were small children, John and William had never showed any sign of wanting to take over the silversmith shop. They were mainly interested in adventures related to sea life and could not imagine themselves permanently tied to a shop. Only the youngest son, William's friend Joseph, had shown a real interest. He had spent many hours in the workshop with his father and had enjoyed it. He liked the mechanical processes connected to making silverware items. So when the father wrote his will, it was only natural that the silverware shop should go to his youngest son Joseph.

This same year, 1795, John Warner and James Hemphill had again returned from a successful trip to Martinique. On their return, John and William Warner had come to their father and begged him to help them start their own wharf business. They were tired of working for others and wanted their own business. John and William wanted to buy the wharf of John Robinson, at the end of Market Street, beside Samuel Bush's wharf. Joseph Warner, Sr. agreed to help them financially, and before the end of that year John and William were running their own wharf in Wilmington.

In his will Joseph Warner, Sr. needed to include two trustees who could take care of his three daughters when he passed away. It had not been difficult at all for Joseph to find two people in Wilmington qualified to handle that obligation. He appointed Bancroft Woodcock, Delaware's best silversmith and a good personal friend and colleague, and his good friend the Quaker and tanner Isaac H. Starr who lived close by and with whom he had spent many wonderful hours.

As William continues to work hard emptying the *Ino*, he remembers the autumn of 1795, when there had been a strong feeling of political disapproval in Wilmington among the federalists and the anti-federalists, when Washington was supposed to sign the Jay Treaty with England. As William saw it, Federalists were people who believed in a strong central governing form of the Union of the North American States, and Democratic-Republicans were people believing strongly that the individual states should run their own business as much as possible.

The Federalists were generally people with an attachment to Europe, or people inspired by the European governing form with a strong central government for each country. Many ship owners and people living off trading with Europe had a federalist approach. Farmers and people who did not have a strong attachment to the European trade, but to trade purely related to the North American agricultural economy, tended to be Democratic-Republicans.

On August 4, 1795, William recalled, the Anti-federalists had called for a meeting in the Presbyterian Meeting House on the hill near the Academy. A committee of nine persons was appointed to communicate with President George Washington, and these Anti-federalists included Joseph Warner, Sr., Isaac H. Starr, Caesar A. Rodney and many other prominent citizens.

That year had been a turbulent one for the Warner family. John Warner took his father's approach and gradually began to share the views of the members of the Democratic-Republican Party. The two eldest Warner brothers successfully worked themselves into the wharf and merchant business, and William Warner became a Federalist when it came to the trade relations between the United States of America and England, that he as a ship owner and merchant depended on. John and William had taken up the Wilmington merchant's and ship owner's old tradition of trading with Liverpool in England, and William Warner saw no need to be hostile to a good trade partner.

As a businessman he strongly felt the need to be pragmatic when it came to trading conditions with England, in order to optimize the interests of his own business. He could not afford the luxury of sacrificing good trade relations with England for issues such as improved rights for the American seamen who were taken out of Americans ships and pressed into service onboard British Royal Navy ships. He understood that it was humiliating to American seamen to be forced to serve in the military of the nation from which the United States of America had liberated itself, but he felt that the American government must sort out these diplomatic problems without putting restrictions on trading.

To William Warner, the Federalists seemed to do most for preserving good trade relations with England. So it was only natural for him to join them. The youngest Warner brother, Joseph, was only 15 years old and lacked the firm convictions[218] of his father and elder brothers, but when asked directly, would answer that his sympathy was partly with the Democratic-Republicans and partly with the Quakers, although the viewpoints of these two groups contradicted in many areas. This didn't feel odd to Joseph at all, because upholding contradictions was almost a daily routine to him, with his family background and time spent around eccentric personalities and characters with different strong political convictions in Wilmington.

William recalled from the many visits he had paid the Warner family in those early years that the family as a whole had become quite successful. In 1798, Joseph Warner, Sr. had been elected Chief Burgess in Wilmington. That was a very honorable position to hold and Mary Warner had been so proud of her husband. In 1777, the Chief Burgess in Wilmington was the honorable John McKinley, who later became the first Governor of the State of Delaware.

To those in Wilmington who took care of the sick, like the Quakers, 1798 had been an absolutely terrible year. Ten percent of Wilmington's population, 192 adults and 16 children, died of yellow fever.[245] Six years earlier, in 1792, when William was five, 20 percent of the population of Wilmington had also died of yellow fever.

That year, John Warner's good friend James Hemphill dropped overseas sailing to become a shop owner in Wilmington. William Watson often visited his shop in the lower end of King Street, near his father's wharf. James ran a wholesale grocery business. The ships connected to John Warner's Wharf delivered a lot of the imports brought to his shop. Hemphill sold old Madeira, port and sherry from Lisbon and Malaga wines, Jamaican rum and sugar, chocolate, tea and coffee, indigo, soap, candles, tobacco and snuff. He also sold gunpowder, shots, flints for shotguns, pork, ship bread, lamp oil, super fine flour from the Brandywine mills, window glass, molasses, gin and brandy.[239]

James Hemphill and his wife had children now, and he had chosen the same safe approach to life that Ann Bush had demanded of her husband. Like Samuel Bush, James compensated for not sailing the ocean by establishing his own sailing route and now ran a packet *Hannah* to Philadelphia twice a week, on Tuesday and Friday. But James had to admit that the fresh water at the quay on the northern bank of the Christina River did not smell as good as deep sea saltwater that had occasionally sprayed into his face when sailing for the West Indies.

From the shop at their wharf at the end of Market Street, the Warner brothers sold more or less the same kind of articles as Hemphill. The gin they imported from Holland, where their ships go to the Frisian island of Texel to trade in the nearby port Den Helder, or they go further to Amsterdam. They sold Spanish cigars, rum from the Danish West Indian Islands of St. Croix and St. Thomas, glue imported from England and plaster from Paris.

William and John Warner also ran a packet, the *Charlotte,* from their wharf in Wilmington to Philadelphia, Monday and Thursday. William Warner named the ship after the wife of British King George III. William was definitely the one with a natural talent for trading and leading the company, when tough decisions needed to be made. He wanted absolute control and to make all the decisions. John had accepted that in the beginning of their partnership, but later it was the main reason they went separate ways with their businesses. They early on earned a reputation in the borough for attending quickly to the orders that came in from the country merchants, and they showed flexibility to their trade partners and accepted country produce as payment[239] for delivered goods. John tried to keep up when it came to making good deals, but in the end there was no doubt that William was much better at trading, because he simply loved to negotiate. William Warner had a much more aggressive approach toward his business, and he was highly ambitious. John and William Warner moved their business to Philadelphia, as many Wilmington merchants did, around the turn of the century.

Joseph Warner, Sr. died on Oct. 11, 1800, at the age of 58, after a short illness. He had been of sound mind until the very last. The father had fully understood when his eldest son John came to his bedside, almost five weeks before he died, and told that he had put his name on the Borough Ticket to run for Assistant Burgess. Joseph Warner, Sr. turned his head toward John and smiled because he knew that this was another sign of his eldest son's affection toward him. Williams's friend Joseph was 20 when he lost his father.

That September 6 both John Warner and Samuel Bush had put their names on the Wilmington borough ticket to run for Assistant Burgess. William Hemphill ran for Treasurer and the ambitious Thomas Mendenhall ran for Assessor.[240] John Warner, William Hemphill and Thomas Mendenhall had to their great joy all been elected. John Warner was so glad that he had been able to bring his father the good news that his son had been elected. Somehow the old Wilmington Quaker Joseph Warner, Sr. saw this positive election result his eldest son had reached as his own final milestone in life. Joseph Warner, Sr. had done what he could as a father, and now it was time for the eldest son John to take over.

As planned, Williams's friend, Joseph Warner, Jr. then took over the silversmith business, which came as a relief to his mother, who greatly mourned the death of her husband and didn't have the strength anymore to assist in the silverware shop.

In the following eight months, William had then offered to help Joseph run the silverware shop and he had accepted the help. The two of them had managed the shop so well, that Joseph had extra time to think about his own future marriage, and he had finally decided to marry his girlfriend Mary. Less than 8 months after his father's death, on July 5, 1801, when he was 21 years of age, Joseph Warner, Jr. married his fiancée Mary, who was not a Quaker and a member of the Society of Friends. They married "out of church"[0], a condition that would not have pleased Joseph's father, if he had lived to witness it. But the mother Mary, who could be stricter than her husband used to be, was pragmatic when it came to an important matter like marriage. She wanted the best for her son, so she completely accepted that her daughter-in-law came from another church society.

This day it was only a little more than four years since his best friend Joseph married, and William remembered the wedding as if it had happened yesterday. The wedding had been beautiful. Because the Society of Friends would not allow the wedding to take place in the Friends Meeting House on Quaker Hill, Joseph and Mary were married in the Old Swedish Church in Wilmington.

Mary, the youngest Warner daughter, also married "out of church" at age 23, to an officer in one of the Delaware Regiments, James Thompson, who belonged to the Presbyterian Church in Wilmington, where William and his family went when he was little. John Warner, who also was active as an officer in that regiment, had got acquainted with James Thompson and finally introduced him to his little sister, and James and Mary had stayed close together ever since. The mother Mary Warner was glad that her husband had not lived to see this, but she accepted it fully as she had when Joseph had married.

People with pacifistic attitudes like the Quakers had become less and less popular in the days during and after the Revolutionary War, when Joseph Warner, Sr. and his generation of Quakers married, but most of them had, as tradition prescribed, married other Quakers. Twenty-five years later, when the next generation married, the tradition broke. The young Warners, like other young people in Wilmington, had a pretty good picture of the ongoing changes in society and the public opinion and many of this generation of Quaker sons joined the army without having any second thoughts. For these two Warner children, Joseph and Mary, members of one of the oldest Quaker families in Wilmington, to marry

28

"out of church" was just a natural attempt for young people to orient themselves toward a more progressive future.

That same year, 1801, the newly married Joseph and Mary Warner decided to move their silverware business to Philadelphia[0] as the elder Warner brothers had done earlier to follow the business trends. They left Joseph's mother Mary, with Ester and Hester, in the Warner residence in Wilmington. Most serious Wilmington merchants, ship and wharf-owners had started branches in Philadelphia.

Then the yellow fever once again swept over Philadelphia, leaving a trail of death in families and homes there. John and William Warner followed the situation closely and, when people started to die in large numbers close to where they had their shop and wharf on the Delaware River waterfront, they decided it would be much safer to return to Wilmington. Therefore, on August 27, 1802, William and John Warner informed their coming Wilmingtonian customers in the local newspaper, *Mirror of the Times,* that they were moving their business to Wilmington, because of the yellow fever raging in Philadelphia.[242]

That same day, James Hemphill had announced the sale of his quarter share of the ship the *Eagle* and his 430-barrel schooner *Delaware.* The elder Warner brothers and James' father, William Hemphill, owned three-quarters of the *Eagle.* Samuel Bush decided to join the other colleagues and buy the last quarter. A fortnight later, Hester Warner died of yellow fever in Wilmington.[0] Their mother Mary Warner was inconsolable and cried for many days. Luckily, she still had Ester to support her and take care of her in that difficult period.

When the yellow fever finally loosened its grasp in Philadelphia, William Warner did not waste a second going back to Philadelphia to try to get his business back to normal as quickly as possible. Wilmington was definitely no longer a large enough place for him to do his business, he had concluded when forced to stay there again. As the Assistant Burgess, the eldest Warner brother John had many obligations to take care of in Wilmington, and even though Ester Yarnall was staying with his mother in the mansion, John felt a deep responsibility to look after her. Personally, he also felt more attached to Wilmington, where he grew up, than to Philadelphia. Like his little brother, Joseph, John had been very close to his father, Joseph Warner, Sr.

In March 1803, when John Warner had stayed some time and done business in Wilmington, while William Warner still wanted to conduct his business from Philadelphia, the two of them decided to separate their companies financially and permanently.

William Warner bought a brig to use for trading with Liverpool in England and named it *Fair American*, loyal to his belief as a Federalist seeking fair and pragmatic solutions to Atlantic trade political issues. Samuel Bush and John Warner, with wharves side by side on the Christina River, found it natural to begin doing business together. They also bought a new ship and named it *True American*, loyal to Samuel Bush's beliefs as a Democratic Republican. Working together on a daily basis, John Warner and Samuel Bush gradually began to share the same political views. Every day that went by pulled William and John Warner further apart.

"That is pretty much the story of the Warner family as I know it," William Watson thought as he rolled a new barrel along the plank to the quay.

Despite William Watson's ravenous appetite for Delaware history, and his great knowledge about the people who surrounded him all his life, his knowledge about his own ancestors is remarkably scant. He has early on directed his interest toward the genealogical family trees of his friends and other people in Wilmington and, of course, the genealogical family tree of all the Watsons in the state of Delaware. William knows that his family descended from a Welsh family and his parents were staunch members of the Presbyterian Society. Most of the neighbors they had known when his parents lived were Quakers, and recognized members of the Society of Friends and belonged to the borough's old families.

These families originally came to Wilmington, or the Christina or Brandywine Hundreds from Chester County in Pennsylvania, just north of the border. Most of these people, like William's own forefathers, had come to Chester County from Ireland and Wales. William Penn had granted their forefathers land in that area.

William had been told that the Watson families in the State of Delaware originally settled in three main areas. The first group, the one William's family belonged to, lived in and around Wilmington in the northeast corner of Delaware.

William Watson believes that his own family line comes from the William Watson who bought 2,692 acres of land in small tracts around Brandywine Hundred, together with Samuel Stewart, John Bird,

William, David and Samuel Talley, and 16 others in May 1760.[170] William never knew his grandfather and his parents never spoke about their families. They had been too occupied with the daily struggle to survive to pay any particular attention to their own genealogical past.

William remembers that in 1695, Isaac Warner conveyed 200 acres to William Talley at Naaman's Creek. Naaman was one of the Indian chiefs who lived with his tribe and ruled the area around Wilmington before the Europeans arrived in the New World. William Watson could not help wondering if Isaac Warner was a forefather of his friend Joseph Warner. But then he remembered that Joseph Warner, Sr.'s parents, William and Christiana Warner, came to Wilmington in 1732, ten years before Joseph Warner, Sr. was born on September 29, 1742.

The second group of Delaware Watsons lived in the northwest corner of Delaware and across the border to Cecil County, Maryland. Like the first group, they belonged to the Welsh Community in New Castle County and were originally from Londonderry or Dublin, Ireland. The British had oppressed their forefathers for generations, first in Wales, in the iron-manufacturing districts, and then after they moved to the northern part of Ireland. Finally, some of the young ones refused to accept their hopeless living conditions and bought one-way tickets to North America, crossing the Atlantic Ocean to the port of New Castle in the Delaware River. Most of them did not have the money to pay the ticket, so when they arrived in America they paid the captain by signing a contract to work for a couple of years for some New Castle farmer, who was impatiently waiting for the new labor force and the ship's arrival at quay.

Some of them worked hard for years before having enough to buy their own small piece of land. When they decided to move inland, they were advised to go northeast. They looked at the horizon and decided to travel toward the highest point they could see. There they saw to their great joy that the soil contained a lot of iron ore, and these new settlers decided to name the place Iron Hill and Pen Cader, meaning 'highest seat." They also found that the hill was wooded, which meant that they had the proper resources for making iron. As experienced iron manufacturers, they could not have been more pleased.

Also called the Welsh Tract, this area's largest part was in Pen Cader Hundred and the remainder in Cecil County Maryland. In 1684, Governor Talbor of Maryland claimed the land around Iron Hill as a part of his territory and succeeded in driving out the settlers. They fled southward, shocked that their families, persecuted for generations by the English, had travelled so far only to be driven from their land here in the New World. When they were allowed to return, they taught themselves how to make weapons for self-defense.[172] This skill would turn out to be crucial in the future.

In the autumn of 1701, some of these first settlers finally obtained a title to the land on which they were living, obtaining a grant for 3,000 acres from William Penn. Some of them had come from Montgomery County in Pennsylvania, where Penn earlier had granted them 40,000 acres.

John Welsh had chosen 1,091 acres, and in 1727, he sold 500 acres to Thomas Lewis. He sold another part to James Sykes, of which executors later conveyed 281 and one-half acres to Robert Faires, who passed the land onto his son William, who passed it on to a descendant David B. Ferris. William often wondered if this Ferris family was related to the Wilmington Ferrises Joseph Warner, Sr. knew so well.

James James, another of the early landowners living around Iron Hill, got land from Penn as early as 1703. Thomas James received 1,250 acres by deed, John Thomas 632, William Jones 2,747, and Howell James 1,040.[172] William could remember this because he had a way with numbers as some people had with faces. Once he had seen one, he never forgot it.

In the first known group of Watsons living in Pen Cader Hundred, Howell James and his wife, Sarah, sold 154 and one-half acres of land on the north side of the Christina Creek to Thomas and Susanna Watson, the grandfather and grandmother of a captain Thomas Watson in a Delaware Regiment. The captain, Thomas Watson had a son John, who now lives in Wilmington as a Gentleman.[247] William has met John Watson and talked to him on several occasions on the streets in Wilmington.

William Watson catches the eyes of the supercargo onboard the *Ino* to see if his break is coming to an end, convinced that he is also somehow related to these early settlers in the Welsh tract in Pen Cader Hundred. The relationship is not straight from father to son, he realizes, but through intermarriage between these Pen Cader Watsons and the Watson family line from the Brandywine and Christina Hundreds. William is proud to believe he is related to this Pen Cader Hundred Captain Thomas Watson, who served in one of the Delaware Regiments in the

Revolutionary War. He died as a Colonel in 1792, 13 years ago. William sees this late Colonel Thomas Watson as a Revolutionary War hero, the same as Colonel Allen McLane. The grandfather of the Colonel Thomas Watson and his wife Susanna had actually founded the Watson family in Pen Cader Hundred.

William supposed that these Watson families had developed strong feelings for their new homeland, where they for the first time owned land, almost automatically becoming patriots who wanted to serve in the army. They had been fighting for generations for everything they achieved in life and they were now willing to defend North America with life and fortune if it should come to that.

The settlements of the New Castle Watsons had spread out though the years and now they lived along the Christina River, which runs across the entire New Castle County. The Christina Creek originates in Cecil County, Maryland and runs through the beautiful White Clay Creek Hundred and the north end of Pen Cader Hundred. It continues eastward, forming the border between White Clay Creek Hundred, to the north of where other Watsons live, and Pen Cader Hundred to the South. Then it runs northwest and becomes the border between White Clay Creek Hundred to the northeast and New Castle Hundred to the southeast. The Christina River grows from a creek to a river at the 'triple point," where White Clay Creek Hundred, New Castle Hundred and Christina Hundred meet.

William knew that the third Watson group in Delaware had a direct English origin. Captain Luke Watson, his wife, Sarah, and their children came directly from New York to Lewes, Sussex County, in 1676. They founded the largest family group, the Sussex Watsons.[250] These English descendants arrived exactly 100 years before the Americans declared their independence and were not especially interested in fighting the English soldiers when the Revolutionary War began. They felt they were heard by the British authorities and did not feel a strong need to improve their situation.

William knew that many believed some of the Sussex farmers actually supplied ships of the Royal Navy with living bullocks and helped them in many other ways during the war. Like most male Delawareans, the Sussex Watson' s men were called in for the military service, but during the Revolutionary War some deserted after only a short period of service.

William is proud that he belongs to the northern group of the Delaware Watsons, the families living mostly in New Castle County.

Now the easy job of rolling barrels along planks has come to an end, and the crew has to work together two or three seamen at a time to get the large wooden boxes up from the half-dark hull. William is beginning to feel hungry after many hours of hard work. He is now desperately looking forward to having dinner with Mary Ann and her mother this evening. Mary Ann and her mother live in Water Street, just three minutes away. The seamen in the hull of the *Ino* put their hands on the last box, and begin to run with it.

William has begun to long for family life recently. Being a seaman naturally forces him to be far away from his hometown for long periods of time, and it sometimes leaves him with feelings of loneliness. Reaching his homeport this afternoon is therefore almost a sacred moment to him and he is eager to spend the evening with new people, especially Mary Ann and her mother.

As he is helping moving the last large box, William thinks of the general conditions for running or working in a business in a port town like Wilmington. It can be risky to be wharf-owner, ship-owner, seaman, port laborer or sea captain. The market can go up and down in a short period of time, and ships often disappear at sea, go down in a storm or get taken by pirates. Ship-owners normally try to spread their economical risk by working together and being part owners of each other's ships. Typically, four peop le will own a schooner.

The economy is good this year, 1805, and has been improving for several years. The increase of the production of flour from the Brandywine Mills and flax seed from the Delaware farms has resulted in an increase in the number of sea trips to Philadelphia or the three other major east coast ports, Boston, New York and Baltimore.

When the merchants and wharf-owners in Wilmington are happy, the sea captains, port workers and seamen are happy, too. The stores owned by the wharf-owners or their relatives then prosper and the positive effect spreads among all the shop owners in the borough. These wharf-owners, seamen and sea captain's families of Wilmington know that the large ship-owners can afford to lose roughly four out of five ships at sea and still make a decent profit. William Hemphill is the largest ship owner these days, with several ships in his homeports Wilmington and Philadelphia. Several deep-sea captains earn their living working for him.

This year, William Hemphill and many of the other Wilmington ship-owners have wisely managed their ocean going ships, William Watson thinks. Any seaman in Wilmington knows that normal trade has more or less been cancelled this year in the Dutch West Indian island St. Eustatia, the Danish West Indian Islands St. Thomas and St. Croix, and the French West Indian Island of Martinique. The British, French and Spanish fleets are around these islands.

The Wilmington wharf-owners and ship-owners have been around long enough to see which way the wind is blowing and to be careful. Therefore they directed their trade directly to Europe[293] this year.

William Hemphill sent his ship, *Benjamin Franklin,* to Holland, to the island of Texel and the borough of Den Helder and to Amsterdam. The other Wilmington wharf-owners— Samuel Bush and John Warner, the Stocktons and the Craigs— sent their ship the *Mercury* to Amsterdam. William thinks how *Mercury* is not a proper name for an ocean-going Wilmington ship, as *The Wilmington Mercury,* a free newspaper occasionally delivered to the patrons of the *Delaware Gazette,* is mainly a list of deaths from the Wilmington Health Board. The ambitious Thomas Mendenhall, by the way, is the President of the Health Board.

The *Eagle* was sent to the harbor of Altona on the Elbe River, carrying high quality skins made by Quaker tanners John Ferris and Samuel H. Starr.

The cooperation John Warner had with Samuel Bush was through his own company named John Warner & Company. This year, in the local *Mirror of the Times,* he advertised Queen's Ware, China that he had imported on the *Maria* from Belfast.[294]

Finally, at 8:00 in the evening, William and his fellow seamen finish unloading the *Ino.* They admire, for a short moment, the mountain of 430 barrels they have created in front of William Hemphill's wharf, before they separate and hurry home.

William carries his sea chest home, walking along the now silent Second Street. John Freed, Jr. is eating with his family this evening so the apartment is empty when William arrives. John Freed, Sr., the father of William's roommate, is a laborer working mostly at the Wilmington port, like many other hard working people living on Second Street. The apartment is cold, damp and sparsely furnished, and looks in every way like a traditional bachelor seamen's flat. William removes his dirty, wet shirt and carefully washes his face and body with a mixture of soap and cold water, standing in front of the basin placed on the living room bureau. He hurries to change his clothes and jumps down the stairs to go to Mary Ann's home.

When Mary Ann introduced William to her mother for the first time, shortly before he went to sea with the *Ino,* they had very little time to get to know each other, but it became quite clear to him that he was welcome in their home. Mary Ann's mother seemed happy to be able to increase the size of her small family and after William had met her a couple of times, she treated him like a son.[12]

When William arrives outside the apartment of Mary Ann's mother at 68 E. Water Street, he can smell roast chicken. After so many months at sea, William has completely forgotten the last time he ate chicken, one of his favorite dinners.

Mary Ann, hearing the steps, opens the door before William can reach to knock on it. She smiles to him with an expression of knowing and kisses him for the first time since his return to Wilmington.

It is so much pleasure to be with her, William thinks. He likes her ability to surprise him time and time again, her mystery. Almost physically wrapped around her body, William closes the door behind him. William is definitely in love with Mary Ann, no question about it, and if you asked his friends, Joseph Warner, Jr., Damian Starr, Enoch Lang or John Freed, Jr.,[12], William lost his senses when he first set eyes on Mary Ann. Having seen many different hydrodynamic well-shaped boats and ships named for wives and girl friends in the Wilmington wharfs or along the Christina River quay, William knows his geometrical preferences, and Mary Ann does not disappoint. His friends think William smiles and laughs too much now, sometimes uncontrollably, when they spend time with him. It's kind of disgusting. Now they have a hard time making long concentrated theoretical conversations with him, like they loved so much, and often used to do earlier on.

They aren't completely wrong about William's mental change. He does have a hard time controlling his feelings and thoughts these days, to an extent that it even annoys him. William likes his thoughts to be proper, continuous and sequential, and his mind to operate one topic at a time. But these days, he finds himself in peculiar situations, suddenly thinking of Mary Ann right in the middle of some other important thought-process. It is very disturbing to him, and a quite inefficient way to process thoughts, but he can do nothing to help it at all. It's simply beyond his mental control. Luckily William has a unique ability to calm himself down when he gets too disturbed by these random thoughts of Mary Ann, by thinking of the rational argument that infatuation is seldom known to last long compared to the total lifespan a young ambitious seaman like William has available for complicated logical and philosophical thinking.

I'll visit the Warner' s tomorrow, William thinks, as Mary Ann's mother asks them to sit down at the table and wait for the dinner to be ready. The Warner family has made it a tradition for William to come to their house as soon as possible after he has returned to Wilmington from a longer sea trip. That might be a problem now that he has met Mary Ann, but William will do what he can to keep his promise to the Warners as always. As they now sit and wait for dinner to be ready, William and Mary Ann hold each other's hands and study each other's faces without talking. In a moment like this it is as though they both still can't believe that they have had the luck to meet each other.

William remembers how lucky he was to find the apartment on 33 East Second Street. It is very close to the harbor and many families of the port workers, seamen and captains found it convenient to live on this area. Frankly, the area between Second Street and the Christina River is not a healthy place to live. In the spring and in the autumn, when heavy rain can last for several days, the Christina River rises and prevents the rainwater from draining from Second, Front and Water Street. The cellars of the houses slowly fill with water, and this stagnant water is an ideal place for mosquitoes to breed in large numbers, which can spread yellow fever in the apartments above.[196] The mosquitoes bite people in their sleep at night and are almost inactive in the daylight hours, as though they are aware that if they cause too much irritation, humans will take action to eliminate them. Then when darkness arrives and people go to sleep, the mosquitoes "seize the night" and attack the defenseless sleeping inhabitants.

Nobody in the borough of Wilmington, or for that matter the whole known world, knows the connection between the mosquitoes and the yellow fever yet. Not even after the terrible loss of lives 13 years ago when 20 % of the boroughs population had died, in the autumn of 1792, in the mosquito-season, had any doctor at the Wilmington Borough

Hospital assumed any connection. The losses in all of Wilmington had been highest on Second Street. Overnight, whole families passed away and were quickly taken to the cemeteries and buried after quick and simple ceremonies.

Mary Ann, her mother and William sit at the table to have their dinner. On the dish in front of them is a large delicious roasted chicken from John Warner's hen house, right next to his wharf. William says grace and they begin eating. William asks what has happened in Wilmington since he left in the spring and Mary Ann's mother looks at her daughter, as she tries to think of special events that might have caught her attention. Mary Ann shakes her head, so William begins to talk. He has been eager to share some of the knowledge he has collected from reading all the old newspapers on the voyage from New York to Wilmington.

Mary Ann looks admiringly at William as with expressive eyes he tells stories he has read, like the one about the excellent accommodations of seamen in Copenhagen. Mary Ann thinks how happy she is, that William seems to be so different from boys she has met earlier. 'Did you know," William continues, 'that the West Indian Islands are very important to any country with colonies there, because the huge trade taking place between Europe and North America passes through this region? In the last quarter of 1799, when George Washington died, American export through the West Indies grew enormously: the Dutch West Indies, Danish West Indies, Spanish West-Indies, French West Indies, and Swedish West Indies, all of them. The port of Altona is the largest American export port in Europe including Bremen.[238]

'It is quite evident," William concludes, 'that the neutral countries, in Europe, are gaining most in their trade in this time of war. With the U.S.A., being neutral like Denmark, I'm sure that William and James Hemphill, John Warner and Samuel Bush and other Wilmington ship-owners are profiting heavily from this war between France and England." Looking around the table William finally realizes that Mary Ann and her mother are tired. He stops talking and begins to eat the delicious food on his plate, which is almost cold. Silence enters the room.

2

The British Commander-in Chief of the West Indian Fleet until 1800 was Admiral Sir Hyde Parker. The Royal Navy's West Indian fleet had its headquarters on the island of Jamaica, in the port city of Kingston in Port Royal. His authority was final on all general policies affecting the impressment of the American seamen in this region of the world and he was known to be a hard liner.[271] In 1799, Parker informed William Savage, the American Agent for seamen in the West Indies, who also had his office in Port Royal, that the only grounds on which he would release American seamen was by executive application through the British Minister to the United States, who lived in Philadelphia, 1,200 miles away, and that the applications had to be accompanied by proof that the seamen were natural born citizens of the United States of America. Slow communications meant that it could take years for an American seaman to be released from imprisonment in Port Royal. William Savage was one of only two American Agents for seamen in the entire world. Admiral Seymour replaced Admiral Parker in office in Port Royal, and has a more liberal policy when it comes to releasing American seamen.

It is now October 21, and the Boston schooner carrying John Brown is cruising southward along the coast of Spanish Florida. Farther north, and on the other side of the Atlantic Ocean, a large sea battle is taking place between the British and French Fleets in the Bay of Trafalgar, on the south coast of Spain. The French fleet was finally lured out of the harbor of Cadiz after returning from the West Indies.

From his flagship *HMS Victory,* Admiral of the Blue Lord Nelson controls the battle. *HMS Defence* has a crew of 525 men, including six Americans forced off American merchant ships and ordered to serve in the Royal Navy. The Royal Navy wins the battle, but Lord Nelson loses his life.

Several days later, the American schooner passes the British St. Luke's Islands [299] (the Bahamas) northeast of Cuba and northwest of Haiti. The wind is from the northwest. Single cumulus clouds in their characteristic cauliflower shapes are passing the firmament, but the air is crystal clear. Although they are on a dangerous merchant trip delivering arms and ammunition to the Frenchmen, John Brown, the captain, and other seamen and officers have no doubt that they are doing the right thing. They have not forgotten the help North America received from France early in the Revolutionary War, when it mattered most. They are just helping their French friends keep their West Indian colonies from the hands of the British. Being well paid doesn't hurt either, the captain thinks to himself.

A 140-foot frigate belonging to the Royal Navy's West Indian Fleet is patrolling these waters regularly to inspect passing ships. The frigate belongs to a small fleet under the command of Rear Admiral Dacres, who has hoisted his flag onboard a second-rater with 98 cannons, three decks and 760 men, the *HMS Hercule,* which has a temporary homeport in Port Royal. *Hercule* was won from the French Fleet in battle.

The lookout on the frigate sees the approaching American schooner and he shouts, "An American schooner, an American schooner!" The captain orders a change in course toward the schooner to make an inspection of the cargo and the ship's papers. The lookout climbs down from the main mast and is relieved of his post as a reward for spotting the foreign ship.[211] Almost at the same time, those on the Boston schooner see the British frigate approaching, and react anxiously. All ships sailing between eastern American ports and the West Indian Islands are manned with mariners to protect the ship, crew and cargo against piracy or attack from ships belonging to belligerent nations in the area. Conditions on ships from Philadelphia and Wilmington are no different. But what is different is that, because this Boston schooner is transporting weapons and ammunition, all the ordinary and able seamen are trained to use guns.

The captain of the Boston schooner briefly considers giving the order to set full sail to escape the approaching British frigate, but he comes to his senses. He knows that captains of British frigates are apt to react violently to any escape attempt when an inspection is going to take place. The much faster frigate will catch up with the schooner sooner or later on the open sea, with no islands to hide behind. The British captain orders a cannon fired at the starboard side, and John Brown watches smoke silently leave the cannon and the front porthole on the frigate. Seconds later, a cannonball hits a wave in front of the schooner, then a loud bang reaches his ears. The captain of the schooner orders it to stop. Fifteen minutes later, the frigate reaches the portside of the American schooner and the darkening shadows of the frigate's sails crawl onto the schooner.

Brown clearly sees the faces of the captain and officers on the quarterdeck. He also notices the cannon crew of six seamen standing around each of three starboard side cannons on the quarterdeck. Their upper bodies are naked and some have tied red scarves around their hair. Brown also counts 13 cannons on the lower deck at starboard side, 16 total.

The captain, two officers and seamen on the schooner stand along the railing on the port side, awaiting their new destiny. The superior force in front of them is too large to ignore, and they show every sign of not wanting to take up the fight. Brown is terrified.

Seamen on the British frigate lower a jollyboat and five seamen, five mariners and two officers head toward the schooner, 'Heave, heave' sounding rhythmical on the sea surface. An officer and the mariners enter the schooner with an air of superiority, clearly masters of the situation. While the commanding officer reviews the ship's papers and speaks to the American captain, the mariners are directed into the hold to investigate the cargo. In only a few minutes a mariner returns to the deck with a clear proof of enemy goods.

The British officer laughs as he looks through the papers, with Dutch St. Eustatia Island as the ship's destination, then throws them into the sea. Everyone hears the outcry from the mariners in the hold, when they find the weapons. The British officer gives the order, 'Press the crew and destroy this prize." He is sure they are all Americans, but has no regrets about taking the crew, even though many of them will not see their families for years, may even be the head of household and a family's sole support. He cares only for his orders. He even knows that some of them will never return. But he has taken the position, along with many officers in the Royal Navy, that these American seamen are the same as Irish and Welsh renegades who, when England is in danger, refuse to take her side against France. Even worse, they have taken over British trade with other countries friendly to France. Although there are severe punishments for not following orders in the Royal Navy, on the open sea, a captain of a frigate, as the highest-ranking officer, can interpret the rules. He can, if he wishes, set Americans with proper papers free[268] but this seldom happens in times of war.

The captain of the Boston schooner is part owner of the ship. He knows that transporting ammunition to England's enemy, France, makes seizure of this ship legal in any British court, but he feels a need to protest somehow. Although he cares little for his seamen, he uses them as a starting point for a discussion with the officer. "Sir," he begins, "You are by no means entitled to take these American seamen and impress them. They are not British."

"Ha, ha, very funny, very funny indeed" the British officer roars. "They do speak the English language quite well, don't they?" The American captain does not reply; he finds the question childish and ridiculous. "Anyway," the British officer goes on, "I have a full right to take any person into British military service who is helping an enemy of England. I do fully encounter this crew so busily occupied with supplying France."

Encouraged by the attitude of their captain and the seriousness of the situation, John Brown asks his captain's permission to show his customhouse Protection Certificate, signed by the port collector in Boston, a handwritten document that proves his American birth and origin and contains a description of his eye and hair colors, and special marks like scars on his body. The Protection Certificate was introduced by the American Department of State to protect American seamen from forced service on British warships.

The American captain nods. All five seamen hand over the certificates they had hidden in their chest pockets for just such a situation. The British officer gives them a glance and notes the seal with the American Bald Eagle used on official American papers. But he tears the certificates apart, shouting, "Any British seaman can buy as many customhouse Protection Certificates as he likes for five pence in New York, Boston or Philadelphia or any other American east coast port." The commanding officer nods his head and the mariner forces John Brown, the other American seamen and two officers onboard the jollyboat.

The British captain is partially right. Serving-conditions on British war ships, or man-o-wars as the seamen call them, are so tough that many British seamen flee when they get the slightest chance at American and English ports. They often take jobs on American merchant ships, which pay five times as much salary as the British Navy.

These English seamen can then buy a false American customhouse Protection Certificate, making it almost impossible for any captain on a

British frigate to prove the seaman's original English nationality. For certificates issued in the late 1700s, the formality was small. An American seaman could get a false certificate issued for an English seaman who worked in the American merchant fleet and even earn some money by handling that transaction. For example, in Philadelphia, an American seamen who could prove he was born in the city might be a witness at the port collector's office and swear that an English seaman who had followed him to the office was his friend, and also born in this city. The port collector would issue a certificate to the English seaman. British captains know this all too well.

The captain of the British frigate is, according to British Laws, laws recognized by the government of the United States of America, in his rights to board and visit any ship in the waters close to the shores of e.g. the British Isles of St. Luke' s. The captain may search for contraband goods encumbered with import or export restrictions, enemy goods, persons in military service of the enemy, and British seamen on American merchant vessels. The captain of the British frigate has also been instructed to impress as many foreign seamen as possible, because of the need for seamen in these times of war with France.

These instructions to impress seamen are issued by the Admiralty Office in London from time to time. Instructions were sent out recently to cover the loss of seamen in the battle between the British and French fleets in the Bay of Trafalgar. The usual procedure for ordering impressments consists first of an order in council, which authorizes the Lord High Admiral or the First Admiral to institute impressments proceedings. Such authorizations may be limited and specific, applying only to certain commands, ships or part of the sea. Or they may apply to the entire navy. The Admiralty issues press-warrants to the officers of the navy based on the order from the council.[267]

The British do not cheerfully submit to the practice, and it is especially hated by the lower classes in England. First of all, it is humiliating, because the Navy forces men to serve without any consideration to their private situations. Press-gangs will for example, arrest wildly protesting fathers, who may have a sick wife and 12 children to take care of at home, but happened to walk the streets when a press-gang passed. A son who is the only supporter of his mother might be arrested and put on a man-o-war, without the mother ever knowing what happened to her son. When press-warrant officers and mariners are busy impressing on the city streets or in pubs, it is common to see groups of wives, mothers, and girlfriends screaming and beating up the mariners and officers to stop them.

A frigate is classified in the Royal Navy as a fifth-rater and, in contrast to ships with higher ranks like the first- rater *HMS Victory*, the crew eagerly volunteers when a frigate is mustered. The expectation of seizing hundreds of foreign ships and collecting prize money drives English and even foreign seamen to serve on these frigates. Morality and ethics are not their guiding principles.

Heading back to the frigate in the jollyboat, John Brown throws a glance back over his left shoulder and sees that the Boston schooner is on fire. Although his situation is grave, Brown feels a strange kind of warmth toward his captain. He can see through the false defense his captain made on their behalf, earlier on, but he knows the captain had not expected this situation, because he paid the American seamen a couple of days ago. American captains have been known to turn over to British captains seamen they consider troublemakers. These seamen are sometimes owed 20 to 24 months of wages. This is a money-saving trick for unscrupulous ship-owners and captains, because it can take years for such seamen to return home and testify[270] against the wrongdoing, if they ever manage to return. The burning Boston schooner proves quite clearly to Brown that all Americans are in it together.

On the British frigate, the five seamen are instantly put in irons. The captain and officers are taken into the officer's resting room. The seamen are told to be quiet. John Brown sits down and notices that frigate is headed southwest. John Pristoff, an experienced or able seaman, is the oldest of the Americans, 30 years old. He has been impressed before and knows what lies ahead. He hates the Royal Navy for its brutal discipline, miserable food and sleeping quarters, and above all, the almost constant risk of danger. But he keeps it to himself. The others will learn soon enough.

Timothy Clark, 27, and William King, 23, begin to talk quietly, but immediately a marine soldier in a classical red suit knocks Clark hard on the left side of his head with a gun and shouts, 'Qui et!' Timothy's vision disappears in a second or two and then he faints. The soldier posts himself beside the American seamen the rest of the afternoon to make sure they make no more trouble. Brown watches the gunner seamen, posted eight around each cannon on the front deck, or the forecastle. The sun is steadily baking their dark brown bodies but the sea breeze helps them keep a comfortable temperature.

After nothing happens for a while, the soldier stops paying close attention to the American seamen. Pristoff looks at the others and whispers, 'They are always rough to impressed Americans, because we are known to protest violently to this kind of unfair treatment. Keep a low profile, don't annoy the soldiers too much, and you will not be punished." The other four nod their heads, glad that Pristoff is with them. 'They will try to keep us together as a group, so just do as I tell you, and you will be better off. Take a look at the quarter deck. See the captain? On his left are two midshipmen carrying messages for the captain. On his right are a master and the two master mates, and at the steering wheel are two quartermates.[213] Never enter the quarterdeck if you are not specifically told to do so, or you will be severely punished." Pristoff lowers his voice as the marine soldier, who has started to walk back and forth, passes them, "All men onboard are keeping watches. In general there is a starboard and a larboard watch for every man working there. A normal watch lasts four hours, except for the two dog-hour watches between 4:00 and 8:00 in the evening. All in all, there are seven watches each day."[212] As Pristoff stops speaking, the petty officer at the steering wheel turns his half-hour sandglass indicating 4 p.m., and rings the ship's bell. At the eighth bell, the crew changes watch for the dog hours. The seamen come down from the rigging aloft.

At 6 p.m., the boatswain's pipe shrills and the marine soldier comes and unchains them. They are taken down to the lower deck where seamen are sitting in groups of 10 on benches among the cannons, at tabletops hanging from the loft. The frigate crew is busy eating and no one pays them any attention. The Americans are taken to an empty table.

It is a Monday, October 21, 1805, and the food served follows the standard weekly food ration for Monday's evening meal issued by the Victualling Board – a half gallon of beer, half pound of bread with two ounces of butter, which sometimes turns rancid in the heat, four ounces of cheese and one pound of oatmeal. The Americans are put on half-rations, because they had not been working all day.

When a seaman rises from his seat to enter the kitchen with a tray, he stares at the strangers onboard. John Brown is asked to pick up a tray and follow the marine soldier to the kitchen.

The American seamen are hungry and as they eat, they look at each other, satisfied. They are not used to being served this quantity of food, so they conclude that the situation is not too dark after all. Once they have eaten, they are each given a hammock by the mariner, and they see that some of the seamen have already put their hammocks in position on hooks in the ceiling. John Brown puts his hammock up too, but it takes him several tries to get into it. He rolls around several times and ends up on the floor, and the other seamen laugh heartily.

At 8 p.m. the ship's bell rings. This is the watch numbered one and after the change of watch, a master mate checks that the lights are out on the lower decks. The hammocks creak rhythmically as the ship rolls in the night. None of the American seamen gets any sleep. Tim is most concerned of all. He has heard of people impressed for several years. Discreetly, the Americans follow the shift of the night watch at midnight as they are still awake.[212]

At four a.m. a shriek of the boatswain's pipe sounds. The boatswain's mate walks through the lower deck and cries, "All hands!" John Brown sees a couple of seamen, who do not tumble out of the hammocks at once, immediately dumped onto the deck, screaming. After they dress, Brown and the other Americans carefully study how the British seaman next to them lashes his hammock, looping the ropes seven times around the heavy canvas. The boatswain's mate checks that everyone is doing it properly. Their hammocks are stowed in special netting along the upper deck's bulwarks to give them some protection against smaller bullets and fragments in battle. After leaving the hammocks in the netting, the five Americans are ordered to work washing down the decks and scraping them smooth of splinters with the holystones, which they know all too well from American merchant ships. Sand is sprinkled in the water on the deck to increase the efficiency of the scraping.

John Brown carefully rolls up the legs on his trousers to protect them from being destroyed too quickly, and the sand on the deck begins to hurt his skin.

At 6 a.m. the boatswain's pipe shrills again and the men take their first meal of the day. They are having ' burgoo,' gruel of water and oatmeal washed down with Scotch coffee, a bitter concoction made of burned biscuits dissolved in hot water[167]. Brown notices again the large quantity of food, and is glad that he feels full after the meal. He has no wife or children back home, so looks on his situation with only mild concern. So far the Royal Navy does not seem as bad as he has heard in the taverns back home.

He wonders why the Americans are off duty more than the British seamen. Pristoff doesn't like sailing through St. Luke's Islands. It is a dangerous place. There are thousands of small islands and hidden reefs in this region and maps are very poor. At noon they take a local pilot onboard, but he seems useless.

After a couple of days, they enter the Windward Channel between Cuba and Haiti. Pristoff is now sure they are on their way to Port Royal in Kingston of Jamaica, the British headquarters in the West Indies.

On Friday November 1, 1805, Pristoff's assumption proves right. The frigate enters Port Royal in very fine weather.[3, 69]

After the frigate is moored, the five Americans are ordered to a jollyboat, which heads toward a huge ship of the line moored on the opposite side of the harbor. As the jollyboat approaches the ship, Brown reads the golden letters written on the rear gallery: *Hercule*. That's a French name, John realizes, then remembers that the Royal Navy has taken a lot of French prizes. This ship might be one of them. Pristoff notices that a Rear Admirals flag has been hoisted onboard.[69] The *Hercule* arrived just the day before, after the dangerous hurricane season ended.

The jollyboat approaches the gangway, entering the long shadow along the port side of the ship. The American seamen are amazed. They have only seen a ship of this size from a distance. Its side rises up from the water's surface, giving meaning to the phrase for Royal Navy ships 'the wooden walls of England." The sight frightens them. All 49 cannon portholes on the port side are opened, but only the cannons on the lower deck are visible.

The five Americans are ordered to climb the gangway to the upper deck. John Brown gets dizzy when he climbs. The bulwark on the upper deck is 24 feet above sea level. John has hardly ever been so high, not even climbing the rigging on American schooners. On the top deck they are ordered by a marine soldier to form a straight line near the main mast. An officer sitting at a table calls them forward one by one. William King is the first to be called. 'Name," the officer shouts, and William King gives his name. "Are you willing to serve in His Majesty's Royal Navy and get the good bounty of one pound?" the officer asks, trying to cheat and flatter him at the same time.

Pristoff had instructed them all not to take the bounty. Receiving the bounty is legally seen as having entered a man-o-war voluntarily, both by the British and the American authorities, meaning that such a seaman can never be discharged unless the Royal Navy officers agrees, which never happens in times of war. "I'm not taking the bounty ," King answers firmly. "You will have the number 1,508 then," the officer commands. Pristoff knows that a second-rater with 98 cannons and 3 decks can have a maximum permanent crew of 760. Any number higher than 1,000 is termed super numerous, and a seaman or mariner with such a high number will not be among the regular staff, but given hard, dangerous, unhealthy or dirty work that no one will do voluntarily. Pristoff decides to keep quiet about this knowledge. No reason to worry the others. The officer already knows they are Americans, and writes this in the column headed 'Place and County Where Born". Then the officer asks "Your age?" "Twenty -three", King answers. "How long have you been a seaman?" "Three years," King answers, and the officer writes 'Ord" in the Qualities column, for 'ordinary seaman." Brown is given the number 1,509. His ten years of experience makes him an "able seaman."

The American seamen are put on a special prison ship anchored just outside Port Royal. These prison ships are mostly discharged second-rate ships of the line, stripped of everything of value. These prison ships are painted black and crossbars placed in every cannon porthole. The ships prepared for officers have been rebuilt with small, individual cabins. An officer is considered a gentleman, and gives his word of honor that he will not escape, so is usually placed in an open and more comfortable prison on shore in Kingston. But the captain and officers from the Boston schooner, as with most American officers, will not give their word of honor to a British officer simply to improve their conditions. So they are taken out to live under reasonable conditions on one of the prison ships, which are anchored with a cable 200 yards between one another in a line, as though lined up for battle. Each is placed in a room with a table and a chair. The separate rooms are painted and have a small window or a porthole to look out of. The captain is allowed to write letters and communicate with whomever he likes. But imprisonment makes it difficult for the captain to file a complaint over the impressments of his crew to the British and American authorities in the area, as he is committed to doing according to American Law. He will be fined $100 if he does not do so.[269] But, like with most captains, he will not do it anyway.

The proper American authority to contact in the West Indian Islands is the Agent for Seamen, stationed right here in Kingston town. His name is William Savage[273] and he was born in England. If you ask American seamen onboard these prison ships in Port Royal, men who refuse to serve onboard British war ships and imprisoned in the unbearable heat and stench, you will not hear that he is doing a fine job.[176] Since Seymour replaced Parker and became head of the British West Indian Headquarters five years ago, the communication route between impressed seamen on prison ships and the British authorities has been reduced considerably. It is no longer necessary to send an application for release with proof of one's American origin through the Agent for Seamen, who then sends it to the British Minister to the United States in Washington D.C. Now, theoretically, impressed American seaman in Port Royal can write the local Agent, right here in Kingston, who then can communicate and sort out the problem with local British Rear Admiral Dacres onboard his flagship *Hercule*.

John Brown asks an elder seamen, who has been onboard the flagship several years, what can be done to escape. He tells the seaman about his customhouse protection, which was destroyed by the officer on the British frigate. The elder seaman nods his head and smiles. 'This is a common experience, and the British officer's usual procedure. They do not recognize these handwritten certificates. Write your family and ask them to take a document that proves who you are to a justice of the peace, who will fill out a printed certificate with a seal of the American Bald Eagle and send it to you. This can take a long time, years, if you are unlucky. After you receive it, you hand the certificate over to the American Agent here in Kingston, when he comes alongside the ship. He should present it to the British Admiral onboard this ship and again, if you are lucky, you will be released. But don't be too optimistic. When your certificate arrives, you might be somewhere else in the world or onboard a ship with another name, making you almost impossible to trace, especially with such a common name as John Brown! And," he looked John Brown straight in the eyes, "even if your certificate somehow gets to the ship you're on, because of that common name of yours, they might compare it to another man with your name and write back to the American authority, 'Sorry, release has been denied, because the subject onboard does not fit the description." The easiest way out of here is to escape. But when the *Hercule* is in harbor, we are guarded every second, and when we are at sea, it is virtually impossible. But look on the bright side. Here on a prison ship outside Kingston, there are no women to disturb us and make us miserable. No woman, no cry. This remote area is no place for a fine women, and you would never imagine one of the beautiful princesses paying it a visit."

When Brown, who has no experience with long-term imprisonment, hears that he will not be free anytime soon, he feels panic, but is man enough not to let it show. To hide his feelings, he laughs and says, 'No, Port Royal is no place for a pretty English princess. But maybe a handsome, intelligent and adventurous crown prince might pay a visit. Any English prince would be more than welcome to pay a visit to Boston or Salem, where I come from. But it is probably as unlikely for a member of the English Royal family to come here as it would be for the French Emperor and his beautiful wife to go to Fort-de-France, Martinique, where I was heading when I was impressed."

John writes to his mother, asking her to go to the Justice of the Peace in Salem. But now he knows that she doesn't have his birth certificate or any papers that identify him. He spends several hours planning to escape[3] with John Pristoff, while *Hercule* remains anchored in Port Royal. But the impressed Americans are never allowed off the ship, and swimming to shore is out of the question, because, like most seamen, none of them know how to swim. The attitude is that swimming will only prolong suffering if a man is unlucky enough to be on a sinking ship. Besides, the anchor chain guard will surely see them, and he will not hesitate to shoot.

The other American Agent for Seamen is stationed in London, in England.[272] Appointed this year, he is former Brigadier General William Lyman, 50 and born in Northampton, Massachusetts in 1755. He graduated from Yale in 1776, served in the Revolutionary War as Major, was a member of the Massachusetts Senate in 1789, and a member of the Third Congress as a Democrat and the Fourth Congress as a Republican from 1793 to 1797.

Lyman replaced Erving, the former American Agent for Seamen. Erving was known to be a conscientious, hardworking ambassador for the impressed seamen who kept accurate records of the impressed seamen who wrote him letters, letters written to him by the American captains, or consular dispatches received from the Department of State.

Driven by strong indignation to unjust behavior toward impressed American seamen, he worked long hours on detailed and correct records. The Department of State was very pleased with Erving' s work, but had other plans for him and replaced him with the very popular Massachusetts General William Lyman.

The first month and a half that John Brown and the other American seamen are onboard *HMS Hercule*, the ship remains moored in the Harbor of Port Royal. Not much happens in the American seamen's lives. Life consists mostly of the same boring routine from morning to night. In addition, it can be humid and hot in Port Royal. British officers and seamen are frequently given shore leave, and Kingston offers many taverns where they can spend their time.

John Brown and the others from the Boston schooner are never given shore leave, though. If for some reason they are taken to shore, they are escorted by marine soldiers and never let out of sight. The Americans are not trusted at all. Local merchants and women are on occasion allowed onboard the *Hercule* to offer their services and give the seamen a chance to spend some of their savings, but most of the time, they crawl through the same routines day after day.

When they are not actually eating during the given hours, they are only allowed to wash the decks, their hammocks or their clothes. One afternoon John Brown stands at the larboard railing on the upper deck, watching the sunset and the life at the Kingston water line of Port Royal, so close by. He feels a deep emptiness inside, realizing his youth is being wasted. To an elder seaman who often stands next to him, he says with longing, 'My God, how I would give my right arm to be off this ship and on the shore right now."

"You want to be off this ship n ow, you say?" the old seaman replies, shaking his head. 'My young man, there will soon come a time where you would die to be off a Royal Navy ship." At John Brown's frightened face, the old seaman laughs. Then he looks John Brown straight in the eyes. 'The re is a nice atmosphere now, but wait until you find yourself at sea for months in e.g. cold Nordic water. The mild climate and the beautiful environment make everybody relax here in Port Royal. The fact that the officers can get new impressions onshore, and get away from each other and the seamen, reduces tensions. This can be seen from the fact that there have been very few punishments." Brown nods and the two of them quietly observe the harbor front.

Wednesday, November 6, John Brown and William King pull up a bucket of water from the sea to wash the upper deck. They see the frigate *HMS Penguin* arriving with the surviving officers and men from the *Aquixo*, which was set on fire. As the newcomers board *Hercule,* the priest is performing a Divine Service.

The Divine Service each Sunday at 10 has become a fixed point in the lives of the five impressed Americans from the Boston schooner. John Brown loves to sing and has a trained and beautiful voice. The prayers and psalms sung are almost identical to those heard in English and American churches, so at the Sunday Divine Service, it is natural for their thoughts to turn to home and their loved ones. The following Sunday, John Brown gets tears in his eyes imagining his mother sitting alone at her usual place in the Salem Presbyterian Church.

November 15 John Brown has been onboard *Hercule* for a fortnight. He watches the arrival of the flagship *HMS Malaba* arriving from England with a convoy of merchant ships. But not much happens these days, except routine work. The seamen are getting visibly bored with the daily routine work, and some of them try to compensate by saving the grog, rum with water, they are served after the hot noon meal, and rum bought in Kingston, where rum is produced. Large quantities are taken on board ships that enter the port here. Seamen onboard the *Hercule* save the rum for when they play cards.

On Friday, November 29, some of the off-duty seamen[69] gather in quiet parts of the lower decks where the marine soldiers seldom come and start playing cards, although it is strictly forbidden. Rum soon accompanies the card playing, and soon the atmosphere is as high as in a Portsmouth tavern full of seamen on Christmas leave from the Baltic Fleet. They are enjoying themselves to the fullest, happy to be relaxing and laughing. Time passes very quickly and suddenly some of them remember, or are reminded by their friends, what time it is, as the 4 p.m. first watch bell sounds. They have to be on duty, but they are too drunk to work and the officers notice it right away. The captain is immediately informed.

These seamen do not sleep at all that night and none of them eat the next morning, lacking an appetite. The crew gathers at the main mast for the punishment, and as 11 o'clock approaches, small talk ceases. The seamen's thoughts are elsewhere.

The petty officer turns his half-hour sandglass and the shriek of the boatswain's pipe goes through the bones of every seaman onboard. A roll of drums summons all hands to the top gun deck. The sound of the drums is frightening. On the quarterdeck and the maindeck, the officers stand on elevated places in formal dress and swords. William King, John Pristoff, and John Brown stand close to the main mast, because they arrived early and have been pushed there by the rest of the arriving crew.

Before them stands the Master-at-arms, several sturdy boatswains mates and, guarded by a pair of quartermasters, the first of the seamen to be punished this morning. 'Do you have anything to s ay?" the captain asks, but the man keeps quiet. 'Strip," the captain orders. The seaman slowly removes his shirt. 'Tie him up!" the captain commands. The quartermasters tie the seaman's hands to a pair of gratings. 'Seized up, Sir!" the quartermasters repo rt back a few minutes later. The captain then reads the appropriate passage in the Articles of War and the seaman hears that none of the eight articles that result in the death penalty has been violated. He is to be punished for drunkenness. The captain closes the book and turns to the boatswain's mate. 'Do your duty!" he orders.

The mate pulls out the knotted cat-o-nine-tails, draws it back and lays on the first stroke with all his strength, grunting from the effort. The crack of the whip reaches John Brown and the other American's ears and their faces twist with revulsion. The blow leaves a pattern of livid red welts along the man's back. His face turns red, but no sound comes from his lips. All the seamen onboard are tense, and the officers watch them closely. The next two lashes cut more deeply, and as the fourth lash lands, the seaman screams so loudly that the sound can be heard on the harbor front. Brown is quite upset. He has never seen anything like this in his entire life. How could any human being, even an officer, order such a cruel punishment? Of course, the seaman was drinking and playing cards without permission, but the punishment is way out of proportion to the crime. John wants to protest, but he keeps silent, as does the rest of the crew.

The lashes turn the seaman's flesh into a bloody, dripping mass. Between strokes, the mate runs the cat's tails between his fingers to clear away the blood, which he flicks onto the deck. Those closest to the gruesome scene have disgust all over their faces, which they try, unsuccessfully, to hide.

As the 12th stroke is reached, the mate is replaced with a fresh new mate with intact strength and the punishment can continue. The 2nd mate is released at the 24th stroke and the 3rd mate finishes the 36 lashes ordered. But at the last 12 lashes, there is no sound coming from the seaman. His head, with eyes closed, is now hanging limp from his shoulder, and it only moves rhythmically as he is hit.

A strong feeling of injustice spreads through the several hundred seamen packed shoulder to shoulder on the top deck. The officers standing on their elevated posts surrounded by marine soldiers strengthen their body position, making it clear that any reaction will be firmly suppressed. Royal Navy officers know all too well that mutiny can happen in situations like this.

The horrible scene he has just witnessed changes something in young John Brown and the other young American seamen. After this day, they will not see the world with quite the same openness and innocence. The natural human instinct that tells them all human beings in positions of power will be just, as they were taught by their parents, has been damaged forever.

The daily routines continue. Decks are washed, over and over again, sprinkled with sand and scrubbed with holystones. Sails are unbent over and over again in an attempt to let them dry so the salt water will not destroy them. Sails are expensive and must be treated well.

On December 5, a seaman is climbing the mainmast and busy unfolding the topgallant sail when his foot slips from the yard cable. He falls 35 yards to the surface of the deck. The experienced seamen onboard recognize the sound of bones crashing into the oak planks and don't have to turn to see what has h appened. Fortunately for the seaman, his head hit the deck first and he was instantly killed. And luckily for the rest of the crew, he did not hit anyone else on his way down. Brown is shocked. On the smaller ships of the American merchant fleet, it is not a common event for a seaman to be killed falling from a mast.

On December 16, *HMS Hercule* makes preparations to leave Port Royal. A fresh breeze is blowing and clouds move on the nearly clear sky above. Fresh beef is taken onboard along with water from the large water tank in Kingston harbor. Other food supplies are also taken in large quantities. The crew is impatient to get out on the open sea after the long stop in Port Royal and they are glad when the captain finally gives the order to pull up the main anchor, set the sails and leave port. John Brown and the other American seamen are amazed to see the crew of about 600 men in busy activity[69] at the same time.

Mariners and seamen gather around the capstan on the second gun deck to help pull in the heavy anchor. On the order "set sail," Brown hears shouts and sees more than a hundred seamen simultaneously climb or run up the cordage connected to the three masts. On the decks, seamen pull ropes to heave the sails. Although he is a bright guy, John has not yet figured out the details of how this mighty ship is organized, but he watches carefully, determined that one day he will know. It has taken a master's mate years to learn, but Brown is convinced he will pick up in a few months.

Eight days later, two days before Christmas Eve, another man falls from the main mast and dies. It is the thankless job of one of the sail maker's mates to sew his earthly remains into a bag made of old canvas, with two cannon balls at his feet. A short Divine Service is held on the top deck at the main mast and the body is buried at sea.

On Christmas Eve, the crew is longing for home and their families. They are served an extra portion of rum. The captain knows that small gestures like this get the seamen's attention. It makes them think that the captain is not so bad after all. Instead, they will direct their dissatisfaction toward the rather ignorant officers who make their lives a living hell.

Though many seamen onboard *Hercule* are experienced seamen who have sailed under many different conditions for many years, they still find it strange to go out on a deck wearing only a light shirt and feeling the warm air on Christmas Evening. John Pristoff and John Brown have a problem despite the nice weather. They have spent most Christmases with their families in Boston and Salem. Brown is worried about his mother, but he knows she will not worry when he has not returned from the West Indies before Christmas, because she does not expect him to be home sometime before the early spring.

The officers dress and dine with the captain this evening in his cabin, doing their best to have a good evening to distract them from their longing for home. They dine with a white cloth on the table and make many toasts, drinking bottle after bottle of red wine or port wine out of crystal glasses, as they do back home in England at Christmas. They discuss wine, the art of warfare, poetry, and navigation – any interesting topic that comes up. Through an open window in the gallery, their toasts and laughter travel into the tropical night and are heard by the marine soldiers and seamen in their hammocks on the lower decks, the guards posted on the ship, and people who promenade along the quay in Port Royal.

In Wilmington, the last week's traditional Christmas preparations have come to an end. It has been a busy December in the borough. Since the turn of the century, a spirit of progress has come to Wilmington, and the local economy has increased each year. The large production of wheat, especially from northern Delaware farms in New Castle County, increased the production of fine flour from the Brandywine Mills. Overseas trade had increased, so the mill, ship and shop owners in Wilmington looked with optimism on the future.

The shops on Market Street, in the Market House on High Street, and in the lower Market House on Second Street have been filled with quality merchandise from Europe even more than normal, because a large number of Wilmington ships went there this year, and demand was equally high. Stores at the wharves saw increased sales, so the storeowners, captains and seamen were also happy.

William Watson feels happy right now. He is home for Christmas this year with many of his fellow seaman from Wilmington, and this year he is going to spend it with Mary Ann and her mother. William looks forward to this kind of family life again. When William walks the familiar streets of Wilmington he meets people he has known for more than a decade, seamen who have been at sea for a long time and now are home.

Joseph Warner, Jr. who has moved his silversmith shop to Philadelphia, now operates the business from here just like his elder brother William Warner. One morning, sitting in his office reading the *Pennsylvania Gazette*, he suddenly says aloud to his wife, 'Mary, have you heard that President Jefferson complains our country's love for peace has generated the opinion in Europe that the American government is now based entirely on Quaker principles[183]? It seems like the atmosphere from this old Capital, this Quaker City of Philadelphia, still has an influence on the way America is governed from our new Capital Washington D. C.. Mary, I think Father would have enjoyed reading that, if he had lived today. At least it will be good for Joseph Tatnall, who knew George Washington, and the other old Wilmington Friends to learn that their ideas are still valued." Joseph's firstborn son, named after his father Joseph, plays at his feet. So William Watson's best friend has become a Joseph Warner, Senior, like his father, and his son a junior like he used to be. William's friend is happier now than he has been the last four years, and William and Mary Ann are delighted with the young Warner's success with their business and private life.

When Mary Ann and William make the trip to Philadelphia, from time to time, to meet Mary and Joseph Warner and see their happy little family, they both think that they want to marry soon and have a child of their own. But they believe they are still too young and so have not discussed the subject with each other.

William Watson reads the same newspaper a few days later at the kitchen table in Mary Ann's apartment. Looking out the window at the different wharves on the northern bank of the Christina River, William thinks to himself that peace between England and France would make it safer for American seamen on the ocean and in European and West Indian waters.

HMS Hercule patrols the waters around Jamaica in these first days of the New Year of 1806. On January 2 it is cloudy and a fresh breeze is blowing. At 4:40 p.m. the watch-out on the foretopmast platform reports a Danish brigantine in sight and a chase begins. The watch-out is soon rewarded, as usual, with leave. The chase lasts almost five hours and at 9.30 p.m. the Danish schooner is finally put in a rope behind the *Hercule*. The crew of 13 Danish seamen is impressed[69]. Brown and the other impressed Americans onboard don't like it. Watching the Royal Navy impressing seamen from an American-friendly and neutral nation like Denmark angers John, but there is nothing he can do except feel as sorry for the Danish seamen as he does for himself.

A fortnight later, on January 16, *Hercule* is anchored at Amba Roads. An officer with a group of mariners and a group of seamen are sent into the harbor to confiscate a schooner, but it has the luck to escape. On January 23, *Hercule* visits another Danish schooner, but this time the commanding English officer finds the ship's papers in order and lets it sail again. From the forecastle, John Brown can see the relieved faces of the Danish seamen, who are waving at the crew onboard *HMS Hercule*. John waves back, thinking that, in a couple of weeks, these seamen will probably arrive in a harbor and spend some time having fun. He is genuinely happy for them.

The days pass. John Brown finds the routines very boring, but recalls the old seaman saying that he shall thank his God that he is bored. The alternative he will probably learn soon enough. The old seaman had spoken specifically about the rough conditions in the Baltic Fleet. Seamen have been known to freeze to death on the yearly convoy out of the summer station in the Baltic Sea to England. Seamen from warmer climates often ask for permission to be transferred out of the Baltic Fleet to a warmer place like the one John Brown is enjoying now. He can't imagine freezing right now. He is, however, concerned that he is wasting his young life for nothing.

Monday, February 17. An experienced seaman falls overboard and disappears. John Brown observes him fall clear of the ship from a bar but he never surfaces again.

Saturday, February 22, the *HMS Hercule* returns to Port Royal and Rear Admiral Dacres hoists his flag.

March 10. A convoy of merchant ships under *HMS Jupiter* arrives and *Hercule* receives a packet with instructions from the Admiralty Board in London.

The days pass without event for the crew. When no punishments are scheduled, it is just routine day after routine day. On Sundays they have Divine Service at 10 a.m., which John Brown and many of the other seamen and mariners look forward to. They sing the beautiful psalms Brown knows so well from the Presbyterian Church back home in Salem, and concentrating on singing puts him in a wonderful state, where he can easily picture his mother and his friends at home. Now and then, they wash their hammocks. Each crewmember has two, so that one of them can dry while the other one is used. Ships come and go from Port Royal. Most of the names are easy to be remembered: *HMS Success, Echo, Fortune*. John Brown makes a sport out of doing so, simply to exercise his brain in these boring days.

April 3 is a beautiful morning with a clear sky and minimum wind in Port Royal. A court martial is in session onboard the flagship *HMS Hercule* and captains from the different Royal Navy ships anchored in the port form the panel of judges sitting at the captain's long table. The court martial is held in the flag captain's cabin at 10 a.m., and prepared statements and witnesses are put forward. These written statements have been obtained at separate interrogations of the seamen and officers involved in the crime, men who belong to the ship where the actual crime took place. These interrogations are done ahead of time to avoid wasting the time of the flag captain and captains from the other ships. In some cases, these early interrogations make it possible to eliminate testimonies that are unfavorable to officers involved in the actual case. At the court martial, the prosecutor will only put the prepared questions forward, questions that can be answered by the common seamen by a simple yes or no. This will also ensure a short session. A seaman from the *HMS Pelican*, a frigate that normally patrols around Jamaica, is found guilty and sentenced to death, to be executed at noon.[69]

The news of this serious verdict spreads to all the ships in Port Royal within 10 minutes.

The time is noon. John Brown thanks the Lord, as do the other crewmembers, standing shoulder to shoulder on the top deck, that the person found guilty is not a crewmember of their own ship. An officer standing next to the flag captain reads aloud the conclusion from the jury, together with the Articles of War.

The flag captain comes forward and orders a master mate to do his duty, and a rope is tightened around the neck of the seaman, who has his hands tied behind his back and a scarf over his eyes. On a nod from the Master Mate, 10 seamen pull the rope and lift the seaman' one yard above the deck. The hanged man desperately kicks with his feet, looking for solid ground, then the body tugs a couple of times and hangs slack, swinging slowly from side to side like a pendulum running out of time.

The body is then taken down on the order from the captain. The ship's crew is silent the rest of that day. It is obvious their sympathy is with the dead seaman, and that the officers will pay for taking part in this cruel deed by being ignored or glared at. The officers have experience and understand that they'll have to keep a low profile the rest of the day. Mutiny has happened after execution of a seaman in the Royal Navy. The following day, *HMS Hercule* leaves the port for a small trip to give the crew an opportunity to exercise their bodies and to get the sails out in the fresh wind. *Hercule* returns to port on April 13.

On April 18, John Brown looks out on the harbor in Port Royal, thinking of his mother in Salem. He is increasingly frustrated about his situation, but sees no way out of his imprisonment. He desperately wants to go home. He is waiting for a letter from his mother in response to his request for her to get him a new protection certificate. He is becoming more and more impatient as the time passes.

This same day, in Wilmington, merchants, wharf-owners, ship-owners, captains, seamen, harbor laborers and the port collector are gathered at the harbor front, discussing new trade restrictions imposed by the British council on neutral countries such as the United States, Holland and Denmark. William Hemphill, his son James, all the Warner brothers, and Samuel Bush are all there. Although they are not in the same social circles and do not express their opinions directly in a mixed crowd, they all agree that a step like this is not good for the United States, Wilmington, or their own purses.

The federalists, who want a strong central administration, are strongly represented in Wilmington. The Federalist leader of the House of Representatives in Washington D.C., the sober-minded James A. Bayard, lives in Wilmington with his family, on the hill at 211 Market Street not far from the Brandywine River. Bayard likes to stay in Wilmington as much as he can, because he finds Washington D.C. dull. It is barely five years since John Adams was the second President, and Washington social life is not yet interesting. William Warner and Allen McLane, both federalists, know Bayard well. In fact, William Watson's friend, William Windell has also become a Federalist. His charismatic boss, the Revolutionary War hero Allen Mclane, has convinced him. When William Watson and his friends working in the revenue service discuss the issue, his roommate John Freed joins his cause and defends the Democratic Republicans against the Federalist Windell.

Allen McLane knows Bayard quite well, and often spends his time discussing politics with him. McLane is often accused by his opponents in Wilmington of having control of the federalist newspaper, the Delaware Gazette.[223] McLane denies this, though he personally makes sure that when James A. Bayard makes a good speech on Capitol Hill, it is printed on the front page. To those who live off the sea, and especially by trade with England, any American government action that provokes trade restriction from the English authorities is seen as plain madness. Many people, especially Federalists, consider President Jefferson unrealistic in his way of dealing with foreign affairs. The group gathered on the Wilmington quay is worried what American backlash there will be this time. Few of them understand the difficult situation President Jefferson is in. In his administration's confrontation with the British, Jefferson has chosen a martyr strategy. Jefferson knows that the United States does not have any effective power to use against the British, and that his trade restrictions hurt the United States economy much more than Britain's. People assembled on the quay know all too well what it will do to their personal fortunes.

William Warner has successfully increased his trading with England from Philadelphia. He has mostly been trading with Liverpool, with the *Fair American.*[162, 235, 236] When discussing restrictions on trade with England, William completely loses his temper. Samuel Bush and William's brother John Warner are also increasing their trade from Wilmington with their ship, *True American,* but they are trading with Denmark, Holland, and other neutral countries through the West Indian islands. This trade is much more independent of government restrictions related to England.

This escalating trade conflict between England and North America is slowly dividing the American people, much the same way it has politically divided Democratic Republicans and Federalists. It boils down to the fact that many Republicans live off business related to the land, while many Federalists live off the English sea trade.

It is obvious that England will not let neutral countries like Denmark and the United States and their merchants gain on the war between England and France, if they can prevent it.

To counteract British actions, the American Congress passed a Non-Importation Act, prohibiting importation of specific articles from England. Jefferson and his administration are convinced that this act will damage the English export business and hit English merchants in the wallets inside their silk vests.

William Warner in Philadelphia and Federalist ship-owners in Wilmington knew that this law was under preparation, as Bayard had kept them informed. But when they read the news that the law has actually passed, they are furious. McLane reads this news with professional interest as Port Collector. No one in Wilmington doubts that he will do this job to perfection. McLane has a good reputation from the Revolutionary War, and he has proven time and again that he can put his country's needs before his own.

This day, William Watson is working at the Warner wharf loading the *True American,* as he has done so often before. The ship is going across the Atlantic Ocean to the harbor of Altona near Hamburg on the southern border of Denmark. William will not sail with the *True American,* he is just helping to load the ship. He loads large pieces of leather made by

John Ferris, a good friend of the late Joseph Warner; Sr. and one of the finest tanners in Wilmington. The Danes and the Germans are getting the finest leather Wilmington can produce, William thinks. He recalls the tannery of the Isaac H. Starr family, whom he also knows quite well. William doesn't think Starr is as good a tanner as Ferris, and Starr certainly has not improved since getting a seat in the Delaware House of Representatives last year.

William Hemphill, Samuel Bush and John Warner watch Watson and the other laborers load the barrels as they discuss Jefferson's reaction to the English law. They try to see the long-term perspective of the issue and accept the regulations, even though it will be bad for their business in the short term. 'Our nation has to show firmness and strength toward England in a crisis like this," Samuel Bush says and the other two nod their heads, agreeing, without feeling the need to add anything.

To William Watson, his friend Damian Starr and other seamen in Wilmington, this act is a threat to their daily earnings, because it means, in general, less trade with England and fewer jobs for the seamen. William knows some merchants will try to trade these articles with England anyway. Restrictions will cause prices to rise, sending profits to such a high level that weak souls will be sorely tempted to import them.

On rare occasions when Watson and Joseph Warner get a chance to speak about it, Joseph makes it clear that he is absolutely sure his brother William will do so. It's just a question of time. William's parents, Josep h and Mary Warner, had always been true to their Quaker belief of loyalty to any sitting government. Therefore, disobedience to the law, as their son was now considering (although he would not admit it, if asked) would be unacceptable to them. Joseph Warner, Jr. knew that. Obedience to God and government and respect for fellow human beings had been the guiding principles for the Warner family, whose lives had been successful so far.

Joseph is not happy about the trade restrictions and his brother William's trade with England. He is glad that their father did not live to see this.

It is a bright and warm spring day, and in the afternoon William is free of work. He has been in a good mood ever since he got up, because after an easy day's work, he is going to spend the afternoon with Mary Ann.

William sings and whistles so much that it annoys his co-workers, but they keep quiet, because they know that they would probably act the same way, if they could sing and find a proper girlfriend.

This afternoon, William and Mary Ann are going to spend their first day outdoors since they met. William has invited Mary Ann to the popular and beautiful tour along the Brandywine River to the Gilpin Paper mill, on the beautiful bank of a quiet forest lake. When he is off work, William likes to get away from the noise and the crowed streets of Wilmington. He knows of no better place than sitting on a fallen pine tree at this forest lake, watching roe deer come to drink from the smooth surface. When he has time, he likes to watch the small circular waves caused by the small noses of the deer.

William and Mary Ann walk uphill in the hot sunlight, along the Brandywine River, then sit down and rest on a couple of rocks at the edge of the lake, in the shadow of the tall pine woods. They silently watch fish jumping at insects hovering over the lake surface. Every time William is near the Gilpin Paper mill, he can't help talking about the mill and some of Delaware's history. He tells Mary Ann that the paper mill was built in 1787, the same year he was born and the year Delaware, as the first of the 13 States of America, ratified the American Constitution. William also tells her a signer of that ratification, Thomas Wattson, could be a relative of William's who fought the invading British Army near Aitken town in Pen Cader Hundred in New Castle County in the summer of 1777. The Royal Marines invaded the peninsula from the bottom of the Chesapeake Bay at the head of Elk River. Thomas Wattson, signing for New Castle County, had placed his signature, Thos. Wattson, right next to that of Allen McLane, signing for Kent County. When he died in 1792, Thos. Wattson held the rank of Colonel. Thomas Watson and Allen McLane were alike in many ways, but as a landowner and farmer, Wattson never found the time to leave the North American continent and was not as open minded as McLane, who had traveled to England when he was young and, as port collector, was used to working with people from abroad. William felt important, being born where the Union had all started and the same year as the young America.

In 1788, a year after Delaware entered the Union, when William was one, the educated men of Wilmington incorporated The Library Company of Wilmington. Joseph Warner, the father of his friend, was a founder, along with Isaac H. Starr, wharf-owner John Shallcross, John Ferris, Thomas Mendenhall and many other prominent Wilmingtonians.

They gathered books on topics such as agricultural techniques, poetry, mathematics and astronomy from their personal libraries and made them available for the education of the young men in the borough. William Watson is proud of all the things his friends' fathers have accomplished. They set a standard for him to live up to.

Although she laughed at the story, deep down Mary Ann is very proud of him.

Mary Ann and William laugh most of the time they are together, and it has been a long time since William has felt so happy and relaxed. When the sun can no longer be seen on the lake surface and it becomes chilly, they head home. William is sailing to Philadelphia early in the morning on one of the Warner schooners, so he wants to go to bed early this evening. Back in Wilmington, they stand close together for a long while in front of the apartment house, looking at each other without saying anything. They feel that they belong to each other. They know days are getting longer and that they will have many spring days to spend together. Finally, they say goodbye for the evening.

On April 23, *HMS Hercule* leaves Port Royal to exercise the cannons again, near the local British headquarters, where enemy confrontations are rarely seen. On May 7, 12 live bullocks are brought from ashore. It takes a considerable amount of time for seamen to get them into their boxes on the first gun deck below. The next day, Brown and a couple of other seamen help slaughter five of them for food for the ordinary crewmembers. Fresh meat is one of the few advantages for ordinary crewmembers when ships are in a harbor or near a shore.

About a month later, on May 21, *Hercule* fires shots at an American schooner sailing from New York to Jamaica, and sends a jolly boat to visit the ship. Brown watches from a bar in the top of the first mast, where he is helping rig the sails. He sees the faces of the American seamen onboard the schooner as they hand over their Protection Certificates to the British boarding officer. The officer soon hands the papers back to the American captain, and from the officer's nodding of his head, John Brown assumes that the papers and cargo have passed the examination. The American seamen are visibly relieved and as Brown observes their delighted faces and hears their laughter, he remembers his own impressment seven months ago. If his ship had been going to English Jamaica and not French Martinique, he would be a free man today.

The next day, May 22, William Lyman, the Agent for Seamen in London, writes to Secretary of State James Madison, telling him that he thinks the situation on impressments has improved.[185]

May 30. *HMS Hercule* returns to Port Royal and port activities are taken up again. Water and food are supplied in large quantities. Brown observes British frigates regularly arriving with confiscated enemy ships. *HMS Fortune* arrives with a French privateer in tow, and *HMS Mediator* arrives with a French brigantine. Fresh beef is taken in. *HMS Hebe* and *HMS Blanc* sail. *HMS Penguin* arrives with a captured Spanish schooner.

On Friday, June 20 feelings among the British crew, from Rear Admiral Dacres to the lowest ranking mess boy, are running high onboard *HMS Hercule*. The Flagship is going to leave Port Royal and the West Indian Islands for the last time this year, heading home to Old England. Some of the elder seamen know this could very well be the last time they see this exotic port. The master mates and the officers need not raise their voices this day to make the crewmembers do their work. Everyone does his duty without hesitation to avoid unnecessary delay of the return to England.

The convoy will go east, south of Cuba. The route east up through the Wind Ward Channel, between Cuba and Haiti and past the southern part of the St. Luke's (Bahamas) Islands before turning east into the Atlantic Ocean, is too dangerous a route. Turning west from that position, up through the Old St. Luke's Channel and the Santaren Channel to reach the Straits of Florida, passing hidden coral reefs, can be deadly, as those who regularly operate in the West Indies know.

A convoy of about 120 merchant ships filled with rum barrels, sugar tubes and other highly desired West Indian produce is forming outside Port Royal. Royal Navy ships will escort the entire merchant fleet safely to England under command of the Master and Admiral Dacres on the flagship *Hercule*. The Master took over command of the *HMS Hercule*, as the captain died recently and was buried at a churchyard in Kingston.[69]

Five days after the departure from Port Royal, four seamen are punished for fighting as the ships pass Grand Cayman Island south of Cuba. On this long trip to England, Brown and the other seamen have plenty of time to strand at the bulwark and search the horizon for new places to talk about. As they pass the Cayman Islands, John finds himself speaking to the old seaman he has had many conversations with. This day they talk about piracy, which is frequent in these waters. Innocently, John says, 'I don't understand this whole concept of piracy. Why would anyone think they could get away with stealing the cargo of someone else's ship? A cargo of, say, 450 barrels of rum is not something you hide in a pocket." The old seaman smiles as he shakes his head several times. 'My young man, you have much to learn yet. Pirates don't take a stolen cargo to their homeport or any large port city. They find a remote island to hide their new property. These beaches of the Cayman Islands we are passing now are an ideal place to dig a large hole on one of the sandy beaches and hide stolen property. Then they come back once in a while to fetch a small amount they can bring back without anyone being suspicious." John's face lights up. "A brilliant idea. They are indeed smart, these pirates. If ordinary people thought this way, the world would be a much richer place to live in."

The convoy proceeds through the Yucatan Roads. On June 29, when *Hercule* reaches a point near Cape Antonia, a small additional convoy of merchant ships and Navy ships going to England joins the convoy.

On the Fourth of July, three of the impressed Americans onboard the *Hercule* are punished with 18 lashes.[69] John Brown hates the officers for being provocative in this way. On this 30-year anniversary of the Declaration of American Independence, he is sad about not being free to celebrate with his fellow American countrymen. He can't help thinking of the celebrations that he knows are going on in every village and town in the United States. People are gathering in public places, parks or big lawns where families can find a nice spot to sit and enjoy their sandwiches, while they listen to speeches by politicians, businessmen, and other celebrities. Thirteen-gun salutes will be fired, followed by 13 toasts, an annual ritual. The subjects of these toasts differ from year to year, depending on the current political situation and political agenda. In the chilly evening, fireworks will illuminate the skies over the villages, towns and cities. Standing on the forecastle at noon, staring out to sea, Brown realizes it may be some time before he gets a chance to attend another Fourth of July ceremony. Damn those British officers, John thinks as he turns in that evening.

The convoy enters the Florida Roads a few days later and continues its voyage north along the Florida coast. On Wednesday, July 16, the officers on the quarterdeck observe the city of Charleston on the coast of

South Carolina. Monday, July 21, they pass 50 miles north and 200 miles east of the entrance to Delaware Bay and Cape Henlopen.

A couple of days later they are north 20 and east 300 miles off Cape Cod. Hearing where they are, John Brown, William King and John Pristoff become silent and sad. They are so near the North American coast, Salem and Boston, their places of birth, and yet so infinitely far away.

On the 25th, the Great Banks of New Foundland appear on the northwestern horizon. The following day, five seamen are punished for disobedience.

As the convoy gets closer and closer to England, the spirits of the English seamen rise, while the Americans John Brown and John Pristoff often wonder whether they will ever see or set foot on North American soil again.

Monday, August 4, some of the seamen, mariners and a couple of officers from *HMS Hercule* save the crew of an American brig in the convoy, which is sinking.

Many of the merchant ships in *Hercule*'s convoy are American ships, now being under the protection of the Royal Navy. John Brown and the other seamen find it hard to face that they, as impressed Americans in the Royal Navy, are forced to protect American ships sailing with British cargoes in violation of the Non-importation Act. This Act is beginning to have a serious impact on American ship owners, and they have found it necessary to enter forbidden trade with England or the West Indian or inter-European trade. The number of ships transporting to and from the United States has decreased much in the last year, and American ship owners are replacing decreasing income on the home market with these new markets. The American captains are paying the British officers for naval escort service, so the British treat the American captains in the convoy respectfully. The Royal Navy officers see this as a perfect role for them in these times of war: England and America side by side and against France.

But the seamen onboard these American ships do not enjoy the same respect as the officers and are not as safe as they might think, under the protection of their American captains. Troublesome or overly independent seamen, or those owed a large salary, have occasionally been turned over to the Royal Navy for impressments. Brown has heard about such episodes in the Salem and Boston harbor taverns. To hear a rumor in a tavern is one thing, actually experiencing it on the open sea, where nothing can be done to prevent it, is another. Some events in life have to be experienced to be fully comprehended, John thinks. He had ignored these rumors when he heard them the first time, because many seamen consider them exaggerated or false. Discipline is strict onboard American ships, but all seamen receive the same treatment and consider it normal. John simply can't imagine any American captain doing such a low thing as turning over a fellow American citizen to the British Royal Navy just to save a few dollars. He wonders how such a person can live with himself afterwards.

On August 8, six seamen are punished for disobedience, one of them, William Rogers, for the third time since the ship left Port Royal. Rogers is fed up with the Royal Navy, but there is little he can do about it. Hopelessness fills him, as he realizes that some of the best years of his youth are wasted and nobody seems to care. This fills him with extreme anger, and he can't help insulting his superior officers. Then he gets punished for disobedience. After punishment, his hopelessness reaches even greater heights, and he joins a small gang of men who drink when off-duty to ease their pains and sorrows. Sometimes the drinking gets out of control, and one or two of them forget the time they are to serve again or can't perform their duty properly. This is exactly what happens to three of them the following day.

On August 11, three more seamen are punished for drunkenness. William Roberts is not among them this time. His back still hurts so much from the last time that he hasn't slept since. In fact, he has a hard time just lying in his hammock. The two first nights, he got his commanding officer's permission to stay on the main deck for several hours to let the cooling night breezes of the North Atlantic Sea relieve his back pain.

August 17, five more seamen are punished for drunkenness, but spirits are generally running high in the British crew because they are close to England and the end of this voyage.

Finally, on Friday August 24, *HMS Hercule* anchors in Cowsand Bay, in the English Channel, on the south coast of England. The sick men on-board are sent to the onshore hospital where conditions are better for taking care of them. A Swedish seaman dies onboard the ship before the others can transport him to the hospital. *Hercule* takes on fresh beef and water.

On the 30th, the flagship sails again, to anchor at the Royal Navy head- quarters at Spithead. Soon after, *Hercule* sails eastwards out of the English Channel to the North Sea, goes north to the Medway River and arrives at the Nore.

On September 11, seventy-nine of the super numerous men who are no longer needed onboard are transferred to *HMS Zealand*, also anchored at the Nore.[69] *Zealand* is a Second-rater now used as a transfer ship, where seamen can stay while waiting to be transferred to another ship in the Royal Navy where they are going to serve. The seamen stay here until their ship arrives from the dock or from a voyage on the sea. The Royal Navy uses this practice to keep ship crews gathered if it is possible, and to avoid trouble. John Brown is one of the seamen discharged to *HMS Zealand*, together with John Pristoff, William King and the others from the Boston schooner. The five American seamen are satisfied as long as they are kept together.

In the autumn of 1806, flax seed is being harvested on Delaware farms. William Hemphill advertises, as usual, in the *Delaware Gazette* to buy flax seed. Local farmers drive the flax seed in their horse-drawn carriages to his wharf on the north bank of the Christina River, where he pays them upon receipt. The farmers return home happy, because the price is good this year, since production has not been overwhelmingly large. This also means that most flax seed produced will be sent abroad and not to the oil mills this year.

William Watson is not helping at the Hemphill's wharf this autumn. Instead he is working for Isaac Hendrickson, Jacob Broom and Summers, who jointly own the schooner *General Washington*. Like Hemphill, these three men are exporting flax seed to Europe. William Watson and a group of harbor laborers are busy loading barrels into the *Washington*. Port Collector McLane and his two assistants show up on the quay to be certain that everything that's going on here is fine. Sometimes, illegal cargo is unloaded from the ships, and regular inspections by revenue officers are the best way to keep these activities to a minimum.

Williams's trip this year is special and he is very much looking forward to it. Until now, he has only sailed the Delaware River or along the North American coast, and always as an ordinary seaman. The *Washington* will go to New York, where William has been before. But this time, William will cross the Atlantic Ocean to Europe, precisely Belfast and Londonderry in Ireland, for the first time.

On Christmas day, 1806, onboard *Zealand* anchored in Chatham Roads, John Brown and the rest of the crew from the Boston schooner are celebrating. They are cold all the time, because the wooden ship's sides are leaky, and when wind gusts hits the ship the draft is heavy on the upper decks. It is much colder here than onboard the *Hercule* in Port Royal, Jamaica, last Christmas, John thinks. As they eat that evening, John Brown turns to John Pristoff and says, 'I am beginning to get the feeling that the old seaman in Port Royal was right, when he told me that staying in the cold Nordic climate can be very tough."

The men onboard ships gathered in New York harbor, waiting for an opportune time to depart for Europe with their flax seed cargo, are preparing Christmas dinner. This will be William's first Christmas away from Wilmington, and he thinks of this several times during the day. He finds waiting time here in these narrow quarters quite boring. New York, of course, is a great experience with its 100,000 citizens, 50 times as many as in Wilmington, and so very different in many aspects. But William has no money to spend here and would prefer to be home in Wilmington with his girlfriend Mary Ann and his friends. Christmas has always been a fun time in Wilmington, William recalls.

Fortunately, a friend of both Mary Ann's and William's, Damian Starr, a member of the Quaker Starr family, happens to be on one of the other ships anchored in New York this Christmas. William and Samuel spend a lot of time together while waiting for spring to arrive. As the days go by, the harbor becomes more and more crowded with ships planning to cross the Atlantic to Europe.

On New Years Eve, Damian Starr and William Watson stand together, around midnight, on the starboard bulwark of *General Washington*, watching the spectacular fireworks displayed in the sky above New York. The beautiful yellow, green, red and blue flowers on the dark sky fascinate the two young men. They have never experienced anything like this before, and it shows them just how much larger New York is compared to Wilmington. William and Samuel conclude that it is possible to judge the size of a city by the size of its New Year's Eve firework.

3

On January 13, 1807, 45 men and 13 boys onboard the *HMS Zealand*, including John Brown and John Pristoff[36,] are transferred to *HMS Defence*. This ship has been waiting on their arrival for quite some time.

The third-rater *Defence* was part of Lord Nelson's West Indies fleet in 1805, some months before John Brown's Boston schooner arrived there. *Defence* was severely damaged in the Battle of Trafalgar, and spent nearly a year at the dockyard in Chatham, under repair. Last December 20, it dropped anchor in Chatham Roads to be equipped with masts, anchors, rigging, and food supplies. To prepare for a voyage in the New Year, the ship was now being supplied with a crew.

On the top deck, new crewmembers are given a choice between remaining onboard *Zealand*, with relatively nice food and good accommodations, until they can be sent to a regular prison ship in the Port of Portsmouth, with its half rations and primitive quartering, or enter the active man-o-war *Defence* voluntarily.

In the four months Brown and the other Americans have been onboard *Zealand*, some of their fellow mates have told terrifying stories about the real prison ships in Portsmouth, where people almost were starving to death or becoming raving mad from being isolated from the outside world for years.

Brown and the others make a calculation from what they have experienced onboard *Hercule* so far. After all, they are still alive and fit. They have experienced real tough conditions, but they know they have to be on an operating warship if they are to have any chance to escape and go home. Being in a prison ship anchored in a harbor will offer no chance to escape and only weaken them mentally and physically. So, they enter *Defence* voluntarily, not knowing that being listed in the Muster book of *Defence* as having entered voluntarily will put them in a very difficult position, when it comes to trying to be released in the future. If a request comes from an Agent for American Seamen to free them as impressed American seamen, even if it contains material proving their American citizenship, the captain of a Royal Navy ship may reply that they cannot be the men they are looking for, because they entered voluntarily. If a seamen has not entered voluntarily, the captain may compare the description to another seaman with the same name and answer that a seamen with that name is onboard, but does not fit the forwarded description. The American seamen don't know that officers in the Royal Navy, an organization with so much dignity and pride that punishes crews for the slightest deviation from regulations, are in a position to systematically lie about the impressed seamen's circumstances. It is hard for them to comprehend that such things take place on ships in the Royal Navy. When experienced British seamen tell impressed Americans that they will never get out of the Royal Navy, the Americans simply don't believe it. They are convinced that it is just a matter of getting proof of their American origin sent to this ship, the agent for American seamen, or the Admiralty in London to be released.

In the following days, 98 men are transferred to *Defence* from *HMS Zealand* and *Ceres*. On January 17 and 18, food supplies are loaded, including 1,387 pounds of fresh beef and 10 tons of beer. A salute of 21 guns is fired on the 18th from each Royal Navy ship to celebrate the 69th birthday of King George III. The captain reads the officer's commissions that same day. On Monday the 19th, the pay commissioner pays the ship's crew.

Driven by curiosity, Brown decides to talk to some experienced seamen from *Defence*'s earlier expeditions, men who fought bravely at the Battle of Trafalgar. The English seamen are proud to describe, over a pot of rum, this now famous battle that unfortunately ended Lord Nelson' s life*Defence* had six seamen killed in that battle. A seaman takes John Brown for a walk along the ship's sides on the lower decks, pointing out places where people were killed or lost their limbs, and the specific places where the toughest action took place. Being part of the first crew to serve onboard *H.M.S. Defence* after that battle makes John Brown proud, even though he is an American. He is not the type of person to run from a dangerous situation, so the English seaman's stories are interesting to him. John plans to tell them to other American seamen when he returns home someday.

On January 22, the Clerk of the Cheque boards *Defence* and pays a bounty to those of the crew prepared to receive it, and to try and convince those who are in doubt about it. Brown recalls what Pristoff told him earlier and firmly refuses to receive any Bounty.

The weeks pass slowly for the ordinary crewmembers onboard *Defence* anchored in its winter camp in Chatham Roads. Nothing special happens to break the boring daily routines. The ship is gradually being fitted out with the materials, with foodstuff the last supply taken onboard. Common seamen are normally not told when a ship is going to depart, but by watching the different types of foodstuff taken in, they can get a pretty good idea how close they are to departure for a long voyage. The more perishable foodstuff taken onboard, the closer they are to departure.

During the short days this time of year, experienced seamen like Brown are doing routine work in the rigging, washing the decks, splicing ropes, or polishing brass. John Brown and John Pristoff complain to each other about the boring work, with so little exercise for their brains, and the cold nights. As newcomers, Americans, and super numerous crew, they were placed in the worst night quarters, their hammocks next to the cold shipside and the cannon ports. Although Brown wraps himself up in the carpet he received at arrival, and puts on extra clothes before entering his hammock, he still wakes up three or four times a night, freezing bitterly.

In daylight hours, when they are off duty but still freezing, they sometimes sneak down to the kitchen and the hot stow in the stem on the second gun deck. The soldiers and purser will not allow anyone to hang around the kitchen for long, because food is known to mysteriously disappear. John Brown now begins to understand how cold it can be onboard ships in the Royal Navy, the cold the other seamen talked so much about back in the West Indies.

Sometimes Brown observes that the atmosphere between ordinary crewmembers and officers are tense. The officers stare angrily and intensely at the crewmembers, looking for signs of dislike and misbehavior. The seamen, landsmen and mariners stare back, and make faces when the officers look the other way. If an officer looks back, the seaman will look down, leaving the officer with the feeling that the seamen only follows his orders because of the officer's position, not because of his personal skills or respect. On a short-term basis, an officer can accept this. But sooner or later, the officer feels frustrated and angry.

Mutual respect between officers and ordinary crewmembers is the ideal. But conditions put pressure on them both. Officers with self-confidence and respect for their fellow man can bring more harmony into a situation. They correct subordinates only when absolutely necessary, and without undue harshness. This kind of officer creates cooperation. But when a seaman is much more intelligent and quicker than his superiors, or an officer maybe has bad manners or a bad memory, conflicts occur, and this can lead to severe and repeated punishment of the ordinary crewmember. Brown long ago realized that he is brighter than any of the officers onboard *Defence*. He can see that officers have a hard time coping with that, so he is careful not to appear to smart.

Time passes by uneventfully on *Defence*. On February 4, some crewmembers are punished for the first time since John entered the ship, and he notices that Captain Ekins is stricter about disobedience and regulations than the flag captain onboard *Hercule*. When crewmembers are punished here, it is not one or two at a time, but four or more, and the maximum of 12 lashes is doubled. "It doesn't look good for the coming voyage, for the common seaman," John says to John Pristoff. But they have made it this far, and John is confident that he can handle the stay onboard this ship, too.

Defence's position on the east coast of England is much farther from home than Port Royal Jamaica, and John thinks of his mother more often now. He and John Pristoff avoid discussing their families. They both find it too hard to talk about, feeling responsible for their families and not knowing how they are doing, while much of the working population on the East Coast is experiencing the negative consequences of British trade regulations and American responses. On days when they are in bad moods because of their captivity, they can only hope that their families are doing well.

On Monday, February 9, 1807 the crew knows that it can't be long before the ship leaves port. Perishable foods like 500 pounds of butter and 1,002 pounds of cheese have been brought onboard. Three days later, John Brown and other seamen and soldiers are busy scrubbing their hammocks when the Clerk of the Cheque comes onboard again to muster the ship's company, look for deserters, and finally pay the crew.

The day after, Captain Ekins receives orders from the Admiralty to release some of his men. Ekins does not receive this news well. For months, he has been concentrating on gathering a well-trained crew, which is very hard to do and badly needed after many months in the dockyard. Five Swedes onboard the ship are to be released. From a distance, John watches the joyous expressions on the faces of the Swedish seamen. They are obviously satisfied to be returning home. The seamen onboard *Defence* discuss reasons for this release, and crewmembers with knowledge of the political situation between England and Sweden come to the conclusion it must be a diplomatic gesture to please the Swedish King and government. This will make it easier for the Royal Navy and the Admiralty in London to negotiate better terms for summer naval stations in Swedish waters.

Sweden possesses the coastline in the southwest part of the Baltic Sea, an ideal place for summer stations for Royal Navy ships. Good relations between England and Sweden are very important to the Admiralty in London, and releasing Swedish seamen is a perfect way to show good will.

England is not self-sufficient when it comes to supplies of oak timber, vital for building and maintaining the many wooden ships in the large Royal Navy fleet, the main guarantor of England's national security in these times of war with France. The Baltic summer stations are therefore very important to the Royal Navy's mission of protecting English merchant ships going into and out of the Baltic Sea with timber and other goods that comes from the different ports and countries around the Baltic Sea.

John Brown understands the strategic plans made and executed by the Admiralty Board in London, but he doesn't want to be a part of this war against France, a country that helped America gain its independence from England. He is grateful to the French for their help. Of course, his decision to try and help the French in the West Indian Islands by supplying weapons and ammunition from Boston is the reason he is impressed on this Royal Navy ship. He is no longer able to defend American seamen or the interests of France, and his intolerable situation is hard to bear in these endless days.

The following day, the ordinary men and officers are served fresh beef and beer for dinner. The next morning, *HMS Defence* unmoors in a fresh breeze to go to sea. She sails south to the Downs and out in a heavy gale with thick snow showers. The nights become increasingly cold, and the men in their hammocks struggle to sleep as *Defence* glides along the northern coast of France near Le Havre in a strong icy wind. The storming shows John Brown clearly how drafty his night quarters near the cannon port are. Even after a day of hard work, John doesn't sleep much because of the cold.

At least more food is served on cold days. Daily meals are the highlight of the day, and John eats with great appetite. From his time on ships in the American merchant fleet onboard ships sailing along the east coast, John is used to cold, humid weather, but he now realizes the cabin of a small merchant schooner holds body heat better than a ship this size. The smell and air on the lower decks are bad at night, but because of the cold, the deck room is not ventilated then.

On the 19th, seamen and officers from the *Defence* save two men from a sinking brig. The survivors run around the upper deck thanking everyone they meet for saving their lives. The men are so happy to be alive that it takes them some time to calm down.

Defence returns to the English Channel near Spithead on a day where the wind is fresh and the sky cloudy. This first, small trip was made to exercise the seamen in the riggings, test the different functions of the sails, fire the cannons and train the men who operate them, and let the soldiers and the mariners shoot the smaller guns onboard the ship. Everything seems to work, so on the 26th, Captain Ekins gives the order to take in provisions for six months for the crew of 525 men. They take in fresh bread, oatmeal, and barrels of beef, hogsheads of pork, barrels of brandy, gallons of Rum, sugar, and lemon juice.

That same day, William and Damian Starr are warming themselves over a cup of hot coffee in the cabin onboard the *General Washington* in the harbor of New York. They discuss how dangerous it might be to cross the Atlantic Ocean. 'Early winter can really be a terrible time to sail to Europe," William says. 'Near the coast, where only constant movement keeps the water from freezing, ships can ice-up in minutes, when seawater is continuously sprayed over the decks. The cold strong winds help the freezing process. The ship's center of gravity ...." William pauses, concentrating on this new theory he has read about. He is pretty sure he has the expression right. 'The ship's center of gravity can quickly rise above the waterline with ice building up on the upper parts, which can cause the ship to turn over and sink rapidly, and no one can prevent it. Regular storms occur often this time of year, destroying ships and dragging them down with men and mice. And besides, American seamen like you and me can be impressed and forced to serve in the Royal Navy," William says, wanting to warn Damian against every foreseeable danger from sailing the ocean. Damian nods his head. He has been thinking of these things as well. They conclude that the most likely danger they might face is impressment into the Royal Navy.

William has often heard stories in the taverns, about entire crews caught by the British and removed from their American merchant ships, even though they had papers and were able to prove their American citizenship. It is quite disturbing to think of.

It is late, so Damian says goodbye to William and the other on *General Washington,* and rows to his own schooner. William and Damian have agreed to meet early next morning and want to sleep now.

William can't stop thinking about the stories of impressments, and these worries keep him awake most of the night. But the next morning he still wakes at sunrise, quickly eats his breakfast and drinks his coffee and rows from *General Washington* to meet Damian. Together, they row from the outer harbor front to the quay in front of New York's customhouse, on the South side of Manhattan, to apply for Protection Certificates.

They identify themselves to one of the revenue officers, and are issued handwritten Customhouse Protection Certificates. It only takes half an hour. They get one certificate to take with them while sailing and a copy is made for the New York port collector to keep. This copy can be forwarded to them if they are impressed. William and Damian thank the revenue officer. Although he is busy, the officer takes the time to wish both of them a nice trip, and William and Damian hurry to the rowboat. William is glad they went to the Customhouse early and avoided waiting in line.

William's Protection Certificate includes a physical description, but because he has no special marks like tattoos or scars, the description is remarkably short. William notices one thing, and can't help bragging about it to the crew on the *General Washington* later that morning. 'The number of my Protection Certificate, dear friends, is surely a number to bring luck, 7777. Did you know that the number 7 is a sacred number? It is the most frequently used number in the Holy Bible, and now that I think about it, the number of red stripes in our flag," William proudly waves the certificate at his shipmates. 'I think all American seamen should have a PC, and the American authorities automatically should give it to them."

When William goes to bed that evening of February 27, 1807, he feels safe and sleeps well.[10]

Going to Belfast with the schooner *General Washington* this year is a clever thing to do. The British Royal Navy is impressing more American seamen than ever before[266], mostly in the English Channel. Many ocean-going American ships go to ports on the English south coast or through the Channel on their way to and from the North Sea or Baltic Sea. It is almost equally dangerous to sail the St. George's Channel, between Ireland and the English west coast, to Liverpool, as William Warner's ships do.

On March 3, crewmembers are again punished on the *Defence*. Eight seamen and mariners are punished at the main mast for drunkenness, disobedience and insolence. A total of 192 lashes are given, and the men scream so much that it is hard for the crew to bear. That much punishment, the men know, risks health and lives.

The next day, an American ship sailing from Bordeaux to New York is inspected. From the forecastle, John observes the relaxed expressions on the faces of the American seamen and remembers that he once loved to sail on the merchant ships, when he was a free man. But that was a long time ago. The cargo and papers onboard the American ship seem acceptable and it is permitted to continue for New York.

Two days later, six seamen are punished for neglect of duty and uncleanness. John is getting increasingly angry about what he sees as random punishments of innocent people almost daily. 'Discipline is completely out of order these days," he complains to John Pristoff after another punishment. 'This type of punishment is too hard on the men onboard. There isn't the slightest motivation to improve your behavior when you're treated like an animal." William King has the same opinion, adding, 'If this kind of severe and lasting punishments was practiced in the U.S. Navy, it would cause mutiny."

On March 15, six seamen are punished for neglect of duty, because they have been fighting. The frequent punishments have created a tense atmosphere between superior officers and the ordinary crew. It is early in the voyage, but already increasing quarrels between the two groups and more individual fights occur between seamen and mariners.

Three days later, the sea and air temperature have risen enough that working in boats on the sea surface is possible, so inspections of the outer ship's sides begin, and some seamen wash the ship's sides. Taking advantage of the nice weather, cannon crews are trained in firing the cannons and using hand weapons. Later that afternoon, the squadron under the command of *Defence's* captain is gathered. In the afternoon a Frenchman tries unsuccessfully to desert, and a seaman and mariner are caught stealing. All of them are severely punished. Theft is the only crime where officers and ordinary crewmembers share an opinion about hard punishment. There is no mercy with theft.

The next day, the atmosphere is tense. Someone has been stealing from the personal belongings of fellow crewmembers on the lower deck, and fingers are pointed. Feelings are running high and a single wrong word ignites an explosion of emotions. In the evening, when officers leave the crew alone on the lower deck, an interrogation begins to find the thief. Natural leaders of the seamen ask crewmembers who might be guilty, and it only takes a short time before two seamen admit their guilt. Although the ordinary crew would normally take care of punishment for theft themselves, because of all the fighting between crewmembers lately, the leaders of the meeting decide to turn the thieves over to the officers. The next day, the thieves are punished along with five men punished for drunkenness.

The *Defence* moves south along the western coasts of France, Spain and Portugal, and is close to the port of Tenerife on March 23, when four seamen are punished for drunkenness and two mariners for neglect of duty. Among them is 24-year-old John Smith, born in Jamaica. He is punished for drunkenness, because he drinks when he longs for home.

John Smith hates the British, the intolerable discipline onboard this ship, the food and the cold climate in the North Sea. He finds the living conditions for seamen in the Royal Navy an insult to intelligent people, and has stated this to the officers. On April 8, his eyes shine with hatred as they sail close to the Canary Islands, which have a climate much like that around Jamaica. He feels very homesick and apparently cannot control himself. The first officer John Smith meets that morning, unfortunately, has the average officer's contempt for an ordinary seaman and Smith explodes in anger. He is a muscular, tall seaman, and very bright, and he has mental and physical control over the officer, lifting him 10 inches off the deck. The officer tries in vain to regain control of the situation, using what he learned at the Naval Academy, but John Smith is positively mad and his rude, hard tone leaves the officer speechless. It is clear from the officer's wide eyes and open mouth that he has never experienced anything quite like this before. John Smith is too agitated to care about the consequences of his behavior. He is responding viscerally to long-term mistreatment.

The officer realizes he is in a life-threatening situation. Hard work has turned Smith's body into pure muscles, and he could break every bone in the officer's body if he wished. Both of them know it.

Since the beginning of the French Revolution, ordinary crewmembers in the Royal Navy have become more and more self-assured, knowing that in a physical test between officers and ordinary men, hard-working seamen and mariners would have the upper hand. Life onboard is in a delicate balance. From the faces of the seamen surrounding them, the officer can see that they are on Smith's side, so he kindly asks to be set down, then quickly withdraws to the quarterdeck.

John Smith has made his point and won a great victory in the eyes of his fellow seamen, but they also know it is for a limited time. He has won a battle, but not won the war. The officer, of course, immediately complains to Captain Ekins, and Smith will be punished, along with five others for neglect of duty and theft.

It is less than a fortnight since John Smith was whipped the last time, and while the thought of the approaching new punishment is hard to think of, he regrets nothing. From the quarterdeck, Captain Ekins reads the appropriate paragraph from the Articles of War and John Smith is seized up at the main mast. Many of the seamen have hateful faces and stare intently at the officers, who stare back. It is a constant war of nerves between officers and men, all trapped in this narrow and confined space.

A seaman who dares to voice his opinion to an officer gains respect from his fellow seamen, so the punishment of John Smith hurts the other seamen's pride even more than usual.

John Smith is whipped so long that he faints, and his mates worry if he will make it this time. But his strength helps him through the punishment, and he walks away with dignity and manages to recover in a remarkably short time.

The following day John Brown is employed on the forecastle and observes men and officers from *Defence* board a Danish ship on its way from Norway to the Danish West Indies. On April 8, *Defence* is around Palma de Majorca and sails into a storm in the afternoon. The main topgallant yard breaks in the strong wind and is carried away.

Four days later, John Smith has once again refused to obey orders and, together with seamen who are found guilty of fighting, drinking and stealing, he is punished for neglect of duty. This is the final test of his strength, and it finally sinks into his mind that these cruel officers can keep on punishing him for the slightest misbehavior for years to come. This realization breaks John Smith down for good. John Brown can see it in his eyes as the last cuts of the whip hit him. From now on, when Smith gets punished, it will only be for drinking too much.

It is April 17 and the infirmary has so many sick people, most of them sick from flogging, that Captain Ekins gives the order to kill a bullock to serve the patients fresh beef to help them recover faster. John Smith's health has been so severely damaged that he has lost faith that he will ever be relieved of this living hell. He eats the food served mechanically and with no enjoyment, in contrast to those fellows who have managed to cheat their way into the infirmary to rest and eat well for a period.

On the 21st of April, the mariners are exercised with the small guns and moving all the fighting ballast to the larboard side of the ship. It is a slight break from the boring routine. Two days later, three seamen are punished for neglect of duty and disobedience, and five days later, six more are punished for neglect of duty. At this point of the voyage, it is evident to everyone onboard that Captain Ekins has a problem maintaining good discipline.

On May 3, Captain Ekins orders to stop the mixing of the lemon juice with the seamen's grog, because the lemon juice is now in short supply. Two days later, Captain Ekins intends to punish someone, but forgets to give the order. The seamen and officers talk about this rare event for months. They see it as a sign of possible change. If Captain Ekins can forget to punish someone, it could mean that punishment to the extent now used is not fair or necessary in the first place.

On the 11th of May, a seaman is punished 72 lashes for having sex with another man onboard the *Defence* and almost dies from the punishment. To Captain Ekins, this is a crime way beyond drunkenness, neglect of duty, theft or any other, and the seaman is punished more severely than any this year. Captain Ekins is actually proud of what he sees as his mild judgement of this crime and thinks to himself that this seaman should thank God he is still alive. The correct penalty for such a severe crime, according to the Articles of War, is death by hanging. But even an English seaman complains to John, " It is all too much, punishing people so severely, whipping them so badly. It's such a part of our sea culture, we even punish our food before we eat it." John looks puzzled and the English seaman explains, "We even whip our cream!" They all laugh heartily for a while and then return to work.

June 12. A pilot is taken onboard in the morning and the ship is slowly taken into Cowsand Bay. John is scraping the upper deck, and notices several ships of the line gathered in this port, the *HMS Prince of Wales*, *HMS Tanuant*, *HMS Pompeii*, *HMS Foudryant*, *HMS Warrior*, *HMS Colossus*, *HMS Achilles* and *HMS Captain*.

He decides to try and contact crewmembers onboard the other ships to get an estimate of how many impressed Americans there are, and to get their personal data. A trusted English seaman who can move easily to the other ships anchored in the port can gather this information, free of surveillance from officers. Brown hopes to gather the names of impressed Americans, their ages, the name of the ship they are on and of the American ship they came from, and the cities they are from. John and the other Americans will remember this information and exchange it when they meet crewmembers from other ships in new ports. Perhaps this way, information about the destinies of some impressed American seamen will slowly but surely make its way home to local authorities in the States and finally to families and relatives.

Defence takes in fresh beef, butter and cheese. During inspections of the ship, some of the rigging is condemned and taken into the dockyard. On Wednesday the 17th, *HMS Mars* arrives. The next day, two chalkers begin chalking the ship, and the clerk of the cheque arrives to muster the ship's company and pay the crewmembers.

In early June 1807, the *General Washington* enters Delaware Bay with linen and glass from Belfast harbor, after a safe journey. As they approach home, William is pleased, because this trip across the Atlantic Ocean paid much more than he would have earned working onboard a ship sailing the Delaware River or along the east coast. He thinks, if he continues to earn this way and saves, he might be able to marry Mary Ann in a couple of years.

General Washington arrives in the Christina River on a beautiful, warm summer day. Many children are bathing in the river, playing and laughing. As William now catch sight of these happy children, he recalls how much he loved to swim and play in the river when he was a boy. As the schooner approaches the quay at Hendrickson's wharf, one of the boys jumps out of the river and runs to the Sign of the Ship to report that a new ship has arrived. The news quickly spreads from the tavern through the streets of Wilmington, and when William jumps onto the quay, he almost lands in the arms of Mary Ann, who has been waiting for his arrival. Mary Ann had even walked to the top of the hill several times that day to look for the schooner, and she had finally managed to spot it sailing on the Delaware River.

For Mary Ann and William, it is delightful to meet again. While William has been on the ocean, Mary Ann has been busy helping her mother nursing, visiting and otherwise taking care of sick people in their homes or at the Wilmington Borough Hospital.

Business activity in Wilmington has been increasing in recent years. William Hemphill's ships have brought home exotic items from India and other ships have brought exciting things from the ports of France, Holland, Denmark and Germany.

William and Mary Ann spend an entire week together in Wilmington in mid-June. It is warm and sunny most of the time, and they enjoy being together and outside.

On June 22, in the Chesapeake Bay where William often had sailed, the British frigate *HMS Leopold* attacks the American *USS Chesapeake* 10 miles outside Cape Henry. Three men on the *USS Chesapeake* are killed and 18 men are wounded. The *USS Chesapeake* is boarded and an English seaman and three American seamen brutally forced off the ship. The Royal Navy apparently intends to impress American seamen along the U.S. coast and not just from the English Channel[266] close to England. The impressment of American seamen in the English Channel reaches a level that summer that is the highest in many years.

As the news of the Cape Henry episode travels up through the Peninsula to Wilmington, it causes a public outcry. The United States of America and England are at peace, and Wilmington residents cannot believe that such an act of war can take place in the very waters where they earn their daily living. Soon the outcry comes from all east coast ports. In local newspaper articles and public speeches, people begin to call for war against Britain. The administration follows the situation closely, and insists that Britain immediately cease impressments of American seamen.

In stores along the harbor front and wharves in Wilmington, the matter is intensely discussed among wharf and ship owners, captains, seamen and port laborers. When William is on the quay on the north bank of the Christina River, it is the first subject to come up. William knows that some people in Wilmington, men like John Warner, Samuel Bush, Allen McLane and Thomas Mendenhall, see this British attack as a personal insult. It makes them very angry.

To seamen like William and Damian Starr, and captains who work onboard ships sailing in the Delaware and Chesapeake Bays, the news causes similar outrage. William and his fellow seamen discuss what can be done to protect them from impressments. William has not made any use of his protection certificate yet, so he has no proof that it will actually protect him when or if he is confronted with British naval officers. But thanks to the Cape Henry incident, Mary Ann and William do not feel that it is safe for him to sail.

Mary Ann, who has heard the story about Ann Bush requiring Samuel Bush to stop sailing the oceans before they got married, wonders if this arrangement can be a condition for her future relationship with William too. She often presents William with arguments against him going to sea again, but she can see the determination in his eyes. He flatly refuses to promise her anything of that kind. William believes it is plain stupidity for a woman to put restrictions on her future husband's work. William recalls in detail the story of Samuel and Ann Bush, but the way William sees it, the story is mostly about Ann Bush's selfishness. He dares not tell Mary Ann this. After all, he wants to marry her eventually.

William has actually spoken with Samuel Bush about the story, and Samuel tells a story quite different from the one Mary Ann tried to give William. Samuel Bush had been helping supplying the Continental Army on a small scale with his sloop, but only sailed along the Delaware River, because of his promise. Although Samuel was considered one of the best pilots out of the Delaware River, and should have been able to maneuver a ship, Ann Bush would not let him take deep-sea trips to the West Indies to fetch supplies during the Revolutionary War, like other Wilmington ship-owners had done, even though he knew that route as well as his own pockets and had sailed it several times with his father Charles Bush. Samuel had given Ann his promise before they married, and did not have the guts to break it. But oh, how he hated himself for it. He spent many sleepless nights during the war, wanting to help supply the Continental Army from the Dutch West Indian Island St. Eustatia and Danish West Indian Islands St. Thomas and St. Croix. But Ann could not bear to be home alone at night, so she would not let him break the promise, and he didn't have the heart to do it on his own.

June 25. John and the others from the Boston schooner are still onboard *Defence* anchored in Cowsand Bay. The Boatswains and carpenter's stores are received onboard, and 1,310 pounds of tobacco. The tobacco is only used for chewing, of course, because smoking onboard is strictly forbidden due to the high danger of fire, especially near the powder room.

Two days later John is painting the inner walls on the ship's lower decks. He loves this work, because it is new to him and after many uneventful days, even the smallest change is welcome. While painting walls a couple of days later, John learns that four mariners have managed to escape from the ship. They have been away for several hours when the officers discover it, and John knows from experience that it will be hard to find the mariners. Captain Ekins comes to the same conclusion and the four mariners are formally discharged from the Muster book.

Escape. John has been dreaming about it almost every night since he first arrived onboard the *Defence*, but because he is never let out of sight, he can't do anything about it. Nobody trusts an impressed American in the Royal Navy. When they are in a harbor, girls and musicians from shore are sometimes rowed out to the ships to entertain the crews for a couple of hours, and young seamen and mariners spend their money carelessly on these occasions. The elder seamen, with family at home and children to bring up, are more responsible and try to save their money.

The next day, a survey of the purser's store is held and a new purser appointed before the old one is discharged.

President Thomas Jefferson finally reacts to the *USS Chesapeake* incident on July 2, issuing a proclamation requiring all armed British vessels to depart from American waters. A few days later, Port Collector McLane receives written orders from Secretary of Treasury Allen Gallatin to increase the patrolling of the Delaware River and enforce the new proclamation.

The *Chesapeake* affair widens the gap between Federalists and Democratic Republicans on the east coast, and the political gap between the two eldest Warner brothers. John Warner now seems to agree mostly

with the Democratic Republicans, and the more he gets to know his new business partner, Samuel Bush, the more he is convinced of his beliefs. The two of them succeed in avoiding trade with England this year. Instead, they direct the *True American* to the West Indies, to St. Croix and St. Thomas. They increase their trade with neutral countries, especially with the Danish port of Altona near Hamburg, and with Ireland. This redirection hurts their business, but in difficult times like these, they are willing to sacrifice to support President Jefferson and their country.

William Warner, on the other hand, has no problem using his ship *Fair American* to continue his profitable trade with England or, more precisely, Liverpool. His only concession to the situation is to be a bit more careful when sailing the Delaware River with illegal British articles. William Warner sees the revenue cutter from New Castle more often as it patrols the Delaware River checking inbound and outbound ships like his own.

Since the time William and John Warner bought the John Robinson wharf back in 1795, they have disagreed more and more in business affairs, because of their differing political points of view. Confrontations between them increased considerably when they both moved their business to Philadelphia, but when John returned to Wilmington things were better. But when the family meets at Mary Warner's residence in Wilmington, one of them usually leaves in anger, because they can't help discussing politics. The youngest Warner boy, Joseph, is sad at this constant mixture of politics and business at family gatherings meant to be for the brothers to spend time with their mother. Obviously, politics have the power to destroy a family, Joseph often thinks at these gatherings.

When Joseph Warner and William Watson broach the subject, William completely understands his friend. Both of them see William Warner as a first class egoist, only concerned about his own business and not paying much attention to the good of other family members or his own country. If Joseph Warner, Sr. had still been alive, William Watson was sure that he would speak with William Warner about the real values in life and how to behave decently. Money seemed to be all William Warner cared about.

Independence Day. *HMS London* and *Dragon* arrive in Cowsand Bay while John Brown is busy splicing two ropes on the forecastle of *Defence*. The impressed Americans onboard ships in the harbor who are not on duty this afternoon will gather to celebrate the independence of the United States by drinking and toasting 13 times, just as they would do at celebrations at home. They raise their cups again and again. Filled with strong emotions and a longing for home they toast their beloved country America, the Stars and Stripes, President Jefferson, their wives, children, and girl friends. The British officers keep a low profile with these Americans this day, well aware that disturbing them might result in violent behavior.

This peace onboard *Defence* doesn't last long. Two days later, crewmembers fight each other and some of the Americans refuse to take orders. None of the crew has heard about the *Chesapeake* affair yet, but still already feel frustrated and that frustration turns into disobedience and fighting. Tension between men and officers increases, and John feels very unhappy about the situation.

This day, Secretary of State James Madison writes to James Monroe, the American minister in London, to settle this affair.

The following day, drunkenness, disobedience and fighting once again result in the punishment of four seamen onboard *Defence*.

Two days later, the seamen are busy loading large quantities of wood and coal into *Defence*. This kind of hard work normally tires out the seamen and makes them less focused on fighting. The weather is very fine that day.[45]

4

Friday, July 10 is another uneventful day onboard *HMS Defence*. A lieutenant and a mariner are discharged to the harbor in the morning; otherwise the day is routine.

This is not the case in Whitehall or the Board of Admiralty in London. A dispatch arrives from Lord Hutchinson, the English general attached to the Russian headquarters, reporting that the French and Russian Emperors, Napoleon and Alexander, have made a peace agreement on the Russian border, on a bridge in Niemen.

English government officials become very alarmed. A genuine peace agreement between these great powers on the European Continent, Russia and France, changes the entire European power balance. Peace. The Admirals in London desire no such peace.

From 1803 to 1806, rumors flew through the Danish Duchies of Holstein, just south of the border to the main Danish Peninsula of Jutland, that French troops stationed just south of Holstein might at any time march north, up through Jutland. Now that France is at peace with Russia, Napoleon is free to concentrate on a Danish operation if he should find it interesting.

France lost most of its fleet in the Battle of Trafalgar, and could use a fleet like the Danish one to blockade vital Danish waters of the Little Belt, the Great Belt and Ear Sound. French troops in Jutland could help enforce such a blockade and thereby cut off the British entrance to the Baltic Sea. To secure Royal Navy convoys in and out of that region, England must control the entrance. To the Admiralty and the government in London, it is conceivable that Napoleon Bonaparte might try to take control of these entrances to the Baltic Sea. There is no time to waste.

Danish Crown Prince Frederik VI envisions this same scenario when he receives the news about the French Russian peace agreement. He has already reinforced Danish troops on Denmark's or Jutland's southern border.

English spies and observers are always present in Hanover, where the family of English King George III originated, to watch the French occupants. These spies have brought information of the French positions in the region to the British government. An attack on the Kingdom of Denmark could quickly become a reality. To the British, the new power balance means it might only be a question of time before Denmark might be occupied by a large number of French troops, severing the British life nerve to the Baltic Sea and vital timber supplies.

John picks up news of these developments from talk among officers onboard *Defence*.

The Danish Fleet is, at the moment, anchored inside the fortifications of Copenhagen, to avoid the negative attention of the British Royal Navy and the Admiralty in London. But the members of The English Board of Admiralty are already busy planning a secret operation to neutralize the Danish Fleet, to keep a step ahead of young, dynamic Napoleon Bonaparte and his brilliant strategies.

On Monday the 13th, *Defence* weighs anchor and sails out of Cowsand Bay, heading south-southwest. Two days later, she moors in the Downs for three days, then returns to sea. The guns are exercised, and grog is served instead of beer, because they have run out of beer. The following day, three seamen and one mariner are punished.

Monday July 20, all sails are set and *Defence* heads east to Yarmouth Roads on the south east coast of England and right on the coast of the North Sea. This reinforces Captain Ekins' suspicions of an upcoming campaign against Denmark. *Defence* is accompanied by *HMS Commodore* and a squadron.

John observes the arrival of *Valliant*, *Leda* and several gun brigs to Yarmouth Roads. Although no one on *Defence* knows it, these gun brigs are part of the fleet that will enforce a closing of the English harbors and the coastline. The English coast is always closed when preparing war operation to prevent foreign or domestic ships from reporting Royal Navy activities to foreigners, and to make it easier to collect war equipment in the harbors.

Defence is supplied with butter, sugar, oatmeal, and fresh bread, enough to make a long voyage to the Baltic Sea. The high level of activity in port continues, and men and officers on the ships in Yarmouth Roads know the Royal Navy is preparing for a large war operation.

The following day the wind is fresh and John, working in the rigging on the foretop mast, observes the Flag of Admiral Gambier hoisted onboard the *Prince of Wales*. He studies the large number of cannons and guns being supplied to the different ships. Even an impressed American not familiar with Royal Navy procedures, can see that war is coming. Rumors fly among the ordinary crews that Admiral Gambier is going to lead an attack on the Danes.

On Saturday, the 25th, *Defence* receives a pilot from the *Prince of Wales*. His arrival creates excitement among the experienced seamen and officers. It is a certain sign that *Defence* will soon leave Yarmouth Roads.

John Brown has never been onboard a man-o-war preparing for war. He listens to off-duty seamen, when they occasionally gather over a pint of beer on the lower deck, describe previous battles like Trafalgar and the Battle of the Nile. The stories are horrifying, and John is not happy about what he hears. It is frightening enough just to take part in cannon exercises. He has no desire to be on the dark lower gun deck when the ship is in action. His current job is to rig the sails, and he doesn't imagine the rigging is a safe place to be when the cannon balls start to fly in great numbers. He doesn't sleep at all that night. He asks John Pristoff whether the Royal Navy can actually attack a small, defenseless, neutral country like Denmark. Pristoff looks him in the eye and answers in a low voice, 'England and France are at war. I'm afraid no one knows exactly what the British are really capable of doing."

On Sunday the 26th, when Divine Service is normally held at 10 a.m., Admiral Gambier gives the signal for his part of the Fleet to weigh anchor, and the flagship *HMS Prince of Wales, HMS Consul, HMS Centaur, HMS Ganges* and the greater part of the Fleet gathered leave Yarmouth Roads, heading east, to cross the North Sea to Denmark. Seamen and mariners who are not on duty find good spots on the upper deck to watch the spectacular departure of the fleet of 26 large ships of the line.

HMS Defence remains in Yarmouth. The crewmembers are disappointed, although none of them long for war. They simply wonder why they aren't taking part in the campaign at this point. *Defence* is known in the Royal Navy as a fair fighter, having done well in the battles of the Nile and Trafalgar. *Defence* is also known as the singing ship, thanks to a crew that enjoys singing at Divine Services.

The following day, the *HMS Superb* arrives and *Defence* receives 160 extra beds and hammocks from the *Minotaur,* indicating that *Defence* will be supplied with more men, perhaps prisoners, and mariners or wounded. No one onboard knows yet.

Wednesday, July 29, *HMS Defence* leaves Yarmouth Roads through the

St. Nicholas gateway, passing Yarmouth Church and heading north and northwest toward the Humber. John Brown and John Pristoff stand along the bulwark on the forecastle as the ship passes the Bay of Wash, on the English east coast. They can see a town, and John Brown hears someone call it Boston. The name fills him with longing for home. His heart is heavy the rest of that day, not knowing what lies ahead.

When *Defence* arrives in Grimsby Roads on July 30, John notices several transport ships holding a high number of troops. Additional transport ships arrive the next day.

Defence and her squadron moor in Grimsby Roads, and Captain Ekins brings the Agents and Masters of the transport ships to *HMS Defence* to give them instructions about the coming operation against Denmark. The *HMS Cyane* arrives that morning, and *HMS Mars* in the afternoon. All ships are made ready for sea. In this grave situation, incidents between officers and seamen have ceased and there is maximum co-operation between the different crewmembers. They are approaching a campaign, where their lives and security depend very much upon the way they are going to cooperate. Now is not the right time for discussions.

Captain Ekins carefully instructs the Masters on the plan to attack Denmark. A war operation like this needs a complete and fully supplied crew to succeed. A lack of sufficient English seamen means that impressed Americans like John Brown and the others are needed.

That same day, General William Lyman writes a consular dispatch from London to his superior, Secretary of State James Madison in Washington D.C. Since Lyman took office in 1805, he has received hundreds of letters each month from miserable and desperate American seamen trapped onboard ships of the Royal Navy. In 1807, he has received more letters than ever before, and he is greatly distressed.

Lyman works long hours trying to help these men regain their freedom. But every time he clears one letter from his desk, two new ones seem to arrive. At parties he attends in London, he hears rumors that the Royal Navy is preparing a large war operation and that the coast has been closed. Lyman is not happy to hear this at all. A new war operation always means more Americans impressed from American merchant ships in the English Channel, the St. George Channel or along the

English east coast.

In fact, at that very moment, Americans are being pressed in large numbers by British cutters and frigates in English ports or along the coast of England. Lyman's name is one of the first things a captured American receives from his fellow prisoners these days, and one of the first things they do is write to him. Impressed Americans are often put on prison ships anchored away from others, to prevent them from disturbing life on the ordinary prison ships with more 'well behaved' prisoners.

The *Chesapeake* affair seems to Lyman a perfect case for settling an agreement with the British authorities on impressments. Therefore, he writes to Madison, "*... Thus you will see on what grounds this event is placed, at this point of impressments, which heretofore does continue to produce. As documents from the office so fully evidence, such are vexations to our commerce, and humiliating and intolerable injuries to our citizens. The time has come to claim and insist on their redress and prevention of this badge of inferiority and submission too degrading longer to be born. This government, or most of its officers, in an unrestrained and capricious exercise of power, seem to claim it as a right to impress and, in very many instances, particularly, when in want of men, to totally disregard every circumstance and evidence of citizenship or national character accompanied with the retort of a disdainful curse for both character and country; and in all cases, the most frivolous pretexts or even 'suspicions light as air are confirmations strong' to set aside the best founded claims. In short the instruments of this brief authority play such fantastic tricks as to 'make the angels weep.'*

Individuals who are impressed are often bound, starved and scourged into submission to serve abhorrent to their feelings and repugnant to their duties. There is not at this time, I believe, a single ship of war in the British Navy, whose crew does not consist partly and, in some distant stations, principally of American seamen."[275]

Lyman reports that 15,000 American seamen are held against their will in the Royal Navy, and that the British are doing everything in their power to keep them there. He charges the British authorities with making it a rule to impress seamen under different names, so that when fair applications are made for their release, a British captain can reply that he has no one of that name. For someone with a common name like John

Brown, release becomes a practical impossibility. The situation has grown worse in the past 20 years, and Lyman is determined to stop it, even if it means war between England and America. [275] 'It is a disrespect to the very principles on which the United States of America is founded," he often says to anyone who will listen.

The following morning *Defence* unmoors and Captain Ekins orders the signal for the convoy to weigh to be given. A pilot climbs the gangway.

By 8:00 that evening, the convoy is heading into the North Sea on a course toward the Skagerak. The officers, seamen, mariners and other crewmembers onboard *Defence* can still only guess what their precise task will be in this operation. The warm sun is standing high over the horizon, and John Brown and John Pristoff stand quietly by the bulwark. Brown shakes his head and says, 'Well, at least we can't complain about the weather on this departure." Pristoff, who has had bad experience with the Royal Navy's behavior on foreign operations, replies, 'John, when you return from this operation, if you're lucky enough to return, I think you will begin to understand what you are a part of. You will have a share in the blame." John Brown keeps quiet, understanding that John Pristoff is sad about their situation.

Monday the 3rd, at 4 in the afternoon, the convoy is gathered, 39 ships. The ship's company is given good treatment on the order of captain Ekins, and one of the things they are served is chewing tobacco. As the seamen sit and chew, John Brown is told that this gesture is always made when the ships are on their way to war, a dangerous battle, or some other important event.

In this way, the captain shows that he cares for the well being of his crew. As the seamen and officers walk the decks and chew their tobacco, a peaceful atmosphere descends for the first time since John boarded *Defence*. Yes, indeed, this will help unite the British crew against the Danish, John Brown thinks. But he doesn't want to be a part of that unity. John can't accept an attack on another small country, which fights to stay as neutral as possible in the war between England and France.

The following day, a Danish brig coming from Norway and destined for Chester is boarded. Nothing unusual is found and the ship is free to go. The Danish crew expresses no knowledge of war to the British officer and mariners who visit the ship. When the boarding officer later reports this to captain Ekins, he smiles and says to the officers at the steering wheel that the Royal Navy has succeeded in keeping its operation a secret, which leaves the navy with an element of surprise. It looks good for the coming operation.

At 10 in the morning, the men at the cannons are exercised in firing, using real shots, and the mariners are exercised with small arms. The ships in the convoy stay close together. At 3 p.m., another Danish ship on its way from Amsterdam to Norway is stopped and asked about news. This crew also seems ignorant about the operation and the Danes speak kindly to the English, treating them as good friends they are delighted to meet.

HMS Gallant and three merchant ships join the *Defence* convoy that day. That evening, a seaman falls to his death from the main topgallant, and his body is committed to the sea shortly after. The convoy and 42 merchant ships enter Skagerrak, between Norway and Jutland.

On August 5, *Defence* signals to the Packet *Auckland,* sailing from Gothenburg to Harwich. In the afternoon, the crew on *Defence* sounds 34 meters on the Jutland Reef close to Hanstholm, or the Holm as Royal Navy officers and seamen call it, on the northwest coast of Jutland. The following day, they sail northwest and observe the land on the Naze of Norway. The wind is strong.

During the night and the following day, *Defence* sails eastwards and, in the afternoon, the crew observes land about the Scaw, the top point of Jutland. At 2 p.m., *Defence* is only 12 to 13 miles from the Scaw Lighthouse. The ship soon passes the Sea of Skagerak to enter the Cattegat Sea separating Jutland and the Kingdom of Sweden. A Danish ship of the line is spotted with a convoy to the north. *Defence* has 140 merchant ships in convoy.

On Friday the 7th of August, nine seamen are punished for neglect of duty. This high number reflects the tense atmosphere onboard related to the coming operation against Denmark. John Pristoff is one of the men punished, because he refused to serve in this campaign. Pristoff considers Denmark a friend of The United States of America, because Denmark helped America gain her own freedom, letting her be supplied with guns and ammunition through the Danish West Indian Islands of St. Croix and St. Thomas during the Revolutionary War.

John Pristoff is no troublemaker, as any seaman onboard *Defence* can attest. Unlike many other American seamen onboard, John was a grown man when he was impressed in the harbor of Liverpool and had not misbehaved at all since boarding the *Defence*. But the demand to fight a small neutral nation was totally against his principles, and he was ready to take punishment for neglect of duty.

John Brown would rather not attend this punishment, but is carefully watched by the officers and dares not look away as the seamen are whipped. John Pristoff is seriously hurt by the whipping, and is finally carried, unconscious, to the sick quarters. John Brown is not allowed to go and visit his friend, as no seaman is allowed in the sick quarters.

As they sail deeper into Danish waters, John Brown recalls that Pristoff often expressed his hatred of England and the Royal Navy for the brutal treatment of men onboard its ships. His hate was not arbitrary, but came from his earlier experience.

John Brown figures that, with Pristoff' s strong aversion to fighting a neutral country, it might be better for Pristoff to remain in sick quarters, rather than behind a cannon. John Brown himself decides that he will not speak up against this injustice and risk being punished. He is well aware one can die from the injuries caused by flogging. It is simply too dangerous to risk being punished.

On August 8, the Danish Crown Prince Frederik VI, head of the Kingdom of Denmark and the armed forces on behalf of his beloved but insane father King Christian VII, receives a messenger from the British Government, Mr. Jackson. The meeting takes place in the Crown Prince's headquarters in Kiel, on the southern border of Denmark. The Crown Prince and part of the Danish State Administration decided to stay in Rendsborg, so they can react quickly to changes in the military situation. Mr. Jackson arrived in the North Sea port Tøningen on the Elbe River the day before.

Frederik VI decides to meet Mr. Jackson, even though he quite improperly demanded to be presented to the Crown Prince immediately. This is a breach of protocol; no one dictates orders to the Danish Crown Prince. But Frederik keeps his Napoleon-like temper under control and says nothing. Mr. Jackson offers Frederik VI two options: An alliance with England, which includes temporarily confiscation of the Danish Fleet and a following transport of the fleet to English harbors, or war.

The Crown Prince orders carriages made ready for a trip to the Danish capital, Copenhagen. He is convinced that the British will soon occupy all of Zealand, the main island in Denmark, holding the capital.

The Crown Prince is quite worried. A British attack could, if things turned out badly, lead to the Kingdom of Denmark's removal from the world's catalogue of nations.

If Denmark loses its military land forces trying to liberate Zealand, and loses its navy too, Napoleon Bonaparte could easily send his forces northward to occupy Jutland. The oldest Kingdom in the world would then disappear forever. The thought is unbearable to the Crown Prince who feels the heavy burden of his responsibility.

He knows that, as head of state, the armed forces and the people, he would be the one to take the blame. He has no time to waste, so he hurries to Copenhagen to do everything in his power to prevent a British invasion of Zealand. His father, King Christian VII, is staying in The Royal Residence Amalienborg in Copenhagen, and the Crown Prince wants to take care of him as well as to put Zealand on military alert.

The following morning, John Brown sees the Island of Anholt and its lighthouse. As *Defence* sails deeper into Danish waters, the wind becomes stronger and the sky darker. Lightning cuts the sky into fragments, and enormous claps of thunder terrify the crew.

Heavy rain follows and the seamen become quite nervous. They are mentally alert, like cats moving outside their territories, knowing that an attack might be waiting beyond the horizon. To the impressed American seamen, the situation is philosophically unbearable. They were well informed by their families about the principles that lead to the Revolutionary War. Many also have personal childhood memories of family members who participated in that war.

They have been told of the hoisting of the first American flag in a foreign port, in the harbor of the city of Charlotte Amalie on the Danish West Indian Island of St. Thomas. When the news of the Declaration of Independence reached the island, the flag went up onboard the Wilmington ship *Nancy*, anchored in the harbor to smuggle weapons into the 13 states in the beginning of the Revolutionary War.

John Pristoff had refused to have anything to do with a fight against the first friend and country that recognized the American Independence, and had paid the price. The British officers did not recognize neglect of duty for an American seaman's principles.

John Brown thinks back to that first hoisting of the American flag in a foreign port. He shouts to William King, a few yards away standing in the bow, "What was the name of the officer who hoisted the American flag onboard the *Nancy* at the Danish island of St. Thomas?" William King answers right away, "Thomas Mendenhall!" When ships enter the Delaware Bay, seamen are told local stories about the Revolutionary War. Therefore, Brown and King have good memories of the *Nancy* incident.

Defence follows a southerly course along the Swedish west coast, heading for Ear Sound. Early in the afternoon, she reaches a position outside Ellsinore, just north of the Castle of Kronborg, and Captain Ekins finally gives the order for the convoy to moor.

The captain and his first lieutenant notice with relief that the flagship *HMS Prince of Wales,* with Commander in Chief Admiral Gambier, and 16 other ships of the line are already anchored here.

Danish Crown Prince Frederik VI is travelling up through Jutland with great speed, and this evening he reaches the Castle of Kolding in the southern part of east Jutland. He orders the First Battalion of the Third Regiment of Jutland and three squadrons of Slesvig Horse Troops to march eastward to the island of Fun to the island's main town, Odense.

General Moltke is ordered to mobilize Jutland's military forces. The sea batteries in Fredericia on the east coast of Jutland, are mobilized, as are the batteries in the Castle of Nyborg on the west bank of the Great Belt.

Monday, August 10. The sun shines brightly and a light breeze still blows around Kronborg Castle. Onboard *Defence,* Captain Ekins sends a signal to the marine lieutenants in his squadron to exercise the men. Onboard *Defence,* 60 seamen and some mariners are trained using hand weapons. John Brown supposes this is for the coming operation.

None of the Americans are exercised for action. John Brown is relieved to see that the Americans are apparently not going to be part of the landing forces. He assumes the officers have considered his situation as an American and want to save him from fighting against a nation friendly to his own country. But then he realizes how naive he is. The real reason, of course, is that a landing operation would give him a very good opportunity to desert. Or even worse, to join the Danish forces against England.

Escape. John Brown has been thinking of it often. He looks with longing toward Kronborg Castle, the beautiful wood of tall oak trees covering the coast from the castle northward.

On the newly washed and yet wet quarterdeck of *Defence*, the combination of the sight of the Kronborg Castle and the present tense atmosphere, results in comments from the Royal Navy officers about the play of William Shakespeare called Hamlet. 'Hamlet, who was Prince of Denmark is supposed to have lived in this Castle," one officer begins, who only knows the play lightly from the subject of dinner conversations. He is instantaneous interrupted by Captain Ekins, who knows his Shakespeare so well, that he is able to develop and extrapolate the stories in the different plays.

Captain Ekins, with a wild, satanic look in his eyes and a bitter smile on his thin lips whispers, as his eyes moves systematically from the one officer to the other on the deck: "As the present King of Denmark, the insane Christian VII can be said now to be only a shadow of himself, a true ghost, the same way the present Danish Crown Prince Frederik VI can be said to be as irresolute as Prince Hamlet himself. Therefore one must expect the night watches, at the sea batteries here at the Kronborg Castle, this very night, by the sight of our great English fleet anchored here, terrified are forced to admit, that the citizens of the Kingdom of Denmark at this crucial moment in its history, is without a real sovereign, and forced to shout out at the top of their longs: Something is rotten in the state of Denmark ."

Ekins has hardly finished the last sentence before a loud raw masculine laughter, coming from all the English officers assembled, roles out on the quarterdeck, crosses the salty water of the Ear sound and the beach and reflects on the great northern tower wall of Kronborg Castle and delayed returns to the quarterdeck of *Defence* again.

Captain Ekins glances shortly at the Swedish coastline, seven miles to the east opposite Kronborg Castle, and wonders if the Swedes will assist the British in this confrontation against the Danes. He laughs again and says to his first lieutenant, 'The Swedes are sweet, it's the Danish we eat." Again the officers laugh long and loud.

John Brown observes the scene from the forecastle, but does not realize what the fun is all about. All he is aware of right now is that they are all in a serious situation, with war rapidly approaching.

Defence is so close to the shore that John Brown can see the faces of the men, women and children who promenade along the beach, and he thinks seriously several times about jumping overboard and swimming to the beach. Then he would be a free man, able to return to North America and his mother. But he notices that the jollyboats are constantly in the water close by, and he knows any attempt of escape will be discovered, and the mariners will shoot to kill.

The other Americans are put to the work chalking the flatboats. John Brown observes the launch boat of *Defence* sent to another ship to be fitted out with a gun.

Crown Prince Frederik VI is crossing the Little Belt in the ferryboat between Snoghøj in Jutland and Middelfart on the island of Funen, on his way to organize the defense of Zealand and Copenhagen.

In the afternoon, the English seamen are exercised once again and the cannon crews are trained in double-shooting and fast loading of the cannons. The citizens of Ellsinore are used to hearing cannons, because the batteries at Kronborg Castle are often exercised in connection with ship warnings related with the collection of the Ear Sound Toll from the Customhouse. But local citizens can tell the shots are coming from the waterside and a more northerly direction than usual. They are alerted but not terribly concerned. Foreign ships anchored here mean profit for local merchants. At the noise of cannons, these merchants begin to gather food supplies they know the English ships of the line are usually interested in.

That afternoon, 60 men and two officers from the famous 43rd Regiment, which specializes in landing operations, join the *Defence*. Ten of the beds *Defence* took in at Grimsby Roads are sent to the *Prince of Wales* south of Kronborg Castle, where the largest part of the Royal Navy fleet is anchored. John, chalking the flatboats, notices several Danish gun brigs arriving from the south, from Copenhagen Roads. The situation is tense onboard all the ships in the waters around Kronborg Castle. As if to match the mood, the sky darkens and the wind increases.

The morning of Tuesday, August 11, the wind is strong around both Ellsinore and Copenhagen, preventing any attacks from the Danish gunboats in Ellsinore Roads. Preparations for battle continue on the Royal Navy ships. The seamen are exercised with weapons and John Brown and John Pristoff are employed washing the lower deck.

The wind remains strong, and at noon it begins to rain, just as Crown Prince Frederik VI and his retinue of carriages passes Frederiksberg's Castle on the top of Valby Hill, just west of Copenhagen. The Crown Prince has been silent for most of the trip, speaking to his traveling companion General Bülow only when he needed to discuss military details. Ten minutes later, the Crown Prince enters the Western Gateway in the Fortification of Copenhagen. The strong west wind pushed his carriage over the island of Zealand to Copenhagen, as though God was giving him a helping hand.

Crown Prince Frederik's carriage passes under his seal above the gateway, into the tunnel in the middle of the building. They stop between the main guardhouses, two small, white buildings with red tile roofs in front of the bridge to Danish Military Headquarters on the islet of Bremerholm. At the gateway, every person, high and low, must identify himself and be entered in the guard book. As the Crown Prince enters his office, he has instructions to his subordinates for the defense of Copenhagen and Zealand ready. When he left Kiel, he gave one of his subordinates the order that Mr. Jackson should be delayed two hours at each horse station along the route. Twelve stops along the dusty road from Kiel to Copenhagen have given the Crown Prince a 24-hour head start.[132-1]

Zealand has two coordinated commanding authorities, the Chief Command of Copenhagen and Kronborg Castle headed by Major General H. E. Peymann, and the Chief Command of the rest of Zealand and larger surrounding islands, headed by the Crown Prince himself. The Crown Prince is also head of the first command should anything fail.

Frederik gives orders to his subordinates and all of Copenhagen and Kronborg Castle are put on highest alert, along with Sea Defense ships in the Roads of Copenhagen. The alert extends from the northern harbor entrance, Toldboden, to the ship lane blockade, eight ships of the line grounded north of the sea fort Trekroner to make the ship lane impassable. Only six years ago, the British Royal Navy was in the Roads of Copenhagen, and the Danes soon after built the blockade because they wanted to be prepared for the next time.

A gunboat fleet is quickly organized from the wharves on the islet of Nyholm and put under the command of Navy Commander Sten Bille. Sten Bille disposed gun brigs from Copenhagen Roads to Ellsinore

Roads twenty-four hours before the Crown Prince arrived in Copenhagen.

Norway, which is administered together with the Duchies of Slesvig and Holstein, is allowed to take its own military actions.

After a couple of hours, the Crown Prince has finished his work. He hurries from the headquarters past Nytorv up Norges Gade into Frederiks Torv, surrounded by the four identical Royal Palaces, Amalienborg. His carriage passes a marble statue of King Frederik V on a horse in the center of the square and enters the gate to the Levenzaus Palace, the southernmost of four identical palaces. From the windows in the palace, the Crown Prince sees three British ships of the line. 'Mr. Jackson was right, there *is* a large British fleet here," he shouts angrily. He rushes to the opposite end of the house and through the connecting building between the Levenzaus Palace and the Moltkes Palace, built to make it easy for him to visit his father without going outside. Old King Christian VII is sitting in a chair and smiles warmly at his beloved son.

There is no time to waste. The Crown Prince hurries to the old King. 'Father, dearest father. I'm afraid we must leave Copenhagen immediately. England is taking Zealand as we speak. There are British war ships in the Great Belt, the Ear Sound at Kronborg Castle and here in the Roads of Copenhagen. Follow me; we can join the army in Jutland. Please, follow me to Rendsburg." Servants pack the King's personal things, and the King and Crown Prince hurry in a carriage toward the west coast of Zealand, to reach Corsør and cross the Great Belt. News of the Crown Prince's travel is communicated by light telegraph, a new and indispensable tool for serious situations, and reaches Corsør before he does.

The following day, Wednesday August 12, there is a moderate breeze around Ellsinore, with occasional rain showers. *Defence*'s cannon crews are exercised, and *HMS Africaine* arrives at Ellsinore Roads. The *HM Sloop Bohetta* is supplied with bread, beef, pork and flour from the *Defence*. The seamen and the mariners are once again exercised with hand weapons to make them more fit for the fight.

From the rigging, John sees a Danish merchant ship approach *HMS Defence*. The Danish merchant climbs the gangway to the top deck, and John watches the merchant and *Defence*'s purser discuss prices of beef. From their faces and the way they shake hands, he concludes that they have reached an agreement. Soon after, 954 pounds of fresh Danish beef are supplied to the *Defence*[45, 46] from this ship. John wonders why a merchant would trade with an enemy of his country, then recalls that war has not yet been declared here.

Ellsinore merchants have often seen British war ships here, passing through Ear Sound to or from the Baltic Sea. John supposed that the Danes think the fleet anchored at Kronborg Castle now is a traveling convoy making a short stop. Yet they must have noticed the British ships exercising handguns and firing broadsides several times, while anchored so close to the Castle of Kronborg. Surely military and navy officers know this is more than just a friendly stop around Ellsinore Roads.

John notices that the Danish frigate No. 6, *Friderichsværn*, anchored at Kronborg Castle when *Defence* arrived, has disappeared. That frigate, at least, must have known something unusual was going on, he figures.

Crossing the Great Belt from Zealand to Funen is less dangerous in the dark, so Crown Prince Frederik VI and King Christian VII wait in Corsør for dark, then sneak out, faces covered, to the ferryboat. Frederik dares not be seen onboard, so he hides in the hold of the ferry. King Christian stays on the open deck. As they slowly cross the Great Belt, they pass a ferryboat coming from the other side, probably carrying Mr. Jackson to meet the Crown Prince in Copenhagen. Hidden on the west side of the island of Sprogø, in the middle of the Great Belt, a British frigate waits to inspect the approaching ferryboat, not knowing of its royal guests. When the frigate catches up with the ferryboat, British mariners and two officers enter the ferryboat. King Christian VII feels the danger and begins to act like a sick Swedish Baron. The British officers know of the complicated Swedish mentality, and are very impressed by this performance. Frederik nervously follows the whole scene from below. When the British officers direct their attention elsewhere, he quickly escorts his father into a jollyboat, which takes them to the island of Funen, unnoticed. As they reach shore, Frederik VI relax, relieved he was able to save his beloved father, King Christian VII of Denmark, at such a crucial historic moment.

The following day, Thursday August 13, Admiral Gambier finally decides which ships will participate in the Copenhagen operation. He orders *HMS Defence* equipped with the 43rd Regiment landing forces. *HMS Defence*, which fought so bravely in earlier battles, would once again be at the center of a large sea operation.

Then Gambier changes his mind about *Defence*. The Copenhagen operation will not be an open sea battle, like the Nile and at Trafalgar, where *Defence*'s easy maneuverability would be a strength. It will be mostly a landing and blockading operation, where ordinary-performing ships of the line will be sufficient. *Prince of Wales* orders *HMS Defence* to send the soldiers of the 43rd regiment to *HMS Valliant*. *Defence* is also ordered to leave its launch and two flatboats for use in the landing operation.

The operation is partly to confiscate the Danish Fleet, and *Defence*'s new task is to guard the Cattegat and Skagerak to prevent any Danish ship from escaping to the North Sea or the fjords of Norway. The ship has performed this task before, and the crew knows these waters very well. At 1:20 p.m., newly chalked boats are sent to the *HMS Prince of Wales,* and *Defence* leaves Ellsinore on a northern course toward the Cattegat, accompanied by *HMS Comus*. Their first task is to hunt down the former guard ship of Kronborg, the Danish frigate *Friderichsværn,* which they now know for certain escaped northward.

At 4 p.m., when Kronborg Castle is six miles to the southwest, John and the lookout observe three Swedish merchant ships ahead. Officers from *HMS Defence* ask the Swedish captains if they have seen the *Friderichsværn* , and the captains of the Swedish merchant ships confirm that a Danish frigate has come this way. There is a moderate breeze, and *Comus* and *Defence* move northward at four knots.

Early in the next morning, Friday, August 14, the breeze is light. At 2 a.m., Captain Ekins sees the lighthouse on the island of Anholt. In a few days, it will be turned off for several years. An English seaman dies this morning. At 4 a.m. they take in the anchor. *Comus* stays close by.

At 8 a.m. Nidingen Lighthouse on the Swedish west coast is observed to the northeast. The body of the dead seaman is committed to the sea followed by a simple prayer by the ship's priest. In the afternoon, the wind has almost disappeared and the sea surface is very calm. *Comus* and *Defence* are together when, to his great satisfaction, Captain Ekins observes the *Friderichsværn* just ahead of them.

But now, with their prize in sight, the wind dies. The ships of the line may as well be glued to the surface of the water. John Brown and John Pristoff are standing at the bulwark on the forecastle, and John Brown whispers "This is definitely the frigate I saw when we first arrived in Ellsinore Roads." John Pristoff nods his head in agreement.

At 8 p.m., a light breeze begins blowing. *Comus* and *Defence* are still close together and with the Danish frigate a small distance ahead. They are between the largest Danish islands in the Cattegat, Læsø and Vinga Sound, outside Gothenburg. At midnight *Defence* stops receiving signals from *Comus*, and the men onboard conclude that the *Comus* has moved far ahead while hunting the Danish frigate. Half an hour later, Captain Ekins receives a report of cannons fired in the darkness ahead, and concludes that *Comus* has caught up with *Friderichsværn*.

John Brown is awake, resting in his hammock, carefully listening to noises in the darkness, when he hears the master mate call "All hands. All hands." Shortly after, all men on duty run to their posts, and the sails are quickly set to make *Defence* ready for action. Those who have managed to sleep through the excitement are awakened by loud shouts as the main decks are emptied of loose items. Captain Ekins' furniture is removed from his cabin and taken down to the hold, so it won't hurt someone if the ship is attacked. The men do not need to throw furniture out the windows as has been the case earlier, when they were in a hurry to clear the ship because they were surprised by the enemy.

Nothing happens for the next four hours. The guards onboard *Defence* are tense, waiting to see the *Comus* and the Danish frigate on the horizon. At 5 a.m., silhouetted against the Swedish west coast and the light, morning sky, illuminated by a glowing, warm raising summer sun, *Comus* appears towing the Danish frigate.

Comus and *Defence* align themselves and the captain of *Comus* boards *Defence* to give Captain Ekins a brief report on the chase the preceding night. *Comus* had slowly but surely caught up with the Danish frigate, then fired several broadsides into her. The English boarded the ship, but it only took a few minor skirmishes before the Danes realized they were outnumbered. *Comus* confiscated the 36-gun frigate and the 230 men onboard. Twelve Danish seamen were killed and twenty wounded, some of them mortally. Only one member of the Royal Navy was wounded, so Captain Ekins and the captain from *Comus* are quite satisfied with the outcome of this chase. Officer Watt from *Defence* is sent to command the frigate number 6, *Fridericksværn*.

On the quarterdeck this beautiful morning, the two British captains quietly discuss whether *HMS Defence* should take some of the captured Danish prisoners. Captain Ekins accepts to take half of them. *Defence* soon after hoists out boats to begin the transfer of 100 Danish prisoners.

Away from the island of Zealand and Copenhagen, the officers and men onboard *Defence* and *Comus* do not yet know that they have participated in the hostile action that started the war between the Kingdom of Denmark and the United Kingdom, at a time in history where both countries theoretically are headed by insane kings: George III and Christian VII.

Watching the Danish prisoners climb *Defence's* gangway one by one, John Brown suddenly feels badly when he thinks about the Ellsinore merchant who supplied *HMS Defence* with Danish beef and other foodstuffs, when they were near Kronborg Castle. Now, as a 'thank you', *Defence* has chased down the guard ship from Kronborg, killed twelve Danish mariners and seamen, wounded several mortally and taken about 200 Danish prisoners. To John this did not seem to be a fair deal to Ellsinore, and as an American, he is not happy about his involvement.

While the *Friderichsværn* had tried unsuccessfully to escape British ships, the Danish King and the Crown Prince have been much luckier, arriving safely in Rendsborg. The *Friderichsværn*, which actually meant 'the protection of Frederich," was used to train some of the bravest Danish officers that fought Lord Nelson's fleet in the Copenhagen Roads six years before, when the ship was connected to the Navy Academy in Copenhagen. Among these men was the now-famous Danish sea officer Peter Willemoes.

The following morning, on August 16 at 3 a.m., *Defence*, *Comus* and its prize *Friderichsværn* are 10 miles southwest of the Scaw Lighthouse. One of *Defence*'s night watches spots the *HMS Cyane* in the Skagerak. At the same time, the *HMS Valliant* and other Royal Navy troop transporting ships have anchored in Ear Sound, along the coast between Ellsinore and Copenhagen, close to the sandy beaches at Vedbæk.

The land here is elevated to the south and wooded, making it an ideal place for a British invasion, because it will be hard for Danish military posts farther south to see enemy activities in the Vedbæk region. The large number of jollyboats, launches and flatboats from Royal Navy ships of the line, including those from *Defence*, are busy transporting soldiers, mariners, weapons, cannons, ammunition and other equipment to the beach.

Among these trained men are parts of the 43rd Regiment which was partly transported to Ellsinore onboard *Defence* earlier.[132-1] The British ships now have a total of 30,000 troops in good order on the shore at

Vedbæk, equal to 30 percent of the total population of Copenhagen.

At 2 p.m., as British infantry troops steadily march south toward Copenhagen, the captain of the *Cyane* comes onboard *Defence*. It is decided that *Cyane* will transport the Danish prisoners to an English prison ship anchored in one of the English east coast ports. *Defence* hoists down its barge and the 100 Danish prisoners from the frigate *Friderichsværn* are now sent in small groups to the *Cyane*.

At 3:20 p.m. the two ships part, and *Defence* resumes patrolling the Skagerak. News of the British invasion of Zealand reaches the Danish Government and the Crown Prince, and Denmark is therefore forced to declare war against England.

Two days later, British land forces are able to make a half circle around Copenhagen, on the landside from Kallebod Strand at the south shore, through Frederiksberg Castle, through the estates of Falconergaarden, Store Vibenhus to the road of Strandvejen on the north shore. The castle is made British headquarters. On the seaside, the fortifications of Copenhagen are half circled by Admiral Gambier's war ships.

Standing at the bulwark, John sees a convoy of merchant ships headed by *HMS Agamemnon* on the horizon as *Defence* passes the Scaw.

Defence again takes up the hunt for enemy ships and in the next 14 days, she steadily cruises the Skagerak between the Scaw and the Naze of Norway. She systematically checks all passing ships, and in this time she boards seven American, six British, six Danish, four Russian and others for a total of 23. Four ships are taken as prizes, two Danish and two Russian. John Brown and John Pristoff especially remember an American brig they stopped, which was headed directly for Boston. What the two of them would have given for passage home with that ship.

On the morning of September 2, *Defence* meets *HMS Clio* south of the island of Flekeø on the Norwegian south coast. The same afternoon, a Danish ship on its way from Spain to Copenhagen is confiscated, and *Defence* takes onboard the Danish prisoners.

In the twilight, John Brown stands on the upper deck gazing at the sunset over the Norwegian south coast. At that moment, the Royal Navy Ships in Copenhagen Roads begin the first bombardment of a nation's capital, as the first bomb hits the pavement close to Vor Frue Church inside the fortification of Copenhagen. The British ships shoot at the church tower to adjust the cannons.

Five days later, on September 7, *Defence* still patrols the Skagerak in a strong gale with rain showers and a cloudy sky, six miles southeast of the island of Flekeø. John again stands at the bulwark, his face washed by the rainwater. He is in a very low mood, realizing that there is little chance of being released in the near future. It has been almost two years since he was forced out of his Boston schooner to serve in the Royal Navy.

In London, the American Minister to England James Monroe sits at his desk writing to the British Foreign Secretary, asking for reparation of the damage England caused in the *Chesapeake* affair. He suggests four items of reparation, the third being *"abandonment of impressments from merchant vessels."*

James Monroe and William Lyman often meet when Monroe is in London, and they are shocked when they hear about the British brutality in Copenhagen, as is President Thomas Jefferson. None of them really comprehend how any civilized nation can act so cruel against a small defenseless nation.

In Lyman's office, Monroe can see for himself the constant flow of letters from desperate American seamen held against their will onboard Royal Navy's ships. Lyman is thrilled as always when someone like Monroe from the American administration has time to come to visit him in London. It lifts his spirits to be able to show someone the results of what he is doing.

Outside the Naze of Norway on September 12, two cannons onboard *Defence* are firing at a brig. Later, a Danish brig bound for Copenhagen is boarded and some of the Danish crewmembers are taken as prisoners. A midshipman and five seamen from *Defence* are sent onboard to take the prize to Yarmouth Roads. In the late evening, *Defence* captures another Danish ship, and Captain Ekins order these Danes taken as prisoners, too, and the prize taken to Yarmouth. Shortly after, *Defence* boards a ship with homeport in Finmarken and heading for Copenhagen.

When John Brown climbs into his hammock that evening, he knows he has experienced just one of many busy days hunting Danish and Norwegian prizes in the Skagerak. He does not feel good about this at all.

Three days later, there is a moderate breeze in the evening. *Defence* is again on a position south of the Naze of Norway when a seaman falls from a top yard. Luckily, he falls to the leeward side and into the water not far from the bulwark. He can swim, so a boat is lowered and picks him up.

HMS Defence and *Clio* spend most of their time hunting prizes in the northwestern part of the Skagerak. On the morning of September 19, long chases have brought the ships so far south to the west coast of Jutland that they can see the cliffs of Bovbjerg.

On September 22, *Defence* is again outside Flekeø, in company with *HMS Spencer, Comus* and *Pelican*. John remembers seeing the *Pelican* before, in Port Royal, Jamaica two years earlier. He recalls this clearly, because he attended his first execution of a man ever, while onboard the *Hercule,* and the executed man came from the *Pelican*. Three days later, *Pelican* goes into the Norwegian shore to attack Norwegian Sea forces stationed there.

On September 27, *Defence* is on its own for a period of time. The *Comus* has gone out of sight, but *Spencer* appears close by. *Defence* and *Spencer* fire cannons at the Danish gunboats, then at 7 p.m., the two ships sail out of the east outlet.

On Friday October 2, the wind is light and it is cloudy. *Defence* burns a blue light to signal its position to the other ships. A Danish ship sailing from Iceland to Copenhagen is boarded and five seamen taken as prisoners. The prize is, as often before, taken across the North Sea to Yarmouth.

October 8 at 10 a.m., a strong gale blows in. Several Danish and Norwegian ships have been boarded in the past week, but no prizes or prisoners taken. *Defence's* main mast's topsail splits and nearly all of the canvas is lost. Even a large group of seamen are unable to hold the canvas down because of the strength of the gale.

Defence is again together with *Comus* and *Pelican* outside the Naze of Norway. The storm grows stronger, and to avoid drifting onto the west coast of Jutland, the British warships go into the Skagerak and anchor in the Cattegat on the east side of the Scaw to ride out the storm. The rainstorm lasts three full days.

The northern point of the Danish Peninsula Jutland, the Scaw, is one of the most dangerous spots to sail along on the long Danish coastline. Several ships go to their graves here every year in autumn and winter storms. The Scaw is the meeting point of two seas, the Skagerak to the west connected to the North Sea, and the Cattegat to the east, connected to the Little Belt, the Great Belt and Ear Sound. Depending on the strength of storms, the sand reef moves from year to year and maps quickly become outdated here, which makes it difficult for passing ships to predict where the ground is along this coast. Experienced Danish pilots are available but passing ships are seldom willing to cover the expense. It costs many of them dearly.

Defence is in Skagerak with *Comus* October 16 in a fresh wind with rain.

In London, King George III issues a proclamation recalling all British seamen from the service of foreign nation's ships and ordering British naval officers to return all natural born British seamen in the service on ships from foreign states. This is actually an order to increase impressments of British seamen into the Royal Navy from American and other countries merchant ships, but it also has the side effect of increasing impressments of American seamen.

This proclamation makes the already bad relations between the United States of America and England even worse.[276] During the remainder of this year, American Secretary of State James Madison requests the release of about 100 impressed American seamen. Some of them are released, but most are held back on the grounds that they have taken the bounty.

When news of the bombardment of Copenhagen and the theft of the Danish fleet finally reaches American newspapers, many Democratic Republicans are outraged.

Samuel Bush reads about the Copenhagen campaign in the local Democratic Republican newspaper, *American Watchman*. He says to his wife Ann, 'To think that a small, neutral country like Denmark has been brutally attacked, it almost feels like America has been attacked. Who can feel safe if England can get away with this kind of crime?" Samuel Bush is clearly agitated, and Ann does not like it when he is upset. She thinks he needs to take better care of his health.

When the sons of Samuel Bush's generation, the young independent merchants, storeowners and wharf-owners in Wilmington, hear about the attack on Denmark, they, too, feel alarmed. James Hemphill and John Warner are also very upset. They have sailed together to the Danish harbor Altona and as children they watched the Revolutionary War fought, nearly in their own yards. Joseph Warner and William Watson are equally frustrated. Given a chance, England might attack the United States again, if this action is any indication.

John Warner assures his little brother Joseph, "If it comes to war with England again, I will not sit and watch as our father did. I'll follow my regiment where it might go to defend our country."

By October 20, the *Defence* has spent almost a week around the Scaw. The wind changes and comes from the north-northeast for three full days, the perfect direction for a ride home to England and Yarmouth Roads. Captain Ekins decides to take this chance to sail with the favorable wind to return quickly. Ekins is quite satisfied and concludes that *Defence* and her crew have done well this year and can return to England with pride.

John is also quite satisfied when he hears they are returning to England. This autumn he has been forced to spend much time aloft rigging the sails, exposed for a long time to all kinds of bad weather. It will be good for his health to reach a harbor soon, he thinks.

Defence comes out of the Skagerak and gets sufficiently far out into the North Sea to clear the West Coast of Jutland before October 24, when the wind changes to the dangerous direction of west-northwest. The following day, they reach the Flamborough Head and have crossed the North Sea in only five days.

Then on October 27, *Defence* drops anchor in Yarmouth Roads and is supplied with large amounts of food.

Soon after, John Brown hears about the bombardment of Copenhagen from seamen onboard returning ships that actually participated in it. John is sad to realize that he participated in this somehow. The bombardment angers the entire world, including the lower classes in England. From that day on, British people are not quite as safe as they used to be on the streets of Copenhagen, and the few American seamen visiting in the following years are thrown out of taverns and otherwise harassed, because they speak a language most uneducated Danes in the taverns find indistinguishable from the British.

In newspapers in Boston and other east coast cities, the British Minister to Denmark, Mr. Jackson, is dubbed Copenhagen Jackson. The name sticks to him for a long time in North America. When President Thomas Jefferson gets the news from Copenhagen, he explodes in anger, and in private parties he attends in the following months, he frequently damns the British to hell.

On October 29, John sees several transport ships arrive, and at 3 a.m., the *HMS Prince of Wales* arrives with the greater part of the Royal Navy fleet from Ear Sound and most of the captured Danish ships from Copenhagen. Transport ships continue to arrive in the port. Seeing the large, stolen Danish fleet in these sad circumstances angers John. There seems to be no limit to what the British will do in these times of war, he says to the other Americans at dinner. They agree.

On November 2, *Defence* sets sail and leaves Yarmouth Roads in a fresh wind. Three days later the ship is moored in the Downs and the North Sea pilot can finally return to shore.

The following day, John sees Admiral Samuel Hook arrive with four ships of the line, including three confiscated Danish ships. *Defence* disembarks her surplus troops to the *Brunswick,* a transfer ship like the one John stayed on earlier.

On November 7, *Defence* leaves the Downs to go west in the English Channel and on Tuesday November 17, *Defence* moors at St. Helen's near the Isle of Wright and Portsmouth. Two days later, the launch is sent to the yard with the carpenter, the boatswain and the gunner.

That day John Brown begins to feel sick. It is as if, now that he has returned from this year's long, stressful campaign and the days have become more easy and relaxed, his body finally reacts to the long-term mistreatment. John is taken to the sick quarters, and because *Defence* has no real surgeon onboard, the ship signals to shore to have one sent onboard to examine John and other sick men and boys.

A strong gale blows up three days later, on November 20, making it impossible for anyone to leave the *Defence* or any of the other ships anchored here. John is still very sick. The surgeon recommends that John and two others be taken to the hospital ship when the weather improves and sailing with the jolly boat is possible. John is now paying for working many days in the riggings this autumn while *Defence* patrolled in the Skagerak, a tough and unhealthy job. He is very sick.

In the late autumn when it is constantly freezing, many British seamen on Royal Navy ships sailing in other northern waters write to the Admiralty in London, asking to be transferred to a ship sailing in warmer climate. John was in a hot climate when he entered the *Hercule* in Port Royal, but after spending the whole autumn in the riggings under the most terrible weather conditions in the Skagerak, his body can't take it anymore. He has had a high fever the last couple of days. He is delirious now and hovers between life and death. John Pristoff worries whether John Brown will ever make it back to Boston.

The following day the wind dies down a bit, so John can be transported to the hospital ship anchored at St. Helens, the *Gladiator*. He seems more dead than alive. John is unconscious and still has a high fever when a strong seaman puts him over his shoulder, walks to *Defence*'s main deck, and carefully climbs the gangway to the jollyboat that will take him to the hospital ship.

At the *Gladiator*, he is put into a narrow, uncomfortable bed, one of many filling up the first gun deck. He wakes up and sees a guard and understands that even here on the hospital ship, there will be no easy way to escape. Before John falls into a deep sleep, he feels for the first time that maybe he will not make it this time.

A doctor and nurses come and look at him once a week, but he is unable to predict when they come. The hospital ship is stuffed with sick people. Seamen are dying right next to John, but nobody seems to do anything about it. Some of the healthier young seamen ask a doctor if things are supposed to be like this, and they are told that treatment here is in full compliance with the Transport Office. But John understands from some patients who have been on other hospital ships that the *Gladiator* is not the best. One young seaman three beds down shouts loudly, so that the nurses and half the patients can hear him, that he earlier stayed on a ship with the most human service. The civil doctors on that ship had kept him there for months to spare him from a return to the terrible conditions on a prison ship.[145] This hospital ship is a bad place, and so is the food.

Luckily, John recovers, and after a fortnight in the narrow bed, is so well that a doctor releases him. A jolly boat takes him up the peninsulas and past a small island close to the mainland toward the west. He observes two rows of the black painted ships of the line, similar to those he first observed in the roads of Port Royal outside Kingston, but in greater numbers. John counts eight ships in each row.[145] All ships have the stem toward Portsmouth harbor and the shore, and even without masts or riggings, they look like war ships lined up for a naval battle. Badly prepared, though, John thinks with amusement, considering the closed cannon ports.

Small individual cottages are mounted on top of each ship, and on the top of the gallery of some of the ships, he can read some of the names: *Guildford, Prothee, Vigilant, San Domaso, Pegase, Suffolk, Assistance, Crown* and in front of them all, a distance from the others, *Royal William.*

The jollyboat sails in a shallow-water region, and he notices several sand banks rising from the sea surface between the rows of ships. This is actually a well-protected, natural harbor. John sees a tall hill further to the west with a castle on top, and another seaman tells him this is the Castle of Porchester. All of this is hidden behind the Isle of Wright, and seeing it for the first time, John begins to understand how well organized the Royal Navy is. Many hundred years of tradition lie behind this great British Royal Navy.

The boat takes him out to the *Royal William,* and from the whispering among the English seamen, John understands it is a prison entrance ship, a ship one has to pass through on the way to another prison ship, a transfer ship, or an active man-o-war. An Admiral's flag is hoisted onboard, and from the men with him, he understands that this whole floating prison camp is under command of an Admiral, just like an ordinary squadron in the Royal Navy. Thick iron bars block the two cannon ports that are open at this moment. As the boat approaches the ship, he notices a wide raft anchored below the gangway. They stop at the raft, and the seamen are taken out. A soldier posted on the raft points a finger toward the gangway without saying a word, and John begins to climb the gangway.

On the top deck, he is met by an officer who carefully writes down the names and date of arrival for each prisoner. Each of them has to change clothes, and are given a yellow suit much too large for most of them. 'T.O." is written on the left side of the chest of each suit, for Transport Office.[145] John feels ridiculous in this new suit. A guard on the poop watches them as they are given hammocks.

A soldier escorts them down to the first gun deck, where they are met by darkness and an unbearable smell. John Brown blinks his eyes to try and see, but it's very dark. Only the reflections of the beam of light from the two open cannon ports provides light. When his eyes adjust, he is surprised to observe, in spite of the smell, a totally clean deck. Seamen's boxes are neatly arranged along the sides of the ship between the gun ports. The deck is crowded with people, sitting and standing everywhere.

The prisoners already on the deck silently watch John and the other newcomers as they walk down the stairs. They stand at the bottom of the stairs for a while until a strong, tough-looking man approaches. He points toward the rear of the ship and says in a loud and firm voice, 'Go place yourself with your things below the gallery." They pick up their boxes and slowly make their way through the crowd of men, who only move when asked directly. Below the gallery, John is surprised to see that the normal ceiling has been replaced by a kind of latticework, and he looks directly into the gallery above, where three guards are posted. Each quarter hour, the guards shout, "All is well."

In the middle of December 1807 it is very cold on the prison ships outside Portsmouth harbor. The prisoners are extremely bored most of the time, and spend their time filling the small and large cracks in the walls of the first gun deck room to insulate the decks. Some of the holes are so large that the prisoners can't find enough material on the deck to fill them. Even though it is very cold in the room, the prisoners also have to consider that the room badly needs ventilation. They can insulate the walls too much.

After a week onboard the entrance ship, John still finds it is very confusing. Every day, new people are coming and going at random hours. It causes a lot of stress and fighting between newcomers and the groups that have already formed of those who have stayed long enough to get acquainted.

From his hammock in the evening, John can clearly hear the guards walk back and forth above in the gallery. In the night the number of guards is increased from three to seven.[145] Eight to ten men are kept in reserve in case something goes wrong onboard the entrance ship. John understands that the guards have not experienced such a large number of prisoners in past years. The Admiralty Board must have ordered impressments on a larger scale, John concludes. Royal Navy frigates are inspecting large numbers of merchant ships right now in the English Channel, the waters around here, and in English ports.

John hears the guards discuss the Bombardment of Copenhagen. One of the guards has recently read in *The London Gazette* that Copenhagen was a massacre. More than 1,300 defenseless citizens of Copenhagen, including 62 children, were killed by shells from Royal Navy ships or by cannons on shore. 'I feel no pride in knowing any Englishman onboard a British ship that participated in the bombardment of Copenhagen," one guard says to another. The other shakes his head and replies, 'It has caused an outcry all over the civilized world. Now the world thinks we British are simple savages. As a normal, decent Englishman I don't like to get that kind of bad reputation simply because of the misbehavior of a few others."

Before the guards began to talk about it, John had almost forgotten the Campaign against Denmark. Now all the horror and questions come rushing back. In fact, he recalls that, while onboard *Defence*, he actually helped transport to Ellsinore the mariners from the 43rd Regiment, which took part in that bombardment. He now understands that the attack by *HMS Defence* and *HMS Comus* on the guard ship of Kronborg, the frigate No. 6, *Friderichsværn* was the episode that started the war between Denmark and England.

Hearing this for the first time makes John feel guilty again, knowing for sure that he had participated. John decides that, from this day on, he will keep it a secret that he had been onboard the *Defence* in the Campaign against Denmark.

After several days, John is transferred to a prison ship named the *Prothee*. Entering this prison ship, he gets a real shock. The prisoners here mostly look like dead people risen from their graves, with deep, sunken eyes, long thin hair, and thin and pale pockmarked skin. Their backs are mostly bent, and a few of them dodder around the deck trying not to step on their beards, which have been growing wildly for several years. In their once yellow Transport Office suits, most of them are terribly emaciated.

John is handed a thin blanket and a mattress. As he walks down the stairs to the deck, an indescribable smell hits his face. It is very dark. Each second cannon port is closed. If a newcomer is so lucky to have gold, he can, in the summertime, negotiate a place on deck near a port, with fresh air and light. Those with no money are put in the darkest place on the deck. Previous stays on English man-o-wars have not exactly made John Brown a wealthy man, so he has to enter an unfavorable place on the deck, which, in wintertime, means close to a cannon port. He earlier slept close to a leaking cannon port in the wintertime onboard the *Zealand,* and that had been very cold.

The *Prothee's* commander answers to the commander on the prison entrance ship, *Royal William,* as do the commanders of the other prison ships in this squadron. The commander of *Royal William* has a small staff of officers, cadets and sub-officers. The guard crew attached to the prison ships, all in all, consists of nearly 50 men.

As boring and eventless months pass by, John figures out that the prisoners mentally divide themselves into two groups with quite different behaviors. One group is full of deep depression and hopelessness, and these men spend most of their time rambling about on the decks like ghosts. The other group is manic and extremely noisy. But there is one thing the two groups have in common and that is their bewildered looks.[145] John understands that he needs to isolate himself mentally from the other prisoners onboard, to avoid becoming part of their raving madness.

Some young prisoners unfortunately go raving mad from the long-term isolation onboard these prison ships. Older seamen think of their homes and loved ones, which comforts them and helps them feel less isolated. It makes the older seamen appear much calmer.

The daily routine onboard the *Prothee* and other prison ships anchored in Portsmouth in the summer period begins with a boat pipe at 5:45 in the morning, and a quarter of an hour later, the men are supposed to be on deck with their hammocks packed and stuffed in the bulwark net.

In the wintertime, they are awakened a little later at 8:00 when a pipe calls them for washing in the morning, which is followed by cleaning of the ship twice a week. Big tubs are placed on the deck to be used as toilets, and some days they are emptied. The ship's cook prepares their food in the kitchen by the stem. They eat at tables and sit on ship's coffins, but the food is insufficient. Sometime between 9 and 10 o'clock in the evening, the lights are turned off. This is the simple, monotonous life John experiences, day after day, a routine that causes some seamen to go mad.

John finds out that the American prisoners onboard have no direct contact with ordinary people on shore. Their only contacts are the British contractor of foodstuffs, the Central American Agent for Seamen from London, and maybe one subordinate in each of the English ports, appointed by the United States Government. The American agent for seamen in London can visit American prisoners on the prison ships anchored in south English ports if he wants to, but mostly the visits are made by the local American subordinate, who then reports to his superior in London. Through this subordinate, prisoners can sell things they have made during the many long hours onboard the prison ship, or buy new things with the money they earn by selling their items. This man also will bring or send them their mail. The mortality rate onboard is high, with death mostly caused by hunger, cold or pneumonia.

One day John pulls himself together and asks an American prisoner who has been onboard the *Prothee* a long time how he can get out of this prison ship. The experienced prisoner explains that he should write to the American Agent for Seamen in London, William Lyman.

The contractor employed under the Transport Board brings foodstuffs to the prison ship. When provisions are delivered, they are carefully controlled by some of the prisoners, to check that they have received what was ordered. But it is always possible for the contractor, who has connections on shore, to deliver the exact quantity ordered, but at a much lower quality.

If he is inventive, the contractor finds a way to "adjust" the products he delivers, thereby earning good money on these prison ships supplies.[145] This reduction in the quality of the food delivered eventually results in more sick prisoners, and even costs some of them their lives.

There is a contractor for each of the different supplies, a potato man, an onion man, a herring man, a meat man, and so forth. Some days the meat and herrings delivered are completely rotten.

One day, they receive a party of rotten herrings and the next time the herring man comes to the shipside with new supplies to sell, the prisoners empty two full barrels of rotten herring onto his head, filling his boat. The herring man then complains about the bad treatment to the commander of the prison ship, but the commander doesn't care a bit.

John observes that some of the elder prisoners have small businesses onboard. When the contractor arrives to deliver his stuff, they buy their own supplies. One of them sells homemade 'Scottish coffee" made out of burned bread boiled in water. In the morning, he walks around the deck and offers this coffee with molasses or brown sugar. Newcomers, who normally have some money and are used to much better living conditions, are easy targets. They do not know how to get extra food themselves to supplement the meager rations offered by the cook, so they will buy in the end.[145]

Some prisoner cooks make expensive but irresistible casseroles of a dish named lobscouse made of onion, beef, potatoes, salt and butter.

When the spring or autumn gales blow over Portsmouth harbor for days, supplies are cut off to the cooks onboard these isolated prison ships. Then the price for a meal prepared by a prisoner cook rises quite a bit.

Onboard these ships, prisoners are constantly thinking of how to escape. Some form a group to try to dig their way down in the front end of the ship, to get out through the side of the ship just above the sea surface. But it is hard to escape without being noticed, and the penalty is death if discovered. Some who have tried have drowned, and some who reach shore are handed over to the British port authorities, if they are stupid enough to contact loyal local people along the shore. Some prisoners do manage to escape, but are later caught by these same prison ships' boats and mariners in the harbor.

Frequently, English officers come onboard the prison ships to kindly ask if anyone will take the gold and the bounty to enter a man-o-war voluntarily, but only seldom are prisoners desperate enough to say yes.

John stays on the *Prothee* outside Portsmouth until early February 1808, when he is finally sent onboard a transport ship sailing east from Portsmouth up the English Channel to Chatham near Sheerness, at the outlet of the River Medway on England's southeastern coast. He has stayed here earlier, when he arrived from Jamaica. Here, John is put onboard a transfer ship named *Namur*. Anchored in this southeastern port, the ship is mostly transferring men in and out of Royal Navy ships belonging to the Baltic fleet.

Conditions onboard *Namur* are much more comfortable than the *Prothee* and the other ordinary prison ships John has entered earlier and he notices this immediately. The quality of the food served is good and the quantity sufficient. The space onboard is large and the seamen are treated nicely, almost like on one of the better British hospital ships.

Chatham is not known as a good place for prisoners from neutral countries like the United States of America and Denmark to end up. Impressed Americans who refuse to serve onboard Royal Navy ships are, in this port, transferred to special prison ships.

Since 1807, the prison ships *Buckingham*, *Sandwich* and *Bahama* have been used to isolate American prisoners, because they protest so violently against being impressed that it is often difficult to have them onboard normal prison ships. The Americans are generally known among British officers to be too independent and to spread a bad mood

119

and discipline among the other prisoners. After experiencing what the Americans manage to get away with, other prisoners begin to neglect their duty, disobey or otherwise cause problems, and so the Admirals think it's a good and necessary arrangement to keep the Americans isolated here.

Fellow prisoners onboard *Namur* tell John about these special ships anchored here, and at the same time, he is told good, sarcastic American jokes, which are produced so easily from the tough environment onboard these exclusive American prison ships. The one statement John likes the most is: 'Oh, it is good to know that in good Old England, it is the privilege of high as well as low to live their lives at Buckingham."

John stays onboard *Namur* eight long, unforgettable months, until November 5, 1808, when *Defence* appears through the portholes as it anchors in the Medway River at the Great Nore. John Brown and 68 other supernumerous men from *Namur* are transferred to *Defence*[38, 47] this day.

When John enters *Defence*, John Pristoff is very happy to see his long-lost friend again. *Defence* has been on a long trip the first half of 1808, patrolling the waters outside Lisbon, then crossing the Atlantic Ocean to patrol around Martinique and St. Luke's, where John was impressed from the Boston schooner three years ago. Then *Defence* passed south of Cuba, sailed along the North American coast and returned to the Downs in late June. In the middle of July, *Defence* reached Chatham, and finally arrived back here this day of November 5, 1808.

The wind is moderate and the weather fine this day, when the pay captain enters the ship. John is given a new job on this voyage, entering the muster books as a yeoman working in the powder room.

Defence came here only to pick up the extra men onboard *Namur,* and on November 11, heads south to its winter quarters in the Downs, where it anchors for the remainder of 1808.

December is cold and a moderate wind blows, generating only small waves around the ship. The carpenters on the ship stay busy repairing the storerooms. John is quite bored and longs for home much of the time.

The American Congress passes Jefferson's Embargo Act on December 22, sending shock waves through Wilmington ship-owners, captains and seamen, in fact, through the whole business community on the eastern

North American coast. The act prohibits all American vessels from leaving American ports.

In the apartment on Water Street in Wilmington, William Watson and Mary Ann receive the bad news. They worry how William will provide for himself, Mary Ann and her mother, and how the small borough of Wilmington will provide for its citizens. When both import and export are forbidden, almost every type of business in a port town is severely hurt.

William Warner and his Federalist friends, who made such profit from their trade with England, consider this Embargo Act the final sign that President Jefferson has lost his mind. How can any president hurt his own country's economy that badly? Tension increases between the Democratic Republicans, who defend their president, and the Federalists.

As both Marshall for the district of Delaware and port collector in Wilmington, Allen McLane is in a tough position. He is in charge at the very front line, enforcing this controversial and unpopular law. But George Washington himself couldn't have chosen a better person as marshal and guard of this port than Allen McLane, and all the ship-owners in Wilmington know that very well.

The Wilmington ship-owners discuss the new situation a lot, and Wilmington ships are slowly moved to smaller Maryland ports like Elkton, on the other side of the border. Maryland still has the English coin system and some port collectors there are a little more lax about records of ships coming in and out of port.

Illegal trading with England takes place. In remote coastal areas, ships load and unload cargo taken to and brought from Europe or the West Indies, unnoticed, in the middle of the night.

Although American merchants who used to trade with England can see that England is wrongly restricting the American-English trade with new unjust laws, this new Embargo Act is seen as 'shooting oneself in the foot." Destroying your largest foreign trade might work for a Philosopher King like President Thomas Jefferson, but is too drastic a step and too large a sacrifice for many pragmatic American merchants and ship owners that live by the sea. William Warner and many other Federalist merchants and ship owners begin to hate Jefferson, now that he has become a direct threat to their daily earnings. But among many Democratic Republicans he is a brave hero.

121

When children and families slowly begin to starve in American east coast ports like Wilmington, it becomes easy for some ship owners to persuade unemployed seamen and captains to make a trip to England, earning a huge salary by sailing on the few ships that dare to go.

Prices on imported goods skyrocket and, for an increasing number of merchants, the temptation of illegal trade becomes too great. The Embargo Act is the main topic of conversation among unemployed seamen and captains hanging around the tiny apartments on Second Street, Front Street and Water Street, or the taverns drinking bad coffee, the only thing they can afford these days.

From fresh stories about new ships returning from England, it seems profits just go higher and higher for each trip. The temptation to sail is great, and too hard to resist for many ship owners, captains and seamen in Wilmington and other east coast ports.

Mary Ann, her mother and William seriously discuss whether William should try to get work on one of those ships going overseas. He could sail in the internal European merchant fleet where salaries are quite high. It is not illegal as long as the ship doesn't use an American port. But their relationship is still young, and Mary Ann cannot bear having the two of them separated for so long right now. 'It should be safe enough," William tells her, trying to be optimistic. 'I have my Protection Certificate, and it is valid on all of the Seven Seas." But when William looks into her eyes, it only takes a second for him to know the answer. William has to stay in Wilmington for the time being, whether he likes it or not.

William Warner and some captains and seamen from Wilmington and Philadelphia decide to begin to trade illegally, the meaninglessness of the situation becoming more and more clear to them. They are restless. They simply can't stay idle for reasons they only see as absurd.

The day before Christmas of 1808, a court martial is held onboard *HMS Christian VII* while the ship is anchored in the Downs with *Defence*. *Christian VII* is a former Danish ship named after the insane Danish King, who died recently, making Crown Prince Frederik VI the new King of Denmark. *HMS Christian VII* was stolen with the rest of the Danish fleet in Copenhagen.

John Brown has now spent most of his thirtieth year onboard a hospital ship, *Gladiator*, a logging ship *Namur,* and now a man-o-war

Defence, while all ships stayed anchored in harbors. His uncertain situation is beginning to drive him crazy. He has been sick, not allowed to sail and not allowed on the shore, and now is forced to work in the dark powder room, which is on the lowest deck below the waterline to protect it against enemy cannonballs and explosions. No natural light reaches this region and the gunpowder he fills into the cartridges is unhealthy for his lungs, which makes him sad. John feels he is an object that belongs to His Majesty's Royal Navy, one the navy can store or use in any way it wishes.

The powder room is artificially lit by tallow candles, placed in outside lanterns to avoid risk of explosion. The cold late autumn and winter days are tough on John. Absolutely nothing interesting happens. Day after day, he fills cartridges with gunpowder, then stores the cartridges. British seamen are on leave for Christmas, home with their families for several weeks now. But John Brown, John Pristoff and the other impressed Americans have to stay onboard *Defence,* because they are not trusted to go to shore on their own.

Early on Christmas morning, John Brown and John Pristoff have left their hammocks because they can't sleep, and now they stand on the forecastle to get some fresh air. Back home in Boston, Christmas night is beginning, and John Brown guesses that his mother is sitting at her usual place on the front left bench in the Salem Presbyterian Church, attending the midnight divine service. She must consider her only son dead by now, certainly if she hasn't received one of his letters. It has been three and a half years since he left Salem and according to the plan she forced him to give her, he should have returned at least three years ago.

As the new year begins, the Admiralty in London has decided to make *HMS Defence* part of the Baltic Fleet this year. The ships belonging to this fleet normally gather in Cowsand Bay in the beginning of the year. *HMS Victory,* with Rear Admiral of the Red James Sammaurez, will be the flagship, which commands the entire Baltic Fleet this year. The flagship and second-rater *HMS St. George III,* also part of this Baltic Fleet, is getting a new Admiral and will be the flagship for the squadron to which *HMS Defence* is attached.

The ships will be made ready, food supplies put onboard, and crew supplied if necessary. As one of the last things before leaving, the crew and great guns will be exercised. In early April, when departure of the fleet is imminent, the Admiral of *HMS St. George* will leave his prosperous estate in Cornwall and travel to Portsmouth to enter his flagship.

In Wilmington and other East Coast ports, the food situation has worsened. The Embargo has resulted in the disappearance of 80 percent of the grain shipment from America. It is tough for port cities as well as other cities.[187, 188]

Wilmington merchants, mill-owners, ship-owners, captains and seamen are really suffering now. From time to time, William Hemphill, Samuel Bush, John Warner and the other wharf and ship owners meet along the quays and discuss the grave situation. Earlier, many people were busy here, loading or unloading different ships. Now ships are all tied up and not a single man is seen onboard any of them. At the Customhouse, McLane can only give them the bad news that more than 500 ships are tied in the harbor of New York. This is very bad for business and the prosperity of all of the American people, Samuel Bush says gravely, and the others simply nod their heads without speaking.

President Jefferson is not at all happy about this grave situation, and when asked, decides early this year not to accept a third term as President when he is asked.

In John's hometown of Salem, soup kitchens feed 1,200 persons a day. At noon, John's mother leaves the tiny apartment she no longer can afford to heat to stand in the soup kitchen line. She spends much of her time worrying about her son, who should be taking care of her in these tough times. She has come to the kitchen for some days and has met another old widow, who also lives close to the harbor and who has a seaman son abroad. Like John, he has not been home for several years. It comforts John's mother to have someone to talk to, and the two ladies develop a close friendship.

Standing in the kitchen line as usual, waiting for food and talking with her new friend, John's mother experiences a feeling of happiness, a feeling she has not had since John's father died several years ago. Since her husband died, she has been mostly alone, because John spends most of his time at sea to earn a living. She no longer had friends, because at her age, all her friends, relatives and family her age had died. She was a proud, intelligent woman, and her husband's death isolated her and made her alone without her minding the change.

The family's few common friends were much younger and had simply stopped inviting her out or visiting her when her husband died. John's father had been the one who spoke, when they earlier socialized with others and now that he was gone, John's mother ended up spending her time alone when John was away. It didn't matter that much to her, because her own small family had been everything she needed, but when the husband died and her son went away for many months, she didn't expect any social events to happen before her son came home again. John was well aware of this behavior, and he felt the same deep responsibility for his mother's social life that his father had for years before him.

But now, forced by circumstance to stand in the soup kitchen line to avoid starvation, John's mother began to speak to the other lady as if they had known each other all their lives. Now she had this new feeling, that someone actually needed her company again, which made her happy. She felt that her new friend was genuinely interested in her and her son's well being.

The two ladies began to meet regularly in their apartments, and gradually John's mother managed to get a social life again. She could now be found talking to anyone she met, even the grocer or the butcher, when she visited their stores to see if they had anything cheap. It was good that these two elderly ladies could help and support each other, with one-fifth of Salem's citizens reduced to virtual beggary these early months of 1809.

William Gray, a wealthy and influential Salem merchant, supports Jefferson's Embargo. He owns approximately 50 percent of all the ships anchored in Salem and Boston, and has lost ten percent of his personal fortune the first six months of the year because of the trade restrictions under the embargo. Gray is highly respected for showing this kind of idealistic behavior, setting his country's needs above his own without question. William Gray could be the owner of the Boston schooner John and his colleagues left Boston in. But Gray's behavior does not represent the majority of smaller merchants and ship owners, who desperately need to start trading again to meet the basic needs of their own families.

American and British seamen who had served onboard American merchant ships now lying idle in east coast ports now try to cross the Atlantic Ocean to get a berth on English ships. Some of them even try to

125

voluntarily enter Royal Navy ships, with the willing assistance of the British consuls. This new traffic of seamen from American to English ships reduces the numbers of impressments of American seamen into the Royal Navy in a way President Jefferson never intended.[189]

Mary Ann, her mother and William are beginning to feel very poor. They go hungry from time to time, because they no longer have money to buy food. But they stick together. Thanks to William's connections with the wharf and store owners, he is occasionally able to find small jobs, just enough to keep the worst hunger from the doorstep of the tiny apartment in Water Street. But none of them are gaining weight these days.

McLane has less and less work to do in the Customhouse. No ships are leaving or arriving, and no customs receipts are made. There is little to do. His superior, The Secretary of Treasury, has a hard time balancing the budget with no customs collected from the ships. John Freed, Jr. and William Windell are also working less and less as the weeks pass by. John Freed, Sr.'s family is also going hungry, because he is a port laborer who normally loads and unloads ships, and now has nothing to do. He is not as lucky as his son, who, as a revenue officer, is on a steady public payroll. John Freed, Jr. shares his income with his father's family.

In the evenings, Mary Ann and William can't always avoid the topic of seamen in the borough who are known to take illegal jobs occasionally on ships that dare to sail to England. One evening, William declares to Mary Ann and her mother, "You will never find me onboard one of these ships. It's dangerous and unpatriotic." Mary Ann agrees, but her mother has a more pragmatic approach to the subject and replies, "William, at least wait to see if things change for the better before you decide what to do when considering your future work."

Discussions around kitchen tables in Wilmington about these illegal trips to England grow louder as time passes. Some family members accept them and some don't. Many of these families can't afford to heat their houses anymore, and some starve because they can't get food.

Implementation of the Embargo destroys national unity, and that of the Warner family far more than anything else during these years.[189] Members of the Warner family are completely divided about this issue. Nobody dares to mention the Embargo when William Warner and John Warner happen to be in the same room. Everyone knows that William

Warner is determined to let his ship *Fair American* sail to Liverpool as usual this year, and they don't support it or like it at all. John Warner and Samuel Bush are equally determined to obey the law and keep their ship *True American* in port. Port collector McLane proudly witnesses this on his frequent walks along the quay, inspecting ships in the harbor.

When William, Mary Ann, Joseph Warner and his wife Mary meet in Philadelphia, or in Wilmington when the Warners are home to visit the family, William gets the feeling that Joseph is sick and tired of his elder brother William's selfish behavior. One day, Joseph Warner says to William, 'I'm just gl ad our father is not around to see my brother act as he does now. It is definitely not part of the Warner character to be so greedy, that you have to go against the law to be satisfied! Why can't he see that, in only a few months, all by himself, he is destroying the good reputation our father and mother have spent a lifetime to build up?"

William quickly replied, 'Joseph, you know very well that we are all on your side on this issue. But you have to understand that your brother has to repay the debt on his wharf and ships! There is really nothing else he can do." As a seaman, William often justifies to himself the illegal trade with England, thinking that under the circumstances, it isn't too bad. One day very soon, he might find himself in a position where he'll have to make such a trip just to survive.

Joseph, guessing the thoughts of his friend, answers, 'William, it is different when it comes to you, because you are an ordinary seaman. You have very few options to support yourself. William, my brother, is not that poor. He is able to work himself through this temporary crisis, just as Mary and I are!" William accepts that point of view, and Mary Ann is relieved when the two couples part that day, that Joseph and William will stay friends even through this great trial.

On February 11, 1809, William Warner announces in the *Delaware Gazette* the death of his half sister Ester Yarnall. Earlier, when William and John Warner were running their business together in Wilmington, they would sign their names side by side when putting an advertisement in a local newspaper. On the occasion of Ester's death, it would have been appropriate for them to cosign as usual, but their political differences had grown to such a degree that if John decided to sign, William wouldn't and vice versa. William regretfully signed alone.

The death of Ester, the oldest daughter in the Warner family, grieves all the Warner and Yarnell family members. William Watson had known her, because she was practically always around in the Warner mansion when he went to visit Joseph. But he had seldom talked to her, and did not know her quite as well as he did Joseph and the rest of the Warners.

When the sad news first reached William, he felt sad for his friend Joseph and his mother Mary, and he thought it unfair that Ester had to die so young. Especially since the Warner family had already paid so dearly by losing the father and two younger daughters earlier.

The following Sunday, the day of the funeral, all the Warner and Yarnell family members and friends gathered in the churchyard outside the Friends Meeting House on Quaker Hill. It is a very cold and humid morning, but at the time of the ceremony, the sun shines from a blue sky, which helps raise spirits.

As close friends, Mary Ann and William attend the ceremony, and it saddens them to see their good friends in such deep grief. The funeral ceremony is simple and beautiful and the priest makes a nice speech. He highlights important events in the lives of both the Yarnell and the Warner families. He begins by telling about the friendship between Ester Yarnell's parents Mary and John Yarnell and the young, promising silversmith Joseph Warner, all distinguished members of the Society of Friends. He speaks of what the Yarnell and Warner families had meant to the borough of Wilmington through the generations, and how this fine tradition was continued through their sons and daughters.

Defence is anchored in the Downs on March 4, 1809, in a moderate wind and clear sky. *Defence* is supplying *HMS Implacable* with water, bread, rice and sugar. *HMS Caledonia, Tonnant, Illustribius* and *Bellona* sail to the west. John sees Admiral Lord Gambier, who had been rewarded with the title of Lord for the successful Bombardment of Copenhagen and stealing the Danish Fleet, onboard the *Tonnant*. *Defence* receives 120 bags of bread, five pipes of wine and four puncheons of rum along with plenty of wood and coal. Then she heaves anchor and sails to St. Helen's to meet the other ships.

These plentiful food supplies delivered to the Royal Navy ships are a big contrast to the situation on dinner tables in most working families of Salem and Wilmington these days. John has not received any letter from home yet. Had he known about the starvation in Salem, he would have known that he is actually lucky to be onboard a man-o-war in the Royal Navy right now.

Mary Ann and her mother have lost weight in these cold winter months.

On this day, the Embargo Act ends and Congress passes a new Non-Intercourse Act to replace it. This act excludes all public and private vessels of Great Britain and France from American waters, strictly forbids the importation of both British and French goods, and gives the President power to renew trade with Great Britain and France by proclamation, on the condition that either should cease to violate the rights of the small neutral countries[278] like the United States of America and Denmark.

Port Collector McLane has, of course, been informed about the new law by the Department of Treasury, and he must now implement it in Delaware. McLane is known to administer laws strictly. Not one single ship has been allowed to leave the port of Wilmington since the Embargo Act went into effect. McLane is well aware of his good reputation and he wants to keep it this way. William Windell and John Freed, Jr., have been ordered to check that the ships anchored along the quay and the wharves on the north bank of the Christina River stay there, and that the port is closed to arriving ships. In the Wilmington Customhouse the employees are used to listening to harsh comments from these wharf-owners, ship-owners, captains and seamen, who have a real hard time accepting that their ships can't get out on the Delaware River and to the ocean, so they can earn their living.

A couple of days later, William arrives at the harbor front in Wilmington and meets William Windell and John Freed, Jr. William says, "You must have had very little to do at work since they introduced the Embargo Act, other than just inspecting ships in our port. Isn't that right?" John Freed, Jr., his roommate, answers, "William, a new law has just replaced the old Embargo Act. The Non-Intercourse Act is less restrictive. Now, in principle, ships in the harbor of Wilmington are allowed to leave the port and sail for trade destinations other than England and France. For example, you are allowed to go to neutral countries like Denmark." William's face brightens at this good news, and he smiles. "John, I'm really glad to hear that ch anges for the better are finally arriving. Families have been starving in Wilmington for quite some time. I only hope the new law will help bring an end to this, which has lasted far too long already."

That evening, William tells Mary Ann and her mother the good news John had given him earlier that day, that the new Non-Intercourse Act makes it possible for American ships to leave port and sail again. William can finally resume earning a salary to support them. During the difficult time of the embargo, Mary Ann has been impressed with William's ability to find new jobs. She likes his naïve, indomitable optimism, and the way he had an almost childlike ability to keep a positive drive no matter how difficult the situation. His ability to get out of even the most severe problem and remain optimistic and unmarked was a unique thing that Mary Ann liked very much about him. But despite his optimism, Mary Ann still thinks it is too early for William to go to sea again. "William," she says, "my mother and I can' t do without you here in Wilmington yet. It is of course a big thing, that you are able to earn well on ocean-going trips again, but I still think it is too dangerous to go." William doesn't try to argue. He loves Mary Ann far too much to see any point in arguing with her at this moment. But as they continue eating, he can't help secretly watching her, and he suddenly understands how difficult it would be for him to live without her. To close the subject for now, William promises himself that before he makes any more deep-sea trips to Europe, he will ask Mary Ann's mother to let him marry her daughter. Yes, William thinks, he will definitely marry Mary Ann soon.

After the new Non-Intercourse law passed Congress, ships that had been anchored for a long time in New York begins to leave in great numbers. Officially, departing ships sail to find a market in the island of the Azores[190], but the New York port collector estimates that 90 percent of these ships are heading for English ports.[191] Still, he gives his permission.

On March 15 His Majesty's Ships *Victory, Defence, Blake, Saturn* and *Monmouth* are gathered at St. Helen's. Since New Years, nothing special has happened onboard. Even the number of punishments has been low, only two. The second time someone was punished was March 3, when eight seamen were flogged. The day before, a seamen who was to be punished jumped overboard and drowned, no doubt in order to avoid cruel flogging.[48]

John Brown stands at the bulwark and points out to another seaman the hospital ship, *Gladiator,* where he spent time recovering the last time he was sick. *Defence* stays a short time at St. Helen's, then goes back to the Downs to join the convoy of ships anchored here and ready for this year's voyage patrolling the coast of the Continental Europe and later going to the Baltic Sea.

Men are punished three more times on *Defence* before the Royal Navy Baltic Fleet leaves the Downs on April 9, heading east for the Baltic Summer Station. The number of punishments on *Defence* is low compared to other ships in the Royal Navy. She is generally known in the navy as a ship with humane leaders.

On April 17, *Defence* is caught in a strong gale and forced to anchor close to the Isle de Goree in 15 fathoms of water, over a sand bank with fine brown sand full of glittering white shells. It is a beautiful sight from the lower deck's porthole. John Brown and William King have their heads out of one of the portholes, and William says, 'I'd give all my savings to be out on that sandbank in a jollyboat right now. It would be perfect for a swim!" Unlike most seamen, John Brown and William King can swim. John Brown tries to cheer William up by saying, 'I know how keen you are on swimming, and I certainly wish you could go."

No one onboard *Defence* knows that today, Mr. Erskine, the British Minister to Washington, is proposing a settlement of the *Chesapeake* affair to the new American Secretary of State, Robert Smith.[277] Impressed American seamen from the *Chesapeake* will be returned to America and British officers punished for the attack. The Americans accept this settlement, but it will be 1811 before this case is finally settled. In the meantime, Secretary of State Robert Smith instructs William Pinkney, James Monroe's successor as United States Minister to England, to delay further negotiations on impressments. So, officials hold up the return of thousands of impressed American seamen onboard Royal Navy ships for the three American *Chesapeake* seamen. American authorities have shot themselves in the foot once again,[278] the first time being the Embargo Act.

John Brown, John Pristoff, William King and other impressed Americans have written to their families, relatives, friends, local port collectors, Justices of the Peace, the Department of State, the West Indian American Agent for Seamen in Kingston, Jamaica and the

European American Agent for Seamen in London, asking for copies of Protection Certificates and other papers to help the men prove their American origin. It has all been in vain.

All the careful reports from American Agents in English ports like Liverpool and Portsmouth to the central Agent for American seamen in London and the Department of State in Washington, with detailed lists of names and identification numbers of impressed American seamen and the ships they were impressed on, had been useless so far.

Onboard *Defence* on April 21, 19 seamen are punished. As often happens, one of them tries to escape the whipping by jumping overboard. He is saved by the jolly boat and brought back to the ship. Captain Ekins is keen on living up to the reputation of *Defence* as a ship that goes by the standard regarding order and discipline in the Royal Navy. A seaman must not be allowed to kill himself to avoid punishment. That might become a tradition and spread to all the ships in the entire Royal Navy. So Captain Ekins, after eight days, orders the punishment of the seaman who jumped overboard to take place.

From May 31 to June 2, *Defence* is anchored outside the island of Texel, close to the borough of Den Helder and the passage to Amsterdam and other Dutch inland cities. *Defence* is still off the coast of Holland on June 14 when 12 persons are punished. Among them is Thomas Lowe, who is punished for the third time this year, for drunkenness.

There is a typical pattern to the punishment of some American and some English seamen. The first time, they are usually punished for contempt to a superior officer, disobedience, or neglect of duty. After being nearly beaten to death, they normally begin drinking to ease the pain. Then they will be punished for drinking. As they recover from that severe punishment, anger builds up inside, anger at being kept against their own will. Then they will be rude and insulting to their superior officers once again, which leads to further punishment. Then the drinking begins again, and the pattern of punishment is repeated.[48]

In the month of June, 72 American ships that left New York arrive in Liverpool[192] in the very heart of Old England, even though the captains gave their word of honor to the port collector in New York that their destination was the Azores islands, in the middle of the Atlantic Ocean. William Warner is not the only east coast ship-owner deliberately breaking the laws of the United States of America these days.

On July 3, *Defence* has left the Dutch coast and is finally on its way to join the Royal Navy Baltic Fleet. The flagship *Victory*, which heads the Baltic Fleet and its own squadron, has already arrived at the summer station in Malkonita Bay, in the middle part of the Baltic Sea near the Gulf of Finland.

In the afternoon, the cutter *Ranger* and a convoy of merchant ships join the *Defence's* group in the North Sea along the Danish west coast. An English seaman standing next to John points out the Cliffs of Bovbjerg, which can clearly be seen from their position on the forecastle, lighted as it is by the sun. Two days later, they are in the Skagerak and pass the Scaw in a fresh wind with rain.

Since Denmark declared war on England two years ago, in August 1807, the Royal Navy has taken full control of internal Danish waters in the spring, summer and autumn months, when they escort their convoys of merchant ships in and out of the Baltic Sea.

So, as *Defence* now progresses through these waters, she occasionally fires cannons to let the Danish batteries and coast militias know that the Royal Navy's well-fitted, ready-to-fight war ships, are passing by, on their way to the Baltic summer station.

On the 8th, John observes the Lighthouse of the Island of Anholt. *Defence* stops here and Captain Ekins orders supplies sent to shore for the Garrison on the island. The British occupied the island of Anholt the year before for use as a perfect naval station in the middle of the Cattegat Sea. It can easily be supplied and defended from the Royal Navy's Scandinavian headquarters outside Gothenburg, where the British base is established at Vinga Sound.

This year, *HMS Dictator* is responsible for patrolling the Cattegat to prevent any attempt by Danish naval forces to retake Anholt, and to keep the passage between the Great Belt and Skagerak clear of any enemy threat. The ship responsible for controlling the Cattegat also takes charge of the smaller frigates and gunboats that control the Danish merchant ships passing the entrance to the Limfjord fjord when sailing between Aalborg and Copenhagen.

On July 10, *Defence* and its boats are hunting several Danish cannon boats. After losing the larger part of her Fleet to England, the Danish Fleet introduced these gunboats in large numbers. They are easily built, operated, and applied to attack the British convoys passing through Danish waters in and out of the Baltic Sea. The Great Belt is an especially advantageous place to attack a convoy, when two conditions are met. The first is no wind, which causes the ships to 'freeze' to the sea surface in the Belt. Danish cannon boats can then maneuver around the English merchant ships to find the best angle of attack, one that will give maximum protection to the Danish gunboats and minimum protection to the English ships. The second condition is thick fog, which provides the cannon boats with an ideal cover, allowing them to come very close to the convoy without being discovered. It typically takes one or maybe two days for the entire Royal Navy fleet, moving at the speed of the slowest merchant ship in the convoy, to pass the Great Belt and enter the Baltic Sea. So both conditions are rarely met at the same time when a Royal Navy convoy passes by.

But this year, when the Royal Navy makes its first passage of the Great Belt, it is hazy in the afternoon with very little wind. *Defence* meets *HMS Ruby,* with Rear Admiral Dixon, who is in charge of the squadron, *Vanguard, Mars, Majestic, Standard, Tribune, Tartarus* and another small war brig. The next day, the convoy of merchant ships and the squadron reach the south end of the island Sprogø, in the middle of the Great Belt. The haze is still there.

Captain Ekins and other British captains in the convoy are well aware that they are approaching Danish Naval Headquarters in the Great Belt, and so, late in the evening, *Defence* and other Royal Navy ships send boats out toward Corsør harbor, to meet the Danish gunboats and prevent them from cutting too many English merchant ships from the convoy. Danish gunboats have been doing everything in their power to revenge the English theft of the Danish fleet, and Danish privateers have made fortunes taking many English prizes.

On July 12, the breeze is fresh, but it is still hazy. *Defence*'s boats are again sent toward Corsør to meet the Danish gunboats. Twenty-seven Danish gunboats are observed in the Belt. John is working below deck, in the powder room, producing cartridges for the cannons, which are fired so often during the days it takes to pass the Great Belt. John is quite nervous. He has heard of cannonballs hitting the powder room of a ship, blowing it up and destroying it completely. If this should happen onboard *Defence*, he will probably never even realize it.

In the afternoon, a seaman watches the fight between the Danish cannon boats and the boats of the British man-o-wars from *Defence's* mizzen top-bar. When John hurries up the stairs to the upper deck from the powder room, he hears a firm knock above his head, a now familiar sound. A seaman on a top-bar has fallen and been killed on the deck right above him. John and the other men onboard feel sorry about this accident, but unfortunately, it happens so often that they have grown used to it.

In Wilmington, Mary Ann and William have had a great time together this spring and summer. William has helped Mary Ann and her mother when he wasn't working on the quay or on local ships. Mary Ann's mother likes William more and more as the time passes. William is flattered by all that she is doing to make him feel home, but at the same time, he reminds himself that a seaman cannot remain in port or along the local coast indefinitely. So, he decides that this evening, he will finally ask Mary Ann's mother for her daughter's hand.

William and Mary Ann have a day off and are planning to walk up along the Brandywine River to the Gilpin's Paper mill after supper. As they sit at the table eating, Mary Ann asks, 'William, why are you staring at me all the time? Is anything wrong?' William glances at Mary Ann's mother, then at his plate of food. Without looking up, he says, 'No, no, not at all. Nothing is wrong, Mary Ann.' He eats for a while, then asks, 'If you are finished Mary Ann, why don't we go to the mill now?'

Mary Ann nods eagerly and begins to collect the dishes to take out to the kitchen. 'Yes, let's do that now.' Mary Ann kisses her mother on her cheek, and she and William hurry out the door and down the staircase. As they walk out onto Water Street, William turns to Mary Ann and says, 'Oh, I forgot something in the apartment. Just wait here for me for a second and I'll be back.'

William jumps up the stairs and knocks twice on the front door. When Mary Ann's mother opens the door, William blurts out, 'Will you allow me to marry your daughter?' He waits, breathless and a bit nervous, for her answer. Mary Ann's mother is quiet for a moment, her hand to her mouth, then she nods her head and says quietly, with a smile: 'Yes, yes, of course. Of course William, you know I would never try to prevent that.' William returns her smile, reaches quickly for her right hand and shakes it. 'Thank you so very much. I promise I will take good care of her." He runs down the stairs to meet Mary Ann.

As the two of them now walk west on Second Street, past the lower Market House toward Market Street, Mary Ann instinctively starts to turn right, up Market Street toward the Brandywine River. Instead, William pulls her to the left. She looks confused and asks, 'William, what are you doing? Aren't we going to the mill?" He just puts his finger to his lips and keeps walking, down to the harbor front and the Christina River. At the river, William heads east, through the lot holding John Warner's wharf to a large black stone. It is the largest of The Rocks, a small group of large stones with a high symbolic meaning for the descendants of some of the first European settlers, who arrived in the New World at exactly this spot many years ago.

William holds Mary Ann pressed flat against the stone. He looks her straight in the eyes and asks, 'Mary Ann, will you marry me?" Her expression makes it clear what her answer is, and William laughs loudly, revealing the excitement that has filled him for several days. 'I think this makes us engaged then." Mary Ann murmurs, 'Hmm. You think so?" Then she laughs, too, and whispers in his ear, 'This means you may kiss me, if you'd like." William looks at her intensely and begins to smile. He gently pushes her up against the rock and kisses her intensely, thinking, 'God, how I love this girl."

From his office in the wharf building, John Warner happens to look out the window at that moment, and he sees the whole scene. Warner smiles and mumbles to himself 'I think I have some good news for my little brother Joseph." Then he laughs so loudly that Mary Ann and William hear it, and see John standing at the window. They wave at him, then run out into Market Street.

'I think it is okay for you to take my hand, now that we have declared ourselves engaged," Mary Ann says, giving William a warm smile. Before William realizes it, the two of them are walking hand in hand up Market Street, as they both had wanted to do so many times.

On July 17, *Defence* catches up with the flagship *Victory* and the rest of the Royal Navy Baltic fleet near Norgen Island in the Gulf of Finland.

On August 5, *Defence* patrols in a region with various reefs, and runs aground on a rocky coast in Malkonita Bay at 8 in the evening. Captain Ekins and the first lieutenant worry about getting stuck here. Being grounded this far north in the Baltic Sea with winter approaching is the same as destroying the ship. Ice can build up to such an extent on these rocky coasts in winter that it is beyond belief for anyone unfamiliar with pack ice. But half an hour before midnight, *Defence* is afloat again. Ekins is very pleased, and calls for a toast among the officers gathered in the captain's cabin. Two days later, the 20-year-old landsman from Chester, Thomas Lowe, is punished for the fourth time on this year's voyage.

On August 17, *Defence*'s boats are lowered and a party of mariners sent to shore in order to destroy an enemy battery at Papskallan. The next day, another party of marines from *Defence* is sent to shore to build and man a new battery there.

Four days later, John observes from the forecastle an attempt by the Finns to retake the battery. He watches the Finnish soldiers run down the hills behind the battery to make a surprise attack on the Royal Navy mariners entrenched in their newly erected battery station. But the Finnish soldiers are instantly discovered by the English lookout and the attack is turned back by the Royal Navy mariners. The Finnish soldiers are quickly finished off.

In early September, while John is onboard the *Defence* in the middle of the Baltic Sea, Copenhagen Jackson reaches Washington D.C. with his American wife. In Republican newspapers, he is systematically called 'Copenhagen Jackson.' He travels the country, giving speeches mostly to Federalists.

In the apartment on Water Street, Mary Ann reads about Copenhagen Jackson in the *American Watchman*, and when she and her girlfriends or her mother's friends gather around coffee tables talking, they circulate horrifying stories about the bombardment of the innocent children and women in Copenhagen. They've never heard of this kind of brutal warfare against civilians used by a nation that call itself civilized and they pray that this kind of warfare will never come to Wilmington.

On September 5, 1809, Allen McLane is sitting at his desk thinking about his age. He is resting after a long walk along the quays on the Christina River's north bank, inspecting the moored ships. He is now enjoying a cup of hot coffee and reflecting on his life achievements. 'I'm 69 and next year I will surely turn 70," he mumbles to himself. 'But actually I'm quite satisfied with what I have achieved so far." Caught up with memories this way, he recalls that this day is a very special one. His thoughts travel back exactly 35 years.

The First Continental Congress is taking place in Philadelphia in Carpenter's Hall this September 5. A group of 68 men, including McLane, people with the same political opinion on the future of the American colonies, gather in the yard outside the State House and solemnly declare that they will support Congress with life and fortune. The moment is impressive, and George Washington, the 6-foot-5 inch aristocratic-looking Virginia farmer and Colonel, has said nothing during the session. His height and charisma single him out, and he shows himself to be a true leader by giving attention to new, unknown and up-and-coming members in the group gathered in the yard, people who have met here but who are not attending the First Congress inside the Hall.

One of these is Allan McLane, 28 years old.

Deep in his heart, he feels a need to help protect Congress and the American cause, and marrying the second daughter of James Wells, a patriot and former High Sheriff of Kent Co., three years ago, strengthened his patriotic feelings. But to McLane, this gathering outside the State House is more than a simple gathering. It is an almost religious experience. He was born right here in Philadelphia on Walnut Street, the very street bordering this yard, just a few hundred meters away, in a simple log house made out of trees cut from the prosperous woods near the Schuylkill River, on August 8, 1740. Standing here on such a solemn occasion for his country, in his childhood environment where he recognizes every smell and knows every corner, almost brings tears to his eyes.

A trip to England a few years ago, from 1767 to 1769, helped convince him that, in the long run, the North American colonies needed to be free from England.[133] When the war was over McLane settled near Duck Creek Cross Roads in Kent County, Delaware as a leather breeches maker.[142]

Looking up from his desk, McLane glances around the room, and then makes eye contact with his subordinate, John Freed, Jr., who has just entered the room with a large handful of ship's papers. McLane proudly says to him, "Are you aware, young man, that this very day is exactly 35 years since the First Continental Congress met in Philadelphia, and I was present outside the building?"

'Oh, is that right, Sir?" John Freed answers, absentmindedly. 'I was not quite aware," He puts the papers on the desk and leaves the room with the same haste as he entered it, appearing rude without meaning to. McLane continues his work.

September 22, the crew onboard *Defence* is preparing the ship to leave the Royal Navy summer station in Malkonita Bay to return to England. Most of the merchant ships under protection of the Royal Navy that trades in this part of the Baltic Sea have arrived from trade stations and ports further north and east, and are ready to be escorted out of the Baltic Sea.

Defence, its squadron, and the convoy of merchant ships leave the summer station and, on October 3, pass the Lighthouse of Øland along the East coast of Sweden on a southern course. On the 7th, they anchor in Carlscrona Roads, outside the Headquarters of the Royal Swedish Navy.

Three days later, 14 seamen are punished onboard *Defence*, among them the British able seaman Joseph Page, whom John knows quite well. Page tries to bear the pain by concentrating on the three church spires in the borough of Carlscrona in front of him, but it doesn't seem to help a lot.

John Brown is beginning to get problems with his breathing after working for such a long time in the powder room. He occasionally complains to his superior officer, but is just told to shape up. His superior officer says, 'When you were sick after our return from the Campaign against Denmark, it was from being outdoors too much working in the riggings. Now you have been allowed to work indoors for quite some time, and you start complaining about getting sick from being indoors. Can you make up your mind?"

John is too weak to answer back. He just coughs a couple of times, and returns to the powder room to continue his unhealthy work. The day after, he begins to feel very sick. All this time in the powder room has done his lungs no good, and now it's too late to try and change it.

Because the Royal Navy convoys are going to depart the Baltic Sea soon to return to England, a lot of provisions are taken in from the Swedish port Carlscrona. Most of the crew onboard *Defence*, including John, are employed taking in and storing away this provision. John must work hard and at a high speed for long hours.

139

Swedish merchants from this port city of the Swedish Navy's headquarters supply the British Royal Navy, which is good for the Swedish economy in these times of war. Sweden needs the money for its own war, because when England stole the Danish fleet and war between England and Denmark broke out, the Swedish government also declared war on Denmark, 'cruising in the slipstream of the navy of the great British Empire' and hoping to claim new Danish territory as Swedish land sometime in the future. Sweden had done this successfully in times past, when its neighboring countries were temporarily weakened. The Swedes therefore figure it is not a bad thing to help England bring Denmark to its knees in this war.

The wind is moderate and the sky is cloudy. At noon, John is on the top deck, and although he feels sick, he notices *HMS Tartar* and the cutters *Cheerful* and *Hero* sail. John sweats heavily and feels uneasy.

The American public reads in the newspapers that Francis Jackson has replaced Erskine as the British Minister in Washington.[234, 277] Copenhagen Jackson is in North America to stay and spends his time hanging around in high society. Many ordinary Americans would rather have seen him stay in England.

The next day, October 12, John is released from work in the powder room and promoted to able seaman. His superior officer has finally admitted that fresh air will be better for John Brown's lungs under the present circumstances. John can't help feeling a little proud about his promotion in the Royal Navy. He is now going to work on the forecastle. But he has already been in the powder room too long. John is definitely not feeling well, and he has a permanent high fever.

As the days pass by, he becomes weaker and weaker. On October 22, when he stands on the forecastle in early morning, panting heavily because he is not able to breathe, he vomits blood over the starboard bulwark. The last things he sees before he faints are the six windows in the old crane in the naval dockyards near the headquarters of the Royal Swedish Navy. He has hardly fallen to the deck before John Pristoff and his colleagues, who have been worried about him for quite some time, are by his side to pick him up. They immediately carry him to sick quarters.

The surgeon who comes to sick quarters to examine John determines that he is seriously ill. The surgeon orders John transferred to the hospital ship *Gordon*[48], which is following the Baltic fleet and is anchored here in Carlscrona Roads.

Three days later, on October 25, William meets Captain Goff at Hemphill's wharf. Captain Goff informs William that the gaff schooner *Ino* is going to leave for New York tomorrow afternoon. They can wait no longer, if they want to safely sail the Delaware River and the ocean before it gets too stormy.

William expected the departure to take place much later this year, because there is no immediate risk of the river freezing. But William also knows that he has to be onboard that ship tomorrow. He and Mary Ann need the money badly after all these months William had low-paying jobs. Although she has not told him directly, William is quite sure that Mary Ann is pregnant. For that reason alone, they'll have to marry before he leaves for New York.

This evening, when Mary Ann and her mother return from the Wilmington Borough Hospital to make supper, William tells them Goff's decision. Mary Ann doesn't like the idea of William leaving Wilmington at all. 'Can't you stay, William?' she begs him.

Mary Ann's mother steps in between them. 'Mary Ann, you must understand he has to go, if he sees this as a right thing to do. You both need the money to take care of the child you are expecting when it comes.' Mary Ann has not told her mother about her pregnancy, and she is very surprised at these direct words.

'Expecting. How do you know I'm expecting?' Mary Ann appears insulted.

'I have eyes, Mary Ann. You must be six months along. And by the way, I think it will be a very good idea that you two marry before William leaves.'

'But moth -'

Now it's William's turn to go between the others. 'Yes, Mary Ann, listen to your mother. We have to marry before I leave.'

Mary Ann loosens up. 'William, since we have so little time left to be together before you leave, let us not discuss it. We will marry tomorrow morning then,' she says.

'There is no time to waste,' says William. 'I'll go and ask the priest at the Old Swedes Church right away to see if he is able to marry us tomorrow morning. Then I will invite William Windell, John Freed, Jr., Damian Starr, Enoch Lang, and Joseph Warner and his wife. Then you can arrange what you need to arrange, Mary Ann." William kisses Mary Ann and quickly leaves the apartment.

He goes east down Water Street, turns left at the corner and walks up French Street. Half a block up on the right is Spring Alley, a block-long alley, where the parsonage of the Old Swedish Church is. William knocks firmly on the door and the Rector of the Old Swedes Church, Joseph Clarkson, opens it and invites him in.

William briefly states his errand, that tomorrow he sails to New York and later Europe, and he and his fiancée have to get married before he leaves. The pastor thinks of the present political situation for merchants and ship-owners, and especially seamen, who risk impressment into the Royal Navy. This can separate young couples for years and maybe for life, if a girl gets tired of waiting and marries another. 'Under the circumstances," Clarkson says, 'I think you are right. It is better f or you to get married before you leave." William, who had been thinking of nothing but the pregnancy since he came to this holy man, blushes, wondering if the pastor knows that Mary Ann is already pregnant, but he says nothing. Maybe the priest has a direct connection to the higher power. "At 10 o'clock tomorrow morning, then. Be there on time," Father Clarkson says and closes the door as William hurries back down Spring Alley.

William goes to William Windell's flat and invites him, his wife and their new child to the wedding. They congratulate him and promise to be at the church on time tomorrow. Then he walks over to ask Enoch Lang and Damian Starr, then Joseph Warner; Jr., who has just moved back to Wilmington from Philadelphia this year. Ester Yarnell took care of the older Mary Warner, and when Ester died, Joseph and Mary Warner found it best for the family to be together.

All the members of the Warner family have warm and positive remarks when William gathers them in the living room of the Warner mansion and brings the good news that he and Mary Ann were going to be married tomorrow. John Warner smiled, genuinely happy that he could finally reveal to his family about the time he, from his office window, saw William and Mary Ann kissing so innocently and romantically at The Rocks, probably for the first time. Everyone laughs heartily at the story. William could kill John Warner for telling it, but he minds his manners and just sends John his worst killer look, a look that seems to have no effect.

John Freed, Jr. is at their flat when William meets him and William invites him to join the wedding. 'That's great William. I'll have to ask Mr. McLane for half an hour off, but I'll be glad to do that, William, and I'm sure McLane is magnanimous en ough to grant it," he says, knowing that it will probably only be a matter of time before the two of them stop sharing this flat. But both bachelors knew this had to come one day. The flat is merely a base they both visit for short periods between trips on the sea. They had not spent much time there together, and had not even thrown a party there for their friends.

The next morning, William and Mary Ann's friends gather at 10 o'clock outside the gate to the cross-shaped Old Swedes Church, at the east end of Broad Street outside Wilmington, between the south bank of the Brandywine River and the north bank of the Christina River. The church has a tiny spire and is built of granite boulders.

Mary Ann walked to the church with her mother, her mother's fri end and two of her own best girl friends. William arrived accompanied by his friends Joseph Warner, William Windell, Enoch Lang and John Freed. Joseph Warner offers to walk Mary Ann to the altar, her father being absent, and she is honored for William's be st friend to do that.

Mary Ann managed to rent a nice white wedding gown this morning, even on such a short notice, and when Joseph Warner begins to walk her to the altar, William thinks he has never seen her look so beautiful. Joseph had said exactly the same about his own bride, when he and Mary got married, so William figures that is the way it should be. Mary Ann is quite nervous now, but not so much because of the wedding. She is concerned about William's coming voyage.

The wedding ceremony is simple and beautiful. They sing three lovely psalms, and the priest makes a short speech addressing William's departure for New York that afternoon, and what the priest finds as the three most important values in life, belief, hope and love.

When the marriage ceremony is over, Mary Ann's mother invites them all to the flat in Water Street for coffee, cakes and sweets lacking the time to arrange a suitable wedding party. They all accept.

As the wedding party walks down French Street, approaching Front

Street with the Customhouse to the left, William Windell stops and says that he has to leave or his boss will be angry if he does not show up at the Customhouse office as agreed upon. But the new bridegroom William says, 'Come on, William, the party is only 30 yards from here. You can keep an eye on the Customhouse all the time from the flat."

William Windell and John Freed, Jr. agree to come along. William Watson feels very lucky and happy this morning that he is finally married to the only girl he has ever loved, and if everything goes well they will be parents in less than 3 months year. His friends Joseph Warner and William Windell have been married for some time now and both of them have already children, so William thinks it is time for him and Mary Ann to have children of their own.

The weather is ideal for departure, with a strong wind from the west. The conditions are perfect for a trip out of the Christina River and Delaware Bay this day.

John Freed and William Windell leave the party first, to go to work. As the only two assistants from the Revenue Service, they are going to prepare papers for the gaff schooner *Ino* that Mr. Goff will captain to New York with William onboard.

William packed his ship's box early this mornin g and carried it to the cabin of the *Ino*. He is prepared and ready to depart anytime. So he relaxes at the party, completely focused on enjoying his last hours at home in the company of his wife, Mrs. Mary Ann Watson, her mother and their best friends.

The party finally breaks up at three in the afternoon. As everyone walks out onto Water Street, they see Thomas Mendenhall standing in the doorway across the street, at his home at 69 E. Water Street. Mendenhall says hello and put his fingers to his hat as he sees the crowd coming out. William proudly announces that he has just been married, and that they all are on their way to the quay to send him off to New York. 'Congratulations to the two of you. May you have a good life," Mendenhall says, smiling, as the party continues down Water Street. From the Customhouse William Windell and John Freed, Jr. rejoin the party, this time bringing the ship's papers for departure.

At the *Ino*, the crew and captain Goff are already onboard and prepared to depart. From his chest pocket, William takes out his Protection Certificate, with his lucky number 7777, to calm Mary Ann down and reassure her that he is as prepared as he can be for a safe journey across the Atlantic Ocean and back. Mary Ann ties the colorful silk scarf around his neck again, and kisses him goodbye.

The gaff schooner *Ino* sails freely on the Christina River outside the quay at the Hemphill's Wharf, slowly carried by the stream toward the outlet and the Delaware River. For a moment, everyone on the quay and onboard the *Ino* is silent, as though trying to seal this moment in memory for the rest of their lives. Then everyone waves and smiles, and laughter echoes across the water. The last eyes to have visual contact are Mary Ann and William's. Mary Ann is frightened, watching this small ship float down the Christina River, heading for the Atlantic Ocean. She promises herself that she will pray for William every day he is away, as she and her mother walk back to their flat in Water Street.

William Windell, John Freed, Jr. and Joseph Warner had been unconcerned the entire morning, but they, too, are beginning to have their doubts about this voyage, thinking it will probably eventually go to England.

McLane is angry about the *Ino* leaving, because he knows all too well that the real destination for many ships leaving Wilmington is England. But he can do nothing, because the ship's papers have a destination of New York.

William feels good about having his feet on the deck of a sailing ship again. The slowly rolling movements thrill him and he has never had a problem with seasickness. He always finds it joyful to be on the open sea. He has been on ships under the worst weather conditions and seen the dramatic change in appearance of his traveling companions, but even in the most terrible storm, William is completely unaffected, sitting at his usual place at the table in the ship's cabin, eating supper with his usual appetite, while other crewmembers are on the open deck, vomiting from empty stomachs for hours. Pausing to regain their strength, sick seamen occasionally look in through the portholes and see William eating his food and having a great time. Some of them wondered if he is somehow out of this world. William's ability to never be seasick earned his colleagues' respect, and William became a kind of inspiration to them all, when their world at sea seems too large and troubled to cope with.

On October 31, the flagships *HMS* V*ictory*, *Africa*, *Nemesis* and other war ships attached to *Victory*'s squadron depart Carlscrona Roads, accompanied by the hospital ship *Gordon,* where John is still lying sick. The Royal Navy squadron is protecting a convoy of 214 merchant ships on the way home to England.

John stays in sick quarters onboard *Gordon* when the hospital ship follows the *Victory* squadron and convoy of merchant ships to Vinga Sound.

The *Ino* arrives in the Port of New York after a trouble-free voyage. William recognizes the port, and knows that he will stay there for Christmas, as he did two years ago. Winter seems to have come early this year, and William's situation is different now. He is just as poor as the first time he arrived in the port of New York, but this time is in the fortunate situation of having a lovely wife. "Yes, indeed, the beautiful, irresistible Mary Ann is finally my wife," William thinks, smiling happily.

Just to be able to think of Mary Ann as his wife while on this journey makes William feel so much better than the last time he came here. Mary Ann will probably spend her time helping her mother on home visits to the sick and elderly people in Wilmington, and working at the borough Hospital.

The following day it snows heavily in the southern part of the Baltic Sea, and in the afternoon the *Victory* convoy passes the small Swedish island of Hanö, south of Carlscrona, with a convoy of 42 merchant ships. The snow in the air is an indication that winter might come early this year.

Captain Ekins and several other captains in the Baltic Fleet have been looking at Hanö for some time, thinking to use it as a Baltic summer station in the future. The island is only four miles from the Swedish mainland, and the water is deep enough that the entire Baltic Fleet and a large convoy of merchant ships can anchor there and be protected properly. The island has another strategic advantage as a summer station. Its position so close to the southern Baltic Sea is a perfect place for the Royal Navy to stay later into autumn in the Baltic Sea, before winter and ice set in. Staying longer in the Baltic Sea increases the navy's ability to escort more merchant ships back to England and hence earn a greater profit for both the navy and the merchant's fleet.

Captain Ekins is quite sure that Hanö will be the perfect place for a summer station. It is also an advantage that Hanö is so close to

Carlscrona and the Headquarters of the Swedish Royal Navy. This will make communication between the Royal Navy and the Swedish Admiralty much easier.

On November 25, the *St. George* squadron to which *Defence* is attached and 187 merchant ships reach the island of Langeland in the south end of the Great Belt. The flagship *St. George* fires its guns to gather the convoy and make it easier to defend. Although it is quite hazy, this time when the English ships pass the Great Belt, Danish cannon boats do not attack them. It is very late in the year, and the British convoy has succeeded in fooling the Danes. Danish military posts along the Danish coast thought that the last British convoy from the Baltic Sea had already left.

The passage through the Great Belt and the Cattegat Sea runs smoothly for the convoy, and early in the afternoon of December 2, it has reached a position in the Skagerak 23 miles west of the Scaw. The wind is changing from west-southwest to east-northeast, which can take them quickly toward England and free of the dangerous lee shore on the west coast of Jutland.

When it doesn't rain and John has time off work, he often spends his time standing at the bulwark inhaling the fresh sea air. With his strong hawk eyes, he can see even the smallest fishing or farming cottage along the rocky south coast of Norway. Alone at the bulwark for many hours, John lets his eyes study the large beautiful sea waves as they rhythmically rise and fall, as if they were huge lungs of the earth. He tries to imagine how these poor Norwegian fisher and farmer families are doing, probably sitting at almost empty dinner tables and eating their humble meals, hoping for better times, where foodstuffs can be transported freely between Denmark and Norway.

As time has passed since Denmark and England went to war in August 1807, more than two years ago, John has seen *Defence* confiscate several Norwegian ships and smaller boats trying to cross the Skagerak Sea, and take their captains and seamen prisoners. These Norwegian prisoners have mostly been hardworking men and boys who were just busy transporting their cargoes of cattles and grain and flour from the rich cornfields of Jutland to the poor valleys along the south and west coast of Norway. After the confiscation of their ships, the Norwegian men and boys were usually sent to English prison ships anchored in southern and southwestern English ports on the other side of the North Sea, where Danish and American prisoners also spent their time in prison ships. These Norwegian men and boys are often held prisoner for years, under conditions of starvation, cold and isolation, giving them plenty of time to think of their poor families left helpless and probably starving in Norway.

Still standing at the bulwark, John honors these brave Norwegian men and boys by forcing himself to imagine the heartbreaking scenes that must have taken place in these small coastal fishing cottages and farm houses, when wives and children received the devastating news that yet another Norwegian ship had been confiscated and that their men were not coming home, but were on their way to prison ships in England.

Being impressed or being a prisoner onboard the *Defence,* for some years now, John had been forced to see this happening from the British side, while he, during the many almost countless days, had stood on the forecastle, when the ship patrolled the Cattegat, or along one of the bulwarks and silently and helplessly noticed the many hollow-cheeked, thin, sinewy and sad looking Norwegian men and boys, while they slowly climbed the gangway of *Defence,* from their ship or boat, to finally arrive on the main deck.

John clearly remembered these sad looks of defeat which had shined so strongly and clearly in their receding and empty eyes, when they stooping, with loosen limbs let themselves walk around on the different decks by the eager and triumphing young marine soldiers, that somehow thought that they had made just another lucky catch, being lucky as if they had been part of an ordinary hunting party, participating in a better fox chase in the countryside, back home.

On December 8, the *St. George* squadron has reached the south end of the North Sea. There is a strong gale and the mizzen staysail is carried away in the heavy seas surrounding *Defence*. The island of Texel is to the west.

On December 18 *St. George, Defence*, the rest of the squadron and the merchant ships anchor in Leith Roads. Captain Ekins is pleased that they made the trip from Carlscrona Roads to Leith Roads with only minor problems.

The *Victory* squadron, including the hospital ship *Gordon,* also crosses the North Sea without any accidents and returns to winter quarters in Portsmouth. John is coughing a lot and his temperature rises and falls as the infected area of his lungs increases and decreases. One week, the nurses and the doctors think they might lose him.

John celebrates Christmas Eve, 1809, in a narrow camp bed with a high fever, lying with sick seamen on the deck onboard *Gordon,* anchored in Portsmouth.

When he wakes from his fevered dreams on Christmas Eve, he can only think of his lonely mother back in Salem. It has been more than four years since he said goodbye to her, and a long time since he last wrote to her, because he lost faith that she would get the letters, since he never received any answers. His mother must be convinced by now that he is dead.

At midnight this Christmas Eve William and a fellow seaman from the *Ino,* 16-year-old, William Freeman from Philadelphia, are standing on the deck of the *Ino* enjoying the spectacular fireworks illuminating the sky over lower Manhattan. It is an extraordinarily beautiful sight to both of them.

Mary Ann and her mother are at the harbor front in Wilmington this evening, walking along the quay to see the fireworks there. It had become tradition for them to go and watch wealthy citizens shooting off their spectacular fireworks. Christmas day, hundreds of ships have gathered in the port of New York. The captains are eager to get their ship's papers made ready for departure, so they'll be ready to leave port early in the new year. The New York Port Collector and his assistants work long hours to get the many ship papers ready.

When ship captains and crewmembers are not nearby, assistants in the customhouse can't help laughing as they check the different papers. Never in the history of the United States of America have so many ships wanted to go to the Azores Islands. The New York Port Collector himself is very angry, as McLane was when *Ino* left Wilmington. The port collectors are angry because they are responsible for making sure that no ship is leaving port to sail to England unless it has a legal reason and permission to go there. Trading with other neutral countries is legal, but trips to these were few and normally carried little trade. Writing small neutral countries as the destination in ship's papers is not that credible.

Captain Goff appears at the Customhouse carrying the papers from the *Ino*. The port collector comes forward and stands quietly behind his assistant as he silently reviews the papers. Then he asks Goff sarcastically if he is sure that the Azores Islands can take all that flaxseed. 'Maybe these islands in the middle of the Atlantic Ocean are made out of flax seed when it comes to a closer look," the New York port collector says loudly, so that everyone in the room can hear. Captain Goff tries to make himself invisible. He is not normally the type to hide when confronted with problems related to his business affairs, but he has no appropriate answer to put forward right now. He just whispers to himself, 'Go ahead and laugh, sitting here with your publicly well-paid position as port collector, with no responsibility for the income from exports that this country lives off. If you are so smart, maybe you can get the British Prime Minister and our President to meet on the Azores and sort the problem out." William Watson and William Freeman have rowed the captain to the quay. When they hear the port collector and the whisper of their captain, they can't help laughing, even through they are standing right next to their boss.

Amos Stevens, a 29-year-old Boston born ships carpenter, is onboard another ship anchored in New York, its homeport. He, like other men here, is waiting impatiently for his ship to be cleared for departure. Officially, his ship is also on its way to the Azores, but as it is the case with many, including William Warner's *Fair American* in Philadelphia, its real destination is Liverpool.

The *Ino* is ready to leave the port of New York, and William finally dares to ask captain Goff, where they are headed. Captain Goff sees no point in hiding the destination from his crew any longer, and he tells William frankly that they are going directly to Portsmouth in the English Channel.

'England can't supply itself with grain or flax seed, and President Jefferson knew that quite well when he started the Embargo," Captain Goff says, trying to explain his illegal voyage to England.

William Watson and William Freeman begin to feel uneasy. But they have no reason to. Both of them knew from the beginning that part of the deal to participate in this voyage was accepting the risk of going to England, in order to receive the high salary offered. William is worried, though, as the *Ino* sails on the Atlantic Ocean heading directly toward the heart of Royal Navy headquarters.

Thanks to a strong and steady western wind, the *Ino* reaches The Solent, the small canal between the Isle of Wright and the English south coast, in the English Channel, on January 6 in the new year of 1810.

It's cloudy and the crew onboard the *Ino* observe a high number of frigates and ships of the line belonging to the Royal Navy on the position known as Spithead. This would definitely be enemy territory number one for an American seaman like me, William thinks to himself as they approach the port of Portsmouth.

As the *Ino* arrives in the Bay of Portsmouth, Captain Goff points toward a group of ships the same size as *Ino*, and orders the masters mate to bring their ship to that position and drop anchor. Captain Goff goes to his cabin to change clothes and make himself look a bit more respectable in this foreign port.

William Watson and William Freeman take a look around the harbor. Freeman points at a jollyboat with 10 mariners and one officer heading directly toward them with great speed from the direction of a large ship anchored at Spithead.

The ship is *HMS St. George*[64] a 98 cannon second-rater named after British King George III on one side and Saint George on the other. The *St. George* is flagship for the squadron in this year's Royal Navy Baltic Fleet, to which *Defence* is attached. The flagship has Rear Admiral of the Red C.W. Reynolds onboard.

At 6 that morning, *St. George* had sent its boats out to search the harbor for seamen to impress. This time of year, when the Royal Navy's ships are rigged out for the Baltic mission, they usually help supply their crews by searching merchant ships in Portsmouth harbor area to find seamen and mariners to bring back.

This misty morning, the focus is definitely on the American mariners, because *St. George* needs a certain number of mariners to serve onboard the flagship. When British officers and mariners want to take men from American merchant ships, they have to be quite tough with them to be successful.

The jollyboat comes along the port side of the *Ino*. William Watson calls captain Goff, and everyone onboard the American gaff schooner is alert. They know that the British marine officer and his crew are allowed to come onboard to check the ship, so they do nothing to prevent it. The marine officer observes William Watson with a gun at his feet, ready to defend the gaff schooner if ordered, and the British officer shouts to his mariners, 'Check the papers of these seamen and mariners."

While he examines the captain's and the ship's papers, William Watson, William Freeman, and the other American seamen are asked by one of the mariners to show their personal papers.

William Watson takes out his Protection Certificate, having what he considers the lucky number 7777 and the English mariner snaps it from his hand and hands it to the marine officer. William Freeman's papers are also handed over. The marine officer sees that William Freeman is 16 and William Watson 22, and thereby probably the youngest crewmembers onboard so he points at them and says, 'I'll take these two English seamen with me to the *St. George*." Captain Goff protests at once, 'These are American seamen, proven by the Protection Certificates you have just seen."

'My good man, these New York protection certificates can be made for any British seaman within minutes. I have seen hundreds of them." The marine officer shouts, 'Take them away!" Two English mariners quickly move toward William Watson while another two grasp William Freeman.

William Watson suddenly understands the seriousness of the situation. With a single stroke of his left arm, he knocks down the Royal Navy mariner closest to him. The mariner falls unconscious to the deck of the gaff schooner. The next mariner who approaches William is knocked overboard, and the British mariners in the jollyboat have to concentrate on picking him up. But two other British mariners on the *Ino* attack William at the same time and succeed in tying him up with a rope. William Watson is carried from the *Ino* to the jollyboat and William Freeman, who is small of stature, follows freely.

As the jollyboat rows away from the *Ino* with William Watson lying in the bottom, Captain Goff shouts at the top of his lungs, 'I'll report this, damn royal marine fools! Be sure I will report this. Has it passed your attention that we Americans are free of British rule? It's that simple, you damn fools."

Captain Goff storms to his cabin and writes to the American Department of State, telling them that two of his best men have been forced off his ship, while he could do nothing but stand by helpless. He asks the Department of State to file a protest with the Admiralty in London against this injustice. Finally, he writes a second letter to The American Consul and Agent for Seamen in London, General William Lyman.

William Watson is pressed against the bottom of the jollyboat with two heavy British Royal Mariners sitting on top of him. He feels like screaming in anger while he listens to the rhythm of the marine mate shouting "Heave, heave, heave."

His thoughts fly wildly, then go back home to his pregnant wife, Mary Ann. "How are you, my true and dearest love?" he whispers to himself, with an empty heart. He misses her terribly in these stressful, unfair moments.

William begins to understand the violent hatred Allen McLane and Samuel Bush sometimes expressed, when the talk back home turned to the British Royal Navy. With this evil act against him, Royal Mariners have become common, brutal criminals to William. He now begins to understand what the three Americans impressed from the *Chesapeake* must have felt, more than two years ago, when taken by the *HMS Leopold* right outside the Delmarva peninsula.

The jollyboat approaches the *St. George* from behind, and William Freeman reads the golden letters on top of the ship's gallery. He whispers to William Watson, who can see nothing from the bottom of the jollyboat. "It's the *St. George…*" William Freeman doesn't finish his sentence before the marine officer orders him to be quiet.

The mariners untie William Watson after what seems like hours, and push him toward the gangway. This is a gigantic ship, William thinks as he climbs the rope ladder. When he reaches the upper deck, a mariner points to the left, and William falls in line with seamen and mariners brought to the *St. George* from other American and British merchant ships in Portsmouth Roads or the harbor.

William Watson and the other seamen now stand silently, hoping for better treatment than they just experienced. An officer approaches quickly from the cabins at the rear, behind the steering wheel. William watches without turning his head by moving his eyes as far to the left as possible. The officer seems friendly, or at least not as hostile as the one in the jollyboat. He says, "Welcome onboard the *HMS St. George*." Then he turns around and walks back to the cabin where he came from, at the same high speed.

The officer in charge of showing the seamen their serving posts onboard the ship musters them to determine their skills as seamen. The young and inexperienced William Freeman becomes an Ordinary Seamen and William Watson an Able Seamen. The two of them are not yet entered into the muster book, because the officers don't know whether they can eventually get them to serve voluntarily.

Each newcomer is given a hammock and a carpet, taken to the lower deck and shown a place to stay for the night, close to a cannon port. It is cold, and William Freeman is now in a very bad mood. As a young, free American he never imagined that he one fine day could be forced to serve onboard a foreign man-o-war. Both Williams observe some seamen working hard, scraping the decks with holystones, but they can't figure out, why they are allowed to walk freely around the deck while the other men work.

The two of them are left alone for a couple of hours, then a masters mate returns and asks politely if they would consider joining this crew onboard the *St. George*. "We serve plenty of nice food and the payment is fair, I should say. If you sign up right away, you will also receive a bounty," he tells them, a warm smile on his face.

William Watson knows from discussions in the harbor of New York that an American seaman should never accept any Bounty offered by any English officer, because this means he can never escape service in the Royal Navy. He and William Freeman are honestly flattered that an English officer is speaking so nicely to them. But William Watson, seeing that Freeman is in a state where he probably would say yes to anything, immediately speaks up. "Sir, we are flattered by your kind offer, but we are American merchant seamen, and we cannot serve in the Royal British Navy. I have a pregnant wife at home who is depending on me to return on time. William Freeman is only 16, and his mother is a widow and likewise very dependent on his quick return. Sir, I ask you to help us get off this ship and back on the American schooner we came from as soon as possible."

The master mate's face turns very dark and angry, and he replies, "A common seaman who asks me favors. Ridiculous." Then he shouts to another lower ranking officer standing next to them, "Make sure you show these new *British* seamen how we work here in the Royal British Navy."

Within three minutes, the two Williams are on their knees scraping the decks with holystones, exactly like the other seamen onboard the flagship *St. George*.

In their first hours onboard, both Williams are amazed at the size of this ship of the line. They have never seen such a huge ship at such short range. The officer's and mariner's uniforms are beautiful, colorful and clean, like nothing they have ever seen. If they look toward the top of the masts and watch the seamen running along the top yards, looking like tiny small men, they get dizzy. Everything seems to be so big on this flagship.

By talking to more experienced seamen, William soon finds out that there are quite a number of impressed Americans on the *St. George,* as is the case onboard any ship in the Royal Navy here around Spithead and Portsmouth.

An American seaman approaches and asks where they come from in America, and they are questioned about the situation back home. They are shown the rules applied onboard and how to put up their hammocks. Being young and new onboard a Royal Navy's ship doesn't feel so bad, knowing that experienced American seamen are present.

William and William are told that they are allowed to buy paper and pen and write home, but that they should expect letters to travel for a while before they reach home.

William Watson decides to write to the Agent for American seamen in London, as an experienced American seaman told him to. None of the American seamen know how to spell the name, so William Watson addresses his letter to 'Mr. Limma[12] in London'.

The same day, William writes a letter to Mary Ann, realizing that this is the first time he has written his wife's new name since they got married. In his short letter, William tells Mary Ann what has happened to him, and asks how she is doing in her condition. He wishes her all luck and hopes to be back at her side very soon, although he has no idea when he will be given the chance to return.

In the middle of January 1810, John Brown is well enough to be transferred from the hospital ship *Gordon* to the lodging and transfer ship *Monkey* anchored in Portsmouth harbor. The idea is that he will stay here until an opportunity comes up for him to be returned to his ship,

Defence.

On January 25, Amos Stevens' American schooner from New York arrives in the busy east English port of Liverpool. As always, when the crew arrives in a foreign port, they work hard, unloading the cargo while they think about the free time on shore that waits ahead.

Amos leaves the ship and jumps onto the quay, glad to have solid ground under his feet once again. Together with one of his good friends, John Wiley, he has a day off work and several days to wait for the English articles to arrive in the port, to bring back to New York.

Like many deep-sea sailors arriving in a new port such as Liverpool, Amos and John and their friends are not wasting their free time. Less than an hour after leaving their schooner at the quay, they are sitting in the pub closest to the quay and having their first drink.

The first round this day is on Amos. He had promised that, with him as the ship carpenter, they would cross the Atlantic Ocean without breaking a single bar. But they ran into several storms in a row, and in the last one, the topgallant bar broke. Amos repaired it quickly, but had to promise to buy the other crewmembers a round of beers when they arrived in Liverpool.

Although it is sunny, it is also quite cold, as it normally is at this time of year when humidity decreases temperature in an English harbor. It is now 3 p.m., and Amos, John Wiley, some other American and British seamen, and some local girls are having a party at a table illuminated by candlelight in the darkest corner of the pub, close to the back entrance.

Amos and his American colleagues are laughing and cheering and enjoying seeing new faces after the time at sea. They are beginning to feel a little drunk, because they have been drinking on empty stomachs. Suddenly a group of seamen standing close to the pub's entrance shouts, 'The Press Gang, the Press Gang!" Before anyone can move, a group of six strong seamen and a press-warrant officer enters the back entrance, close to the table where Amos, John and three other American seamen sit. They are immediately grabbed and taken out into the street. Amos tries hard to get free, protesting wildly, 'Release us at once!" He asks the two mariners holding him "What the hell do you think you are doing? We are Americans, American born citizens. You are holding us against the law."

The press warrant officer shouts, 'Take them to the *Rendezvous.* They are British all right, cowards trying to escape the duty of serving their country and His Majesty's Royal Navy." Amos, John and the others from the New York schooner are dragged to the *Rendezvous*, a house on the harbor front in Liverpool, where newly impressed seamen are gathered temporarily. They are locked up with a lot of other American and British seamen[72] from other newly arrived ships in harbor.

They are kept there for two days, until January 27, when they are taken in small groups out to the prison ship *Princess,* anchored just outside the harbor of Liverpool.[72]

Princess is an overcrowded prison ship, and while they stay here, Amos, John and the other newcomers ask some of the old prisoners what they can do to be released. They are told to write to a kind of American Agent for seamen here in Liverpool, Captain Carter[8], who deals with this matter in the harbor. He comes onboard the *Princess* occasionally, and they can hand him a letter with information on themselves, or give him their names and Protection Certificates, if they have them.

Amos and John write a letter to Captain Carter, and when they get the chance to meet him, the next time he comes onboard the *Princess*, they give him their information[8]. To Amos, he seems to be a noble and kind man. He looks like a man of honor and dignity and a man who can be trusted. Captain Carter promises to include their names on the lists reported to the Department of State in Washington every quarter.

Then on February 4, Amos and John are discharged from the *Princess* and sent onboard the transport ship *HMS Espegle* for transport to the south coast of England and the entrance prison ship, *Salvador Del Mundo*[60], which is anchored permanently in the port of Plymouth. On February 22, Amos and the other men from the New York schooner climb the gangway to enter *Salvador Del Mundo*.

The commander of *Salvador Del Mundo* tries to make a joke with Amos and the other newly arrived prisoners, while they stand in a line on the upper deck, by paraphrasing quotes from the Holy Bible in his own strange way. He produces the same joke whenever new prisoners arrive, and even his subordinates do not find it amusing when he says to Amos and John, "Welcome to His Majesty's Ship *Salvador Del Mundo*, The Redeemer of the World, a former Spanish prize. Ha, ha, yes, they surely save the world these days, these Spanish lovers of our archenemy France. Don't they? They even claim to have found the New World way back and to have helped it gain independence from our great British Empire. Well, let me say with a clear and conscientious mind to you, Let the American prisoners come to me, for You may not hinder them therein. To those belong the Kingdom onboard this, His Majesty's *Ship Salvador Del Mundo,* and in those I find great pleasure. For those prisoners not exactly like these humble American prisoners shall not be allowed at all to enter my kingdom onboard this all mighty ship." The commander bellows with laughter, which is heard for a long time on the upper deck, where the entering seamen silently wait in a line while the commander walks around on the deck, punching his subordinates in their stomachs and smiling at them while he is amusing himself. He long ago accepted that his subordinates do not even try to laugh at his jokes anymore. It doesn't matter to him at all. Like any lonely naval sadist, he knows all too well how to amuse himself during the long voyages on the oceans so far from home.

A few days later, Amos is sent to one of the other prison ships in Plymouth, anchored behind the entrance ship. It is a Danish prize, *Prince Frederich*[40, 48, 60] named after the former Danish Crown Prince, now King of Denmark. Amos does not wish to enter prison ships or work as carpenter on a foreign country's war ship. But after speaking with more experienced prisoners and making some considerations, he accepts to enter a man-o-war simply to increase his chances of escaping one fine day.

He stays onboard the prison ship *Prince Frederich* a month and is then sent through the entrance prison ship *Salvador Del Mundo*[42] again.

Throughout February of 1810, the American Department of State works very hard to produce a draft report on impressments of American seamen in the Royal Navy, listing all known cases. The final report is to be presented to the members of the House of Representatives. William Watson's letter to Lyman has been forwarded from Lyman's office in London to the American Department of State, as has Captain Goff's letter to Lyman and his letter directly to the Department of State. These letters are used to document William's whereabouts.

The information on Amos Stevens, John Wiley and their comrades has also arrived at the Department of State, even though the report for the first quarter of 1810 from Captain Carter in Liverpool has not been sent yet. Amos' captain from the New York schooner wrote a letter to the Department of State, as he was supposed to, immediately after they were taken to the *Rendezvous* in Liverpool.

Department of State employees are drafting their first internal document on impressed seamen as a simple list with only the last names, the name of the ship on which a seaman is impressed, and a registration number given to each seaman.

The Agency for American Seamen in London is efficiently organized under Lyman. He and his secretaries work hard, long hours to organize and file the many letters and documents they receive, and to write accurate lists and quarterly reports to the Department of State that can, they hope, help release some of the many pressed American seamen.

The Admiralty in London sometimes makes it clear to officers in the Royal Navy that they must release American seamen found onboard the English man-o-wars who have been entered in the muster books and where correct identity papers have been presented. But it seldom happens because the seamen are highly needed.

Onboard the *St. George,* the atmosphere between the officers and the newly arrived American seamen is tense. From what he has heard in taverns or read in the newspapers, William knows that impressments of American seamen into the Royal Navy is one of the main diplomatic topics discussed between the United States of America and England. He also knows that some Congressmen and much of the population consider it a war issue. William and the other American newcomers onboard know that it is illegal to hold them here, especially those who showed correct Protection Certificates on their arrival. They refuse to take the offered Bounty and, in fact, to serve in the Royal Navy at all. This confuses the British officers, because *St. George* is busy preparing for this year's trip to the Baltic Sea, and in a month, the officers will need to have mustered a complete crew of at least 500 men and boys.

The British officers do not realize that each day that passes, they meet and muster more and more well-informed American seamen, men who know their rights and protest vigorously against impressments.

St. George's officers deal with these troublesome and overly independent American seamen by chaining them to the decks on arrival. The tactic is to keep them onboard the *St. George* until they have cooled down, then the officers offer them a bounty. If they take it in a weak moment, they are considered volunteers, enrolled in the Royal Navy as long as the Royal Navy wants. Here, the callous laws of nature rule, and smart officers can feel free to cheat American seamen kept in the dark or just plain stupid.

But as he has already shown, William knows the rules, and after some weeks, before *St. George* leaves for to the Baltic in April, the officers finally gives up trying to get William Watson and William Freeman to serve voluntarily.

In his cabin on the *St. George*, Flag Captain James is discussing with his subordinates why the American seamen will not serve. He gets no answer, and becomes angry and confused. 'It hasn't even been 25 years since the Americans got their independence from England. Why can't they serve now when England needs them?" he shouts.

James then orders the Americans taken to the entrance prison ship in Portsmouth, the *Royal William*. The next morning, William Watson and William Freeman are ordered to climb down the gangway to a waiting launch together with other Americans who have refused to serve in the Royal Navy. From Spithead, they row toward Portsmouth and southward along the peninsulas. At a small island close to the mainland toward the west, William Watson observes two rows of black painted ships of the line, and the entrance prison ship *Royal William*.

On February 18, John Brown is transported back to *Defence* from the transfer ship *Monkey* to work as an able seaman. *Defence* is anchored in the Roads of Hamoze at Plymouth, and the transfer ship *Monkey* has come from Portsmouth. *Defence* has come here to pick up seamen who have been sick and stayed in Plymouth's Hospital, a hospital with a great reputation.

Not much happens onboard *Defence* in the winter months. It is dark, boring, and very cold onboard. Looking out the portholes, John Brown imagines that he is free, gazing at Mount Edgecumbe with the castle on top. His feeling of light optimism evaporates as he realizes the borough's strong fortification. This is not a place to escape.

On March 5, 1810, The American Department of State communicates its final 'Report on Impressed Seamen' to the House of Representatives. This report includes an alphabetized list of impressed seamen on the ships of the Royal Navy. In this final report, the seamen are again listed by last name, name of the ship where they are held captive, and unique identification number. Amos Stevens is listed as onboard the *Egeria* and William Watson onboard the *St. George*. There is no John Brown on the list. John's captain did not file a report with the local American authority and Department of State about the impressments, as did the captains for William and Amos.

Former President and now Congressman Thomas Jefferson has seen the report and genuinely feels sorry for these many seamen and their families and loved ones. He did not have that kind of dark future in mind for his countrymen back in 1776, when he sat at his portable desk and carefully wrote The American Declaration of Independence, which should set all Americans free.

When Thomas Jefferson is asked if it is true, as the Federalists claim, that Britain can be trusted to show good faith compared with France, Thomas Jefferson gets very angry. He later writes to a good friend, John Langdon, "*Her good faith! The faith of a nation of merchants! ...of the friend and protectress of Copenhagen! Of a nation who never admitted a chapter of morality into her political code.*" [266]

Jefferson had been the ambassador to France and stayed in Paris not that long ago. It had been a very nice stay indeed, and he even had had the chance to do a little scientific work. Jefferson loves the French. Based on recent English actions on the international scene, Jefferson is not particularly impressed with British diplomacy. His deep affection toward France has not changed.

Defence receives its sails on March 14 and March 22 Amos is finally sent from *Salvador Del Mundo* to *Defence*.[39] Both are anchored in Plymouth harbor. Amos sees this as an improvement with respect to his chances of escape and return to his home and the United States.

The barges and jollyboats of prisoners arriving at the gangway of *Defence* with new crewmembers is, as always, followed with high interest by the crew already onboard.

The young seamen live boring and routine lives onboard *Defence,* and are constantly looking for news and new experiences. When new crewmembers come onboard, it is an excellent opportunity to get some news. The news quickly spreads out that an American ship carpenter from Boston has arrived. When John hears this, he searches for Amos Stevens and finds him that evening after Amos has found the place where he is going to sleep.

Salem and Boston, where the two of them come from, are so close to each other that information is frequently exchanged and becomes common knowledge for people living in both port cities. John Brown is very glad to find this new American friend, who understands his background, and with whom he can speak when he longs for home.

On March 28, *Defence* unmoors and moves to Cowsand Bay to meet with the rest of the squadron going to the Baltic Sea this year.

Three days later, Captain Carter compiles data on impressed American seamen he has learned of since the new year, and finally makes his counts, for the first quarter of 1810, of men who had been pressed from Liverpool during the past three months and who had convinced him of their American citizenship. On this list, he writes the name and data for Amos Stevens and John Wiley, together with approximately 50 other American seamen who have arrived at this port. He encloses his lists in a letter and sends it to the American Department of State.[8]

On April 7, *Defence* is in the Downs. Mr. Ekins is commissioned captain for *Defence* in the coming Baltic mission, and for some reason, he changes the rules for punishment that were applied in the years before he entered the ship. Offenses like neglect of duty and drunkenness were previously punished with 12 lashes. Now the number is doubled, tripled or made even higher. Maybe Captain Ekins had been talking to captains or Admirals from other ships that punished more severely, because today, ten seamen are punished with 36 or 48 lashes each for neglect of duty. A seaman also receives 30 lashes for desertion.

Almost all the logbooks of the ships in the Royal Navy Baltic Fleet this year are handwritten in the layout. Only the second-rater *Cressy's* ship log is in printing. The Royal Navy lag resources.

John Brown works on a bar in the foretopmast onboard *Defence* on April 14, when he observes that Admiral Dixon hoists his flag onboard the *Dictator*. This year, Dixon's squadron is going to guard the Cattegat and the Great Belt as they did successfully the year before. Two days later, Dixon's squadron leaves the port.

Seamen onboard *Defence* see new proof of the tougher discipline introduced onboard Royal Navy's ships, when a seaman belonging to

HMS Lynx is punished 25 lashes in a jollyboat anchored beside the *Defence's* gangway on April 24. Afterwards he is sent around to receive the same punishment at the gangway of each ship in the squadron, a feared punishment called Flogging through the Fleet. This is the first time John has seen this cruel form of punishment, which seamen often don't survive without being crippled. John Pristoff says to John, after the jolly boat with the seaman is rowed to the gangway of the next ship, 'He will get 24 lashes at the gangway at the side of each ship in the squadron. The ship's doctor from *Lynx* will be in the jollyboat with him to make sure he doesn't die directly from the actual flogging. He will proba bly get 300 to 400 lashes total."

Three days later, eight more seamen are punished with 24 lashes each. The following day, *St. George* leaves Spithead, without William Watson and William Freeman onboard, to sail for the Baltic summer station.

On May 1, while *Defence* is still moored at the Downs, John and Amos and other seamen and mariners wash their clothes and hammocks. The air is full of haze and in the high humidity, the clothes dry very slowly.

Onboard the *Royal William* in Portsmouth harbor, William Watson and William Freeman become more and more frustrated, knowing that they may rot in this place if nothing is done soon. Escape seems impossible at the moment. But they are glad, at least, that they are here together. They stick together, because they see seamen who do not belong to a group, especially the younger ones, going more and more crazy, because of the isolation in these long stays onboard.

This day, the American Congress finally passes the Macon Bill, which provides for non-intercourse with both Great Britain and France.[48, 278]

Diplomats from The United States of America and Great Britain make no hard effort these days to take up negotiations on impressments. Of Amos, John, and William, only John, who has been impressed the longest, for more than four years, is realistic about their chances to be released. They are, he knows, presently non-existent.

May 15. Eleven seamen are punished 24 lashes each onboard *Defence*. Simon Lee, a seaman from New York is punished for contempt. As a true New Yorker he knows how to use his mouth, if you ask one of the British officers, and he always answers back if provoked.

Now he will pay bitterly for his oratorical talents.

Finally, on May 19, a little late this year, the signal is given for 'Prepare for Sea." Once again, *Defence* will take up the patrolling of the Dutch coast outside Texel and Den Helder, controlling the entrance to the seaway to Amsterdam. As usual, *Defence* will later that spring join the Royal Navy Baltic Fleet. Harassing ship traffic along the Dutch coast and around Texel might also result in the disturbance of ships sailing from Wilmington.

Lyman reports to the Department of State that press-gang activity is increasing in the streets of London and South English ports. This spring and summer of 1810, impressments are 'carried out to an extent beyond all former examples"[185] Lyman writes.

May 25, *Defence* is anchored outside Cappelern as it exercises the large cannons and mariners with the guns. The brig *Raven* is here, and the *HMS Theseus*. All in all, *Defence* stays 11 days around Cappelern this year. On Friday, June 1, when hoisting in the barge, two seamen fall overboard and drown.

Thirteen seamen are punished June 9, among them William Alexander, who is punished for the second time this season for desertion, and Simon Lee from New York, for skulking. Simon Lee has not changed his habit of being a big mouth, and he is extremely lazy. *Defence* returns eight days later to Cappelern.

Port Collector Allen McLane stands at the window in his office in the Customhouse, watching the heavy carriage and pedestrian traffic on Front Street below. It is June 15, and his thoughts go back to exactly 35 years before.

"In the year between the two Congresses, Allen McLane put actions behind his patriotic words and was appointed a Lieutenant in Colonel Caesar Rodney's Regiment of the Delaware Militia.[170] *To his grief, his father died in Philadelphia that same year.*[133]

On June 15, 1775, Delegates of the Second Continental Congress gather in the white-paneled Counsel Chamber of the State House on a square in Philadelphia.

The Delegates of the Second Continental Congress have been there since May 10 for discussions, and have just, by unanimous vote, appointed Colonel George Washington to be Commander of all Continental forces.

John Adams is satisfied that his oratorical gifts have been put to good use, persuading many of the Yankee congressmen to shift from their first choice, the New Englander favorite Artemas Ward, to the southerner Washington, effectively removing internal jealousies and strengthening the unification of the northern and southern states.[208]

Many gathered in the room is convinced that, in this farmer and Colonel George Washington, they have made the most forceful choice to meet the British wherever and whenever necessary, to free the colonies from England once and for all. McLane is not present on this solemn occasion, but the 32-year-old Virginia lawyer Thomas Jefferson is a delegate. "

McLane returns his thoughts to the present as a horse-drawn carriage transporting barrels of fine flour from the Brandywine mills to a ship at one of the quays loses a wheel. The horse panics as the barrels roll out into the street.

June 25, 15 more men are punished severely onboard *Defence*. The ship stays a fortnight anchored at Cappelern again. *Defence* continues patrolling along the north coast of Holland until July 24, then returns to the Downs for a short stop and then returns once again to the waters west of Cappelern. By September 5, the crew is annoyed because life has, for far too long, been nothing but simple, routine work. Sixteen seamen are punished this day.

John has been insulting to his superior officer this morning. He is increasingly frustrated after almost five years of impressments in the Royal Navy. In fact, he is sick to his stomach of it. For the first time, John loses his temper and talks back to his superior officer. "You little fat ass," he sneers. "If you are just half as stupid as you appear to be, I find it hard to find words to express how sorry I feel for you! Why don't you go and hang yourself and make my day?" It takes the confused officer several seconds to realize that he has been verbally attacked. When his slow brain finally comprehends, and he understands the meaning of the many words spoken so quickly by this angry seaman, he runs like a scared chicken to inform the captain. As a result, John will receive 12 lashes from the Cat-o-Nine Tails at 11 o'clock at the main mast.

As Captain Ekins orders John's shirt removed and has him seized up, John begins to regret his actions. He has witnessed the punishment of hundreds of seamen in the five years he has been in the Royal Navy, and knows all too well how badly it hurts. He has seen many seamen crippled for life at these regular punishments. As the first stroke hits his back, it is as though a huge hand is grasping his body and trying to tear his lungs out. He tries to count the lashes to keep his mind off the pain, but it is hard. His pain increases with each stroke and at the tenth stroke, he almost screams. Knowing only two strikes remain, he keeps silent and wins respect of both officers and ordinary crewmembers. When the punishment finally comes to an end, John realizes that he is hurt, but not so badly that he has to go to the sick quarters.

Five days later, seven more seamen are punished.

August 8 is Allen McLane's 70th birthday. Early that morning, the entire staff at the Customhouse in Wilmington gathers in McLane's office before he comes to work that day. When he walks in, they call out 'Congratulations, Sir." McLane responds with one of his characteristic warm smiles. 'Thank you my friends, thank you very much," he says, delighted. McLane has much to celebrate this day, having played a fine role in the United States' struggle for independence. Throughout the day, many prominent citizens of Wilmington come by to pay respects to their local national hero.

William sits on his ship's coffin beside a cannon porthole, trying to get some fresh air and sun on his face. The thick, black bars in the porthole block his view of the sea surface in Portsmouth Roads. He feels absolutely no reason to celebrate this day. He longs desperately to be free, back home in Wilmington with his wife, Mary Ann. But he is in British captivity onboard the entrance prison ship *Royal William*, anchored right in the heart of the headquarters of the British Royal Navy.

It is now August 28 and a fine day. Onboard the *Royal William,* William spends another day sitting on his ship's coffin, staring at the water through a cannon porthole and thinking about his home state and its great history. As the almost endless, uneventful days pass, with nothing important or interesting happening to distract his mind, William focuses on the people he loves back home.

A ship named *Nancy* is anchored in its homeport of Wilmington this day, exactly 35 years after a ship with that same name anchored here, too. The day is indeed special.

William wonders if Mary Ann received his letter. Is she still worrying about him, not knowing where he is? Is Mendenhall celebrating this day? William let his thoughts roam over the different wharves along the quays on the north bank of the Christina River. William knows that, if Thomas Mendenhall is attending to his usual business at his wharf, and McLane happens to be out checking ships at the harbor front today, and the two of them meet and see this new ship *Nancy,* they will surely recall the day 35 years ago.

McLane has just arrived at work on this beautiful, sunny August morning. John Freed, Jr. and William Windell are already there. McLane enters the building with a loud, "Good Morning" and instantly hears the answer, "Good Morning, Sir."

"William, please hois t the Stars and Stripes," McLane asks.

"Yes, Sir I'll do that right away," William Windell answers quickly. Everyone knows this is indeed a special day. McLane leaves the customhouse building and walks toward the harbor and the wharf buildings. He spots Thomas Mendenhall in a crowd of people around his wharf and walks toward him. All the men and boys turn to McLane, who shouts, "Thomas Mendenhall, Thomas Mendenhall! May I congratulate you, Sir, on this special day?" Mendenhall looks into the smiling f ace of McLane and smiles back. McLane continues, "Sir, I have just asked my revenue officer William Windell to hoist the Stars and Stripes on the flagstaff of the Customhouse building on this beautiful morning. But my God, it would be a great privilege if you, Mr. Mendenhall, would have honored me and Wilmington, and for that matter all of the United States of America, by doing it yourself."

As the crowd cheers Thomas Mendenhall, his thoughts go back 35 years. He has, on occasion, spoken to people he knew back then in order to make an exact reconstruction of the important event that took place that special day.

The sky is darkening in the northwest of Wilmington over the wooded hill, and the first serious cold gusts have just started to blow, indicating the beginning of the autumn. At 10 o'clock Sunday morning, August 28, 1775, in this religious borough of 1,200 inhabitants, the largest town in the Three Lower Counties with six churches or meeting houses ringing bells, the streets are beginning to fill with people in their best suits, heading to their churches or meeting places.

Joseph and Mary Warner are walking, with their son John, on their way to the Quaker Service in the Friends Meeting House. Mary Warner is holding her husband's hand on her right, and on her left, the daughter Ester Yarnall. Both children are from her previous marriage[0] to John Yarnall.

The quays, storehouses and wharves on Christina River's north bank, between Orange Street and Walnut Street, are normally empty in the church hour, but an extraordinary activity is going on today.

The Philadelphia-Wilmington ferry, a 30-ton sloop, named Ann after the wife of Samuel Bush, is moored at the fourth berth from the east part of the river. This is right in front of the wharf of Charles Bush, an Irish born cabinetmaker and father of George, Lewis, and Samuel. Freight to Philadelphia has been loaded and the passengers have already entered. The captain is preparing for the first of the Ann's biweekly trips, Sunday and Thursday, to Philadelphia.

At the first berth close to Walnut Street, in front of the wharf of Joseph Tatnall, there is a high level of activity. The 38-ton brigantine Nancy is fitted out for a voyage to Lisbon on the Portuguese southwest coast. The plan is to stop at the Azores on the return, then at the island of St. Christopher and back to Wilmington. The cargo and owners of the Nancy are Joseph Tatnall, Joseph Shallcross, John Morton and Thomas Lea. The ship's captain is Hugh Montgomery.

Joseph Tatnall, turning 35 in nine days, is a member of one of the four early Quaker miller families in town. These families, the Shipleys, Canbys, Tatnalls and Warners, came to Willingtown (Wilmington) from Buck and Chester Counties in Pennsylvania, just north of the Brandywine Hundred, soon after Thomas Willing staked out the city 44 years ago. The Warners came from New Jersey. Edward Tatnall and John Morton built mills on the south side of the Brandywine River. Three years ago, Joseph successfully built his on the north side of the river, where the many rocks made it very difficult to establish the raceways to the wheels.

The Brandywine millers had for years discussed the possibility of establishing mills on the north side of the river, but always concluded that it was impossible. Young Tatnall had now proved them all wrong and established his mill on the north side. Now conversations about the mills often said that if anyone was capable of doing such a difficult job, it was this bright young man Joseph Tatnall.

Buck's Tavern is located in the oldest house in town. It has a marble tablet in the western wall bearing the initials "IWS" and the year 1732. The tavern is on the northwest corner of Market and Water Streets, close to the wharves and the lading places for the ships in the harbor front. From the tavern people are watching the carriers load barrels of superfine and ordinary flour. This last quarter of the ship's lading, belonging to Thomas Lea, is hurried noisily from the Mills down to the Brandywine Ferry, across the river and down Market Street and finally, around the corner at Market and Water Streets to reach the Nancy.

The lumber part of the Thomas Lea's quarter of the cargo were already loaded, and only the 25 barrels of ship's bread wait on the quay to be taken onboard.

Captain Hugh Montgomery is restless and wants the ship to depart as soon as possible. They have to stop at the Customhouse in New Castle before they can head toward the Atlantic.[222] There is no Customhouse in Wilmington, as the number of ships here is too few. Port Collector Charles Bush operates most of the time from the port at New Castle. George and Lewis Bush, brothers of Samuel Bush, are helping their father. George Bush especially likes his father's job as Port Collector and hopes that he will be allowed to take over one day. Finally, the Nancy *is ready to depart and Thomas Mendenhall, a young officer onboard, passes the order from Captain Montgomery to the anchor seamen to loosen the moorings.*

The families of the crewmembers have gathered at the berth and eagerly wave goodbye.

When the Nancy has traveled the two miles down the Christina River to the Delaware River, some Wilmington children run up the hill to the top of French Street at the Academy. From here they can, in fine weather like today's, follow the ship clearly down the Delaware River past the point of New Castle.

Sometime during the winter of 1775, the financier of the Second Continental Congress, Robert Morris, Esquire, chartered the Nancy. *A contract is made with the Spanish Government to sell arms and ammunition to the Americans. From Europe, Nancy returns to the West Indian Island of Puerto Rico and drops off Don Antonio Seronia to procure the arms and the ammunition. To avoid suspicion, the Nancy sails between the different islands for some time. At the Danish West Indian islands of St. Thomas and St. Croix, they take in ordinary supplies in the daylight hours and ammunition at night. The ammunition is sent over to the Danish islands in small boats from St. Eustatia, a Dutch island[197].*

On the night when the cargo is nearly loaded, the Nancy *is anchored outside the roads of the main city of St. Thomas, Charlotte Amalie, where the Danish Governor of St. Thomas lives. The crew of the* Nancy *receives news of the American Declaration of Independence and a description of the flag flown over Washington's Camp. Thomas Mendenhall immediately secures the necessary materials and produces a flag with 13 red and white stripes and 13 white stars on a blue square background in the upper right corner.[222]*

The number of men onboard is increased and the brig is armed for defense. On the day they sail to return to the U.S., Captain Montgomery and Mr. Antonio Seronia invite the Danish governor and 20 other gentlemen on board to dine. A sumptuous dinner is cooked and sea turtles prepared, making it a great turtle feast.

As the Customhouse barges approach from Charlotte Amalie with the Danish guests, they are ordered to lie on their oars while a salute of thirteen guns is fired. Amid the firing Thomas Mendenhall is ordered to haul down the English flag and hoist the American flag, the first ever seen in a foreign port.[198]

And so this new nation, The United States of America, hoists its flag, "the Stars and Stripes" for the first time in a foreign port, on the territory of Denmark whose flag, Dannebrog, is the oldest national flag in the world. Dannebrog is a white cross on a red background, symbolizing the Kingdom of Denmark's attachment to the Christian World. The Dannebrog is also the inverse of the St. George's Flag, the flag of England, from whom the Americans are finally liberated. Dannebrog had fallen down from the sky on a battlefield in 1219 outside Tallin on the south coast of the Baltic Sea.

As the Stars and Stripes is hoisted by officer Thomas Mendenhall for the first time onboard this floating ship Nancy *in the Danish port at Saint Thomas to celebrate the U. S. Independence, as declared by Thomas Jefferson, it feels to the Americans and Danes present, that an almost divine Trinity of Thomases has been united in this single act representing: The United States of America, the Stars and Stripes and the Declaration of Independence. Then the people gathered on the* Nancy *proudly shout "Cheers for the National Congress, down with the lion King and up with the "Stars and Stripes."[198] At this solemn moment in Thomas Mendenhall's life he is feeling more happy and free than he has felt before.*

The whole scene causes great excitement among the crews on the numerous vessels gathered in the harbor. When the party onboard the Nancy *is over, the company of Danes returns to Charlotte Amalie in their boats and the* Nancy, *carrying this "first foreign American flag" and busy carrying out her obligations to Congress, quickly heads for full sail on her way toward the coast of North America.*

When the Nancy *finally arrives outside the Delaware Capes, in a dense fog, a fleet is observed. Whether it is American or English is hard to tell from a distance, but soon enough the crew sees two enemy frigates and their tenders. There is no way to pass into the Delaware River and escape engagement. Captain Montgomery gathers his crew and states his determination to defend their important cargo at all costs.*

He gives his crew a chance to go, saying, "If there is a man, fearful and faint-hearted, let him go. The boat is ready to take him to shore. These public stores must be protected to aid our destitute country in the dark hour of need, in the noble cause of liberty." There is a moment of solemn silence onboard, then Mendenhall steps forward and says, "I will stand by you, Captain."

The crewmembers give three cheers. The enemy is superior and the Nancy's *only option is to strand and try to save some of the ammunition she carries. The Nancy is run ashore on the Cape Island, in the Turtle Gut Inlet, and a barge filled with men sent by Capt. Week, the Commander of the Continental Fleet in the Delaware Bay, arrives to look out for the Nancy. [198]*

The arriving soldiers are sent to shore to protect the ammunition and weapons saved, because this shore is Tory territory. The British men

171

onboard the Royal Navy frigates fire their long guns, but they cause little damage or excitement. Mendenhall can see that there is no time to save more ammunition, and they are forced to leave the Nancy. *John Hancock jumps overboard from the boat to approach the* Nancy *one last time, determined that if they can't carry away all the valuable content of the* Nancy, *at least they can save the most important thing she holds, the 'first foreign American flag', fluttering so freely and proudly in the wind. He shouts to the other men in the boat as he jumps overboard, "To save the beloved banner or perish in the effort."*

Hancock ascends the shivering mast, unfastens the flag, plunges to sea and bears it to the shore. The enemy shoots down Nancy. *The remaining ammunition explodes, and enemy boats have come too close, thinking that the removal of her flag was is a sign of surrender and intending to take her as a prize. The explosion, which could be heard 40 miles away, also takes down those in the small boats surrounding her. The saved cargo was later brought to and distributed in the Capital by men onboard another good ship, the* Wasp.[198]

When Thomas Mendenhall and Allen McLane finally part this morning, McLane walks back to the Customhouse, caught up in events taking place ten years ago, when he and Thomas Mendenhall had become the most terrible enemies.

Thomas Mendenhall had been a revenue officer working in the Customhouse building in Wilmington under the command of Allen McLane. In 1801, shortly after Thomas Jefferson's inauguration, Mendenhall initiated a trial against McLane to have him removed from office, of hoping that he could win the office himself.

Mendenhall had originally been a Federalist like McLane, but changed his political philosophy and became a Democratic Republican like President Jefferson.[133] The attack on McLane's integrity failed. Although he was a Federalist, McLane's status as a hero in the Revolutionary War saved him. McLane had served long and fought with the Commander in Chief of the Continental Army, George Washington, in the most crucial battles of the war, and walked the most exhausting miles with him. In 1797, Washington had appointed Colonel Allen McLane Marshall for the District of Delaware and Port collector, as one of his last Presidential acts before he withdrew to his Virginia farm at

Mount Vernon, weary of all the continuing troubles and the mentality of city folks.

Shortly thereafter, when Thomas Jefferson was presented the proposal to remove McLane from his office, he flatly refused. Jefferson made the comment, "... To the victor belongs the spoil..." McLane felt proud. He thought how suitable it was to call President Thomas Jefferson 'The Philosopher King." There was more to the President than an administrator, and he was not the kind of president who misused his power, just because he was given the chance.

The whole incident was a tragedy, in a way, McLane saw now, because Mendenhall is quite a hero himself, written into American History by being the first to hoist the Stars and Stripes in a foreign port, Charlotte Amalie at St. Thomas. Mendenhall must have forgotten that when he took McLane to court, so focused on his hate against his former boss and the chance to take the job of port collector of Wilmington. Mendenhall did not have the faintest idea that it could backfire and damage his own reputation severely.

At that time, when Thomas Mendenhall had been working in the Revenue Service in Wilmington, McLane decided to have a new revenue cutter constructed at one of the Wilmington wharves. Mendenhall clearly expected to be appointed commander of this new revenue cutter, but McLane passed him over, because he did not trust him[0]. It demands the highest degree of personal integrity to be in charge of collecting the duty from arriving ships. Customs duty was one of the largest basic tax sources of the United States of America.

Joining the Democratic Republican Party might have led the former Federalist Mendenhall to believe that he and Jefferson had somehow joined a common cause against the Federalist McLane. But Mendenhall was wrong.

At the time of the trial, Joseph Warner and Jesse Zane took the side of McLane. Mendenhall was angry with them, apparently thinking that these men were leading a counterattack on his personal integrity that followed the slipstream of the trial. Zane and Warner questioned Mendenhall's integrity not so much because he had been a Federalist and later became a Democratic Republican, even though that seemed

173

fickle and irresolute. No, the real reason was that Zane and Warner believed Mendenhall had helped the Royal Navy occupy the neutral Dutch West Indian Island of St. Eustatia.[0]

This was unforgivable to any patriotic American. Mendelhall had helped transport ammunitions from that island himself in the Nancy. How could he then help the Royal Navy occupy the island?

Dutch St. Eustatia, and Danish St. Croix and St. Thomas constituted the center of the American West Indian trade during the Revolutionary War, and these three islands kept that position until this day of 1810.

Because of the strong dependence between the east coast communities like Wilmington and these West Indian Islands, the Wilmington wharf-owners, Brandywine millers, local Wilmington store and ship-owners, seamen, and captains had a hard time forgiving any American who dared assist the British in occupying St. Eustatia.

McLane thought that, in his heart, Mendenhall knew that he, Zane, Warner, or for that matter any other prominent citizens of Wilmington, would never forgive him.[0] When rumors about the event first arrived in Wilmington, Wilmington wharf and ship-owners seriously discussed putting forward proof or witnesses before a legal court related to this St. Eustatia incident. Thomas Mendenhall would without doubt have been convicted for treason and executed.

McLane also recalled that Joseph Warner himself was in no position to raise his voice against Mendenhall at the time, because for a period, he was unfoundedly accused of treason related to selling cattle to the British enemy.

But, McLane thinks, we all have to discipline ourselves and try to be civilized, so we'll be able to forgive without forgetting these unfortunate episodes during the war that might divide our local community. If not, it could prevent us from moving forward and prospering, he realizes. Then he speaks aloud, 'Especially on a solemn da y like this, we have to move on and forgive to get business and work back to this port again." McLane speeds up his walk and soon reaches the Customhouse building.

On September 14, *Defence* leaves a position near Cappelern off the North Frisian coast and goes north. Ten days later, she is patrolling outside Horns Reef on the South west coast of Jutland, with the white, illuminated church tower of Flø Church on the coastline in view. They cruise here several days, but meet few Danish enemy ships here, so *Defence* returns south to guard the entrance to the seaway to Amsterdam.

When *Defence* is patrolling close to the coast, John and Amos often spend their free time on the forecastle, looking for people and events on the coastlines they sail along.

William stays in the prison ship until late September. He has finally reached the conclusion that he will probably never get a chance to escape unless he is out of the prison ships. Great hope has built up inside him during the many months onboard the *Royal William*, and he is now convinced that it will be easier for him regain his freedom onboard an active man-o-war. His fellow prisoners have told him that. He is now transferred to a prison on land, where he is kept under better conditions until he can enter a man-o-war.

On October 1, *Defence* returns to the Downs. On the 5th, 12 seamen are punished. Rolf Teazel, a 24-year-old landsman from New Castle, England is punished with 36 lashes for drunkenness. John has teamed up with Rolf several times and is beginning to know him well.

Defence is back outside the North Frisian coast near Cappelern on Oct. 15, and on October 24, returns to the English coast and the Downs. *Defence* has been accompanied by the former Danish prize, *HMS Christian VII*.

On November 1, a group of 17 seamen are punished 24 to 36 lashes each.

On November 28, 11 men are punished 24 to 36 lashes each. Amos Stevens, the 29-year-old ship's carpenter assistant, who has wrongly been entered into the muster book as a seaman, receives 12 lashes for disobedience. Amos has become sick and tired of constantly being told off by people who seem to have half his brain size. He hates it. He has absolutely no intention of serving in the Royal Navy. He was a free, independent American ship carpenter, used to a free life at sea, where he could organize his time all by himself. Now he is surrounded by discipline around the clock and it makes him extremely mad. What do they think he is? A toy soldier? Amos is a strong man, with a compact, muscular body, and even though the flogging hurts his back, he quickly recovers. His wounds do remind him that he will have to be more careful about expressing his feelings about the Royal Navy and its officers. Amos doesn't know that his behavior is very common for newly impressed American seamen onboard Royal Navy ships.

Defence is moored in the Downs once again. *Monmouth* is there too. On December 2, *Christian VII* sails and a British admiral leaves his flag onboard the *Monmouth*. Amos and John really hate to see the *Monmouth* carrying a flag belonging to the Royal Navy. But the Royal Navy is in possession of ships of the line from several neutral nations like the United States of America and Denmark.

While they talk about the French-English and English-Danish war one day, John passes on to Amos some of the details he has collected about the Bombardment of Copenhagen, information available only to crewmembers of ships in the Royal Navy. This information only adds to Amos' anger against the British. "They are simply not civ ilized people," he tells John. Why do they need to control the whole world?"

On December 3, a court martial is held onboard the *Monmouth.*

The flagship *Victory,* holding Rear Admiral of the Blue James Sammaurez, the Commander of the Royal Navy Baltic Fleet, arrives from Vinga Sound outside Gothenburg, at the end of this year's voyage to the Baltic Sea. He will also head next year's Royal Navy campaign to the Baltic Sea.

The American crew onboard *Defence,* and those few British crewmembers who have not been given leave to go and celebrate Christmas with their families ashore, stay onboard *Defence* in the Downs. So, this Christmas, John and Amos spend much of their time together longing for home.

On the second day of Christmas, the *HMS Den Helder*, a former Dutch ship with the same name as the harbor city south of Texel, where *Defence* spends much time patrolling, arrives. John is convinced this ship came from this city and that the Dutch seamen were taken as prisoners and later transported to prison ships in the English ports. He has seen this happen to many seamen from Denmark, Norway, and Slesvig-Holstein. John spends many hours studying the arriving merchant ship seamen from different countries who climb the gangway from time to time and enter the main deck.

On December 29, *Defence* sets sail again, and on the last day of the year it arrives at Cowsand Bay.

On the last day of the year of 1810, *Defence* is in Cowsand Bay, where next year's Baltic Fleet will meet. There is a fresh bre eze and John Brown, John Pristoff and the other seamen on his shift are busy scrubbing the hammocks. Amos has learned most of the different working routines that are normally followed by an assistant carpenter onboard the *Defence*. He has mostly been making small repairs around the ship until this point in time.

5

On the first day of 1811, it is snowing. The snow whirls above the sea surface on a light breeze as *HMS Defence* takes over the guard in the bay from *HMS Saturn*.

John, who has been onboard *Defence* since his reentry on September 4, 1810, has caused no further negative remarks from his superior officers since his punishment. The simple reason is that he has been impressed for so long now the he has resigned mentally. He is not trying to escape anymore, having already concluded that it is impossible.

Seamen like Thomas Lowe are quickly broken down psychologically. They don't have John's ability to mentally withdraw from the many harassments from superior officers in this rough environment. The break down is caused by being forced into an environment that may be controlled by lunatics or even semi-psychopathic officers.

These ordinary seamen swing between deep melancholy and dreadful anger at having no say in their own lives and being under constant, strict control of others. This often leads to yet another series of punishments, first for contempt, then for drunkenness, then again for contempt, and so on.

Those whom the officers successfully break down eventually end up being punished for drunkenness time after time. This is where Thomas Lowe is now. He no longer gets punished for fighting, being insulting, or neglecting duty. Only for drunkenness, typically in connection with a stressful period, such as when the enemy is approaching. At these times, everything becomes unbearable to him.

John has been working as an able seaman onboard *Defence* up until January 1, 1811. He has been onboard Royal Navy man-o-wars for more than five years. His hot temper has cooled to a reasonable level, and he has resigned himself to a destiny shared with his ship. He tried to escape for some years earlier on, but without any luck, since as an American, he is constantly watched. John has noticed that seamen who have no strong feeling of justice, who do not protest against unjust and brutal behavior, get along very well with the British officers. Some time ago, he chose to present a calm front, just to make life easier.

This new approach seems to have paid off. On this first day of the year, John is appointed Captain of the Forecastle, in charge of seamen working there. John has spent almost 20 years onboard ships. It is a step up to be Captain of the Forecastle of a third-rater in the Royal Navy. Now he doesn't have to work in the rigging all the time exposed to the cold weather that caused health problems earlier.

Most of the month of January 1811, *Defence* stays in Cowsand Bay, and it is extremely quiet.

On January 21, the American Department of State receives an internal document, *"Cases of impressed seamen how and when disposed of "*[7] listing the name of Amos Stevens, with a note attached stating, *"the original papers were sent to General Lyman."*[7] William's papers are not connected with these lists.

At that moment, Amos is inspecting the woodwork in *Defence*'s hull, searching for even small cracks that might grow and endanger *Defence* when she meets the next strong storm or enemy cannonball.

The quarterly report on impressed seamen from Captain Carter in Liverpool to the American Department of State has, on this January 21, 1811, been included in the Department of State's internal draft document on impressed American seamen. The Department of State sends the original papers received on hundreds of other impressed American seamen to the American Agent for Seaman in London, General William Lyman.[10]

In late January, the flagship *St. George* is anchored at Spithead. *St. George* has been a part of the Baltic Fleet in 1809 and 1810. The previous year, Baltic headquarters were outside Carlscrona on the Swedish southeast coast, and inward and outward-bound Royal Navy convoys passed the Danish waters with ease. Fresh winds and high waves in the Danish belts last year prevented Danish privateers and cannon boats from successfully attacking the passing convoys.

The *St. George* squadron returned to Spithead in late December, as usual, and everything had been routine so far. In early January, large numbers of the crew begin to get sick. In a period of one week, from January 11 to January 18, 118 of the crewmembers become very sick. *St. George* has been hit by an epidemic. Fortunately, they are still in harbor, and the sick men are quickly sent to the hospital in Portsmouth.

Flag Captain Daniel Gurion orders the ship to be carefully

disinfected. Groups of seamen carry buckets filled with coal that was sprayed with detergent and then lit around the decks. The vaporized detergents spread out in the hull of the ship, on the decks, and in the Admiral, flag captain and officer's cabins. This is supposed to efficiently eliminate any disease. The current belief is that disease is only present in the air, and that filling the air with vaporized detergent will kill it. The floors and the walls of the ship are not really disinfected, so it is just a matter of time before a new epidemic will develop on the ship.

When Flag Captain Gurion concludes that he has the epidemic under control, he requests the Admiralty in London to send more seamen[64] to replace the sick men before the departure for the Baltic Sea. Many of the man-o-wars in the Royal Navy are consistently undermanned so supplies of new crewmembers come mostly from transfer ships or prison ships these days. All the sick seamen cannot be replaced that quickly. The war with France has lasted almost nine years now, and war with Denmark and Norway more than three. The Royal Navy ships are permanently undermanned.

In Wilmington on this day, John Freed, Jr. sees Allen McLane sitting and staring out the window, but decides to leave him alone. William Windell and John Freed often speak about how absent-minded the old Port Collector has been lately, and it seems to just get worse every day. McLane is thinking of January, 1776, 35 years before, when he volunteered for a battle against Lord Dunmore, at Norfolk. Later he joined the minutemen of Maryland and Virginia, and for a short period returned to his wife Maria and their home in Duck Creek Cross Roads in Kent County. [142]

While supplying the *St George* with new crewmembers on January 27, the officers decide to enter both William Watson and William Freeman, who had shortly been onboard earlier, in the muster book[63, 64]. The officers initiate the process of getting the men from the prison on shore to the flagship.

The days of February 1811 generally hold fresh or light wind and rain, mild weather for winter. *Defence* is steadily made ready for this year's mission. The rigging is repaired and food supplies are delivered in large quantities. To the relief of the common crewmembers, there have been no punishments for quite some time.

On the quarterdeck of *Defence,* Captain Charles Ekins walks restlessly around, feeling somewhat sad. He will no longer be commander of *Defence,* and must leave the ship before this year's cruise to the Baltic Sea begins. He can't help feeling nostalgic the remainder of the time he stays onboard the *Defence.* The officers and the ordinary crewmembers notice their captain's change in spirit. He is quite a different person, as though his function and title onboard has been half his identity, and now that his title is about to evaporate onboard, so is his personality.

He is almost as kind as an Admiral, but all too kind for a flag captain. He has never spent much time among his officers, which has gained him their respect. To some of the officers, it therefore seems awkward now, when Ekins walks around the quarterdeck, asking them personal questions and trying to get to know them. The seamen, however, like it much better. They are used to being among people who show their real emotions and intentions directly, and they like their "new" captain. One positive result of the captain's nostalgia is fewer punishments.

On Sunday February 3, *Defence* is still anchored in the Downs. The wind is strong and the air hazy at the same time. The ships are mustered by divisions. *St. George* is anchored at Spithead in strong wind, rains, and heavy swell. At noon, her crew is mustered and Divine Service held, two hours late.

Defence stays in Cowsand Bay with Esq. Charles Ekins as captain until February 23. Then, in a ceremony held at the main deck, he is replaced by Captain David Atkins, a very good and trusted friend of Rear Admiral of the Red C. W. Reynolds, who is in charge of this year's *St. George* squadron to which *Defence* is attached.

Two days later, *Defence* leaves Cowsand Bay under the new captain's command for the first time. The ship is unmoored and sails at 8 a.m. toward the Downs. On February 28, they reach the Downs.

After a month in prison on shore, William Watson, now 24, and William Freeman, now 17, are transported to the HMS Service spot on the shore at Spithead. Early on March 4, the jollyboat from *St. George* fetches Watson, Freeman and ten English seamen.

An officer on the top gun deck asks William Watson, "Will you take our good bounty?" William Watson decides to answer for himself and Freeman. 'Sir, as impressed American seamen, we will not take the

Bounty." The officer th inks to himself that these Americans only want to enter *St. George* to increase their chances of escape.[63] But the officer also concludes that these newcomers will soon be wiser. There will not be any opportunity to escape on this year's expedition to the Bal tic Sea. The superior officers will see to that.

At Spithead, a fresh breeze is blowing. Both seamen and officers are variously employed. In the harbor John observes *HMS Fantome* leave. *Princess Caroline* stays.[64]

The following morning, as Watson and Freeman get out of their hammocks after a restless night's sleep, they find out that they are onboard to work, and that they will be under strict discipline most of the time. The men onboard are concentrated on preparing the flagship for its participation in the voyage to the Baltic Sea. Some of the seamen are ordered up in the riggings, and William helps an able seaman fixing the many ropes on the deck.

A boat with two officers and a group of mariners is sent to one of the other small ships anchored at Spithead to assist with the punishment of a seaman. The wind is moderate and it is cloudy. The boats are busily bringing supplies from the shore.[64]

On March 6, William and several other seamen onboard the *St. George* are painting the Admiral's cabin, so it will be ready for the arrival of Rear Admiral of the Red C. W. Reynolds. Reynolds is, at the moment, enjoying a stay on his family estate in Cornwall, not far from the Royal Navy headquarters in Portsmouth. Reynolds does not intend to leave his estate one minute too soon. He awaits a letter from Flag Captain Daniel Gurion telling him that *St. George* is made ready to go to sea, and a letter from his superior, Rear Admiral of the Blue James Sammaurez, Head of the entire Royal Navy Baltic Fleet, with orders to enter his Flagship *St. George*.

William is a super numerous, and therefore helps with odd jobs onboard, such as painting a cabin or other special work that is not part of the daily routine. It isn't too bad being a super numerous, beca use there is great variation in the daily work performed.

The following day, sail makers begin to repair some of the ships many sails. On the 10th, water and beer are supplied from shore and the day after, the rigging is tarred. William Watson and William Freeman are allowed to wash their clothes for the first time since they arrived. The Clerk of the Cheque musters the ship's crew, and the seamen are paid.

On the 12th, the hospital ship *Gorgon* arrives. As often before, *Gordon* will follow the Baltic Fleet to its summer station at the island of Hanö, near the southeast coast of Sweden.

On Sunday the 17th, the ship crew is mustered and a simple but beautiful Divine Service is held. William Watson likes the services, because they remind him so much of home. He loved to sing at services in the Presbyterian Church and in the Friends Meeting House in Wilmington, when he had the opportunity to go there.

Preparations for the departure of this year' s Baltic trip continue. It is evident to William that they are preparing for a huge operation.

On March 20, he observes that ships for the Baltic Fleet, *Africaine*, *Tremendous*, *Princess Caroline* and *Ariel,* have begun to arrive. That same day, Rear Admiral of the Red, C. W. Reynolds arrives in Portsmouth with his retinue of carriages and servants. He is quartered in Royal Navy Headquarters in Portsmouth, where he opens letters sent to him here. His personal secretary James Railton, who will follow him to the Baltic Sea this year, is constantly at his side. First, Reynolds opens a letter from his superior Rear Admiral of the Blue James Sammaurez, who informs Reynolds that he will arrive later this spring to board his own flagship, *HMS Victory.* Sammaurez is looking forward to commanding the entire Baltic Fleet this year.

Sammaurez and *Victory* will establish headquarters for the Royal Navy Baltic Fleet at Vinga Sound outside Gothenburg, where they will stay from late spring to late autumn. This Baltic headquarters will constitute a base for the different Royal Navy Squadrons escorting convoys of merchant ships in and out of the Baltic Sea through the season.

James Sammaurez states in his letter that he wants Reynolds to send two or three ships of the line to Vinga Sound as soon as possible. He asks Reynolds if his squadron also is going to protect Anholt Island this year. It is clear to Reynolds that Sammaurez has already received intelligence reports that the Danes will probably try to recapture Anholt this spring, before the British fleet can arrive and prevent it.

The Danish island Anholt, strategically placed in the Cattegat, was taken by the Royal Navy after the Bombardment of Copenhagen. When Denmark lost its fleet, it also lost its ability to defend its islands far from shore. The Royal Navy soon took over Helgoland Island on the southwest coast of Slesvig-Holstein and later occupied Anholt Island in the Cattegat. Both islands are now kept and supplied as permanent Royal Navy Naval Stations.[129]

Reynolds begins to consider what can be done. Concerns about Anholt are well founded. The Danish Admiralty at Gammelholm in Copenhagen plans to retake Anholt Island in early spring, and has already given the orders to do so. One of the Danish officers who will take part in this operation is sea lieutenant Wigelsen.

The same day, at 5 a.m., *Defence* unmoors to go on a mission. The squadron is composed of the ships of the lines *HMS Monmouth, HMS Christian VII, Aboukir, Bedford, St. Domingo, Nymphen, Partian, Raven, Bermuda, Skylark,* and several other smaller ships.

The 22nd of March, boats from *St. George* are sent to shore to take in more prisoners. The following day, preparations to go to sea continue.

Then finally, on March 24, Rear Admiral of the Red C. W. Reynolds comes to his flagship *St. George III* from Portsmouth harbor, from the very quay where Lord Nelson left to sail the *Victory* to the Battle of Trafalgar that unfortunately cost him his life. The entire crew lines up on the main deck, on the order of Flag Captain Daniel Gurion, to welcome Admiral Reynolds. As he stands on the quarterdeck he smiles kindly as he put his right hand to his hat and awaits the hoisting of his Admiral's flag onboard.

Both William Watson and William Freeman are impressed by the handsome Admiral's uniform and hat, but then realize it looks a little old-fashioned, compared to the smart uniforms of the Navy of their own country, the United States of America.

After this short ceremony, Reynolds quickly moves to his Admiral's cabin. As he opens the cabin door, he is met by the smell of new paint, as expected, and he admires the work. It is nice and neat, just as he wants it to be. A new floor carpet with the classic black and white diamond pattern looks exactly like the top floors in the Admiralty building in London. Sixty years of age demands some comfort[108], Reynolds thinks to himself.

Two days later, on March 26, *St. George* unmoors for a small trip to St. Helens. *Victory, Infatigueable, Piobe, Ethalion* and *Princess Caroline* arrive that day.

On March 28, before the Baltic Fleet has sets out, while the garrison of Royal mariners on the occupied Anholt is weakest, the Danes attack the island, just as Sammaurez feared. But the operation is far from successful. Some of the Danish mariners never leave the beach. The resistance from the English mariners is too strong and some Danes are taken prisoners and others are wounded. The major part of the Danish forces are soon forced to retreat and leave the island.

Wigelsen, the sea lieutenant from Jutland's Naval Headquarter in Fladstrand, on the northeast coast of Jutland, is participating in this unsuccessful attack on Anholt.[89-0]

The following day, Admiral Reynolds receives a letter from Admiral Sammaurez, asking which ships they should send to the Baltic this year. Should it be *Conquestrator, Porition, Princess Carolina and Platagenet*?

On April 2, *St. George* is anchored at St. Helens, and five seamen are punished. It is the first punishment William Watson and William Freeman have experienced, and it fills them with disgust.

Three days later, the entire squadron attached to the flagship *St. George* leaves Hosely Bay.

This year, neutral American merchant ships sail to the Baltic Sea in larger numbers than ever, to take advantage of Russia's break with Napoleon's Continental System. This system was supposed to isolate England by forbidding English trade with countries on the European Continent. As a consequence, Napoleon orders the confiscation of all American ships.

This order introduces a large conflict between Denmark and the United States of America for the first time since America's declaration of independence. It is hard for Danish privateers to separate American merchant ships from English ones, because they seek protection in the same Royal Navy convoys going in and out of the Baltic Sea through Danish waters. Providing protection for American ships sailing in and out of the Baltic is a profitable service that the British Royal Navy is happy to offer.[195] Another problem is that Denmark officially takes Napoleon's side in the war between England and France, and becomes trapped between loyalty toward its American friends and its French allies.

American seamen on Royal Navy ships in the Baltic Fleet are angry to hear about the many American merchant ships in Royal Navy convoys. William Watson, William Freeman and the other Americans onboard *St. George* are at first angry and then depressed when they receive the news. Here they are, American seamen enslaved on war ships of the Royal Navy, protecting American merchant ships mainly trading for the British against the first friends of the United States, the Danes. It is difficult for Watson and Freeman to keep their spirits up under these strange circumstances.

On the 6th, *Defence* is again patrolling outside Texel when President James Madison appoints James Monroe as Secretary of State. Monroe's mentor is Thomas Jefferson, and Monroe also knew the late George Washington well. Former Secretary of State Robert Smith has been removed from office this day, because he led a chaotic administration, to put it mildly.

Letters from wives and families of impressed American seamen piled up for months in the Department of State, together with complaints from merchants, ship owners, and captains who have had their ships confiscated, mostly by Danish privateers when they passed through Danish waters. This situation developed because no appropriate orders were given to bring the chaos to an end while Robert Smith was head of the department.

James Monroe, the former minister to England who negotiated impressments with the English Government, will bring order to the state administration and, others hope, help impressed seamen like John Brown, William Watson and Amos Stevens gain their freedom.

The two letters William wrote to Lyman from the entrance prison ship in Portsmouth, the *Royal William,* had been ignored. Lyman faithfully entered William's information in his leather-bound *Book for Impressed Seamen,* then sent the letters to the Department of State.

In those letters, William Watson asked Lyman to send a copy of his New York Protection Certificate to him onboard the *Royal William* in Portsmouth. But the letters, and many others from American seamen, had just been piling up on the desks in the Department of State without even being read.

The quarterly returns from the American Agents in London and Kingston and the lists of impressed seamen carefully made by Department of State employee for the House of Representatives, were not used to acquire customhouse Protection Certificates for any impressed American seamen. This is why William and many others have never heard anything from the authorities back home, and why many of them have remained in anxious captivity for months and even years.

The new Secretary of State is a bright, caring and responsible administrator, and soon the Department of State requires copies of Protection Certificates sent to impressed individuals onboard Royal Navy ships like *St. George* or *Defence.* From his own previous work on the issue of impressed Americans, Monroe is fully aware of the tough conditions these seamen endure.

On April 9, ten seamen are punished 24 to 36 lashes onboard the *St. George.* The number of lashes given onboard the *St. George* and other Royal Navy ships has greatly increased. There is a constant need for more seamen in the Royal Navy, caused by the long war with France, and the understaffed crews must work harder, and need tougher discipline. The impressed Americans clearly see this. Verbal and physical fighting between ordinary crewmembers and officers occurs more and more often. William looks upon this kind of behavior with disgust.

The following day, the *St. George* loses its best bower anchor in a fresh breeze with a heavy swell. Preparations are made for sea. In the afternoon, the small sails are weighted. William is still amazed at these tall sailing ships. He has never seen a sight as impressive as when many ships of the line are gathered at such close range.

On April 12, *St. George* enters Hoseley Bay while the crew washes hammocks and clothes. It is fine weather, and William observes that the greater part of this year's Baltic Fleet has already arrived. William is going to be a mariner onboard the *St. George* for the voyage to the Baltic Sea. He doesn't like it at all, and protests violently, accusing his superior officer of breaking a promise. But William realizes, as so many other American seamen have before him, that the promise of an officer in the Royal Navy is only kept as long as it is to the Navy's benefit.

The following day, Rear Admiral of the Red Reynolds receives a letter from Rear Admiral of the Blue, James Sammaurez, telling him that provisions can be taken in from the supply ships from Harwich.[108] Another letter says that Sammaurez is still in London, but will soon be on his way to Portsmouth harbor, where his flagship *Victory* should soon be ready to go to its summer station at Vinga Sound. Sammaurez asks Reynolds to meet him there.

Sammaurez mentions that Anholt is a pleasant place to stay and an excellent camp. Reynolds is ordered to visit the consuls in Gothenburg and to send the usual post and to prepare for the arrival of the Fleet under the command of *Victory* and Sammaurez.[129]

Finally, Sammaurez gives a strategic evaluation of the war situation in the Baltic Sea. Sweden is expected to be less hostile this year. Sammaurez asks if Reynolds has heard about Rear Admiral Dixon's attempt to marry last year. Dixon is going to guard the Cattegat and the Great Belt this year. Sammaurez is a little worried that his flagship has not yet returned from a trip to Portugal. He cares for Lord Nelson's old flagship from Trafalgar.

During the morning of the 14th of April, *St. George* sets out its launch alongside the merchant ships *Bush* and *Dragon*. William, on his guard on the top deck, observes the ship name *Bush* and can't help thinking about his wife Mary Ann, the Warner and the Bush families in Wilmington. He then becomes angry. Why is he forced to be here, when he should be home?

The following day, Reynolds is ordered by Sammaurez to sail at last, and to serve as Rear Admiral of his own squadron, the *St. George* Squadron.[108] The same day, Reynolds receives a condition list from *HMS Platagenet*.[131]

In the afternoon, in fine weather, William observes a small fleet of ships arrive, including *Courageaux*, *Platagenet*, *Les Loire*, *Bellephoon*, *Defiance*, *Thesus* and *Defence*. Now most of the ships in the Baltic Fleet have arrived, and William sees the *Defence* for the first time. Amos and John, onboard the *Defence,* see the flagship *St. George* for the first time also. Even though they are held against their will, these three Americans can't hide the excitement of being a part of this g iant fleet. *St. George* salutes with 11 shots.

The Royal Navy Baltic Fleet is finally ready to sail on the morning of April 16. By four in the afternoon, the whole squadron is gathered and is on its way. Even though it is cloudy and raining, the ships are a beautiful sight. William has never seen anything quite like it. The off-white sails across the sea surface do, indeed, look like "grey geese" as Nelson called them, William thinks.

The day after, sail-makers are employed and a division of mariners, including William Watson, exercised at the cannons and guns. When he learns that their position is west of the island of Texel, close to the borough of Den Helder, his thoughts go to his friends and employers in Wilmington. The Warners, Hemphills and Bushes have frequently sailed here. William Watson tells William Freeman where they are, and they look for the land, but can't see it. "John Warner, the big brother of my best friend Joseph, has sailed here many times."

"Yes, it is a common place in Holland to sail," William Freeman answers. "A lot of my friends in Philadelphia go there, too."

The two of them look to the western horizon, but no American merchant ships are approaching now. "It would surely make me glad, if we could get *St. George*'s jollyboat and row to the harbor of Den Helder. We could hop on an American merchant ship and be home in a month or so," William Freeman says.

"That would be great," William Watson replies. He sighs. "At least we have each other's company, until we are able to return."

The whole squadron is visible in the afternoon. Then a thick fog settles over the water. Each hour, the *St. George* fires a shot to let the other ships know where the flagship is positioned.

On April 18, while *Defence* is anchored in Hoseley Bay, it receives two superb pilots to pass on to *Victory*. Admiral Dixon, who is going to guard both the Cattegat and the Great Belt this year, hoists his flag onboard the *Vigo* today.

The convoy runs into a strong gale with heavy seas on its way to Vinga Sound. They are 40 miles south and 223 miles west of the Cliffs of Bovbjerg on the North west coast of Jutland. They keep a safe distance from the dangerous lee shores of Jutland and the Jutland Reef. This is easy to do as long as the wind is from the east-southeast. In the afternoon, the storm staysails are bent. This is William Watson's first real storm in the North Sea, and he begins to understand how dangerous it can be to sail here. Right before his eyes, some of the lower starboard sails are ripped off the masts and washed away in only a few seconds.

William Watson and William Freeman know that there will be no hot food served in this stormy weather. It is too dangerous to light the stove and risk a devastating fire. They are standing on the top deck when the starboard gangway breaks off as a wave hits the ship. William Watson cries out, "Watch out!" to his friend William. In the past half hour, many seamen and mariners passed on that gangway, and William is relieved that it broke off without hurting anyone. An incident like this reminds them all that weather in the North Sea has to be taken seriously.

On the 20th, four seamen are punished onboard the *St. George*. On the 23rd, St. George and its squadron are still in the North Sea. Admiral Sammaurez forwards a letter to Admiral Reynolds that he received earlier from Glasgow. The letter is from W. J. Gamber and J. W. Grakes, two rich merchants who own many of the merchant ships in this year's convoy. They want a permanent station with war ships established in Billard Bay, in the central part of the Baltic Sea, to establish permanent protection of their trade.¹⁰⁸ The Royal Navy is not prepared to offer these two merchants that concession, and will not set aside funds nor provide any naval resources for such a project. "That would cost us a fortune," Admiral Reynolds says to his personal secretary, James Railton, after reading the letter once again.

He puts the letter in one of the two chests in his cabin. One chest is for official letters from the Admiralty in London, his superior Admiral Sammaurez, subordinate captains in the squadron, and letters to the chief gunners, pursers, chief carpenters, surgeons and other letters of official business. The other chest holds letters from his son, who is also in the Royal Navy, and from his wife and daughter in Cornwall or London. In this personal chest, he hides letters dealing with the prizes and prize money relating to his work as an Admiral of a squadron. This makes sense to Rear Admiral Reynolds, because he finds the paperwork related to collecting prize money more like pleasurable family letters, and not like real work.

On the 24th, the squadron is 52 miles north and 67 miles west of the Cliffs of Bovbjerg in a fresh breeze. The Cliffs of Bovbjerg is one of the highest points visible on the North West coast of Jutland.

Three days later, in the afternoon, the weather is fine and they have almost passed the Skagerak when the Scaw Lighthouse is seen seven miles south-southeast. Passing such a short distance from the Scaw can be very dangerous. Every experienced officer and seaman knows it, and the pilots constantly keep an eye on the coastline while passing.

By 6:00 in the morning, they have passed the Scaw and the lighthouse is eight miles to the southwest. For the first time, William can see a greater part of the coastline of Denmark at a close range. The beaches around the Scaw remind him of the beaches at the entrance to the Delaware Bay on Cape Henlopen. William hopes that fewer ships wreck here at the Scaw than back home, where a lot of ships are known to strand. He notices that the lighthouse here is quite different.

Standing at the bulwark the next morning, watching the calm sea and the Danish shores, he can't stop thinking of Mary Ann. She was pregnant when he left. He must be the father of a girl or a boy right now, a child at least one-year-old, maybe sitting and playing on the floor in the apartment in Water Street. Maybe Mary Ann is teaching their child to walk. He wonders if she is well. He tries to image the faces of Mary Ann and her mother laughing as they watch his son crawl around the floor making funny faces. He imagines the reactions of their friends Damian Starr, Joseph Warner, John Freed, Jr. and Enoch Lang, when they visit and see his child for the first time. Perhaps the child reminds them all too much of him. It has been almost one and a half years since he left the borough of Wilmington. God knows how he longs to go home at this moment.

Near 10 a.m. William observes that the air has becomes quite hazy. He is concerned. The *St. George* will be going through the dangerous Great Belt, where Danish privateers in great numbers are waiting for them. As a mariner, he is forced to go out in the small boats. It is firmly against William's belief to fight a friend of the United States of America, but he cannot prevent it from happening, only wait to see what happens.

On April 28 *Defence*, *Cressy* and *Dictator* are still in Hoseley Bay.

A thick fog in the Cattegat makes it difficult for the *St. George* squadron to advance. It is as though God is on the side of the Danes, a British seaman next to William says. 'Every time we are in Danish waters, it is hazy with very little wind," the seaman complains. "These Danish privateers sneaking in on our convoy and cutting out single merchant ships are like hyenas hunting on the plains. Luckily, we do not usually meet Danish cannon boats this far north in the Cattegat. They like to hide behind islands in the Cattegat, like Læsø. We'll have to get further south before there is any real risk of being attacked." William is relieved to hear this.

The next day, the weather has improved quite a bit, and the officers onboard the *St. George* can get an overview of the number of warships in the squadron and merchant ships in the convoy. At 8 in the evening, they are close to Marstrand on the Swedish North West coast, north of Vinga Sound.

On April 30, the part of the trip most dangerous for the merchant ships is over. But for ordinary crewmembers onboard Royal Navy ships,

192

the time for punishments has returned. Punishment does not normally take place when the ships are in danger of being attacked and cleared for action. But now that the ships are in safe waters again, near the Swedish coast, they resume.

One seaman who knows he is going to be punished jumps overboard and drowns. Ten minutes later, eight seamen are punished for neglect of duty and insolence. William Watson is shocked seeing such cruelty. He thinks it is a kind of madness that makes absolutely no sense. English able seaman John Anderson, who is punished for neglect of duty, just hates the Royal Navy even more, and from now on, spends much of his time thinking of escape. He knows, though, he will likely never succeed in escaping the iron grip of the Royal Navy. In the afternoon, *St. George* finally arrives and anchors at the headquarters of the Royal Navy's summer station at Vinga Sound.

On May 1, *Defence* prepares for sea and the next day, five seamen are punished.

Next morning, *Hero*, *Vanguard* and *Helder* arrive in Vinga Sound and, in the afternoon, the flagship *Victory*, with James Sammaurez onboard, arrives, together with *Tremendous*.

On May 4, John Brown and Amos Stevens finally see Vinga Sound, the *Victory* and the other ships. The fast ship *Defence* made the trip from an English port to Gothenburg in only four days.

While most of the Baltic Fleet is gathered in Vinga Sound, Sammaurez gets new intelligence about the situation in Denmark. An English agent, Mr. Fenswick received intelligence that this year, the number of Danish cannon boats and ships armed with cannons has been doubled. Sammaurez makes sure that this information is passed on to the commanders of the other ships.

When he receives this information, Reynolds makes a quick decision. *St. George* is undermanned by almost 200 men and has few mariners onboard, thanks to the epidemics onboard the ship in February. So he decides to transfer some of the super numerous Able Seamen into Mariners. William Watson, Able Seaman number 1224, is 'promoted" to mariner, much against his will.

William Watson is concerned now. Experienced seamen report how dangerous being a mariner can be when the convoy passes the Great Belt.[201] There, mariners go out on the water in tiny jollyboats, looking for and fighting Danish cannon boats, to prevent them from taking merchant ships from the convoy.

To the Royal Navy ships of the line themselves, the Danes are no threat. In fact, to provoke the Danes, the seamen onboard the ships of the line in the Royal Navy are ordered to wash their clothes as they pass through the Great Belt. This is their way of showing Danish military observers at Nyborg on Fuen, or at headquarters for the cannon boats in the Great Belt, Corsør on Zealand and other places, that they do not take the Danish military seriously.

On the 6th of May, while the *St George* is still anchored in Vinga Sound, Reynolds receives an order from Sammaurez to pass through the Cattegat as quickly as possible this year, because the Russian Fleet may threaten[113] his convoy.

The next day, John Brown observes from the forecastle of the *Defence* that *St. George*, *Hero*, *Courageaux*, *Tremendous*, *Ethalion*, *Tartar*, *Rose*, *Ranger* and *Buizer* sail with a convoy toward the Great Belt and the summer station in Hanö Bay in the Baltic Sea.

On May 9, *St. George* and its squadron take in anchors and leave night quarters in the Cattegat in a fresh breeze at 5:15 in the morning. At 8:00, it is calm and cloudy, and 147 merchant ships are in sight from the quarterdeck of the flagship. The unlit Anholt Lighthouse is visible to the south.

A division of mariners, including William Watson, is exercised in using cannons and small arms, and training is conducted to prepare for possible enemy confrontation. The squadron is slowly approaching the Great Belt in a light breeze, and the weather is fine, making it possible to keep track of Danish cannon boats.

In the afternoon, William notices that they are seven miles south of Anholt, and the island of Hjerm can be seen to the southeast. At midnight, the Squadron is anchored close to Hjerm.

William Watson doesn't sleep that night. He has heard so many stories about fighting in the Great Belt between Royal Navy mariners in jollyboats and Danish cannon boats. In close combat, many mariners are killed or severely wounded, if they are not lucky enough to be captured.

Sometimes experienced mariners can neutralize a Danish cannon boat, but it is always a bloody mess.

William still have not received his protection certificate, even though he has written twice to General William Lyman, asking for a new one.

What William Watson and the other impressed Americans in this year's Baltic Fleet do not know is that Lyman has fallen ill and is unable to work as hard as he used to for the release of impressed American seamen. Although assistants do most of the hard work, Lyman's illness has slowed down the whole process.

So just when the process of addressing release of impressed American seamen has sped up in the Department of State, it has slowed down in the office of the American Agent for Seamen in London.

If he is lucky enough to be taken prisoner by the Danes, William Watson worries that he will not be able to prove that he is American, and so won't be released. The Americans onboard *St. George* talk about escape often while passing through Danish waters. A neutral nation friendly to America would be an ideal place to escape, but Royal Navy officers know this too, and when they sail in Danish waters, they watch the Americans closely.

Among British seamen who think of escape are some mariners who do not share the same positive feelings toward the Danes. Most of these seamen have taken part in raids against small Danish merchant and fishing boats. They have even been sent to shore to attack fishermen working peacefully on the shores.[262] These English mariners know that they can hardly expect nice treatment, if they should ever fall into the hands of the Danes.

On May 11, Amos is standing at the bulwark onboard *Defence,* anchored in Vinga Sound, and sees the *Gluckstadt, Arehn* and *Accute* depart. *Raleigh* arrives. *St. George* and the squadron are near Romsø Island in the southern part of the Cattegat, near the entrance to the Great Belt. They anchor here for the night. They have seen no Danish cannon boats yet.

On the 13th, the squadron is at the entrance to the Great Belt. The weather is fine and a division of mariners is exercised using cannons and rifles. They are preparing for fighting again. William Watson and the other mariners try to fire a blank cartridge for the first time. The closer they get to the Great Belt, the more William Watson rejects the whole idea of fighting the Danes. He is an American seaman, not an English mariner. But he is aware that no complaints are accepted. Still, fighting friends of America will never make sense to him at all.

The following day Admiral Reynolds receives from Admiral

Sammaurez orders for the captains on the ships in Reynolds's squadron, and is asked to pass them on.[121]

Two days later, when a moderate breeze is blowing and the visibility is good, the crews make a general exercise at the cannons. They fire against a mark visible on the sea surface some distance from the *St. George,* so they can adjust the cannons and be prepared to fight.

A merchant ship *Elisabeth* from Londonderry is supplied with water. A boat is sent out to look for Danish cannon boats, but none are in sight at the moment.

The Royal Navy makes itself heard while sailing in Danish waters, with the frequent shooting, and the Danes along the coast have no problems figuring out that the Royal Navy has returned.

This night, as *St. George*, its squadron, and the merchant ship convoy are anchored in the Great Belt, everyone sleeps tight except the watches onboard and the mariners sitting in jollyboats in the Belt.

An hour before the first watch onboard the *St. George* is called at 2 a.m., when most of the men are still fast asleep, off the Capes of Virginia the *HMS Little Belt*, a frigate the British stole from the Danes in 1807, meets the frigate *USS President* before sundown. They meet at Cape Henry, only 10 miles from where the *USS Chesapeake* and *HMS Leopold* met back in June 1807.

William is sitting in the *St. George* jollyboat with William Freeman and other *St. George* mariners. He whispers to his friend, 'Here we are, on our first night as mariners in action, Americans in a jollyboat protecting a British convoy against attack from cannon boats from Denmark, one of the first friends America ever had. It's almost feels too strange to be true." William Freeman nods his head slowly, so as not to attract too much attention from the British mariners surrounding them. William Freeman, who has a bad memory and very little interest in history, asks William, 'What was it that President Jefferson said about England's credibility after the Bombardment of Copenhagen?"

William Watson remembers very well. "…Her good faith! The faith of a nation of merchants! Of the friend and protectress of Copenhagen! Of a nation who never admitted a chapter of morality into her political code…" William Watson had read the Wilmington newspapers back home, and other newspapers while sailing along the U.S. coast and had read about his president's feelings. It gives him a special satisfaction to be able to inform people about things they ought to know about, but perhaps had forgotten.

The two Americans look at each other and smile without saying a word. The Royal Navy may have their American bodies right now, no doubt about that, but it didn't have their American souls.

They sit silently for a long time, their faces directed toward Corsør, waiting for the sun to rise. The horizon over Zealand is already red.

William Freeman knows a seamen and a mariner from Philadelphia onboard the *USS President*. William Watson sailed between Wilmington and Philadelphia countless times and visited his friend Joseph Warner often, so he also knew the *USS President*. But sitting here in a jollyboat in the Great Belt just before sunrise, they don't know that the *USS President* is, at that moment, fighting the British crew onboard the *Little Belt* as the sun goes down outside the Capes of Virginia.

The *Little Belt* finally strikes her colors, but at the same time fires a shot that hits the main mast on the *USS President*.[300]

The *Little Belt,* under the British command of Captain Bingham, suffers 10 men killed and 20 wounded, and the *USS President* has a single boy wounded.

This war episode close to the US coast causes the same kind of public outcry in the United States of America as the *Chesapeake-Leopold* episode had done, and even the Boston Federalist paper the *Columbian Sentinel* now begins to support the recovery of impressed American seamen. This incident causes ordinary Americans, and especially seamen, to call for a war against England. Americans feel that they have suffered enough humiliation. The *Chesapeake* affair has not even been settled yet, and here it is 1811. How long will relations between England and the United States of America continue to grow worse, without any consequences?

Friday the 17th, the following evening, William Watson is again part of the mariners in the night watch team on the sea surface in the Great Belt. The row guard normally consists of the jollyboats from the different ships of the line in the squadron.

As the crews from each ship sit in jollyboats this warm spring night, staying close together and near the anchor cable of the most northerly ship in the convoy, they can clearly see the beautiful town lights in the port of Corsør on the island of Zealand. Watson and Freeman are both sitting in the *St. George* jollyboat thinking to themselves, as they watch the distant light, how nice it would be if this jollyboat was filled with only Americans. They could row the seven miles to Nyborg and turn themselves to the Danish night watches, and probably be released after a short while. William Watson knows the penalty for escaping is different for mariners than it is for ordinary or able seamen in the Royal Navy. A failed escape attempt would mean the death penalty for mariners. And the mariners in the other jollyboats would shoot them if they were discovered trying to escape to shore. Ordinary seamen involved in an attempt to escape from a British man-o-war would only be flogged.

Rear Admiral of the Red C. W. Reynolds receives a packet from *Victory*, brought from England to the ships under his command[126]. The seamen and other crewmembers are always very exited when an unexpected packet is received. It might hold personal letters to the men.

Two days later, the Sunday Divine Service that William is looking forward to never takes place. The breeze is light and the weather fine, and at 8 o'clock Flag Captain Gurion gives the order to clear the *St. George* for action.

William and a group of seamen help remove the furniture from Rear Admiral Reynolds's cabin, and store it away in the hold. *St. George* approaches the island of Sprogø, in the middle of the Great Belt, between Nyborg and Corsør.

The Royal Navy squadron officers are watching the convoy of merchant ships closely. Shots are fired repeatedly from the man-o-wars to order the merchant ships to assemble, to make it easier to protect them.

News about the *USS President* and *HMS Little Belt* episode travels through the Delaware-Maryland-Virginia peninsula the same way the information on the *Chesapeake* affair did almost four years ago, when William was with Mary Ann in Wilmington, enjoying their summer walks along the Brandywine River. When the news arrives in Wilmington this time, wharf and ship owners like Samuel Bush, John Warner, William Hemphill are just as disturbed as before.

Revenue officers John Freed, Jr., William Windell, and many seamen who had appeared in the port in the weeks since, are much alarmed. When Mary Ann received the news, she became very worried, as she has often been. This time, it is more severe than ever, because she lost her child and her husband William should have been home a long time ago.

He has been away for more than a year now. Mary Ann's mother coped with her daughter's almost permanent sadness after William left, and Mary Ann finally began to get better. But Mary Ann was not well at all, and she still needed protection against the world's random cruelty and injustice for some time to come.

At noon the sails are trimmed on *St. George*. They are now fully prepared to meet the Danish cannon boats. Let them attack, the English seamen and mariners think. They are excited about what is going to happen.

They exchange few words, and even William begins to feel a little nervous. He sends his thoughts to Mary Ann. What would she think, what would his Quaker friends think, if they knew that he was about to take part in war actions against one of America's first true friends among the nations in the world? Would they ever be able to forgive him?

As an American, William feels so ashamed in these tense minutes. How will he ever be able to explain to his friends and family that he ended up in this situation? It will be hard enough to explain that he was impressed from the *Ino* in the harbor of Portsmouth, when it was obvious to everyone that it was illegal to trade with England. They may ask what he was doing there in the first place. Then he would have to explain how he ended up on a second-rater flagship in the Royal Navy's Baltic Fleet, to build British warships that fight the friends of the United States of America and even the United States itself. William is seized with a melancholy sadness. He has surely got himself mixed up in some quite heavy troubles.

At half past one, William sees two strange ships on the horizon, but they disappear again. At 6 o'clock in the evening, all the guard boats of the squadron are gathered around the rudder of the flagship *St. George*. The mariners onboard the guard boats have developed a strong friendship that will last for life, however long, or short, that might be. This is one of the few moments when they can relax and enjoy themselves. They talk and tell jokes.

As the boats wait on the calm sea surface in the Great Belt for Danish attacks, William looks up the huge shipside and sees the gallery of the *St. George*. Rear Admiral of the Red C. W. Reynolds and his secretary James Railton are standing together close to the windows, discussing an issue.

William looks at the houses on the coasts of Fuen and Zealand, and the warm spring air and the fresh smell of the sea make him long for home.

He closes his eyes and pictures how Wilmington would look on a spring evening, as though it is the last time he is allowed to have such thoughts. He is convinced that he will not live through the night to see another dawn. Every mariner knows his life depends on others in a critical situation like hand-to-hand fighting with the enemy, in small boats in the dark. So they keep an eye on each other all the time, looking for any sign of weakness that might be life-threatening to them all. William Watson likes that part of being a mariner, the part that helps shape his own strong character, and he likes the comradeship. He found it natural and easy to defend his own country, and would gladly accept it as his duty. What he doesn't like, here in the Great Belt, is being impressed and forced to fight for a foreign nation, one that might become an enemy of the United States, and against a friend of the United States of America.

Mary Ann is dining with her mother in the apartment in Water Street. Mary Ann is quite depressed. She doesn't talk much, and she eats less and less each time she and her mother sit at the table. As a consequence, she grows thinner and thinner. Her mother is aware of her daughter's critical situation, but is afraid that saying something will make things even worse. So she keeps her worries to herself.

Mary Ann lost her child just 17 days after William kissed her goodbye and sailed toward the Atlantic Ocean. She had been deeply concerned about William being away on what she considered to be a dangerous trip to Europe, and is convinced that her own worries for William caused the stillbirth.

As a nurse, Mary Ann's mother helped her give birth to the dead child in the bedroom in the apartment in Water Street. Joseph Warner came on the day of the funeral to fetch the little white coffin and take it to Old Swedes Church. It was as if the spirit of life permanently left the apartment with him that day.

Mary Ann's mother is used to being mentall y strong, as a widow who worked hard every day at either the borough hospital or in Wilmington homes, helping the sick or dying and sometimes assisting a healthy child into this world. She arranged the funeral alone, because all Mary Ann could do was lie on her bed and cry.

All of Mary Ann and William's friends showed up at the funeral, and the Old Swedes Church was so stuffed with mourning people that many had to stay outside in the churchyard. Grown men and women cried at the ceremony, because the whole situation was more than anyone could bear. They came to bury the child of a wife married hardly two weeks before, in this same church, to a man who had been forced to go to sea to support his little family.

The priest, Joseph Clarkson, had married Mary Ann and William, and, like most of the congregation, had trouble holding back his tears, when he saw Mary Ann with bent head and folded hands standing beside the white coffin as the first benches in the church filled up with her friends, with their own lovely children sitting on their knees. But the speech he held for Mary Ann and William's dead boy, which Mary Ann had named after William's father, had been as moving as the wedding speech.

Joseph Warner's wife, Mary, and the wives of John Freed, Jr. and William Windell understood the sad situation exactly as the priest had, and loud sobbing from these first church benches occasionally drowned out the noise from the rest of the nave.

Mary Ann had received her first letter from William last spring. In that letter he had told her that he was being held prisoner on a ship in England. This news, on top of the loss of the baby had been too much too soon for the young bride. Mary Ann had had a happy, trouble-free life before her just a few months ago, and now every dream had fallen apart. Her mother insisted that she eat something, and Mary Ann followed her mother's suggestion, having no will of her own to protest it.

Shortly after, Joseph Warner came to the apartment in Water Street to inform Mary Ann of the death of their friend Damian Starr. Samuel had been killed the very day he returned to Philadelphia, on a ship that might have carried restricted articles from Liverpool. This new news certainly did not improve the general mood among these Wilmington friends. It deepened Mary Ann's depression for a long time, and increased her conviction that her husband's life too could be in danger. She worried herself sick at night, imagining how easily he could be slaughtered on return from an English port, or how he could go down with a ship in a storm in the middle of the deep ocean. William should have been home last summer. Why hasn't he arrived?

Since the new Macon Bill came into force, trade with England had been strictly forbidden. The Hemphill and the Warner families had been trading for generations with England, the land their forefathers originally came from. Many other Wilmington ship owner families had traded with England for just as long, and it had been tough to stop such a profitable tradition on such short notice, just because of some laws - laws that looked completely stupid to American ship owners, captains and seamen.

McLane is widely known as a great patriot, and every captain, wharf or ship owner knows that, as Marshall for the District of Delaware, he will do anything he can to catch every unlawful trade appearing in 'his waters". Some Wilmingtonian shipowners are determined to continue to trade with England despite the new situation. They move their business to Philadelphia, where they try to hide among the much larger numbers of ships going in and out of the port, or they go across the border to Maryland.

But the port authorities in Philadelphia are skillful and persistent, and do a good job spotting arriving ships that might be involved in illegal business. Some times, when they are discovered, dangerous hand-to-hand fights occur between port authority personnel, and captains and crewmembers from the ships.

Damian Starr, like his good friend William, decided to take a risk and go on a trip to Europe, first to Londonderry and Dublin, and then passing Liverpool on the way home. Then Samuel was killed in the harbor of Philadelphia on arrival. An American seaman who takes part in illegal foreign trade takes a real risk these days.

Joseph Warner dared not tell his brother John about Damian Starr. John had been fighting so much with his brother William Warner about this kind of trade, and felt no mercy for those who disobeyed the law and received their punishment for doing so. Luckily, Samuel had not been killed on one of William Warner's returning ships.

John Warner knew that his brother continued steady illegal English trade, going to Liverpool with his ship the *Fair American,* and John disliked him for doing so.

John Warner felt loyal to his business partner Samuel Bush, and when John heard the story about Samuel's brother, Lewis, who had been killed in the Battle of the Brandywine September 11, 1777, he felt deeply touched. In that same battle, the French General Lafayette was wounded by the British and taken care of by James Monroe, who is now Secretary of State. John had only been three years old at the time and has no personal memory of it, only the stories he has been told. Through those stories, he knew that the British soldiers singled out Lewis on the field just north of the Brandywine River and killed him. Although Samuel Bush was already a patriot at that time and supported the Continental Army the best he could, the killing of his brother made him almost a fanatic.

The two wharf owners seldom talked about the war, but when they did, it was in few, expressive sentences. Samuel Bush never left John Warner with the impression that an attitude toward the British could be half-hearted. This had not at all improved the bad relations between the brothers John and William Warner.

At midnight, the weather is fine in the Great Belt. As William quietly sits in his guard boat, surrounded by other guard boats on the dark and silent water, he again observes the bright lights of Nyborg and Corsør. The sky is clear, with the Milky Way and many sparkling stars right above their heads. A small wave occasionally gurgles along the side of a merchant ship, but otherwise everything is quiet. It's just another peaceful, warm spring night.

When will I ever see Mary Ann again? William thinks over and over while watching for approaching Danish cannon boats in the night. Will I survive this war and return to Wilmington? Many of the English mariners have similar thoughts about their hometowns in England.

At 4:30 in the morning, William and his guard boat return to *St. George*. He climbs the gangway, tired but relieved that he is still alive. The sun has just come up and the sight from the forecastle is so beautiful. Half an hour later, the squadron weighs anchor and makes sail. At noon they are on their way south, out of the Great Belt toward the north end of the island Langeland.

On Wednesday May 22, well past the Great Belt battle zones, it is again time for routine activities, and Flag Captain Daniel Gurion orders the punishment of seven seamen. Gurion feels very pleased that *St. George* has passed the Great Belt with no loss of lives, boats or merchant ships in the convoy. Because of his good mood, he decides to order mild punishments for the seamen, who violated the rules while they were passing the Great Belt. He orders 12 lashes for each of them, quite mild for this year of 1811, and definitely mild for the *St. George*. Admiral of the Red C. W. Reynolds is known as a hard-liner when it comes to punishment of his subordinate crews. Some have been drinking to steady their nerves and some have been disobedient.

William looks at the flat green landscape that surrounds them, so very similar to the landscapes along the coasts of Delaware. Beech woods on the coast look very much like the ones in Sussex County back home. From onboard ships, he has often seen many barges loaded with timber as he was leaving the natural harbor near Millsboro and sailing through the Indian River Bay, through Rehoboth Bay and into Delaware Bay. He would then continue sailing north along the coast, passing Cape Henlopen and the coasts of Sussex, Kent and New Castle Counties. He would pass the borough of New Castle and finally end up at the wharves in Philadelphia. Here they would normally transfer the timber to an ocean-going ship.

William now wonders about the Danes. Their mentality cannot be that different from the prevailing Quaker mentality in Wilmington, he concludes, standing on the *St. George* forecastle and silently studying the landscape of the Island of Langeland.

William and most of the crewmembers are sleeping when the night watch observes a thick fog coming in with the wind from the direction of Funen Island, half an hour before midnight. The captain and officers are glad that this fog did not arrive while they were still in the Great Belt. It surely has allowed the Danish cannon boats to sneak out in great numbers and successfully cut out several merchant ships from the convoy.

On May 26, the squadron is south of Lolland and Gedser Lighthouse is observed. *Tartar, Den Helder, Ethalion, Rose, Ranger and Ariel* accompany St. George.

Two days later, *Defence* receives 17 prisoners from *Censor*, which has been busy hunting Danish merchant ships in the Cattegat.

May 29. *Defence* is still anchored in Vinga Sound. Six seamen are punished, some of them for drinking. The crewmembers find it very boring here.

On this day, Admiral of the Red Reynolds receives a letter from Admiral of the Blue Sammaurez concerning merchant ships belonging to the company Sally and Sons. They are employed by the government for transport of merchandise, and are to be protected.[123] According to Article 8, chapter 2, Admiral Reynolds is going to present a health report to the Admiralty concerning all men on the ships under his command.[124] Many men have been dismissed from the Royal Navy's ships in recent years because of sickness, which is becoming more common onboard. The Admiralty wants to monitor the health situation on ships more closely now.

Secretary Railton reads the letter aloud to Admiral Reynolds, who stands on the port side in front of the gallery windows, with a clear view over the southeastern part of the Swedish coast of Skaane. The Rear Admiral of the Red turns around, smiles, and nods his head, quite satisfied with himself. The inward bound trip from South England through the Danish Waters to the Baltic Sea had been a success this year. *St. George* is now 67 miles north and 36 miles east of Bornholm, within hours of its destination, Hanö Island.

Admiral Reynolds walks to the quarterdeck and stands beside his flag captain Daniel Gurion. Together, the two officers observe that *HMS Hero* and the frigates under its command, which are busy hunting potential prize ships in the waters around the flagship. At 7:30 in the evening, the flag captain and the admiral have the luck to observe that the *Hero* successfully boards a sloop. The weather is fine and the sight clear.

Around midnight on May 30, *St. George* finally arrives in the Royal Navy's Baltic summer station, at the island Hanö in the Bay of Hanö. The flagship *St. George* anchors on a position on the west side of the island, between the Swedish mainland and Hanö. A ship from His Majesty's Service with Naval correspondence and personal post from seamen to their families is sent to Hanö on arrival.

The *St. George* crew is allowed to wash clothes. Washing his hammock on the top of the deck, William observes the few buildings that have been erected in the little harbor of Hanö, and the Union Jack fluttering in the eastern wind from a flagstaff on a small hill in the middle of the island, near the small Royal Navy cemetery.

President James Madison sends a letter to the Danish King Frederik VI, announcing that George W. Erving, the former American Agent for Seamen in London, has been appointed as the new Special Minister to

Denmark and will arrive in Copenhagen this day. He is Minister of *"Captures made under the Danish flag."* Erving's arrival in Copenhagen is necessary because American ships, which had begun to participate in the Baltic trade when Russia broke with Napoleon's Continental System, began to be captured in large numbers the previous year. The Non-intercourse Act forbidding trade between England and America had given the American ships, captains and seamen no other alternative besides participating in inter-European trade.

Some American ships seek protection under the Royal Navy's Baltic Fleet when sailing from England to the Baltic ports and back to England. The protection is mostly needed against Danish privateers, who have a hard time distinguishing American merchant ships from English ones in the same convoys.

Denmark has good relations with the United States of America, and the Danish authorities will do whatever possible to help American captains and crews who have their ships confiscated and wrongly deemed as prizes in the Danish prize courts. The arrival of Erving in Copenhagen is intended to speed up the process of releasing confiscated American ships in Danish ports.

King Frederik VI and his administration are doing what they can to help the Americans, but they cannot actively forbid Danish privateers from bringing in American ships, because Napoleon has ordered confiscation of all American ships. King Frederik VI and his administration must 'play on two horses" in this delicate and urgent matter.

The large number of American ships taken as prizes in Danish waters the previous year and this year has resulted in many American ship crews being held in prisons in the Danish port cities. Unfortunately, they sometimes have to stay for months or even years until their case can be presented to a court and they find out whether they are allowed to leave onboard their ship or, if their ship is confiscated, sent home some other way. The courts are burdened with the many cases, causing many American seamen and captains to stay in prison much longer that necessary.

In the Kingdom of Denmark, no foreigners, whether friend or enemy, are allowed to travel on their own through the country. So American ship crews are typically imprisoned in the port where they are first brought with their ship. If the ship is later confiscated, usually the American captain and crew are sent to Copenhagen to the Danish Military Headquarters prison at the islet of Gammelholm, until the Admiralty decides when they can be sent out of the country under escort of a Danish officer. They normally have to wait for a transport until a larger group has been gathered. Then they will be sent to the Danish port of Altona, near Hamburg on the south border, where most American ships arrive in Northern Europe. In the port of Altona, local Danish authorities will make sure that the American captain and seamen get on a ship to transport them back to their hometowns in the United States.

Just before the Americans leave Copenhagen in stage carriages to cross Zealand to Fun and down through Jutland to the port of Altona, they are visited by the North American Consul in Copenhagen, Mr. Hans Rudolph Saabye, who takes them to the new Travel Office in police headquarters, in the former castle of Charlottenborg. Mr. Saabye lives in a house in Amaliegade 10 and is a personal friend of King Frederik VI, whose residence is only 50 meters farther up Amaliegade. The Royal Palaces Amalienborg are located in the District of Frederiksstaden (Frederik's City). Mr. Hans Rudolph Saabye is also an influential Copenhagen merchant.

At the Travel office, the captain has to wait to be issued a passport, normally only valid for a departure from Copenhagen within three days.

In most of 1810, the outcry from ship-owners in Salem, Boston, New York, Philadelphia and other east coast ports is regularly in the east coast newspapers. The American ship-owners were angry at the Danish prize courts, and the opinion of those in Wilmington was no different. The seizure of American ships in Danish waters is straining the relationship between the two old friends, The Kingdom of Denmark and The United States of America, for the first time.

These angry public complaints from east coast ship owners and merchants help to convince President James Madison that it would be a good idea to send a U.S. minister to Denmark, in the middle of 1811 to try and sort out these problems. That is the reason Erskine has arrived in Copenhagen now.

This same day, Admiral of the Red C. W. Reynolds is ordered to bring the Portuguese Ambassador, who is going to the Royal Court in St. Petersburg, onboard *St. George* for a transport to Hanö Island.[122] At

Hanö, the Portuguese Ambassador will continue his voyage on a frigate going to St. Petersburg.

At Hanö, Rear Admiral Reynolds sends a letter from the *St. George* with a horse courier across Sweden, to his superior Rear Admiral Sammaurez onboard *Victory* anchored in Vinga Sound.

On June 4, *Defence* is still in Vinga Sound. John and Amos spend most of their free time on the forecastle studying ships passing by or looking at the fortification of the Borough of Gothenburg to the east.

In Hanö Bay, there is a fresh breeze and a clear sky and the seamen are employed in the rigging. William and a group of mariners are sent to the island of Hanö to exercise the rifles for the first time since arriving here. He is looking forward to putting his feet on solid ground and smelling the green grass that he has observed from the *St. George*.

As his company marches uphill to the small Royal Navy cemetery, they hear cannons fired from the bay and observe smoke coming from the portholes of the *St. George*. Twenty-one shots are fired now. William asks one of the British seamen about this and he is told that the old British King George III, who gave had given name to the flagship *St. George III,* together with the Saint George, is celebrating his 73rd birthday this very day.

King George III does not have a pleasant birthday this year. He has entered the final stages of insanity, from which he shall never recover. His servants have to tie him in a chair to feed him. His son, the Crown Prince William, Prince of Wales, will reign now.

Even the Americans have known King George III for a very long time. He was King of England when the Americans declared their independence from the British throne in 1776.

At 8:30, that evening, Flag Captain Daniel Gurion orders the boats taken in and William and his company of mariners return from Hanö to the *St. George*.

William talks with an old English seaman this evening, and learns that the entrance prison ship he had been a prisoner on, the *Royal William*, was named after the English Crown Prince, and the flagship *St. George* he is now on was named after the King. William laughs to himself and sarcastically says to William Freeman, 'Now we can tell our American countrymen if we ever return what it is like to be ruled by both the English King and the Crown Prince."

At the Royal Navy Baltic summer station, Captain Gurion has firm control over the men in crew, and punishments are resumed for the first time since arrival here. Four men are punished for drunkenness with 24 lashes each.

On June 6, Rear Admiral of the Blue James Sammaurez sends a report to Rear Admiral of the Red C. W. Reynolds concerning the condition of the Swedish Fleet.[119] The following day, the American William Alexander is again punished for contempt onboard *Defence.*

On the 7th, a seaman drowns and four others succeed in escaping when the launch of *St. George* is on shore on Hanö Island. This exciting news spreads through the entire crew very quickly. The crew is relieved to realize that escape is actually possible and each of them, in their own thoughts, prays that the four seamen will succeed in getting away.

William's brain is in high gear now. This is exactly why he entered the *St. George* instead of sitting in a prison ship in the Roads of Portsmouth. William wants that same kind of opportunity to escape, and wonders if the time has come. He knows damn well how dangerous it might be. A seaman who tries to escape and is caught will be flogged. But the nonnegotiable penalty for mariners who try to escape the Royal Navy is death. So William cannot afford one single mistake, *if* he tries to escape. The British mariners hold Hanö Island, a small island and very easily overlooked. It is four miles from the Swedish mainland, too far to swim but close enough when rowing a boat. So William concludes that escaping to Hanö makes no sense, at least while the boats are watched so closely.

St. George sends its mariners to Hanö for exercise on June 17. It is a fine sunny day. William has looked forward to a new chance to exercise his muscles on solid ground, and to be outdoors after all this time onboard ships. The rocky Hanö Island has only small trees and grass, and no civilians have ever lived there because the winter climate is too harsh. Local Swedish fishermen occasionally use the island as a dump for their fishing tools when they are fishing in the waters near the island, but they never built houses to live in. The surrounding Baltic Sea freezes and the island is packed with snow and ice in the winter season.

As William marches with the other Royal mariners, he tries to recall the last time he had been walking in the nature at home. It was when he walked along the Brandywine River with Mary Ann two years ago.

This same morning, *Defence* is still anchored in Vinga Sound as *Orion* arrives together with *Vanguard, Shieldrake,* and a large convoy of merchant ships from the Baltic Sea. The merchant ships are on their way back to England, and *Defence* uses the chance to get rid of all the prisoners collected from the many prizes it had taken while patrolling in the Cattegat. The prisoners are now transferred by boat to *Vanguard* so they can be sent to prison entrance ships when convenient. Then at 9:30 a.m., *Defence* goes down in the Cattegat with *Cressy, Gordon, Shieldrake, Buizer* and a new convoy of merchant ships that are inward bound.

The following day John and Amos observe Anholt Island covered in haze. This is not ideal weather for the convoy to pass the Great Belt and Danish privateers' cannon boats.

Despite the unfavorable weather, *Defence* manages to return two ships taken by the Danes back to the convoy.

The sloop *Ranger* is anchored at Danzig Bay on the south coast of the Baltic Sea. She reports to Rear Admiral Reynolds that a new group of French privateers has been observed, but because they all have their sails down, they do not look fit for fighting.[119] The French privateers entered the Baltic Sea through the thin Kiel Channel and avoided the time-consuming voyage into the North Sea and around Jutland to reach the Baltic Sea. The French privateers are looking forward to capturing American ships, as Napoleon ordered earlier this year.

On June 20, *Defence* is in the Great Belt and at 2:30 a.m., loosens the topsail and signals to the convoy's merchant ships to weigh, then repeats her signal by firing several guns to gather the convoy.

At 5 a.m., the launch is sent to assist ships that might be in trouble. Amos and John are at their posts. As Captain of the Forecastle, John is in a good position to overlook the entire battle scene in the Great Belt, between the Royal Navy mariners in their launches, barges and jollyboats on the one side, and the Danish mariners in their cannon boats and Danish privateers in their schooners on the other. John is thankful of his new post now it is summer time, because last time he passed the

Great Belt, he was below deck, in the powder room. But John doesn't like what he sees now. He is definitely on the side of the Danes, but this is not the time or place to express his thoughts, which would be considered quite radical by the officers on the quarterdeck of *H.M.S. Defence*.

As assistant carpenter, Amos is alert and ready to repair any new holes made in *Defence's* hull during the fight by Danish cannon balls or rifle bullets. He and his crew are also ready to repair damages to the woodwork in the rigging. Because the Danes no longer have any real Navy third-raters, it is unlikely that *Defence* will be severely damaged. The officers told the ordinary crewmembers this, so Amos is alert but calm, standing on the deck and trying to follow the battle.

The following day, *Defence* is still in the Great Belt. At 9:30, Danish gunboats make preparations to attack the convoy of merchant ships. The convoy is ordered to gather around *Defence,* and *Shieldrake* weighs to go and meet the cannon boats. *Dictator* has put down anchor in an attempt to turn the ship around to set out the launch with several Hawsers for the counterattack. But they are rushed, and one of the wires strikes the heavy launch with Hawsers and men, which sinks in very few seconds.

On June 23, the sky above the Great Belt is filled with thundering and lightning. *Defence*'s carpenters, including Amos, are sent out in the boats to repair a gunboat. Amos is nervous on the sea surface in a small boat in the middle of the Great Belt, with thunder and lightning all around him. It is not a pleasant experience. Amos knows from English seamen onboard the *Defence* that they can easily be surprised and attacked by Danish cannon boats here. At 9:00 p.m., Amos and the other carpenters finally return to *Defence*.

The following day, *Defence* is still in the Great Belt and is met by *Hero, Platagenet, Woodlark, Fly,* and a convoy of merchant ships going north and coming from the Baltic Sea.

June 24, there is a fresh breeze over Hanö Bay and dark clouds cover the entire sky. The bad weather that *Defence* experienced yesterday in the Great Belt has moved east, over Zealand and Skaane, and is now slowly approaching Hanö Bay. A party of seamen is sent to shore at Hanö Island from the flagship *St. George* to assist the building of a slaughterhouse for cattle. It's easier to transport dead meat to ships anchored in the in the bay, than living cattle in small boats.

Around midnight, it is raining heavily in the bay, and the storm is increasing in strength. Lightning bolts lighten up the dark sky over the bay and one strikes the main mast on *Den Helder*, anchored close to the flagship *St. George*.[114] The flash is followed by an enormous rolling bang that temporarily deafens William and others on the upper deck on the ships close to *Den Helder*. The noise is so loud that Rear Admiral Reynolds and the captains and officers on all the ships set down their wineglasses and rise from their chairs. They rush to the gallery windows or onto the bridge to find out what has happened.

As the lightning illuminates windows in the galleries of these ships, officers and captains stand with the watch crews on the upper decks and look silently at the fire burning on *Den Helder'* ssplintered mast. The mast sustained much damage. From the deck of the *St. George*, William watches the surprised guard crew onboard *HMS Hero*. All the men are frightened and see the mast damage as a bad sign.

It has been more than 130 years since Isaac Newton published his theories on the fundamental governing equations of the universe's basic natural forces. Knowledge of these fundamental physical equations should refute superstition among these educated officers and ordinary crewmembers, but deep in their hearts they still fear signs and omens. These are still valuable concepts in the human search for deeper understanding of otherwise incomprehensible phenomena occurring in life.

The following day, Reynolds stands on the poop deck and enjoys the fine weather following the awful night. He quietly follows the loading of 7,187 pounds of good Swedish potatoes that are received onboard the *St. George* this day.

On June 26, *Tremendous* arrives with two prizes taken in the Baltic Sea and good fresh Swedish beef is received onboard *St. George*.

6

William has found a pleasant spot on the main deck of *St. George* in the fine weather of June 28. He enjoys the sunshine as his hawk's eyes carefully inspect the coastline of the Swedish mainland, looking for farmers working in the fields. He tries to recall Wilmington and the beautiful early morning view from the top of the hill near the Academy. In weather like today, it is possible to see miles away over the Christina River despite the light summer morning haze.

He had enjoyed the breathtaking view of the many turns in the river from the Christina Bridge downstream to Wilmington, where it flows lazily past the wharves and harbor front on the northern bank. On a warm summer morning, mosquitoes dance in chaotic patterns above the long, wet grass close to the southern bank, opposite John Warner's wharf. From the Academy, the view of sunrise over Delaware Bay, to the northeast over the Brandywine and Delaware Rivers, was always magnificent.

William hopes he will soon be able to stand on the top of that Wilmington hill again.

He has decided what to write and begins his third letter to his wife Mary Ann in Wilmington.

Hanö Bay June 28th, 1811.
Onboard His Majesty's Ship St. George

My dear wife Mary Ann Watson,

Since I wrote you the last time, when I was imprisoned onboard the Royal Navy's Entrance prison ship, anchored in Portsmouth, much has happened. In order to give myself a chance to escape, I volunteered to serve on a man-o-war. In late September 1810, I was transferred from a prison ship behind the entrance ship to a prison on shore. Then on March 4 this year, I was mustered on the flagship HMS St. George.

I have written twice to Mr. Limma, the American Agent for seamen in London, to inform him about my situation and to make him send me a protection certificate, because I have lost the one I had myself. I have received no answer. The same way, my dear wife, I have received no letters from you. I hope you are well and hopefully also our child to whom you must have given birth.

I will ask you to go to the Port Collector Allen McLane and ask him to make me a protection certificate and send it to me.

Dear wife, I send you my love.

Mariner William Watson
Onboard His Majesty's ship St. George.

William puts the letter on the warm deck for a couple of minutes so it can dry. Then he takes it up and reads it twice. He has not written much in the past few years, and feels it best to check the content of the letter carefully. Finally, he folds it and puts it in an envelope. He writes Mary Ann's name and address on the front of it and goes to deliver it to the mail officer for shipping.

As often before this summer of 1811, a whole week goes by with no wind and a clear blue sky in the northwestern part of Europe and along the US east coast. The fine weather allows the officers and the seamen onboard the Royal Navy Ships in Hanö Bay to relax. Sometimes it is extremely hot. It is hot in Wilmington, too.

This warm morning, Allen McLane sits on a barrel on the harbor front at the Christina River and enjoys the sight of the slowly floating cool water. He occasionally smiles to himself. It's funny how he always remembers the important days in his life during the Revolutionary War. Today, exactly 33 years ago, he fought so bravely in the Battle of Monmouth.

In the apartment in Water Street close to the river, Mary Ann has completely recovered psychologically from her stillbirth, and now can concentrate her concerns on William. She spends much time wondering where William and his ship the *St. George* are right now.

He will certainly not be happy when he discovers that his good friend Damian Starr was killed, she thinks. Mary Ann had made it a rule to visit Samuel's grave in the graveyard surrounding the Old Swedes Church when she visits the grave of William's and her child. Since the funeral, the grave has been covered with fresh flowers every time she comes by for a short visit. Some of their friends visit that grave, too.

This summer, William Lyman reported back from London to the Department of State that far from being impressed, many American sailors were actually appearing "on the beach" in British ports. [185] They are unable to find jobs onboard arriving merchant ships, which already have full crews, so these American seamen are sometimes forced to think about entering a Royal Navy man-o-war just to make a living. As far as the Royal Navy is concerned, they can stay on the beach until they decide to enter a man-o-war voluntarily, as William Watson and William Freeman were forced to do, to get a real chance to escape.

On June 27, *Defence* is still sailing in the Great Belt, in a thick haze and a light breeze. Eight seamen are punished this day.

Two days later, the butchers from *St. George* are sent to the Hanö shore to slaughter some bullocks, which have been delivered to the newly erected slaughterhouse.

On June 30, *Defence* is at the north end of the island Langeland. At 4:20, in the early morning light, several Danish gunboats are observed near land. John and Amos have just been assigned their posts this morning, and both of them follow the situation intently. It seems as though the Danish boats await the appropriate time to come close to the British convoy.

At 3:30 in the afternoon, the squadron's small boats are sent against the Danish gunboats, which begin to fire heavily.

A battery manned with Danish mariners is observed on the island of Langeland, but the Royal Navy officers know that the fortifications of these Danish batteries along the shores are normally well manned. They will never dare to send in landing forces to try and destroy the batteries in close fights. It is simply too dangerous to the royal marines.

At 7:30 in the evening, John notices that the Royal Navy boats return and two wounded royal mariners are carried to sick quarters. The whole scene makes John and Amos sad. That evening, when the two of them stand at the bulwark on the forecastle, they speak mostly of Boston and people they know there. Without any special expression of emotions, John says, "Amos, are you aware that it's been more than six years sin ce I left Salem to sail from Boston harbor? I haven't had any contact with anyone from home since that day. My mother must be convinced that I'm dead now."

"Yes, it's kind of unreal. I hope for both of us that an opportunity to escape comes along soon. Maybe when we finally arrive at the summer station at Hanö," Amos answers. 'It will definitely give us a better chance to escape," Amos continues, trying to encourage his friend.

It is now July 1. Rear Admiral of the Red C.W. Reynolds has seriously considered the preparations necessary before his squadron of the Royal Navy Baltic Fleet and its convoy can return to England[110] later this autumn. He now orders all the ships anchored in Hanö Bay under his command to take in food supplies in large quantities and make other necessary preparations. At the same time, he orders the ship carpenters to go ashore on the island to help build another house, to be finished for the winter. This will establish Hanö as a Royal Navy station to other nation's ships that might pass by in the winter season, when the Royal Navy's ships and crews have returned to England.[64]

The following day, *St. George* begins to take in supplies. She receives 1,840 pounds of good beef and 2,300 pounds of fine potatoes from the Blekinge area from shore. Then *St. George* supplies the hospital ship *Gordon* with some of the Blekinge potatoes.

The Swedish merchants at Matvik harbor can earn a lifetime's income on summer trade with the Royal Navy, and are extremely happy that the Royal Navy has chosen to make their summer station here in Hanö Bay. The Swedish merchants stand silently and laid-back on the quay, with their hands in their long trouser pockets, eagerly surveying the many small boats on the bay that are transporting articles, for which they have been well paid, to the Royal Navy ships.

The following day, Rear Admiral Reynolds receives from the Admiralty the permission to sign a contract with the merchant company Sally and Sons, and the Naval Stores that cover the protection of their ships back to England.[111]

This July 4th is another mighty fine day with a clear blue sky. William Watson and William Freeman stand on the forecastle of *St. George* and follow the many activities on the island of Hanö. William is not as happy on this Independence Day as he has been on previous ones. He is aware that it is exactly 35 years since the United States of America declared its independence in Philadelphia, just 40 miles north of his hometown, Wilmington. William is sure the day will be celebrated properly at home and in other villages in the United States.

He is sure that Mary Ann, her mother, and all their friends with their families will be out celebrating this important day. But he and the other American prisoners onboard the flagship *St. George* and other Royal ships in the squadron are in British captivity, with nothing to celebrate. Still, William sincerely hopes that all the people he knows and cares for back home will have a good day.

Official America is also seriously celebrating today. President James Madison, the 'father of the Constitution," is making a fine speech to a large crowd, including Secretary of State James Monroe.

Congressman Thomas Jefferson is also very proud this day. It feels like hardly yesterday that he wrote the Declaration of Independence, and now 35 years have already gone by. Allen McLane is also participating in the celebration of this day, together with Thomas Mendenhall and many other prominent citizens of Wilmington. All over the country, the traditional 13 toasts are made over and over again in large and small crowds gathered all along the U.S. east coast.

Any child would see happiness on the faces of the men and women gathered this day, but one who looks closely would also see small signs of worry. Some of the men and women present live or work in east coast port cities, and they know that the United States of America is not truly independent and free this day. Many American seamen are still impressed onboard the British Royal Navy ships, and many American merchant ships are still routinely and wrongly confiscated on the open sea or in European ports. They know this through their official work or the stories told by family members working in the ports, from revenue officers, wharf-owners, merchants, captains, seamen, and port workers. Many get their information on impressments from local newspaper articles describing in detail the narratives given by quite a number of captains or seamen released from impressment.

On this July 4, there is no doubt in President James Madison's mind that a majority of the American population will call for war against England if the situation on impressments does not improve radically very soon.

Joseph and Mary Warner and their children are in Wilmington today visiting his mother. John Freed, Jr. is with his wife and kids, as are William Windell and Enoch Lang. But Mary Ann and her mother are not really celebrating this day, as William imagines. They prefer to stay at home in the apartment in Water Street. Mary Ann can't keep her thoughts from William.

Onboard *Defence,* Amos and John are standing at the forecastle, enjoying the fine weather this day. They look at the island of Sprogø in the middle of the Great Belt, where *Defence* is trying to locate some Danish cannon boats to fight. The boats have somehow managed to keep out of sight.

After a period of silence, Amos says, "I'm quite sure my family is having a fine picnic on one of the lawns in Boston this fine day."

"Yes, you are probably righ t," John Brown replies. "I would almost give my right arm myself to be back in Salem this day. Since I was a kid, it has been a tradition to celebrate this honorable day to the fullest. I hate to miss the fireworks at midnight."

"It's only seven mile s to shore. Why don't we take a swim and go celebrate this thirty-fifth anniversary of our independence with our good friends the Danes?" Amos jokes, trying to get his thoughts away from their depressing state of captivity. John doesn't answer.

In Boston, Amos Stevens's large family is indeed celebrating this Independence Day. The family members occasionally cheer Amos while they picnic, to show each other that he is not forgotten. Because they have each other, they are much less worried than John Brown's mother. They received a letter from Amos describing his impressment onboard the *Defence.* He informed them that he is still employed as a ship's carpenter, as was the case when he worked on the New York ship that took him to Liverpool. In the letter, Amos told his family that it was considerably more work assisting the chief ship carpenter, as they were sent out in a boat to work on the man-o-wars and merchant ships within the entire fleet.

Further up the coast, in Salem, John's mother is not having m uch fun this day. She can't keep her thoughts from her only son, whom she has not seen in more than six years. She is convinced that he must have drowned. Her friend from the soup kitchen line also has a son who is impressed, and this woman tries to comfort John's mother, but she is becoming more and more depressed with each year that passes. She has tried several times to ask about him at the port collector's office in Salem, but each time is told that searching for a man with a common name like John Brown among the many Royal Navy ships is like searching for a needle in a haystack. She should forget all about it, they tell her. The name is simply too common.

When the friendly, obliging Salem port collector carefully and respectfully explains this to her, she has no problem understanding how difficult it might be to find her son. But a few hours after she returns to her flat, she finds it unbearable that nobody in the world can tell her if her son is even alive, now that he has been missing for more than six years.

Until July 5, *Defence* spends most of its time cruising in the Great Belt, with very few enemy confrontations. At 1:15 a.m., several lights are observed on the sea surface by the lookout, and all officers on duty on Royal Navy ships in the convoy are alarmed. In the Great Belt, you never know what is approaching. It could be a few cannon boats or many. *Defence* quickly sends out its armed boats to assist and protect the merchant ships. When daylight finally breaks a couple of hours later, it reveals no less than 22 well-armed Danish gunboats attacking the convoy from different positions. The fight between the Danish and English boats goes back and forth for several hours.

In the early afternoon, *Defence*'s exhausted mariners are forced to return, because a thick fog once again covers the Great Belt, making it impossible to see and attack the enemy gunboats. This is ideal for the Danish gunboats, but officers on the English ships and the mariners in the boats are cursing heavily.

Captain Atkins is visibly irritated when he speaks to the officers on the bridge. 'It seems as though this thick fog arrives right on time, every time we manage to get our boats in position to attack the enemy." Atkins is increasingly frustrated. 'The Danes alre ady have the advantage of being in well known waters, and now our battleships and the convoy we're supposed to protect are helpless, glued to the sea surface. And there's nothing we can do about it. How come God decided to take the Danish side every time we pass the Great Belt?"

At 4:20 a.m., a gust of wind swirls around *Defence*'s hull, pushing the fog back for a few minutes, long enough for John to see, from the forecastle, that a Danish gunboat full of aggressive mariners prepared to fight for their lives is sneaking in on *Defence*'s boats.

The bridge is alerted and Captain Atkins immediately orders three cannon shots fired. The gunboat is struck and several Danish mariners severely hurt. John sees boats from the *Dictator* rapidly approaching the Danish gunboat. British mariners soon board the cannon boat, and 54 Danish prisoners are taken to the *Cressy*, which is sailing on its own for the time being, chasing several other Danish gunboats.

Cressy catches up with one gunboat at 11:00 a.m., and at the same time *Sheldrake* meets another. Ship's carpenters, including Amos, are dispatched to a merchant ship in the convoy to repair damages on the mast and the rigging. The Danes successfully shot at her, but have not been able to take her yet.

An hour past noon, *Defence* has the Danish gunboat, taken as prize, in a tow. At 9:30 p.m., Amos and the other tired ship carpenters and sailmakers return to their ships after a long busy day. *Defence* withdraws to the northern end of the Great Belt near Hjerm Island to find a quiet place to anchor for the night, and to avoid danger from the presence of the many Danish cannon boats further south, near their headquarters in the port of Corsør.

Before they turn in that evening, Amos and John stand for half an hour at the bulwark on the dark top deck of *Defence*. John whispers, "Amos, the *Defence* and I were involved in the Campaign against Copenhagen in the autumn of 1807. Did you know that? As an American, I'm not particularly proud of this. Participating in today's attack against Danish cannon boats in their own waters is nothing to be proud of, either." John stares down toward the cold dark water for a minute or two, then continues, 'See the lights in the houses along the Danish shore? Most of the Danes are sleeping peacefully now. It's a friendly nation in there, and I don't like being part of this occupation force at all. The Royal Navy has no high moral ground to stand on, being here in the Great Belt. Unfortunately, escape is out of the question under the given circumstances." Suddenly an officer shows up behind them and demands that they return to their hammocks. John and Amos slowly walk toward the staircases to go and get some sleep. They are both very tired and fall asleep within minutes of climbing in their hammocks.

The next day, at 4:00 a.m., Amos and other carpenters from *Defence* are up early and sent onboard some of the damaged merchant ships in the convoy to assist the local carpenters repairing masts and riggings. Admiral Dixon and his flagship *Vigo* are also present now.

A Danish sloop joins the convoy and the sloop answers a signal from *Cressy*'s Captain Charles D. Pater. Shortly after, the Danish sloop receives a new set of hammocks from *Cressy*. If military personnel on the Danish mainland discover such a co-operation with the enemy, it will be cause for a stiff penalty for that Danish captain.

Sunday July 7. *Defence* has, over a period of time, gathered a lot of prisoners taken by British gun brigs and frigates in the fighting against the Danish gunboats. All super numerous men and Danish prisoners onboard the *Defence* are sent to *Cressy*. *Dictator,* which spends most of its time patrolling in the Cattegat this year, and *Vigo,* which takes care of the Great Belt now, are both anchored outside the British station at Anholt this day.

Onboard *St. George,* Admiral Reynolds receives a short note from one of his subordinate officers reporting that six men have escaped from the fleet in Hanö Bay. Every time Royal Navy seamen escape, it's an eve nt of great interest to all the other ordinary crewmembers onboard ships in the navy. The news spreads like wildfire.

When William Watson and William Freeman get the news, they both began to consider making an escape themselves. But they see the increased surveillance that is applied onboard the *St. George* almost immediately after the escape of the seamen was known, and they drop the idea right away. But it was still quite heartening to both of them to realize that escape from a Royal Navy ship is possible after all.[111] Just the idea that escape could be possible makes captivity much more tolerable.

On July 10, Rear Admiral of the Blue James Sammaurez sends a letter to Reynolds, informing him that a convoy of 70 merchant ships has departed Vinga Sound, on its way south toward Hanö. The convoy is presently approaching the Great Belt.[125]

The following day, *Defence* is anchored at Anholt and four seamen are punished severely for drunkenness. Thomas Lowe is once again among the punished men. This war is simply too much for a man with his kind of intelligence and sensitive mind.

In Hanö Bay, the gunner onboard the *H.M. Sloop Ranger* asks Rear Admiral Reynolds for a yearly account of his arms and ammunition.[108] The captain of *HMS Helder,* sailing near Falsterbo, sends Reynolds a letter informing him that a Danish ship has been taken as a prize and sent to Hanö. The main mast on *Den Helder* is not in good condition since it was struck by lightning that midnight on the 24th of June.[115]

On Sunday July 14, the body of a dead seaman is found in the water close to the *St. George*. The seaman drowned in an attempt to escape from *Den Helder*. His body is shortly after committed to the sea once again after a simple Divine Service.

The following day the butchers from *St. George* are sent to shore to continue to slaughter bullocks. The large fleet demands huge amounts of meat.

In his office in the customhouse building in Front Street, Allen McLane sits at his desk staring out the window. He has done so frequently this summer. It is too hot for him to stay outside in the sun today, and so he prefers to spend time at his desk in the cool office room.

The room is quiet, making it impossible for him to keep his thoughts from wandering back, to the summer of 1776.

"It is July 1776, and with some difficulty he is crossing the Delaware River on his way to General Washington's camp outside New York. The Delaware Militia is being fitted out at the moment in New Castle and Kent Counties. That militia will be under the command of Delaware Colonel John Haslet, under order of the Congress in Philadelphia. This militia is ready to march to Washington's camp in late July, early enough to arrive before the fighting with the British begins.

McLane is not part of the Delaware Regiments, but knows one of the captains in the First Company, Joseph Stridham[1], a descendant of the surgeon Tymen Stridham from Wilmington. Tymen Stridham was one of the earliest European settlers in Wilmington. McLane arrives just south of New York in August and celebrates his 30th birthday there on August 8.

He thinks about his wife, Maria, a lot this day, and hopes that this war will soon be over so he can return home and they can start a family.

He knows that 30 is long past the average male age for having one's first child. But then he recalls that, having given his Oath to defend Congress and his country with life and fortune, he will not put children into this world before he considers it safe enough for a child to live in.

He hopes that his wife isn't too affected, seeing the many adorable children of their friends while he is away fighting to achieve independence for the country and freedom for its people. She never speaks of it when they are together, and he guesses that she understands that his oath holds him to a promise that he must fulfill. Someone has to take the lead in the world, he thinks to himself and now he had partly done that himself.

Washington, other leaders of the Continental Army, and other patriots, like him, are fully aware of the strategic possibilities of the area around New York. New York itself poses serious problems for its defenders, surrounded as it is by many bodies of water that invite the Royal Navy to get into strong positions with its man-o-wars.

Washington sends one of his trusted and experienced generals, Charles Lee, to establish the defense of New York. He estimates that New York can't be held in the long run, but well fortified, it can cause serious losses to the British. Before completing the fortifications, Lee is sent south to help save Charleston, leaving Washington's Army, which has just arrived from Boston, alone. Washington has begun to build Fort Lee on the west side of the Hudson River and Fort Washington on the Manhattan side to guard the entrance to the North or the Hudson River.

To make any kind of an effective fight for New York City, it is necessary to make a dangerous division of the American Army. Large contingents of men and quantities of artillery have to be ferried across the East River to Long Island where the heights of Brooklyn is a central strategic point for the defense of lower Manhattan.

The Royal Navy's ships have already poured more than 12,000 troops onto Staten Island. McLane and other men are ferried over to Brooklyn, along with the Delaware and Maryland regulars under the command of Sterling.

Every soldier, from the lowest rank to the highest, is frightened by the thought of the massive number of Royal Navy's ships anchored outside Sandy Hook, and the huge numbers of mariners that are expected to invade Long Island at any moment. If the Royal Navy's ships then choose the available solution of a quick entrance to the East River, the Brooklyn regiments will be exposed to great danger.

For once, McLane is afraid although not directly scared. Commander in Chief George Washington and others swore, that day in Philadelphia, a few blocks from where McLane was born, that they would protect Congress with their life and fortune, and he still feels comfortable with that decision.[133] Washington states the seriousness of this New York situation in a letter to a Connecticut colonel: 'Since the settlement of these colonies, there has never been such just occasion of alarm or such an appearance of an enemy, both by sea and land".

The lines are finally assembled. General James Grant's soldiers are on their right, against Sterling, who claims he is of Scottish earldom and is known to be a hard drinking officer, and the Delawareans and Marylanders.

At the center, Sullivan fights against General Von Heister' s Germans. Clinton, who has made the plan, together with Howe, makes a sweep into Sullivan's rear flank. Sterling and his men fight heroically and, though greatly outnumbered, hurl back the soldiers under Grant's command. To raise the spirit among his own men, Sterling tells them that General Grant "...has boasted before Parliament, that he can march from the one end of America to the other with only 5,000 men."

In the center of the battle scene, the brave American men are resisting fiercely, but are beginning to give way when the British, right after a night-long march over the Jamaica Road, crash down upon Sullivan's rear flank. Sterling's Delaware and Maryland regulars deliver a tough fight, even after they are surrounded on three sides. As George Washington happens to see this he exclaims, 'Good God, what brave fellows I must this day lose."

Sullivan and Sterling are finally captured and the American losses are roughly 1,500 against less than 400 British. McLane thinks that the British have, unfortunately, shown themselves as more professional soldiers.

Howe now has total control. The American survivors stream back to the Brooklyn entrenchment in panic and Washington shouts furiously to the retreating fearful soldiers, 'Remember what you are contending for!" To everyone's surprise, Howe gives no order to charge and two days later Washington has escaped back to New Jersey, where, to their luck, no British fleet stops them from crossing the East River. On August 29, they escape successfully under cover of an American fog. In less than nine hours, 9,000 men are ferried to Manhattan in flat-bottomed boats. In the fighting on Long Island, McLane and the other Delawareans find themselves fit and their efforts noticed.

A conference is held on Staten Island between the Americans and the British. John Adams, Benjamin Franklin and Admiral Howe are there, among others, but as the Americans demand recognition of independence as a prior condition to negotiation, the two parties soon split with no results.

New York cannot be held and burning it down is out of the question. Washington and Howe act slowly in the days to come. Howe is focused on using New York's docking facilities to establish a base on the mainland for use of his fleet, and purposely overlooks Washington's troops on Manhattan.Washington and his men somehow ignore that they are in just as much danger on Manhattan, accessible from all sides by the British fleet.[208] Maybe both the British and American leadership just want to achieve their goals without losing too many men." [208]

McLane's thoughts are suddenly brought back to his Customhouse office, when John Freed, Jr speaks to him. 'Sir, I brought yo u a cup of hot coffee."

'Oh, thank you very much my young man," McLane replies, genuinely surprised, giving him an encouraging smile, 'That was certainly a kind thing to do."

Every one in the Customhouse office has noticed how absent-minded McLane has become. William Windell and John Freed, Jr. discuss it from time to time. They both know that McLane is recalling great moments in American History. They know he played an important role in the Revolutionary War, but can't help thinking that McLane wasn't involved in that many battles. But they don't know for sure. They have to trust his words.

The following day, Rear Admiral Dixon and *Vigo* are outside Rostock, in the south end of the Baltic Sea. He informs Rear Admiral Reynolds by letter that *Censor* and *Diligence* from his fleet have been ordered to go to Hanö to help escort the convoy of merchant ships back to England. *Diligence* will go directly for Hanö, and *Censor* for Bornholm.[108]

This same day, *St. George* mariner Thomas Simians, whom William knows very well and who has been punished several times before, is being 'flogged through the Fleet."

A seaman dies at 4:30 in the morning of July 26 onboard the *St. George*. At 10, his effects and clothes are sold at the main mast and, at 6:30 in the evening, the body is sent with a boat to Hanö to be buried the following day in the small Royal Navy cemetery on the island. *St. George's* priest performs the simple ceremony for the funeral of a common seaman in the Royal Navy. A mariner ends the ceremony by blowing the rhythmically simple 'the last post" in his horn, and the small group of men returns to the *St. George*.

July 31. Rear Admiral Reynolds is informed that the carpenter on the hospital ship *Gorgon* had been crippled by a fall from the main mast, and they request a new carpenter sent from England. Reynolds temporarily sends *Gordon* the carpenter from *Sirius*.[109] It is so late in the year, that a new carpenter from England might arrive so late that the fleet would already be on its way home. The same day, Flag Captain Gurion orders the punishment of seven seamen.

On August 6, *Defence* is still anchored in Vinga Sound as *Cressy*, *Mars*, *Orion*, *Vanguard*, and *Grasshopper* depart with a convoy heading for Hanö. *Woodlark* arrives in Hanö Bay.

On Monday the 7th, the seamen and the mariners onboard the *St. George* exercise using the cannons and rifles, and the mariners try to fire blank cartridges. William much prefers going to Hanö Island for the exercise, to get solid ground under his feet. He loved these trips, and looked forward to each and every one of them.

The squadron ship crews are beginning to get restless, preparing mentally for the dangerous trip home to England, escorting the convoy of valuable and fully loaded merchant ships through Danish waters. The impressed Americans are kept onboard now and constantly monitored to prevent escape. Escape is difficult from the small Island of Hanö, but it is more likely to succeed this time of year, because many boats and ships are appearing in the bay close to the island, making it easy to steal one if they are let out of sight for a short moment.

Port collector Allen McLane is celebrating his 71st birthday this day of August 8. Revenue officer William Windell hoists the Stars and Stripes over the Customhouse building before McLane shows up at work this morning. As he approaches the entrance of the building, they all shout at the top of their lungs, 'Congratulations, Allen McLane, congratulations." He replies, smiling, "Thank you, all of you." H e looks honestly flattered. The customhouse is small and has few employees, so they never forget each other's birthdays.

Friday August 9, *Defence* unmoors in Vinga Sound, and at midnight is in company with *Princess Caroline*, *Prince William*, *Tweed*, *Cocuette,* and a convoy of merchant ships heading south through Cattegat toward

Hanö. Two days later, *Defence* meets a convoy of merchant ships under the command of the captain of *Den Helder.*

At the same time, William Lyman sit in his London office, coughing heavily as he writes a consular letter to Secretary of State James Monroe.[185]

Lyman tells him that there is a problem with the American administration with respect to impressments. The net flow of seamen out of American ships is negative now, meaning that British seamen flee from Royal Navy's ships to American merchant ships outnumber Americans impressed into Royal Navy ships. As long as the American merchant ships are allowed to freely pass on with their cargo, this situation is in the favor of the American economy. So Secretary of State James Monroe and Pinkney, in ongoing talks with the British administration, make no further objection to impressments from British ports.[126] In effect, in order to protect the American trade and the merchant and ship owners, the administration gives up a strong position on impressed American merchant seamen onboard the Royal Navy ships. The topic of impressments is still not negotiated.

Lyman himself is beginning to feel that he might be seriously sick, and that this is not helping the impressed American seamen who send him letters in the hope of being released. Lyman has been working too hard for far too long, and now it has apparently become pay back time.

The release of seamen like William Watson, John Brown and Amos Stevens demands a firm attitude toward human rights by employees in the American States administration, rights so deeply founded in the American Constitution. In the scales of justice, Congress and the President are forced to balance one scale holding the freedom for impressed American seamen against the other scale, with American foreign trade. It is a delicate balance between the rights of seamen and the rights of merchants.

The seamen, sons of those who fought so bravely to liberate America and earn its independence, are now deprived their personal freedom. Even two nephews of George Washington are impressed onboard Royal Navy ships for a time.

On August 12, the weather is fine in Hanö Bay and *St. George* is rigged with colors. All ships in the Royal Navy fire a salute of 21 shots to commemorate the birthday of his Royal Highness, the Prince Regent

William. News of King George III's insanity, the reason the Crown Prince has taken over, reaches the Bay of Hanö and the Royal Navy ships there. The crew of *St. George* sees this as a bad sign for their flagship. They worry that the return to England will not be safe. It is a good thing that no one onboard recalls the myth about the destiny of the Saint George for which the flagship is also named.

Allen McLane sits at his desk and reads a two-day-old copy of the *American Watchman and Delaware Republican*. This reminds him that it has been 35 years today since he took part in the Battle at Long Island.

"Although skeptical, King George III does not want to interfere in the decisions made in Parliament. It is now August 12, and both the Howe brothers leading British forces in North America have gathered a military force around New York on a scale never before seen, in order to take the city and make it a base for British military activities in North America.

As early as June 29, General Howe's 10,000 troops from Halifax moved south and are spotted outside Sandy Hook. Admiral Howe arrives 10 days later with 150 troop transport ships convoyed by a naval squadron, followed on this August 12 by the bulk of the European reinforcements, mostly Hessians. They are thoroughly nauseated from a long sea voyage with wormy biscuits and rotting pork.

William Howe seeks 20,000 men in addition to his Halifax detachment, and now has more than 32,000 troops all in all, as well as mountains of supplies and equipment. Admiral Howe simultaneously can engage the enemy with 73 warships manned by 13,000 men, nearly 45 percent of all the ships and men on active service in the Royal Navy. With the assistance of his brother, the general, Admiral Howe is to assault coastal towns, shelter loyalists, dismantle American merchant ships, destroy armed vessels, and impress rebel seamen. Carleton's army in Canada adds up to 13,500 troops.

Howe genuinely hopes that George Washington and his men will retire inland, but the political pressure from the New York Provincial Congress on the Continental Congress in Philadelphia makes Washington eager to defend New York. The surroundings of New York therefore become the natural battle scene [208]. *In a quiet moment, George Washington thinks to himself that one certainly needs the ability to concentrate on fighting this war, knowing that to fight the British King George III, whose family comes from Hanover, Germany, means to fight the Hessians from Germany too."*

On August 20, *Defence* is at Vinga Sound. Eight seamen are punished, including Thomas Lowe, who, as often before on this voyage, receives 24 lashes for drunkenness.[44]

On its way to Hanö, *Defence* helps escort a convoy of merchant ships from Vinga Sound south through the Great Belt and to the Baltic Sea. The Danes have been waiting for this convoy to pass the belt, and every night the convoy stays here, the Danish cannon boats attack with great force.

One mariner from *Defence* is killed and one wounded in these fights.[28] Thanks to the determined captain Sir A. Dickson onboard the *Orion*, the Danes are constantly kept frustrated.[44]

James Monroe is quite satisfied with his achievements after only four months as Secretary of State. His staff has finally gone through several large piles of letters requesting copies of protection certificates for impressed American Seamen onboard the Royal Navy's ships.

Laid back in his desk chair, he lets his thoughts go back 35 years.

He had been appointed Lieutenant in the Third Virginian Regiment a year before. Now, in August 1776, Congress has ordered his regiment and a number of state infantries to New York. They arrive too late. The city has already been lost to the British. The commander in chief, George Washington, and his men are at the Harlem Heights." [208]

This same evening, Allen and Marie McLane sit quietly at the dinner table and eat their supper as they have done so often. The sound of silverware against china is all that breaks the silence. The two of them exchange looks once in a while, but Allen McLane's thoughts are also on the day 35 years ago.

On September 15, 1776, Howe finally lands a force at Kipp's Bay midway between New York City and the Harlem River. The Connecticut militia that is manning the coastal fortifications and two continental brigades soon flee in panic. To raise the morale of his men, Washington takes the lead, exposing himself to enemy bullets. He comes close to being captured. The British drive the Americans into the woods of Northern Manhattan. Howe afterwards spends a month in New York with a mistress, and Washington uses that time to evacuate his troops to the Bronx peninsula.

McLane march long miles with different foot regiments and is ferried over at Kingsbridge. Howe sends his ships up the Hell's Gate and the East River and Long Island Sound and disembarks troops at Pell's Point south of New Rochelle. Washington soon sees the danger and moves his troops northward, from Kingsbridge along the Bronx River, to White Plains in the state of New York. General William Howe arrives there five days later. [208] *McLane follows a regiment the 25 miles north from Kingsbridge to White Plains."* [133]

On September 21, Admiral Dixon's Flag Captain Gibson from *Vigo* reports to Admiral Reynolds that a new flotilla of French cannon boats has entered the Great Belt from the channel of Kiel.

The following day, September 22, 1811, William Lyman dies in Cheltenham, Gloucestershire England. He is only 56 years old. He is later buried outside Gloucester Cathedral in England. In Northampton, Massachusetts, where he was born, a cenotaph is made to his memory at the Old Cemetery. These two Williams never made contact, despite seaman William Watson's two letters to Agent for Seamen William Lyman, and although they had so much in common. William Watson was born in 1787 in Delaware, the first state to ratify American Independence and become the first state in the Union, on December 7, William Lyman's twenty-second birthday. Lyman was a democratic member of the Massachusetts State House of Representatives. Lyman had done all in his power, as head of the Agency for American Seamen in London, to help impressed American seamen. Now he was dead, and William Watson and other impressed American seamen could only pray that someone else would take over in London and try to protect their constitutional rights in the same way that William Lyman did.

A week later, on September 29, the captain onboard *HMS Hero*, who captured the captain of a merchant ship that stranded at the island of Læsø, asks Admiral Reynolds for permission to release the captain of that ship, who claims that he has a wife and six kids at home.[108]

The gunner onboard *Defence* asks Rear Admiral of the Red C. W. Reynolds for a yearly account of his stocks.[130]

It is the last day in September, and a breeze is rising, indicating that the first severe autumn storm will soon reach Hanö Bay. Flag Captain Daniel Gurion observes the ordinary crewmembers on the upper deck of the *St. George* washing their clothes at 10 o'clock in the morning. He stands on the quarterdeck with his hands behind his back, as William has often seen him do. William can see Gurion smile. Gurion is indeed satisfied as he stands and follows his crew working for some time. In a month or so he will have to break up the Royal Navy summer station here at Hanö and begin the voyage to escort the convoy of merchant ships and his squadron back home to England.

The captain stands with a stiff body as he rocks back and forth on his feet while he continues his reflections over the *St. George* squadron's voyage to the Baltic Sea this year. First, he addresses the discipline of the crew onboard the flagship. Gurion knows very well that his good friend Rear Admiral of the Red C. W. Reynolds is a true believer in hard discipline and exercises as the most important tools to produce a squadron of men fit for fight.

The first nine months of this year, 129 crewmembers on *St. George* have been sent to the hospital, 114 have been punished, some several times, 10 have died, and five managed to flee. This means that 253 crewmembers have suffered severely in these months, even before the return through the Great Belt and the North Sea begins. Gurion is very satisfied as he looks over the Swedish mainland, and has no second thoughts about the hard discipline applied onboard the *St. George*. The Baltic squadron's ships need to have very tough conditions. He is sure that he will experience mutiny at some point onboard ships under his command if he does not rule with a firm hand. The 253 persons out of an initial total crew of 730 means that 40 percent of *St. George*'s crew have something interesting to tell their fellow seamen at tables in the taverns or their families, when they return to England for Christmas. This includes those men who are so fortunate as to have returned alive from the hospitals, but he'll have to disregard the 10 who will never experience a Christmas again.

Gurion knows that his conduct onboard the *St. George* is in full compliance with how Rear Admiral of the Red C.W. Reynolds wants his

Baltic Squadrons run - with a firm hand. Reynolds is 60 years old, and his personality was formed a decade before the American and the French revolutions. His strong views on discipline at sea were formed and consolidated in the Royal Navy under the crack of the whip in his youth, and he has no respect whatsoever when it comes to disrespectful crewmembers onboard his ships. Reynolds likes the system just as it is, with him on the top of the pyramid, taking 50 percent of all prize money earned by the ships in his squadron. He honestly thinks it's fair.

The time for the Royal Navy Baltic Fleet to return to England is rapidly approaching. At a meeting between Rear Admiral of the Blue Sir James Sammaurez and the merchants William and Phillip Emes, owners of a large portion of the merchant ships in the convoy the Royal Navy will escort to England this autumn, November 1 is chosen for departure.

Sammaurez knows all too well that units of the Royal Navy, and the merchant fleet presently operating further north in the Baltic Sea, need to be out of these waters before the winter and the ice sets in the Baltic Sea and the narrow Danish Waters. The Rear Admiral clearly remembers a catastrophe three years ago, in December 1808, right here at Vinga Sound where his flagship *Victory* is anchored now. A large number of ships were smashed by heavy pack ice and went down, and when the second-rater the *HMS Crescent* tried to cross the North Sea, it went down on the sand reefs of the North West coast of Jutland. These events are still fresh in his mind, and he doesn't want to see this kind of disaster repeated, if he can do anything to prevent it.

Sammaurez told the two merchant ship owners that he wished to depart no later than October 1, to prevent the weather from bringing any unexpected surprises that might endanger the return to England. The Emes brothers argued strongly for November 1, so that all of their merchant ships would be able to return from the North Baltic Sea to Hanö Bay before the departure. But Rear Admiral of the Blue James Admiral Sammaurez finally gave in and accepted the November 1 date for the convoy of merchant ships and the Royal Navy military escort to depart the Baltic Sea[200] this year of 1811.

Unofficially, Sammaurez asked the Swedish government to agree that, in case of bad weather, the ships would be allowed to anchor for the winter in the little Swedish harbor of Matvik, on the mainland close to Hanö, if necessary. Officially, Sweden is trying to remain neutral, but the

King of Sweden and the administration in Stockholm look upon the Royal Navy's fight against Denmark with great admiration, and of benefit to Swedish interests in Norwegian territory.

If the Emperor Napoleon Bonaparte and his small Danish ally lose this ongoing war in Europe, then Sweden, by helping the British Royal Navy get good naval stations in Swedish waters, might be able to negotiate a takeover of the control of Norway from Denmark.

Rear Admiral of the Blue Sir James Sammaurez is worried for his ships and his men and fully aware of the risk he is taking by delaying the departure from Hanö. He takes his responsibility very seriously. His many years of service in the British Royal Navy are marked by great determination in many difficult situations, and so it is here, when he can see that it is of the greatest interest to England. Besides, Sammaurez is actually fond of staying here in the waters of Vinga Sound outside Gothenburg. Both the Danish consul and the Swedish authorities like him very much because of his personal character, and because of his strategic naval skills. Before England stole it, Denmark had the sixth largest fleet in the world, so mingling around the British Royal Navy's Commander of the Baltic Fleet is indeed honorable for both Danish as well as Swedish diplomats.

On October 6, Charles D. Pater, the captain of *HMS Cressy* is rowed to the flagship *Victory* to meet his superior, Rear Admiral of the Blue James Sammaurez. At the meeting, Captain Pater receives the order to depart immediately for Hanö to meet Reynolds' squadron and assist the return of this year's last convoy to England. Pater is also informed about the large number of armed Danish ships appearing in the Danish waters this year. From the flagship *Victory, Cressy* receives an enforcement of 40 mariners. Sammaurez gives Pater the last intelligence updates about the Danish Naval situation, that in the harbor of Kalundborg, on the Zealand side just at the entrance to the Great Belt, a large number of Danish cannon boats and armed ships have been observed lately and are probably waiting for their arrival.

On October 19, the gentleman John Watson is out for his regular walk along Market Street in Wilmington. He doesn't notice that he passes Mary Ann, who is on her way to Lower Market House to shop. From his late father, Colonel Thomas Watson, John Watson knows that this day 35 years ago was a very special day to both of them. John had been a boy then, but he remembers how proud his father had been when the two of them talked about that day later on. John lets his thoughts go back to the time when he lived on a farm with his family near Aitken town in Pen Cader Hundred, in the southwestern end of New Castle County.

"Exactly three and a half months after the Declaration of Independence in 1776, Captain and farmer Thomas Watson sold part of his land to his Colonel in the Delaware Militia, a farmer, Thomas Cooch. Cooch was a neighbor living with his family on a farm on the south side of the Christina Creek near the bridge that bears his name, Cooch's Bridge, just west of Iron Hill, where the first Walesian settlers made their homes many years ago."

Four days later, on the morning of October 23, a young Wilmington postman jumps easily up the stairs and knocks on the door to the apartment on the first floor in Water Street. Mary Ann opens the door. "A letter for Mrs. Mary Ann Watson," says the young postman, who knows her. He is well aware that this letter has been wanted for a long time. 'For me? A letter for me? Thank you very much, that is indeed a surprise," Mary Ann replies gladly. She exchanges a few more sentences with the postman, then closes the front door and hurries into her room, eagerly reading the front page of the envelope.[12]

From Mariner William Watson
Onboard His Britannic Majesty's Ship
St. George, On the 28th of June 1811

To Mrs. Mary Ann Watson
Wilmington
Delaware
United States of America

From the kitchen, her mother has curiously followed Mary Ann's short conversation with the postman and now shouts, 'What is it? Who is that letter from?"

'It's from William," Mary Ann answers absentmindedly, look ing on the desk in her room for a hairpin or other sharp object with which to open the envelope. A few seconds later, her mother is standing in the

234

doorway, quickly drying her hands on her apron as though she was going to open the letter herself.

"Please, mother, please!" Mary Ann says angrily. "It's from *my* husband." Mary Ann closes the door to her room quickly, almost right in the face of her mother. Mary Ann sits on her bed as she slowly and carefully opens the envelope. She takes out the letter, unfolds it and reads it.

When Mary Ann has finished, she feels sad to realize that William is still held by the British. She begins to doubt she will ever see him again. She has been so worried for such a long time, and now she has an answer she is not quite prepared to receive or accept. Mary Ann begins to cry hard, and her mother knocks on the door to her room.

"Mary Ann, Mary Ann what is it? Let me in now. Please." Her mother slowly opens the door and approaches the bed, where Mary Ann lays, sobbing. "Mother, William is still imprisoned onboard the British Royal Navy ship *St. George.* He is well, when you consider the circumstances. He asked me to go to Allen McLane to have a new Protection Certificate sent to him. He has lost the one he had with him when he left Wilmington."

Mary Ann's mother now understands her daughter's reaction. "You better go to the Customhouse right away and meet Allen McLane as quickly as possible. Take your Marriage Certificate with you to prove who you are."

"Yes, I'd better go right away." Encouraged by her mother's suggestion, Mary Ann stands up and walks quickly to the bureau, where she pulls out the top drawer and takes out her Marriage Certificate. She dresses in her finest dress, and walks to the Customhouse. As she enters, she is met by William Windell, her husband's good friend.

"Hi, William. Could I please speak to Mr. McLane?" She is almost begging.

"Certainly, Mary Ann, just follow me, I'll take you to his office right away," William Windell answers, quickly leading Mary Ann to McLane's office. McLane sits at his desk staring out the window waiting for a cup of coffee he asked Windell to bring him earlier. Once again, his thoughts have wandered to war memories of this day in the month of October 1776.

"The Continental Army manages to post itself strongly, and General

Howe and his men seem satisfied with capturing a hill at White Plains, just on the right side of the American troops.[208] *In this engagement McLane involves himself deeply and makes an honorable contribution. He is quite satisfied with his own effort and is aware that his superior officers have noticed his fearless and courageous behavior."* [133]

'Sir," William Windell says, approaching the desk together with Mary Ann. "You can just put the cup on my desk. Thank you very much," McLane answers absent mindedly, without looking up from his desk. He is too caught up in his own war memories to be disturbed.

'But, Sir," Windell insists, 'I have brought the wife of seaman William Watson, Mrs. Mary Ann Watson."

McLane sits up, surprised. 'Oh, Mrs. Mary Ann Watson." McLane comes to his senses. Women seldom come to the Customhouse building, so this catches the interest of the always-curious port collector. 'Tell me, what can I do for you, Mrs. Mary Ann Watson?"

'My husband, William Watson is a good friend of John Freed, Jr., and Mr. William Windell. In the last letter I received from him, he asked me to contact you to ask you for a favor. You might know him."

'Oh, yes," Mc Lane exclaims. 'Your husband worked from time to time onboard the ships of John Warner, Samuel Bush or William Hemphill. Isn't that right, Mrs. Watson?"

'Yes, yes that's correct," Mary Ann answers eagerly, trying to be helpful as she smiles one of her winning smiles.

'I know who he is. What can I do to help you?" McLane asks.

'William is impressed onboard a ship in His Britannic Majesty's Baltic Fleet, the *St. George*, which was anchored near the coast of Sweden on June 28, this year, when he wrote me. William asks that you send him a new Protection Certificate, so he'll be able to identify himself and be released and hopefully return soon. Unfortunately, he lost the one he took with him from New York," Mary Ann explains. McLane smiles, realizing that he will actually be able to help her. 'Certainly, Mrs. Watson. I'm very sorry to hear that your husband William is impressed in the Royal Navy. I will make sure that a certificate is issued as quickly as possible and sent this very day."

"Thank you, Mr. McLane." Mary Ann answers, delighted to hear these promising words. 'May you have a nice day, Sir." She smiles shyly as she turns to leave.

'Have a nice day, too, Mrs. Watson and good luck," McLane replies.

As Mary Ann is on her way down the stairs to leave the building, William Windell and John Freed, Jr. notice how sad she looks. John Freed, Jr. decides to speak up to try and comfort her. 'Mary Ann, we are so sorry to hear what has happened to William. If you write him, will you please send him our regards?"

'Thank you for your concern. I will send him your regards in my next letter, I promise you. I know he will be happy to receive them. Goodbye." Mary Ann shakes their hands and walks home to her mother's apartment.

That same evening, when Mary Ann and her mother sit at the living room table and quietly eat their dinner, Mary Ann feels happier than she has for many months. It was a good experience after all, getting that third letter from William, showing that he is actually alive and eager to come back to her although still imprisoned. He was alive. And being able to help him by going to the port collector definitely cheered her up. Now she felt that she could lighten up and direct her thoughts toward a much brighter future. Her mother saw Mary Ann's mental change for the better, and she couldn't be more pleased.

Secretary of State James Monroe is sitting and dining with his wife Elizabeth in their Georgetown home this same evening, when he thinks back to what he had gone through 35 years ago.

"He is at White Plains, New York, and before he leaves there, together with the Commander of the Continental Army George Washington, he participates in successfully defending it.

After this half-hearted attempt to beat the Continental Army, the Howe brothers give up on the idea of winning the war with the Americans this year of 1776. The two Howe brothers decide to disperse their troops by seizing Newport, Rhode Island to get good winter naval stations for part of Lord Howe's Fleet." [208]

McLane likewise can't help thinking about the battle at White Plains that evening.

"He had fought well, but it was late autumn, and General Washington and the Continental Army had to think about going south for a safe,

237

warm winter camp."

A couple of days later, Mary Ann happens to meet Joseph Warner and his wife Mary outside the Water Street apartment. They have just arrived from Philadelphia with one of John Warner and Samuel Bush's packets and are on their way to visit Joseph's old mother in the mansion on Shipley Street, behind the family's old silverware shop, Sign of the Can, on Market Street.

Mary Ann tells them about the letter from William and the difficult situation he is in, and Joseph Warner's face turns grave as he listens. 'Damn those British fools, damn them," Joseph says angrily. 'Sorry, Mary Ann, but I can't help it. It makes my blood boil, when I hear of these brutal attacks on innocent fellow American seamen and especially now, when it's my best friend William. How are you? It must be hard to handle the uncertainty."

'Oh, I'm quite well myself. After all, William is well. I have asked Allen McLane to send William a new Protection Certificate, because he lost the one he had. Then perhaps he will be able to return soon," Mary Ann replies, trying to sound optimistic.

'Promise you'll give him my regards, when you write him," Joseph Warner asks.

'Yes, I will do that, I promise you Joseph. I know William will be more than happy to receive greetings from you. You are, after all these years, his best friend," Mary Ann says. They say goodbye and Mary Ann goes to do some shopping for her mother in the Lower Market House, before it gets too dark. The days are beginning to get much shorter, and before they realize it, winter will arrive.

The following day is October 26. John Quincy Adams, 44 years old and son of the second US President, professor at Harvard, former US Senator and present Minister to Russia, and fierce opponent of impressment of American seamen, is very angry. He is constantly receiving intelligence that American seamen are being impressed into Royal Navy ships in great numbers. The Royal Navy has begun to impress seamen from American merchant ships, in US home waters, when they return from Europe. In the first six months of 1811, the number of impressed American seamen has increased to a number never seen before.

Adams writes a letter to a friend, *"The practice of impressments is the only ineradicable wound, which, if persisted in, can terminate no otherwise than by war. But it seems clearly better to await the effect of our increasing strength and of our adversary's more mature decay, before we undertake to abolish it by war.*

    For as I have no hesitation in saying that at a proper period, I would advise my country to declare a war explicitly and distinctly upon the single point, and never afterwards make peace without a specific article expressly renouncing forever the principle of impressing from any American vessel, so I should think it best to wait until the time shall come, and I think it not far distant, when a declaration to that effect would obtain the article without needing the war." [279]

John Quincy Adams does not at this moment know how involved he will later become in this topic of impressments. But right now, it makes him so angry that it spoils the day for him.

On October 28, four months after William wrote his third letter to Mary Ann from *St George* anchored outside the south east coast of Sweden, at 11:00, Mary Ann is at home in the apartment on a break from work. She decides to write to her husband William.[12] She has received three letters from him so far, but before this third letter came with a return address, she has not been able to figure out how to write to him. She sits at the table in the living room near the window, where she can follow the busy traffic down on Water Street. There is enough light here for her to write.

She dips the pen in the black ink box on the table, leans over the paper, and starts writing.

Wilmington Oct. 28, 1811

Dear Husband,

I am well and hope this letter finds you in good health too. I have received 3 letters from you since you left. The last letter was received this month. I am very sorry to hear what has happened to you. I would be very happy to see you, but I am afraid it will be a long time before I do. I have applied to Mr. McLane for your protection and he sent one to you Oct 23rd. I would have written to you sooner, but I did not know where to

239

send my letter. My Dear, it does make me feel much better to write to you. I have had more difficulties the first 9 months since you left than ever before in my life.

Damian Starr came home, but I was not able to see him, as he was killed the day he arrived at Philadelphia. Eleven days after you left I gave birth to a dead child. I believe the stillbirth was caused due to the trouble concerning you. I have recovered, Thank God, and I am doing as well as one can be in my situation. Dear William, all I want in this world to make me happy is to have you with me once more. I would be unhappier if not for my mother. She has been everything to me that a mother could be. I believe that if she was your own mother, she could not miss you more. Joseph Warner, William Windell & John Freed and Enoch Lang send love to you. Enoch Lang has been married. If you cannot return when this letter reaches you, write as soon as possible. I end with my love and respect, and likewise my mother's. I remain until death your affectionate wife.

Mary Ann Watson[12]

Mary Ann folds the letter twice and wraps a piece of paper around it as an envelope. On the front of the envelope she writes,

From Mary Ann Watson of Wilmington, Del U.S. America

William Watson
Mariner
On board his Britannic Majesty's Ship
St. George on the
28th of June 1811 perforce[12]

The next evening, Rear Admiral of the Red C. W. Reynolds decides to gather the officers from the *St. George* and the captains from the other Royal Navy ships anchored in the Bay of Hanö. At the table in his cabin, they carefully plan the departure of what is intended to be the last Royal Navy convoy out of the Baltic Sea this year. The first issue to address is the arrangement of the signals to be used within the convoy.

The weather is clear with a fresh wind coming from the southeast. This is not a favorable wind for departure. But two days later, on

October 31, the mariners of the Royal Navy quartered in this year's newly erected buildings on Hanö Island are given the order to prepare the closure of the Royal Navy summer station on the island for the winter.

Before leaving Hanö, the British hold a short commemoration at the cemetery on Hanö Island. Reynolds and Gurion are present. So is William, who is one of the guards in the barge that brought the admiral and the flag captain to the island from *St. George*.

At the flagstaff with the Union Jack fluttering in the cold eastern wind, a marine sergeant blows "The last post" on his brass horn over the graves of the dead bodies of their comrades, as an icy wind gust hits the crowd and rain begins to fall.

William is standing with his face toward the Admiral and the flag captain and he looks toward the Swedish mainland. It is getting cold here at four o'clock in the afternoon. Royal Navy activities have now ended here in the Bay of Hanö. All ships in the bay are ready to leave for England.

William knows that the officers onboard *St. George* say that they depart tomorrow for winter camp in Portsmouth.

As they now all stand silently and listen to the monotone, melancholy sound of the brass horn, William thinks about the letter he wrote Mary Ann on July 28, that hot summer day more than four months ago. Now the *St. George* is leaving this summer station, and he has not yet received a letter from Mary Ann. In fact, he has written her three letters in all since he was impressed and he has never received any answer. Why has she not been writing to him? From his letters, she must know how hard it is for him to be held captive here without any contact with the only person he has ever loved. Just a few words from Mary Ann would do him good. What is going on in Wilmington? What is she doing right now?

On the southern part of the island of Hanö, the trees of the original Nordic kind, lime trees, ashes, elms and hornbeams, stand naked. All the leaves have already blown off.

The men onboard the most recently arrived merchant ship from the northern part of the Baltic Sea report that ice is starting to form there. It is definitely time to go. The atmosphere in Hanö Bay is not pleasant any more, and the memories of the many extraordinary weeks with warm weather this summer are all gone.

On November 1, the day for the convoy to depart, the gale is blowing from east and northeast.

This wind direction is optimal for leaving Hanö Bay and entering the southern part of the Baltic Sea. The time limit is past and Rear Admiral Reynolds decides to order the convoy to set sail. In the middle of the day, the signal is given to heave the anchors and four cannons are shot from the quarterdeck of Rear Admiral Reynolds's Flagship *St. George.*

Swedish farmers and merchants on the mainland have earned much more than usual by trading with the Royal Navy here in the bay this year, and they watch with gloomy eyes as the fleet leaves Hanö Bay. They are already looking forward to a reunion next summer. The departing fleet is truly an amazing sight. A couple of Swedish pilots watch the same spectacular scene from the pilothouse at the entrance to Matvik harbor.

At the time of departure, this last homeward bound convoy consists, so far, of the flagship *St. George*, the third-raters *Defence* and *Dictator*, the brigs *Ethalion* and *Woodlark,* the gun brig *Earnest,* and a total of 130 merchant ships.

At this time of year, wind strength and direction are very unstable in this region of Scandinavia. Late in the afternoon, the sky grows dark on the southeastern horizon and the wind suddenly comes from the south. A storm is quickly building up in front of the convoy and some of the smaller merchant ships already have damage to their rigging and masts. Flag Captain Gurion is informed and orders the ships in the fleet to diminish the sail areas. But it's too late. It's early in the evening when the storm reaches the fleet, and Reynolds realizes there is no alternative but to give the order for the fleet to return to Hanö Bay.

He is furious and frustrated right now and the other *St. George* officers try to keep away from him to avoid becoming an arbitrary target of his anger. Reynolds is a perfectionist and he is mad now, because he realizes that earlier, he predicted this situation. In the spring, when he and Sammaurez discussed the time for departure from the Baltic Sea, he wanted October 1, in order to secure stable weather conditions. Sammaurez had agreed, but then the merchants and ship owners, William and Phillip Emes, wanted a month's delay and Sammaurez ordered it to please the merchants. Now Reynolds has the full proof that he was right, as he usually is. But that is all to no avail now. Since Reynolds can't direct his anger at the Emes brothers, the officers onboard do everything to get out of his way to avoid taking the roles of the Emes brothers. A return to Hanö Bay now can mean that some of the ships will have to stay the winter in Matvik Harbor, where ice could pack around the ships and maybe destroy them.

The convoy returns to Hanö Bay and the ship carpenters and sail makers get busy working in the harbors of Matvik and Karlshamn to repair the ships as quickly as possible. Amos is working hard assisting on the smaller merchant ships. Some of the ships are fixed with jury masts, because they don't have new ones available. This will make them vulnerable on the coming voyage through the Baltic Sea, the Femmern Belt, the Great Belt, the Cattegat, the Skagerak, the North Sea and finally the English Channel on their way to their English homeport.

The next day, the storm keeps its strength until noon. Then it reduces, but changes direction to the southwest, bad for a departure. If the wind stays in that corner it can substantially increase the total distance to sail, and the time needed to return safely home. The fleet might be forced to beat up against the wind down to the coast of Pommern, before setting course toward Rügen in the western Baltic Sea, where they are actually heading.

On November 5, five days after the convoy should have left Hanö, *Defence*'s captain David Atkins forwards a request from the ship's carpenter to Reynolds, to get a yearly account of his stocks.[127] In the same letter, Captain Atkins reports that *Defence* has only six living bullocks and hay for four more days. If more bullocks are going to be taken in, more hay needs to be delivered.[127]

This day, *HMS Hero*, *Rose*, *Bellette,* and *Cressy* are located off Treminien at Kiel, between Rostock and Femmern.

The atmosphere among the officers onboard the *St. George*, *Defence* and other ships in the convoy becomes more and more tense, as days go by without any significant change in weather conditions. Winter could come early and prevent them from getting a chance to return to England at all.

This same day, President James Madison is speaking to the assembly at the Twelfth Congress. In the months before, he has spoken frequently to Secretary of State James Monroe, as the impressments of American seamen from American ships along the US east coast was at its highest in many years.

James Monroe's appointment had not been by chance. He had earlier been the one who negotiated with the English government on impressments. Monroe visited William Lyman when he ran the London office. So when the letters from unhappy wives, families, east coast port collectors, Justices of the Peace, and the impressed seamen themselves began to arrive at the Department of State in previously unseen quantities, Monroe knew all too well what this was all about and what to do.

James Monroe personally signed some of the letters that accompanied copies of Protection Certificates sent from the Department of State to some American seamen impressed in the Royal Navy, in order to put pressure on the British captains to release more American seamen.

Therefore, President James Madison has been sufficiently briefed about the present situation on impressments as he speaks this day. As Madison speaks to the assembly, he is not lacking in war-like sentiment, but he deliberately avoids mentioning the sensitive word *impressments*, because he knows that it might cause an outcry for war among the suffering American people.[279]

On November 8, in the afternoon, the strength of the wind finally reduces and its direction changes to the northwest. After a short consultation with captains on the other ships of the line in the squadron, Admiral Reynolds decides to give the order to prepare the sails for departure for the second time this autumn.

The next morning, the weather is fine with a light northeast wind – a favorable wind for leaving. Around 10 a.m. a signal is given from the flagship *St. George*, and the convoy is homeward bound once again. Six of the 130 merchant ships are left back in the harbor in Matvik. This time, the Royal Navy has been enforced with the third-rater *Rose*, the gun brig *Ranger,* and the gun brig *Carnest*, which have arrived in the meantime in Hanö Bay. It is a powerful squadron that now heads for meeting the Danish cannon boats and the Danish privateers.

Some of the merchant ships that were part of the returning convoy and which had been visiting St. Petersburg, Memel, and other trade stations this summer in the northern Baltic Sea actually came from Salem and are now on their way back there. Similarly, one ship is returning to Philadelphia and several to Boston. If William Watson, Amos Stevens, John Brown and other impressed American seamen from Wilmington,

Boston or Salem knew this, they would probably try to get onboard these ships. Under cover of darkness, they could try to hide in the hold of these merchant ships to return to freedom.

Captains of American merchant ships under the escort of the Royal Navy would never run the risk of taking American seamen escaping from the Royal Navy ships onboard their own merchant ships. If discovered, it might cause the American ship to be expelled from the protection of the Royal Navy on the way home through Danish waters.

At the time of the second departure on this November 9, Rear Admiral of the Red, C.W. Reynolds has under his command the following Royal Navy ships:

Second-rater, 3 decks, and 98 cannons: *St. George.*
Third-rater, 2 decks and 64 cannons: *Defence, Vanguard, Ethalion, Consagente, Loire, Gorgon* and *Vigo.*
Sloops and brigs: *Platagenet, Couraseux, Couragense, Tremendous, Shieldrake, Bunesser, Helder, Censor, Diligence, Sirius, Mars, Formidable, Ariel.*
Gun brigs: *Earnest, Carnest, Rifleman* and *Nightingale.*

As the convoy sails toward the Great Belt, the third-rater *Hero,* sloops *Ranger* and *Rose,* and gun brig *Carnest* join the convoy.

The convoy finally is homeward bound, and the first part of the voyage is successful. The first two days, the convoy manages to sail 110 miles. In the late afternoon the following day, the convoy anchors south of Møn Island in the Femmern Belt. In the early evening, the wind suddenly increases to storm strength with snow and hail showers in addition to strong, unpredictable wind gusts. Many of the merchant ships break loose and drift by their anchors. Giving a ship more anchor cable is not always successful.

Lookouts on the bridge of the flagship *St. George* can see distress signals from several merchant ships, and during the night about 10 of the smaller merchant ships go down. Flag Captain Daniel Gurion is informed of these events and orders it written in St. George' s logbook. The surrounding ships are in no position to assist because of the high seas and can only watch the tragic events taking place in front of their eyes.

The following day, the 11th, the storm continues with equal strength. Early on the 12th, *St. George* gives the signal to the convoy to continue. The course is now south-southwest, and by noon, the third-raters *Cressy* and *Hero* and the brig *Bellette* join the convoy. They have been waiting with a small number of merchant ships a few miles east of Femmern, where it had been arranged that they should meet.

On the 12th and 13th, foodstuff is reloaded from some ships to others within the Royal Navy. *Woodlark* delivers rum, raisins, pork, sugar, and flour to *Cressy*.[35]

On November 13 at 10:00 p.m., *Dictator* sends two boats to the row guard.[49] The next morning at 7, ships in the convoy take in anchors, and when they lower them that evening, they are on a position along the south east coast of Lolland near Nysted, a few miles south west of the hard sand bank at Rødsand (red sand). *St. George*, *Defence*, *Cressy* and *Woodlark* are in company.[67]

At 11 a.m., *Cressy* supplies *St. George* with 398 gallons of rum and 458 pounds of cacao.[35]

Normally, a row guard of a couple of row boats is considered sufficient to protect a convoy during the night, but to increase the protection this night, Flag Captain Gurion orders the frigate *Woodlark* to keep up the sails.[67]

At 10:00 p.m., *Woodlark* observes and hears cannons fired to leeward. *Woodlark* begins to sail through the convoy and its officers speak to the crew on several ships, to get intelligence about the alarm.

Back in Matvik, the schooner *Ariel* arrives after hunting prize ships. Some have been taken.[29]

During the night, a dramatic change in the weather takes place. The wind direction changes to the southwest and the strength of the wind increases. There are occasional strong rain showers and wind gusts. The convoy faces troubles again, and the officer on the bridge of the *St. George* observes distress signals from the relatively new ship *Cressy*. The next morning, it is observed that a ship has lost all of its masts, and some merchant ships have had their sails severely damaged.

By 8 a.m., the wind has decreased and *Woodlark* is ordered by Reynolds to assist a ship with a distress flag hoisted. The carpenters and some men from *Woodlark* assist the merchant ship by making a jury mast, and afterwards take her in tow.

A Second Lieutenant and seven men from *Cressy* are sent in a boat to help one of the merchant ships fix her rigging. Before the team gets back to *Cressy,* the wind increases in the afternoon. A Danish privateer comes from the borough of Nysted and captures the boat with the *Cressy* team. The team is taken to Nysted as prisoners.[107] During that evening and night, a great storm develops.[35]

At midnight, *Woodlark* still has the dismasted merchant ship in tow. There is a thick haze, as seems to be the case almost every time an English convoy is passing Danish waters. At 3 a.m., *Woodlark* burns a blue light so it can be seen and to help the merchant ships to keep in company.

At the same time *Cressy* is suddenly drifting, and she fires two shots to warn the other ships about the danger of collision. Several lights are lit onboard the *Cressy* in order to figure out how fast the other ships are drifting.

The main fleet, with the heavy second-rater *St. George* and the third-raters *Defence*, *Cressy* and *Hero,* begins to drift northeast toward the shore and the Rødsand sand bank. At the same time, some merchant ships in a group at Rødsand are blown off their anchors and eastward toward the Baltic Sea, where they initially came from. *Woodlark* and her merchant ship in tow follow that path.

It is November 14. The *Cressy* sends its carpenter to a brig.[35] At the same time, *Censor* has steadily drifted all the way back to Hanö Bay. Because the harbor in Matvik is already closed for the winter, they are forced to anchor outside and send a boat to the shore to get a pilot[74-1] onboard.

The next morning, the 15th of November, the weather is beautifully clear. Rear Admiral of the Red C. W. Reynolds stands at the windows in his cabin onboard the *St. George*. He looks tired this morning and swears several times as he talks to himself and thinks about the unpredictable weather conditions in these waters at this time of year. He is sick and tired of still being on this southern Baltic position. Reynolds is a firm believer in intelligent, careful planning. He loves systems and precision on his sea voyages, but this whole situation is beginning to look badly arranged, because of the delay in departure, caused by the way merchant fleet owners eternally worry about profit optimization.

The closer the time of departure is to the arrival of the stormy and icy wintertime in the Baltic Sea, the better it seems for the merchant fleet owners. If the convoy had just been allowed to leave when he and Sammaurez had suggested, Reynolds thinks, they would have been a safe distance from the Danish shores right now - somewhere in the middle of the North Sea, safely heading directly for the English Channel and Portsmouth. The wind continues to come from the southwest, and the ships in the fleet are forced to throw out the anchors near Rødsand to avoid drifting toward the lee shore and a stranding.

Although some of the crew onboard the ships in the Royal Navy's Baltic Fleet has been shifted since 1808, these crews are still filled with scary memories of the icy winter that arrived early that year.

William Galey, one of William's English marine colleagues, is one of them, and he is distressed now. He remembers clearly that it was extremely cold, with large blocks of ice floating around the ships in Vinga Sound, where they are now heading. The men onboard the ships now experience the same kind of coldness as they sail here in a thick fog and William Galey is convinced that it's just a question of time before they'll hit an iceberg. Shortly after all the seamen begin to wonder if maybe all the internal Danish waters are already filled with ice. The crewmembers are quite scared.

Before they turn in that night on the *St. George*, the seamen take in all the sails. They know a storm can build up during the night, because the liquid in the storm glass hanging from a beam on the bridge is already packed with large crystals. But as the first guard team is relieved at 8 p.m., the crew onboard the *St. George* doesn't have the faintest idea what they will all be going through before the dawn.

The situation onboard is tense for other reasons. The mariners know that the convoy is on the border to enter the Great Belt, the most dangerous water for them to pass. They expect that the Danish cannon boats are waiting for them right now.

The speed of this year's Royal Navy Baltic convoy is limited by the weakest link in the chain, the smallest merchant ships. Information on the progress of the convoy is signaled from each Danish fleet station to the next along the coast of south Zealand, actually the island of Møn and the island of Lolland.

The crews on the Danish cannon and privateer boats walk restlessly back and forth in their houses in the Danish harbor cities, just waiting for the signal that the British convoy has arrived at their specific position and they have to go. If, by luck, the wind disappears and fog covers the water, not even jollyboats and barges filled with Royal Mariners can prevent the much faster Danish cannon boats from cutting merchant ships from the convoy and taking them as prizes. It will be like seagulls sitting on fishing net poles in the open water, attacking a shoal of fish passing by in the waters below.

At 8:00 p.m., the officers on the bridge of the *Cressy* observe several dismasted merchant ships[35] around her.

The first guard onboard the *St. George* is awakened at 9:30 p.m. and ordered to put out more anchor cable. Shortly afterward, a masters mate shouting "All hands, all hands!" awakens all the men. The storm has now reached the level of a hurricane. Before the anchor cable can be loosened, the entire upper deck is covered with water pumping in through the low hawseholes. The anchor cable passes through one of these holes in the bow of a vessel. Now, the violent movements of the ship throw chairs, tables, coffins and loose parts around on the decks, making it dangerous for the crew to stay there. For on-duty crewmembers forced to stay on their posts, it is very stressful.

The crew on duty has not finished giving out the extra anchor cable when screams come from a large merchant ship headed directly toward the bow of the *St. George*. William and several other seamen standing near the railing see the bow of the approaching merchant ship hit the anchor cable of the *St. George,* which drags down the bow of the merchant ship to a very low position. At the same time, a huge wave sweeps over the merchant ship. It instantly goes down, and nothing more is ever seen of the ship or its crewmembers. The collision also breaks the anchor cable of the *St. George*.

William and the seamen and mariners onboard *St. George* who witness this scene are deeply shocked, and can't help letting out cries of compassion and despair at the terrible sight. But they have little time to worry about the other ship, though, because suddenly they realize that they and the *St. George* are in the utmost danger themselves.

They had anchored for the night at a depth of 20 meters, the depth beneath the keel of the drifting flagship, but with the broken bow anchor cable, the ship has drifted to a depth of only 12 meters. The crew on duty is busy doing its utmost to prevent the *St. George* from running aground.

Flag Captain Daniel Gurion orders the 'heavy anchor" to be dropped on the seabed to try and stop the ship's dangerous drifting, but it is no use. The drifting *St. George* has gained such speed and momentum that it seems impossible to stop it, and the heavy anchor breaks loose after only a few minutes. The combined forces of the strong wind on the sails and the heavy sea on the hull transferred to the anchor cable, stretching it, making the anchor ring open and the anchor break off as if the ring was made of pure butter. The situation onboard the *St. George* has become extremely dangerous, because the flagship continues its uncontrolled drifting toward land through in the dark and stormy night.

The officers on the bridge are silent for some minutes, then they initiate a new attempt to stop the drifting of the ship. A new cable is put out of one of the hawseholes, but before the crew can drop the duty anchor, the cable has to be attached to it. The officer on the bridge is informed that the depth under the keel has reduced to only 13 feet, and water is reported on the *St. George's* lower deck.

The officers and men onboard the drifting *St. George* are convinced that it will only be a matter of time before the *St. George* will strand. Under these uncertain circumstances, the only reasonable thing to do to save the ship is to set the sail and try to veer, to get the bow up against the wind and regain the sail forces that will make it possible to take the ship away from the dangerous coast, and out into the open sea.

Some seamen climb the rigging to loosen the topsail and the forestaysail, but the wind takes the sails and snaps them out of the hands of the seamen, who are trying to keep their balance on the tows near the bars and unfold the sails at the same time. Within minutes, the sails are blown to pieces in the strong wind and carried away.

The water depth beneath the *St. George's* keel has now reduced to eight feet. In the meantime the duty anchor has been attached to a cable, and with a great effort from many seamen and mariners, it is thrown overboard.

The duty anchor plows steadily over the seabed for a short while, but finally it, too, breaks free. William Watson and William Freeman are astonished to observe this right before their very eyes. The duty anchor has a weight of nearly four tons, but it just broke as easily as a match.

The *St. George* continues steadily to drift toward the shore. In this increasingly stressful situation, the ordinary crewmembers get dizzy and begin to hallucinate, imagining that they see waves as high as mountains as the gusty, icy wind, filled with snow and sleet, howls around them. Flag Captain Gurion stands next to the steering wheel and speaks to his officers, seamen and mariners. He tells them that the only way they can save the *St. George* now is to cut down the masts, one by one. That will make the ship lighter, and eliminate some of the sideways forces on the hull causing the ship to tilt and take in more water than normal. Gurion dares not wait any longer and gives the order to cut down the masts, and some of the seamen go and find axes to begin the job.

The strong emotions felt by most of the men onboard the *St. George* in these crucial hours, and caused by the uncertainty they experience about their destiny, are indescribable. Seaman William Galey has a feeling that he shares with most of the men onboard. Galey says that, even though he has participated in many tough sea battles and hand-to-hand fights on enemy territory during his long service in the Royal Navy, and even though he has been stranded earlier with another ship, he has never experienced moments quite as scary as these.

Dictator, Rose, Hero, Defence, Bellette, and Cressy lay undamaged at their anchors.

Filled with deep fear, the crew onboard the *St. George* can only wait for the masts to fall. It is 2 a.m. William is not sure, as he carefully follows what is happening, if the masts are going to fall into the sea or hit the ship and break it to pieces. At the moment the foremast falls, a high sea lifts the ship and to William Galey, William Watson and the others, it feels as though the *St. George* will be taken up into the sky. In the next moment, the hull of the *St. George* rushes down toward the seabed with extreme force, and a large bang sounds as though all the individual planks in the ship were breaking. A moment of total silence follows, then the wind howls again and the crew realizes, with great relief, that the main mast has fallen free of the ship.[200]

Flag Captain Daniel Gurion, who carefully watches the men cut down the masts, now shouts encouragingly, 'The main mast has fallen, boys, all men at the pumps. Throw out the cannons and anything else that can lighten the ship. Keep an eye on the foremast, when it falls. If we live until dawn, we may, by the help of God, hope to reach the shore.' After a short pause, where the only sound heard is the howling wind, Gurion continues. 'Or at least some of us, while sitting on the remaining ship sides.”[200] This is a moment of truth, a time to be absolutely realistic and not sentimental, and Gurion shows the kind of courage he is expected to show to his men as a leading officer and Flag Captain in the Royal Navy.

At 4:00 a.m., several shots are heard from the bridge onboard the *Dictator*. *Dictator*, *Bellette*, *Cressy*, *Rose*, *Defence*, *Hero,* and *St. George* are gathered together with only 77 of the merchant ships.[49]

St. George's rear end now suddenly hits the ground hard, several times in a row, breaking the rudder loose from its hinges. The rudder hangs from the rudder chains, which break an hour later, at 5 in the morning. The *St. George* is now severely damaged, but because the rudder broke completely loose, it prevents further damage to the rear end of *St. George*. As the crew sees it, it is miraculous that the *St. George* does not take in water at this point. The experienced crew finds this situation strange, because the ship is damaged but they are happy.[200] After all, God still seems to be looking their way, they think.

At 6:30 a.m., dawn finally breaks, and to their horror, William and the rest of the crew get visible proof that they are grounded on a sandbank four nautical miles from land to the northeast. The masts, which could have been used to make rafts to reach the shore, lay broken to pieces alongside the ship, removing any hope among the men onboard about any rescue. Further destruction is quite imminent unless God chooses to enter the scene and save them all somehow.[200]

At this crucial hour on the morning of November 16, *Woodlark* has been drifting eastward along the Swedish south coast of Skaane for some time, accompanied by some of the other merchant ships. The lookout onboard observes the north end of Bornholm to the south-southeast. In one night, they have been blown back half the distance to Hanö Bay. At 2 p.m., *Woodlark* is in a position to signal to *Pyramus,* already anchored in Matvik harbor together with *Ethalion*, *Ranger*, *Ariel,* and *Censor*.

At the same time, an officer onboard *Bellette* observes that the *St. George* is dismasted, as are several merchant ships. *Bellette* takes in the anchor and sails next to *St. George* to assist her any way the flag captain wants. The *Bellette* captain takes a boat to *St. George*. It is evident that *St. George* needs towing if the convoy is going to continue its voyage toward Vinga Sound, and *Bellette's* captain offers this service to Gurion.

About this time in Wilmington, Allen and Maria McLane are eating breakfast in their kitchen before the port collector leaves for his office. Allen McLane takes a sip of his coffee and looks at his wife, whom he loves very much. He looks over the edge of his cup, and says aloud, 'It is November 16 today, Maria!"

Maria McLane recalls very well this day in the autumn of 1776. It was a time of great trials, retreat and depression for the disillusioned men in the Continental Army, and her husband has spoken of it many times since. That year, 1776, had been very special compared to the other years in the war, she admitted willingly. Maria Bache McLane has fully accepted that her husband speaks more about the war this year than he ever has. Allen McLane lets his thoughts go back 35 years.

'Washington begins to move his troops southward from White Plains, and divides his army in two. He leaves 5,000 New Englanders and New Yorkers under the command of General Lee at Northcastle, and 3,000 under Hearth at Peekskill. McLane follows Washington's troops, 2,000 men who cross the Hudson River. General Nathaniel Greene thinks that Fort Washington, on north Manhattan, can be held, and on Nov. 16, he and Washington cross the Hudson River to make an inspection of the fort. At that time, Howe has followed them back from White Plains and started an attack on Fort Washington. Before their very eyes, they see the defense crumble and they succeed in escaping back to the New Jersey side just minutes before the American garrison of 2,900 men attached to the fort surrenders. Howe, delighted by his success, sends General Cornwallis over the Hudson River to see if they also can take Fort Lee on the New Jersey side." [208]

Sitting in his office in the Department of State, Secretary of State James Monroe takes a break and lets his thoughts go back, too, to the height of his military career, when he was only 19 years old, in late 1776. He and the Third Virginian Regiment had followed George Washington and the Continental Army on a depressing retreat southward toward Pennsylvania. It surely had been tough times back then.[208]

The wind has decreased a bit now and the height of the seas is less than it was a few hours ago. An emergency flag has been hoisted onboard the *St. George*. During the day, the three third-raters *Cressy*, *Bellette*, and *Defence* have come as close as possible to the flagship to make it easy for their boats to assist the damaged ship.

At 3:15 p.m., *Cressy* sends its carpenter to the *St. George* to help fix the damaged rudder region.[33] The convoy of merchant ships is at anchor outside the island of Langeland. Around 4:00 p.m., *Dictator's* carpenters are busy producing a jury rudder for the *St. George*.[49]

St. George continues to roll quite a bit in the heavy waves for most of the day, but at 8:00 p.m., the movement stops. Realizing this, William Watson, William Freeman, and William Galey can't help thinking that now the flagship is probably stuck on the Danish beach. Then at midnight, an indescribable joy sweeps through the crewmembers, when they learn that the stem of the *St. George* has turned toward the land and the water depth has increased three feet since 8:00 p.m. As if by miracle, the *St. George* is suddenly free of the ground!

It is now after midnight, Sunday the 17th, and *Dictator* receives a message from *St. George* to send over all its boats to help the *St. George* to sea as soon as possible. Soon after, several boats are towing *St. George*[49] to keep the flagship free of the ground near the sandbank at Rødsand. *Cressy* sends its carpenter to the *St. George* to help make a new jury rudder. All the carpenters involved in this process work hard around the clock.

Boats are also sent to *St. George* from *Bellette* at 4:00 a.m. At 6:30, *Bellette* takes in her anchor to place herself in front of the *St. George* to begin towing her so they can continue the voyage toward Vinga Sound. By 8:00 a.m., *Bellette* is towing the *St. George*.[30]

At 8:15 a.m., the carpenter onboard the *Cressy* is still working on the jury rudder for the *St. George*.[35] At 9:00 a.m., the hawser connecting the *Bellette* and the *St. George* is taken by the wind and sea current, and St. George is forced to sail by itself for a while. Half an hour later, crews in the small boats have a new hawser out to connect the *St. George* and the *Bellette*. But the seas are still quite large, and the hawser breaks once again.[30] Another half hour passes. Then the officers onboard the *Cressy* see the *St. George* set sail and pass the *Cressy* on its own.[35]

At noon, the blacksmith and the carpenters from *Cressy* and other ships are busy working on the jury rudder for the *St. George*.[35] Amos and his boss, the chief carpenter from *Defence,* have been brought to *Cressy* to assist. Amos is glad that he is able to help. Making a jury rudder is an interesting and rare job.

St. George has now been in a state of shipwreck for almost 30 hours.

She is free from danger and, after a jury mast is made, they anchor at the old position at 8:00 in the evening.[200] Flag Captain Gurion and Admiral Reynolds are waiting for the many carpenters gathered onboard the *Cressy* to finish the jury rudder.

Now that the men onboard are calmed down, Rear Admiral of the Red C. W. Reynolds inspects the damages at the rear end of his flagship. William sees him walk down the stairs to the middle deck, a place the Admiral seldom comes.

After inspecting the rear end, Reynolds walks to his cabin and writes a dispatch to Sammaurez in Vinga Sound. He reports that, of the original 130 merchant ships that left Hanö, only 76 seem to remain. Twelve merchant ships can be seen stranded on the Danish coast, unfortunately near the enemy position at the borough of Nysted. Two ships have collided and several of the smaller merchant ships have lost their masts in the storm. Because the seas have been so heavy, it is feared that many of the missing ships have been dragged down at their anchors. Many merchant ships are severely damaged and it is doubtful that they can be repaired, even with assistance from His Majesty's Ships.[200] Reynolds also reports that a second lieutenant and mariners from *Cressey* have been taken prisoner by a Danish privateer.

On Monday November 18, *Woodlark* lays at its anchor in Matvik harbor on the Swedish mainland, and the officers observes two new ships from the *St. George* convoy arriving. The crew onboard *Pyramus,* also anchored in Matvik harbor, is busy making ice saws to prepare for future tough winter conditions and heavy pack ice. The British crews have never been here in the Baltic region so late in the year, and they are scared that winter will set in any moment and cause the sea to freeze overnight.

The ice saws they make must be ready for when the ice packs around the ships in the harbor. Then, when the damaged ships from the *St. George* convoy are repaired and ready to return to the open Baltic Sea, they can saw themselves out.

Wood is taken in so they'll be able to keep themselves warm while waiting here. The crew watches several more ships from the *St. George* convoy arrive in Matvik harbor, ships that previously lost their anchors. In the Matvik harbor, the returned merchant ships are tied to stones. *Pyramus* assists them.

This day, at 10.30 a.m. *St. George* passes the *Cressy* and anchors.

From *Defence*'s inward cruise from Vinga Sound through the Great Belt to Hanö, the *St. George* convoy now knows that a large number of Danish cannon boats and privateers are probably waiting for them. Three sailmakers from *Cressy* help fix the new rigging and sails onboard the St. *George*. Admiral Reynolds does not want to waste any more time anchored here. They have to go north now, because the convoy was delayed in the first place.

St. George is also equipped with a new anchor chain and anchors, and to strengthen the defense of the ship in its new and more vulnerable condition, 60 muskets, 60 sables and 60 bayonets are brought onboard for the use of the mariners. The 60 muskets come from *Dictator*.[49]

Rear Admiral of the Red C. W. Reynolds has many strategic issues to discuss with his superior, and is looking forward to getting the *St. George* to Vinga Sound so he can meet Sammaurez, who might help him determine whether *St. George* can cross the North Sea to return to England, or if she should stay on the Swedish west coast during the winter.[200]

In Matvik harbor at 4 p.m., the officers onboard the *Censor* speak to the men onboard a merchant schooner, whose captain informs them that 27 merchant ships from the *St. George* convoy are heading back to Matvik harbor and *St. George* has lost her masts.

While the returning merchant ships get their riggings and anchors fixed in Matvik Harbor during the following days, Royal Navy ships waiting for them in the harbor go hunting for Danish and Swedish fishing boats and merchant ships belonging to a variety of different nations[74-1].

This day, Rear Admiral Reynolds receives the *State and Conditions* list from *Hero,* together with a list of 17 prizes taken or destroyed from October 10 to November 9. Thirteen of these prizes are Danish[128]. His blue eyes study the list of the prizes taken, while he sits at his table in his Admiral's cabin. He tries to loosely calculate his profit. 'It is a lmost only Danish ships on the list," he says to Gurion, who is drinking rum from a tin cup. He grins from ear to ear, 'It is such a shame that we were not allowed to take one single, noble Swedish prize, now we have been in Swedish waters all summer. It would have been so very easy to do, and they obviously don't dare to give us one by themselves." Reynolds laughs loudly for several minutes. His flag captain and bold admirer Daniel Gurion instantly adopts the behavior of his superior and laughs as well. At the same time, he thinks to himself that it doesn't matter. It is only the total number of prizes that counts, and one prize can be as noble as another, at least when it comes to his wallet.

On the night of November 18, *Dictator* sends armed boats to the wind side of the convoy to protect ships here[49] against Danish cannon boats. In the morning, *Cressy's* carpenters are sent to *St. George*[35] and *Bellette* sends a boat to *Cressy* to assist when the jury rudder is finished and ready to transport to the *St. George*.[31]

The jury rudder, or Pakenham rudder, named after its inventor Admiral Pakenham, is transported the next morning and hoisted down to the waiting boats from *Cressy*, *Dictator,* and *Bellette* to be taken to the *St. George*.[31, 33, 49]

While the men and officers have concentrated on getting the damaged ships in the convoy in a condition so they can proceed on their voyage toward England, Danish privateers on the shore and people from the borough of Nysted have been emptying the nine stranded merchant ships from the convoy.

That same day, the town bailiff in Nysted makes an inquiry of the Second Lieutenant, other officer and seven seamen taken as prisoners in the storm from one of *Cressy's* boats. The youngest of the English seamen is 22 and the oldest 35. They tell the Danish bailiff that they come from *Cressy,* under the command of Captain Charles D. Pater. They were in a convoy with the flagship *St. George* and have been under way from Hanö for six to seven days.[108]

In the chill but clear weather, the officers and captains on the anchored Royal Navy Ships stand silently in small groups, watching the Danes so busy emptying the stranded merchant ships. They can do nothing to prevent this. It would be suicide to send the marines to assist these ships stranded so near a Danish borough. Any approaching Royal Marines would be greatly outnumbered.

One of the younger officers who is not too bright, is standing on the bridge of the *Dictator.* He tries to break the silence present by being funny and says, 'I don't think we should be so ashamed this morning for not being able to stop ourselves from being so humiliated and plundered by these enterprising Danes. Look at it this way. They are just attending to business the same way we are. After all, better they should take the content of these few ships than try to retake the entire fleet we stole from them four years ago." The superior officers on the bridge start to laugh, and the young officer, feeling encouraged, continues. "You laugh? This is serious. Don't you think the Danes can come and take their fleet back, if they get angry enough? Recall their forefathers, the Vikings. They managed to pour great numbers of fearless troops into the very heart of England, and mess up the place pretty badly, something that Napoleon has spent an entire war and half his career trying to do without any success. Remember these generous Danes gave our country the name England, meaning 'the land of meadows" in Danish. These far -seeing, fearless Nordic Vikings found North America and met the native Americans more than 400 years before Columbus ever heard of India. Our English city of York was controlled and greatly influenced by these Danish Vikings, who brought their superior ship building traditions from Roskilde, where all the Danish Kings are buried. That city of York again gave its name to New York!" Some of the younger British officers are rolling around on the quarterdeck now, laughing hard and holding their stomachs, a thing they never tried onboard this ship before.

The captain of the *Dictator* shakes his head at the whole ridiculous scene. To close the mouth of this young officer, the captain poses a question. 'Well, if the Danes or the Nordic Vikings really obtained such honorable and brave achievements, how come the World hasn't heard about it?" The young officer has a quick answer ready. 'Because it is Viking tradition never to brag about your achievements." The captain looks very tired as he addresses what he considers a very young and naïve officer. 'If you continue to try and be so funny this way, my good man, I'm afraid we might actually be able to get rid of our bad reputation as a tough ship to serve on."

The items the Danes take from the stranded ships are later sold in local auctions[200] to the benefit of the Crown and to supply a poor war economy in this unimportant and remote corner of the kingdom, at least according to the Danish central administration.

In the late afternoon, Reynolds gives the order to fix a cable between the *Cressy* and the *St. George* so towing can resume. As a second-rater, the newly built *Cressy* is a much better ship to be used for towing than *Bellette*.

As soon as dark falls that evening, Danish privateers begin to plan new attacks to cut more merchant ships from what they now see as an unorganized, weak British convoy, when the chances are the best.

That evening, Captain David Atkins from *Defence* orders shots to be fired, and an hour later shots are regularly fired from different Royal Navy ships. Boats stuffed with mariners are rapidly put in the water from *Cressy* and other ships of the line. The *St. George,* too, sends out boats with armed mariners to assist in protecting the convoy during the night[200]. William is in one of these boats. He has built up a routine for meeting the enemy at an arms distance on the dark sea surface. He is not scared anymore, just highly alert. Only, on a philosophical level, William is sad to be here assisting in a fight against a nation that helped his own country obtain its independence.

In the daylight of November 21, the crewmembers onboard the *St. George*, Admiral Reynolds included, conclude that they are forced to leave the missing merchant ships behind, because none of them has shown up in the meantime and must have gone down. Reynolds sends a courier ship northwards to the *Victory* and Sammaurez at Vinga Sound with a dispatch telling him that they will be ready to continue the voyage this day. At 9 in the morning, the convoy is ready to sail. *Dictator* is now in charge of the larger part of the convoy of merchant ships, because *Cressy* is held ready to tow the *St. George* when needed. Before the convoy has passed the Great Belt and the Cattegat and reached Vinga Sound, the 76 merchant ships have grown to 94 including the prizes taken.[27]

Dictator observes several shots fired at 9:30 p.m. and sends two boats filled with mariners to the row guard.[49] At the end of the day, they anchor 10 nautical miles east of Femmern to wait for a better wind direction.

That day, in Matvik harbor, *Ariel* and *Woodlark* receive fresh beef from the *Pyramus*. Direct trade with the Swedish merchants is still possible.

A group of seamen from *Woodlark* is sent to shore to cut wood and bushes near Matvik on the 22nd of November. *Woodlark*'s captain Dashwood writes to Admiral Sammaurez to inform him that some of the merchant ships originally in the *St. George* convoy have returned to Matvik Harbor. These ships have been tied up to rocks and trees, having lost their anchors in the previous storm. Captain Dashwood is uncertain whether it is possible to get these merchant ships back to England this year. In his dispatch, he pessimistically concludes that it is not likely that these ships can be repaired this year before Matvik harbor is closed by ice.[200]

Defence's rudderstock was damaged in the storm and as a ship carpenter assistant, Amos is helping to supply the ship with a new rudderstock from *Cressey*.[35]

Five days later, Sammaurez receives Captain Dashwood's dispatch in his cabin onboard *Victory*. Looking at the borough of Gothenburg on the eastern horizon, he becomes absolutely furious. What does he mean by not returning the last merchant ships to England? Of course these ships are returning this year! For what does this Captain Dashwood think they are being paid?

Admiral James Sammaurez has promised the owners of these merchant ships, in person, that they will return this year, all of them! Sammaurez quickly writes a new dispatch to Dashwood, ordering him that the last part of the convoy has to come back to Vinga Sound as soon as possible. He includes an instruction to Dashwood to receive an acting lieutenant from *Cresent* in order to strengthen the leadership onboard the *Woodlark*, to make sure that all merchant ships in the convoy will return safely home.[67]

When he receives Sammaurez's dispatch, Dashwood understands clearly that others will take over the command of his ship if he doesn't pull himself together. Dashwood now quickly hands out instructions to get the anchors fixed on these merchant ships so they can sail for Vinga Sound.

The following day around 8 a.m., the convoy is at the north end of the Island of Langeland, in sight of the unlit Langeland Lighthouse. To the northwest is the flagship *Vigo,* with Rear Admiral Dixon standing on the quarterdeck, and a convoy of merchant ships going south in the Great Belt. *Vigo* is with *Orion*, *Wrangler*, *Cresent*, *Bruiser,* and 38 merchant ships.[49]

Two hours later, Rear Admiral Dixon and his flagship *Vigo,* heading south, salute Rear Admiral Reynolds and flagship *St. George*, heading north, as they pass each other in the Great Belt. Rear Admiral Reynolds answers the salute.[49]

Bellette's captain is onboard *St. George* at 5 p.m. and Gurion and *Bellette*'s captain agree that it is best if *Cressy* continues towing the flagship. *Bellette* will now go ahead and escort some of the faster merchant ships to Vinga Sound, to minimize the time these ships are exposed to attack in Danish waters.

Cressy sends the hawser to the *St. George* by two boats and takes the flagship in tow. When Reynolds and Gurion are convinced that the towing seems to be working, *Bellette* leaves *Dictator, St. George, Cressy* and the main convoy to take its own convoy of merchant ships to Vinga Sound.[35] The main convoy with the damaged flagship moves slowly northward. The jury mast and rudder on the *St. George,* being towed by *Cressy,* will soon let Danish privateers and cannon boats in the Great Belt know that a storm-damaged and slow moving Royal Navy fleet is returning home now.

William is standing on the main deck of the *St. George* beside William Freeman this late and dark autumn afternoon. They are looking for Danish cannon boats and privateers in the Great Belt. Back in the Customhouse in Wilmington, Allen McLane is looking out the window of his office and thinking of his war memories.

Secretary of State James Monroe is also looking out of one of the windows in the Department of State and recalling the days and nights he experienced 35 years ago.

General Washington's army is now on the New Jersey side of the Hudson River and the Commander in Chief is convinced that General Howe's men will go south toward the Capital, Philadelphia. Washington and his men begin to retreat from the Manhattan area, down through New Jersey to the Delaware River, with Cornwallis and Howe's men following them. It is late November and the weather is wet and cold and the regiments are moving slowly. The soldiers are in low spirits moving along the muddy roads, and supplies and shortage of carriages have hampered both armies. General Washington is searching for supplies and more militiamen along the way, and the troops stop for several days each at Camden and New Brunswick.

Washington thinks of offering Howe battle points on several occasions, as he is convinced that Howe heads for Philadelphia, but Washington's army is only traveling at its minimum due to desertions and expiring enlistment. He finally gives up the idea. Lieutenant Allen McLane tries his best to keep up the spirits in his own company, but some of his men desert under the pressure of these hard conditions. As McLane is able to figure out, it is almost 40 percent of the privates that leave. But McLane is not one who gives up easily. He will fight for what he believes in and fight to the bitter end if that is needed.

The morning of November 24, the boats filled with mariners return from the night row guard and slowly approach the gangway of *St. George*.[49] William Watson, William Freeman, and the other mariners are freezing. It can be extremely cold sitting in a small boat with no chance to move and exercise for so many hours. They are tired and hungry, too. Haze covers the Great Belt. The convoy is heading toward an anchoring position near Nyborg.

Only one and a half hours after the mariners return to the *St. George,* the lookout observes rapidly approaching Danish privateers on the horizon. Gurion orders five shots fired and burns a blue light to warn the merchant ships in his convoy to gather as quickly as possible. *Cressy* immediately sends the armed guard to assist a new row guard. Thick fog once again covers the Great Belt, and the privateers again escape the staggeringly superior English sea force.

The alarm is finally called off at 10 a.m. and the yard taken in. Captain Charles D. Pater from *Cressy* sails to the *St. George* to talk to Rear Admiral Reynolds. Pater returns to *Cressy* at noon with instructions about the fleet, and finally succeeds in anchoring at Nyborg.[35]

The boats to the row guard are sent out from *Dictator* again[49] at 2:30 p.m. and half and hour later *Dictator* sends out another group of armed boats to assist a single merchant ship which has it's distress flag hoisted.[49] Shots are heard from *Cressy's* bridge at 3.30 p.m. and coming from west-southwest, the landside near Nyborg and *Cressy* fires several shots in that direction.[35] Different Royal Navy boats are returning at 4 p.m. after they have recaptured the ship *Johan Henrick* from the Danes. Ten Danish prisoners are taken from that ship[49] on that occasion. The late autumn dark covers the Great Belt at 6:00 p.m. and officers onboard *Dictator* clearly observe several blue lights and several muskets fired.

The captain of the *Dictator* orders two boats to be sent to assist the convoy's row guard for the evening and n ight[49]. At 7.30 a.m. the boats return[49] because there is no more risk of the convoy of merchant ships being attacked.

Later that morning, November 25, Captain Pater pays Admiral Reynolds a visit at 9:00 a.m. Twenty minutes later, William stands on the forecastle and, in the morning light against the eastern horizon, sees a Danish 'Flag of Truce" come out from Corsør Harbor, cross the Great Belt and approach the gangway of the *St. George,* anchored some miles outside Nyborg. He sees what he considers a strange event. The Danes in the boats climb the gangway and a few minutes later, there is direct contact between the Danish and English enemies on the main deck of the *St. George.* Danish and English prisoners and diplomatic letters are exchanged.

William does not consider himself a sophisticated philosopher, but even so, he has a hard time comprehending what he sees. He wonders how these Danish and English enemies can fight each other day and night, and then suddenly stop the conflict and have a friendly conversation and exchange mail and prisoners in the most civilized way. Then why can't peace be negotiated?

The Royal Navy fleet and the convoy of merchant ships are still anchored at Nyborg[35, 49] around 3 p.m. An hour later, 29 newly taken Danish prisoners are transferred from *Dictator* to *Defence* and *Cressey.*[49] Soon after, *Cressy* fires a cannon and several muskets at a ship with an American flag. The merchant ship *Elosine*, which is on its way to Jutland to Kolding Fjord, is boarded and the cargo taken.[35]

On November 28 at noon, *Ariel* moors at the pilothouse in Matvik harbor and finds here the brigs, *Pyramus, Cresent, Ethalion, Ranger, Woodlark, Wrangler, Censor* and approximately 28 merchant ships.

On November 30, *St. George* has been towed steadily by *Cressy* for some days now. At 8:00 a.m. they have reached a position north of the Great Belt and William can see the unlit Anholt Light House[33] to the north. Admiral Reynolds, Flag Captain Gurion, the officers and the rest of the St. *George* crew feel very much relieved. They know for sure, now that their damaged flagship has made it so far north in the Cattegat, they will be able to arrive safely at the Royal Navy Baltic Headquarters in Vinga Sound.

7

St. George and *Cressy* finally reach Vinga Sound with *Dictator* and a convoy of merchant ships on December 1. *Diligence* is in the area patrolling the northern Cattegat. Rear Admiral of the Red C.W. Reynolds gives the order to his men onboard *St. George* to fire a salute to announce his arrival, and soon after, Rear Admiral of the Blue James Sammaurez onboard *Victory* returns it with 11 shots. From his Admiral's cabin, Sammaurez observes the jury masts on the *St. George*[73] that he had been told about.

Cressy's captain, Charles D. Pater, is so satisfied with the successful towing of the *St. George* to the English Baltic Sea headquarters that he opens a new cask of rum to celebrate with his men.[33] After all the troubles and hard work they had been through the past month, he thinks, the men honestly deserve a good time with a cup of rum.

The small convoy of merchant ships under the surveillance of *Woodlark* is still anchored in Matvik harbor at this late time of year. The following week, the *Ariel* and the gun brig *Carnest* have the nerve to go hunting prizes in the water south of Hanö. The merchant ships are being repaired and the Royal Navy ships supplied with additional foodstuff. The admirals in London are convinced that the Baltic Sea is already frozen.

When they arrive at Vinga Sound, the *St. George's* crew and officers, including Admiral Reynolds, are still convinced that they have lost nearly 50 merchant ships in the storm at Nysted.

But onboard the *Victory,* Sammaurez has already received better information about this convoy's destiny.

The remaining ships are now being repaired and then *Pyramus* will escort them to Vinga Sound. There are no larger ships of the line in the small convoy in Matvik Harbor, so Sammaurez has instructed Captain Dashwood to take the convoy up through Ear Sound instead of passing up through the Great Belt. This will take the Danes by surprise, because no military person would expect a Royal Navy convoy to sail from the Baltic Sea so late in the year, and certainly would not expect a returning convoy to come up through Ear Sound.[200] Sammaurez knows that the Danish Navy and Military think that the Royal Navy convoy has already anchored in Vinga Sound, where it is preparing for the last part of the voyage - crossing of the North Sea to England.

Sammaurez was amused at his brilliant plan as he wrote the letter to Captain Dashwood. In Vinga Sound, several merchant ships have gathered to join this newly arrived convoy for the passage through the North Sea to England.

At 11 o'clock this December 1st, every single person on the flagship *St. George*, from Admiral to mess boy, is very excited when the ship's bell sounds for this day's gathering at the main mast. They have heard rumors that a parcel with mail for the crewmembers has been taken onboard.

First Lieutenant Francis Rogers now stands at the main mast listening to an officer who loudly reads the names on the envelopes and hands them out to the men onboard. It is completely quiet as the officer speaks, as each and every man listens for his own name. The officer steadily calls names for 10 minutes, then suddenly says, 'William Watson, Mariner!" William Freeman is standing next to William Watson and pokes him in the side with an elbow with a genuine look of surprise. "William, William there is a letter for you."

William Watson looks confused, then says, slowly, "Yes. It must be from Mary Ann. She has finally written me after my three letters." He pauses. "Or it could be from Port Collector Allen McLane." William's blood rushes to his face and he feels dizzy. Someone has finally heard the almost endless calls and prayers he has put forward regularly for more than two years. He steps forward and the officer quickly hands him a letter. William takes it and as he walks back, he realizes, to his surprise, that the letter is not from Mary Ann or Allen McLane in Wilmington. It is from the American Department of State in Washington D.C. William is breathing heavily as he thinks, 'From the Department of State! A letter to *me* from the American Department of State! This is incredible!" He tries to breathe deeply and slowly, wondering why the Department of State would send him a letter. When he has come to his senses, he opens the envelope very carefully to avoid damaging to the letter. The envelope contains two pieces of paper. He unfolds the one. On the top of the page is a symbol he knows so well, an American bald eagle. He reads the date and the short note. *"On the request of the American Agent for Seamen in London, General William Lyman, the*

Department of State hereby sends You, William Watson, an American Mariner onboard his Majesty's ship St. George, a copy of your protection certificate numbered 7777 and issued in New York on February 27, The year of our Lord 1807."

The signature at the bottom of the page is illegible to William. He unfolds the second piece of paper and smiles as he recognizes a copy of his Protection Certificate. He studies it carefully and feels great relief. Now, finally, he is able to prove who he is - an American. William Freeman observes the whole scene with amazement, his mouth wide open. William Watson turns to him and smiles. "There, you see, I told you 7777 is a lucky number. It is almost holy. The number 7 is the number most frequently occurring in the Holy Bible." William Freeman smiles. "I didn't know that, William. But it's certainly a good thing that your Protection Certificate has come back to you."

William Watson's thoughts race. He is not at all certain what this means. Maybe he can be released sometime in the near future. Then he stops for a few seconds and lets his mind linger on the wonderful thought that at least he knows for certain that someone back home in America is thinking of him and knows his difficult situation. This new knowledge strengthens him tremendously. Everyone onboard *St. George* who knows him can see the change in him immediately.

Right away, William's attitude and look become that of an important person who believes strongly in himself. He keeps reminding himself that it is not just anybody who wrote to him, but actually the American Department of State! William wonders who is the Secretary of State right now, and recalls the name Robert Smith, not knowing that James Monroe took over the office on April 6 this year.

The letter cheers him up a great deal, and reconfirms what he used to believe, deep down in his heart: that in times of trouble, his beloved country will come to his rescue. That is what America has always been about, William thinks, and he smiles to himself, feeling warm inside.

News of William's letter spreads over the entire flagship, and instantly creates a new mood of optimism among all the impressed American seamen there - a mood that was not there before. Later in the afternoon, when William Watson and William Freeman stand at the starboard railing looking in the direction of Gothenburg, William's mind is set on his beloved country, the United States of America. He feels restless and can't wait to be released, so he can rush home to the wife he loves beyond comprehension and his child, whom he has never seen.

Encouraged so much by receiving his letter, William finds new, extra energy to help the younger William Freeman keep up his spirits. He says, "William, I have decided to tell you a story while we sail on our return to England. It will keep our minds off this horrible ship."

William Freeman can't read, and he is happy to have the opportunity to educate himself with a good story. "Yes, William, it will make me extremely happy if you would do that." William Watson's eyes seek the eastern horizon, with the view of the borough of Gothenburg, as he begins.

"It is a late November day in the year of our Lord 1637. In the bottom of the scurries of Sweden's only large west coast harbor, two three-masted ships are anchored on the roads outside Gothenburg. The strongly fortified borough is surrounded by Danish waters to the west, the Norwegian fief Bohus to the north, the Danish fief Halland to the south, and some minor Swedish territory to the east. One of the two ships is the Key of Calmar, armed with 12 cannons. The other ship is Bird Griffin, armed with 10 cannons. Boxes with the last supplies of fresh vegetables are handed up from a rowboat at the gangway on the port side. During the past three days, they have taken in a cargo of several hundred axes, spades, knives, hatches and adzes among other things.

The crew is well paid, but they are not of the normally good standard found in a harbor town like Gothenburg, which has a proud seaman tradition as far back as anyone can remember. These seamen are busy checking the rigging and the nine sails each ship carries - as many as the bastions in the fortifications of the city. They are all experienced seamen from coastal traders and fishing boats.

Peter Minuit is a 52-year-old man of great energy, an officer and the former Governor of the newly established Dutch North American Colony, New Amsterdam. He was also Director General of the Dutch West Indian Company, which established the colony in 1621 on the lower rocky banks of the Hudson River on the island of Manhattan. He is a contradiction to the rest of the crew on the two ships he commands, as he becomes more and more calm and self-satisfied as the departure approaches for this first Swedish expedition to the New World.

He hasn't felt this happy in five years, when on his return to Holland, he was so disgracefully dismissed as Governor on what he believed were false accusations of mismanagement of the New Amsterdam colony. Patrons along the Hudson River who felt secure being so far away from the government in Amsterdam, had finally succeeded with their enterprise, and had him removed from the Governor office.

He was convinced that he had been a scapegoat, caught between the dissatisfied patrons on the one side of the Atlantic Ocean and dissatisfied investors on the other side. The patrons were not able to generate the outcome in the New World that the investors had been promised at the patron's departure from Holland. On the other side, the investors were dissatisfied with themselves for having so foolishly made these investments that obviously gave no returns. He had then been the one to pay.[219]

On his return to Holland in 1632, he had been filled with bitterness and thought that he had seen the New World for the last time. But that year, two things happened that made the voyage he was going to start in a few minutes possible but delayed.

First, Samuel Blommart, one of the directors of the Dutch West India Company had contacted him. He was feeling dissatisfied with his returns from the Dutch North American Company in New Amsterdam, and wanted Minuit to pursue an opportunity that had emerged from the work done in the last 30 years by Blommart, Minuit, and a Dutch businessman named William Usselinx. In the 30 years before the final establishment of New Amsterdam, Usselinx had spent his time and fortune establishing a trade route between Holland and North America. He soon found out that he received little reward for his services and left Holland angrily and went to Sweden.

In the Swedish Capital of Stockholm, Usselinx succeeded in interesting the Chancellor of Sweden, Axel Oxenstierna, in a plan for establishing a Swedish colony in the New World. He then gained an audience with King Gustav II Adolph in the Royal Palace on the protected islet Ridderholm (Knight Island), just opposite the home of Oxenstierna in the inner Stockholmian scurries. He presented to the king the benefits such a colony would be to God, the King and Sweden. The Christian religion would be planted among the heathen, the king's treasuries would be enriched, and the burden on the shoulders of the people of Sweden would diminish, Usselinx had argued.

The king himself was a busy and successful commander of the Swedish Army in the demanding and wasteful 30 years war, which involved almost every nation on the European Continent. He was head of a nation that had risen from one of the weakest and poorest nations in Europe to leadership of this war. It was easy to convince the king of both the moral and economical advantages of establishing a colony in the New World

The king, being busily occupied with warfare in the northern part of Germany, allowed a trade company to be established. On June 14, 1626, when the Swedish trade company was chartered, ladies of the court, the king himself, nobles and bishops bought large shares in the new company.

On November 6, 1632, while commanding the Swedish Army of infantry and cavalry west of the village of Lützen in the northern part of Germany, Gustav Adolf II was separated from his soldiers and fell from his white horse, shot to death.[154]

His beautiful 6-year-old daughter, Kristina, succeeded him on the throne, but Oxenstierna, had no natural talent for keeping in the background, and took over state affairs. He had no time for colonial thoughts. Blommart then persuaded Peter Minuit to write to Oxenstierna and pursue the idea of establishing a colony. Peter Minuit did so, specifically mentioning in the letter that his plan was to go to the South River near Virginia, where the English had established their colonies close to those of the Netherlands, and to call the Swedish colony New Sweden.

Preparations for this voyage had been overwhelming, and expenses far exceeded the original estimate. But that is all of no concern now, Peter Minuit thinks happily. He is filled with strong masculine energy and thankful that, at the age of 52, he will again be allowed to conquer the New World."[154]

William Watson smiles, exhausted from telling the long, complicated story he once learned in school. 'I think that will be all for now, William!" William Freeman doesn't want him to stop now, and begs, 'But William, please continue. It is such a living and interesting story that you are telling me – a story that the world needs to know about.

What happens next?"

William Watson walks away with his final words, 'Don't ask me anymore questions about it. You will learn soon enough!"

William Watson decides to wait until the next day to contact his superior officer about possible release based on the firm evidence he now has that he is an American. He is quite confident that he will be set free when Flag Captain Daniel Gurion is confronted with the official letter from the American Department of State and the copy of his Protection Certificate.

The North Sea weather can be dangerous to the Royal Navy at this time of year, but from a military viewpoint, there is no danger. Cannon boats can't operate in the rough autumn and winter weather. So mariners like William Watson don't have to go out in boats and risk their lives in dangerous man-to-man fights, as was the case when they passed through internal Danish waters.

The English crew onboard the Royal Navy ships anchored here at Vinga Sound is desperately looking forward to the return to their families for Christmas.

It is good for Admiral Reynolds to be anchored with his fleet here in Vinga Sound, because it gives him a chance to dine with the captains in his Fleet. During the first two dinners arranged in his Admiral's cabin onboard the *St. George,* the subject of return to England is discussed rather intensely.

Reynolds is generally in a good mood on these occasions, happy that they have already come so far, and he is firmly convinced that his flagship *St. George* is well prepared to make the challenging trip cross the North Sea, especially since it can call on the assistance of *Cressy.* The successful towing of the *St. George* up through the Great Belt from Nysted to Vinga Sound is clear evidence to him that *St. George* can make the rest of the trip, too. Most of his captains are loyal to Reynolds in everyday matters, and at this crucial moment, they stand behind him. David Atkins from *Defence* is probably the most loyal captain Admiral Reynolds has, and he backs up his good friend and superior completely.

Commander Sammaurez has dinner with his subordinates, Rear Admiral Dixon from *Vigo* and Rear Admiral Reynolds from *St. George,* on different evenings and they, too, discuss the matter of *St. George's* return. As commander in chief of the Royal Navy's Baltic Squadrons, Sammaurez is concerned about letting the *St. George* pass the dangerous North Sea with jury masts and rudder. The North Sea is not at all like the internal, narrow Danish waters. He argues with himself for a long time. One moment, he is prepared to let the flagship *St. George* scuttle in the scurries in Vinga Sound, to prevent the Danes from taking it when the winter sets in and the *Victory* and the rest of the Royal Navy fleet have returned to England. Then the next moment, he worries about his reputation as commander of the Royal Navy Baltic fleet and thinks that it looks much better if he returns a complete fleet to Portsmouth.

Reynolds strongly opposes scuttling the *St. George*. At dinner onboard the *Victory*, Reynolds, Gurion and Atkins completely reject the idea. Reynolds refers to the successful towing of the *St. George* from Rødsand, and *Cressy's* captain Charles D. Pater backs him up. Sammaurez finally agrees that the *St. George* will be allowed to return to England. But the following night, he can't help becoming more and more worried about the safety of the *St. George*. He reopens the discussion the next time they meet, but Reynolds and Gurion stand their ground, so Sammaurez finally relents.

The *St. George* is now prepared to go to England, with *Cressy* towing her when necessary and *Bellette* and *Defence* escorting her closely.

In the month of December 1811, the Danish Admiralty and King Frederik VI decide that 14 Danish ships are going to take part in the combined Danish-French Baltic Fleet. The part of the Royal Navy convoy still anchored in Matvik Harbor risks meeting this combined fleet[79] if it stays.

The next day, *Cressy's* foretopmast is taken down on the forecastle to be repaired. The mast received some minor damage during the many days of towing the *St. George*. Some days later, the rear starboard cannon on *Cressy's* first gun deck is strengthened to ready the ship to continue towing the *St. George* across the North Sea[200], if the decision is made to tow again.

William Watson decides that the time has come to contact his superior officer regarding his release from serving in the Royal Navy. He walks to the main deck and addresses the first officer he sees on the quarterdeck, 'Sir, I would like to seek permission to speak to Captain Gurion."

'On what grounds?" the officer answers sharply, seeing no point to the conversation.

'I have received a copy of my Protection Certificate from the American Department of State and I would like the opportunity to present it to the captain personally," William Watson replies.

"Yes, of course, and I would like to have dinner with the Admiral and receive all his prize money," the officer answers sarcastically. "As you might know, we are in a foreign port right now, and under no circumstances will we release anyone here. If you need to address this issue, you will have to wait until we have arrived in Portsmouth."

William is quite familiar with the rough tone officers use to answer questions posed by ordinary crewmembers. He is dejected. The officer is telling him, quite frankly, that he will not be released at any point, whether he has a Protection Certificate or not. William feels sad at first, but after a couple of hours, his good mood returns. William simply refuses to let an officer in the Royal Navy dictate how he is going to feel. After all, he is so delighted that he received a letter from the Department of State, that it's hard for him to hide his happiness.

While anchored outside Gothenburg, there is a good possibility to send letters, so the English seaman William Galey decides to write to his wife in England. He tells her about the horrifying days and nights they experienced around Nysted and Rødsand, and ends the letter in a way that shows how optimistic most of the English crewmembers are regarding the last trip home to get their Christmas leave: *'Despite all our hardship, we did not lose one single man and none was wounded. For this and every other grace, that the almighty God has given us, I ask you, together with me, to offer up the most heartfelt thanks in His holy name. We shall all sail to England with the first favorable wind. We have a fine ship to escort us the new* Cressy. *When we return to England people will say, Here comes the old* St. George *in leading strings like a little child."* [200]

The following day, December 3, *Dreadnought* supplies *St. George* with a main topsail[51] as part of the preparations to return *St. George* to England.

In Wilmington, Allen McLane is unable to sleep. Maria is fast asleep next to him as he recalls the events of December, 35 years ago.

His own company and the rest of Washington's Army reach Trenton on this day of December 3, and spend some time placing obstructions in their tracks to delay the enemy. The British main goal this autumn was to secure eastern New Jersey as a winter camp - a goal they had already achieved.

McLane recalled that Washington had ordered his troops to be ferried over the Delaware River at Trenton. When Howe receives this message, he decides to station some of his troops at Princeton, Pennington, and along the east side of the Delaware River at Trenton, Bordentown and Burlington!

In early December, Washington and McLane march down the Pennsylvania roads with their different divisions, regiments and companies. Their spirits are at the lowest since the outbreak of the fighting. Washington is kind of depressed, because he has finally understood that traditional fighting, with each army lined up in front of each other, will never leave the Americans as winners in one single battle. This year's confrontations had clearly shown that.

McLane, on the other hand, is not that pessimistic. As an earlier military scout, he is used to fighting man against man, when surprised on his observation post in the landscape by the enemy. He had come out of these hand-to-hand fights as the winner every single time. As Lieutenant McLane saw it, the British soldiers were much less independent than the Americans, making the individual close combat situation an advantage to the Americans.

As so often happens in such a situation, the Commander in Chief regards the bad position the Continental Army is in as his own personal fault. But McLane, as a loyal lieutenant in a good mood, is quite optimistic and feels he has to cheer up the superior officers. And as forces of General Lee and Gates gather with them, Washington's own optimism rises. But here in the middle of December, the retreating George Washington has to devise a plan soon, because all but 1,400 of the Continentals end their enlistment at the year's end. Washington does not waste any time in planning his next stroke.

A loud snore from Maria brings McLane's thoughts back to their bedroom. He thinks to himself that Maria has always been a loud sleepyhead and it was a good thing that she was not with him, George Washington, and the rest of the Continental Army during the war. That would certainly have made it impossible to hide from the enemy at night.

In the following days, Royal Navy ships arrive from the Baltic Sea and are supplied with large quantities of food and rum, beer and water. *Cressy* is running out of flour and bread, and the next day Captain Charles D. Pater is forced to put his men on half rations.

The 6th of December, a launch brings a shroud from the *Dreadnought* to the *St. George*. A court martial onboard *St. George* has sentenced a seaman from the *Dreadnought* to death and the *Dreadnought*, also called 'the living hell" by ordinary seamen and mariners in the Royal Navy, is obligated to supply the shroud.[51]
 William Watson is not happy about being forced to stand at the St. George's mainmast to see the seaman hanged, now that he knows he is not going to be released soon. Both William Freeman and William Watson are feeling quite sad, wondering if they will ever see the United States of America and their loved ones again.

Two days later *Dreadnought* supplies *St. George* with two topmasts.

The following day, on December 9, Sammaurez writes a letter to the General Auditor in the Military Headquarters of Copenhagen at the islet of Gammelholm in Copenhagen, discussing the release of war prisoners. He wants to negotiate the release of 10 Danish prisoners from *Cressy*. Although Denmark is an enemy, Sammaurez is a diplomatic man, which is why he is liked so much by the Danish Consul and Swedish representatives in Gothenburg. When he visits Gothenburg on occasion, he is invited to dinner parties. He writes this letter on nice, golden-edged paper to show the proper respect he thinks must be present in diplomatic communications even in these times of war.
 Sammaurez asks for release of a midshipman from the *Cressy* jollyboat who was taken prisoner by Danish mariners in Nysted, where *St. George* lost its masts.
 As a correct gentleman, he addresses another issue of great concern. The Danes have apparently observed English mariners stealing fishing

nets in the northeast end of the Great Belt. Sammaurez promises his Danish counterpart in the letter that these mariners will be properly punished, when the guilty are found. It is very important to Sammaurez to distinguish between regular war actions and improper ones.

The following day, the Anholt schooner that regularly sails between Anholt and Gothenburg with supplies anchors in Vinga Sound with a convoy of 12 sails of transport.[59]

The next day, the Danish General Consul in Gothenburg writes a report to Danish military headquarters, informing them that the wind is from the east and he expects Sammaurez and *Victory* to leave any minute for England. He also reports that Sammaurez is an honest man who greatly admires the Danes and wishes them all the best, while he is provisioning here. Although they have military cooperation with France in the Baltic Sea, the Danish military leadership still wants to have good relations with England. The General Consul also gives the information in his letter that *HMS Hope* and two other British ships of the line will stay at Vinga Sound for the winter.

On the morning of December 14, the remaining small British convoy is still anchored in Matvik harbor.[67] At noon, the captain of the *Ariel,* who is in charge of part of the convoy, is ready to give the signal to weigh anchor. *Ariel, Crescent, Ranger, Woodlark, Censor, Ernest* and 34 merchant ships sail toward Vinga Sound. *Wrangler* and *Ethalion* will stay in Matvik during the winter months.[29] The weather is clear and the breeze fresh from west-northwest on this day of departure.

Three days later, on Tuesday December 17, the wind is from the southeast and the weather fine, with a light haze that covers the Vinga Sound region.

Rear Admiral of the Blue James Sammaurez stands, as often before, at a starboard side window in the gallery of his flagship *Victory,* silently admiring the many ships from his battle fleet and the merchant ships under his protection. He is becoming increasingly restless. All these ships anchored in front of his eyes are fully provisioned and ready to leave. Even the wind comes from east, perfect for a passage home to his beloved England.

Rear Admiral Sammaurez plans to let the large fleet depart Vinga Sound and return to England in three different sections. The first group to leave Vinga Sound, escorting the largest convoy of merchant ships, is his own flagship *Victory,* which will be accompanied by three other ships of the line and a couple of gun brigs.

Then the plan is to let the *Cressy* sail with *St. George III* in tow, escorted on each side by *Defence* and *Bellette.*

Finally *Hero,* the brig *Grasshopper,* the sloop *Egeria* and the armed merchant ship *Prince William* will leave Vinga Sound with a third convoy of merchant ships, the last part of this year's final Royal Navy convoy from the Baltic Sea.

Sammaurez finally hoists the flag for the fleet to depart at 10 a.m., and soon after *Victory* and the first group departs Vinga Sound with a favorable eastern wind and heads for England.

Two hours later, at noon, *Cressy* and the *St. George* fleet section follows on a northwesterly course, sailing as close to the wind as possible. Captain Charles Pater stands on the bridge beside the steering wheel onboard *Cressy,* while Admiral Reynolds stands on the quarter deck of the *St. George* with his arms gathered behind his back, rolling up and down on his toes, as he always does when the navigation of his flagship lives up to his high standards.

Admiral Reynolds smiles to himself, enjoying the sight of the many full sails on the western horizon. It will be an exquisite pleasure to return to England and enjoy the Christmas days with his family, Reynolds thinks to himself. This year he will have some exciting personal experiences to tell his son about, knowledge that he hopes will be of use to his son in his own career in the Royal Navy. Reynolds especially looks forward to telling him about the smart jury rudder invented by Admiral Pakenham, which they are using now.

William Watson and William Freeman enjoy the quiet moments that can be experienced onboard this busy flagship now and then. They are standing at the railing on the forecastle, listening to the sound of the waves that rhythmically hit the stem on the starboard side. William Watson says that it is time to continue with his story, and William Freeman, who has been looking forward to this moment, eagerly agrees. William Watson slowly turns toward the rear of the *St. George* to watch the scene around Vinga Sound and the Borough of Gothenburg for the very last time.

From the rear end of the Key of Calmar, on the small 'eight deck', the roof of a small cabin for the captain erected in the rear end of the quarterdeck, Peter Minuit places himself between the two lanterns astern. A large blue and yellow Swedish flag on a pole 10 feet above the deck snaps loudly over his head, indicating the presence of the strong eastern wind. It is time to leave. He shouts a final salute to honor the Almighty God, the 11-year-old Queen Kristina and the Kingdom of Sweden, then gives the signal for departure to his two Dutch captains. The anchors are quickly raised. Minuit takes a final glance at the borough of Gothenburg, so nice and orderly looking from a distance and arranged inside the strong fortress walls. The windmill on top of the hill on the east side of the borough, with its rotor directed toward the east, is producing at maximum level in this strong wind. Peter Minuit considers it a good sign for the coming long and uncertain voyage. As the two ships are slowly escorted out through the scurries by a lot of smaller boats, Peter Minuit keeps eye contact with the spire of the new Gustav II Cathedral, consecrated four years ago, the year following the king's death.

As the two ships sail out through the outer scurries and pass Vinga Sound, they are saluted from the cannons of the batteries of the Castle of Aelfsborg, which protects the entrance to Gothenburg. They pass the Swedish islands of little Denmark and Vinga Sound before they head into the Cattegat Sea toward the Skagerrak."[140, 154]

William Watson finds this a proper place to interrupt his story. William Freeman, on the other hand, is noticeably disappointed and begs William Watson to continue. But William Watson says, "William, you are not interested in knowing the rest of the story right now. Trust me and you will later be able to conclude that I was right in doing so."

About this time this very same day, there is a debate in the House of Representatives in Washington D.C. about impressments of American seamen on British Royal Navy ships. One of the men speaks at length about England in angry terms, finally declaring loudly to those assembled, "*I would rather see that fast anchored isle, that protector of the liberties of the world, swept from the catalogue of nations, than have that one American, one natural born citizen against his will being torn from his family, his country, and kept in a state of the most horrible slavery.*[266]

The section of ships under the command of the flagship *Victory* and the section under the command of the flagship *St. George* are now "flying" smoothly westward across the Cattegat waves, homeward bound and close to each other. The crewmembers onboard both the merchant ships and the Royal Navy ships are in a relaxed, good mood. With this favorable wind, they will all soon see the beautiful coasts of Southeast England on the horizon and before they know it, will be with their families and friends celebrating the Christmas holidays. The many large and grey sails gathered on this occasion are always a magnificent sight.

Even though the convoy is on its way to the fleet's winter camp in Portsmouth harbor, *Bellette* still finds time, the following morning, to board a sloop under Danish colors in Cattegat bound for Jutland. An officer and 14 men are sent to take the prize back to Vinga Sound. Five of the Danish prisoners are taken onboard the *Bellette*.[31] Two hours later *Orion* boards another Danish brig.

Lookouts see the Lighthouse of the Scaw at 11 a.m., and *Victory*, *St. George*, *Rose*, *Bellette*, *Vigo* and *Orion* are sailing close together. Half an hour later, *Rose* boards yet another Danish ship. From the bridge of *Victory*, the officers see a merchant ship from the convoy strand on the shore near the Scaw. They discuss this every time it happens. Some merchant ships try to save distance by passing close to the Scaw, but because the motion of two seas meeting here constantly moves the sand reef, some of those ships are bound to end on the reef or the shore.

On the order from Admiral Reynolds, *Cressy* puts *St. George* in a tow at 11 a.m., and even though the two ships are in this emergency situation, Captain Pater orders seven men onboard the *Cressy* to be punished with 18 lashes each, for neglect of duty and drunkenness.

Some of the seamen had apparently decided to celebrate Christmas in advance and too much. Because of the towing, *St. George* is sailing just be½hind the *Cress*y, and Reynolds has a good view of the punishment from his quarterdeck of the *St. George*. Admiral Reynolds is very pleased with what he sees as natural enforcement of strict discipline, which must be applied in a squadron of the Royal Navy Baltic Fleet under his command. The keen, servile Pater is fully aware of and responding to that.

In the afternoon, the *St. George's* section of ships has crossed the Cattegat Sea and is free of the Scaw. *Cressy* is still towing the *St. George*. The two ships hold a steady, fair speed, despite the few sails set on the *St. George* and its limited abilities to maneuver, because of the jury masts and jury rudder. Gurion orders the tow to release. The *St. George* is going to sail down the Skagerak Sea to the North Sea on its own.

At midnight, *St. George*, *Defence*, *Cressy* and *Bellette* are sailing in the Skagerak and the small convoy left in the Baltic Sea during the storm is now headed by *Pyramus*. The Royal Navy ships and 32 merchant ships are seven to eight miles southeast of Møn Island. *Pyramus* burns a blue light to gather the merchant ships[74-2] behind her.

At twilight on November 19, *Cressy* and *Defence* sail behind the *St. George,* and *Victory* is two miles ahead. The weather is fine now and a light breeze fills the many sails. The mood among the English crewmembers is quite optimistic, because they know that every hour that passes brings them and the fleet a bit closer to the coasts of England. There are 34 different nationalities among the crewmembers onboard the *St. George,* though, so not everyone onboard is happy and homeward bound.

All through the night of the 18th and morning of the 19th, *Defence* and *Cressy* stay close to the *St. George* when the flagship is not being towed, as Sammaurez ordered them to do at their meetings in Vinga Sound, before they all left. Captain Pater makes sure that his crew is constantly prepared to make a transfer of the hawser to the *St. George* to continue towing if the order should be received. *St. George* has done well so far, although it becomes more and more difficult to keep the flagship up in the wind, the wind now coming from the north, because to the south is the coast of Jutland. The officers on the bridge are interested in changing course to the southwest.

The fragile jury masts on the *St. George* make it difficult to increase the sail area to a normal level, and the jury rudder has a problem handling the increasing rudder forces from a course change toward southwest.

Boats transfer the hawser to the *St. George* at 9:10 a. m. and *Cressy* again takes up towing of the flagship.

As Captain Pater eats his breakfast this morning in the officers' mess, he decides to punish a seaman while they still have the Admiral's flagship in tow. He finds it important to use any opportunity that comes along to try and impress an important superior officer like Reynolds. The seaman receives 24 lashes for drunkenness and neglect of duty.[62] As Pater expected, Reynolds observes the punishment from his quarterdeck onboard the *St. George*. Reynolds is genuinely delighted that *Cressy's* captain shows such initiative to keep the good discipline in the Royal Navy.

Bellette shortens its sails occasionally in order to stay beside the *St. George,* as demanded by Sammaurez.

At noon, the four ships have reached 57 degrees 48´N, 08 degrees 57´E, in Skagerak, somewhere between the village of Hirtshals on the west coast of Jutland and the town of Kristianssand on the south coast of Norway. They are now fairly far down the Skagerak and coming closer and closer to the North Sea. The weather has changed from a wind direction and speed ideal for a passage to England, to strong gales and squalls. Many of the seamen and mariners onboard the *Defence, Cressy, Bellette* and *St. George* are already sitting on sea chests on the lower gun decks, enjoying themselves as they talk and have some rum to keep them warm as they celebrate Christmas leave in advance. Rear Admiral Reynolds really doesn't mind this year. After all the difficulties his crew has been through this year, he is very satisfied with their performance, which resulted in his flagship *St. George* being able to return to England.

Reynolds and Gurion stand in the Admiral's cabin looking out of the gallery at the high waves. The Admiral is the first to break the silence. "As you might know, captain, I am very pleased with this year's trip to the Baltic Sea. Despite the fact that the number of cannon boats in the Danish Fleet and the number of Danish and French privateers was double that of last year, I think we did all right. Don't you, Sir?"

Flag Captain Gurion gives his best career smile and looks at his superior, whose position he admires so much. He is genuinely delighted to answer honestly, 'Dear Admiral Reynolds, I couldn't have said it better, I couldn't agree more. We showed the Danes and the Frenchmen again this year, that Britannia rules the waves." Captain Gurion lifts the tin cup of rum he is holding in his right hand and says, 'Cheers to God, King and England!"

'Cheers," Admiral Reynolds returns, then states solemnly, 'I hope the new King George IV will be as good and long-lasting a King as his father King George III, who ruled us for more than half a century. It is so sad, that his destiny should be insanity. Hopefully this is not a sign for us to observe onboard the *St. George III*, named after him." They sip the strong Cuban rum from their tin cups, and remain silent for a while, then Reynolds continues. "And there is the interesting story about his sister Caroline Mathilde, who married the Danish King Christian VII. They were the mother and father of the present Danish King Frederik VI. King Christian VII also developed insanity, which, I guess, lead to the Queen having an affair with the private doctor of King Christian, Mr. Struensee."

"What happened?" Captain Gurion asks, always curious about high society gossip about European Royal circles. "Oh, that was really not a pretty sight, I should say. The entire Danish state administration in Copenhagen, promptly living up to its reputation, ganged up against this defenseless German Mr. Struensee. He was convicted for treason, executed and cut into small pieces for public display in Copenhagen. The Queen, the present King Frederik's mother, was expelled from the Kingdom of Denmark. How would you like to be the Crown Prince in such a country? How would you like to sacrifice your life completely to serve your mother country, only to discover late in life that that same country had destroyed your family? Likewise, this present war between Denmark and England stays in the Royal family. Maybe that is what caused the insanity of our king to develop, seeing his dear sister treated that way and knowing that war between countries in Europe always means war between Royal family members. For any ordinary person, family and the family members constitute a core unit that every member will defend naturally to obtain maximum security and benefits for themselves. But for the Royal family members, that individual first and foremost has the obligation to stay loyal to their duty to the country they serve, while having their family members living in different countries in Europe. They become fragile and these Royal families can so easily be torn apart."

Seamen onboard *Bellette* report to the bridge that the ship is beginning to take in 10 inches of water per hour now. This is critical, and the captain of the *Bellette* immediately orders the seamen to the pumps. Like *Defence* and *Cressy, Bellette* has a standing order to assist the flagship

St. George whenever needed, but now has its own severe problems.

The wind increases rapidly, and in half an hour, a strong gale is blowing from the west-southwest. The wind holds heavy hail and rainstorms. The resulting high waves that surround the flagship cause the *St. George* to pitch severely on the towrope. This is immediately observed from the bridge onboard *Cressy,* and Captain Pater orders a decrease in the area of the sails.

Around 3:00 p.m., *Cressy* is pressed very hard to the starboard side and the storm staysail tears apart. Men are sent up in the rigging and the sail is tied up quickly. Another sail is set and later the storm staysail is replaced. The men standing on the moving ropes at the upper bars tying up a loosened sail in a strong icy wind and hail showers need a steady nerve and a good physical health.

At this hour, the delayed *Pyramus* squadron and the convoy of merchant ships anchor northeast of Dars Head in the western Baltic Sea. The course has been west-southwest for some time now. It is very late in the year to still be in Danish waters. With the steady wind coming from the south-southwest, *Pyramus* now easily goes north and heads for Ear Sound in order to avoid a passage through the Great Belt.

At 4 p.m., a decreased wind strength is observed on the bridge onboard the *St. George. Victory* is a half-mile to the northwest, *Vigo* in the same direction, *Dreadnought* to the southwest, and to the leeward of *Cressy* are the *Bellette* and *Defence.*

The sea swells higher and higher, making it extremely difficult for Captain Pater to keep *Cressy* on course when towing *St. George.* The high weight and low sail area of the *St. George* makes *Cressy,* with its low weight and large sail area, fall off from the wind in the direction of the northeast – toward the dangerous lee shore of Jutland. They now head toward the northeast when they want to go southwest. It's an unstable situation in the long run. Captain Pater signals his troubles to Admiral Reynolds, who fully understands the seriousness of the problem. He gives the order for the ships to return to Vinga Sound and stay clear of the northwest coast of Jutland. *Cressy* veers at 4:30 p.m. and all the ships are now sailing on a northeastern course, on their way up the Skagerak, where they just came from.

Reynolds signals Sammaurez at 6:00 p.m. that *St. George, Cressy,*

Bellette and *Defence* are forced to go back to Vinga Sound. Sammaurez understands that the time has come to split up the three original fleet sections of the Royal Navy Baltic Fleet. He burns a blue light to gather his section under command of the *Victory*.

Sammaurez looks through the rear windows in his Admirals cabin, silently contemplating the diminishing silhouettes of the four Royal Navy ships of the lines on the northeastern horizon. He wishes them all well, recalling the discussions he and Reynolds had before they left Vinga Sound. He knew then that Reynolds might get into serious trouble trying to cross the North Sea, and said so several times, but because of his democratic nature, Sammaurez had given in to Reynolds, Gurion and Atkins, with a majority of votes, that they should return to England with the *St. George*. 'Now, see what a fine mess they've got th emselves into," Sammaurez says aloud, angry. He walks back to his desk to take up his paperwork.

Sammaurez now decides to exchange all Danish officers and men taken from merchant ships in the Cattegat by the Royal Navy this year with English midshipmen[96] taken by the Danes. Yes, that must be a fair deal, he thinks to himself as he writes a letter to the Danish Admiralty in Copenhagen about this proposal.

The following morning, December 20 at 4 a.m., *St. George* is still towed by *Cressy*. The wind has reduced to only fresh now.

St. George cuts the towrope to *Cressy* later that afternoon. *Bellette* veers later and signals to *St. George*. The officers on the ships are interested in finding out how far east they have gone into the Cattegat, to get an estimate of how close they are to the rocky Swedish west coast. Sailing in a dark sea near a rocky coastline is not the best way to steady an officer's nerves on the bridges. *Bellette* now receives an order from the flagship *St. George* to sound every half-hour on her larboard bow.

Finally, at 11 p.m., the crewmembers relax, because *Cressy* has signaled an observation of land to the south-southeast. At midnight, *St. George* is put in tow again, so Reynolds and Gurion knows where they have her, increasing the possibility of keeping *St. George* of the rocky Swedish coast.

The four ships of the line are close to Sälø Island, three or four miles to the southeast and north of Vinga Sound the next morning at 6:30 a.m. The wind now comes from north-northeast, a perfect wind direction for a passage home to England.

The officers onboard *Bellette,* the smallest of the four Royal Navy ships present, see the Sälø Beacon and run toward it to signal to the island for three Swedish pilots.

At 11 a.m., the seamen who were punished two days ago for drunkenness onboard the *Cressy* are again punished for the same crime, but this time each of them only receives 12 lashes. *Cressy* is close to the *St. George* again and Reynolds observes the punishment with satisfaction from *St. George's* quarterdeck. Reynolds is again very pleased with what he sees, and Captain Pater knows it. Not one captain, marine officer, seaman or anyone else in the *St. George* squadron has any doubt that Rear Admiral of the Red C.W. Reynolds is a hardliner when it comes to discipline.

Half an hour later, a Swedish rowboat from the coast stops at *Bellette's* gangway and the ship receives three Swedish pilots. It is squally and raining, and *Bellette* immediately sails toward the other three Royal Navy ships, anchored further out on the beacon, to get this fleet section homeward bound as quickly as possible now that the wind direction is ideal.

At noon, the *Hero* section of the convoy is between the Naze of Norway and the town Hanstholm, or the Holm as the Royal Navy officers and seamen call it, off the northwest coast of Jutland. *Hero, Prince William, Egeria, Grasshopper* and 50 merchant ships are sailing together.

Two hours later, *Cressy* receives one of the Swedish pilots from *Bellette*[33] and *St. George* receives another.[31]

Pyramus, Woodlark, Crescent, Ariel and the convoy of merchant ships have reached the entrance to Ear Sound at 2:20 p.m. The breeze is strong and from the west-southwest, and the sky is cloudy. *Pyramus* orders the squadron and merchant ships to anchor east of Saltholm Island, which divides the southern part of Ear Sound into a channel to the west between the Danish island of Amager, just outside Copenhagen, and the Malmö Channel to the east between Saltholm and Sweden. Anchoring here on 11 fathoms of water should protect the ships against the strong western wind and from the Danish cannon boats from Copenhagen to the west.

Around 3:10 p.m., the captain from the *Pyramus* observes that *Ariel* is stuck on the Swedish shore at Barsebæk. *Pyramus'* boats and *Ranger's* prize are sent to assist the *Ariel*. In the evening, *Pyramus* observes 37 merchant ships. At 10 p.m. *Ariel* fires a rocket to make its position known to the *Pyramus'* officers and to call for help.

Cressy, *St. George*, *Bellette* and *Defence* are now sailing together with a good speed and on the preferred western course, homeward bound for the second time within a week. *Bellette* adjusts sails to stay on the *St. George's* starboard side, as ordered by Sammaurez. In the late afternoon, they pass the Scaw.

During the night, they sail steady on a southwestern course along the southern Skagerak and everything seems to be running smoothly this time. Captain Pater on *Cressy* decides to shorten the sails like *Bellette*, to reduce speed to stay close to the *St. George*. In the morning, the wind is coming from the perfect northeastern corner.

The morning of December 22, as the ships approach the entrance to the North Sea, outward bound for the second time, William Watson and William Freeman are once again standing on the forecastle enjoying a moment of rare silence. They feel no wind here and enjoy having a quiet rest after breakfast. William Watson decides to continue his story to William Freeman.

For the Bird Griffin and the Key of Calmar, it is important to keep a northwestern course to avoid the Scaw Reef, but getting too northerly in the Skagerak can be fatal, too. A strong eastern wind like the one occurring now, or worse, a south eastern wind, can make it impossible to avoid the rocky coastline and the hidden scurries of the coast of Norway before entering the North Sea, one of the most dangerous waters in the world. Passing the Scaw at too short a distance, close to the northwest and western beaches of Jutland, in a western or northwestern storm that so often appear at this time of year, can send the ships into the sand banks and breakers of the coast. It can literally tear them to pieces within a couple of hours, with no chance for any living creature onboard, to survive. Any skilled skipper, captain or pilot always takes quite seriously a pass through the Cattegat, Skagerak and the North Sea. Very few of those who did not are left to tell about it.

William Watson pauses to catch his breath and William Freeman interrupts. He has been surprised for some time. "William, my friend, do you realize what a unique story you are telling me? It sounds as though you know the history of the Kingdom of Sweden, and these treacherous, troubled waters we are now sailing, better than the Swedish pilot we just took onboard. How is this?" William Watson smiles his frequent secret smile. "The story is over for now, and do remember that we have an agreement. No questions or no more story telling!" William Freeman nods his head. "Yes, William whatever you say. Your words are the law to me."

At 8 a.m. this same morning *HMS Hero* signals to the ships under its command. This third section of the convoy has reached a position 66 miles northwest of the Cliffs of Bovbjerg. The merchant ships are going directly to Leith now, and before they separate here in the North Sea, *Hero* signals *Egeria* to take over the lead of the convoy that is now going to Leith. *Nightingale* decides to follow that merchant convoy.

Daybreak comes and *Pyramus'* captain and crew observe with delight that *Ariel* has succeeded in coming off the Swedish ground. At 3 p.m. the *Pyramus* squadron and merchant ships are anchored in the Copenhagen Steeples to take shelter from the strong western wind.

On a position southwest of the Cliff's of Bovbjerg*Hero, Grasshopper* and 18 merchant ships, all government transports[200] are, at 4 p.m., heading south on course to reach Portsmouth. The armed merchant ship *Prince William* goes toward the Humber and loses sight of the *Egeria* convoy, heading for the same place.

The *St. George* is now entering the North Sea. William Watson and William Freeman stand on the port railing of the forecastle and try to identify landmarks along the northwest coast of Jutland, but they are too far out at sea. William Watson smiles to his younger friend and announces, "William, I'll now continue my story."

The Key of Calmar and the Bird Griffin have crossed the Cattegat, the Scaw and the Skagerak all right, but as they reach the entrance to the

287

North Sea, the strong wind jumps to the northwest and a few hours later, strengthens to a regular storm and jumps to the west. Minuit and his Dutch captains can clearly see the white chalk-painted church tower at Hanstholm. They have deliberately avoided going into the Jammerbugten (Bay of Misery), where ships, captains and seamen have so often experienced tragedy. They are heading dangerously eastward toward the coast and the lee shore. Rearranging the sails has no influence on their course and the sounding line becomes shorter every time they try to measure the water depth. At the low depth of 19 fathoms, the captains are in a near panic.

The Cliffs of Bovbjerg are known to any seaman sailing along these coasts for their steep slopes, which on a sunny day, can be seen from afar. They can be very dangerous. The slopes continuously feed the North Sea with more sand, earth and clay, creating new, unknown reefs running farther out into the sea than any other place along the coastline. Luckily, the captains of the Key of Calmar and the Bird Griffin manage to turn the ships onto a safe southwestern course heading for the English Channel.

William suddenly ends his ongoing story with a mysterious smile. 'That will be all for now William."

William Freeman tries to come up with a reasonable protest, feeling injured. 'But William, this is really not fair. You give detailed names of places appearing on this remote coastline, places that should be unknown to you as a young American seaman who has never sailed these waters, and so far away from Wilmington and Philadelphia. I can see by your strange smile that it is probably a real story you have been telling me all the time. Now, what is going on? Please tell me the rest of the story now!" William Freeman is quite upset now, because he feels he is deliberately being fooled time and time again.

'No, I'm sorry but I can't do that." William Watson feels satisfied with himself. He thinks that this arrangement of an ongoing story will give young William Freeman something to look forward to, and let him forget all about the depressing situation they are experiencing right now, impressed in the Royal Navy onboard the flagship *St. George III*.

William knows that he will be able to keep his story going and William Freeman' s mood up until the day he knows for certain that they can put their feet on North American soil again. An officer gives them the order to go below deck.

The wind direction has moved from the ideal northeast to the less favorable north, forcing the convoy to take a more southern path, which takes them closer to a lee shore, the coast of Jutland. The wind is fresh now. To keep the same speed as the flagship *St. George*, *Cressy's* Captain Pater orders the sails shortened at 10:50 a.m.

All four ships are together now. At noon, the convoy has reached the bottom of the Skagerak, 18 miles northwest of Hanstholm. In just two hours, the wind has moved to an even more dangerous direction and is now coming from the northwest, keeping its strength. It is cloudy as the convoy is forced to sail even closer to the lee shore of Jutland.

Bellette adjusts sails to keep her station on the starboard side of the *St. George*. At 3 p.m., they clearly see the land around the Hanstholm. A sounding shows that the water depth is 25 feet here. The four ships keep the course and are all kept together until after midnight.

The breeze is moderate and it rains at 4 a.m. on this new day of December 23. Five hours later, *St. George* receives a signal from *Cressy* asking if she should take up the towing again. Gurion, standing next to the steering wheel, shakes his head. The wind still comes from northwest and the breeze is fresh. *St. George* can handle her own trip home to Portsmouth, if the wind direction does not change to a more western or south-western direction and the strength does not increase too much. Dark clouds are wandering over the firmament, but the air visibility is fine.

In Ear Sound, the *Pyramus* convoy is progressing up along the Swedish west coast. The gale is fresh with squalls. Mentally, the men in this small squadron of the Royal Navy prepare themselves to pass the feared batteries at Kronborg Castle.[74-2]

Close to the flagship *St. George*, Captain Pater observes from the quarterdeck of *Cressy* that one of the ropes of the Pakenham jury rudder apparently has broken and the sail and rope makers and carpenters are busy trying to repair the damage. It's obvious that strong forces must be acting on the jury rudder, and Captain Pater wonders if it will hold until the *St. George* has reached Portsmouth. The seas are heavy now, and large seas heave up and down. *Defence* has traveled out of sight of *St.*

George's quarterdeck, although there is a standing order from Sammaurez that the four ships must stay together as they go England.

Bellette is still taking water in. The carpenter has not been able to identify or stop any single leak in the hull. At 10:00 a.m., the water intake has increased from 10 to 20 inches an hour. *Bellette's* captain orders more seamen to the pumps.

An hour later, Captain Newman of *HMS Hero* signals to Fanshave, the captain onboard *Grasshopper*, to bring *Grasshopper* within hailing distance of *Hero*. Newman thinks they are on a position somewhere off the southeast coast of England near Silver Pitts, and he signals Captain Fanshave to take a course of southwest after noon. The order is obeyed and the course is changed, even though Fanshave and his lieutenants have a feeling that it is a dangerous course to sail. Fanshave and his men have a feeling that they are near the west coast of continental Europe, which makes a western course fatal, but they dare not and are not supposed to question their superior officer from *Hero*.

The orders of command earlier given by Sammaurez cannot be changed or questioned at all. The 18 government transports, *Grasshopper* and *Hero* all follow that given course the rest of that day of December 23.[200] The *Hero* convoy is now running about 9 knots an hour.

At noon, *St. George's* first mainsail is taken down to reduce her speed. What Reynolds and Gurion feared for some time now has become reality. The wind direction has changed to the west-southwest and the strength increased. *St. George* is heading north now, back toward the Skagerak, as it had already done once before on this journey. *St. George* is now sailing as close to the wind as possible to avoid getting closer to the lee shore. They are on the course away from England again. The only good thing Captain Pater can say about the new situation is that the sail makers and carpenters have finally succeeded in shifting the damaged rope of the jury rudder this morning.

At noon, the wind is fresh and it is hazy in Ear Sound where the *Pyramus* and its squadron are at anchor. All members of the crews know that if the wind decreases more, they will probably be attacked by Danish cannon boats. They might lose some merchant ships.[74-2]

Onboard the *Defence*, the storm staysail is taken down so *Defence* can stay close to and on the lee and west side of *St. George*.

An hour later, at 1 p.m., *Defence* lays hove to the wind with most of its sails tied up. The wind direction is still west-southwest. By deciding to tie up all the sails, the captains of *Defence*, *Bellette* and *Cressy* all follow the same order from their superior officer Gurion to reduce speed drastically. Reynolds and Gurion decided not to try to let the four ships go up in the Skagerak this time, the way they did before when the wind was not favorable for a passage directly home to England. This might be a dangerous decision, and all the captains and officers know it, because even though the sails are down, they are still close to and drifting toward the shore.

Half an hour later, *Pyramus* orders the ship made clear for action and the decks are quickly emptied. The small squadron in Ear Sound is preparing for a confrontation with the Danes.[74-2]

At 2 p.m., the officers and flag captain on the bridge of the *St. George* observe that the wind has jumped 90 degrees, from southwest to northwest, within the past two hours. This has stopped their drifting northwards toward the Skagerak, and it forces the four ships on a south-south-eastern course. The wind strength and the direction are now both the worst thinkable. The ships are so close to the lee shore that it's impossible to sail north to the Skagerak Sea because the wind comes from northwest. But they are also so close to the lee shore that it will be necessary to veer or else the ships will all strand on the west coast of Jutland.

The *St. George* carpenters keep an eye on the jury mainmasts and jury rudder they repaired earlier, looking for even the smallest signs of weaknesses. But as far as they can see, when the sails are down, everything seems fine.

An hour later, the mainsail area of the *St. George* is reduced and the first mainsail tied up.

Onboard *Defence,* one of the sails for the main mast is taken down. Because *Defence* only carries one main sail, Captain Atkins finds it wise not to expose it to unnecessary danger. He orders it put under deck, where it is kept ready for when the weather improves. The officers on the bridge and the ordinary crewmembers are optimistic. Despite the tough weather conditions and all the connecting troubles, they are all very much aware that the Christmas holidays are approaching. The wind now mostly comes from the west, but occasionally jumps to northwest or even southwest. The *St. George's* course is not altered.

   St. George's forestaysail is hauled down at 4:30 p.m. and placed under the mainstay sail. Shortly after, the one thing that must not happen, happens. The upper of two hangers on the jury rudder breaks with a loud, frightening noise, and all men at the rear of the flagship instantly realize that they have just witnessed a very serious event. The news spreads through the ship quickly, and soon reaches the bridge. Now the whole crew, including Gurion and Reynolds, knows that the ability to steer the *St. George* has been lost just when it is very crucial. They are totally dependent on the wind strength and direction and, to a minor extent, on the sea currents along this coast of Jutland.

The *Pyramus* squadron and its convoy of merchant ships are slowly heading north to pass the Kronborg Castle. They know from experience to sail as close to the Swedish coast as possible here, to avoid the Batteries of Kronborg. The Danish soldiers and officers manning the batteries have spotted the Royal Navy convoy approaching from the south. The western wind in Ear Sound is increasing.[74-2]

Onboard the *St. George* flag, Gurion gives the order to haul down the mainstay sail at 6:00 p.m. and the seamen put it under the mizzen staysail. *Defence* and *Cressy* follow suit, although the men are quite worried whether the *St. George* can maintain its slightly northeastern course. *Bellette* loses sight of *Cressy* and, ten minutes later, loses sight of the *St. George*. After another ten minutes, *Defence* is also out of sight of the *Bellette*. There are now strong gales with heavy squalls. *Bellette* sounds occasionally to check whether she is on course, away from the dangerous lee shore of Jutland.

The gales keep strength during the evening and night, and the wind still comes from the northwestern corner with a heavy sea. The *St. George* is leading the little convoy, now consisting of only the three Royal Navy ships, *St. George, Defence* and *Cressy*. They are currently in the North Sea 53 miles northwest of the Cliffs of Bovbjerg, drifting to the east-southeast toward the dangerous reefs of Jutland. One of the lads busy helping heave some sails in the rigging on *Cressy* slips from the tow at a top bar just when a strong wind gust hits him, and he falls down and overboard to disappear in the large dark sea. The quartermaster confirms this to Pater ten minutes later.

That evening at 9:30, *Defence* is hove to the wind but keeps its storm staysail up. *Defence, St. George* and *Cressy* are sailing close together but alone in this deserted part of the North Sea. The officers and captains of the three ships are worried, and so are the seamen and officers. William Watson, William Freeman, and their colleagues are preparing for the night. They silently hang up their hammocks; none of them feel like speaking. The English crew should already be home celebrating Christmas with their families, but somehow the weather and the North Sea want it differently.

Captain Pater is more worried now than he has been in a long time. His face looks calm, but his thoughts are a complete mess. He is quite aware that he can't keep *Cressy* on this dangerous course toward the sand reefs much longer. But because of his expected loyalty to his superior officers, Captain Pater does not even consider changing this dangerous course on his own. But he does wonder why nothing is done to take them all out of the increasingly dangerous situation. It must be obvious to anyone onboard that this cannot continue for much longer.

Confused, Pater sits down in his cabin and writes two letters, asking his subordinate officers if they can confirm that in order to save the *Cressy* from a stranding on the west coast of Jutland, they have to veer right now. The officers quickly read and sign the two documents and Pater orders a sounding to be made. Shortly he is informed that the water depth is now 8.3 meters and decreasing to 6.3 soon.

Captain Pater asks his officers to watch carefully for any signals from the *St. George,* but they observe none. Pater knows that *Cressy* will have to veer soon, but he feels guilty giving such an order if it implies leaving *St. George* and *Defence* behind to an uncertain destiny, without communicating with his superiors onboard *St. George* first.

He finally gives the order to veer at 9:15 p.m. and *Cressy* slowly passes the lit-up galleries of *St. George* and *Defence*, pointing to the southwest, so *Cressy's* lights can be seen clearly by the Admiral and the flag captain. Captain Pater then orders it written in *Cressy's* logbook that the Cliffs of Bovbjerg are only 24 to 27 miles to the east. It's a very dangerous place to be. *St. George* is now to the leeward of *Cressy*. Captain Pater observes that *St. George* has its main mizzen staysail and the topsail set. Captain Pater then orders *Cressy* placed on the larboard, or south, side of the *St. George* for a long period of time. This would give Reynolds and Gurion a fair chance to send signals if they have something to say, but still no signals are received.

At 10:00 p.m., *Hero* gives the night signal to *Grasshopper* and tells her to alter course two points to starboard. They can see the lights of four of the government transports, but soon after the heavy squalls of snow and sleet make it impossible to see any ships from the *Grasshopper*.

One and a half hours later, *Bellette* loses its mainstay sail. She is quite alone now, having had no other ships in sight since she left *Defence*, *St. George* and *Cressy* at 6 p.m.[31] Despite the problems with her mainstay sail, she is at a safe distance from the lee shore of Jutland.

Captain Pater and *Cressy* pass the *St. George* completely now, to show Admiral Reynolds that *Cressy* has veered for the last time to be homeward bound. They are leaving for England, and Reynolds, seeing *Cressy* pass by the windows of his cabin, has a chance to send contrary orders if he disagrees about Cressy leaving. But he and Flag Captain Gurion do nothing to prevent *Cressy's* departure. Rear Admiral Reynolds thinks to himself that the *St. George* is very likely to strand soon, and nothing seems to be able to change that. But there is no need to drag *Cressy* to that same fatal destiny.

Ten minutes before midnight of the 24th of December 1811, the men onboard the *Cressy* finally lose sight of the lights from *St. George* and *Defence*. Pater thinks that *Bellette* is still with them, because they were ordered to stay together when they left Gothenburg. But she is not. Pater takes breaking his order from Sammaurez very seriously, but he has no alternative if he wants to save his ship and his crew.

Onboard the *St. George*, Reynolds looks out the windows in the gallery in the direction of London, on the other side of the North Sea, where his wife and daughter are right now. He also gives some thoughts to his son, who has served eight years on the *HMS Piobe* and now is on another ship in the Royal Navy. Reynolds is now very worried about the outcome of this trip. It does not look too good right now. How will his son's career progre ss, if his influential father leaves the Royal Navy and this earth for good? It is as though the willpower slowly disappears from Rear Admiral Reynolds's mind in these crucial moments, as though, against his normal habit, he has given up fighting a fatal destiny.

Reynolds recalls the letter he received from his son, when he was onboard *Piobe* three years ago, congratulating his father for the new title of Rear Admiral of the Red. That letter had pleased Reynolds very much. At least if he is going to die now, he will die as a Rear Admiral, a lucky circumstance that will throw glory on the whole Admiral family, at least if a court-martial does not expose any misconduct on his part on this trip.

Reynolds begins to speculate about the insanity that once again possessed the former King George III earlier this summer of 1811, this time, unfortunately, for good. Reynolds began to see this sad event as an alarming sign to him and the rest of the crew onboard his ship named after the king. A cruel idea almost materializes in his mind, as he stands silently at the window of his cabin. Maybe *St. George III* will also, in the end, lose its ability to control and govern itself, represented by the death of him and the other officers onboard. Reynolds shakes his head hard to get rid of these dark, depressing thoughts, and then says to himself repeatedly that it is ridiculous to speculate this way. For a second or two, he thinks that he must have been carried away by his great imagination. Anyway, he must keep that kind of impossible thoughts to himself under any circumstance, to avoid scaring the crew he commands.

Defence's Captain David Atkins has not given up yet. He is now sailing on this clearly deadly course by his own free will. He was appointed captain of *Defence* for this year's Baltic operation, and loyalty to both of his superior officers makes him proud. He wants to perform his duty and stand by the side of the *St. George* in this difficult situation. There is no doubt in his mind about this. When he saw *Cressy* veer and leave earlier this evening, he gave the order to make everything ready for the *Defence* to veer. Then he asked his first lieutenant, Phillip H. Baker, if the *St. George* has veered yet and received the answer he expected: No, the *St. George* is on the same fatal course.

Before he goes to his cabin to rest, Captain Atkins glances at the wild looking sea surface. The huge seas that separate *Defence* and *St. George* impress him. He says to Baker, 'I want the *Defence* to hold the same course as the *St. George* and make no veering before she does." Shortly after, Baker passes the order to the master's mate at the steering wheel, putting his mouth directly to his ear to be heard over the roaring storm surrounding them. Baker thinks to himself that Atkins probably just gave them all a death sentence, but he is also very much aware of the strict discipline in the Royal Navy, and of what would happen if he tried to counteract the orders of his superior officer. The other officers carefully and silently watch every movement in the face of their captain, as he walks the quarterdeck before he goes to his cabin, and they all know that his stubbornness and misdirected loyalty may have cost them all their lives. Instead of speaking out about their worries, they just silently wish they were onboard the *Cressy* now, or that *Defence* had a self-assured, independent captain like *Cressey's* Pater. *Cressy* is now out of sight, on a steady safe southwestern course toward England and Christmas holidays for its crew.

Amos Stevens is busily working at this late time of the evening. Together with some assisting seamen, he is checking the planks in the hull of the *Defence* for any weaknesses that might cause water to break in. But *Defence* had been well repaired in the Royal Dockyards after the Battle of Trafalgar and this good carpentry work can still be seen here five years later.

Some of the seamen on duty onboard the *St. George* get the order to walk and check each cannon on the decks to make sure that the towlines that hold the cannons are properly tightened. One cannon breaking loose in a confined space like a closed room of a gun deck would be a minor disaster. A cannon weighs more than 3,000 kilograms, and a loose cannon can kill and cripple several seamen in few minutes, before anyone gets the chance to tie it up again.

8

At the beginning of the day of Christmas Eve, the strong gale is getting even stronger. *Grasshopper's* Captain Fanshave tells the officers on the night watch that he will go to his cabin to take a nap. He instructs them to call him if any signal is made or anything else unusual occurs. He orders them to sound every second hour and to report the result to him. He then goes to his cabin and lays down on his bed, wearing all of his clothes, to rest for a while.[18]

The silent, darkly dressed officers standing on the open bridge of *Defence* next to First Lieutenant Phillip H. Baker, and the officers standing next to First Lieutenant Francis Rogers onboard the *St. George* all watch the sky and the many white clouds that run quickly over the firmament. A clear moonshine is present most of the time and it illuminates the contours of the roaring dark sea, the light-reflecting foam, and the two ships of the line accompanying each other on a lonely, unknown position along the west coast of Jutland. Because the ships have been drifting to the southeast for some hours now, the crews have the idea that they must be somewhere outside the southwest coast of Jutland. But this is not the case. They are exactly 25 nautical miles west of the Cliffs of Bovbjerg, on the northwest coast.

There is a pronounced feeling of excitement among the officers on the quarterdeck of the *Defence*. Captain David Atkins is convinced that Rear Admiral of the Red C. W. Reynolds must give the order to veer any minute. It is not possible, in a strong northwestern storm like this, to go so close to the reefs of Jutland and keep the ships safe. A few minutes later, captain Atkins observes that *St. George* burns a blue light from its lee or starboard side.

This is what they have been waiting for onboard *Defence,* and captain Atkins, without hesitation, gives an order and the pipes call "All hands." The guard and the back guard immediately begin to prepare the veering of the *Defence*. Both Amos and John are awake now and jump out of their hammocks, as do the rest of the sleeping crewmembers. Amos is quite tired because he worked hard the previous day and had hardly slept an hour when he was woken up.

St. George still has its stem pointing to the northeast, and with the wind coming from north she is given a much better chance to veer. Flag Captain Daniel Gurion finally decides to give the order to veer and a group of seamen on the forecastle are quickly sent up in the rigging to set one of the foretopsails. While near the top bars, the seamen also try to twist the topmast fore staysail, but it is stuck under the pressure of the strong wind, and they must give it up. They have enough trouble just keeping themselves from falling. The jib is hauled up, but is hardly halfway to the top before it blows away in the strong gale. William can see pretty well because of the reflecting moonlight, and observes that the jib blows quite a distance over the sea surface before it is finally absorbed by the water. William understands that the men have no success in this attempt to get the flagship to veer.

Half an hour past midnight, First Lieutenant Baker is still standing on the bridge onboard *Defence*. He is quite nervous about the whole situation, because no orders seem to be given anymore, and he sends a master mate to the captain's cabin to ask Atkins when they are going to veer. Atkins only repeats what he has said before, that he doesn't want to give the order to veer before the flagship *St. George* has. Captain Atkins knows that his ship *Defence* is very capable of making a quick veering, when ordered. The problem is only onboard *St. George*. The crew onboard *Defence* is now very worried. Amos and his small group of assisting seamen are constantly running around checking the individual planks of the hull and therefore they have little time to worry about the real, great danger they might find themselves in. John, who has been captain of the forecastle since January 1 this year, is worried and he constantly keeps an eye on the rigging and the sails on this position of the ship.

Onboard the flagship *St. George*, the crew now tries to haul up a new jib by pulling it up by the strings to one of the foremast sails. This method seems to work, but it does not make the ship able to veer. The jury rudder with a broken upper hanger is unable to transfer forces perpendicularly to the long axis of the ship to let the ship make a natural turn. The forestaysail is lowered a little to help the veering, but this is also in vain when it comes to veering. The *St. George*'s position in the roaring sea, with its stem pointing toward the northeast, seems very stable and not easy to alter at all.

To support the broken upper hanger of the jury rudder, a stick is put through the third rear portside canon porthole, with a nine-inch cable to fix the rudder in the upper bearing. But this is no success at all.

It is now 1 a.m. The storm is still very strong and the wind from west-southwest. The hammock cloths are removed from their positions along the bulwark and fixed in the rigging to save them. The storm staysails are set, but quickly taken down again, except for the one on the mizzenmast, because of the still-increasing wind forces. The jury masts are laced up with more tow to strengthen them further. *St. George* is still lying with the stem pointing to the northeast, parallel to the incoming waves from west-northwest. She rolls rhythmically from side to side, making it difficult for anyone on duty to stay on their feet on the wet, smooth decks. In the hammocks on the first and second decks, several hundred crewmembers are also rhythmically rolling from side to side. Few can sleep because the rolling movements are too strong. But nobody wants to leave the hammocks, because it is difficult to stand up on the decks. This makes it very difficult for men on duty to carry out orders. It takes much longer to carry out an order now, at a time when a quick response is urgently needed.

William Watson and William Freeman are lying in their hammocks side by side, together with a lot of other ordinary crewmembers in the total darkness on the second gun deck. Both are admittedly afraid now. Some of the seamen and mariners in the hammocks next to them get seasick and throw up, creating a mess and a disgusting smell that are carried around the entire deck by the rolling movements of the flagship. This makes even more crewmembers throw up. Master mates order crewmembers to clean up the mess, but most of the ordinary seamen are too sick to follow these orders, well knowing what risk they might take. William would rather be up in the fresh wind on the main deck now, but this is not allowed unless one has a specific duty to carry out.

Finally, a little before 2 a.m., the wind direction jumps from north to west very rapidly, which causes the stem to change position from northeast to northwest. This causes some of the cargo to be displaced to the starboard side of the hold by the extraordinary strong rolling of the *St. George*. The movement of the hull also causes a couple of cannons to break free, which makes the hull lean permanently to the leeward, starboard side. Normally, this would press all the lower deck mariners and seamen on the wet deck onto this leeward side of the ship, but many of the men are still in their hammocks.

Later, the wind direction changes from west to southwest and back to west and northwest again, a more favorable position for the flagship to veer. Flag Captain Daniel Gurion gives the order to make another attempt to veer.

On the bridge of the *Defence,* the officers carefully watch the *St. George,* hoping to observe the flagship make a successful veering.

Captain Gurion now gives the order for the sheet anchor to be keelhauled from the northeast leeside, the starboard side, under the rear end of the *St. George* hull, to try and turn the ship's stem from northwest to west and southwest. The cable connected to the sheet anchor is drawn in through the third cannon porthole from the rear on the port side.

William Watson and William Freeman and the other men have been out of their hammocks for some time now. They are among the men called to the second gun deck to work at the cable wheel on this deck. There are about 60 other strong seamen and 10 of the strongest of the mariners working at the wheel now to pull in the cable and turn the flagship's stem to the more favorable southwestern position.

This seems to be successful. The stem of the *St. George* slowly turns toward west and the optimism among the officers and ordinary crewmembers rises. Slowly but steadily, the stem of *St. George* now twists westward and, despite the strong wind and huge waves coming respectively from northwest and west, the stem moves toward the southwest. The increasing cable forces make the cable stretch more and more.

Captain Gurion and Rear Admiral Reynolds know that the survival of the ship is in the hands of these seamen working the cables, wheel and anchor. While working hard, William observes Rear Admiral Reynolds himself walk down the stairs to the second gun deck and toward the wheel to encourage the men working with the cables. He says, 'My good men do your best. What you are doing is very important to all of us. I count on you. Keep up the good spirit.'[20] William sees the Admiral pat some of the seamen on the shoulders. He smiles to them, and William can see that an honest smile is returned. They are all very much aware of their responsibility in these crucial minutes.

William knows that this might very likely be the last attempt the Lord ever gives them to save His Majesty's Flagship *St. George III,* the crew and their own lives. Suddenly a huge wave from the west hits the hull of *St. George* hard and the ship is slowly elevated. William and the other men at the wheel feel the resulting decrease in force in the cable and the wheel sticks. This movement of the hull loosens the cable underneath the rear end of the hull just enough for it to move through the water by the force of the sea current around the hull. The cable is quickly swept backward and free of the hull, but then it is stuck beneath the bottom of the jury rudder, which is only properly fixed in its lower bearing. As the huge wave passes underneath the keel of the *St. George*, in its top vertical position above the seabed, the cable is stretched to its maximum over the sharp lower edge of the jury rudder. When the wave has passed, the rear end of the hull lowers so much that the jury rudder and cable break at the same time.

When the cable breaks, the 70 men at the wheel, including William and William Freeman, are instantly thrown to the deck. William feels both a physical and mental breakdown when he sees all these good men spread chaotically around the deck. Their hard work has been in vain. Slowly but steadily, the stem of *St. George* now turns back from the newly obtained southwestern position to its former position pointing northwest. The sounding depth reported to the bridge is 12 meters, which tells the officers that they are rapidly and irreversibly moving toward the dangerous, shallow sand reefs of the west coast of Jutland.

A Midshipman on the forecastle reports to the bridge that the distance to shore is now reduced to 20 miles, and the seaman who look out in the foremast can see nothing telling them where they are along the coastline of Jutland. They are 20 miles west of the Cliffs of Bovbjerg, a point they actually know well. Most of the seamen on the main deck agree that it is only a short time before the *St. George* runs aground.

Captain Gurion listens to the different arguments put forward by the officers and men standing on the bridge and makes the conclusion that his flagship *St. George* is beyond saving. He orders two of the guards to go below deck and pass the order to make the anchor chains ready for use. Before the last guard leaves, he is told to pass the orders to the captains of the masts to cut loose the lower yards and the topmasts to make the preparation for quickly cutting loose the masts when the ground is met.

Additionally, the order is given to open the cannon port holes on the upper deck, cut the cannons free and throw them overboard, and then

301

close the portholes again, to make *St. George* as light as possible when the ground is met. Captain Gurion decides to save a cannon on each side of the ship on the main deck.

Onboard *Defence,* the storm staysail is ripped apart by the increasing gale at 2:30 a.m. As a consequence, the forestaysails are hauled down to save them. *Defence* is hove to the wind by the mizzen staysail. The storm coming from the northwest is now tremendously strong.

    Defence is now only 10 nautical miles from the shore at a point south of the Cliffs of Bovbjerg on the shore where the small Danish village of Fjaltring is located. It is a village with less than 200 citizens, who mainly live in houses along a small road and on farms lying close to the village church.

Captain Fanshave has rested peacefully in his cabin onboard the *Grasshopper* since he went to take a nap, but now suddenly wakes to the penetrating loud cry of "All hands, all hands." All crewmembers are being called up to the main deck. At the same time, a midshipman knocks on the door and walks right in to inform Fanshave that they are in shallow water. Fanshave, already dressed, hurries up on the deck and finds that *Grasshopper* is stuck on a sandbank. The pilots are wrongly convinced that they are stuck on Smiths Knot on the English southeast coast. Fanshave listens to the pilots, then orders the ship steered to the south-southeast, not knowing that he orders the ship directly toward the Dutch coast of the island of Texel.

    For a long period, Fanshave and his officers think that *Grasshopper* is stuck for good. Fanshave almost gives her up, but then he is informed that the sounding now shows that the ship has 3 meters of water below her keel. Fanshave thinks that they have been lucky and found a deep hole in the seabed, which means sand banks now surround them. He immediately orders the anchor to go, in order to keep the ship on that safe position. From the bridge, Fanshave and his officers try to locate the ships in the convoy. They observe *Hero's* lights and think she must be at her anchor too. *Hero* fires several guns and burns a blue light at that time.[18]

Baker, the first lieutenant onboard *Defence,* notices that the time is now 4:30 a.m. He orders John Page, an English seaman, to send four men up to the foremast top yards. Page knows how difficult and dangerous this can be under the present tough weather conditions and with a ship rolling, so he leads the men up in the rigging. Just as Page reaches the top yard, his feet get a small puff upwards, which tells him that the *Defence* must have hit the ground. He looks down and, in the moonlight that shines along the shore, clearly observes the white breakers to the leeward and starboard side of the ship. Ralph Teazel, another English seaman, who has just reached him in the top of the rigging, shouts to Page "We must have hit the ground." The storm is wailing and whining loudly around the masts and the bars and it's almost impossible for John Page and Ralph Teazel to keep up their conversation near *Defence's* foremast top yards.

"Yes, I think you are right," John Page shouts back. He has hardly finished his sentence when *Defence,* slowly falling from the huge wave into a trough in the sea, shivers and hits the ground very hard.

The forestaysail is half wrapped up in tow when the first large sea sweeps the main deck and over the men standing on the deck to the leeward bulwark. This prevents the seamen from hauling up the forestaysail. As Captain Atkins realizes how impossible the situation is, he gives the orders to fire shots, burn a blue light and send up two rockets[257] to tell the surrounding world that *Defence* and its 503 crewmembers are in a very grave emergency situation.

It is early morning now along this remote northwest coast of Jutland, and still pitch-dark. The time is 5:45 a.m., and onboard the *St. George*, Rear Admiral of the Red C. W. Reynolds, Flag Captain Daniel Gurion, First Lieutenant Francis Rogers, and the other officers and ordinary crewmembers, 502 persons in all, hear these shots and observe the rockets light up a part of the previously dark northwestern sky. The men onboard the *St. George* know at once what has just happened. *Defence* is stranded.

The signals are also noted by a single Danish night watch and coastguard, who just happens to be awake in a tent where he is staying with three other coast guards, who are asleep, four miles south of the small Danish village of Fjaltring. These men, local coast guards, farmers and wreck masters who live on farms just south of the village of Fjaltring, are Peter Dahlgaard, owner of the farm Dahlgaard; Jens

Gadegaard, owner of the farm Gadegaard; Peter Ruby Christensen, owner of the farm Sønder Sønderby; and Christen Weie, owner of a small farm. They have been staying the night in this tent they built of canvas and wrecked timber from the cargo of the newly wrecked Norwegian bark with the German name *Die Liebe*, which they carefully guard to prevent anyone from stealing the timber.

Peter Dahlgaard is the night watch on duty, and from inside the tent is the first on the shore to hear a shot fired from the seaside and to the northwest. He quickly wakes up the others, who are sleeping tightly after having been drinking brændevin, strong Scandinavian snaps, most of the previous evening. Soon after, Peter Dahlgaard walks out of the tent and into the dark storm, with the three other men closely following him. They had wisely built their tent on the east or land side of the grass-covered dunes, to shelter it properly from the strong North Sea gale that occasionally carried large quantities of hail, snow and rain.

As the four men stride uphill to the top of a dune, they hear another shot and observe a glimpse of a blue light in the northwest. From their experience as coast guards, they instantly know that it can only be a signal coming from a ship in the utmost trouble. The walk over the dunes has made them all feel fresh and fully awake, and they feel their full strength in the present situation and are ready to act if needed. Standing close together on the beach to shield themselves against the wind, they look at each other, their eyes saying that only a miracle can save any of these poor souls onboard that unfortunate ship in the dark on the edge of the forceful and destructive breakers. They have seen for themselves, and heard through their fathers, grandfathers and friends, many sad stories about ships stranded here through the years, and they cannot offer any hope to the poor souls out there on the dark North Sea at this moment.

When *St George*'s Flag Captain Daniel Gurion hears the shots fired from *Defence* at 4:45 a.m., he makes a quick decision. He is convinced that it's a question of minutes before the *St. George* will also hit the ground, and therefore, he orders the bow anchors and the main anchor to go.

The bow anchors pull out one-and-a-half cable lengths of tow on each side of the ship before they finally hit the seabed. Gurion asks Lieutenant R. Watson to send the carpenters down into the bottom of the ship to listen to the well, to get an idea if any water is coming in. *HMS St.*

George is now stranded, too.

Reynolds is informed about the dangerous situation his flagship is in. Being awake so early and receiving such bad news is not a good beginning of what should have been a special day, exactly nine months since he entered his flagship *H.M.S. St. George* in Portsmouth. Half asleep, Reynolds think to himself that the number 24, this day's date, leads to the birthday of Jesus Christ and ought to be positively connected to this flagship named after Saint George, because it's the exact number of persons originally members of the highest English order, *Order of St. George*.

The last movement the flagship made before it stranded was to turn around the anchor cable turning the stem 90 degrees from northeast to northwest, almost performing the veer the crew had worked so hard to achieve during the night but without success. The veer was obtained at the very moment it was too late to make any use of it to leave this lee shore coast and return to England. The *St. George* was stuck immediately after the veer. But the tough effort made by William and the other men on the second gun deck was not all in vain, as the stem of St. *George* now points to the favorable position of northwest, in contrast to *Defence*, which stranded with its stem pointing northeast and the hull parallel to the incoming, destructive waves. *St. George's* stem pointing to the northwest will allow the hull to resist the destructive waves and provide shelter for the men onboard from the storm coming from that same direction. *Defence*, on the other hand, has little hope of avoiding destruction unless the strength of the storm diminishes considerably or disappears in the next few hours or so.

The carpenter onboard the *St. George* soon returns to the bridge to report that water in the hold has already reached a level of 10 feet. Half an hour passes and the carpenter reports that the water level has risen to above the lower deck – the second gun deck.

William and William Freeman are still together with their comrades on the lowest deck, which so far has protected them against the cold seas and the icy winds that buffet those higher up in the ship on the open decks. Reynolds, Gurion and First Lieutenant Francis Rogers receive continuous messages from the officers on the bridge, transferred from the reports from the carpenters, who regularly keep their eyes on the intake of water in the hull. They are fully aware that it is just a matter of time before they'll have to move the crew on the lowest gun deck upward in the ship. Finally, Gurion orders William and the other seamen and mariners on the lower second gun deck sent up to the first gun deck.

The mariners and seamen on the first gun deck begin to feel distressed as they realize that the men from the lower deck are coming up to the deck where they stay. Men on the first gun deck have sustained much less physical abuse, well-protected as they are against the tough weather, compared to the other seamen and mariners on the open top decks. But it demands a strong mental capability to remain calm, knowing that you are stuck down inside a ship that is being destroyed.

Defence lays parallel to the incoming waves, so that the waves pass the upper portside bulwark then free fall across the deck's width. The icy water gains momentum and speed as it falls, finally smashing the defenseless feet and bodies of the frozen men fighting to keep a hold at the lower leeward bulwark. Each large wave hits several dozen frozen men who have icy, senseless fingers. These men gradually lose the ability to hold on to each other or to the bulwark or tow and are swept off the *Defence* and into the sea. Most of them send up a prayer for the storm to end, but the constant sound of the wind howling in the masts and riggings does not indicate any change of the wind conditions in the near future. William and William Freeman are still below the open decks.

Almost every man on the first gun deck is scared now.

On the stormy beach south of the village of Fjaltring, Christen Øster Mærsk is quickly walking southwards. He walks close to the waterline, where the wet sand makes an ideal flat solid ground to walk on, in contrast to the dry, soft sand that covers most of the beach, which is much harder to walk in.

He is walking from the Mærsk Farms, a small group of farms located two miles south of Fjaltring to meet the other wreck masters and night watches and replace one of the men who has spent the long, cold night watching over the Norwegian bark *Die Liebe*. He walks on an isthmus that separates the Bøvling Fjord and the North Sea. In the first morning light, Christen Øster Mærsk observes the *Defence* stuck on the first sand reef, on a position along the isthmus where the tiny Tranholm peninsula is located in the fjord. Knowing how many ships have stranded here through the years, Christen thinks to himself that maybe the tiny, wide Tranholm peninsula holds some extraordinary, mysterious topographical conditions that create a dangerous siren song when a storm builds up on the coast. It might be a song so absolutely beautiful that it could be heard even far out on the open North Sea, attracting many inexperienced seamen to strand on that specific place, only to experience a fatal destiny.

Christen Øster Mærsk is normally a stout -hearted west coast farmer with only simple thoughts, so he knocks these crazy thoughts out of his head as he concludes that this huge ship cannot have been stuck for long, because it still has all three masts standing.

Ten minutes later, as John Page, Ralph Teazel and the two other seamen are on their way down from the top yard onboard *Defence*, First Lieutenant Baker gives the order to begin cutting loose the masts. As John Page and the other seamen reach the deck, the main mast, mizzen mast and foretopsails yard, where they have just been seconds ago, are falling overboard.

Christian Øster Mær sk continues to walk southward, keeping his eyes on the tall, dark ship. He sees four tiny persons near the foretop yards and wonders how they dare to stay there in this tough weather. A few minutes later, he sees the masts fall into the sea. He is not quite sure that those people in the rigging got off the masts before they left the ship. Poor souls, he thinks to himself.

Six or seven shots have been fired by 6:30 a.m., as far as John has been able to count. Amos is busy checking the inside of the hull of the *Defence*. It worries Amos and the chief carpenter a lot that they have to take care of the ship in this very difficult situation.

The pumps are constantly working now. Suddenly, the rolling of the ship breaks several cannons loose on the top deck, and several seamen are killed instantly when a wave hits the hull and sets some of the cannons on the upper deck adrift. The loud screams of many dying people fill *Defence*. Other heavy things have broken loose on the deck and injured more seamen.

Some have their arms and legs broken when hit by heavy, flying objects. When forceful, huge seas sweep over the main deck, groups of men are swept down through the hatchways. At the forecastle, John Page and John Brown observe the chief carpenter's wife, hol ding a little girl's hand, trying to run over the main deck to reach safety at the staircase to the quarterdeck. But a large wave breaks over *Defence* in these very decisive seconds and sweeps the two females, together with some men on the deck, down the nearest hatchway. It is saddening to both of them[289] to see and to be unable to help.

At this time, Captain Atkins is on the main deck, sitting on and tied to a Howbitzer cannon, which has been fixed rear of the place where the main mast had been. Many officers and men are now clinging to different wrecked parts of the *Defence*. The small boats are gathered down at the leeward gangway. In one of these boats, 20 men sit quietly, awaiting the breaking up of the ship, but suddenly a large wave sweeps over the main deck and the boat is swept overboard and turned upside down. The boat sails this way for some time along the leeward, starboard side of the ship, before it finally disappears in the sea.

The time is 7:00 a.m., and John Page, Ralph Teazel and John Brown decide that they want to leave the ship. 'We better leave now," John Brown says, and the two others nod their heads again and again. The ship is now breaking down with a speed that makes it possible for the men still onboard to get a clear feeling about when it will be all over. This will be soon. As John and Ralph Teazel pull them together and jump overboard and into the roaring sea, *Defence* finally gives in to the many rhythmical and forceful punches to the hull from the waves and sea floor. The ship breaks into two pieces and separates just in front of the captain's gangway.

John, John Page and Ralph Teazel are now swimming in the huge, icy waves and manage to get up onto the mizzen top yard few minutes after they have jumped. Sitting on the mizzen top yard, John Page happens to look toward the wreck as it breaks, and he watches the sheer anchor cast from the front part of the main deck onto the forecastle by the combined forces of a heaving wave and the breaking of the ship. It kills several men standing there. John Brown, captain of the forecastle, notices that none of the seamen he captained seem to be among these men.

The men on the wreck of the *Defence* are now screaming constantly and so strongly that Christian Øster Mærsk hears it where he is walking on shore, only 800 meters east of the wreck. He feels a deep sadness, realizing he is the only person present on this wide shore, so close to the

Defence and yet unable to help any of the many distressed men.

About 100 seamen, mariners and officers of the *Defence*'s crew sit on two bars tied together and lying on the main deck. They all silently wait for the final disintegration of *Defence's* two parts. Suddenly a huge wave sweeps this deck region again, and this time it manages to lift the raft consisting of the two bars and carry them out into the open, troubled sea.

Huge waves hit the mizzen top yard almost every ten seconds and have been forceful enough to sweep John Page, John Brown and Ralph Teazel off the yard because they have completely frozen fingers. But the two do not give up. They try to fight their way back to the mizzen top yard from one small wreck piece to the other, which happens to float along the shipside in the icy cold water, but without success.

A huge wave manages to throw Ralph Teazel back onto the deck of the *Defence*. Luckily John and John Page manage to get on the raft just as it happens to sail away along the side of the ship. At this time John Platt and Ralph Teazel are the only persons left onboard the wreck of the *Defence*. John Platt had also jumped into the sea earlier, but was swept back onto the deck of the ship twice by the large waves, as though God was giving John Platt and Ralph Teazel a sign to stay onboard the wreck for a while. When the raft with the many men sailed along the shipside, both John Platt and Ralph Teazel jump into the sea and get on it at the first try.

Now there are only 40 men sitting on and clinging to the raft. With cold bodies, completely frozen fingers and no ropes to tie themselves to the bars, it seems as though it will only be a question of time before most of these men are swept off for good to disappear in the cold sea. Suddenly a huge wave hits the raft and all but four men are swept off.

John Page is one of the many men swept off on this occasion, but he manages somehow to get back on, and observes that John Brown is already sitting there. John Page takes a look around the horizon to get an overview of their situation and says to John, 'Don't you think we are approaching the beach?' John looks and answers, "Yes, I think so." More men have managed to return to the raft and there are now 20 frozen men sitting on or clinging to it.

As the raft drifts in through the breakers and experiences the strong southward sea current, one wave after another rhythmically sweeps over the men and the raft every ten seconds. As the raft gets very close to the beach, only six people are left on it.[20]

Christen Mærsk, still walking southward on the beach, hears a weak moaning but cannot locate which direction the sound comes from. In the rough sea a distance from the beach, he sees many small parts of wreck drifting toward the beach. He increases his speed and hurries south to his own strand fief to see if some of the many wreck parts have landed there. Christen is a very practical man and quite economical in his way of thinking, which seems to be the case for most of the farmers and coast guards living on the poor farms along this part of the west coast of Jutland.

Peter Dahlgaard, Peder Ruby Christensen, Jens Gadegaard, Christen Weie and a fourth coastguard, Mads Liisbye, who arrives from Fjaltring to release one of the other night watches, are now all moving northward from the tent toward the stranding when they observe several parts of the shipwreck in the water close to the beach. On top of one of these wreck parts, they observe a single person lying flat out, and he seems to be alive! Peder and Mads quickly wade out into the icy water, well aware that the cold water, forceful breakers and undersea currents can carry them away at any time. They hurry toward the wreck piece that holds the surviving seaman and they manage to grab the small raft in their first try.

The wreck piece is heavy, but the two of them manage to drag it onto the shore a safe distance from the breakers. Christen arrives just in time to watch this scene. The man they have saved is not a seaman but the Englishman and Second Masters Mate David McCrobb, but he is too weak to tell them.

Peder Ruby Christensen now quickly takes off his canvas and gives it to this first man from *Defence* who has managed to reach the shore alive. In this winter storm, a wet and cold man will die if not soon protected properly against the cold wind. Christen observes that the seaman looks very weak and he takes off his canvas to cover him as well. Christen then helps McCrobb to his feet, so they can find a shelter in the tent.

The Danish coast guards on the beach split up at this occasion and Peter Dahlgaard, Jens Gadegaard and Christen Weie continue to walk northward to reach the actual stranding place of the *Defence*.

As Christen Øster Mærsk and David McCrobb reach the tent, they are amazed to see a wet seaman already sitting there. None of them saw where this man came from. He must have known he was walking on enemy territory and decided to hide in the dunes temporarily, Christen thinks to himself. Then when the coastguards decided to leave the tent to go north, in the direction of the wrecked ship, this seaman finally dared to enter the tent to seek shelter for the icy storm.

This man is Amos, and he seems remarkably well, considering that he has passed the dangerous, cold sea between the wreck of the *Defence* and the beach all by himself.

Mads Liisbye and Peder Ruby Christensen left David McCrobb and Christen Øster Mærsk to walk for the tent, to go for help and to change their wet clothes.

They are planning to go to Peder Ruby Christensen's farm, Sønder Sønderby, to fetch horses and carriages that can be used to transport the many wet and exhausted seamen they are sure will soon end up on the beach from the huge shipwreck. Peder and Mads decide to walk directly east to quickly pass the dunes and seek shelter from the cold storm, which has soaked them both. When they reach the east side of the dunes, they walk north toward the small group of farms located south of the village of Fjaltring.

As they walk along two sandy trails on the ground, all covered by lyme grass, they try to figure out how many crewmembers are onboard this tall ship and how many will have enough strength and luck to reach the shore alive.

This wrecked ship is a size that no one along this coastline has ever experienced before. They dare not even try to guess how many men could be onboard such a huge ship.

While Peder and Mads move north along the two sandy trails on the east side of the dunes, Dahlgaard, Weie and Gadegaard move north along the beach on the west side of the dunes.

They now see the raft, which now has only five men sitting on it. At the same time, the coast guards take a good look at the wreck stuck about 800 meters from the shore, just as the poop, which holds the captain and the officers' cabins, falls into the sea. They take a closer look at the wreck and clearly see that no more men seem to be onboard the wreck or in the sea nearby. Only a very few men can be seen sitting on or clinging to some of the wreckage parts.

It is less than two-and-a-half hours since the well-functioning third rater Royal Navy ship *Defence* hit the ground, and now it is in such a wrecked state that it does not seem to hold any living creature onboard.

With his life in danger and with a great effort, Peder Dahlgaard enters the roaring sea and breakers and succeeds in dragging the first four men to the shore one by one without any problems. But the last man on the raft, John Page, is not able to leave by himself. He is very weak and one of his feet is stuck between the two bars. This has actually saved his life so far by preventing him from being swept off the raft when it went through the forceful breakers.

As Peder walks out into the breakers once again, all of his body disappears under the sea surface several times and prevents him from reaching the raft again at his first try. John Brown, Ralph Teazel, John Platt and Thomas Mullins are now safely on the shore, and they closely follow the attempt to save John Page. John Brown and Ralph Teazel get up to assist Peder, but Jens Gadegaard and Christen Mærsk ask them kindly to sit down again. The two Danish coast guards try to explain in their best Danish, but with a West Juttish accent much like an English dialect, that they, the Danes, are much stronger and fit to perform these demanding rescue attempts. Despite the fact that he is quite exhausted, John has no problem understanding the facial expressions and body attitudes of Christen Øster Mærsk, so he just nods his head and sits down again.

John begins to relax. He is beginning to realize that he is one of the few men able so far to reach the shore alive, and as an American he is not on English territory, but on that of Denmark – a neutral kingdom and a friend of the United States of America. He realizes that there might be a good chance that he soon can be a free American again.

Finally Peder Dahlgaard manages to get out to the raft. Using both hands and a considerable amount of physical force, he frees John Page's foot, and carries him safely to the shore.

At the same time Peder and Mads have come so far north that they have passed the first group of farms on their way to the north, the Mærsk farms, where Christen Øster Mærsk lives. They continue along the road and pass close by the pond Tuskjær (toad pond). Tuskjær is a large pond, normally filled with toads and thousands of loud croaking frogs in the late springtime. The pond and the frogs provide food to a loyal couple of storks staying here each summer. The pond is also inhabited with one or two pairs of swans during the summer, which vigorously defend their nests and cygnets from anyone who dares to come too close.

As Peder and Mads pass the pond this stormy Christmas Eve, it takes more imagination than they are able to muster now to imagine how nice this spot is on a mild, warm summer day. The pond is now covered with ice, hail and snow.

The sand road turns east west of the pond and around the west end of the barn of the Tuskjær farm. Then it is 100 meters to the farm Sønder Sønderby.

When Peder and Mads arrive in the yard of Sønder Sønderby farm, Mads is quickly sent to a neighboring farm, Gadegaard, to borrow a horse and change his clothes to ride with a message of the huge stranding. He will take the message to the district Bailiff, who normally resides in the borough of Lemvig 10 miles northeast, but who is spending the Christmas holidays with his and the baron's family at Rysensteen Manor, four miles east of this farm.

The farm Sønder Sønderby consists of the traditional four, red brick buildings with straw on the roof, straw harvested in the wintertime in the Bøvling Fjord, close to where *Defence* has now stranded. The straw grows in the fjord just few hundred meters from the roaring North Sea without any difficulty. Mads Liisbye heads for the farm Gadegaard and Peder Ruby Christensen enters the yard of his own farm.

He opens one of the two doors to the entrance room and walks into the bedroom where his wife and two kids are still fast asleep. He silently and quickly takes off his wet clothes and finds a new dry shirt and pair of pants. Peder's wife wakes up and he tells her about the terrible stranding.

The coast guards still on the beach are impressed and shocked by the size of the wreck of the huge ship *Defence*. The stranding of smaller schooners and brigs is a weekly or at least monthly experience during the winter months around here, and they constitute a welcome contribution to the poor living and harvest that are the normal standard here. But larger war ships like the *Defence* are very rare on this coastline.

These families living close to the North Sea have often taken care of entire ship crews, or single seamen or captains who managed to get off stranded ships, reach the beach alive and walk across the dunes to knock on the door of one of the farm houses when autumn and winter storms raged wild for many days. But the farmers Jutland have not established any permanent rescue service to look to help any stranded person.

The only reason a farmer or coastguard would stay on or near the beach during the night, as Peder Ruby Christensen and his colleagues had been doing this very night, was when shipwrecks or stranded cargoes needed protection from local people looking to supplement their poor income. But no coastguard or night watch would be established for the sole purpose of looking for survivors coming in from the North Sea.

After changing his clothes, Peder Ruby Christensen leaves his farmhouse to enter the eastern of the three wings of his farm, the wing holding the cows, calves, pink pigs, red and white hens and black horses. His eldest son, Christen Ruby Pedersen, has been awakened and fetches the harness hanging on the wall in the big barn, helping his father make a carriage ready to leave for the beach.

Each time one of them hurries through one of the doors leading to the center yard, the open door is grabbed by the strong wind and smashed up against an outer wall with a big bang. In the wind shelter close to the western wing, they have managed to get the carriage ready faster than ever before, and Peder now jumps onto the driver's seat and gives the signal to go. As he drives, he looks toward the farmhouse building and from his elevated position in the driver's seat, looks through the kitchen window for a few seconds, where his wife is busy cutting slices of bread and preparing food for the men who might be brought to her house from the beach. She has plaited her golden hair into a slack ponytail at this early hour of the day. The sound of the iron fitting on the wooden carriage wheels on the hand-sized beach stones in the farmyard makes her look out of the window, and the two of them make an eye contact. She nods, saying Yes, Go do your duty.

In the meantime Mads Liisbye has reached Gadegaard, borrowed dry clothes and a horse and arrived in the yard outside the Rysensteen Manor. His horse gallops along the long stable buildings with the roof gables, and continues over the small bridge, crossing the moat encircling the white L-shaped chalked mansion with the red tile roof. He jumps off the horse almost before it stops and runs up the stone staircase to the scullery. A maid from the kitchen, who has heard and seen Mads coming, meets him at the door, then quickly runs to deliver the message about the huge stranding to the men in the house, who are still in bed at this early hour of the day. The hosts and the guests on the Rysensteen Manor had celebrated the traditional Little Christmas Evening the evening before and had all found the need to sleep a little longer.

The District Bailiff for the Skodborg-Vandfuld District, Mr. C.F. Schønau, and the owner of the Rysensteen Manor, get up immediately at the sad news about the stranding, and a servant immediately gets the order to saddle their horses.

Shortly, all three men are galloping against the strong western wind and along the long earth road that leads to the North Sea beach and the Rysensteen Foreshore just south of the village of Fjaltring, where the wreck of the *Defence* is being destroyed by the roaring North Sea.

Around 7:50 a.m., Peder Ruby Christensen arrives with his carriage at the tent holding the surviving men. Mads Liisbye and the two gentlemen from Rysensteen Manor arrive at the tent at the same time. District Bailiff C. F. Schønau, the highest representative authority in charge of this district, takes over command.

He orders the survivors taken to the nearest houses or farms south of the village of Fjaltring as quickly as possible. Peder Ruby Christensen and Christen Øster Mærsk help the survivors from the tent onto the open carriage.

The Second Masters Mate David McCrobb is very weak and appears to be unconscious from time to time. Peder and Christen lift him cautiously and carefully place him in a soft place in the carriage, with a lot of hay underneath him. Ralph Teazel, John Page and John are weak too, and they are also carried to the carriage by the strong West Juttish coast guards, wreck masters and farmers. The survivors are quite cold and have many bruises on their limbs and bodies from the wreck pieces that were cast around in the breakers while they were striving to reach the shore.

John Page tries to listen to the words of the Danes in order to find out where the *Defence* has stranded and where they are heading now. From the words of Christen Øster Mærsk, who several times points to the north, John Page picks up the name 'Sheldon'. Christen Øster Mærsk has talked about the small village of Fjaltring, which, when pronounced with his local dialect sounds like Sheldon. It is import for the Englishman John Page to pick up a place name here where they had stranded,

315

because he knows Denmark is enemy territory and he will probably have to participate in maritime inquiries, when or if he one day returns to England.

At daybreak, north of the northern entrance to Ear Sound, the officers on the bridge of *Pyramus* observe one of the merchant ships in the convoy totally dismasted.[74-2]

A new carriage now arrives at the tent from the farm Gadegaard to assist transporting the surviving men to one of the farms. Mads Liisbye told the people from Gadegaard about the stranding, when he changed clothes there and borrowed a horse, before he rode on to Rysensteen Manor to talk to the bailiff.

The cold wind keeps cooling down the weak bodies of the surviving men as they lie in the carriages outside the tent, and they cannot stay there for much longer if they want to stay alive. Therefore, Peder Ruby Christensen leaves for the Sønder Sønderby farm south of Fjaltring with the first four survivors from *Defence*: John, John Page, Ralph Teazel and David McCrobb.

Thomas Mullins and Amos are, at the same time, helped onto the second carriage from Gadegaard, which soon departs to follow in the tracks of the first carriage.

As the two carriages travel at maximum speed along the thin sandy tracks laid out in the lyme grass, heading toward the farms, John tries to keep an eye on his comrade, the weaker and weaker McCrobb, to make sure that he keeps up his spirit. But they have not been riding more than 10 minutes before McCrobb silently dies.

John feels very tired and helpless when he realizes that one of the very few survivors from *Defence* didn't make it, and he reaches out to close David's eyes for the very last time.

As they continue northward, John notices the difference between the stormy, cold and salty environment on the beach side of the dunes, just 10 meters from where they are driving, where not one single green blade of grass grows, and this side, where the wind is relatively weak, there is no sea salt, and the temperature is considerably higher.

Here, the rain keeps the zone vigorous in the form of a thick carpet of long lyme grass, ordinary grass and a few other plants. John looks at the water and the fjord to the east and realizes that they must be driving on a narrow isthmus. He does not understand how it is possible for nature to preserve such a narrow tongue of land so close to the wild, roaring, foaming North Sea to the west - a sea whose forceful breakers had managed to break the *Defence* apart in only a couple of hours.

As they slowly approach the coast farms, where the sandy tracks transform into a regular gravel road, where the Mærsk farms are, they pass a small stooping figure wearing a headscarf and slowly walking north in the sandy trail. As the figure steps aside and the carriage passes, John sees it is an old woman. From the driver's seat, Peder asks if she has any snaps or brændevin with her. She smiles a big toothless smile and eagerly nods, glad that she is able to help, and draws out from beneath her coat a clear bottle with what looks like water. She hands the bottle to Peder, who passes the brændevin to John then nods his head toward the other men in the carriage, to encourage them all to take a large sip of the brændevin. John Page and Ralph Teazel are almost unconscious and John works hard in the bumbling carriage to pour some of the liquid into their throats, finally succeeding.

Ralph begins to cough as he tastes the strong liquid and he has his eyes wide open for several seconds before he goes back into a deep sleep. The brændevin is very strong and quickly improves his blood circulation, keeping him warm. John takes another large sip and immediately observes positive changes the brændevin has on his own body. His body begins to feel warmer and much better, and he is deeply grateful that someone is trying the best they can to help him improve his condition. I have definitely not been pampered in this way in the Royal Navy the last six years, John thinks.

The first carriage reaches the Strandgaarden farm just on the north side of the gravel road, where the Sønder Sønderby farm is. It is a farm with the traditional arrangement, the farmhouse located to the south, the stable wings to the west and east, and the large barn wing to the north. The wreck master Thomas Wang temporarily runs the farm on behalf of the owner Captain Conrad Falkenberg. Falkenberg is the administrator of the Rysensteen Foreshore where *Defence* has stranded.

The carriage turns into the sea-stone paved courtyard and stops by the western daily entrance door, so it will be easy to get the seamen into the house. Clack, clack, clack, the horses loudly mark their entrance in the yard. Peder Ruby Christensen waits for Thomas Wang to come into the courtyard and tell them which rooms he wants the survivors brought to.

317

At the same time this morning, *HMS Hero* is on the coast off the island of Texel, just north of the harbor of Den Helder. Captain Fanshave and the other officers and men onboard the *Grasshopper* witness horrifying scenes as the dawn finally breaks. *Hero* has stranded and is totally dismasted. She is lying on her larboard beam end, with the stem pointing to the northeast, exactly the same way *Defence* stranded earlier. In the early morning hours, *Hero* has also gone through the same kind of emergency procedures that *St. George* and *Defence* did 400 miles further north on this same continental North Sea coast. *Hero* is stranded a mile from *Grasshopper* at the Haaks Sand.

The crew of the *Hero,* who quite soon after the stranding were forced to leave the water-filled lower decks, are now packed closely on either the forecastle or the quarterdeck. People gathered on the beach and on nearby ships can clearly see them. In between these two separate and elevated decks are only waves of icy seawater. *Hero* has hoisted a Flag of Truce and it is obvious to everyone watching that she and her entire crew are in extreme distress. *Hero's* captain Newman orders a cannon fired, which Captain Fanshave orders his men onboard the *Grasshopper* to repeat. The signals are observed and the Dutchmen on the beach hear the shots. Several large groups of men, women and children are fearfully watching the seamen struggle to survive onboard the *Hero*. A logger, two brigs and several smaller vessels can now be seen flying out from the beach on the island of Texel to try and assist *Grasshopper* and *Hero*[18] in their almost hopeless situation.

Thomas Wang's wife, Thyra, and one of the maids, Mette Cathrine Madsdatter, now come out in the yard in Strandgaarden and take a look at the freezing seamen stretched out half dead in the hay in the bottom of the carriage. Peder jumped down from the driver's seat the instant the carriage stopped, and now stands at the end of the carriage next to Thomas Wang prepared to help to carry the seamen to the house. The two farmers first carry in the unconscious John Page, and because he is unconscious, Thyra asks them to put John Page directly on the bed in one of the small, low-lofted western chambers, close to the warm kitchen where she and the maids are busy cooking and preparing for the Christmas holidays. Thomas Wang and Peder Ruby Christensen have known each other for quite some time and just nod their heads without saying a word as they carry the dead body of David McCrobb into the north wing, the large barn. Most farmers on the west coast of this part of Denmark have been brought up with the forceful commanding language of silence. They do not need to speak to each other in order to communicate. Through the many years they have spent together, they have learned to 'read" each other's body and facial expressions carefully and accurately. Thomas and Peder return to the courtyard and carry Thomas Mullins in to the same chamber and bed where John Page now lays.

Peder returns to the courtyard, quickly turns the carriage around and drives the 30 meters across the gravel road to the yard of his own farm, the Sønder Sønderby. Here John helps Peder get the unconscious Ralph Teazel into a bed in the house. Peder's wife has been waiting with the food she made and a stone-preheated bed.

Mrs. Christensen asks one of the maids to take off Ralph Teazel's wet clothes and dress him in dry woolen underwear. John is given the same type of underwear. He changes his clothes and enters the large bed to try and get some sleep.

In one of the two western chambers in the farmhouse in Strandgaarden, John Page is lying in a warm soft bed beneath a thick duvet that goes right up to his ears. He is still very weak and tired, but he is conscious now.

He can't stop thinking about how well these farmers have been treating him so far, and he smiles back without being able to talk to them. The maid Mette Cathrine Madsdatter, while having a break doing the Christmas preparations, silently opens the door to see if he is getting any better. John smiles one of the sweetest smiles he is able to produce but without saying a word. John Page wants these people to understand how grateful he is for being taken care of this nice way. These farmers and Danes are supposed to be enemies of his native country England, but he has met no hostility yet.

The Englishman John Page is coming from a situation of many years of tough, disciplined service in the Royal Navy. After experiencing this terrible, inhuman stranding and his own miraculous survival, he now finds himself in a nice, warm bed in a farmhouse with such decent, modest people that it leaves him speechless and thankful beyond words. In contradiction to how he would normally react after extreme long-term stress, he is now so touched and moved that he almost get tears in his eyes. Onboard the wrecked *Defence,* they had all been well aware that they had stranded on enemy territory, and that they could expect bad treatment, if they were so extremely lucky to be able to reach the shore alive.

John Page had sailed long enough in the Royal Navy Baltic Fleet to know that English mariners had made several raids over the years on the fishermen working along this shore, stealing their equipment and boats when one of the Royal Navy's ships occasionally passed by here and had the time for such attacks. Now it was crystal clear to him, that if it hadn't been for these modest, helpful Danes, he would not be alive now. He is also convinced that if it hadn't been for the brændevin that he had been so kindly offered in the carriage on their way to the farm, he would probably not have lived to think about it now.

In the meantime, Amos and John Platt have been carried from the beach in Jens Gadegaard's carriage and brought directly to his farm Gadegaard, 800 meters north east of Strandgaarden.

Amos, who had felt so fresh after he had fought his way in through the breakers all by himself and arrived at the beach from the wreck, now realizes that he is actually badly hurt, with large bruises on different parts of his body and limbs. He feels quite exhausted. On his way to shore, he was heavily beaten up by some of the smaller wreck pieces adrift in the breakers. Lying in bed, Amos suddenly recalls the sad sight of the carpenter's wife and daughter grasped by the heavy sea and swept down the stairs in the ship from the main deck, and it renews the strong despair and desperation that had obsessed him in the long minutes following, when he realized he was unable to do anything to save his boss's wife and their young girl.

Amos and John Platt have been packed up in the same bed in Gadegaard to help them warm each other. That is the traditional way to arrange stranded, weak seamen in beds in the wreck master farms along the coast to secure an optimal condition for recovery of these men. Many years of experience treating survivors from shipwrecks in the North Sea had taught the farmers that putting two men in one bed allowed the strongest of them to warm the weakest. This was found to be very important, when a seaman was unconscious and stiff.

While the surviving seamen from *Defence* were transported to the farms south of Fjaltring to be taken care of, District Bailiff Schønau stayed on

320

the beach to help organize handling of the wreckage that already had reached the shore, and the much larger amounts that could be expected to arrive on the beach later on.

Because Denmark and England are at war, well-trained military troops have been stationed on strategic points along this Danish North Sea coast. Therefore, a company of soldiers from the Zealand's Hunter Force has been quartered on a farm just northwest of Strandgaarden, named Dahlgaard for the owner Peder Dahlgaard, the coastguard and wreck master that earlier this morning stayed as night watch in the tent near the beach, the first to hear that *Defence* was in great distress. Peder Dahlgaard is still on the beach, together with an officer in the local coast militia, officer Peder Høegh, owner of Rammegaard Manor four miles north east of Fjaltring.

The District Bailiff orders commissioned officer Peder Høegh to take charge of the arrangement of the incoming wreck pieces. As Schønau and Høegh discuss what can be done, they see a horseman on a shiny, black horse galloping on the beach close by the water's edge to the south, coming directly toward them. As the horseman rides north and the wind whips around him, his long, dark coat flutters wildly behind him like a long tail. He reaches the two men and stops his horse abruptly. Still sitting in his saddle, he tells them that another and much larger ship has stranded five miles to the south. All three shake their heads in silence and then the horseman rides south with the same fast speed as he came.

The District Bailiff takes up the business of arranging the collection of the huge amount of wreck pieces. Officer Peder Høegh is told to make sure that the pieces are gathered in larger piles along the beach, and when this job is completed, to report it to his superior, the commander of the local coast militia A. Von Schurnhardt, who has his local headquarters at Peder Dahlgaard' s farm. Schurnhardt will then make sure that military guard posts are stationed by each of the piles of wreckage along the beach.

Schønau then rides north, because he has received information since he arrived that another and smaller ship has stranded further northwards on the beach. He has to inspect that site, too, before it gets dark.

It has been more than four years since Denmark declared war on England, and the Danish coastguard had in the meantime installed some small guard cabins along this windy west coast beach to protect the guards against the very rough weather conditions that appeared much of the time here. One of these guard cabins is quite conveniently located on this beach between the Mærsk and the Tuskjær farms.

It is now 8:00 a.m. The water level onboard the flagship *St. George* has reached just above the middle, first gun deck. The heavy ship is slowly rolling with each wave that hits the hull, and it is sinking deeper and deeper into the sand. This is reported to Captain Gurion.

He tries to think of a way out of this hopeless situation, but ends up only shaking his head, realizing that there is really nothing that can be done. The seamen have been working hard and constantly at the pumps for several hours, hoping the storm will decrease or simply end, so they can have a fair chance to empty the ship of water. But water continues to pour in, more than the quantity they can pump out. It's just a question of time before the ship is full of seawater.

Gurion has gathered some 350 men on the inclining upper deck, if he overlooks the few who are from time to time swept overboard by the huge waves, disappearing in the sea for good. Calling the 125 men on the first gun deck up to the main deck will certainly add to the already high death rate on the main deck. He orders First Lieutenant Francis Rogers to call up all men to the main deck.

William, along with many of the seamen and mariners waiting on the first gun deck, has put on as many of the clothes he had in his sea chest as possible. Poor as they are, the men know that they will have to leave the few things they own onboard the shipwreck, except what they are able to carry on their bodies or in their clothes. William now puts his Protection Certificate inside his clothes, directly on the skin of his stomach. He still has a few things left in his sea chest, but he understands that he will have to leave it here and concentrate on saving himself.

Around his neck, William tightens the silk scarf Mary Ann gave him when he left Wilmington, and now he realizes that it really serves a purpose here. It will be extremely cold on the open main deck, and he knows that the time will come when wave after wave of icy saltwater will sweep over the deck and soak him to his bones. William hopes that sufficient clothes and this silk scarf will keep him warm and alive.

William hears talk among the other seamen and mariners that this lee shore is very dangerous, and the only hope he can cling to, in order to survive, is that he may be lucky to get in one of the very few boats onboard. This seems quite impossible, because entering a boat requires permission from the captain. William thinks that maybe he and William Freeman can be lucky and get onto one of the two masts when they eventually are cut down, or maybe he can hang onto some of the cargo that might sail along the ship. William is confident that a small chance of survival actually exists.

This kind of reasoning has put William in a good mood, and he still firmly believes in his luck when troubles seem to pile up in front of him. Under normal conditions, many of the elder officers, seamen or mariners onboard Royal Navy ships, who consider themselves tremendously experienced, would consider William naïve. If William expressed his belief to these men, despite the difficult situation, they are willing to invest quite a lot of energy and time in trying to convince him that this is certainly the case. But though their tongues speak with self-assurance and they can confirm each other's words loudly again and again, William can see clearly in their eyes that many of them have given up hope for a rescue and, therefore, the hope to live. These over-experienced men know too many horrifying stories about the Reef of Jutland and lee shores in general to mobilize hope for a rescue. They consider themselves wise men who have sufficient wisdom and knowledge about life to be capable of predicting the possible outcome of this difficult situation. Getting off this shipwreck and reaching the shore alive at this stage is definitely not an option to them.

In general, the morale onboard is pretty low, although Rear Admiral of the Red C. W. Reynolds and Flag Captain Daniel Gurion constantly encourage the many ordinary crewmembers and the officers onboard the flagship, as they are supposed to do as superior officers.

When William thinks more about it, he believes that very few of the seamen onboard the *St. George* can swim, which means it is impossible for them to get away from the wreck of the *St. George,* unless they are on a piece of wreckage the entire time. Trying to swim from one wreck piece to another in the open sea is not a real option for most of the men onboard now.

William knows how to swim all right. He learned in the Christina River on hot summer days, where he spent much of his time playing as a child. It was the only place in Wilmington one could stay in the summer time with some kind of pleasure, because of the constant heat.

William Freeman had also learned how to swim in pretty much the same way as William. Freeman grew up in Philadelphia and learned to swim along the Delaware River banks there.

Now the two of them stand close together discussing what can be done to get off the ship and reach the shore alive.

Most of the seamen remain silent. They do not try to talk at all to discuss options. They look very pale, in a kind of trance and without any sign of wanting to take initiative on their own. They are blindly counting on orders from their superior officers - orders that they are absolutely sure will finally save them. They are so used to getting orders by self-assured superior officers for even the slightest thing, that they have stopped questioning that condition a very long time ago. They do not spend much time wondering why God gave them the same ability to think for themselves as their superior officers and why they hardly ever used that ability.

The time is now 9:00 a.m. Finally an officer, on the order from Gurion, runs down the stairs to the first gun deck and orders all men here to slowly move up the stairs to the upper open deck.

This will be the end of order and the beginning of chaos, William thinks to himself, and he shouts to William Freeman 'Stay near me, William, stay near me and you will be just fine!" William Freeman only nods his head, looking very scared and saying nothing. William Freeman does not have the same amount of self-confidence as William has. On top of that, William Freeman is only 17 and he is quite nervous about the uncertain situation onboard this shipwreck.

The seamen and mariners on the first gun deck carefully, as always, follow the orders received, slowly moving toward the staircases. As they approach, they begin to hear the increasing sound of the wild wind howling in the rigging and the jury masts above them.

As they finally reach the bottom of the staircase, their legs mechanically move from one step to the other while they constantly look down to avoid falling and dragging other men down with them.

When their heads pop up on the main deck, a terrible sight meets the two Williams, and as they stand on the deck, most of the seamen from the lower deck seem to instantly lose their spirit as they observe corpses lying along the lower leeward bulwark. Watching the expression on the living seamen's faces does not help to increase the newcomer's own mood.

Besides being a man-o-war, the flagship *St. George* is also a permanent place for the education of the young officers. Therefore there are more than 50 boys onboard this flagship under the age of 15, many of them only 11 and 12 years old. Although the elder officers have tried to protect them against the strong, freezing wind, the boys have begun to die in large numbers, some of the first to die onboard the flagship.

Soon all of *St. George's* lower decks are filled with saltwater, and at 10:00 a.m., all men off duty are sent from the main deck to the quarterdeck, where normally only officers are allowed to stay.

It is still storming wildly and the single clouds are drifting fast over the firmament. The air is so clear that from the top of the rigging the land and some people on the beach are easily seen.

One seaman standing near the top yard on the rear mast, the one closest to the beach, clearly observes a small group of houses and farms about three miles to the south behind the dunes. They also observe a large are of water behind the dunes. The lookout is observing the village of Fjand, the Nissum Fjord and the ten-mile long, narrow isthmus separating the fjord and the North Sea. He observes the village of Fjaltring, to the north at the north end of the isthmus, and Fjand in the other end, to the south. Two-thirds down the isthmus is a narrow channel connecting the sea and the fjord. The *St. George* has stranded only 600 meters from the shore. Only 600 meters! But the breakers in between the stranded flagship and the shore seem very turbulent, and this fact alone makes it clear how dangerous, if not impossible, it will be to cross these 600 meters of water.

The foremast was cut down an hour ago. The yards on the rear mast are now covered with dozens of seamen and mariners desperately trying to get an impression of the environment along the shore. The many seamen in the rigging of the rear mast yards have helped to create a better space on the quarterdeck, where most of the men and officers have gathered.

Although his ship is stranded, Flag Captain Gurion still upholds strict discipline onboard. The discipline is more needed than ever. Since the quarterdeck is now filled with seamen and mariners in addition to officers, it gets the former status of the main deck. Water now completely covers the first gun deck, where William Watson and

William Freeman stayed only a couple of hours ago. The few men still on the main deck constantly have their feet swept over with icy seawater, and William observes that now and then, the water also manages to wash into the captain's cabin, where Reynolds, Gurion, Reynolds' secretary James Railton, First Lieutenant Francis Rogers and half the officers are gathered. Although they are protected against the strong, cold storm, the men in the captain's cabin are freezing pretty much the same as the rest of the crew onboard.

Since dawn, Reynolds, Railton and Gurion have been following the situation of the wreck condition closely from the captain's cabin.

Some time has passed as they have been waiting impatiently, unable to do anything to improve the situation for the men onboard. The gallery of *St. George* is pointing directly toward the sand beach near Fjand. Most of the people in this small village gathered on the beach after dawn, to see this rare, spectacular sight the local wreck master had reported. From the beach, they can easily read the name *St. George* written in tall, golden letters on top of the gallery.

The same way, the Rear Admiral and captain have a perfect view of the beach. Admiral Reynolds sits at the captain's table in an armchair pointing toward the gallery, with the captain in a chair to his left and Railton in a chair to his right. They all sit with their feet resting on the deck and an inch of seawater around their feet.

From time to time the three officers get the courage to lift their heads and look out through the windows, toward the beach. What they see frightens them. Between the wreck of the flagship *St. George III* and the beach, it's not Britannia that rules the waves but the huge and strong Danish breakers. Looking at this view, the three officers are quite aware that few of the men onboard will survive a passage through these breakers, so they can only hope for better weather conditions before it is too late. Without a word, they silently observe the foaming green sea and the huge hills of water that periodically rise outside the windows and beneath their feet. Large amounts of foam break loose from the sea surface occasionally and fly over the sandy beach to abruptly disappear over the dunes.

When Reynolds, Gurion and Railton manage to distract their diffuse thoughts from the danger in the breakers appearing just outside the gallery windows, they admire the many different light colors in the scenery - the chalk-white foam, light green water, yellow-white sand and green, lyme grass-covered dunes. Most of the areas in their field of vision are covered with light colors and only disturbed by small groups of tiny, darkly dressed people who seem to move constantly back and forth along the beach, studying the wreck of the *St. George*.

In one of these groups are the wreck masters Anders Andersen and Jens Dahl, both from the village of Fjand. They also carefully study the *St. George* and for quite some time, but have a hard time estimating how many men are onboard, because some men stay on the main deck at this early hour of the day and are therefore hidden behind the poop when seen from the beach.

The three officers are now listening to the wind gusts that pass the ship's hull and masts from time to time. The wind gusts constitute regions with the highest concentrations of energy in the wind, and therefore also radiate the highest levels of noise to their environments.

If Reynolds listens long enough to the wind, he gets an idea whether the level of noise tends to increase or decrease in the wind gusts that pass his ship. If the noise level tends to decrease, the energy level in the wind gusts also decreases and then the average wind speed, which he is interested in, also decreases.

So, while at sea no idea of the actual wind speed can be estimated by listening to or watching trees and the bushes, as can be done on land, Reynolds, Gurion and Railton, know how to judge whether the average speed of the wind on the sea is decreasing or increasing. For the time being, the passing wind gusts leave the three men with the impression of a noise level that is periodically going up and down, indicating a constant average wind speed that will probably stay so for many hours.

The constant cold in the cabin is steadily weakening 60-year-old Rear Admiral Reynolds, and Railton notices it. The burden of responsibility for all the men onboard now feels heavy and is clearly present in the faces of both Gurion and Reynolds, who look grave and pale.

In this same Christmas storm that began two days ago, a small English ship in great distress managed to survive sudden destruction by passing through the narrow, short channel connecting the sea and the fjord, named Thor's minde. The crew survived. That made the local small fisher community very happy, because they knew all too well, from experience, what the North Sea was capable of doing to ships in a storm, when it was in a bad mood.

But even though the lookout on the *St. George* had observed this small channel when they still were at sea, the flagship was too large to pass through it.

It is now clear to everyone onboard the wreck of the *St. George* that if anyone manages to survive, it will be by clinging to one of the few wreck pieces in the water, when the destruction of the ship goes far enough. The storm has now lasted for two full days and seems not to come to an end. From the reports that reach the deck from the seamen at the top yards, men onboard conclude that they cannot expect to be saved from land. It seems quite clear to the lookout that no ships can safely come out from the shore in this weather, and none of the small fisher boats on the beach near Fjand seem to be big enough to go out in the sea safely in rough weather.

Late this morning, the military leader of the coastguard here, A Von Schurnhardt, orders his troops quartered in Dahlgaard to post themselves along the beach south of the *Defence* wreck, at positions where piles of wreck pieces are being gathered by the local wreck masters and their assistants.

Several barrels of gunpowder and wine that have already come to shore from the wrecked *Defence* are immediately removed from the open beach and transported by carriage to the Rammegaard Manor five miles to the northeast. This is where the King's representative will be quartered, when he arrives to inspect the stranding of these large British warships.

Items like these barrels of gunpowder have high value to the Danish Military in these times of war, and they especially are taken into custody by the local commander of the coast militia officer Peder Høegh on his Manor.

It's noon. *Bellette* is 23 miles northwest of Horn's Reef on the south west coast of Jutland, not terribly far south from the *St. George* and *Defence* stranding places. From the time she left *St. George* and *Defence* yesterday evening, *Bellette* has not been able to get away from the dangerous lee shore of Jutland, but has been forced to drift southwards. Now the captain of *Bellette* realizes that she will actually make it past the Horn's Reef and finally begin the last part of the voyage to England. [30]

At the same time, on a position at sea north of Hven Island, where the astronomer Thyco Brahe earlier had his observatory, in the middle of Ear Sound, *Woodlark* is fighting Danish privateers again. She manages to take one of them as a prize and one is lucky to escape into the Copenhagen Roads.[67] In the following days, *Woodlark* remains in Ear Sound to continue hunting Danish privateers in order to increase the protection of the *Pyramus* convoy as it sails northwards to reach Vinga Sound outside Gothenburg[67] as soon as possible.

A logger from the island of Texel has successfully fought its way out through the breakers and is trying to go up against the wind and the high waves to reach the *Hero* and try to rescue some of the men. But the flood tide and strong gale from north-northwest prevents the Dutch logger from getting any closer than two or three miles from *Hero*.

Captain Fanshave, standing on the bridge of the *Grasshopper*, watches helplessly, knowing that no ship seems to be able to reach *Hero* from land. He orders a boat from *Grasshopper* hoisted out in the sea to try to get near the *Hero* and assist her. But the surf and the waves are still so high that the attempt must be dropped to avoid losing seamen unnecessarily.

The crew onboard the *Grasshopper* can only watch the death struggles of more than 500 men onboard the quarterdeck of the *Hero*. At the same time, the *Grasshopper* suddenly meets the ground. Fanshave now has no other alternative than to try and lighten his ship, and despite the fact that they are very close to the Dutch coast, he gives the order to throw most of the 32 cannons overboard.

The master is then ordered to sound in every direction around the ship to see if he can find a safe path the *Grasshopper* might follow. But escape seems impossible now. The soundings give nothing more than two-and-a-half meters. Fanshave discusses the situation with his officers, and because of *Hero*'s distressed situation, they decide that it is wisest to surrender to the first Dutch ship that manages to get out to the *Grasshopper*.

On the bridge of the *Grasshopper* they helplessly observe as man after man is swept off or falls from the quarterdeck of the *Hero* to quickly disappear in the rough seas.

Not a single man reaches the shore alive or survives otherwise among the 550 men in the crew of the *Hero*.

Fanshave sees that five miles to the north of *Grasshopper* one ship is on the shore with the foremast standing and another is located some distance from her. He is convinced that the two ships must be government ships from his own convoy. Eight to ten ships are later reported by the newspaper, *The Telegraph,* to have stranded and wrecked on the beach northward from Den Helder.

The *Centurion* carrying eight cannons is one of the ships sharing the *Hero's* destiny in this Christmas storm. The *Flora* transport is lost with 1,500 barrels of gunpowder and 250 chests of arms, but part of her crew is saved.

The *Rosina* in ballast flounders and the captain and 17 of her crew perish.

A brig is stranded between Campen and Bergen on the coast south of Den Helder.

The coast landscape of Texel and Den Helder is very similar to the coast landscape around Fjaltring and Fjand.

Ocean-going American ships are in the Harbor of Den Helder and the men onboard are the first Americans to get news about this dreadful event. But they are not aware how many impressed American seamen had been onboard the *HMS Hero.* Here along the Dutch coast as along the Danish coast, losing so many men of the sea is a tragedy that goes right to the heart of any person living by the North Sea.

The weather is getting worse now, and the increasing wave heights force Fanshave to order the anchor cables cut to avoid the ship being dragged down by its own anchors. At the same time, the logger that earlier came out to assist now approaches the *Grasshopper* successfully. The logger shows the route to sail and finally *Grasshopper* manages to reach the harbor of Den Helder[18] safely.

As they reach Den Helder, Fanshave recalls when the same kind of bad weather and lightning appeared in Hanö Bay, midnight on June 24, and destroyed the mast on one of the merchant ships named *Den Helder,* when the *St. George* Royal Navy squadron and many merchant ships were anchored there, - exactly six months ago.[107] It must have been a sign given then, Fanshave now concludes with conviction. All the men who had watched that scene in the Bay of Hanö six months ago had felt very bad about it at that time.

All in all, 147 persons are saved from the *Grasshopper* and the many wrecked ships belonging to the Royal Navy ships and the government transport ships near the island of Texel and the borough of Den Helder in this Christmas storm.[25]

The *Arcimedes* manages, with a lost rudder, to save her crew of 20 men, and they are made Dutch prisoners, like the men coming from the *Grasshopper*. But the crews who stayed onboard the many wrecked transport ships are all gone. The highest Dutch authority in the harbor of Den Helder, Admiral De Winter, now makes it clear to Captain Fanshave and his crew of 120 men from the *Grasshopper* that they will be taken into custody as prisoners, which they all accept. The men and officers from the Royal Navy ships are treated nicely while in Dutch custody.

The time is now 2 p.m., and the wind is still howling at undiminished strength along the west coast near Fjand. After *St. George* entered the North Sea, William returned to his duties as able seaman, because there is no need for many mariners where they will meet few enemy ships.

In the flag captain's cabin there is now 10 inches of seawate r. Gurion stands up and walks slowly to open the door embedded in water. He presses himself out through a small opening, then quickly closes it and begins to wade forward to the stairs leading up to the quarterdeck. There is too much water now on the main deck so all the men are now on the quarterdeck.

Gurion walks the last few yards from the bridge through 20 inches of water, reaches the stairs and goes up to the quarterdeck. There, he orders First Lieutenant Francis Rogers to open the skylight and get some of his men to help the now very weak Admiral up through it from the table he is standing on below them in the captain's cabin, where Railton stands at his side supporting him.

John Anderson, captain of the foretop, William, William Rie and William Freeman immediately walk over to help drag the Admiral up through the skylight. When Admiral Reynolds stands safely on the quarterdeck, he thanks the seamen warmly for their help. He takes a look around the crowded quarterdeck and then walks to the rear of the deck in the starboard side to remain in that corner.

With the stem of the *St. George* pointing to the west-northwest, the corner the Admiral now stands in is the nearest he can come to the beach while still onboard the *St. George*.

William is honestly glad that he has been able to help Admiral

Reynolds, but under the circumstances, he considers if this goodwill can be used for the benefit of some of the seamen. In contradiction to many of the seamen on the quarterdeck, William is not paralyzed by fear and helplessness. He shares the feeling of sadness that comes from being in a very difficult situation like this one, but he has not given up hope of rescue. William never gives up. He has always fought problems showing up in his life quite professionally by struggling, 'to the last drop of blood' if necessary.

As the seamen now stand packed and almost in fixed positions on the quarterdeck where they physically can do very little, William recalls the story he has been telling William Freeman to help him through the tough times onboard this ship. The situation is definitely too serious to continue to tell the story now, so William decides to keep quiet. But he can't help thinking about the story to himself.

Heavily delayed on Christmas Day 1637, the Key of Calmar and the Bird Griffin enter the harbor of Den Helder. Here they are supposed to take in the second half of the Dutch investors' cargo to be used for the trading with the Indians that Peter Minuit has already met, in that special place in the New World. Some of these investors, Peter Minuit thinks, have been found by Blommart.

This stop near the island of Texel is kept on a very discrete level so as not to raise the anger of the Dutch authorities, who have their own clear interests in the New World around New Amsterdam at the North River. They do not approve of this new mission to the South River headed by this dismissed and former Dutch Governor of New Amsterdam.[154]

William's thoughts are back on the quarterdeck a few seconds later. He is a rational man and has always been. He is quite aware that special initiatives need to be taken in order to try and survive this very difficult situation. To William, waiting without doing anything only means certain death.

About 50 boys and men have already frozen to death on the quarterdeck, which is totally unprotected against the strong, cold storm coming in from the northwest. The dead bodies are put one by one outside the captain's cabin, as long as the space can contain them.

The remaining men and officers stand shoulder by shoulder on the quarterdeck, stomach by back and packed as one large group in order to keep warm, like penguins in an Antarctica winter storm.

There are approximately six persons for every square yard on the quarterdeck. From time to time, the outer row of seamen, having taken the stress of the cold for a period, walk into the middle of the group to warm themselves up again, leaving new men to form the outer thermal boundary of the group. The tilting, wet deck makes it increasingly difficult for the men to stay onboard. Very high pressure is put on the men forced to stand closest to the lowest, larboard bulwark.

William nods toward John Anderson and the two other seamen who assisted Admiral Reynolds onto the quarterdeck. It is time to make an attempt to leave the wreck. They all walk to the corner where the Admiral stands. John and William ask permission to take the jolly boat back on the main deck, the only boat not already destroyed by the heavy waves. Reynolds looks at William and John Anderson, then slowly nods his head, meaning yes. The Admiral finally says, "You are permitted to take it, if you are convinced that it is of any use to you."[20]

The four seamen quickly walk down the staircase from the quarterdeck and wade over to the jollyboat that is moored to the portside bulwark on the main deck. The water is quite calm here, protected from the huge open sea waves that keep sweeping over the deck from the wreck's starboard side.

As William stands at the portside bulwark holding the line to the jollyboat, the eyes of almost every man onboard the ship and near the front bulwark on the quarterdeck, follow every single movement William Rie and William Freeman make as they enter the jollyboat. Not a single word is said, but most of the minds connected to those eyes think that they are now going to witness a short, dangerous voyage leading to certain death. When John Anderson has entered the jollyboat, William unmoors the boat and jumps in.

Gurion and Reynolds have also followed the whole scene from the quarterdeck, and suddenly they both get second thoughts about this idea. Gurion quickly asks the crowd to make room for him and he hurries over to the bulwark, where William and the other men already sit in the jollyboat. The flag captain shouts at the top of his lungs, 'Don't do it. I'm convinced that when you get the jollyboat out in the open sea, you will not survive this attempt, because of the height of the waves."[20]

From the jollyboat, William looks up at Gurion on the quarterdeck. He and the other seamen sitting in the boat are quite willing to take risks to try and leave the *St. George* for good. To William there is no doubt that it is a friendly beach they will reach. He already has plans ready for when he arrives. He is going to write to the American Consul in Denmark and also ask the Danish authorities not to hand him over to the English until he can make sure that he can return to the United States of America as a free man.

But in order to succeed with his plan, he must survive these first 600 meters of sea between the wreck of the *St. George* and the Danish beach. He makes eye contact with John Anderson and the others sitting in the jollyboat, looks at Gurion once again and then nods as he shouts back, 'I think we agree with you captain, we will not make the try now." William then moors the jollyboat again, and the seamen in it return to the quarterdeck, joining the many other men standing there.

Anders Dahl, the 11-year-old son of a local wreck master, Jens Dahl from Fjand, is warmly dressed, running along the beach near the wreck of the *St. George,* his body bent into the steady, strong wind from the North Sea. The wind makes it quite difficult for the young boy to stay on his feet, so he stumbles from time to time.

Anders reaches the point on the beach the shortest distance to that northeast corner of the *St. George* where Reynolds stands stiff like a stone pillar, looking toward the beach. Anders has been on the beach most of the day watching this ship, much larger than any he has ever experienced in his lifetime at this beach. With his young, strong eyes, Anders clearly observes the Rear Admiral, who wears his golden gilt-edged uniform with the sign of his title, Rear Admiral of the Red, the Admiral's Silver Star, 3 inches long and 2 inches wide, mounted on his lower left chest against the background of his dark uniform.

Reynolds now stands in 'his usual northeast corner" of the quarterdeck with a lonely Admiral's dignity, looking toward the sandy beach, silently following the boy running along the beach with his eyes. Reynolds feels very tired now. It is depressing to him to be a kind of prisoner onboard the wreck of his own Flagship *St. George III,* without being able to give any useful orders, as a responsible, superior officer is supposed to do onboard an operating ship in the Royal Navy. In this miserable situation, it somehow helps him keep up his spirits, watching this fresh, young boy running and playing so carefree along the sandy beach, stopping only for a few moments to study the many men on the shipwreck of the *St. George*. To Reynolds, this boy looks so innocent, young and free as he runs around playing, able to do whatever he wants to do.

Reynolds finds it utterly impossible to think so far back to when he was a boy. Under the current grave circumstances, Reynolds simply can't recall a time when he did not feel a heavy burden of duty lying on his shoulders.

But suddenly he remembers when his own son was that exact same age.

The other officers are gathered on the south, portside part of the quarterdeck, to the left of Anders on the beach.

Reynolds waits, with a stoic calmness, either for his rescue from land or his death at sea.[257] His stone face shows no sign of emotion at this time.

The time is now 4 p.m. The icy wind still howls constantly, and the seas systematically hit the poop on the starboard side, spraying the men on the quarterdeck with icy salt water the entire day, with the weather showing no sign of change.

The men notice that it is beginning to get dark now, so close to the shortest day of the year. The hope for a rescue from land seems to vanish in the minds of these men at the same speed as the disappearing daylight. The icy seawater constantly coming in has frozen about 100 people to death now onboard the wreck of the *St. George*.

In his bed in the western chamber in Strandgaarden, John Page is awakened from a long, deep sleep at 5 p.m. by the feeling that somebody is standing next to his bed and touching his shoulder. Page notices a tall man wearing a military uniform, and is frightened for a moment. He is well aware that they now reside on enemy territory. The officer and gentleman standing by his side is the local commander of the coast militia, A. Von Schurnhardt, and he is the first person John Page has met in Denmark who speaks English. The officer smiles at him and says, "We have brought a dead officer to this house. He is in the barn, and I want to ask you, if you think you are strong enough, to get up and come and help us identify that person."[3]

John Page and Thomas Mullins, who also has woken up, both feel enormously tired and are convinced that they are too tired to stand properly on their feet. Despite this firm conviction, they answer, 'Sure, we will do anything that is in our power to help you, Sir."

'Fine," [3] Schurnhardt replies. He pauses for a minute and then continues, 'You see, we have received the news today that a three -deck ship has stranded to the south." When John Page and Thomas Mullins hear this, they know at once that he can only be talking about the flagship *St. George*.

Schurnhardt asks Thomas Wang and his stable boy to support John Page as he walks to the barn. Page has hardly managed to cross the courtyard and enter the large gateway to the barn when he is able to recognize the dead body of his late captain, David Atkins from *Defence*. He nods his head slowly as he approaches the dripping body of his former captain, who looks like he is sleeping, stretched out on an old house door placed on two trestles. 'There is no doubt in my mind. This is *HMS Defence*'s and our captain, David Atkins," [3] John Page says with a soft voice as he look at commander Schurnhardt.

After Page has identified the captain of *Defence,* he is helped back into his bed and the maid, Mette Cathrine Madsdatter, puts the two seamen close together and then packs the sleeping quilt tightly around the two bodies, giving them ideal conditions for quickly warming up.

As John Page has returned to his bed and Thomas Mullins is more awake now, Schurnhardt looks at both of them and notices that they are still in quite bad condition. He says shortly and a little worried, 'I'm sorry, we are not able to provide you with a doctor this Christmas Evening, but you will be offered the best food this house can provide." [3] Schurnhardt studies the two Englishmen once again, this time more closely. They look very pale and weak and he decides to leave them alone so they can get the rest necessary to recover. He has a couple more questions to ask them, to try to pick up any important pieces of military intelligence to forward to his superior officers in the Danish military headquarters at Gammelholm in Copenhagen.

Before he walks out and closes the door behind him, he says, 'I will leave you now and come back tomorrow morning, when you might be in better health and able to speak. You shall consider yourself war prisoners and remain calm until further notice." [3] John and Thomas nod their heads as they smile and Schurnhardt walks out of the door, thinking about what the two of them might be able to tell him tomorrow regarding the present Royal Navy's conditions in the Baltic Fleet. He is firmly convinced that *Defence* and the other three-deck ship must belong to the Royal Navy. [20]

This kind of military information is of great value to the Danish military headquarters.

The last thing John Page manages to think before he falls into another deep sleep is that he forgot to ask the gentleman if anyone else survived from *Defence*. John Page and Thomas Mullins go into a deep state of coma-like sleep in the beds in the farmhouse in Strandgaarden, as the strong wind howls through the small and highly bent trees just outside the chamber windows.

The maid opens the door to the chamber occasionally to see if the two seamen are still alive. It is sometimes hard to tell, because their sleep is so deep that they hardly ever move their bodies, and because the noise from the roaring sea and the storm in the trees outside tends to drown out the sound of the men's breathing.

Schurnhardt fights his way through the dark storm to cross the sand road to the south, almost blowing into the courtyard of Sønder Sønderby where he is going to see what he believes are the next two English prisoners of war from the shipwreck. Schurnhardt takes a firm grip on the door handle to the scullery and as he opens the door, a wind gust tries to rip it out of his hand. He quickly bows his head as he enters the low door of the farmhouse leading directly to the scullery. Mrs. Ruby Christensen has heard his steps in the yard outside and meets him in the doorway of the kitchen. 'I have come to see the war prisoners,"[3] he states shortly. Mrs. Christensen nods her head toward the door to his left and he walks over and opens it silently.

John Brown and the Englishman Ralph Teazel are fast asleep as Schurnhardt enters the room. They have both been sleeping deeply since they were put in the bed this very morning. Schurnhardt gently wakes them up one by one to ask them who they are. John is very happy to see an officer in a Danish uniform, which is very different from the British uniforms he had been forced to look at for the more than six years he had been impressed. John has been waiting for this moment for so long, that he has lost track of when his wish first originated.

John is quite aware that the stranding of the *Defence* on the beach of a country friendly to the United States of America and his own miraculous survival have put him in a unique position, and that all his wishing to escape from the Royal Navy might actually come true now. When this Danish officer addresses him in English, he is happy to be able to quickly answer the question posed and at the same time say that he is an

American born in Salem, north of Boston. Ralph Teazel tells Schurnhardt that he is English and from the City of London.[3]

Schurnhardt gives them the same message he gave the other survivors, that they shall consider themselves war prisoners, and remain calm until they have received further notice. They will be served the best food the house is able to provide, and although a doctor unfortunately can't see them this evening, one will come tomorrow, when he will return.[3]

After Schurnhardt has left, John is awake for the first time since he went to sleep in the bed, and realizes that he is actually in a real, comfortable bed with a nice, thick sleeping quilt - an experience he no longer seems to have any fresh memory of. But logically John can calculate that it has been more than six-and-a-half years since the last time he was lucky enough to sleep in a real bed. It was summer of 1805, just before he left his mother's apartment in Salem to go to Boston to enter the Boston schooner transporting weapons to the French troops in Fort-de-France on the West Indian island of Martinique.

This new realization becomes a deeply spiritual moment for John, now that distant and very weak memories over which he seems to have no control are revealed to him once again. He is so very grateful in these solemn moments, knowing that he is alive and on his way to recover to become all fresh and sound again.

John feels he has been well treated here from the very moment they arrived on the raft close to the beach. Both seamen fall into another deep, relaxing sleep in this comfortable environment on friendly territory.

Schurnhardt exchanged a few more words with Mrs. Ruby Christensen before he finally left the Sønder Sønderby farm to go further east to Gadegaard, where the two last surviving persons from the *Defence* are quartered. On arrival, Schurnhardt gives Amos and John Platt the same information he had given the others. When he walks out of the yard of the Gadegaard farm, Schurnhardt finally leaves the day's interrogations behind, and can't help speeding up, walking in the middle of a storm the 500 meters to his military headquarters at Dahlgaard. He is very much looking forward to enjoying the Christmas dinner that will be served to him and the other officers and soldiers from the Zealand Hunter force. They are all, because of the war with England, quite extraordinarily quartered as coastguards here on the Dahlgaard farm.

An hour later, at 6 p.m., the sweating and panting black horse carrying the District Bailiff Schønau manages to fight its way back to Strandgaarden after riding south along the beach close to the waterline. It is no problem for the Bailiff to ride at high speed here in the pitch-dark early evening, because the noisy, roaring breakers in the North Sea, in a safe distance from the water's edge where he has been riding, are a well defined sound wall that he very easily parallel. Schønau is returning from a long day of inspection of the stranding of a smaller ship that took place earlier this morning further to the north on the beach.

He rides into the yard in Strandgaarden, where he meets Thomas Wang. Because it is so pitch-dark along the beach, Schønau has not been able to make his own overview of the work done piling up the wreckage from *Defence* on the beach. Thomas Wang has this information ready for him and proudly reports that the men on the beach have worked very hard all day under the difficult and tough winter storm conditions.

The amount of wreck pieces that have come in so far have been so overwhelmingly distributed that much of the wreckage still needs to be piled up properly. As commanded, permanent coastguards have been stationed along the beach to protect each pile of wreckage. But the most surprising news Wang is able to give, news astounding even to highly experienced old wreck masters, is that virtually nothing is left of the *Defence* out on the first reef [252] only 13 hours after the ship first met the ground.

Schønau has a problem controlling his nervous horse, which moves restlessly from side to side, nodding its head and being very noisy as its metal horseshoes hit against the pavement of beach stones that covers the yard. Schønau is in a hurry, too. He wishes Thomas Wang a Merry Christmas and quickly leaves the courtyard to ride east along the road, with the strong wind in his back helping him, to go and celebrate Christmas Eve with his family at Rysensteen Manor.

He rode out from the manor early this morning and is now looking forward to returning and be with his own family again, which has been awaiting his return at the Rysensteen Manor all day.

In Strandgaarden, Christmas preparations are pretty advanced at this time, because the Christmas Evening dinner is expected to take place at 7:30 p.m. as usual. Thomas Wang and his wife normally live on a small farm north of Fjaltring in the parish of Trans, but Wang is for the time being wreck master for the Rysensteen Foreshore attached to the farm Strandgaarden, where *Defence* stranded.

Therefore, the Wang family spends Christmas Eve this year at Strandgaarden under the same roof as the Englishmen John Page and Thomas Mullins. Wang has temporarily been appointed wreck master for the Rysensteen Foreshore because the real owner, the former military captain Conrad Falkenberg, had earlier fallen out with the District Bailiff Schønau. The District Bailiff himself had some years ago been removed from the post of local commander of the coastguard in a district further north along the coast. Since that day of dismissal, he had developed a very strained relationship to any military officer he came upon, such as Falkenberg.

Falkenberg stays in the vicarage of Fjaltring Church this Christmas Eve, where he is a welcomed guest of the priest Søren Rømer and his wife. The Wang family has found it proper to celebrate Christmas at the Strandgaarden farm so they can also take care of the recovering stranded seamen. Every time a dish or a bowl is filled with steaming hot ingredients at the low, black Morsø cast iron stove along the kitchen wall, a small portion of that food is also put on each of two large plates on the kitchen table.

When Christmas dinner is served on the large dinner table in the dining room, Thomas Wang asks the maid, Mette Cathrine, to wake up the two seamen, who are still sleeping in the chamber next to the kitchen, as they have done most of the day, so the seamen won't feel alone on this stormy Christmas Eve, when they are so far from home. When this is done and the maid has returned, Thyra and Thomas Wang and Mette Cathrine finally sit down at the table and, before they eat, they pray a special grace on this Christmas Eve of 1811.

With bent heads, they pray for the many souls that, they are quite sure, are still onboard the other ship stranded on the reefs further south. Then they pray for the late captain David Atkins of *H. M. S. Defence* and the two dead seamen that have come in from the sea so far and are now in the barn. They also pray for their families and, finally, for a quick recovery for the six surviving seamen from *H.M.S. Defence* resting in the beds in these three farms south of the small village of Fjaltring. As they finally lift up their heads after praying, Thomas catches the eyes of the maid and nods his head, and she goes to the kitchen to take the plates to the two seamen, who are eagerly waiting, already sitting up against the high bed head, concentrated on their own prayers.

At 8 p.m., the long case clock in the corner of the living room in Strandgaarden strikes eight clear, loud strokes as Thomas Wang and the two women silently eat. Only the clink of silverware against the china, the background noise of the breakers at sea and the stormy wind outside break the silence. Here, as well as eight miles to the south, along the beach, the gale is still blowing at full strength over the foaming, icy sea and near coast landscape.

Sleet and snow snap the senseless faces of the calm group of crewmembers standing on the pitch-dark quarterdeck of the *St. George*. William is feeling very cold now and has for quite some time. He is at the same time very sad. William Freeman died an hour ago. He had been unconscious for an hour before he peacefully passed away and left the known world. William Watson had been at his side to the last moment and promised him that if he, William Watson, survived this stranding and reached North America alive, he world personally go and tell William Freeman's parents in Philadelphia what happened to their s on.

At the same time, the six seamen, four Britons and two Americans are sitting up in bed on the farms and served the best food they have had for years. None of them can clearly remember the last dinner they had, or when they tasted fresh pork, beef and milk, so easily provided even on a holiday like today on farms like these, but not easy to serve to common seamen onboard a man-o-war in the Royal Navy, out on the open sea.

John Brown almost gets tears in his eyes, as he sits, supported by two large pillows behind his back as he eats and lets his thoughts go back on the many years he was impressed onboard the Royal Navy's ships.

He tries to imagine the last time he was so close to Denmark. Thinking of it, he blushes and feels very shameful. On August 2, 1807, he was onboard *HMS Defence,* participating in transporting a large group of mariners from the 43rd Royal British Regiment from Yarmouth Roads to Elsinore - soldiers who were going to be used for the attack and bombardment of Copenhagen.

That had become an act of war, which he knows every common Dane, American and Frenchman finds utterly disgusting. Sixty-two innocent, defenseless children were killed in Copenhagen on that horrible occasion. John felt that he indirectly helped the British destroy the capital of Denmark, a true friend of The United States of America, and he also helped hunt down the guard ship at Kronborg Castle, the frigate no. 6 *Friderichsværn*, where 20 Danish men and officers were killed and many wounded, and 200 Danes taken as war prisoners.

As thanks for his part in this disgusting episode to start the war between Denmark and England, his life has miraculously been saved by these friendly, poor Danish coast farmers here on the northwest coast of Jutland. This new situation might lead to him regaining his freedom from six years of impressment in the Royal Navy, while in a country friendly to his own. On top of that, he has now been served this delicious Christmas dinner and cared for by these friendly, shy men and women.

The emotional stress of suddenly realizing this rare connection of events, one very few human beings ever experience personally, is almost unbearable to John, and he looks down on his sleeping quilt for several minutes to avoid crying. Then a blond, blue-eyed and beautiful maid knocks on the door and comes into the bedroom, smiling so genuinely at him as she serves him more food. This must be heaven, John thinks, and Jesus surely must be in it on such a nice Christmas Evening. He smiles back the best smile he has ever learned.

The strong and icy wind howls continuously. From time to time, the moon comes out from behind the clouds and can be seen clearly. On these occasions, William gets a look at the other men standing on the quarterdeck, and can see their tortured, expressive faces.

A small group of officers are still in the captain's cabin, which is illuminated by candles. It is cold in the cabin and the floor is now flooded with water to a level just below their knees, and their breath is visible. Still, it is considerably warmer in the cabin than outside in the storm on the unprotected quarterdeck.

On the dark shore 600 yards to the east, men and boys have grouped on the beach near the water's edge to get the best position to peer through the breakers toward the wreck, when the foam from the waves is not hitting their faces and preventing them from seeing. The local wreck masters, including Jens Dahl, are able to observe that a light is still burning in the upper gallery of the wrecked *St. George*. From the occasional flashes in the windows when an officer passes the table and candles, the men on the beach feel the presence of living men onboard the wreck.

James Railton, Reynolds' personal secretary, is still in the cabin. He is the only one in the room sitting on a chair at the table in the middle of the room, his face directed toward the dark windows in the gallery. A fifteen-inch tall, five-armed silver candlestick with lighted flicker candles stands on the middle of the table. None of the men have spoken for several hours. There is no hope in the room anymore.

None of them have the slightest hope of being rescued from the shore. They are perfectly aware that no small boats will be able to go out from the beach to reach the *St. George* in this steady, wild gale. Railton's seat is only one inch above the waterline. In the glimmer of the candles, he is writing a letter, one he is convinced will be the last letter he'll ever write to his lovely wife. Occasionally he stops writing just to stare at a random point in space in front of him. Then, still absent-mindedly, he begins to move his body again as he dips the long, white goose quill in the ink box beside his right hand.

Secretary Railton has put all his valuables in the pockets on the jacket he now wears, to carry them with him to the shore, dead or alive. Railton's idea is to put the letter to his wife in his jacket pocket and hope that a person who might find him on the beach of this enemy coastline will be so thankful for the money he finds that he will feel bound to send the letter to Railton's wife in London.

In the small kitchen in the low-lofted farmhouse east of the stable buildings in the small village of Fjand, protected against the storm and hidden behind the tall dunes, wreck master Jens Dahl's wife and the eldest maids are busy preparing Christmas dinner, running between the kitchen and the larder in the coldest corner of the farm house.

The dinner will be eaten a little late this evening, because of the Christmas Feast. Large pots and small casseroles have been passing over the hot stove since early this morning, and the air in the kitchen is moist and the thin window glass virtually opaque with condensed steam.

At the water's edge, Jens Dahl shudders slightly in the cold and then gives a last glance through the breakers toward the illuminated gallery on the wrecked *St. George*. He is aware that it will become a very special Christmas Eve in the small village if something happens out on the wreck to force the many men to leave the ship and try to reach the beach. So far, not a single man has been observed trying to leave the shipwreck during the day, as far he knows.

Then he walks eastward on the beach toward the dunes, where his 11-year-old son Anders is restlessly waiting on the beach, freezing and wanting to go home. The father and son head for home, because they know that Christmas dinner must be almost ready, as is the case every year.

The whole group of wreck masters, farmers, fishermen and their boys slowly turn around, listening to Jens Dahl's words, and as they begin to walk home, they are almost blown eastwards over the dunes by the strong wind. Anders is very fond of good food and as usual, his thoughts have concentrated on Christmas dinner almost all day. When Anders was thinking about good food it was almost impossible to distract him. Now he looks forward to finally getting his reward for many hours of restless waiting for dinnertime.

Living close to the sea, these west coast men and boys are very concerned about the poor souls left helpless in the cold, dark evening on the quarterdeck of the *St. George*. At the same time, they are filled with a humble and grateful joy thinking of Christmas dinner, the culinary highlight of the entire year in this remote, poor region. When they reach the first house in Northern Fjand, the four wreck-masters who had stayed on the beach - Jens Dahl, Jens Mikkelsen, Anders Ibsen and Mikkel Sand - and the strand knights Anders Andersen and Jens Højbjerg decide to meet again after Christmas dinner to form a team of night watches to stay on the beach through the night, to look after possible survivors from the *St. George*.[252]

While the men from Fjand have reached their homes, 14 of the men standing on the quarterdeck, a group William does not belong to, gets Reynolds' permission to make a new attempt to reach the shore in the launch.

Reynolds is definitely weak now, and so is Gurion. There is a general feeling onboard the *St. George* that it is only a matter of time before the two highest officers are incapable of making any more decisions. Generally, the officers are in much worse health than the ordinary seamen and mariners in the crew. The seamen, most of them small with slim muscular bodies, are used to staying out long hours, unprotected in tough weather on the open decks, and the hard work they perform, scraping the decks or running up and down the rigging, makes their bodies fit. This hard work and regular exercise keeps most of the seamen and mariners in excellent condition. This circumstance is beginning to have an effect now on the many men onboard the shipwreck.

Most of the officers look pale now, and relative to their number in the total crew, many officers have already passed away. Just as when John Anderson and William asked Admiral Reynolds to take the jollyboat, the initiative for this action also comes from the brightest of the seamen and not the superior officers. The officers are simply too weak now to put any action behind their words, if they tried to take any action.

An increasing number of men have frozen to death since the first attempt to reach shore by boat was made, in the daylight six hours ago, and the death rate is beginning to increase to an extent that the general feeling on the quarterdeck is that something must be done soon to try to save at least some of the men.

William and the two remaining seamen from his group are not interested in making a new attempt to reach the shore, now that William Freeman has passed away. Freeman's death somehow put a damper on their wish to take any action or risk for the time being. Besides, the cold wind, sleet, and saltwater they are constantly exposed to gradually weakens them, and William is also firmly convinced that it is not a terribly good idea to attempt to reach shore at this dark hour, when they can't see what they are doing. John Anderson agrees, so they decide to stay in the background now.

As the wreck masters and their families are eating Christmas dinner around the long tables in their dinning rooms, the 14 seamen have managed to climb one by one into the launch and find their seat. The signal is given to loosen the mooring line so they can attempt to get free of the shipwreck and try to reach the sandy beach.

But the launch has hardly moved 15 yards along the port side of *St. George* on the south lee side before a huge wave grasps it and turns it upside down in one single movement. The launch instantly goes down while heartrending screams come from the dark for several minutes.

Nothing more is ever heard of these 14 seamen. The remaining men onboard the wrecked *St. George* have been silent all the time and now only the loud, constant howling of the wind is heard on the quarterdeck.

The men just stand there, packed shoulder by shoulder in their dark blue woolen long coats, the wind steadily howling in their ears and the waves washing against the wreck, periodically spraying icy saltwater over their frozen hair and blue-cold bodies. They all fight an individual, lonely battle of not falling asleep or, worse, fainting, which means sudden death before Christmas morning ever breaks.

William's little group of seamen who almost left the *St. George* in a jollyboat some hours ago now think, poor souls. Here a few hours after sundown several of the men and boys are already frozen half-dead with no real feeling in their feet, lower legs or in their faces. As their heads cool down from the icy water that sweeps over them, some of them simply can't prevent fainting. The high inclination of the quarterdeck presses the many men and boys so hard together in the lee side, that even dead and unconscious persons are kept standing.

Despite the generally depressing situation experienced by these men onboard the dark quarterdeck of the wrecked *St. George,* William's own spirits are remarkably high. Since he received the copy of his Protection Certificate outside Gothenburg, he has been convinced, unrealistically self-assured like a naïve, childlike young man, that he will succeed against all odds and make it home, where, he is convinced, he is desperately needed by his small family. He had chosen to see getting the Protection Certificate with the lucky number 7777 as a clear sign that he would manage to return to Mary Ann, his child, Wilmington and his beloved country. As ice-cold water sprays over William's head this dark Christmas evening, threatening to make him faint several times, he just has to recall that letter from the American Department of State. Then he instantly regains his full psychological strength to keep on fighting.

His young wife Mary Ann and their child, whom he preferred to think of as a son, would definitely soon see him at the doorstep to the flat at 68 E. Water Street in Wilmington, he was convinced. His remarkable self-confidence has been unbreakable since they left Vinga Sound outside Gothenburg.

At first, he had wondered why the certificate was sent by the Department of State and not by Wilmington's port collector Allen McLane. William figured that Mary Ann must have received his third letter too late in autumn, which meant that the copy he received could not be a result of her contacting McLane, as he had requested in his letter. He concluded that it must have been one of the two letters he wrote earlier to General William Lyman, the American Agent for Seamen in London, which must have been forwarded to the Department of State, which then requested a copy of his certificate from the port collector in New York and forwarded it to him onboard the *St. George III.*

The almost unbelievable, uplifting message that this letter brought William, and that instantly penetrated to the very core of his heart, was that The United States of America took care of its sons and daughters after all when they were abroad and exposed to great distress and troubles. That moved William more than anything else he could think of right now. He clearly remembered that after his first outburst of laughter in Gothenburg, caused by a feeling of pure joy, he had been so touched that he had kept silent for half an hour, so as not to be overwhelmed by emotion. He saw it as a sign from God that he must have been chosen to return to his native country soon, however stupid that might seem to others.

As William stands on the quarterdeck surrounded by many other crewmembers, as the wind noisily howls and the icy seawater mercilessly adds more and more ice to the hair of their heads, William sometimes disconnects from this all to unreal world that surrounds him.

He is still filled with the naïve belief that, with the lucky number 7777, 7 being the most frequent number in the Holy Bible and the number of red stripes in his country's flag, the God of the Stars and Stripes will show good will and set him free on the very day of the birth of His own son. William is firmly convinced that, when he has passed the 600 yards of troubled waters between the wreck of the *St. George* and the Danish beach, he will be able to present his Protection Certificate – which, in his present situation he could call his personal Declaration of American Independence - to the proper Danish authorities.

Then he expects that the Danes, friends of his own country, will declare him what he really is, an unlucky impressed American with the right to be set free from serving onboard war ships in England's Fleet, and to return home to America to his constitutional right to pursue happiness - happiness he is convinced he planted there more than two years ago with his dear wife Mary Ann and their child.

There is no doubt in his mind now. In the endless rows of seamen standing on the poop of the *St. George* with grave faces and with empty eyes, only William's and a dozen others are smiling warmly. He becomes more and more self-assured as the time passes by this Christmas Eve. He sees this difficult situation he is in as an enemy he has to fight. Instead of being sad and resigned, he is angry.

No, he thinks several times during the evening, they are not going to get him in this attempt. God has made a plan here, William is sure. He does not see himself as any ordinary person. God would not let him go through these many tough trials just to let him die. He was born in the

State of Delaware in 1787, the year Delaware was the first state in North America to ratify the Constitution. The Constitution written by James Madison, now the sitting President, the year William was born, and who was called 'the Father of the Constitution." And it was not just ordinary men who signed that ratification on December 7, 1787. No, it was the farmer and Colonel Thomas Watson from Pen Cader Hundred in New Castle County, to whom William felt he had a family link, and who had signed for New Castle County. And Colonel and port collector Allen McLane, one of the signers for Kent County. William is all caught up with these rare and unique thoughts now. These thoughts might be utterly indifferent to most men onboard *St. George III*. But no, this can't just be a coincidence, William thinks again and again. God definitely has a plan here. William ignores the pain from his frozen feet and the wet and icy hair that embraces his blue frozen face. William's mind is all set on the shore now.

At 8 p.m. on Christmas Eve, William is in the large passive group that just stands and watches to see if an opportunity for rescue occurs. The weakened Reynolds and Gurion are sitting on the quarterdeck with their backs against the skylight in the wind and starboard side. They are both too weak to stand. Because the *St. George* has been sinking deep in the sand, the incline of the icy, wet quarterdeck is now at such a high angle that it becomes impossible for many men to remain standing.

William is in the middle of the crowd, his lively eyes a contrast to his own pale blue face and the many other blue faces beside him. His Protection Certificate is still safe on his stomach and the beautiful silk scarf from Mary Ann still tightly knitted around his neck, helping to keep the water out and the heat inside. The English seamen surrounding him are not in quite the same good mood. They don't share Williams' strange optimism and deep feeling of hope. Psychologically, the Englishmen are too burdened with bad war memories. They know that even should they miraculously be able to fight their way in through the breakers, perhaps on primitive pieced-together rafts, and reach the shore alive, they will as Englishmen end up on enemy territory and in a prison for sure.

They know all too well how badly foreign seamen are treated onboard English prison ships to expect any better treatment themselves, when or if they reach an enemy shore like this one. Many of these experienced English seamen have been through so many unreasonably tough war experiences that there is no more room in their heads for the kind of naïve hope that obsesses William. Hope is so important in a deep personal crisis like the one William experiences now, when normal logical thinking would only lead to a conclusion of sudden and total failure.

As Christians, they believe in a higher order of justice, which logically and automatically leads them to draw this sad conclusion regarding their own destiny. As Christians, they know that one must treat other human beings the way they want others to treat themselves. Because they have earlier made commando raids along these shores, they therefore now expect the same kind of bad treatment, if they manage to reach the shore alive. The Englishmen had their hope taken away from them, while William got his hope strengthened, from being here along a Danish shore.

To William, this becomes a rare religious moment. He asks himself over and over as the minutes pass whether God will save them on this Christmas Night or the following days as a genuine thanks for the birth of his son. Will the storm finally decrease and make it possible for lifeboats to come out from the shore and save them?

In the beams in the flag captain's cabin, three lights now hang to signal the position of the ship. Officer and night watch Jens Højbjerg has ridden eight miles south along the beach from Dahlgaard, and is sitting in his guard cabin on the beach at Fjand around midnight as night watch. He decides to walk out to check the situation along the beach, where *St. George* is wrecked.

He observes that the lights in the gallery of the captain's cabin are still on and is convinced that until now, nobody onboard the *St. George* has tried to reach the shore. Because he is a local member of the coast guards and lives not too far from the beach, he is aware that the strong southern sea current will carry the bodies of those who try but fail to reach the shore alive. Since nobody has reached the shore yet, he concludes that the survival strategy of the men onboard the *St. George* is to wait on the wreck until the storm has decreased.

Most of the families in the coast parishes of Fjand and Fjaltring have gone to bed. It takes constant hard work to earn a living on this poor farm land so close to the sandy North Sea beaches, and everyone has to get up early. Even the six survivors from *Defence* are sleeping well now in the beds in the farms of Sønder Sønderby, Strandgaarden and

Gadegaard.

John wakes up from time to time only to hear the wind howl wildly outside the windows. On these occasions he thinks of his fellow seamen onboard the *Defence*. Have more men come in and managed to survive? What about the *St. George*? He knows she is stranded seven to eight miles south of this place. He is quite worried that they will not make it, but is too exhausted to worry in the middle of the night. The cows and calves are lying in the warm, thick hay in the stables, well protected against the storm by the thick, half-timbered walls.

The many other animals on the farms, chickens, hens, geese, and pigs are asleep too, except for a couple of white-black cats using the high noise level the storm provides to increase their chances to sneak in on some of the fat mice in the barns.

9

At midnight Christmas Night, the remaining crew is still calm on the quarterdeck of the *St. George,* or the remains of *St. George*. Most of the English seamen direct their thoughts toward their wives and children at home. Their families have no doubt gathered at home in Portsmouth, London and the different small villages they come from. Despite their own difficult situation, most of the Englishmen on the quarterdeck know that their families must be worried sick. They should be home now, ready to celebrate Christmas morning with their families.

William has never experienced such a dramatic Christmas Night in his entire life. He often lets his thoughts go to Mary Ann, her kind mother and his many friends in Wilmington as the tough hours pass so slowly. Joseph and Mary Warner and his family and their mother Mary have probably been to the divine service at the Friends Meeting House on Quaker Hill this evening to prepare themselves for the Christmas holidays. Maybe they are eating now or just preparing to go to church.

William is sure Mary Ann must be terribly worried about his absence this evening. Is she with their child? Is it a boy who looks like him? He needs to get home now and it suddenly can't be fast enough. How will Mary Ann and the child manage to take care of themselves now when times are so tough in America? He just has to cross these roaring 600 meters of icy, troubled waters between the quarterdeck on the *St. George III* and the Danish beach to the east. Then he will be safe and together with friends of his native country, the United States of America, people who will probably release him from this long-lasting hell.

William learned in school, and from Thomas Mendenhall at the harbor in Wilmington when they talked, that the Danes are true friends of America. They helped the Wilmington wharf-owners smuggle guns back home from St. Thomas in the Revolutionary War, among other things. William knows everything about the famous ship *Nancy*.

It is six o'clock in the evening in Wilmington, and the borough homes are preparing for the coming Christmas. Allen McLane, his wife Maria, his sons Louis and Allen, and their wives and the grandchildren are gathered in the McLane home. The port collector restlessly walks around in the living room. The other family members notice it, but they are used to it. It happens every Christmas Eve. They all know that Christmas is very special to Allen McLane.

A storm has hit Wilmington and Delaware this year, indeed the whole east coast of America, just as it is the case in all of Western Europe. A gust with snow and sleet suddenly hits the window near the desk where McLane stands in the living room. He is quiet for some time, then says aloud, "Maria, do you know that this night it is exactly 35 years since George Washington, I and the Continental Army crossed the Delaware River? Look, the weather it is exactly the same this evening. Isn't that strange?" Maria has been waiting all day for her husband to address that specific subject that comes up every year on this day, like clockwork. "Yes, Allen, we are all aware that this evening is special to you. It has been every year since The Declaration of Independence." The similar weather takes McLane's thoughts back 35 years.

They had been fearful that night, as never before or since. Which side would God be on this night? The place they plan to attack on this Christmas Eve 1776, Trenton, on the New Jersey side of the Delaware River, is under the occupation of the Hessian Colonel Johann Gottlieb Rall and 1,400 men. Washington moves north along the west side of the Delaware River with 2,400 Continentals to attack Trenton from north.

General James Ewing with several hundred Pennsylvania militias is going to cross further downstream to cut off the British from Bordentown, a possible escape route. The attack plan is flexible. If Trenton shows to be too hard a nut to crack, the Continental forces are prepared to move on to Princeton and New Brunswick. A strong cold gale is blowing. Colonel Glover and his Marblehead men, who successfully evacuated the Continental Army from the entrenchment at Bronx to Manhattan and fought heroically at Pelham Bay, now prepare several six-foot flat-bottomed Durham boats, big enough to transport an entire company, to ferry General Washington, McLane, other officers and their companies across the Delaware River. These boats are normally used to transport grain and iron ore along the Delaware River. At 11 p.m. when the ferrying of the troops is at its peak, the snow has set in, and when it turns to wet sleet it ruins many of the gun flintlocks. At midnight, it is time for McLane and his men to be ferried over. The storm has churned the surface of the Delaware River and ice swirls around the boats. The crewmen push the ice away with oars and poles to get the boats to move forward. It is difficult to cross the Delaware River this Christmas Night.

As Port Collector, McLane is in charge of the control of each ship going in and out from New Castle or Wilmington. He keeps a mental record of each ship, captain or seaman with a home port in Wilmington, and whether they are present in the borough or at sea.

This year, a considerable number of captains and seamen attached to ships from Wilmington, New Castle and Philadelphia are overseas. Some of these ships and men are illegally transporting import-restricted goods to the United States from continental Europe or England, which is a very dangerous business. But many young seamen from Wilmington and other east coast ports are unable to find jobs on the American coast right now. So they are forced to leave their country to sail this Christmas on foreign ships between European ports. McLane is also quite aware that some of the Wilmington seamen who are not home with their families this Christmas are impressed onboard ships in the British Royal Navy.

In their Georgetown home, Elizabeth and James Monroe are having a nice Christmas Eve dinner. James keeps losing his concentration, looking out the windows all the time. The howling wind disturbs his thoughts over and over again. 'Elizabeth," he says sh ortly as he looks at her. 'Isn't it strange? Tonight it is exactly 35 years since I crossed the Delaware River with my Regiment and the Continental Army and George Washington and…" He pauses.

"Yes, James, what is it, my dear?" Elizabeth asks.

"The weather is the same today as back then," he says, as though he has told a long-kept secret. His eyes stare at the content of the crystal wineglass in his right hand as he tries to follow the wave of red wine around the upper inside of the glass, as he tilts and rotates the stem of the glass. His thoughts wander back to that special stormy Christmas Night of 1776, too.

McLane, still standing at the window, continues to think of the seamen and captains from the borough of Wilmington who are on the seas this Christmas Night. He recalls most of them. He knows William Watson, or who William Watson is in relation to his family. He had been fighting with the fathers of some of these men in the Revolutionary War. As a

Revolutionary War Hero himself and a man of the sea, he knows very well that the combination of seamen and soldiers in the many Delaware families was a deadly cocktail. Whole families had been destroyed within a generation.

He personally knows fathers and brothers, heads of households, who died in the war. They left widows with small children who grew up to be sailors and captains, leaving their mothers early in order to supply income to their families, only to drown in storms, with their families never knowing what became of them.

Mary Ann's William is around the age of McLane's own sons, and McLane knows that another William Watson of that same age is also impressed on a ship in the Royal Navy this Christmas Eve. The second William Watson comes from Duck Creek Cross Road in Kent County, where McLane and his wife lived when his eldest son Allen was born, just after the end of the Revolutionary War.

It saddens McLane to think that these Wilmington captains and seamen are prisoners on this special evening. Standing by a window in the living room, McLane bends his head and sends up a prayer for the American seamen impressed onboard Royal Navy ships this Christmas Eve.

As he stares out the window, he remembers the beautiful but sad wife, Mary Ann Watson, who came into his Customhouse office two months ago. He had estimated her age to be about 18. He already knew her family, one of the old families in Wilmington, but he had not talked much to her in person before. He had often seen her around the lower Market House in Second Street close to the custom office when she was out shopping, and from her response he could see that she knew who he was. But then, everyone in Wilmington did, so that was no surprise. She had asked him, almost begged him, to send a Customhouse Protection Certificate to her husband William Watson, onboard the Royal Navy ship *St. George*. McLane had asked for detailed information on her husband, which could prove who he was. She had shown him their marriage certificate issued in Delaware, and had stated when he made a copy, that this copy was correct according to the original. McLane then sent the papers to the Department for Treasury, with whom he normally corresponded as port collector. The Treasury Department afterward sent it to the Department of State so they could ask for a copy of William Watson's original Protection Certificate from the port collector in New

York.

McLane knows that William Watson cannot have received this copy of his Protection Certificate yet. So he is quite sure that William Watson must still be onboard the *St. George* this evening, and from what Mary Ann Watson had told[12] him in his office, *St. George* was in the Baltic Sea when William wrote her on June 28 this year. This means that *St. George* must be a part of the Baltic Fleet, of which McLane is well informed. The Warners, Hemphills and other Wilmington ship-owners often sail to Europe, especially to Texel, Den Helder or Amsterdam in Holland and the large port of Altona near Hamburg lying in the Elbe River on the Danish border. On their return to Wilmington, the captains often come by his office and have spoken to him about the patrolling Royal Navy ships of line or frigates they frequently met on these trips to Europe. Many of these ships were somehow attached to the Royal Navy Baltic Fleet as they patrolled the Atlantic Ocean or the English Channel, or sailed along the coast outside Texel. They also patrolled the North Sea, the Skagerak, the Cattegat and the Baltic Sea itself.

McLane is aware that at this time of year, most of the Baltic Fleet is likely at home in England, anchored in the ports of Plymouth, Portsmouth, Sheerness, and Yarmouth. He is, therefore, confident that Mary Ann's husband William is safe onboard the *St. George* in a south English port this Christmas Eve.

Perhaps from there, William can be released before the Baltic Fleet sails in spring, if he can present to his superior officer the certificate that McLane ordered sent to the *St. George*.

The moon is shining clearly at the moment and it illuminates the chalk-white, bloodless faces of the silent men on the quarterdeck of the *St. George*. The sea continues to sweep over them again and again. This, combined with the increasing frost in the clear night air, is causing men to die in larger numbers now.

The death screams from dying officers and men are heard through the rest of the night, and it deeply touches the hearts of the still living men on the deck.[20]

Rear Admiral of the Red C.W. Reynolds is frozen to the bone and half dead, sitting with his back against the skylight. He slowly turns his head toward Flag Captain Daniel Gurion and asks, 'My good man, what is it the legend says about the good *Saint George*?" The flag captain bends his head toward the Rear Admiral in order to hear the words over the howling wind. The Captain's sad eyes now meet the Admiral's. Head to head, so as to hide his weighted words from the officers and men surrounding them, Gurion whispers to Reynolds, 'I'm afraid, Sir, that the legend clearly says *St. George* shall die under the cruelest and most terrible suffering that can be imagined by mankind." Reynolds, well-educated and historically interested, already knew the answer but wanted it confirmed. He nods his head slowly, then leans his head and back against the skylight.

As happens to all men and women, Reynolds, at his advanced age of 60 years, is beginning to spend much time thinking back on his youth. His was marked by the fact that he had witnessed what English aristocrats often called the two damned revolutions: the American Revolution and the French Revolution. The first one, Reynolds hated of a good heart, because that was the one he had participated in himself and he had lost.

He had been a captain on a ship in the great Royal Navy fleet that the English Admiralty sent to Sandy Hook, just outside New York, in the summer of 1776. The Americans had attacked the ship from the coast, and it caught fire and they had been forced to abandon it.

Reynolds had actually stayed around Sandy Hook and New York at the same time Allen McLane, George Washington and the other officers and men in the Continental Army had been there. Reynolds hated these American upstarts, who had caused suffering and defeat for the British forces, which he represented and was so very proud of, and in the end had caused the British Empire to lose its North American colonies. Therefore, it felt good for him that now, later in his career, as a Rear Admiral of the Red in the Royal British Navy, he had the opportunity to pay back a little of that suffering to impressed American seamen under his command.

Reynolds slowly glides down on the deck from the upright position supported by the skylight, and he moves in and out of consciousness, babbling in incoherent, crazy sentences relating to his war memories. 'The American Revolution was the father of the modern revolutions, mature and considered in its expression, headed by country folks and self-contained when it had reached its goals. The French revolution was like a son, impulsive, occasionally randomly violent if needed, partly unjust in its mode of expression, and headed by city folks".

The dimmed expression in Reynolds's eyes disappears as if he had received a revelation. Gurion sees that the Admiral has found the energy to lift up his body from the deck, leaning on both his elbows with wide open eyes and mouth, as if to say something very important. But then he gabbles on in what sounds like complete insanity "...the third and final revolution will be like the Holy Ghost. Transient and indefinable in its substance and diffusive as long as it serves its purpose.... and partly started by suppressed seamen, like the impressed Americans here onboard *St. George*. It is as though these damned Americans shall get to me a second time, here on my home base, the quarterdeck of my own flagship the proud *St. George III*."

As Reynolds speaks these words, he recalls his own Revolutionary War memories from Sandy Hook and New York, and clearly envisions the Commander of the Continental Army George Washington and his subordinate General Stirling heading his extraordinary tough soldiers from Delaware and Maryland on the battlefield just south of New York.

Reynolds with a last effort manages to quote the famous words from that battlefield, as pronounced by Washington. He shouts, "Good God, what brave fellows I may this day lose." Reynolds' body then falls limp to the deck, while Gurion sadly shakes his head and thinks to himself that a vicious insanity must have caught the Admiral here in his last hours as it had caught King George III earlier this year.

On this day, Lieutenant Louis Tuxen is sitting at his desk in the Admiralty on the islet of Gammelholm in Copenhagen. He receives a report from a spy who successfully observed the English convoy in the Ear Sound, which was previously located between Barcebäk and Salt Holmen along the Swedish coast. The spy has seen *Woodlark*, *Pyramus* and *Ariel*, plus 50 merchant ships and a few cutter brigs.[89] The little convoy weighed on a south-southwestern wind and a wind to the contrary had soon taken the ships back to Hven Island, where they had been forced to anchor temporarily.

A Danish privateer confiscates one of the merchant ships from the convoy. The spy reports that he has observed no trading between the shore and the ships, but he had no doubt that they could get whatever they wanted delivered through their old agents in Elsingborg. Some of the English ships had been on shore.

The convoy finally passes Ear Sound by sailing close to the Swedish coast to avoid the batteries at Kronborg Castle. The Danish commander of those batteries cursed as the batteries fired cannons several times, but in vain, as the range of the cannons was too small. The Danish commander, the officers and soldiers at Kronborg Castle could only stand and watch the convoy pass, heading for safety in Vinga Sound and perhaps a meeting with the Royal Navy Baltic Convoy they had been with when it left Hanö Bay, back on November 9.

The screams onboard the *St. George* continue during the next three hours. The Danish night watches and wreck masters on the beach at Fjand, Jens Dahl and others, can clearly hear these screams, carried by the strong western wind from the quarterdeck to the shore. They are saddened to realize that they can do absolutely nothing to help. More and more men die as time passes, and dead bodies begin to fill up the quarterdeck, making it difficult for the living men to hold on to the ship.

Therefore, First Lieutenant Francis Rogers, who took over command when Reynolds and Gurion became unconscious, gives the order to stack the bodies of the dead, or those thought dead, along the portside bulwark, to protect living men against the waves sweeping in at the front of the quarterdeck. The Rear Admiral and the captain are put side by side on the quarterdeck in the portside behind this human barrier. This provides the two superior officers with some of the warmth from the many dead but not yet cold bodies. But it is too late. At 2:00 a.m., Reynolds cannot stand the physical or mental stress of lying on the ice-cold quarterdeck any more, and he passes away.[20] Death screams are heard time and time again from men onboard, until dawn.

It is horrifying for wreck master Jens Dahl and the other Danish coastguards and night watches to listen to. This night is an absolutely terrifying experience for William, in a way he had never been able to imagine, and for the other conscious men on deck, it is the same.

Despite the high mental stress on the dark quarterdeck during this entire Christmas Night, William is able to concentrate on his wife Mary Ann. Unfortunately, he spent almost no time with her after they got married in the Old Swedes Church in Wilmington more than two years ago. But almost every minute of the little time they did spend together had been memorable. It warmed his heart, eased his pain and lifted his spirits to be able to direct his thoughts to something very positive, Wilmington and Mary Ann, during this terrible Christmas Night.

At the same time, 8:30 p.m. in Wilmington, the large McLane family is sitting around the dinner table enjoying their meal.

Mary Ann and her mother are also sitting around the dinner table in their apartment in Water Street, eating without speaking. After some time, Mary Ann looks at her mother and says, "Mother, I do sincerely hope that William is well this Christmas Eve. It's terrible weather outside and I really hope that it is much better in England." "Yes, dear Mary Ann, let us hope that our beloved William is in good hands on this Christmas Eve."

In a deserted, dark office in the Department of State in Washington D.C., Mary Ann Watson's letter to her husband, Mariner William Watson onboard his Britannic Majesty's ship *St. George,* is lying in a huge stack of similar letters from families and relatives to American seamen impressed onboard Royal Navy ships this Christmas Eve. Letters addressed to an American man like Mariner William Watson onboard a foreign warship, like the Royal Navy flagship *St. George,* always end up in the Department of State, because all military related foreign post has to be controlled.

This same Christmas Night, on a desk in the Headquarters for the Danish Admiralty at Gammelholm in Copenhagen, is a drawing of a new invention, a new type of sea mine invented by the celebrated American landscape painter and inventor Robert Fulton, who was born in Pennsylvania to poor Irish immigrants. This sea mine could be helpful out in the Great Belt, the Little Belt and Ear Sound, to hinder the passage of Royal Navy ships to and from the Baltic Sea.

Fulton earlier developed and tested a submarine in the river Seine when he stayed in Paris. With the help of the American minister to Paris, Livingston, he was able to make a British machine manufacturer produce him a steam machine, which he took back to New York to continue his work.

In 1807, the very same year Denmark's Royal fleet was stolen by the British Royal Navy, Robert Fulton was busy testing his new "product," the sea going steamship "Clermont" on the Hudson River just outside New York. The invention of the steam ship was the beginning of all nations losing their great navy fleets of sailing ships.

359

For introducing the seagoing steamship, the American Minister to Paris Livingston and Robert Fulton were awarded a 30 year monopoly for sailing steamships in the waters around New York.

So, just as Samuel Bush had been the first to establish a sailing ship route between Philadelphia and Wilmington, Robert Fulton and Livingston became the first to establish a steamship route in the waters around New York.

In years to come, submarines were also seen anchored in the port of Wilmington in the Christina River.

Robert Fulton had met the Danish minister to Philadelphia, Mr. Petersen, at parties held by the President's wife, when the American states administration stayed in that city. Fulton's military inventions like the sea mine, which could be used to fight British Royal Navy ships trying to pass Danish waters, began to be transferred after these parties in Philadelphia.

Flag Captain Daniel Gurion dies an hour after Reynolds, at approximately 3:30 a.m. Until their last hours, Gurion and Reynolds performed their duty as superior officers to perfection, and encouraged the ordinary crewmembers and subordinate officers to keep up the men's spirits in this difficult situation.[20]

By now, some 302 of the total crew of 502 have frozen to death, leaving only approximately 200 still alive. The dead bodies are lying all over the wreck, both in the captain's cabin and on the quarterdeck.[4]

William, John Anderson, and two other seamen have managed to stick together despite the increasing chaos on the wreck. The group is standing somewhere in the middle of the quarterdeck.

In Georgetown, Secretary of State James Monroe and his wife Elizabeth are still sitting at the dinner table, sipping wine without talking. Because of the terrible weather this evening, it seems impossible for the normally rather determined James Monroe to keep his thoughts from the events of 35 years ago.

McLane and his family are at the dinner table in their home in Wilmington. Secretary of State James Monroe and Port Collector of Wilmington Colonel Allen McLane simultaneously let their thoughts go back 35 years to Christmas Night 1776, where they both were lieutenants under the command of the late Commander in Chief of the Continental Army, George Washington.

It is three o'clock and the last of the guns have been ferried over the Delaware River. When the companies are ready to start the nine mile trek through wind and sleet, Washington is visibly annoyed and shouts in anger over the storm, 'For God's sake, keep by your officers,' whereafter McLane's men instinctively gather closely behind him as do Monroe's men.

At this point, McLane and Monroe are both calm compared to their superior officers, because they don't carry the same heavy burden of responsibility. They are all looking forward to what they are beginning to see as a possible turning point of the war. Washington is more doubtful than Monroe and McLane, as evidenced by the fact that he has made an alternative plan of attacking Trenton. If Trenton can't be taken, the troops shall quickly proceed northward to Princeton and Brunswick.

What the American officers have been taking into account while planning the attack is that it is tradition for European mariners and soldiers, when far from home, to celebrate Christmas Night with a heavy consumption of beer and rum, if it is available.

The British officers had long ago given up controlling the alcohol consumption among the soldiers on Christmas Eve and a night like this one, because the men tend to get quite sentimental on such a solemn event and begin to long for home. Drinking a cup of beer or rum, or twenty for that matter, is an acceptable thing to do to comfort these soldiers this special night.

Being drunk is not acceptable for soldiers on duty for any reason, but if a soldier can manage his duty all right, no officer will intervene and punish him for drinking.

In fact, because of the poor quality of the drinking water onboard ships, drinking it can actually be life threatening. For that reason alone, it is acceptable that crews on the ships drink beer and rum now and then.

Around 3:45 a.m. William, John Anderson and the two others are stacking dead bodies on the quarterdeck. It is exhausting work, but they talk to each other to help keep up their spirits. The heavy work warms up their bodies. They are tired when they take a break, but their bodies are actually now more warm and alive than before they began the work, and they have become more resistant to the stress of the icy waves.

At 5:00 a.m., First Lieutenant Rogers gives the order to completely empty the quarterdeck of dead bodies. So many men have died that the deck is floating with bodies[20], which could hurt those who are still living because of the incoming waves.

The group of men William is with begins to organize that task of clearing the deck of bodies. Stacking them was one thing, but actually throwing dozens of heavy bodies in wet clothes into the open sea demands a lot of energy of men who have already been exposed to inhuman stress.

Passive, weak seamen silently observe William, John Anderson and the others as they pass by, fulfilling the task of stacking bodies given by the first lieutenant. Some are thinking that what William and John are doing is stupid. Why use your last bit of energy cheering up others and arranging better conditions for those still living? Why work so hard, when total destruction seems to be their destiny? Their efforts seem foolish when it seems clear that they all are going to die in the end anyway.

Anyone on the deck with any common sense can see that clearly. But what seems obvious to most of the men does not appear to make any sense to the small group William belongs to, which continues to work very hard.

William has a faith and a hope that have always been a part of his character, which means he will never give up as long as he is in control. His hope has grown gradually stronger since he received the copy of his protection certificate. William is in the same sad mood as anyone else onboard. But he also feels mentally prepared to take action in split seconds if a chance of getting out of this hell suddenly comes along.

At the same time, strand knight Anders Andersen, who had stayed in one of the small farmhouses in Fjand for the Christmas feast and slept there for the night, has risen early in the morning and walked to the beach. As he passes the dunes, he sees that the last rear mast of the *St. George* is still standing.

The time is now 11 p.m. in Wilmington, and Allen McLane again finds himself standing near a window, when he observes two flashes of light across the night sky, followed in a second by two large bangs. He jumps and is immediately alert. Combat scenes from the Revolutionary War run through his head as a horse gallops down the street outside, very close to the window.

Then McLane recalls the Christmas midnight tradition in almost every borough and village across the country. People are out in the street firing their guns and crackers. As he realizes the reason for the extraordinary loud noise, he calms down. But the episode still has left him with an uneasy feeling he cannot get rid of the rest of the night. He can't say why. These shots indicate the start of the celebration of the Christmas Holidays and McLane loves it. He is very much looking forward to the many visitors the McLane home will receive in the days to come. As he has grown older, McLane especially looks forward to spending time with his sons, Allen and Louis. He is very proud of them, and as the years pass, he has discovered more and more similarities between his sons and himself when he was their age.

At sunrise Christmas morning, the commander of the coast militia, A. Von Schurnhardt, has been up for a long time. He returns on horseback to the farms where the seamen are recovering south of the village of Fjaltring from Dahlgaard, where he spent a good Christmas evening and night with other quartered members of the coast militia from the Zealand Hunter force.

He is riding with Judge Claudi, whom he has just met. The two horses slow down as they cross the small wooden bridge over the brook that leads to the pond of Tudskjær, then they speed up again.

They rapidly approach the farms south of Fjaltring, striving in the still strong northwestern storm. Where they ride, so close to the shore, it feels like a sandstorm.

Schurnhardt has planned to attend to his duty very early this Christmas morning and begin an inquiry of the six war prisoners and survivors from *Defence*. The judge of the jurisdiction of the Manor of Rysensteen, Bendix Ahlefeldt Claudi, happens to be in this region for reasons other than the stranding of the English ships. But the idea is that Claudi will work as an interpreter at the inquiries, and write the inquiry reports.

John Page and Thomas Mullins wake up as Schurnhardt and Claudi enter the room where they have been sleeping in Strandgaarden. John Page watches the two men bend their heads to avoid knocking them against the low transverse lofts beams in the chamber. The two arriving men find a couple of chairs standing along the northern wall and move them close to the bedside to get on with their business.

Commander Schurnhardt can see that John Page is not too well yet, and he decides to make this first inquiry very short. He poses his first question quickly and Judge Claudi translates. 'How ma ny cannons were onboard?" [20] Judge Claudi moves his chair closer to the night table to get a blotting pad to make it easier to write the proceedings. John Page answers, 'Seventy -four, Sir."[20]

Schurnhardt asks, 'How large a crew was onboard?" Page answ ers without hesitation: 'The highest number, Sir, is 550." He is close to the real total of 503 men. When Schurnhardt hears this very high figure translated, he is very shocked, realizing what a huge catastrophe he is confronted with at this humble place on this remote coastline.

This number is far beyond the number of men lost from any stranding he has ever experienced along these shores, and, for that matter, higher than any he ever heard about. In his heart, Schurnhardt honestly feels sorry for the many men and their families, and he says with a low voice, looking Page in the eyes, 'Oh, I am very sorry to hear that such a large number of souls have been lost." When Claudi has translated the words, John Page nods.

Then Page recalls what he wanted to ask yesterday. 'Sir, can you tell me if any besides the six of us have come to shore alive from the *Defence*?" Schurnhardt closes his eyes for a moment to get the strength to answer. He looks tired and rests his outstretched arms on his thighs and shakes his head from side to side. 'No others besides you six have come to shore alive!" Schurnhardt states shortly, speaking loudly over the noise from the storm outside. He and Claudi keep looking down and no one speaks for about thirty seconds. Only the howling of the wind outside and the occasional sound of the creaking of the wooden loft beams are heard. Then Page looks intensely at Schurnhardt and says, "We would like to express to you our great gratitude for saving our lives, and we do deeply regret the loss of our lost shipmates."[20] John Page searches his mind to find other positive things to add. He then recalls the *St. George* and asks, 'Can you tell us, Sir, if anyone from the *St. George* has reached the shore alive?" [20]

The day before, Schurnhardt had in fact tried to send a horseman down the isthmus, Bøvling Klit, to where the *St. George* stranded, but the Thorsminde Channel connecting the North Sea and the Nissum Fjord had been impossible to cross. The messenger had returned to Schurnhardt at his local headquarters in Dahlgaard without any news about the destiny of the *St. George*. Schurnhardt clearly looks disappointed as he tells John and Thomas, "I cannot give you a number of persons surviving from the *St. George* because the river that runs to the North Sea from the fjord is preventing anyone from getting further down south to get the information."[20]

Schurnhardt informs the two men that he will personally make a new attempt to cross this river. He promises that as soon as he gets any relevant news, he will come around the farmhouse to inform them on his return to Fjaltring.[20] Again silence fills the bedroom and all the men present look grave, feeling no need to break the silence.

Commander Schurnhardt decides to end the inquiry, but before he and Claudi leave the room, John Page adds the names of the other Royal Navy ships with the returning convoy and how many cannons each of these ships carried. Then Page stresses that he has no idea what happened to the *Cressy,* which had followed them so closely, from when they sailed in the North Sea until the time of the actual stranding.[20] Before the two Danes leave the room, John Page once again thanks them warmly.

The two Danes drag their horses across the gravel road and enter the yard to Sønder Sønderby to talk to the other survivors from *Defence,* John Brown and Ralph Teazel. The conversation in the west end chamber in this farmhouse is pretty much the same as the one that just happened in Strandgaarden.

Lastly, Schurnhardt and Claudi ride to the farm Gadegaard to speak to Amos Stevens and John Platt to continue gathering relevant information to send to military headquarters in Copenhagen.

John Platt is still feeling so sick that he has a hard time speaking. Amos, on the contrary, is feeling quite fresh and is the one who answers the questions. When asked about his position onboard the *Defence,* Amos says that he was a carpenter.

Judge Claudi then asks what type of cannons were onboard. Amos understands the question, but instead of answering, he decides to write a note to be sure that he hands over the correct details about the many different types of cannons. He asks for a pen and a piece of paper, which Claudi quickly hands him. Amos has not spent a lot of time writing, and spelling is not one of his strengths. But on the right side of the paper, he writes, 'The 74 guns upon *Defence*, some of iron, other was there some of them of brass...'' On the left side of the paper he writes a list of the different cannon types:

28 twenty-two-pounders
28 eighteen-pounders
8 thirty-two-pounders
8 twelve-pounders
2 eighteen-pounders for the boats
1 brass hoeter thirty-two-pounder.[4, 77]

During the entire inquiry, John Platt stays hidden under the thick duvet and it is hard for the other men to tell if he is asleep, dead or just unconscious.

Amos is feeling fresher and fresher now, despite the fact that he has several large bruises and large spots with accumulations of blood covering his body. Amos suddenly remembers the loss of his boss, the carpenter and his wife and daughter, which saddens him again. As Schurnhardt and Claudi realize that Amos does not feel well any longer, they end the session.

Judge Claudi then returns to Strandgaarden to await the return of Schurnhardt, who will attempt to ride south and cross the Thorsminde channel for information about the *St. George*. Judge Claudi will send this information to the Admiralty in Copenhagen.

The howling wind is still strong coming from the northwest and showing no sign of losing strength. Now the light has come and made it possible for them to see what they do, William and John Anderson feel it is the best time to try and reach the shore.

This Christmas Night has been indescribably tough to the surviving men still on the quarterdeck and they stand more dead than alive, very much aware that none of them will survive another night onboard this wreck.

William and John Anderson decide to try to make a raft together with Gregory Robertson, William Rie, and six other men. From what they can judge, the strength of the wind will probably not reduce during the coming day and nothing is gained by waiting any longer on what they now see as a sudden death onboard the wrecked *St. George*.

The breaking of dawn has given them the advantage of making it possible to see what they are doing. They begin to search for material on the wreck that can be used for making the raft.

The only spans left on the wreck are a main topsail yard and a crossjack yard. They begin to work but with frozen hands and fingers it takes them a considerable amount of time to tie the two yards together and then to get the raft overboard, because all of them are so weak and feeble.[20]

All four seamen climb out onto the swinging raft one by one. As the first men on the raft, they have plenty of time to tie themselves carefully to the raft, to protect them from being swept off by the wind and heavy seas as the raft passes, they hope, through the breakers on the way to the beach.

This takes a long time, because of their frozen and senseless fingers, while the others hold the raft. As the seas rhythmically pass the portside of the wreck of the *St. George*, the raft goes up and down, which makes it difficult for them to keep the raft steady. William concentrates the last of his energy on tying the rope and himself to the raft, but has a hard time keeping the balance, when the raft tilts too much.

When William is sure that all four are properly fixed to the raft, he glances at John Anderson. When he sees that all four men are ready to go, William gives the sign for the others to enter and they immediately climb onto the raft. William and John try to keep the raft steady as the newcomers concentrate on tying themselves to the raft.

But because William and John are already fixed in their positions, they cannot hold onto the wreck for long, and the raft breaks adrift and heads toward the open sea before the final six men get a chance to fix themselves on. The first large wave that hits the raft seconds after it is free of the *St. George* leeside washes over the 10 men. As the sea withdraws completely from the raft, William notices, to his dismay, that five of the men who had not succeeded in tying themselves properly to the raft are gone. The five remaining men on the raft are scared as the raft slowly moves south and eastward. There is absolutely nothing they can do now to influence or improve their chances of surviving this dangerous trip. They can only hope. With a northwestern wind, there might be a strong southerly sea current near this west coast. Will this current be able to carry the raft away for such a long distance that they all freeze to death before they reach the shore? Will the high waves turn the raft upside down, leaving these men tied firmly to the raft to drown?

Here in the first hours of Christmas Night, Secretary of State James Monroe is sitting in an armchair in his library, the only one awake in his Georgetown home. He can't sleep because of the howling storm outside.
  For the same reason, Allen McLane is the only person awake in his Wilmington home at this early hour. McLane sits at his desk at the window in the living room. Both of them now rest their thoughts on 35-year-old memories from Christmas Night, 1776.

Halfway to Trenton, the army divides in two. General Sullivan continues with one wing on the road to the left of the North bank of the Delaware River. With the other wing, General Greene swings to the left. About 8 a.m. they manage to overrun the unsuspecting Hessian outposts and the two columns of men race toward the center of town. The sleepy Germans, with their tradition of drinking large quantities of beer, stumble out of their quarters still half asleep just as the artillery begins raking King and Queen Street. The roaring wind, the booming cannons and the wild confusion among the Hessians give Henry Knox a feeling of trumpets sounding on the Day of Judgment. Colonel Johan Gotlieb Rall has also been drinking heavily until after midnight, and it is quite difficult to wake him up. [208]

Elizabeth Monroe can't sleep either, and can't understand why her husband doesn't come to bed. She decides to go downstairs to find out what is going on and finds her husband sitting in an armchair, staring absent-mindedly into space. The sound of the howling wind frightens both of them.

Maria McLane has the same problem with a husband who has not come to bed. It is way past his bedtime. She finds him still sitting at the desk where she left him several hours ago, when she said goodnight. She approaches slowly and sees that he looks frozen into a position like a marble statue of himself. But she is getting used to it. As he grows older, it happens more and more often.

Monroe and McLane are both recalling memories of when they were with George Washington and the Continental Army on Christmas

Morning 1776, 35 years ago.

Dressing in haste, Colonel Gotlieb Rall tries desperately to form his men, many of them only half-clad, in an open field, and he orders his band to strike up a martial tune. Washington, however, has no intention of sparring with his adversary in a game of drill field evolutions. Henry Knox's guns bombard the hapless enemy, while American riflemen, from the upper windows of houses, hit them with deadly fire.[208]

Icy wave after icy wave washes over the raft and William faints several times, as do some of the other seamen, because of the cold water. William knows that this trip on the raft might be his final test.

After the long night standing on the freezing quarterdeck, only 50 seamen remain alive on the wreck of the *St. George*.

Wanting desperately to stay on this raft, half frozen to death, knowing that any wave that hits it wrong will tilt it and put an end to their lives, William focuses his will. He concentrates on what might be ahead and not what he has been through. He keeps repeating "I am desperately needed at home by my wife and child, and I have to return to Wilmington as soon as possible."

With icy water constantly sprayed in their frozen blue faces and hair and the howling wind in their ears, William and John realize that the raft has drifted southeast and they have successfully passed the breakers. On their way through the breakers, floating wreck parts have hit their bodies, bruising them severely. Finally, the raft bumps into the beach where it follows the movement of the water while four senseless bodies and one dead man lie completely still. None of them have enough strength to untie themselves from the raft to get onto the beach.

In his armchair, Secretary of State James Monroe puts his left hand to his right shoulder to feel the deep scar he is so familiar with. He still clearly remembers the fighting at Trenton.

In the daylight, Lieutenant Monroe leads a column of troops in a victorious race to the arsenal. During the action, a ball strikes his shoulder, hitting an artery. He is wounded. Monroe is not really in any pain, but finds himself in a difficult situation. His body is covered in blood, and he doesn't know whether he will slowly bleed to death or live,

369

and worst of all cannot help himself. He is very disturbed to realize that he is in a position where his life depends on other people's mercy, and from this moment his way of thinking changes.[208]

Lying on the raft with three living seamen and a dead one, William keeps his focus on the best thing that has ever happened to him in his young life: Mary Ann.

William is not giving up the spirit now. He is just weak and passive, concluding that there is nothing he can do to bring himself out of this terrible situation.[20] After all the suffering, and all his fighting, this will be the end, he thinks, exhausted. He concentrates what he thinks are his last thoughts on what will happen to Mary Ann and their little child when he dies on this beach so far from home.

Strand knight Anders Andersen and wreck master Jens Dahl have been sitting in the guard house on the beach near Fjand, looking out the small window in the door, watching the seamen's risky attempt to escape from the wreck of the *St. George* and try to reach the shore. The Danish coastguards saw their chances as minimal.

The coastguards have many years of experience with local weather and sea conditions, living here by the sea, and after studying the raft, they figure out where it will probably hit shore. They quickly run for that place to be ready to assist the men if needed.

So when the raft hits the beach, they are already ready to help, although the seamen on the raft don't see them at first. Jens Dahl sh outs to Anders Andersen over the noise of the breakers and the storm, "Anders, let's go and bring these men safely onto the shore." They wade out into the huge breakers, the sea sweeping over their bodies, which quickly feel very frozen.

Jens, the stronger of the two, makes the first attempt to grasp the raft but he is washed backward by a huge wave and in the process falls and swallows a lot of saltwater. William and John Anderson can now feel the closeness of the two rescuers and even though their own bodies are senseless, they feel an inner heat. Perhaps they can be saved after all. Jens makes several tries to reach the raft but is washed backward each time. He is as strong-willed as William, though, and keeps trying until he finally succeeds in getting a good grasp on the raft.

Anders Andersen has saved his strength while he observed Jens's many attempts to get to the raft. He now forces himself out through the breakers, blinded by the foam cast off the wave tops and hitting his face. But he has set out right and quickly gets a hold of some of the rope on the raft.

In his attempt to rescue the men, Jens has focused on the dark-haired man with the red scarf [256] so clearly visible in the early morning light. Jens can see that this seaman seems to be very weak. Now that Jens can see the seaman's face, he realizes that the man's eyes follow every move he makes, even though he is not able to help himself.

Jens gets a good hold of the rope tying the man to the raft and after some work, gets him loosened from the raft. William feels weak but very happy when this man, who has been fighting so hard to save him, finally drags him through the breakers onto the beach in a safe distance from the waterline.

For the first time, Jens makes eye contact with William, who manages to smile weakly. Jens pats William's shoulder gently to indicate that he should stay on the beach. This is unnecessary, as William is going absolutely nowhere in his weak condition. Jens asks his son Anders to keep an eye on William while he tends to the other men on the raft. Anders is still in the sea, making sure that the raft doesn't drift off. Jens wades out into water and quickly heads toward the raft.

This time he drags John Anderson onto the shore, then William Rie, and Anders then brings in the last living person, Gregory Robertson. Finally, Jens carries in the dead seaman and carefully lays him in the sand.

Most of the 200 or so living seamen onboard the wreck have silently followed the raft's dangerous drift toward the beach and the rescue attempts made by the Danes near the beach. The risky struggle to go from the wreck of the *St. George* across the roaring sea to reach the shore fills the men on the quarterdeck with a deep respect. After all, they now knew for certain that it was possible to cross this inferno of breakers and live.

But more than 28 hours after the stranding, the men on the quarterdeck are so weak that their spirits regarding their own chance to survive are extremely low.

War commissioner Henning G. Lassen, on the farm Aabjerg in the borough of Vedersø, seven miles south of Fjand, has been alerted about the stranding of the *St. George*. He arrives early this morning to take charge over the coastal militia stationed here, another company of visiting soldiers from the Zealand Hunter forces. He orders Jens Dahl and the other wreck masters to bring any surviving seamen to the nearest houses in Fjand, so they can quickly get optimal conditions for recovery.

A carriage driven by two horses has arrived on the beach and is parked near the group of survivors from the raft. Anders fetched it as soon as he and Jens Dahl had brought in the men from the raft.

The four survivors are carried to the hay-filled carriage and laid in it. They are covered by extra canvas to warm them up. Anders jumps up and takes the driver's seat and Jens sits next to him. It's time to find some warm beds. 'Let's go to my farm at once," Jens demands, to avoid any time-consuming discussion about where to take these men. Anders nods and starts the carriage. They cross the beach and drive south along the same sandy trails that the survivors of *Defence* traveled. But this time the survivors are taken south toward the village of Fjand.

As the carriage arrives at the spot where the isthmus ends at the south end of the Nissum Fjord, they reach two farms close to each other and sheltered from the western storm by the tall dunes. Then they ride about half a mile to the southeast to another group of houses in Sønder Fjand, where 14 houses and farms are located.

The first and most western farm they come to is owned by wreck master Jens Dahl himself. The carriage stops here and Gregory Robertson and William Rie are carried immediately to a bed. They get new, dry clothes at once and Jens Dahl's wife, who has waited for their arrival, helps them into the bed. The carriage continues to the first farm in Sønder Fjand[20, 200] with William and John Anderson. As the carriage approaches the farmhouse, the wife and husband have seen the arriving carriage through the kitchen windows and are standing outside to meet them. When Anders stops, the couple already knows what this is all about. Rumors travel fast in this remote western part of Jutland, and it has been easy to figure out that survivors from the large shipwreck are being transported southward from the stranding place.

The man now standing next to Anders is not a wreck master and therefore will not earn a dime from this stranding. Because of this, the man is jealous and is not going to do anyone any favors. Anders looks at him directly and asks, 'We have rescued four men from the wrecked ship. Two of them are right now recovering in Jens Dahl's house and therefore we thought you could take the last two survivors into your house for the Christmas days. Will you do that?"

The man has been looking down and now, confronted with a question, raises his head slowly and for a split second looks at Anders Anderson with an attitude any man familiar with West Juttish tradition could tell means negative words will come out of his mouth.

Like a dog that is deeply ashamed, the man keeps looking at the ground as he speaks. He has seen the two weak, almost dead seamen in the carriage, and still he has the nerve to answer, 'I'm sorry, but we can't take them. It is forbidden to have anything to do with the enemies of the country." Anders does not yet know, because he has not spoken to William or John Anderson yet, but William is, of course, American and therefore *not* an enemy of the Kingdom of Denmark.

If Anders had known this, he would have thrown it right in the face of this bitter, jealous person. As is the custom here, the man would have been unable to refuse taking William Watson into his house. Anders has no time for long discussions right now, at least not the typical West Juttish kind - very few words spoken over a long period of time, carefully performed in an attempt to outsmart the other, if he loses his concentration, so when he feels forced to break the silence, he might have forgotten what the discussion was all about and say something foolish that can be used against him.

The men in the carriage are getting colder and weaker and desperately need a warm bed as quickly as possible. Anders is aware of the difficult situation and turns the carriage around and hurries back to Jens Dahl's house. As the carriage arrives outside the house, Anders hurries into the scullery, where he meets Jens's wife and explains the situation. She nods her head and William and John Anderson are carried into the farm house.[257]

As Jens and Anders carry William into the scullery, he looks into the eyes of the wife standing in the kitchen. The smell of hot food reaches his nose and his skin feels the comfortable hot air in the room and he instantly thinks of Mary Ann and her mother. Thoughts of these two women always bring him great pleasure.

At the same moment, Mrs. Dahl is looking at something she has never seen before, the beautiful red silk scarf[256] around William's neck. She has never been out of this region of Denmark, never even been in a village with more than 50 inhabitants. It is the first time she has seen such a scarf.[256] And, if Mrs. Dahl had heard the long story about the travels of this silk scarf before she saw it, she would have valued it even more. It was made in Wilmington from silk transported from East India to the West Indies and then to Wilmington, where Mary Ann bought it. Since then, it has been through William's tough experiences of the two years he has been away from Wilmington.

Mary Ann's female intuition led her to give her husband this red scarf for just such a situation as this one, William meeting a foreign woman on a sea trip abroad. But Mary Ann had not calculated on a poor but proud Danish farmer and wreck master's wife in a remote village of Fjand. Mrs. Dahl was far more interested in the scarf itself than in Mary Ann's husband William.

As Mrs. Dahl helps William and John remove their wet clothes, she observes the many bad bruises the two men received coming through the breakers. They are given dry, warm clothes and quickly put in a bed Mrs. Dahl pre-warmed with beach stones placed in the fireplace for some time.[257]

When they are in the bed sitting up, Mrs. Dahl serves them some of the delicious food she had prepared for Christmas. William and John fully enjoy the hot meal of goose meat, white potatoes with a thick tasty brown sauce and finely sliced red cabbage. It has been a long time since William and John had such a delicious and filling meal. Weak as they are, they smile the best they have learned while eating to try and show their gratitude and thankfulness to these kind coast people, who stand silently watching the foreign seamen eat.

War Commissioner Lassen enters the bedroom, and John and William immediately turn grave at the sight of his military uniform. As an Englishman, John is very well aware that they are now considered prisoners of the Kingdom of Denmark. Lassen smiles and succeeds in making them both relax. He carefully speaks in his best English, which is not very good, his west Juttish accent very similar to some English dialects.

The communication made by sailors across the North Sea through the centuries, since the age of the Vikings, has given the coastal people on the west coast of Denmark and the east coast of England a language with the same kind of accent and with some words alike.

Lassen begins by asking William and John what they can tell him about the *St. George*. William informs Lassen that Rear Admiral of the Red C.W. Reynolds is still onboard the wreck, that *St. George* has 98 cannons and is a part of the returning Baltic Fleet.

War commissioner Lassen then asks William, "Who are you?" William looks Lassen straight in the eye to stress that what he is going to say is very important to him. William is well aware that this man is some kind of military commander of Denmark. William knows his history. He answers, 'Sir, my name is William Watson. I was born in America, in the State of Delaware, and was pressed into the service of the Royal Navy. I was a gunner and a mariner onboard the *St. George*."[257] Although William's thoughts are constantly on release, at this early stage of his contact with Danish authorities, he dares not ask about being released or at least avoiding exchange as a prisoner of war with England. He is convinced that he just has to be patient and it will only be a question of time before he has the chance to show his Protection Certificate to the right authority and finally be released.

William can't help smiling to himself as he concludes that his Protection Certificate number 7777 really had provided him with all the luck he needed to survive the stranding. By God, it *is* a lucky number!

Studying the faces of these tired seamen, Lassen sees that they need rest, so he quickly ends his inquiry and leaves the room. Before he leaves the house, he asks Mrs. Dahl to take good care of them. Lassen then returns to the beach to follow the situation still on the wreck.

After they finish eating, William and John warmly thank Mrs. Dahl and when she leaves the bedroom and closes the door behind her, they are both fast asleep.

In the bed in Jens Dahl's farmhouse in Fjand on the Danish west coast, William dreams about his lost friend William Freeman, whom he misses so much, and the story he had not been able to finish before William Freeman died. In his dreams, William continues his story.

They took in mirrors, chalk, tobacco pipes, gilded chains, finger and earrings and several hundred yards of cloth. On the last day of the year, they finally set out from the borough of Den Helder[140] for the New World. To ensure a skillful crew onboard, they had taken in 25-30 good Dutch sailors. The planned sailing route was through the south end of the North Sea, through the English Channel. From there, they would continue past the northwest point of Normandy in France, toward northwest Spain, avoiding getting too far into the dangerous Bay of Biscay, then along the coast of Portugal to the Canary Islands, finally reaching the coast of America with St. Luke' s Islands (Bahamas) on the starboard side and Bermuda on the port side.

Then, in the last days of March 1638, when most of the snow had melted on the south sides of the valleys in the creeks along the bay south of Hudson River, called the South River (Delaware Bay), the Kalmar Nyckel and the Fågel Grip passed Cape Henlopen to enter the South River. On March 28, they entered a river in the north end on the portside bank of the bay and went upstream two miles into Minquas Creek, as the Indians called it, where they anchored. On their starboard side they observed a natural wharf of stones, the Hopocohacking, at an ideal place on the river's north bank, where the water depth was 2 fathoms. The Indians, the true Americans, had used this wharf of stones for council fires for generations. On the shore behind the stones was an extensive flat area encircling a hill to the northwest.

On their arrival, they were met by curious and friendly Indians, who had watched them from the top of the hill since when they were still out on the bay, before they went up the creek and anchored at the Hopocohacking, which William knew as The Rocks. Peter Minuit knew very well, and had explained to King Gustav II before he left Stockholm, that the Dutchmen had already established a fort in this region a few years after they had established New Amsterdam at the entrance to the North River. The Dutch fort was located on the east side of the South River, on the south side of the Timber Creek (Glouchester, New Jersey), around 1623.

As governor of New Amsterdam at that time, Peter Minuit himself had authorized negotiation of an agreement with the Indians to build fort Nassau. In the nine years it had existed, while he was the governor, he had visited the place by ship several times. Minuit now realized that the small group of Dutchmen from Fort Nassau had finally abandoned the place and withdrawn to New Amsterdam to be less isolated, because they felt terrorized and outnumbered by the Indians. Minuit therefore knew that the South River could be the basis for a peaceful Swedish colony of farmers who were able to live off the land and not compete directly with the Indians for vital hunting territory, as had the Dutchmen who wanted furs.

Minuit and some of the other officers went ashore and immediately started to negotiate rights to the land from this place down to a point on the bay's southern coastline, which had a natural harbor (Duck Creek). Five Indian chiefs were present, Mattahorn, Mitatsimint, Elupacken, Mahomen and Chiton. When they rowed to shore, Minuit had asked the soldiers to bring with them some of the mirrors, tobacco pipes and gilded chains.

Minuit and his men now stood surrounded by the five chiefs and a large circle of curious children as they handed over the chains to the chiefs. All the children were naked, but the chiefs were dressed in skirts of tanned skin, Minuit observed. When Minuit handed over the mirrors, the chiefs looked in them and smiled, not at surprise in seeing their own faces, but because the mirrors gave a much more colorful impression than the surfaces of a forest lake.

When the long, white chalk pipes were handed over, Minuit could clearly see that they were valued. The chiefs turned them and studied them carefully and were fascinated by the beautiful, simple design, although compared to their own long and strong wooden pipes that could hold a entire fistful of tobacco, these chalk pipes were very fragile and small.[154]

But their good Indian manners had taught them politeness, and they decided that they would not complain right away, since these guests seemed friendly. They were not surprised to see these white men, because all of them had been in contact with crews of boats from the first Dutch trade station, when those men tried to buy skins.

During this meeting, Minuit eagerly pointed south, trying to describe what land they were interested in. But the chiefs were far more interested in the gifts they had just received, so Minuit stopped, seeing no point of pushing things too far.

The following day, Minuit invited the five chiefs onboard the Key of Calmar to finalize the sale of the land from Duck Creek in the south up to this place, by signing a contract.[220] *The chiefs did not understand this signing procedure at all, but agreed to the ceremony, which obviously meant so much to the guests, because they were interested in keeping a good atmosphere with these men who had traveled so far to visit them, and because of the gifts they had received and more they expected to come. The pot of good Swedish copper they just received had delighted them. But how these pale men thought they could own the land and nature that belonged to and were filled with gods, was a mystery to them.*

They knew one thing for sure, and that was if this new group of pale people raised the anger of the gods as the first group had so many moon shifts ago, they would have to kill them or expel them exactly the same way. The chiefs remained calm, as they noticed that these pale people were so few in number they were not a real threat, and they seemed only to have good intentions with all their gifts. Yes, they seemed friendly and not clever enough to have hidden plans, as some of their hostile neighboring tribes did.

The leader of the guests (Minuit) served them small pots filled with a crystal clear liquid that looked like water but burned their throats and gave them a nice feeling afterwards. Then they accepted this whole new situation. Minuit had served the chiefs the traditional Scandinavian liquor, snaps or brændevin, which was distilled on almost any farm in Norway, Sweden, Finland or Denmark.

A cheerful atmosphere now quickly spread in the warm captain's cabin onboard the Key of Calmar, and one of the chiefs, Chiton, thought to himself that maybe his people should have an immigration policy for these pale people from the far side of the Ocean, now while everything seems in control.

As soon as the land treaty was signed between the Indians and the representative of the Swedish Crown, the soldiers started to build a fort on the north bank of the river, Fort Kristina (Christina), after their young beloved queen. The fort was built on the riverbank between two brooks running into the river, with origins on the top of the hill toward the northwest. The fort walls were built of wooden poles with a sharp upper end and corners made like arrow heads, and covered inside with wet earth and clay."

William turns in the bed as it strikes him that this Fort Christina[134] must have been on the border of Wilmington's Second Street, in the very region where he, Mary Ann, her mother and all their friends and relatives lived. He then continued the story in his dream.

When the fort had been erected, the soldiers dug a canal on the east side and connected it to the brook on the west side, creating an artificial island of the fort. On the top of the hill, they erected wooden houses where the farmers could live in times of peace. They named this tiny village Kristinahamn (Harbor of Kristina), named after the harbor they had dug in the brook east of the fort. On the east side of the fort was the large swamp. This area and the whole area beneath the hill was occasionally flooded by the tides, creating an ideal environment for the millions of mosquitoes that irritated the people and animals around or in Kristinahamn in the summer, and that unfortunately would cause disasters through the years to come.

The soldiers, farmers and seamen had worked hard from the first day they arrived and the weather for outdoor work had been perfect so the new Swedish colony was established in only three and a half months. Then, on a July day 1638, the Key of Calmar left Kristinahamn to go to the West Indian Island of St. Christopher heading for Sweden, with Peter Minuit onboard.

This first Swedish expedition left 25 settlers, among them Israel Holm and the appointed deputy governor Mads Nielson Klint, behind the secured walls of the fort.[134]

When the Key of Calmar reached St. Christopher Island, named after the Italian discoverer of the New World, Peter Minuit visited the Dutch vessel The Flying Deer. After all, he has good memories from his native country Holland and a visit to this Dutch ship would remind him of these good old days. The captain of the Flying Deer is very honored to have his countryman, the former Governor of New Amsterdam and the present Governor of New Sweden, onboard his ship and he decides to show his guest the Flying Deer's good sailing qualities. Minuit is likely to return to Sweden to a hero's welcome and, after all these years of hard work, finally receive the reward he so fully deserves.

Unfortunately, the Flying Deer leaves St. Christopher Island in a hurricane, which drags the ship out on the open sea, where it goes down. Peter Minuit and the other men onboard struggle hard in the huge waves, but he drowns.

The Key of Calmar, anchored on the other side of the island, sustains heavy damage to her masts and rigging, but it is repaired and the Key of Calmar returns to Gothenburg to the great celebration Peter Minuit should have had.

Time passes by.

On August 16, 1642, the fourth expedition to the new Swedish colony is ready to leave Stockholm on a warm and sunny summer day. It carries the new Governor of New Sweden, Johan Printz, a former Lieutenant

Colonel who fought in the European Thirty Years War. Unfortunately, he was dismissed from service because of misconduct, and he was living on a small farm in Finland, a Swedish territory, when Finland's Governor General Per Brahe recommended him to the Swedish Chancellor Oxenstierna.

It was necessary to send a former officer from a distant district in Finland as Governor of New Sweden because no highly placed Swedish officer with a good life in Stockholm could be persuaded to give up his privileges for an uncertain life in the New World. The motivation of most of the other settlers had been the same. They all had their very specific reasons for going. Tymen Stridham, a surgeon, was one of these who left for New Sweden in one of the first four expeditions to Kristinahamn in New Sweden.

Preparing for another expected expensive war with Denmark, the authorities in Stockholm were looking for ways to increase the Swedish Crown's income. They expected this new expedition to New Sweden to help.

When Minuit arrived with his crew, he knew that a former Dutch Governor of New Amsterdam establishing a colony on the South River would not be looked upon favorably in either New Amsterdam or Holland in general. The Dutch governor replacing Minuit in New Amsterdam made a complaint to Minuit back then, but the Dutch had not been able to spare forces in New Amsterdam to attempt to recapture the Dutch position in the South River.

The New Governor of New Sweden knew that it was just a matter of time before the Dutch would be in that position. That was one reason he brought an extra squadron of soldiers on this expedition. Chancellor Oxenstierna had been realistic and understood that the New Swedish colony, its small trading of furs and skins with the Indians, and the agricultural products they could produce would never bring a huge income to the Swedish Crown, especially since Minuit had told him the small returns from the much larger Dutch colony at New Amsterdam near Manhattan. Therefore, a search for metals would be established to increase the income. To create even more income, Governor Printz had secretly been instructed to introduce a new instrument in the New World, an economical success copied directly from the Danish Crown - The Ear Sound Toll!

The Danish Crown was charging a Toll, to be paid to the

Customhouse of Ellsinore, just south of Kronborg Castle, for ships passing the Ear Sound, transporting cargo in and out of the Baltic Sea. This Toll had now been in existence for more than 100 years and had been the main income to the Danish Crown since it was established.

The charges from Swedish ships were low, because the Swedes used their own west coast harbor of Gothenburg north of Ear Sound as often as possible, but the Dutch ships and ships owned by the merchants of the Hanseatic towns in North Germany at the south coast of the Baltic Sea, for example, had no real alternative and therefore paid large sums to pass the cannons of Kronborg Castle. This income had made it possible for the Danish King to conduct his own expensive and successful wars against the long-time Danish enemy, the Kingdom of Sweden.

The profitable Ear Sound Toll therefore naturally became the subject of great and furious jealousy at the Royal Swedish Court and among the leaders of the Swedish State administration. Printz was therefore to copy this successful concept in New Sweden in the South River, which had the same geographical advantages as Ear Sound with respect to controlling the passage of the ships and collecting the toll.

Printz and two ships, the Swan and the Fama, were finally prepared to leave Stockholm. Many of the citizens of Stockholm had gathered on this beautiful summer day along the harbor front on the islets of Ridderholmen and Skeppsholmen to watch the expedition's departure. It was the first time some of these soldiers and new colony settlers had been onboard such large sailing ships, and the first time they saw their country from the sea, at the very time they are leaving it for good. Many were overwhelmed by melancholy when the scurries that separated Stockholm from the open Baltic Sea disappeared in the rear on their southwest course heading toward the New World.

They anchored on the roads of Copenhagen on September 6, 1642, to take in water and fresh food supplies. Danish immigrants in pretty much the same conditions as the Swedish ones were taken out from Copenhagen in rowboats and put on the Swan. They left the following day, September 7, and arrived later that day at Ellsinore roads. A boat was put in the water and an officer sent to the customhouse to pay the Toll to pass Ear Sound.

If a ship failed to pay the toll and tried to pass anyway, the batteries on the Kronborg Castle would fire a cannon ball to the rear of the ship to make it stop. If the ship continued, a cannonball would be fired ahead

381

of the ship. If that was ignored too, a third cannonball would be fired into the rigging and masts, which would normally stop the ship. The ship then had to pay the duty, as well as for the three cannon balls used and a tip to the crew at the batteries on the Castle.

Printz now stood on the quarterdeck of the Swan *looking at Kronborg Castle, its batteries and the customhouse, waiting for the boat to return, and he was suddenly carried away by an uncontrolled jealousy. He now completely understood the jealousy of the members of the Royal Swedish Court and the Swedish States administration, when they thought of the Danish Ear Sound Toll.*

The other officers standing next to Johan Printz on the quarterdeck occasionally wonder why this normally grave and proud man bursts into laughter now and then.

One moment Printz looks grave, and the next moment he giggles like a little boy who has a hard time keeping a big secret and being afraid of revealing it. Despite his giggling, he manages to keep secret this incredible coincidence of events he is experiencing here at Kronborg Castle – that he is on his way to copy and introduce this Ear Sound Toll in New Sweden and the Danes don't know about it.

On November 1, they pass Vinga Sound to enter the harbor of Gothenburg. They leave Gothenburg and arrive at the South River on February 15, 1643, after a voyage without any troubles. Protected by the extra military force, superior to the Dutch at Fort Nassau, the Swedes establish a new community, New Gothenburg, on the west side of the South River on Tinicum Island (outside the present Philadelphia), a few miles south of Fort Nassau, so they can watch the Dutchmen closely.

Soon after arrival, they also build Fort Aelfsborg and the borough of Elsingborg, copied after the borough opposite the coast of Ellsinore in the Ear Sound. It is farther down the South River where the bay narrows (present Salem, New Jersey) exactly the way the Ear Sound narrows between Ellsinore and Elsingborg. This new Aelfsborg was named after the castle controlling the entrance to Gothenburg.

The Dutch, New English and Indian traders on the South River must now pay a toll to pass this point of the river, just as the Swedes, Dutch, and everyone else pays a toll to pass Ellsinore and the batteries at Kronborg Castle in Ear Sound.

The Indians, unaccustomed to such a practice, will only pay a symbolic amount, the way the Swedes did in Ear Sound, but every single ship passing stops, thereby acknowledging Swedish superiority on the South River.[134, 221]

On May 19 that same year, the 16-year-old Swedish Queen Kristina participated in her first state counsel in Stockholm, meeting with the regent and Chancellor Axel Oxenstierna. At that meeting, he presented an unannounced attack on the Kingdom of Denmark. The young, goodhearted and God-fearing Queen Kristina wanted to remain friends with the Kingdom of Denmark, her neighbor, and was sad when presented these evil Swedish political thoughts. But there was nothing she could do to change it at the moment.

Governor Printz knew, from the tough practice the Danes applied on the Ear Sound Toll, that firmness was necessary when administering the South River Toll. Not one single ship should be allowed to pass without anchoring at Aelfsborg in the South River and paying the toll. The Swedish Crown needed every shilling for the war against the Danish Crown. Hopefully, income to the Crown from the South River Toll would back up Sweden's war against Denmark, the same way the Danish Crown had the income from the Ear Sound Toll.

One of the first times Printz had stood on the top of the new Aelfsborg and overlooked the ships that stopped to pay the toll on the South River below him, he again giggled uncontrollably like a child, just as he did when he earlier passed the batteries at Kronborg Castle on his way to the New World. This South River Toll was such a good idea and so far from Kronborg, that the Danes never would find out where the Swedish Crown got the extra income to finance the war against Denmark.

All the Swedish officers at the new Aelfsborg laughed heartily when Printz finally told them his secret, how this secret income from the New World would fool the Danes in such a way that it would probably go down in history. In the summer evenings, Printz and his officers spend many hours standing in one of the western towers in the fortification of the new Aelfsborg, watching the sun set over the South River and dreaming of the increasing numbers of ships that would pass here and pay the South River Toll. Yes, they were convinced that soon, the same number of ships that passed the batteries at Kronborg Castle would also pass here.

Unfortunately, the New England colonists began to complain bitterly of the seizure of their vessels on the South River, and on September 19, 1643, it was necessary to call the first International Conference held in the New World. It was held at Fort Gothenburg to discuss trade and toll problems on the South River.

The New Swedes showed great diplomatic skills at this conference and managed to get a New England ship owner to pay the 40 shillings for the cannonball the New Swedes had fired to stop his ship.[221] When the New Swedes debriefed that evening after the conference, their joy regarding this success was great, and Printz thought to himself that a new era in the history of international diplomacy had been founded by the Swedes that very day at Fort Gothenburg. The future suddenly looked bright, the men present thought.

William turns in his bed once again, feeling the aching wounds on his body while still half asleep. John Anderson is fast asleep. William shortly registers the howling wind outside. He is relieved that the story he had promised to tell his friend William Freeman had come to a natural end in his own thoughts. It makes him calm. He had intended the story to go on just until they reached Wilmington or Philadelphia. But it now ends here on the Danish west coast, where William Freeman passed away.

The time is now 10:00 a.m. The crowd on the foreshore near Fjand and the wreck of the *St. George* is growing. The teacher from the local village school in the village of Sønder Nissum, five miles east of Fjand, heard the rumors about this great stranding and came to the beach near Fjand. He stands on the shore near the waterline and observes a huge wave building up to the west of the *St. George*. It hits the wreck hard and the entire wreck shivers as this huge wave sweeps over the quarterdeck, washing the dead bodies and most of the living men overboard.[20]

At the same time, a poor houseman, Mr. Lassen, has located the body of an officer washed up on the beach, and he walks over to drag him onto the beach a safe distance from the water. Mr. Lassen searches the officer's clothes for papers that might identify the man, and he finds a wallet in his chest pocket and notices that the officer is Admiral Reynolds' personal secretary, James Railton.

Mr. Lassen sees an address included on a ticket. There is a drawing of a woman and she looks very beautiful, dressed in a more fancy manner than seen around here. He finds a note and tries to read it, but does not understand it because it is written in English. It says: 'To the finder of my body. I would ask you, Sir, to kindly inform my wife, who lives in London at the given address, about my death. Your most obedient servant, James Railton."

In Railton' s pockets Mr. Lassen also finds raw pearls, 31 coins of gold and 99 coins of silver. Mr. Lassen's honesty and integrity are inversely proportional to the size of his personal fortune, and without a second thought, he delivers his findings to wreck master Jens Dahl, in the pious hope of receiving a small reward later on[252] for his service.

From the shore, the people from the village see the horrifying sight of a huge wave that suddenly hits the *St. George,* sweeping the seamen and officers off the quarterdeck and into the sea in one giant movement. The group gathered on the beach stands paralyzed, as though trapped in a nightmare they can't leave. Horrifying screams of fear from the men onboard carry directly to their ears on the wind. The screams drown out the noise from the breaking waves.[257]

War commissioner Lassen, who has been on the beach since he talked to William and John Anderson, also sees the many men swept of the wreck and understands the great danger the crew onboard the *St. George* is in. Through the years, he has experienced countless strandings here on the foreshore of the Rysensteen Fief. He knows that the northwestern storm makes it almost impossible to reach *St. George* with boats from the shore. But he decides to ask the local coast militia commander Højbjerg if, for an appropriate sum of money, he will take a boat out to try and save the Rear Admiral and some of the other men onboard the wreck. Lassen is willing to be in that boat himself.

Lassen thinks that taking a Rear Admiral from a Royal Navy Baltic Fleet flagship as a prisoner of war would promote him faster in the Danish military than anything else he can think of. Commander Højbjerg looks at the fishermen, who shake their heads. Højbjerg concludes that it will be suicide to send out a boat in this terrible weather, and he says no.[257]

A part of the quarterdeck is loosened when another huge wave hits the wreck, and a lieutenant and 10 foremast men decide to try their luck. They climb onto the deck part, but before it leaves the *St. George*, the lieutenant is washed off and drowned. The commanding order onboard this wreck has been reduced to the laws of nature in its basic form, survival of the fittest.

The wind moves from northwest to north, which makes it virtually impossible to reach the shore from the wreck on any kind of raft. Both the wind and sea current operate together to carry drifting objects on a direct southern course, parallel to the beach and the coastline. This wind shift also considerably increases the time a raft will have to float from when it leaves the wreck until it arrives at the beach, increasing any survivor's exposure to the waves of icy saltwater and the cooling wind. This time can be extended so much that any hope of reaching the shore alive can be ruled out.

Now the second raft, consisting of the quarterdeck part with only ordinary crewmembers onboard, has sailed far enough south that it is completely free of the protecting wake of the wreck, and the seas take hold of it and turn it around, casting the men on it into the sea.

Five of the men fight their way back to the raft and onto it again. A dead seaman does exactly the same without using any energy. They have hardly arranged themselves on the raft before another huge wave washes them all off again. All the men get back on the raft once again, except for the dead seaman, who disappears in the sea.

A wave washes over the raft every 10 seconds, and for two of the men, it becomes too difficult to keep themselves on the raft. They are finally washed off and disappear. When this second raft reaches the beach, only the heavily beaten up bodies of three English seamen, Michael Collins, Thomas Rees and William Donald, are on it.

The time is now 11:00 a.m. and the mizzenmast is still standing when First Lieutenant Rogers finally gives the order to cut it down. The seamen report to Rogers that they can find no more axes onboard, and Rogers orders them to use their knives. While they are cutting off the land yards in the rigging, a heavy sea hits the flagship and breaks down the mizzenmast. It falls, gaining momentum, and as the sea sweeps over the poop and hits it, the mizzenmast breaks loose. It removes most of the remaining men on the poop, including the dead bodies of Reynolds and Gurion. Their bodies are immediately carried southward parallel to the coastline by the strong coast current, and they are never seen again.

Rogers, who has been in charge onboard the wreck ever since Reynolds and Gurion became unconscious, now gives the order to heave even more of the dead bodies overboard, because this might save some of the living men. But this time, he finds it impossible to mobilize any of the exhausted men. The few survivors are so weak and frozen by now that they can hardly help themselves.

Now that the poop is gone, the frozen seas have an easy angle of attack and the seamen realize that there is no protection onboard the wreck anymore. This knowledge, in their stressful state, knocks the senses out of these few tough survivors still onboard, and as they are washed off two or three at a time by huge waves, they scream in despair and helplessness.

There are now about 30 men alive on the wreck. Six of them, knowing that staying onboard will lead to certain death, begin to build a third raft. While five of them concentrated on building the raft, they do not notice a large wave coming from the starboard side. Seaman William Rogens, who is sitting on the raft to the leeward, observes this incoming wave, as it washes off all five of the other men. Rogens is the only one to reach shore on this final raft from the wreck of the flagship *St. George*.

The English seamen John Tiney and Daniel McCloud come on shore all by themselves, having grasped onto individual pieces of wreckage as they floated by.

Finally, English seaman William Hampson comes to shore by himself, around noon. He is the last of the 502 men onboard the wreck of the *St. George* to reach the shore alive.

As these survivors arrive on the beach, they are immediately taken care of by the local wreck masters and taken to houses and farms in Fjand for a meal and a warm bed.

Near dark that evening, a part of the poop from the *St. George* washes up on the beach. After that, it becomes pitch dark on the beach and along the coast, and no more sounds are ever heard from the wreck of the *St. George*. By 9:00 that evening, the last 20 men give up their souls. Where the destruction of the *Defence* could be counted in minutes, that of the *St. George* must be counted in hours, because of the different stem positions when they struck ground.

The strength of the storm will not decrease. Wind gusts howl eastward and foam is continuously cast from the top of the waves and carried several miles inland, catapulted up over the dunes.

The local military commander quartered at Dahlgaard, A. von Schurnhardt, rides south from Fjaltring and finally manages to cross the channel of Thorsminde. He learns from wreck master Jens Dahl and the other wreck masters on the beach near Fjand that only 12 men survived from the *St. George*, and one of them died soon after he reached the shore.

In the late afternoon, von Schurnhardt leaves Fjand to ride north in the dark to Strandgaarden, south of Fjaltring, to inform Judge Claudi, as expected, about the *St. George's* sad fate. As he rides north in the darkness along the long isthmus to Strandgaarden, the 8-meter high dunes on his west side, covered with lyme grass, protect him against the cold western storm.

When he reaches the point on the beach where *Defence* stranded, he is aware that he is one of the first men confronted with both of these large ship catastrophes. The only object he can see in the darkness is the white chalk-painted tower of Fjaltring Church to the northeast. Schurnhardt finally reaches the farm Strandgaarden and talks to Claudi, who then quickly rides through the small village of Fjaltring to return to home to Lemvig, 15 miles northeast. Safe at home, the first thing Claudi does is write to the Admiralty in Copenhagen. In this letter, the first from the stranding place to the authorities in Copenhagen, Judge Claudi gives too high an estimate of the number of men onboard the *Defence* and the *St. George,* respectively 550 and 850 persons.

At noon, Secretary of State James Monroe sits with his family at a well-provided table in his Georgetown home, and does justice to the food, sitting and eating for a long time. He has always loved good food, and if there is anything that makes him happy, it is definitely the good Christmas food traditions and the time spent in the bosom of his family. But even as he sits eating and drinking and surrounded by his dear family, he still has a hard time showing a mental presence in the room.

Time after time, he is distracted and it is very easy for him to lose his concentration when other people talk around the table. His thoughts are elsewhere, the storm outside forcing his thoughts 35 years back.

In his attempt to fall back in an orchard, the German colonel Johan Gotlieb Rall falls from his horse, mortally wounded. In the south end of the city, General Sullivan is taking position, placing heavy weapons in order to control the bridge, the only escape route available over the Assanpink River. Unfortunately, 400 German men manage to escape before the control of the bridge is brought into effect.

The Christmas storm keeps howling along the coast of Europe and the east coast of North America. In Wilmington, the waves on the Christina River are much higher than usual. Water is continuously sprayed onto the quay and the wooden wharf buildings belonging to John Warner, Thomas Mendenhall, William Hemphill, Samuel Bush and other Wilmingtonian ship and wharf-owners that William knows so well.

In the homes of Wilmington, the small apartments in Second Street, the Warner mansion and the other houses, families are gathered to celebrate Christmas Day. People are happy to be indoors in this rough, stormy weather and the extra sweets and cookies served this special day make the contrast to outdoor life even more pronounced.

The Warner family is gathered in the mansion on the lot next to the silverware shop, John, William and Joseph Warner, their wives and children, Mary and her husband, James Thompson and their children.

Although it has been more than 11 years since the father Joseph Warner, Sr. died, he is always remembered with gratitude during an occasion like the Christmas Holidays. The whole family gathers in the living room and Joseph Warner claps his hands to quiet the children down. 'Dear family, let us all pray that William Watson, my best friend, is in good hands this Christmas Day, as he is obviously not in a position to be with his wife Mary Ann and her mother here in Wilmington. Unfortunately, he is kept impressed onboard the Britannic Majesty's ship *St. George* this Christmas as I speak." The children have become silent and watch the grown ups pray that William will soon be able to return to Wilmington and Mary Ann.

On Second Street, William's roommate, John Freed, Jr. is with his family in his parent's flat. As is the case in Secretary of State James Monroe's home, the lunch table in the Freed family is also stuffed with a Christmas feast. All the Freed family members are fond of good food. The male family members work hard every day, and they are used to building up a hunger before they sit down at the table and eat. It's the kind of good, natural hunger caused by the tough, physical work that is denied office workers, who mostly spend time sitting at their desks.

Food therefore has become a rallying point in the Freed family, and they are not ashamed of reaching for the dishes on the table at dinnertime. None of them have any memory of any family member being denied food. They know that the fattening food they now consume with great pleasure soon will be burned out of their well-trimmed working bodies and therefore never reach that late stage, where it actually sticks to their ribs. They are all slim people.

William always thought the Freed family seemed happy when he met them. He thought this was a result of their simple living and their uncomplicated relations to other people. They all seemed self-contained, which was probably promoted by the fact that they lived a simple material life, which could not give other people reason to envy them. The friendly relations they had with other people were real, because from the very beginning of a friendship it was crystal clear that one could not rub against them to increase one's own social status. The only reason to hang around the Freed family was that you actually liked them.

Despite the fact that each of the family members possesses great and numerous talents, the family tradition taught them not to appear wheedling, oily or fawning toward anyone to promote these talents, which is normally crucial to improve social status. They all just wished to live in good harmony with their surroundings, using the lowest level of energy not to be mistaken for laziness. From the very first day William entered the Freed home, he liked them especially because of their understated lifestyle.

Any person, rich or poor, intelligent or dumb, who entered the Freed family circle with a false appearance or one based on a fragile, false foundation would quite soon feel unpleasantly exposed and would never come visit the family voluntarily again.

William's other good friend, William Windell, is also enjoying the day with his family, and both friends can't help sending William a thought from time to time during the day. Enoch Lang and his new wife are also praying these days, that William will be safe, wherever he is. Mary Ann had to attend their wedding alone.

But Mary Ann is sad this Christmas. Her mother spends a lot of energy trying to comfort her daughter, as she has often done since William left Wilmington two years ago. This is not a Christmas to remember for Mary Ann or her mother. But as with all the other families William knows in Wilmington, they faithfully sing Christmas carols, which do the healing work of comforting Mary Ann in this difficult time of her young life.

It is past dinner time in the coast farmhouses in the villages of Fjaltring and Fjand and on the island of Texel in Holland. While the storm rages outside, peasant families are seated in living rooms stuffing themselves with Christmas candy while they sing Christmas carols and play games.

Outside, along the dark and deserted beaches of Texel and as far south as Camden, wreck pieces of the *HMS Centurion, HMS Hero* and the 10 wrecked merchant ships, including *Flora* and *Rosina,* are scattered among the bodies of more than 600 drowned English seamen, soldiers, ordinary crewmembers and officers. Among these bodies are several dead impressed American seamen.

The English prisoners from *HMS Grasshopper* are lucky to be able to enjoy good Christmas food in their Dutch captivity in the borough of Den Helder, under the command of Admiral de Winther.

The 10 English survivors from *HMS St. George* in beds in the coastal farm houses in Fjand, and the American William Watson in Jens Dahl's farm house in Fjand with three other English seamen, all sleep heavily as the Danish families in the houses are gathered singing Christmas songs.

Once in a while, one of the seamen wakes up and hears the songs, and the familiar melodies fill them with a kind of warm comfort that makes them recall their own childhood Christmas holidays.

No one along these coasts this evening knows that the total loss of souls this Christmas is about 1,805. Losses include the Flagship *HMS St. George, HMS Defence, HMS Hero* and *HMS Centurion,* plus 10 merchant ships. There were 1,005 people from 34 nations on *St. George* and *Defence*, 550 on *HMS Hero,* approximately 50 from *Centurion,* and some 200 from the 10 merchant ships. This is the greatest loss a Royal Navy convoy from the Baltic Sea has ever had in a single stranding episode on the beaches of Continental Europe. An estimated 50 impressed American seamen were lost.

The three formerly impressed American seamen, John Brown, Amos Stevens and William Watson, are the only Americans from the British Royal Navy convoy who are lucky this Christmas of 1811.

On the bedside table near William's head, his Protection Certificate is spread out to dry. When William wakes up from time to time due to the pain from his bruises, or from hearing the Christmas songs, he feels inexpressibly glad, knowing that he is with Danish farmers and has his American Protection Certificate by his side. It is now possible that he will actually be freed from His Majesty's Royal Navy.

In Georgetown, Secretary of State James Monroe remembers an afternoon when he was in Trenton on Christmas Day 1776, 35 years ago.

He is lying wounded on a bed in the hospital belonging to the Continental Army in Trenton. One of only three Americans wounded at this important battle at Trenton, he is recovering slowly. He knows that this battle on Christmas night and morning has been a great victory that has finally turned the fortune of war for the American cause, Commander-in-chief George Washington and the entire Continental Army. He is tired after the loss of blood, but happy. He knows he is in good hands now and will be taken care of as he is recovering.

The Hessians had lost 30 men and 918 were taken prisoner, and only three American soldiers wounded - two of these officers Captain William Washington and Lieutenant James Monroe. It only took an hour and a half to win this battle.[208]

McLane is also allowing his thoughts to go back to Christmas Day 1776, knowing that at this time of that day, he had felt that the long expected American fortune of war had finally arrived.

He had gone through the battle at Trenton without getting hurt, and was of course extremely happy for that. But the most important thing was that the Continental Army had passed the battle without heavy losses. Now they were ready to head on with fresh energy. This first victory was the reward for the many years of tough trials. Commander of the continental army George Washington walks around to inspect his troops after the battle, and McLane can see that he is proud and satisfied. It is clear to the men that the heavy burden of winning the first battle against the British was finally lifted off Washington's shoulders. This great victory at this time is indeed priceless. [208]

Caught up in these memorable historical moments, McLane speaks to his wife. 'Maria, do you recall the Swedish settler and surgeon Tymen Stridham, who arrived at The Rocks in Wilmington with one of the expeditions from Sweden, and who ended up owning half the land this borough is build on?" 'Yes, Allen I know, what about him?" Maria answered, with a minimum interest in these, to her, mostly irritating historical details.

'I thin k he is the forefather of the Joseph Stridham[1] the captain who fought so bravely in one of the Delaware Regiments in the Revolutionary War," McLane says. 'I find it quite interesting that the descendants of these first Swedes that arrived here in Wilmington were up front helping the United States of America gain its freedom." He continues enthusiastically, 'They were all descendants from Sweden, like you my dear wife. Well, they can't all have been made out of crisp bread, can they? But did they come from the same region in Sweden, Maria?"

'I think so. They probably came from near Gothenburg, where the first ships departed, and a lot of them from around Stockholm. Bache, by the way, means hill in Swedish," Maria adds.

'Oh, is that so. How interesti ng." McLane again becomes absentminded, the way he has so often this year. He could suddenly be caught up in an idea or a specific memory and then minutes later completely lose interest.

The stranding of the *St. George,* just like that of *Defence*, calls for the district bailiff to come to the stranding place. A horseman had been sent to the town of Ulfborg in this County of Ringkøbing, and at 8:00 p.m., the district bailiff for the Ulfborg-Hind District, Mr. Grønlund, arrives at Jens Dahl's farm house in Nø rre Fjand. William and John Anderson have been fast asleep most of the day, only awakened gently by Mrs. Dahl for meals. They hear when the district bailiff enters the living room of the farmhouse. War Commissioner Henning G. Lassen is also present, having returned from the beach. He tells the district bailiff and Jens that no sounds of human activity are coming from the wreck of the *St. George* anymore.

Two hours later, the owner of the foreshore Ammidsbøll and the Customhouse inspector Fæster from Rin gkøbing also pass by Jens Dahl's farmhouse. The two of them represent the private and public economic interests in the wreck pieces from the two ships that might end up on Ammidsbøll's foreshore. Therefore, they have both hurried to get to Fjand.

Jens asks them to sit down and gives a brief explanation of what he thinks has been going on near Fjand since the *St. George* stranded. Then the two guests pay William and John a visit in the low lofted bedroom. Jens gently wakes them up. As William is introduced to the customhouse inspector, he automatically thinks of port collector Allen McLane back home in Wilmington.

William and John once again tell their personal stories to Ammidsbøll and Fæster, who stands along a wall listening silently and respectfully. The two Danes have a hard time believing that so many men were lost on the *St. George'* wreck. They realize more men had been lost, in what must have been hell out in the breakers on that wreck, than the entire number of persons living in Ringkøbing, the largest city in this county. Barely two handfuls of weak men kept themselves alive and reached the beach, and two of them are sitting here and talking calmly right in front of them. That somehow felt very unreal to the two stout men.

Half an hour later, Fæster and Ammidsbøll leave William and John, shaking their hands and smiling, and make a trip to the beach to meet with the local wreck masters gathered there. The wreck masters inform them that everything has been done to save these few men who managed to come from the wreck of the *St. George*. The children in the small parish silently follow everything that is going on, getting memories that they will never be able to forget. It is not every day that both a customhouse inspector and the district bailiff pass by their remote corner of the county.

Late the following morning, on the second day of Christmas, the bailiff of the Fjand parish, Hans Baunsbæk, and shore bailiff and wreck master Jens Dahl are on the beach and witness district bailiff Grønlund, who stayed overnight in the village of Fjand, announce an expert appraisal of the wreck pieces that have come to the shore so far. Again the children are present, and 11-year-old Anders Dahl is convinced that this is an important event taking place here where he lives, because the district bailiff slept here in one of the houses overnight. Authorities who visit this remote dune parish seldom stay the night, heading east, away from the sea, before sunset.

Time is not wasted here in Fjand these Christmas holidays, when it comes to the extraordinary possibility of earning income from these unexpected wreck pieces of a huge foreign enemy warship.

Almost every parishioner, young and old, who can get out of farmhouses and fishing cabins, are on the beach attending this extraordinary event, the stranding of the mighty *St. George*.

William wakes up at 8 a.m. and realizes that his limbs are feeling better than the day before. He and the other seamen have laid virtually senseless[4] until now. Among the six survivors from *Defence* and the 11 from *St. George* recovering in these coastal farmhouses, William is definitely the one in the best condition.[257]

William has always felt that he was healthy, but this morning, when he feels mentally fresh and ready to leave the bed, he has to recognize, regretfully, that he is still too weak, and so is John Anderson. Recovering completely takes time. William opens his eyes and meets the gentle blue eyes of Mrs. Dahl. She has taken her assignment as house nurse for the recovering seamen seriously, the way she handles every problem she is confronted with. 'God morgen," meaning good morning, she says with a smile. William smiles back. He smells the hot oatmeal porridge on the tray Mrs. Dahl has put on his bedside table, and realizes he is quite hungry after a long night, a deep hunger that he has seldom felt in his 24 years. He slowly sits up, guided by Mrs. Dahl. She puts a pillow behind his back to support him. She puts the tray in front of him and pours milk all over the porridge from a pitcher. William is not used to so much food containing milk. Milk is expensive in Wilmington and grown up seamen seldom get it. During his two years of captivity on prison ships or man-o-wars in the Royal Navy, he has never been served milk. Such perishable food is seldom taken onboard, and when it is, it is not available for the ordinary crewmembers.[97] Finally, Mrs. Dahl hands him a small glass with a clear liquid like water. William swallows the content of the glass and it makes him cough several times, like it is burning his throat.

Mrs. Dahl laughs as though she had expected this strong reaction of surprise and then she says repeatedly and loudly, 'brændevin, brændevin." William is amazed at this familiar word. Didn't she j ust say Brandywine? How the hell does she know where I come from? He is astonished, unable to figure out what is going on. This is really strange to William. First he miraculously survives an extremely tough stranding that killed almost every man onboard the *St. George,* and is cast away on this remote western shore in the Kingdom of Denmark, where he knows he has never set foot before. Now he hears a very special word from a woman in this remote place, a word that bring out the absolute best memories he can think of, he and his dear wife Mary Ann on a beautiful spring evening walk along the Brandywine River.

He is confused and a little dizzy and not up to exciting or exhausting word games. He will never be able to make clear to this woman, who speaks a different language, what confuses him the most: How does a poor Scandinavian farmer woman, who has probably never been out of this parish, know anything about the Brandywine River in Wilmington, Delaware in the United States of America?

From the beach just west of Fjand and many miles south, the foreshores are being sprinkled with wreck pieces and bodies as the days pass by. Only a handful of men are alive in the hull of the wrecked *St. George*, where the light body of the flagship cat was washed from the quarterdeck and down through all the hatches and stairways to find rest in the very bottom of the ship on the upper side of the keel.

Foreshore owner and assessor P. H. Ammidsbøll is sitting on his horse on the beach, directing the men working for the local wreck masters as they arrange horses and carriages to gather all the wreck pieces. The pieces are spread over a large area of the beach, in piles at carefully selected locations where the carriages easily can cross the tall dunes, to make it easier to transport the wreck pieces to the village.

Ammidsbøll knows that when darkness comes, it will be very difficult to guard the valuable pieces spread out on the long beach. Ammidsbøll knows that they are working against the time. He is well aware that to the men working here, the wreck pieces on the beach are worth fortunes.

District bailiff Grønlund announces to the many people lured to the beach by rumors about the stranding of this gigantic English warship, that none of the dead men on the beach must be touched in any illegal way. If an officer is found, it shall be reported immediately, and if the body of the late Rear Admiral of the Red C. W. Reynolds should be found, it shall be treated with the utmost respect. The one who finds the admiral and reports it shall receive a big reward of 50 rigsdaler (50 £).

Knowing that the greatest number corpses will reach shore further south, because of the northern wind direction, Grønlund sends a couple of horsemen south along the beach to inform all wreck masters along the coast from Thorsminde and down to Nymindegab, 80 miles to the south.[252]

396

On the third day of Christmas, Commander Von Schurnhardt returns to Strandgaarden as he has promised and informs John Page and Thomas Mullins that 11 men from the *St. George* reached shore alive, all in such bad shape that they couldn't help themselves off the rafts.

Schurnhardt tells John and Thomas that the plan is to take the survivors from the *Defence,* as soon as they feel able to be out of bed and outside, to join the survivors from the *St. George,* now quartered now in Fjand.[3]

This evening, foreshoreowner Ammidsbøll, who has been busy and working hard to pile up all the wreck pieces, concludes that he is almost finished with the work. Under his command, the wreck masters can concentrate on picking up some of the more valuable and easily transported items to be put in barns, where they can be guarded until a stranding auction can be arranged.

There is a great variation among the wreck pieces that has reached the shore so far. All kinds of material seem to have come in on the beach.

Because of the strong force of the breakers, even material that doesn't float has been cast up on the beach. Flakes of the different decks, part of ship sides, wood pieces, hatches, parts of spars, sails, ropes, iron cannons, carriages with or without wheels, barrels with gunpowder, flour, fish, rollers, boxes, seamen's coffins, barrels with water, clothes, linen, shoes, bolts, chains, spikes, and more are there.

Knight of Dannebrog Lieutenant Wigelsen, the Danish King Frederik VI's personal representative to the stranding of *H.M.S. Defence* and *H. M. S St. George*, has arrived at his temporary residence at Rammegaard Manor. Shortly after his arrival, he decides to inspect the beaches by himself. He rides southwest on his black horse for half an hour and reaches the farms of Strandgaarden and Sønder Sønderby to go south to the wreck places. On this day of the 27th he reaches the beach to make sure that his orders regarding the stranded ships are handled properly.

In these times of war between the Kingdom of Denmark and the Kingdom of England, all ropes, guns, gunpowder, ammunition and metal, from these English man-o-wars are strictly reserved for the use of the Royal Danish Military Service. Lt. Wigelsen is here to make sure that complete lists of all the items relevant to the military are correctly listed and the items held back for military use. When this work is completed, Lt. Wigelsen sends a copy of these lists to the Admiralty at the Gammelholm islet in Copenhagen.

On this day, after Mrs. Dahl served William Watson his breakfast, he feels well enough to sit up for a longer period of time. While he is eating, she brings him his silk scarf, which she has washed, dried and ironed carefully so as not to harm it. She unfolds it in front of him on the bed and from her expression he can see that she finds the silk scarf extremely beautiful.

William thinks briefly of Mary Ann, then looks at Mrs. Dahl, his body trembling all over, going through his memory of all the good things Mr. and Mrs. Dahl have done for him. He is filled with such an intense, warm feeling that he wants to hug Mrs. Dahl to thank her, but he gets hold of himself, and settles for a warm smile while he firmly regain his self-control.

Then William realizes, for the first time since he arrived on the Danish beach, that he might actually see Mary Ann within a reasonable period of time. He is in Denmark, a true friend of America.

Like the other recovering seamen staying in the village of Fjand, William concludes that these local farmers and fishermen and their wives have saved his life[4] and to him, Mrs. Dahl is unquestionably a better part of what he considers that rescue team. He takes the silk scarf that Mary Ann gave him and that is so dear to him, because it is the only physical thing he owns that reminds him so much about her. He firmly hands it to Mrs. Dahl and nods his head, meaning: "Yes, you can have it." Mrs. Dahl resolutely returns the silk scarf to him, shaking her head several times. She manages to express that she is not able to receive such a nice gift. In her eyes, it is not proper to receive a present from William, a strange and handsome young man, not her husband. What would people thinking in this small west coast parish? The local people would soon begin to talk and gossip. When they got started they would never stop in her lifetime.

William understands that Mrs. Dahl doesn't want the scarf and he ties the silk scarf around his neck just as Lassen enters the room once again. Lassen asks William if he is able to come with him to help identify officers among the corpses found on the beaches in Fjand and Sønder Nissum parishes and brought to the farmhouses. William accepts, and tells Lassen that he will be with him when he gets dressed. William gets out of the bed and stands on his feet for the first time since he was carried to the bed, and he feels a little dizzy. As William dresses, he observes that John Anderson is still asleep and in pretty bad condition.[257]

As William steps out into the farmyard from the scullery, he is forced to blink his eyes several times against the strong sun, meeting it for the first time in a long time. Then he walks out into the fine weather.

There is no wind now and this feels very strange to him because he recalls that the cold wind was present all the many hours he and the other men spent on the wreck of the *St. George.*

For the first time since he arrived on the beach at Fjand, William gets a chance to see the environment that he miraculously survived in. He takes a look at Jens's little four-wing thatched roof farm built of red clay bricks, and observes the other small farms close by. William thinks that in a windy spot this close to the sea, it makes good sense to place the farm houses so close to each other, to minimize the time one is out during the cold wintertime, walking from one building to the other.

In the distance, he can see another group of houses and farms farther to the southeast. He sees the large, shining Nissum Fjord to the north, flat and calm water as far as any human eye can see. To the east and southeast, the dark moor unfolds and to the west, close by, the high, thickly covered lyme grass dunes.

William follows Lassen to the barn where 34 bodies found on the beach are laid out in one long row on a think layer of hay. Lassen asks William to try and identify the officers among these men, because the local authorities need to know. He has received the order that English officers are to be buried in coffins, when the time comes.[257] The seamen, mariners and other ordinary crewmembers are not.

William quickly identifies one of the officers as Admiral Reynolds' secretary James Railton. Later, Railton is carefully stripped of his uniform, so it can be washed and cleaned, because it represents a high value. Before the funeral, Railton is dressed in simple clothes. The uniform is handed to wreck master Jens Dahl, who takes it home to his wife to wash and iron and have it ready for when the foreign seamen leave the village.

After William assists with the identification, the body of Railton and the other 33 bodies are transported in a long cortege of carriages to the village of Sønder Nissum, four miles east, where local teacher Jens

Sørensen is ordered to make the appropriate numbers of coffins needed for the officers.

Jens Dahl, sitting in the driver's seat, and William are on their way to one of the first funeral ceremonies related to the stranded English war ships. The ceremonies will take place in the village church and the cemetery in Sønder Nissum. William, an American, is the only man representing the many English seamen onboard His British Majesty's Flagship *St. George III* on this occasion. The ten English survivors are still in their beds and feeling weak.

He enters the Nørre Nissum Church and sits on a church bench next to Jens Dahl, surrounded by silent Danes, and listens to the sermon given by the local priest. William's thoughts w ander back to his own home borough of Wilmington, and this time his thoughts are for once not directed toward Mary Ann, but to a Gentleman John Watson who also happens to live there.

William met John Watson several times in his life and felt somehow related to him. They talked several times outside the Lower Market House, shopping on Second Street, or at services in the Presbyterian Church on the top of the hill. William recalls that today is exactly 35 years since an episode he know about in John Watson's life.

John was a young boy and a fifer in his father Captain Thomas Watson's Delaware Company, when the company entered the Continental Army in Dover, Delaware on December 27, 1776, after the Americans won their first victorious battle at Trenton. That battle had been the turning point of the war and accelerated the efforts to recruit more soldiers and finally obtain American independence.

On that day, both Thomas Watson, who had a farm in Pen Cader hundred near Aiken town in New Castle County, and his son John joined Allen McLane and the other Delawareans who much earlier on entered the Continental Army in the struggle to get the British forces off the North American continent.[0]

William listens to these humble Danish farmers and fishermen with their small black hymnbooks held between their bent and tar-spotted fingers, singing, with badly trained voices, Christmas songs whose melodies he is so familiar with. His thoughts move back to Wilmington and the people he cared for there.

William recalled the good times when his parents were alive, when he was seven years old. Back then he spent so much time playing outside the church, waiting for his parents and the other adults to finish talking after Sunday service, until he could get down by the river and play with the other kids.

Ever since the Indians lived here in great numbers, this strategic spot on the top of the hill, above where the Delaware, Brandywine and Christina Rivers meet, had been a favorite playground, together with the rocks on the riverside.

William and his playmates also spent a lot of their summer on the top of this hill watching for arriving Wilmington ships still on the Delaware River. When they spotted one, they eagerly ran down French Street to excitedly tell a ship and wharf owner, many he personally knew like the Bushes or the Warners, that their ship was approaching the small harbour.

He and his good friend Joseph Warner had also played outside the Presbyterian Meeting House, when Caesar A. Rodney, Joseph Warner, Sr. and Isac H. Starr headed the meetings, where the leading anti-federalists in the borough of Wilmington had tried to communicate with the first President George Washington about the Jay Treaty. So a lot of important memories were connected to this place.

After the divine service and the funeral ceremony were finally over, William and all the other men, women and children who attended from the parish of Fjand, sat silently as their carriages took them back to the coast village of Fjand.

The following day, December 28, the first real inquiry on the stranding of the *St. George* is held at wreck-master Jens Dahl's farmhouse in Fjand. Parish bailiff Hans Baunsbæk is present and so is the judge from the Rysensteen jurisdiction, Bendix Ahlefeldt Claudi, who earlier attended the inquiries of the survivors of *Defence* and who happens to be in Fjand for other reasons. He is outside his own jurisdiction, but is only functioning as an interpreter between the court and the rescued English and American seamen.

Judge Claudi has brought his son along as he travels in his carriage. They are the only two people living on the west coast of Jutland who have met all the surviving seamen from both the *Defence* and the *St.*

George. Claudi's son is deeply marked by this experience, a melancholy event on a scale beyond comprehension for a child. Later, he becomes the founder of the publicly established Sea Rescue Service along the Danish west coast.

As the 11 survivors sit packed on chairs placed closely along the walls in the living room, they are presented to the court one by one. They all declare that they are English, except for William, who proudly declares that he is an American. He states that his name is William Watson and that he had been impressed in Portsmouth harbor.[257] William adds that his Protection Certificate is dated February 27, 1807 and was issued in New York. Judge Claudi misunderstands and writes in the inquiry records 'ship's patent' and Jan. 27 1804 instead. [252]

In the dark morning, around 5:00 a.m., Allen McLane sits at his kitchen table in Wilmington, drinking the morning's first cup of hot coffee. McLane enjoys these early hours, when he can expect some peace around the house and think clearly. As the Christmas storms seem to finally have ended, he feels more relaxed and happy. He is always worried about the local people at sea. So now he's calm.

In these first Christmas days, when nature had flexed its muscles, it had been almost impossible for him to keep his thoughts from his revolutionary war memories. Now he is again able to focus on other things. But because Maria is not there to distract his mind, he finds himself back in Trenton 35 years ago.

This day, the British reaction to the loss at the Battle of Trenton is strong. As the horse carrier reaches British headquarters in New York with the message of the first real British defeat, Cornwallis and about 6,000 men are dispatched and they hurry back to New Jersey to try and meet General Washington at the battleground in Trenton.

But General Washington does not want to meet the British troops now, and in an impulsive and wild maneuver, in the middle of the night, the Continental Army wraps the artillery wheels in heavy cloth to muffle the noise, and turns south and east, swinging behind Cornwallis. They leave the campfires burning to distract the enemy, and move toward Princeton as planned earlier.

Burdened with captives, General Washington and his units decide to cross the Delaware River again and retire on the Pennsylvania side.[208]

This same day, *Woodlark* finally arrives in Vinga Sound outside Gothenburg and joins Admiral Hope's squadron, which is supposed to guard Vinga Sound for the winter. *Pyramus* continues with the convoy of merchant ships home to Portsmouth in England.[67, 74-2] As it leaves, *Pyramus* fires several shots over the convoy to gather the ships for better protection. Finally, the last part of the last Royal Navy convoy out of the Baltic Sea this year of 1811 is on its way to cross the North Sea to England.

At the inquiry in Jens Dahl's house, the district bailiff Grønlund heads the second examination of survivors from the *St. George* in the hot living room. He poses a new question to each of the surviving men "Are you all seamen?" One by one, they confirm this with a short "Yes."

John Anderson, who is the best formulated among these survivors, heads the talking for the seamen. He explains that the stranded ship is named the *St. George*, that it carries 98 cannons and that it belongs to the English King. Rear Admiral Reynolds had been onboard and the ship was under the command of Daniel Oliver Gurion. Among the crew were also 10 sea lieutenants, one marine captain and three ordinary lieutenants. *St. George* was a ship that, fully manned, could carry 760 men.[4]

They had come from Gothenburg with *Victory,* with 102 cannons under command of Admiral Sammaurez, *Defence* with 74 cannons and 550 men under Captain David Atkins' command, *Dreadnought* with 98 cannons and 750 men under captain Valentine Collard, *Vigo* with 75 cannons and 550 men with Admiral Dixon, *Orion* with 74 cannons and 550 men with Captain James Newman, several more English warships and 150 merchant ships. Their destination was Portsmouth[4] in the English Channel.

The room is silent for quite some time. One of the English seamen coughs now and then, while the men in the living room wait for Claudi to finish writing in his report so he can translate the next question posed by parish bailiff Hans Baunsbæk.

Judge Claudi puts forward the next question, "What caused the ship to be stranded here?" and again, John Anderson does the talking. "It is partly because the original masts had been cut down when *St. George* was stuck on the sand reef of Rødsand, and partly because the rudder was broken at the same place about a month ago."

Admiral Sammaurez ordered the captains of *Cressy* and *Defence* to stay near the *St. George*, because of the bad condition the flagship was in when they left Gothenburg. Sammaurez several times tried to convince Gurion and Reynolds to let the flagship stay in Gothenburg for the winter, but they had refused. Then Sammaurez finally gave in, accepted that the flagship could return to England, and ordered *Cressy* and *Defence* to escort the *St. George* all the way home.

Then on the voyage home, *Cressy*'s captain, Charles D. Pater, consulted his officers on the night of Dec. 24, when Cressy was in the sea outside the Cliffs of Bovbjerg, and made the tough decision to leave the damaged flagship *St. George* to its own destiny. That was also the real reason why the other captain responsible for the escort of the Flagship, captain David Atkins from *Defence,* decided to stick to Sammaurez's order, to the fullest consequences, a stranding of his own ship.[4]

Baunsbæk asks if they all have given a full statement, and all 11 seamen agree. They are all asked to swear an oath according to their own religious beliefs. William, a Presbyterian, swears to his God Almighty, the same as all the other Christians present in Jens Dahl's f armhouse.

Baunsbæk announces that from now on they shall all consider themselves prisoners of war. The local Danish authorities confiscate everything that belongs to the *St. George*. All the seamen are ordered to remain calm until they receive further notice.[4]

When Baunsbæk has ended his part of the inquiry, he takes a deep breath and glances at the War commissioner to give him a final opportunity to make his own inquiry of the prisoners. Lassen just shakes his head, and states that it will be sufficient if he can get a transcript of the inquiry report.

Everyone is now free to leave the court set in Jens Dahl's farmhouse. The surviving seamen enter the yard outside the farmhouse and, for the first time since they left the wreck of the *St. George,* all 11 are together and able to talk to and comfort each other after their miraculous survival of this terrible catastrophe. The relaxing atmosphere among these humble Danish people has pleased them tremendously and it helps them to recover much faster than expected.

As they stand close together in the yard, John Anderson feels a need to say a few words about their newly obtained right to walk around freely, in contrast to the strict discipline they knew onboard the Royal Navy ships. Walking around freely gives each and every one of them a deep satisfaction, but to William it is indescribable. He is suddenly able to experience the clear difference between the narrow, confined space of an English man-o-war and the wide-open spaces along this remote west coast

John Anderson says, 'I think it is quite interesting what confidence the local authorities in this small village have in common prisoners of war like us. After we have given our words of honor to the court and accepted our status as prisoners of war in Denmark, we're allowed to walk around on our own. If we were back home in England, where war-prisoners are taken by the thousands on a daily basis, only officers would have the opportunity to give their word of honor and remain in an open prison."

William smiles at John's words and can't help commenting. "Yes, it is surely a good thing to stay friends with the Danes, as we Americans have ever since the United States declared its independence in Philadelphia. That's 40 miles north of where I live back home in North America." The English seamen can't help laughing at how their American friend William uses even this strange opportunity to promote his little country. But it feels good to all of them, American as well as Englishmen, to get their thoughts off the horrible nightmares they had been forced to go through in the months or even years onboard the *St. George*.

The following morning, five of the survivors from *H.M.S. Defence* gather outside in the courtyard with wreck master Thomas Wang and his wife, the commander of the local coast militia Von Schurnhardt, and servants on the Strandgaarden farm.

The western wind has decreased so that it is unnecessary for the men to hold on to their hats. The women have tightened their headscarves to make sure that the typically strong wind does not release a single hair from their hairdos. They are, as usual, darkly dressed for the day's divine service in an hour in the Church of Fjaltring, three miles north of Strandgaarden.

Three carriages drawn by glossy black horses have been made ready by the stable boys and are parked along the barn in the stone paved yard. Irritated by too much waiting, the horses kick their horseshoes against the stones, making loud echoing sounds in the small yard.

Thomas Wang nods his head and the group gathered in the yard moves toward the main gate. In the barn, several wreck pieces from *Defence* are spread out along the inner walls. On the middle of the floor is an oak coffin on trestles with a simple pinewood coffin on each side.

The group gathers in a half circle in front of the three coffins. They fold their hands and bend their heads to pray The Lord's Prayer led by Thomas Wang. The oak coffin is open and in it is the late captain of the late *Defence,* David Atkins, looking peaceful with his eyes closed and hands folded. His face is pale in death, like the faces of John, Amos and three of the four English seamen from the *Defence* attending this ceremony in the barn.

In the coffin to the left of captain Atkins is English Second Masters Mate David McCrobb, and to the right the Irish ordinary seaman John McCormick. The three bodies in the coffins and the survivors are all that remain of 502 men onboard the *Defence* who lost their lives along this Danish beach. It feels sad to these few survivors to be gathered for the first time since they arrived on the beach, on this occasion of praying for their late captain Atkins and two other dead crewmembers. As they stand in the half dark barn with these dead crewmembers, they can't help crying. For several minutes, they cry as though whipped. Tears run down the chins of the tough seamen from the British Royal Navy and they can't do anything to help it.

John has been through the toughest physical and psychological stress imaginable in the last six years of his life onboard Royal Navy Ships, and not once had he given in to self-pitying. Not in the darkest hours, when the hopelessness of escape was crystal clear to him, he had allowed himself to release his soul from the responsibility of living, giving up as some of the other men onboard had finally done.

Now he finds himself among friendly people who seem to care for his well-being, and with high hopes of being released soon to return home to a brighter future. All that has kept him together through many unfair times in his 33 years disappears and in this simple barn he releases his unhappiness in tears.

After the prayers, the coffins are closed and the five seamen are asked to carry their captain's coffin to one of the waiting carriages in the yard. John and Amos place themselves at the first handles and Ralph Teazel and John Page at the rear handles of the coffin, and a crew of Americans and Englishmen carry the coffin of the late captain David Atkins of *H.M.S. Defence* out of the barn and onto a carriage for transport to the Church of Fjaltring.

The pinewood coffins are carried out by John, John Page and two other seamen and put in another carriage. The carriage with Atkins's coffin goes first, followed by a carriage with Thyra and Thomas Wang, and finally the servants in the last carriage holding the pinewood coffins.

Another survivor from a small merchant ship that stranded near the Thorsminde channel, master mate William West, also attends this funeral.

Commander of the coastguard von Schurnhardt and a couple of soldiers ride in front of the entire procession. The procession passes the coast farms between Strandgaarden to the south and Fjaltring Church to the north. These farms are closest to the North Sea in this region of Jutland. First they pass Dahlgaard to the west, then three more farms to the east before they reach the Rubygaard, a farm built in 1780.

At this point, they can all hear the church bell in the tower of the Church of Fjaltring as it begins ringing. They pass other farms before arriving outside the church. John Brown takes a quick look at the white, chalk-painted church with the lead roof, the chorus and the tower to the west, and finds it quite beautiful in its simplicity.

A granite boulder dike fences the Church of Fjaltring and the surrounding graveyard. The two Americans, John and Amos lead Atkins's oak coffin from the carriage and in through the main western gate leading to the churchyard. They slowly pass a large freshly dug grave as they walk through the tower door to enter the small porch.

To enter the church ship, they bend over the coffin and walk through the two narrow doors to walk up the narrow aisle between 15 rows of low-backed wooden benches on each side. The benches are already filled with local farmers, fishers, wives and kids and, on the back seats, the servants.

As they approach the altar, they see the strict-looking priest Søren Rømer. He is not well liked among most parishioners in the Parish of Fjaltring because of his strictness and his sometimes violent and unpredictable temper. He is known to engage in unpremeditated acts like beating up people from time to time.[262]

On his normal scale of temper, the priest is in a good mood today. He has been looking forward to leading this funeral of such a distinct person as a captain of a second-rater ship of the line attached to the Royal Britannic Navy. People of such high rank are seldom buried in the parish of Fjaltring. Today Søren Rømer has decided, quite extraordinarily, to look with mild eyes on his church community.

Generally, he considers them ungodly and free from any kind of independent moral thoughts, which, according to him, define one of the key characters in a human being. These coast people seldom speak to strangers, which he considers himself to be in this church community. He has had a hard time trying to get to know his parishioners individually. A priest like Søren Rømer is too different to be accepted in the small village of Fjaltring, and the inhabitants do all they can to keep him out of their circles.

Søren Rømer has not lived here long enough to figure out what moves these silent coastal people, if anything does. This irritates and annoys him desperately, and even makes him furious. As John, Amos and the English seamen carefully put the coffin close to the altar, Søren Rømer points to his left at the first bench in the side building to the south, and John, Amos, the four English seamen and the masters mate follow the priest's directions and take a seat.

The small, broad church singer looks the priest in the eyes a final time before he begins to sing the first psalm. He sings with a clear and high voice, his self-confidence making some of the local men who seldom come to church uneasy. The farmers, fishers, servants, wives and children in the rows of benches sing with timid voices.

To the foreign guests, who are from much larger city communities, it is obvious that many local people dare not single themselves out on purpose in this house of God, where they seldom come. Each is careful not to sing with a higher voice than the person sitting next to him. This constrained, false solidarity is unconsciously forced upon the parishioners by their own bad experiences, which tell them that it is far safer not to stick out in a crowd.

Rømer, well aware of his congregation's constrained behavior, normally walks back and forth in front of the first benches, his eyes sweeping over the bent heads as they sing, trying to single out one or two of the most self-asserting and self-satisfied farmers, so he can stare at them and measure the psychological basis for their appearance. If they are found to be weak, he sends them several strong killing looks. Here in the house of God he is on his home base, as everyone sitting on the benches knows all too well.

In the Royal Navy, *HMS Defence* was known as the 'singing ship.' John, Amos and the four Englishmen are the only men there who actually enjoy very much being at a divine service again. Services were the single most important event that kept John and Amos' hopes high through the endless days onboard Royal Navy ships like the *Defence,* and what had time and time again helped them recall memories from Salem and Boston.

The melodies of the psalms chosen for this Divine Service are similar to the ones used in American and English psalms, and the seamen hum the tunes they know and love so much from home. Amos and John, sitting in the Church of Fjaltring, feel a warm gratitude for the treatment they have received in the coastal farmhouses, convinced that there will be an opportunity to avoid being handed back to the British Royal Navy.

The priest stands up quickly as a psalm ends and approaches Atkins's coffin. He folds his hands, bends his head and prays the Lord's Prayer. Then a second psalm is sung and the priest walks up the noisy, wooden stairs to the pulpit. Søren Rømer feels comfortable standing on the pulpit, an almost perfect position to look down on all the members of his congregation.

His speech is well prepared this Sunday. He has not spent so much time preparing any other speech this entire year. He knows and shows it and most of all, the parishioners of Fjaltring know it. This service is unique and the church is filled to bursting. The Danes and the foreigners are sitting perpendicular to each other, and whenever the situation allows it, the local parishioners study the pale faces of the foreigners, the American and English seamen in their beautiful dark blue uniforms.

The moral authority in this remote village of Fjaltring is the priest and he is expected to advise from his pulpit when new administrative procedures are introduced to this local community. So far, Rømer has not received any instructions regarding the English ship *Defence*, so he simply informs the congregation that His British Majesty's Ship *Defence* stranded on Christmas Evening six miles south of the church. Further south, the flagship *St. George* stranded simultaneously. He folds his hands once again and asks the congregation to pray with him for the many souls whom God, according to his knowledge, had taken home from these ships.

While they all are praying with bent heads, the most curious can't help secretly observing the mysterious seamen, these messengers of mass death, with profound awe. There is no doubt in the parishioner's minds that these six survivors are among God's few chosen people. They have survived a heavy and long-lasting storm, on a scale no one remembers experiencing around this shore for decades, and have the respect and admiration of these west Juttish fishermen and coast farmers. The fishermen themselves are used to losing brothers, fathers, sons and good comrades in the dangerous North Sea so they knew what these survivors had been through.

Two more psalms are sung, then Rømer nods to John, Amos, John Page and Ralph Teazel to carry out the oak coffin. Danish soldiers from the local coast militia, units from the Zealand Hunter force under the command of A. Von Schurnhardt, carry out the two other coffins to the large grave dug on the south side of the church.

The coffins are lowered side by side in this large dark and cold grave.

Rømer prays, shouting to be heard by everyone around the grave, as he throws earth down onto the three coffins with a shovel. 'Earth to earth, ashes to ashes, and dust to dust." Each sentence is followed by a shovel of earth that hits the coffins with a loud and hollow sound, emphasizing the importance of the words.

The funeral has ended and the people from the farm of Strandgaarden who brought the three coffins to the Church of Fjaltring now slowly move toward the western gate of the churchyard. Soon after, they return in the carriages, driving along the sandy coast road southwards.

Now that they have overcome their injuries and are allowed to stay outdoors, the seamen decide to go to the beach to look at the pieces of wreckage from *Defence*, which are gathered in large piles. There are no dead bodies along the beach, and the local wreck masters suggest that the strong southern current close to shore during the storm must have taken most of the bodies farther south on the coastline.[3]

On December 30, District bailiff Schønau takes up the inquiry related to the stranding of the *Defence* in the farmhouse at Strandgaarden, trying to get an accurate overview of the events that took place on the morning and day of Christmas Eve.

The inquiry has been delayed because Schønau was too busy securing the enormous valuables from the wreck of the *Defence*.

Night watch, coastguard and wreck master Peder Dahlgaard is interrogated first, followed by Peder Ruby Christensen. Schønau also wants to make a new interrogation of the survivors from *Defence*, but because he has to tend to other important business, they all decide that the continuation of the inquiry shall be postponed to January 9, 1812.

On this same day, American seamen and captains arriving in Amsterdam onboard ships from Philadelphia, Boston, Wilmington and other American east coast ports, receive information about the loss of *HMS Hero* and the many transports attached to the convoy.

Local port workers in Amsterdam who had read about the terrible stranding in the local papers bring the sad news to the ships. Of special interest to the men from Baltimore was the information that the *Beckman*, from Baltimore had foundered and the captain and 17 of the crew had perished.[25]

Meanwhile, now that the storm has subsided, a small sea going boat is sent out from the beach at Fjand. The men in the boat going out to the wreck of the *St. George* include wreck master Jens Dahl, nine other men from Fjand, John Anderson, and William. It feels strange to John and William to be on their way back to the remains of the *St. George*. The sea surface is calm and it takes little time to reach the wreck, where a very sad sight meets their eyes.

The captain's and all other cabins are completely gone. The entire upper deck and half the mid-deck are gone, too. The two ship sides stand, but are so loosely anchored in the seabed that even the small waves hitting the ship cause them to move. The men in the boat search the wreck carefully but find no one dead or alive, only bits of rope and parts of sails. As Jens and the other men from Fjand slowly climb down into the boat to return to shore, John and William are allowed to spend a few minutes alone on the wreck, knowing that they are the only two of the entire 502 men who have the opportunity to enter the wreck of the *St. George*.

William sends up a prayer for the many comrades lost, then thinks of Mary Ann before he climbs down to the boat. Caught up in his own thoughts, William hears Jens shout something incomprehensible in his coastal west Juttish dialect as the boat is rowed to the beach: 'Hoen aer tee I teer Je. Pass no ooee tee æ ræav o æ sæjl at ryer oenbors så tovli såm I rower."

At the same time, Secretary of State James Monroe walks restlessly back and forth in the living room of his Georgetown mansion, letting himself be overwhelmed by memories of 35 years ago on this very day.

He is still hurt after he was wounded on Christmas morning in Trenton, and this particular day he does not participate in the armed confrontation with the enemy. But he later talked about this episode with his fellow soldiers so much that he almost felt he had taken part in the actions himself.

It was now clear that vital information on the British positions in Trenton had come from John Honeyman, who had posed as a loyalist butcher and cattle dealer right in the middle of town in the days before the battle.

Some of Rall's men succeeded in reaching Bordentown and alerting the Hessian colonel Von Donop, who decides to move and retire in Princeton. The enemy soon panics as the rumors of the battle of Trenton spread, and the British camps along the New Jersey side of the Delaware River are quickly abandoned.[208]

Allen McLane walks outside John Warner and Samuel Bush's wharf looking for fish in the clear water of the Christina River, recalling how he and the Continental Army crossed the Delaware River to Trenton 35 years ago.

On December 30, Washington and his men crossed the Delaware River again and stopped at Trenton. He urged his veterans to remain in military service for another six weeks in return for a bounty of 10 dollars. McLane accepted but stayed for another and more honorable reason than the payment. He still felt bound by the oath he had given, to protect Congress with life and fortune, when he and other patriotic Americans had gathered in his childhood neighborhood outside Carpenters Hall on Walnut Street in Philadelphia one and a half years ago.[208]

Later that day, the administrative and personal papers of Rear Admiral of the Red C.W. Reynolds, which he had kept in two large caskets in his cabin, are found, soaked with salt water and randomly mixed together, spread along the long sandy North Sea beach west of Fjand.

In the evening, these wet papers are carefully treated and investigated under the living room table light in Jens's farmhouse. To War Commissioner Lassen's irritation, they do not seem to hold any further military information about the *St. George*. Lassen is obviously disappointed, that while they have been so lucky to collect most of the many letters and orders received by the Rear Admiral himself, no valuable information to the use of the Danish military could be found.

Because of the fine sunny weather this day, an auction of the huge amount of wreck pieces from the *St. George* has been held on the shore west of Fjand.

Ammidsbøll, the happy and lucky owner of the foreshore, states to the many men present on the beach, that according to the law, he is entitled to half of the auction price, but he is willing to accept only a third if more wreck pieces are coming in.

The *St. George* is a wreck of such gigantic proportions that Ammidsbøll has never experienced anything like it in his entire life, and probably never will again.

Such a tremendous fortune cast upon his foreshore, even taking place in the holy Christmas days, makes the already well-off foreshore owner and assessor Ammidsbøll extremely humble before this crowd of mostly poor farmers gathered on the beach, as only money can make some wealthy men humble. His extraordinary good emotions make him put forward this generous offer of reducing his share by his own free will.

As the auction is in progress on the beach, Ammidsbøll silently surveys from a distance, thinking of the Danish proverbs he knows that suit this rare occasion, this huge, lucky stranding, the best. He recalls two: "The Lord takes and the Lord gives" and 'Nothing is so bad, that it's not good for anything." He smiles to himself, concluding that God indeed had rewarded him amply this year of the Lord 1811, with such a unique, huge Christmas present.

The following day, the last of the year, the citizens of Copenhagen are finally informed of the loss of the *HMS St. George* and *HMS Defence* in the Copenhagen newspaper *Dagen* (The Day). The number of persons listed as being onboard, 830 and 550, is even more exaggerated here than the authorities had reported on the west coast of Jutland. They listed the same numbers as if counting, without corrections, the total number of names in the now perished crew lists of the two Royal Navy Ships. On these lists a name can be found twice or even three times if the person on the voyage has changed occupation, for example changing from an Able Seaman to Mariner, as William himself did on this last trip. But no one in Denmark has information available about the exact number of souls lost, not even the few survivors.

The British Royal Navy has no direct interest in correcting these numbers, because in these times of war with France, it will be fine if the French get the idea that Royal Navy ships are well-manned. This is not, of course, generally the case at this late stage of the war.

Reading about this tragic stranding deeply touches the citizens of Copenhagen and leaves them with sympathy for the families of the lost crew[24] and England. The news even moves the Danish King Frederik VI.

This same day, barely two days after Captain David Atkins was buried in the churchyard in the village of Fjaltring, King Frederik VI issues a Royal Resolution that Captain David Atkins is to be put in a double oak coffin and placed in an open grave until further instructions are forwarded regarding transportation of the coffin to England.

Knight of Dannebrog Lieutenant Wigelsen, appointed the King's personal representative at the stranding place of the *St. George* and *Defence*, leaves the Manor of Rammegaard to return to Fladstrand, the headquarters for the Danish Navy in Jutland, on the northeast coast of Jutland.[75]

The same day, Vice-Admiral Murray, at Yarmouth Roads on the English North Sea coast, receives a letter directing him to send a sloop off the coast of the island of Texel to obtain information regarding the ship supposed to be lost there, communicating with Dutchmen on the beach, if weather and circumstances permit, by means of a Flag of Truce.

10

At the New Year's Divine Services, on January 1, 1812 the priest Christian Siersted announces from the Sønder Nissum and Husby village church pulpits that it is strictly forbidden for anyone to remove anything from the bodies washing up on shore from the *St. George* and the *Defence*. If or when the admiral or any other officers are found, it must be reported immediately to the local authorities and no one must touch them.

This day, the wreck survivors at the wreck masters' farms in Fjand have recovered enough that they join William as he attends the funeral of more of their dead comrades, this time in the small Sønder Nissum Church.

They are transported to the Nissum Church by carriages and, after a time in the fresh, cold air, are seated on the gray church benches listening to the beautiful church organ's opening tones, tones that, thanks to long naval service, some of them have not heard for more than a decade. Their eyes fill with saltwater that, for once, does not come from the sea.

The seamen also feel the pain from the many bruises that have marked their bodies, and sad emotions come easily and they all cry as though whipped with the cat-o-nine-tails they so often saw onboard the *St. George*.

The local people surround the survivors, who are dressed so differently, sitting on separate benches and singing in their own special way, their genuine sympathy for these survivors fueled by their own hard-earned experience of human loss.

William separates himself mentally from his English comrades as they sit in the church. William has already recovered completely physically, feeling no more pain from his body at all. As his English comrades mourn deeply, he is far away, in the process of putting a healthy mental distance between himself and this terrible stranding catastrophe.

Every hour that passes by, William thinks less and less on his earlier constrained life onboard the flagship *St. George III* and the Royal Navy prison ships. He is able to completely relax with these kind people while he is temporarily forced to live in this quiet coastal village of Fjand. This allows William to concentrate and generate new, and after so long, positive thoughts, and to focus energy on his long-term future.

How can he get home to his native country as soon as possible? What are the options? To William it is quite amazing how quickly he has regained his normal good mood after only a few days here. Knowing that he probably will be released in the end makes all the difference.

William is happily looking at a clear, achievable goal now – returning to his beloved country, the United States of America. He can see, from time to time, his British comrades secretly observing him, visibly surprised how rapidly he has changed from moody and slow in his reactions to a healthy, curious and quick young man, like they have never experienced. Before their very eyes as if by a miracle, has unfolded a free and happy young American man in his best young age.

John Anderson, who spent so much time with William onboard the *St. George,* is truly delighted that William's future looks so positive, after his American friend's miraculous survival of the stranding.

Lloyds Insurance Company in London sends a letter the following day to the British Admiralty with intelligence received from the port of Harwich that a vessel has arrived there bringing an account of the loss of *HMS St. George* off the coast of Jutland. The same day, a letter from Vice Admiral Murray in Yarmouth Roads, including a letter from Captain Faguhar of the *HMS Desiree*, gives an account of wreck pieces of a battle ship of the line found floating south of the island of Texel. The captain supposes it is one of the homeward bound Royal Navy Baltic Ships lost near the Haaks.

The letter, dated December 30, includes a description of the pieces of wreck. The captain was sure that the pieces that could only be separated from a complete wreck and not carried away or lost overboard by pure accident.

Allen McLane is out for a walk this day of January 3. He slowly moves along the quay in Wilmington, as his thoughts wander back 35 years.

"At sunrise on January 3, he is outside Princeton with the Continental Army when they run into the 17th and the 55th British Regiments, who seem astonished to see an American army rapidly approaching.

General Hugh Mercer, a former apothecary, takes post in an orchard. The British colonel Charles Mawhood quickly orders up the 40th and guard regiments in the village, and they open up with a cannon and send the men of the 17th regiment forward to fight with their bayonets. The violent charge hurls the Americans back into disorder and leaves Mercer mortally wounded. George Washington, seeing the general wounded, fears a rout, and he rides up front and personally re-forms the Virginian troops.

McLane has the pleasure to distinguish himself in this battle, fearless as he normally is. Washington shouts, "It's a fine fox chase, my boys."

The battle takes only 45 minutes all in all and the British lose 10 times as many men as the Americans, who lose 40. [208] Lieutenant Allen McLane is rewarded for his continuous and energetic efforts with a promotion to Captain this day.

McLane was so happy that day, and when he looks back, he realizes that his personal success parallels that of the new nation that he and the other soldiers were helping get established that day in Princeton.

Later that day, McLane arrives at John Warner and Samuel Bush's wharf and turns up Market Street, where he runs into gentleman John Watson. Knowing very well who John Watson is, McLane says, 'Good day, Good day, Sir. Are you aware, Sir, that I was promoted to Captain in the Continental Army 35 years ago this very day?"

John Watson smiles and replies, 'I'm very well aware, Sir, as you surely know that I entered the Continental Army in my father Captain Thomas Watson's Company on December 27 as a fifer. The Battle at Princeton was the first we were fighting in, and with some success I might say." They shake hands, allowing war memories to overwhelm them for some time. Then John Watson, trying to find something appropriate to say on this solemn moment, states, 'One could say that in the same way you, sir, and my father, Thomas Watson stood side by side fighting the British at Princeton, your signatures now stand side by side on Delaware's Ratification of the American Constitution, signed in Dover in Kent county on Dec. 7. 1787, the same year William Watson was born and where my father and I enrolled in our Delaware Regiment. My father, Thomas Watson, signed for New Castle County on the line next to your signature for Kent County."

417

McLane, impressed by this young man's way with words, replies deeply touched, 'Indeed, indeed we signe d." McLane is quiet for some time, while he thinks. Then he gets tears in his eyes. 'But I'm informed the William Watson you just mentioned is impressed on the *HMS St. George*, according to his wife, who came to my office last year.

Many American seamen are impressed on British men-o-wars as we speak. I'm afraid we must control our personal happiness over our Revolutionary War achievements some time yet. The sons of the fathers who fought successfully in that war and gained victory and independence from the English Empire are still kept in captivity by the Royal Navy, and if something is not done quite soon, I'm afraid it will lead to a second war against England."

The mood has turned bleak and further conversation seems pointless. John Watson decides to go home for a cup of tea and leaves McLane with the words, 'Indeed, indeed you are so right, Mr. McLane. Good day, Sir."

The English consul in Gothenburg sends a letter to the Admiralty in London on January 5, reporting the total loss of *St. George* and *Defence*, except 12 men from the former and six from the latter.[22]

Three days later, William is sitting at the living room table in Jens Dahl's farmhouse, writing a letter to the North American Consul in Denmark, Mr. Hans Rudolph Saabye, a wealthy influential merchant, who lives in Copenhagen and is a personal friend of the King.

As far as he knows, William is now completely physically restored. He therefore has decided to try and use his own influence to seek release as Danish prisoner of war so he can return home.

It has been some time since he wrote letters, and to avoid errors, he forms the letters and sentences very slowly on the paper Jens Dahl has given him. He writes,

'January the 8 th, 1812

Sir, I, William Watson, an American will take this opportunity to inform you of my being cast away on the southwest (northwest) coast of Jutland in an English man-of-war named the St George. I was forced out of the half-schooner. The Captain is John Goff. I am sorry to inform you that I

*have lost every article of clothing. My Protection certificate and I are
safe, Thanks to God.*

*Sir, I would like to know if it is possible for me to be set free without
going to England. Please send me an answer and tell what is to be done,
for I am determined never to return to serve in a man-of-war again.*
I have written two letters to Mr. Lyman without getting any answer.
I am married in the state of Delaware.
The No. of my Protection certificate is 7777
I am, Sir, your humble servant
Wm Watson

Nørre Jylland, Ringkøbing Amt, Fjand, i Sønder Nissum Sogn."[5]

The Danish King Frederik VI is very popular among ordinary people in
Denmark and rules his Kingdom by the motto: 'The love of the people,
my strength." He has the final word in every subject having his interest,
and this day writes a letter to the Danish military headquarters, stating
that the war prisoners in Randers from *Defence* and *St. George* have to
stay in prison until further notice.

The plan is that the foreign prisoners shall be released in the end
through the island of Anholt, one of the exchange places for Danish-
British prisoners of war. [99-0] Because news and gossip still travels at
horse speed in the northwestern part of Jutland, King Frederik VI has not
yet been informed that these war prisoners are in the west coast village
of Fjand. But the moment has come for the surviving seamen from *St.
George* to leave the coast village of Fjand for good.

The following day, January 9, two closed carriages are ready to leave
Fjand with the ten English seamen. The drivers wait impatiently outside
Jens Dahl's farmhouse for William, who is saying goodbye to Jens and
his wife. The three of them stand silently in the half-dark living room,
smiling to each other, lacking the ability to exchange understandable and
meaningful words. Then William remembers the one word he heard here
at his very arrival, a word he knows he will never forget. He says it out
loud. 'Brandywine – I will now try to get home to where I was born
near the Brandywine River." Jens laughs, then shouts happily to show
William that he understands, 'Brændevin, ja det er godt med brændevin
(brændevin, yes it's nice with some brændevin)," as he thinks to himself,

419

that here in Fjand was probably the first time this American seaman tasted the brændevin, since he became so surprised when Mrs. Dahl served it to him when he was first brought to their house.

Now the three of them shake hands, and Mrs. Dahl hands William the uniform that once belonged to Rear Admiral Reynolds' secretary, James Railton. William hands over the letter he wrote to the North American consul in Copenhagen, so Jens can pass it on to the proper Danish authority. Jens later gives William's letter to the district bailiff Grønlund, who passes it on to the County Prefect Mr. Rosenørn (Rose eagle), who files William's letter in his archives, because he knows King Frederik VI will have the final word regarding release of the prisoners of war.

This same day, District Bailiff Schønau returns to the farmhouses south of the village of Fjaltring to take up the inquiry regarding the stranding of the *Defence*.[3] This time, the inquiry is held in the farm of Gadegaard because John Platt is still sick in a bed there. At 10 o'clock in the morning, the six seamen are again presented to the court. An English translation of the inquiry proceedings from the 25th of December are initially read to the court by a Danish ship captain, Jens Peter Schmidt, whom Schønau brought for this purpose, because he speaks better English than judge Claudi. Captain Schmidt questions the seamen while Judge Claudi concentrates on writing the proceedings.[3]

Amos Stevens is the first of the foreign seaman asked, and he tells the court that he is an American, born in Boston and impressed in Liverpool on February 28, 1810.[3]

Now it is John Brown's turn, and he states that he is an American, too. He was taken prisoner as early as 1805 and put on a former French ship in Kingston, Jamaica, where he was forced to serve in the British Royal Navy. In November 1806, he was put onboard the *Defence*[3]. He further states that ten prisoners had been taken onboard the *Defence,* from a schooner named *The Little Devil*, from Danzig, on the convoy's return to England from the Baltic Sea. Four of these men were Danish, two were Swedish and four were German.

District Bailiff Schønau now makes it clear that the English and American seamen shall consider themselves prisoners of war from now on and must respect that. All six men from *Defence* immediately confirm that they will respect this.[3]

Amos and John, who like William have spent most of their time here in Denmark considering how they could avoid being turned over to the British, ask the court if their cases can be presented to the proper authority, showing that they are not English or enemies of Denmark, but were pressed into service in the Royal Navy.

John Page and the three other English seamen confirm that John and Amos actually are Americans, as they say, and that they were pressed into English service.[3]

Before the inquiry is brought to an end, the proceedings are read to the six seamen by Captain Schmidt and they are asked if they find these notes correct[3]. They all confirm this by nodding and Amos, eager to get a complete and accurate record made on his case, adds that he had taken a berth on an American ship in the harbor of New York. The ship was destined for England, where he was impressed. Amos then tells the court, that since the time of his impressment, it had been impossible for him to escape English service, because the few times they were given shore leave, the officers followed him closely and he was constantly under watch.[3]

John, listening to Amos, feels the need to add something to correct his own written record. He tells Schønau that he was born north of Boston in Salem and initially had taken a berth on a ship in the harbor of Boston. On one trip, the ship carried a French cargo. Near Jamaica, the ship had been burned and he was, against his will, forced to serve in the British Royal Navy.[3] John informs the court that he, too, had no chance to escape when on shore because of the careful watch and because the punishment for desertion was severe. John adds that he spent a year on this French ship before being transferred to *Defence*.[3]

Finally, both the British and the American seamen declare, for the record, that their Danish rescuers assisted them with all possible help, even giving them their own clothes. John Page, representing the British seamen, added that none of them expected to be treated so nicely in an enemy country. They now express their utmost gratitude for this treatment.[252] They also declare that they had seen the bodies of Captain David Atkins and the two seamen that came in from the sea. The inquiry finally ends and Schønau asks all men in the courtroom, including the five healthy foreign prisoners of war, to walk with him the 400 meters from Gadegaard to Anders Mærsk's farm to the southwest.

As they arrive at the barn in Anders Mærsk's farm, they observe a fourth body that was supposed to come from the *HMS Defence*. The five seamen unanimously declare that it is not anyone from the crew of *HMS Defence,* but the boatswain George Middleton from the British station at Anholt. He had been taken onboard as *Defence* passed the Anholt Island in the Cattegat in late November.[252]

After the identification of the boatswain, the men split up, and John, Amos and the English seamen return to the farms where they are quartered, for lunch.

That day the Danish newspaper, the *Altona Mercury,* brings a letter that has arrived from the borough of Ringkøbing. The letter is dated December 27, 1811. Without mentioning the names of the *St. George* and the *Defence,* it describes the stranding event, 'On the 24th and 25th two English men of war's were lost at this place. One had a crew of 575 and the other one nearly as numerous. We understand that seven men were saved from the former and thirteen from the latter."

This information to the outside world is the most accurate given publicly regarding the number of men lost from the two ships.

It also states, incorrectly, that Admiral Reynolds' body was cast on shore. The letter also wrongly concludes that *Bellette* likewise ran aground and got free again, but seemed to have received so much damage that in all probability, she was lost.[25]

On January 11, a Copenhagen newspaper prints information that, between the beaches of Oxbøl Strand and Nymindegab on the west coast of Jutland, the bodies of two females, two black persons, 77 seamen, 11 soldiers, one civil and one military officer were cast on shore. One of the female bodies is supposed to be Admiral Reynolds' daughter, but this is not correct.

The following day, January 12, the sexton attached to the Church of Fjaltring is working hard this cold morning. He is fulfilling his part of the Royal Resolution issued by King Frederik VI regarding the late Captain David Atkins from *Defence,* digging up the captain's coffin from the churchyard grave.[3, 4] With the help of a couple of strong stable boys from the parsonage, military commander A. Von Schurnhardt, Father Søren Rømer and the sexton heave up the coffin from the grave with a couple of thick ropes. The coffin is roughly cleaned and carried into the mortuary northeast of Fjaltring Church to be properly cared for until further orders come regarding its transport to England.

Early the following morning, two horses and a carriage from Dahlgaard take Commander Von Schurnhardt and a couple of soldiers to the mortuary. Schurnhardt, the priest Rømer and the soldiers make a short ceremony. The oak coffin is moved onto the carriage, saluted by the soldiers and commander Schurnhardt, and returned to Strandgaarden.

The carriage leaves behind for good the graves of the two 24-year-old men from *Defence*. Both men had originally entered the *HMS Defence* and appeared in the ships muster book on August 1, 1810, with the numbers 679 and 881, the Irish and ordinary seaman John McCormick and the English Second Masters Mate David McCrobb. These two men from *Defence*, two of four total that came to shore in this remote coast parish of Fjaltring, were buried side by side to rest peacefully at the Fjaltring Churchyard forever.[44]

In Strandgaarden, all six survivors from *Defence* have recovered fully, as John Platt, the last one, is feeling well again.

The survivors, farmers, their wives and some of the servants from the three farms gather in the yard outside the farmhouse of Strandgaarden for the last time. The survivors are preparing themselves to leave this small village of Fjaltring for good.

It becomes an emotional goodbye for all of them. John Brown and Ralph Teazel say goodbye to Peder Ruby Christensen and his wife and thank them once again for the kind treatment they have received. Although as tough seamen in the Royal Navy, they are used to avoiding deep emotions, they can't help feeling very touched on this occasion.

John Page and Thomas Mullins also use the opportunity to say goodbye to Thomas Wang and his wife and the maid Mette Cathrine Madsdatter.

John Platt and Amos Stevens get a farewell from Jens Gadegaard and his wife. William West, the Masters Mate who stayed with Thomas Wang, is the last of the men to say goodbye.

In Wilmington, Allen McLane stirs next to his still sleeping wife. He is having trouble sleeping, and his thoughts are forced back to the Revolutionary War.

On this day of January 13, the newly promoted Captain Allen McLane is assigned to Colonel John Patton's Additional Regiment, where he receives his commission directly from George Washington.

He recalls his oath to protect Congress with life and fortune, and decides to pay his company of 98 men himself for the year of 1777. Washington, a wealthy landowner, can afford to pay some of his men with his own money, but for Allen McLane it is a great expense that will seriously affect his life when the war ends. Recalling that he has no small children to take care of makes the difficult decision much easier to him.

Knowing that Cornwallis probably is racing toward Princeton right now, and that his own army is exhausted, Washington moves northward into the hilly forest landscape around Morristown to make his winter camp. [208]

McLane and his company decide to move southward, because no confrontations with the enemy are planned at this point.

The six survivors from *Defence* leave the farms south of Fjaltring the same way they arrived, along the two sandy wheel tracks on the east side of the dunes, heading south on the isthmus, Bøvling Klit.

The carriage with David Atkins's coffin is first in line, followed by the six seamen from *Defence* and the master's mate, and finally a carriage with a military escort consisting of coast militia soldiers and two officers.

As the procession leaves Strandgaarden heading for the pond of Tuskjær, the six seamen turn around and wave for some time. Sitting high in their carriage seats, they smell the fresh North Sea air, and watch the beautiful landscape, flat as far as the eye can see. John and Amos experience a renewed feeling of freedom in a way they haven't for some years now, and they are happy to realize that they might have begun the last part of a journey toward freedom.

The wreck masters and farmers stand in the yard waving back as long as they can see the diminishing carriages. The carriages turn left between the pond of Tuskjær and the Mærsk farms and soon are heading for the neighboring village of Fjand 12 miles south.

One-third of the way down the isthmus, the carriages pass the place where the *Defence* went down. The seamen briefly recall the tough and wild experience onboard the wreck stuck in the breakers outside the beach here.

Now that they all have made a complete physical and mental

recovery, the most pronounced feeling is a deep sense of happiness at being alive. The drivers of the carriages make a short stop, and the survivors walk to the top of a dune to take a final look out to sea.

As John and Amos stand next to each other looking at the water, to their complete surprise, they can't find one single sign of evidence that the *Defence* had ever been here. Not one single small wreck piece sticks up over the sea surface.

It is hard to believe that they are survivors from the *Defence*.

Two-thirds of the road down the isthmus was the channel of Thorsminde connecting the North Sea and the Nissum Fjord. A few days earlier, the storm succeeded in filling up the channel with sand.[20]
So it is now possible to pass the channel and drive between the two villages of Fjaltring and Fjand on land. Hearing about these extraordinary geographical conditions makes John think that what he experienced was almost like a scene from the Bible.

Just as Moses once divided the Red Sea to allow the Jews to cross it, weather here at Christmas gathered the broken isthmus, the Bøvling Klit, into one piece, so the chosen few survivors of the stranding of *Defence* can pass and join their soul mates, the survivors from the St. *George,* quartered in the village of Fjand to the south.

John Brown just notices this, without making any statement at all, because he is in a mental state where nothing surprises him, or any of the other survivors. One mile south of the Thorsminde channel, they observe a lot of wreck pieces spread out on the beach and understand that they are passing the place where the *St. George* must have hit the shore. They clearly see the two sides of the wreck sticking up from the sea surface about 600 meters from the coastline.

As the procession of carriages finally reaches Fjand, only a couple of men and boys are outside, and none of their fellow survivors seem to be around. The carriages take off again and turn east, away from the sea, to travel along the road toward the village of Sønder Nissum.

They travel through areas of sand, moors and groups of small, low pine forests. They pass the Sønder Nissum Church, surrounded with a churchyard and a dike of the same type of granite boulders that surround Fjaltring Churchyard.

The church roof is covered with lead on both the ship and chorus buildings and the church has a porch on the south wall covered with red tile roof. From the carriage, John and Amos can easily look over the low dike and they see several large fresh graves. They instantly know that these graves must contain some of the dead bodies from the *St. George*.

They also notice the beautiful grave of Rear Admiral Reynolds' secretary, James Railton.[257] Railton can now rest in peace, because he had got his last earthly wishes fulfilled to the very detail. The letter that he wrote to his wife in London from the *St. George*'s captain's cabin was sent to his wife as requested, and he had a funeral that fully complied with the standard demanded by a British officer in the Royal Navy.

They continue another two miles east, through more moors and low pine forest. No one speaks. On the south side, they now see ahead of them the lead roof of Husby Church. This church looks similar to the Church of Sønder Nissum, we just passed, John thinks to himself, trying to occupy his brain since no one in the carriage feels the need to talk. This church also has a porch covered with a red tile roof, but John notices an extraordinary three-beam cross in the brickwork of the porch just above the door.

They notice that a lot of local people are assembled outside on the churchyard. They arrive just as a large group of people gathers and surrounds a single grave. As John, Amos, the others from *Defence* and the master mate step down from the carriage, the local people enter the churchyard and the newcomers decide to join the outer circles of the crowd.

For the first time, John makes eye contact with one of the survivors from their commanding flagship *St. George III*, and it doesn't take him very long to identify all of them. From their dress, he counts the 11 he has been told survived from the *St. George*. The six newcomers are allowed into the inner circle near the grave, and John sees that those who were here when they came are crying heavily.

Priest Christian Siersted is making another beautiful speech, as he has done at the previous funerals over men from the stranded Royal Navy ship. A seamen next to him whispers to John that they are burying the Anholt boatswain, George Middleton, whom he himself helped identify in the barn at Anders Mærsk's farm south of Fjaltring.

John figures that they must have sent the coffin with the boatswain in advance. To his left, he observes a larger, fresh mass grave, where some 200 dead men found on the shores in the parishes of Sønder Nissum and Fjand were buried earlier that day. At that ceremony, soldiers from the coast militia guard and the Zealand Hunter force fired their guns several times over the grave in honor of these brave men of the sea who found their last earthly resting place here on Husby Churchyard.

After the funeral ceremony, John and Amos find William in his group of seamen and quickly walk over to talk to him. When William realizes that he has met two other Americans, he is very glad.

These three Americans begin to exchange news from America and try to figure out how they can be released as quickly as possible.

William informs John and Amos that he is afraid it has been decided already that they are all going to be sent back to England. Hearing this, John and Amos become worried. This is indeed bad news. The two of them were convinced that they were on their way to being released.

William asks if they are in possession of Protection Certificates, but John and Amos answer no. William takes out his own Protection Certificate from an inner pocket to show them and proudly says, 'I've got a copy of mine. It was sent to me from the American Department of State, in a letter I received when the fleet stayed outside Gothenburg on December 1." William folds out his Protection Certificate with the lucky number 7777 and lets John and Amos hold it and admire it. They both think that it's good that William has this. If they are lucky, it might be useful to all of them.

William is visibly proud and self-confident and before the two others can put forward a word, he continues, 'Five days ago, just before all eleven of us from the *St. George* left Fjand to come here to Husby, I wrote a letter to the North American Consul in Denmark, Mr. Hans Rudolph Saabye. He lives in Copenhagen. I wrote that I was stranded on the west coast of Jutland and asked him if there was anything I could do to avoid being sent to England. I left the letter with Jens Dahl to hand it over to the right authority." John and Amos nod, and John explains that they asked the exact same question during the inquiries held in the farmhouses in Gadegaard and Strandgaarden south of Fjaltring.

What the three of them don't know is that their fate is not in the hands of local authorities. It is only for the King to decide. John and Amos are interrupted in their conversation when the seamen from *Defence* are asked by the priest to carry Atkins's coffin into the mortuary. As the coffin is carried along the aisles over the churchyard, soldiers from the local coast militia once again fire their arms as Honors of War[4, 20] to the late captain Atkins.

After they leave the village of Fjaltring, the stranding survivors discover that they are getting a very special treatment as they travel along the road.

News about who they are travels ahead of them, so the local people they meet along these deserted roads treat them like heroes. Someone who managed to survive a North Sea stranding onboard a ship the size of a second rater is automatically a hero in this rough coastal region.

The good treatment they get traveling these roads is a huge contrast to the tough daily Royal Navy life with its strict discipline. These seamen are sure, when they enter bed at night, that never in their entire lives have they felt so appreciated.

In Husby the *St. George* seamen are quartered in the houses of Laust Mærsk, Kristen Mosbye and Jørgen Andersen's son. Kristen Vang has one of the seamen from *Defence* staying with him[252] in his house.

On the same day, the Admiralty in London orders the captain of the *Princess Carolina* to take the sloop *Plower*, with three or four of the best North Sea pilots he can get, to the west coast of Jutland to gather reliable intelligence about the destiny of the *Defence* and the *St. George*.[23] *Princess Carolina* sails from the port of Plymouth and the *Plower* leaves from Leith.

The following day, January 15, Major General Carl Von Tellequist, the Commander of the Military Headquarters for the Northern part of Jutland, located in the borough of Randers, writes to the First Department in the State Administration in Copenhagen and confirms that the 17 prisoners from *St. George* and *Defence* are going to be kept in captivity, as earlier requested by the King.[97]

Before orders came from the King, Commander Tellequist had informed War Commissioner Lassen that the war prisoners were going to be sent southward, along the west coast of Jutland, to be exchanged, at the British-occupied Danish island of Helgoland, with Danish prisoners held in English captivity.

After the King's order arrives, Commander Tellequist forwards the new order to Lassen, who is with the war prisoners in Husby, to cancel the first order he received and instead to send the prisoners to his own headquarter in Randers.

The next morning, the three Americans, William, Amos and John, and the 15 Englishmen say goodbye to the people they have been staying with in Husby. They enter two closed and dark carriages, nine men in each.

Under military escort, the prisoners of war head northeastward 100 miles along the deserted roads to Randers.

This day the Admiralty in London must finally have received information about the fate of *H.M.S St. George* and *H.M.S Defence,* because instructions are sent to the British Governor of Anholt to send a small vessel to the North Sea to recall the *Princess Carolina* and the *Plower*[23], which are busy searching for the missing Royal Navy ships.

John, Amos and William have arranged to ride in the same carriage. The three Americans have a desperate need for any news about the United States of America. They talk a lot as they travel toward Randers. As the carriages head for the first village, Staby, six miles to the east of Husby, William tells his personal story, as they all look out on the moor and the surface of the Lake of Vedersø.

In Staby they make their first stop. It still feels strange to these seamen, so long at sea, to be on shore. In their bodies they carry the rhythm of the sea and the waves and it still sometimes feels awkward standing on solid ground.

They stop at the inn to feed and water the horses, and while they wait impatiently, they are brought some bread and milk, which they eat in the carriages. A crowd of local people soon gathers outside to silently study these interesting, rare foreigners.

After a while, William says to John, studying the white chalk-painted Staby Church to his right, 'I think we can conclude that all of the churches in Denmark are white ones." As he speaks, he recalls that he had come to that conclusion six months earlier, studying the flat Danish landscape from the forecastle of the *St. George.* The church towers, because of their visibility, provide good points of navigation for the ships at sea. In almost every logbook onboard the ships of the line in the Royal Navy, one is able to read the names of all the churches the ship has passed sailing along the shores.

Foreigners, like these surviving British and American seamen, so seldom travel along this road that every contact they might make with the local people, speaking a few words or giving a single smile, will be remembered and talked about for a very long time afterwards.

What is extraordinary about these seamen from the stranding catastrophe is that the news of their presence has preceded them for quite some time, spreading out through all of Jutland, in fact all of Denmark.

After the stop in Staby they continue their travels three miles before they reach the first town, the town of Ulfborg. They reach the inn in Ulfborg in the late afternoon, and decide to let the prisoners stay there for the night. The prisoners enter the taproom for supper. The inn owner points a finger toward one of the long tables, and they quickly take a seat.

At the same time, this January 16, Secretary of State James Monroe makes an important speech before Congress in Washington D.C., presenting the final Report on Impressments.

While making his speech, Monroe feels very indignant, thinking of his own situation 35 years ago, when he had been wounded fighting for what he believed in and what his mentor Thomas Jefferson had written in the Declaration of Independence: Personal freedom and the right to pursue happiness for individuals on the North America Continent. He thinks of impressed American seamen, kept against their will onboard British Royal Navy ships, and the personal letters and reports piling up in the offices in the Department of State through the years, and he becomes extremely angry.

As he sees it, the United States of America has certainly not achieved for its sons and daughters what their fathers and mothers, and he himself, fought so hard for 35 years ago. As Minister to England, he had personally negotiated the subject of impressments with the British without useful results, and now, like many ordinary Americans who lived by and from the sea, he believes enough is enough.

As John Brown, Amos Stevens, William Watson and the other prisoners of war are having supper in the inn in Ulfborg, Monroe tells Congress that 6,257 Americans have been impressed since 1803, and he adds, disappointed at the lack of accurate data,

"It may be proper to state that from the want of means to make their cases known, and other difficulties inseparable from their situations, there is reason to believe that no precise number or accurate view is now or ever can be exhibited of the names or numbers of our seamen who are impressed into or detained in the British Service." [266]

Monroe waves the report in his left hand from side to side, emphasizing that it contains the important names and numbers of many of these missing Americans. For a split second, the pages in the report with the names, among them John Brown, Amos Stevens and William Watson, are visible to the congressmen, who unfortunately are not in a position to free them for the time being.

As he ends his speech, Monroe puts the report on the platform table and drinks a glass of water.

In this report are also the names of those impressed Americans who were onboard *Defence*, *St. George, Hero* and the other British ships in the Baltic convoy, who unfortunately did not survive the Christmas storm.

Many of these men were in their late twenties and had been impressed for more than 10 years, prisoners on man-o-wars for more than one third of their lives. Wives, fathers and mothers had written the American authorities like the Department of State for help, but the subject of impressments had been stalled for quite some time in diplomatic negotiations between England and the United States of America, and few seamen have been released in the past decade.

The following morning, on January 17, the seamen are called up early for breakfast, and served oatmeal porridge drenched with milk. William, John and Amos slowly eat without complaining, but to be honest, none of them really like this kind of food.

Like these poor but proud farmers, seamen in the British Royal Navy are used to hard work from very early in the morning. A farmer normally gets to work at 5 a.m., earning his breakfast with hard work before he sits down to eat.

He begins his working day by feeding the animals, collecting their waste in a wheelbarrow and transporting it outside. He milks the cows and feeds the small calves with some of the fresh milk before he returns to the farmhouse where his wife is waiting with breakfast on the table. These coastal farmers literally live by the words, 'first you give, and then you take."

A seaman in the Royal Navy on the first shift gets up at 4 a.m. and he also works a long time before his first meal of the day. A farmer's breakfast is often oatmeal porridge with a lot of milk. But a seaman will eat bacon or some kind of meat with bread and butter for breakfast.

The Royal Navy seaman normally prefers food containing meat and fat. The kind of breakfast a West Juttish farmer eats simply offers too little energy for a seaman. The seaman will soon feel hungry again after that kind of meal.

But today it is not likely that William or any of the others will do any kind of hard work. They will be sitting in carriages all day, as they did the day before. Therefore they all accept the breakfast without complaint. As he eats, William begins to look forward to traveling through more of this Kingdom of Denmark, a country which so miraculously has saved his life.

So far, their surroundings look pretty much like the landscape around Delaware Bay, near Cape Henlopen, with sand, moors, flat farmland and a creek now and then. William enjoys this new situation, where he can sit quietly study the landscapes and not do hard work, as he was forced to do onboard the *St. George.*

For a while, William can rest his body completely and concentrate on eating, sleeping and speaking with his fellow travelers as they are transported to Randers.

They are ready to leave Ulfborg and each of the men shakes hands with the owner of the inn, before climbing into their carriage to continue the trip. They travel some miles that day before they pass a small creek, the Little Creek, and later reach the inn near a small village, Idum, that same afternoon.

Even though their daily journeys are quite short, they still normally leave early in the morning. This also happens the following day.

The British seamen are beginning to enjoy the trip along these deserted Danish roads. They are aware that they are most likely on their way to be handed over to the Royal Navy to re-enter service onboard a man-o-war.

William, Amos, and John, on the other hand, can't move fast enough. They are eager to meet with the Danish authorities in Randers as quickly as possible to find out if they will be set free and can return to their families and friends in the United States of America.

The two carriages pass the Store Åen creek and pass through the town of Holstebro, where they make a short stop. People from the small town gather around the carriages and stare while the horses are getting water and hay, carefully studying the faces of these foreign seamen from the Royal Navy strandings.

They stay the night at the Mejrup village Inn, east of Holstebro.

This same day, a letter dated January 3 arrives at the Military Headquarters for the General Staff at the islet of Gammelholm in Copenhagen. The letter states that two women were onboard the *Defence* or the *St. George* and orders are given to immediately transfer these women to the British quarters on the island of Anholt.

Information is later received at the headquarters that such women have not been seen after all.[99-0]

If anyone had asked Amos at the inquiries, he could have confirmed that there had been two females onboard the *Defence*, the wife and daughter of his boss, the carpenter, and that he saw them carried away and drowned. If the General Staff had cared enough about this issue, they could also have read the Copenhagen newspapers January 11, and found that two women's bodies had been found on the beach between the towns Oxbøl and Nymindegab on the west coast of Jutland, and made their own conclusions.

On January 19, the English administration is beginning to confront the high number of casualties related to the Christmas stranding of the British Royal Navy ships along the European Continental coast.

Vice Admiral Thomas Murray writes from his office in Solebay in Yarmouth Roads to John Wilson Brooker, Esquire in the Admiralty Office in London, and includes a letter from the captain of *HMS Woodlark*. The letter included a list of eight men from the *St. George* who had been lent to the *HMS Carnest* May 1811 and transferred to *HMS Woodlark* in Matvik harbor on December 2 the previous year. These men were supposed to go back to the *St. George,* but were never transferred, because *Woodlark* was separated from the *St. George* convoy in the storm at Rødsand, and later went with its own small convoy of merchant ships through the Ear Sound on the way to England.[19]

When *Woodlark* crossed the North Sea and reached Yarmouth Roads, the eight men from the *St. George* were sent to transfer ship *HMS Namur* anchored in the harbor of Sheerness. Murray carefully examined all the weekly accounts left at his office since December 1, hoping to discover more crewmembers from the *St. George*, the *Defence* and the *Hero* who had been lent to other ships in the Royal Navy and lived. But Murray unfortunately had no success at all.

The two carriages with the survivors from *Defence* and *St. George* travel between the villages Mejrup and Vivtrup, in the middle of Jutland, where they stop that evening.

The following day, January 20, William, John, Amos and the Englishmen get up early as usual and eat the 'milk food', as they named the breakfast they are served. They long for the ordinary navy food they are so used to.

The following day, the two carriages stop somewhere along the gravel road, and William suddenly begins to feel uncertain about their situation as war prisoners. He walks over to one of the guards. Knowing that the guard probably speaks little English, William speaks very slowly. 'Sir, could you please tell us who we should talk to at headquarters in Randers, to find out how we Americans can avoid being handed over to the British?" The Danish soldier does not understand any of his words, but from the facial expression and movements of William's arms, the guard, who knows that William is an American, guesses the question. He shakes his head, irritated because he can't answer properly.

The soldier thinks of the answer he would give if he could make himself understood to William, "You will have to speak to the Major General, Carl Von Tellequist, Commander of the Second Infantry Regiment of Jutland and for the entire district of Northern Jutland. He is the one who decides what prisoners of war might be set free." The guard points to the two carriages and William and the others climb back in to continue the trip to Randers.

As they ride along the deserted road, William takes a look at John and Amos and says, "It seems like we'll just have to wait some time yet to see if we will be set free."

In his office in Military Headquarters in Randers, Major General Carl Von Tellequist is thinking about the surviving seamen and the loss of *H.M.S. St. George* and *H.M.S. Defence*. Although England and Denmark are at war, he believes the loss of these ships and so many young people was a real tragedy. Tellequist decides to write to the British Governor of the island of Anholt, Maurice, to express his sympathy.

The island of Anholt is 60 miles east of the opening of Randers Fjord.

England had occupied the island since 1809 and the Danish Navy almost succeeded in getting it back in March the previous year.

Tellequist had exchanged war prisoners with Anholt when the Commander of the Royal Navy's Baltic Fleet, Admiral of the Blue James Sammaurez, was on the island. Tellequist is not well informed about the details of the stranding, and he writes,

"Sir,
Even though the tragic accident, which has happened to the British Majesty's great warships on the Danish coast already, might be known to your Excellency, I allow myself hereby to inform you about this tragic event, as I express my deepest sympathy.

On the night of the 24th last month, the English ships of the line St. George and Defence were wrecked and the violent waves made it impossible to assist the stranded crews. From both ships only 13 who were cast on shore by the sea, together with wreck pieces, were saved. Some of them are sick and for the time being under treatment."[19]

As Tellequist pauses, the two black carriages holding the 17 survivors from the two ships are approaching the village of Ravnstrup on the way to Randers. They are 45 miles east of their destination, Randers.

Tellequist continues writing, *"Some of the dead have come to shore and have been buried with as great a ceremony as the circumstances allowed. All possible attempts have been made to find the officer's bodies with the intention to show them military honor at the funeral in the cemetery. Two lost officers have been found and buried with military honors. Among them was the body of Commander Atkins, who had the command of Defence. He has been interred in a church until I receive further instructions from my gracious superior.*

I regret very much, that the body of Admiral Reynolds has not yet been found, in spite of all the efforts that have been made. In harmony with the Danish nation's deepest emotions, the population has been seized with sorrow, by seeing the British seamen in such great distress without being able to help them.

I, Sir, also regret deeply that I cannot give your excellency a less melancholy narrative of this accident. I remain, Sir, with high esteem, Yours, Tellequist."[19]

The following day the survivors are transported from the village Ravnstrup to the borough of Viborg. The soldiers there are happy to receive such distinguished foreign guests, and invite them all to come in and stay for a while in the main guard building. The Masters Mate, William West, as an officer, stays here in Viborg, where prisoners who are officers are normally quartered.

The Danish soldiers send a young soldier out to buy a bottle of brændevin so they can celebrate this honorable visit by the survivors from *Defence* and *St. George*. As William, Amos, John and the other Englishmen had experienced so often before, rumors had run ahead of them and the soldiers knew very well who they were.

The three Americans and the fourteen British seamen are invited to sit on chairs placed along the walls inside the guard building. The brændevin is served in large glasses. On behalf of the entire D anish guard team, one of the Danish soldiers salutes the American and British seamen, raising his glass and making a toast with a loud: 'Skål."

After they have tasted the drink, John Page says to the seamen sitting next to him that the British would call this kind of liquid snaps. It is a rare drink in England, where they are more used to drinking gin when they are served liquor. Hearing this, William looks at Amos and John and says, 'It is really strange. When I was at Jens Dahl's house, his wife served this kind of snaps, too. We seldom drink this in America, but I know this by the name snaps, too. Mrs. Dahl called it brændevin and I thought she was talking about the river I grew up near, the Brandywine River north of Wilmington in Delaware.

Alcohol was first brought to Wilmington or Kristinahamn, as it was named when the first Swedish settlers arrived there in 1638. I found out that the river where a Chief Namaan lived when the Swedes came renamed Namaan Creek the Brandywine River, after the brændevin the Swedes brought to him and the other natives. Brændevin was not easy to pronounce and the Americans changed it to Brandywine." William is silent for a moment, and then all the English seamen laugh loudly. Then John Page says, 'Well, William you h ave a great imagination when drinking your snaps. When you go home, I'm quite sure you won't find any American who will believe this incredible story you just told us." John Page holds a new full glass of snaps, and he raises it high above his head and shouts 'Skol."

The other seamen and soldiers in the room lift their glasses and return the toast, shouting 'SKOOOOOOL."

They all drink a couple more glasses of brændevin, and then one of the soldiers asks William in Danish to follow him out on the middle of the floor, waving his hand several times.

William is put on a chair. A white cloth is tied around his neck and a think layer of soap-foam carefully smeared on his chin. It looks like he is going to be shaved and the Danish soldier takes out a big knife. The atmosphere in the room is cheerful with a lot of loud laughter. The soldier plays with the knife close to William's chin, in a very professional way. It flies around William's ears with such speed that William is unable to he follow the knife' s movements. But he is completely relaxed and confident that this Danish soldier will not hurt him.[200]

There is a genuinely happy atmosphere in the room and William, John, Amos, John Page, John Anderson and the rest of the English seamen are enjoying themselves for the first time since they arrived on the beaches of West Jutland.

John can't remember when he has been so amused, knowing that it has been almost seven years since he has been with friends in a tavern and served any kind of beer, rum or snaps on shore.

That same evening, John, William, Amos and the fourteen English seamen arrive in the village of Løvskal to stay the night in private homes. The three Americans are restless and uncertain about their future, and William tries again to ask a guard when they will arrive at the military headquarter in Randers.

A guard, picking up the word Randers, says, 'Randers, three days," as he shows three fingers.

The Prefect for the County of Ringkøbing, Mr. Rosenørn, receives a letter from his superiors in the General Command in Copenhagen, ordering him to forward an order to the District Bailiff Grønlund. Wreck masters for individual parts of the beach shall be instructed that any money found on the bodies must be sent to the nearest Royal Money Safe. A list of the dead bodies found with indication of any special personal marks must be returned to the General Command in Copenhagen.[252]

District Bailiff Grønlund travels in his closed carriage to visit all the wreck masters along the coast, from the village of Nymindegab in the south to the village of Fjand, 60 miles to the north. He fulfills the order of gathering the requested information by making inquiries about bodies from the *Defence* and the *St. George*.

Two days later, on January 26, Grønlund has reached the village of Haurvig and a court is in session. The local wreck master, Jep Enevoldsen, tells a lie to the court that, if discovered, would have sent him to jail for a long time and ruined his and his family's life forever. Jep Enevoldsen humbly explains that in his strand fief, 16 bodies have been found on the beach. Only the upper part of one of the bodies remained. A single leg and a thigh also came in individually. The bodies are simple mariners and seamen. To Mr. Enevoldsen' s knowledge no one has stolen from the dead or taken any of the wreck pieces.

To make his lie appear more reliable, Mr. Enevoldsen tells the court that the beach has been filled with soldiers from the coast militia and guarded all the time, making it impossible to take anything from the beach unseen. Except for a seamen's jacket, a pair of trousers and a shirt, which he now hands over to the court, nothing has come in.[252]

The District Bailiff Grønlund accepts Enevoldsen's presentation and ends the session shortly after. When Enevoldsen returns to his farm that evening, he is happy that he decided to hand over to the court the trousers and other belongings of a single seaman.

If he had presented nothing, he concludes, the court would probably not have believed him. What Enevoldsen had not told the court was what he and his family had been busy doing since the time of the stranding of *St. George* and *Defence*. Enevoldsen and his son had been busy locating many bodies on the beach in his fief and taking them to his barn. Mrs. Enevoldsen was meeting the father and son and telling them where to put the bodies.

The Enevoldsen family normally kept hay and sheep in the barn in the wintertime. The sheep heated the barn to some degree, which thawed the many bodies brought to the barn. Mrs. Enevoldsen, having quite an inventive nature, had put a couple of large train lamps in the barn to add to the heat. To further speed up the thawing process further, Mrs. Enevoldsen turned the stack of half-frozen bodies while her husband and son were bringing more bodies to the barn. As individual bodies became sufficiently soft, Mrs. Enevoldsen removed the valuable clothes and boots.[256]

This way Mr. Enevoldsen, wreck master and local authority near the beach of Haurvig, who was supposed to set an example for others to follow, stole the clothes and boots of 15 bodies from *St. George* and *Defence*.

Some of these bodies stacked in Jep Enevoldsen's barn were being stacked for the second time, as they earlier had been stacked on the *St. George*'s quarterdeck to protect their living comrades against the stormy weather, in the last hours onboard the wreck of the *St. George*.

As Enevoldsen returns from court in the village of Haurvig, he feels good about the lie he told, knowing that now nobody will find out how the Enevoldsen family illegally and immorally enriched itself from the stranding of the *St George* and *Defence*.

He later buried the 16 bodies beneath six feet of sand in one of the dunes near the beach at the isthmus, Holmsland Klit, not far from his farm.

That day, the two carriages carrying the surviving seamen from the *St. George* and *Defence* arrived at the village of Over Hornbæk, only eight miles west of their destination Randers.

Two days later, Commander Tellequist sends the usual monthly list to his superiors in Copenhagen with the names and numbers of foreign prisoners held in Randers and Viborg, and who had been taken into custody in the Region of North Jutland.

Although this region covers no more than 20 percent of the Kingdom of Denmark, the total number of foreign prisoners on the list is only 25. They are all survivors from four ships stranded on the west coast of Jutland in the Christmas storm. They include 11 survivors from the *St. George* stranded near Fjand on Christmas Eve; six survivors from *Defence* stranded near Fjaltring at the same time; four survivors of the Danish ship *Waangsaa* at Nymindegab, stranded 60 miles south of Fjand on Christmas Eve; and four survivors from a ship stranded at the channel of Thorsminde, around Christmas. The master mate William West belonged to that ship.

They are all Englishmen except the three Americans and a single Portuguese.[97]

On that same day, the two carriages holding Amos, John, and William and the 14 English seamen rolls over the paving stones in the main entrance to Military Headquarters for the Northern part of Jutland in Randers. To the guard, the 17 seamen state their names and nationality, and the names of the ships they arrived in. This information is written in the entrance book and they are detained in the Prison of Randers.

The Kings representative, Knight of Dannebrog Lieutenant Wigelsen, who deals with the stranding of the *Defence* and the *St. George*, has returned to his local west coast quarters at the Manor of Rammegaard, to find out what has been going on since the ships stranded a month ago.

In the evening, he writes a report to his superiors in the Admiralty in Copenhagen.

This afternoon, he had returned from the beach just west of the village Church of Fjaltring, with information from the local wreck masters that the western winds present since the stranding of *St George* and *Defence* have decreased so that pieces from the *St. George* could be taken.

Wigelsen also reports that at 11:30 a.m. this day, he personally observed an English brig to the southwest anchored for some time at some wreck pieces of *Defence*. At 13 p.m., the brig left in a northwestern direction and disappeared.[91]

Lieutenant Wigelsen does not know that he observed the English gun brig *H.M.S. Rifleman* - a brig earlier under the command of Rear Admiral Reynolds and the *St. George* in the Baltic Convoy. It had returned safely to England.

In England, Admiral Otway had been instructed December 31 to send the *H.M.S. Rifleman* to the west coast of Jutland and do anything in his power to determine the fate of the *St. George*.[23]

On February 3, the American Department of State sends a packet to the new American Agent for Seamen in London, Reuben Gaunt Beasley, the late General William Lyman's successor.

The packet contains papers on several impressed American seamen, including William's original identification papers that Mary Ann had given to Allen McLane in Wilmington October 23, 1811.

The packet also contains a new copy of William's Protection Certificate, issued in New York. When this is received in the Office for

440

the American Agent for Seamen in London, the information in the Protection Certificate is carefully copied into the leather-bound *Register of Seamen Impressed.*[10]

This same day, the double oak-coffin holding the body of Captain David Atkins is fetched from the Chapel of Husby Church by a couple of local men and transported south, to the borough of Ringkøbing.

A new ceremony to honor the late captain is held before the carriage heads south.

11

An inquiry into the Christmas stranding of the British Majesty's Ships *St. George* and *Defence* is held in the Military Headquarters for the Northern part of Jutland in Randers[20, 96] on order of the commanding Major General, Carl Von Tellequist, the cold winter morning of February 5, 1812. Lieutenant Bang has been appointed by Tellequist to lead this inquiry.

As before, the surviving seamen are asked to give their personal version of the dreadful events. William is questioned first and tells Lieutenant Bang who he is. While doing so, he finally has the chance to hand over his Protection Certificate to a Danish authority, as a proof of his American citizenship.

While William speaks, Lieutenant Bang carefully studies the paper William handed him, without saying anything. Then William sees, to his relief, that the lieutenant is smiling, showing that there is no doubt in Lieutenant Bang's mind that this Protection Certificate is genuine.

William hardly slept the previous night, knowing that today he would attend a new and important inquiry. The earlier one in Jens Dahl's farmhouse in Fjand had not led to his release, and during the long night, he had doubts that he could avoid being handed over to the British Royal Navy again.

But now that he sees the relaxed smile on Lieutenant Bang's face, he feels much more optimistic, convinced that he has a good chance of being set free this day.

Amos and John come forward from a bench in the rear to the elevated table where Major General Tellequist sits judging the inquiry. Lieutenant Bang questions both of them carefully.

The two of them state that they are Americans, too, but unfortunately do not have identification papers like William to prove this. John Brown requests that he and Amos Stevens be presented to the proper authorities as Americans.[96]

John Anderson, who had been the spokesman for the English seamen on earlier occasions, is asked by Lieutenant Bang to approach the bar to be questioned. He is asked if he had been treated correctly during his stay here in Denmark, and confirms that he had. John Anderson feels that the atmosphere in the courtroom is pleasant and relaxed, so decides to be honest about his feelings related to his stay. He adds that he and the other seamen have been served too much milk food. But he must admit that, for dinner, they were served food of the same quality as when they were at sea onboard the flagship *St. George*.

Roelff Maeven, one of the seaman from *St. George,* also feeling comfortable in the courtroom, makes it clear to the court that, if the prisoners are going to stay in Randers, they should not be spread around in different houses, as they were earlier. He would be more comfortable if they are quartered in the same house. He also takes the liberty to complain about the food and asks that, in the future, they not be served the kind of bread and milk food they have been served so far.[96]

Tellequist and Lieutenant Bang look at each other and then to the local members of the military court, saying without speaking that the seamen from the *St. George* and the *Defence* have obviously recovered well if they now feel that they can put forward demands and complains on the food and the quartering.

That's good, they all think, that's how it should be around here.

One of the English seamen tells about the convoy they were in from Gothenburg, headed for Portsmouth, England.

As the inquiry approaches its end, Lieutenant Bang consults with his superior, military judge Major General Carl Von Tellequist and informs the court that the 14 English seamen and the two Americans Amos Stevens and John Brown will be kept in Randers prison until further notice.[96]

Lieutenant Bang has everyone's attention as he ends the court session with the words, spoken in Danish, "The American, William Watson, who has put forward his Protection Certificate as a proof of his American citizenship, is hereby going to be released, and can leave this courtroom as a free man."

Everyone in the courtroom is looking at William, who does not understand a word of the Danish spoken. But a few minutes later, Bang translates for William, who he is deeply touched and can' t speak for several minutes.

After all, this innocent and neutral Kingdom of Denmark, so brutally attacked in 1807 by the British, was a true friend of America. Denmark, which 35 years ago helped America obtain its independence from England, and which, thanks to Thomas Mendenhall, was the first Kingdom or country to recognize the independence of the United States of America.

This fifth day of February, the Kingdom of Denmark and the Commander for Northern Jutland, Carl Von Tellequist, had helped William gain his freedom from a cruel impressment. William realized that this moment was touching and solemn in his own and Wilmington's history.

As the people rise from the benches and everyone leaves the room, William walks over to thank Major General Tellequist and Lieutenant Bang for helping him regain his freedom. Seconds later, his thoughts go home to Wilmington, Mary Ann, and their child. There will be a lot to tell his friends and his little family when he finally reaches home.

Later that day, Major General Carl Von Tellequist sits in his office and writes a letter about the court session to the Danish Military Headquarter in Copenhagen in the first Department, The Royal Danish General Auditoriet.

He writes, *"To the Royal General Directorate...is officially to announce that the three imprisoned Americans named in the letter dated January 28 have stated the following. William Watson has identified himself as American and as a consequence of this; he has been released from the prison. Hereafter the two others Amos Stevens and John Brown have been requested to put forward an explanation to the inquiry held of which I include in this letter the minutes.*

Signed The General Commander of North Jutland, February 5, 1812, Tellequist."[96]

As Tellequist writes his letter, William stands in the yard outside Randers prison breathing the fresh air as a free man for the first time since he was forced off the *Ino* in Portsmouth harbor more than two years ago.

He is finally a free man! William is so happy, and he feels a strong desire to tell his lovely wife Mary Ann about this extraordinary moment in their lives.

He has not seen Mary Ann in more than two years and three months, and it feels to him like more than 100 years. How was she? What was she doing back home in Wilmington right now?

John and Amos have not been released like William, and they are disappointed. On the other hand, they are optimistic, because they have seen with their own eyes that, if proper identification papers can be put forward to the court, a real chance to be set free exists.

John is the most concerned of the two. He has been impressed for more than six years, and still convinced that his mother back in Salem must consider him dead. Amos has been in prison for more than two years and is very eager to return to Boston.

The two of them fully understand the strong and warm emotions running through William's joyful head right now.

Amos and John are told after the session ends that Major General Carl Von Tellequist will write this very day to Military Headquarters in Copenhagen about their situation. Copenhagen will decide if their statements that they are Americans will be enough to release them from prison, since they have no Protection Certificates for identification.

Major General Carl Von Tellequist gets orders from the General Staff in Copenhagen on February 7, that the English prisoners, the officers held in Viborg, and the ordinary men staying in Randers shall be given new clothes, and the expenses paid by the Danish State Administration.[96]

On February 10, Major General Tellequist receives a letter from His Majesty the King Frederik VI. The King orders the Americans Amos Stevens and John Brown to be released from Randers and escorted out of the country by a 'parliamentary person."

Recalling William's reaction when he was released, Tellequist wants to see the faces of John Brown and Amos Stevens when they are given the news that, by Royal Resolution directly from King Frederik IV of Denmark, they are released and can return to America as free men now.

Tellequist walks out of his office and into the sunshine that illuminates the yard, where the English seamen, John Brown, and Amos Stevens are sitting quietly on benches, talking.

He keeps watching them as he approaches the benches and notices that they all turn toward him when they hear his steps. They know that the Major General would not come to them unless he had a very important message to bring.

As he stops in front of them, not a single sound can be heard in the yard. Major General Tellequist pronounces the names 'John Brown and Amos Stevens," and when he has everyone's attention, he continues, 'By order of His Majesty King Frederik VI, you are hereby made free men, who will be given the opportunity to leave the country soon. You will by first convenience be escorted out of this country, to return to North America." Hearing these wonderful almost unbelievable words the Englishmen stand up and shout at the top of their lungs: HURRAAAHH, HURRAAAHH! They slap John and Amos roughly on their shoulders to show their recognition.

For John and Amos, it is hard to believe that they are finally free, after all they have gone through, but they quickly put out their hands to show their gratefulness and to thank Tellequist for bringing such good news himself.

John says, delighted, 'Sir, I'm afraid you don't have the faintest idea what this means to me. I have not seen my family for more than six years now. My mum probably thinks I'm dead." His eyes fill with tears as he continues to speak, 'Sir, I will always keep this great moment in my heart, thank you so much."

Major General Tellequist can't help smiling, feeling genuinely flattered. He is growing old, approaching his retirement, and he is genuinely happy to be able to release these American seamen, who still have many years of hard work in front of them, when they return to the United States of America.

Four days later, on February 16, Major General Tellequist reports to his superior in Copenhagen that John Brown and Amos Stevens are going to be released.

He adds in his letter that the Portuguese prisoner Joseph Jutland is to be escorted to Altona, the Danish harbor close to Hamburg, where the local Danish Quartermaster Mr. Haffner will take care of his further travel.[96] Mr. Haffner also gets the job of finding an appropriate ship to take Amos and John home to Boston and Salem.

Finally, on February 20, Amos and John leave the prison in Randers to be transported to the military headquarters in Copenhagen. They are put in a closed carriage and have an officer to escort them. The plan is to travel between the different military quarters in northeast Jutland, where they will eat and sleep, and then pass the Little Belt to the island of Fun, past the Great Belt to Zealand, then across the island of Zealand to Copenhagen.

This early in the year, they will not need to pass the Great Belt at night, as they would after ships from the British Royal Navy's Baltic

Fleet arrive and take control over the Great Belt, generally in the middle of March.

William has been traveling for several days since his release from Randers prison. He and his military escort have been resting, eating and staying overnight in military quarters between Randers and Snoghøj, the place on the coast of Jutland where they took the ferry from Jutland to cross the Little Belt to the island of Fun.

William was transported from the town of Middelfart, where the ferryboat arrived on the Fun side, to Odense and then Nyborg Castle on the east side of Fun.

During the crossing of the Little Belt, the officer who escorted William tried to tell him about the battle of two ships *The USS President* and *The Little Belt* on May 16 the year before, outside the coast of Virginia. William lit up as he heard the name Virginia, and he understood the connection between the ship *Little Belt*, previously a Danish ship, and the belt they crossed. He realized that May 16 the previous year, he had been sitting in a jollyboat in the Great Belt when *HMS Little Belt* was attacked not far from the Delaware peninsula, in waters he had sailed.

He rested a night at the Military Quarters connected to the Castle of Nyborg. From the top of the castle tower, he had been allowed to look out on the Great Belt, where he previously had sailed on the *St. George*. He understood that technically, as an impressed American on a Royal Navy Ship, he had been an enemy of Denmark then. But how he sees the Great Belt from the Danish side, and more importantly, as a free American.

They crossed that Great Belt and arrived by the ferryboat at Coersør on the Zealand side. William then stayed the night in the military quarters in the towns of Næstved and Slagelse.

Finally, on this day of February 26, 1812 in the late afternoon, his carriage passed Frederiksberg Castle, driving down the hill of Valby Bakke to the west gate of Copenhagen -the capital he had heard and read so much about.

They entered the city through the gate of Vesterport and finally the main gate in the yellow Admiralty building on the islet of Gammelholm, Danish Military Headquarters.

William leaves the carriage and enters the guardroom holding the main guard. He explains to the officer in charge, Lieutenant Tuxen, that he needs permission to stay in Copenhagen as long as it takes him to receive a new copy of his New York Protection Certificate from America, before he can travel home safely.

The Protection Certificate he had with him when he arrived on the beach west of Fjand he handed over to Lieutenant Bang at the court session in Randers, and Lieutenant Bang had kept it. William thought it was quite stupid that he had to deliver his Protection Certificate in Randers and was not allowed to have it with him.

These Danish military officers obviously have no idea how much time could be wasted waiting for a new certificate to arrive from North America.[96] But William kept silent. After all, he is still thankful that he is free again, after his miraculous survival of the stranding of the *H.M.S St. George.* Being delayed in his return to the United States of America now seems to be of minor importance.

Lieutenant Tuxen listens carefully to William, then informs him that he can stay in Copenhagen until he has received his new Protection Certificate.[96] William takes Lieutenant Tuxen's right hand and thanks him several times for his kindness. Then he leaves the islet of Gammelholm, walking out through the main gate and through the yellow and white Admiralty building with the black shiny tile roof.

William stands outside the Admiralty building for a couple of minutes, silently observing the Copenhagen citizens walking by or passing in their carriages. He feels free and relieved.

For the first time in more than two years, he is really on his own. He doesn't know what he wants to do right now, but his options are limited by the small amount of British money he has. William is not even sure if the Danes will accept this enemy money at all.

William decides to find a landlord so he can get a roof over his head before the cold night sets in. He walks down the street and passes the somewhat ugly Royal Theater, which looks like a bank to him, with its three different sizes of windows and a large marble inscription, in the center of the four Doric pillars, mounted above the entrance door.

William, always hunting logical connections in everything that meets his senses, gets the idea that maybe this theater was constructed by a talented Mongolian architect, who simply knew nothing about making a simple, provincial theater the way the average Dane would like it. Well, it was none of his business anyway, William decided as he continued his walk.

A few minutes, later he passes the Police Headquarters at Charlottenborg, where law and order are taken care of, and just next to the harbor front of Nyhavn, with many taverns on the sunny side of the water. On warm summer days, Nyhavn is crowded with people, but this winter day not a single person is outside the taverns.

William hopes that he will soon be able to find a job, so he'll be able to pay for a night in a bed.

Outside one of the taverns along the harbor front, William speaks to two happy, slightly drunk Danish seamen out having a good time and asks them about the area in Copenhagen where 6,000 mariners and their families live. He had read about it six years ago in the *American Watchman,* onboard the gaff schooner *Ino* as it approached the Wilmington wharves on the north bank of the Christina River near The Rocks.

Postscript

While working intensely with the archive research material, found in local and national archives in the U.S.A., England and Denmark, the following new findings emerged and were applied in this novel:

1. Identification of Thos. Wattson, signer of the Delaware Ratification on December 7, 1787 of the American Constitution, signing for New Castle County. Research shows that he is the same Colonel Thomas Watson who died 1792 and came from New Ark in Pen Cader hundred in New Castle County.

2. Identification of HMS Comus and HMS Defence as the two English ships of the line that participated in the attack on the Danish Frigate No. 6 Friderichsværn, the first war episode between England and Denmark in the 1807 war between Denmark and England.

3. Identification of the number of crew killed on the ships HMS St George and HMS Defence in the 1811 Christmas stranding of these ships south of Fjaltring and north of Fjand on the west coast of Jutland, Denmark, as 1,005 and not more than 1,300 as assumed until now.

4. Findings that among the first European settlers in the Delaware River, who were Dutchmen, Swedes, Finns and Englishmen, were also Danes from the former Danish territories of Skaane, Halland and Blekinge, and maybe some from Zealand.

The project to research local and national archives in Holland, Denmark, Norway, England and the United States of America, and to obtain historical literature from libraries and analyze the relevant material, and then finally write the 1st edition of this novel, lasted from January 1997 to July 8th 2001.

Researching and analysing archive and library material have been coordinated by me but collecting the archive material would have been impossible without the following people, who assisted me with the work in the different archives:

I would like to thank Dr Thomas P. Doherty, former President of the Genealogical Society of the State of Delaware, who among many things recently has been the editor of the Delaware Genealogical Research Guide. Dr. Doherty has been the key figure to try and make the genealogical puzzle of most of the three Delaware County Watson families living in the period from 1782 to 1830. A puzzle that has not yet found its final form, in the sense that the connection between William and Mary Ann Watson's ancestors and possible descendants has not been established completely yet.

A special thanks to Roger E. Nixon independent researcher for kind assistance considering the research in the Public Record Office's (PRO) huge archives in London. Roger has spent countless hours in the PRO archives over the years the research went on, and almost precisely on the hour of 21.00 every evening reported back to me in Copenhagen via E-mail.

I would also like to thank Marie Velman Melchiori, Vice Director of the National Institute for Genealogical Research in the USA for her two hours of research in the National Archives in Washington DC, that in January 1998 led to the finding of the key document: Mary Ann Watson's letter to William Watson onboard the *HMS St George*.

Also thanks to Allan Rypka, researcher at Focused Research International, Inc. for his kind assistance researching the National Archives in Washington DC and The Pentagon Library.

Thanks to Doris Moyes, from Genealogical Search Services, Utah for the assistance regarding the genealogical research on John Brown and Amos Stevens in Salem and Boston.

Thanks also to Palle Sigaard and his colleagues for the kind assistance I received researching the National Archive in Copenhagen.

A special thanks to Danish author Palle Uhd Jepsen, for the great inspiration that lay in his book *"St George og Defence"* and in its list of references on earlier published material by e.g. P. Storegaard og Arne V. Frandsen.

Zimmerman's unique Ph.D. thesis "Impressments of American Seamen" from Columbia University, 1941 has also been very useful as a reference for the general information on impressments of American seamen.

The work: "The War of The American Independence, Military Attitudes, Policies and Practice, 1763-1789," by Professor Don Higginbotham has been very valuable as a reference in order to place Allen McLane in the proper Revolutionary War context. The quotations of Higginbotham's work are correct for most parts except where quotations from Allen McLane's biography mix in. I hope for the author's forgiveness for applying this trick in order to make the description of Allen McLane's exciting life come more alive to the reader. I thank Professor Higginbotham for allowing me to quote his book.

I would also like to thank:

Tom Hughes, Independent Researcher, Public Record Office for his help; Michael Phillips, Naval Museum, London; N.M. Brandt, Algemeen Rijksarchief, Holland for providing the archive material on *HMS Hero* and *HMS Grasshopper.*

The always kind staff on the Danish Public Archives of: Landsarkivet for Nørrejylland, Viborg; Landsarkivet for Sjælland, Copenhagen and Lemvig Lokalhistoriske Museum.

A special thanks to diver Gert Norman Andersen, responsible for locating and partly excavating parts of the wreck of *HMS St George* and his ship diving team for assisting me on my trip to the wreck of the *St George* in the North Sea in the summer of 1998.

Thanks to Hans Eelman, Texel, Holland, who located the wreck of *HMS Archimedes* in 1980 and *HMS Hero* in August 1982, for his kind information regarding these ships.

Also thanks to the head of Ringkøbing Museum Jens Aarup Jensen and Morten Sylvester former head of the St. George Marine Archaeological Center, in Thorsminde, where the excavated remains of the *St George* wreck can be seen.

If I inappropriately have violated any rights of an author of a reference applied in this novel, I sincerely apologize for that. Please be so kind to contact the publishing company at www.rockbysea-books.com, and we will do our utmost to correct any such errors in future editions of this publication.

I grew up in the village of Fjaltring, neighboring the farms of Gadegaard, Sønder Sønderby and Strandgaarden, where John Brown and Amos Stevens and the four English seamen recovered after the stranding of H.M.S. *Defence,* and close to Fjand where William Watson recovered after his survival from the *St George.*

The archive and literature research on which the writing of this novel is based therefore initially had its origin in local material. The idea was to learn as much as possible from original archive and literature sources to get the best foundation for writing the novel.

As a Dane I had initially only a little knowledge of the American Revolutionary history and early colonial history when I began researching to write my 'ordinary' novel about three seemingly ordinary American seamen that stranded on the coast where I grew up. Therefore it was like rediscovering America for me to realize, that whom I thought was an ordinary small town port collector, Allen McLane, mentioned in Mary Ann's letter to her husband William Watson (found in the National Archive in Washington), really was a local Revolutionary War legend.

When Dr. Doherty and I tried to solve the puzzle of the 1700-1800 Delaware Watson families and I, sitting in my small roof office on my west Juttish farm in Denmark, found Colonel Thos. Watson as a signer of the Delaware Ratification of the American Constitution, when I compared a deed with his signature with the ratification, I did not believe my own eyes. It was quite funny to realize that a person who has never been in the State of Delaware is actually able to identify one of the persons, Thos. Wattson, who helped it become the first state in the union. But that is a new unique ability the Internet has given us.

When I later found out that John Brown, one of only three American survivors from *Defence* and *St. George,* had been onboard *H.M.S. Defence* when this ship and *H.M.S. Comus* attacked the guard ship from Kronborg, frigate No. 6 *Friderichsværn*, the war episode starting the 1807 War between Denmark and England, it was hard to believe, because I thought I investigated the life of three ordinary seamen.

When I investigated the names of the early Swedish colonial settlement, arrived at (Kristinahamn) Wilmington, DE, I found that some of these early names had an origin that was *not* Swedish, Dutch or English. Many Swedish, Dutch and Danish names are alike, but some names have a specific origin from one country.

When I noticed the name *Alice Kirke* who died and was buried in 1732 (three years *before* the Englishman Thomas Willing staked out the modern Wilmington) on the churchyard of the Old Swedes in Wilmington, DE, I found out that kirke (Alice's last name), the Danish name for church, is spelled different in Swedish (kyrka) and Dutch (kerk). Did Alice or other early settlers in Wilmington have a Danish origin?

The fourth Swedish expedition to Kristinahamn (Wilmington, DE) in the New World with the two ships Swan and Fama, which left

Stockholm on August 16, 1642 made a stop at Copenhagen Roads on Sept. 6. Did some Danes enter these ships? Seventeen years later in 1659, the Danish territories of Skaane, Halland and Blekinge were, after a Danish-Swedish war, taken over by Sweden. Halland is the region just south of Göteborg, where the first Swedish expedition to the New World sailed out in 1637.

Did some of the young Danes in this new Swedish territory leave their homes to travel to the newly established (21-years-old) Swedish North American colony, New Sweden, on the south bank of the Delaware River, to live in the free New World, far from their new Swedish oppressors back home in Skaane, Halland and Blekinge? I think yes.

Copenhagen, July 24, 2003

Henrik F. Christensen

Original letters from

Mary Ann Watson
and
William Watson

From Mary Ann Watson of Wilmington Del. U.S. Ame.

William Watson

Mariner,

On board his Britannic Majesty's Ship

St. George on the

28th Jan. 1811 — perforce.

Wilmington Oct 28 1811

D'r Husband

I am well at Present hoping that these few
Lines may find you the same I Rec'd 3 Letters
from you since your absence the last I Rec'd this
Month I am very Sorry for to hear what has
Happened to you I would be very glad to see
you but I am afraid it will be Long before I do
I Applyed to Mr McClane Respecting your
Protection and he sent one to you 23 of this Month
I would write to you before but I did not know
Where to Direct My Dear it Does Releive me
Very Much to write to you I have seen
More trouble the first 9 months after you
Left Me than ever Did before For when Damin
Star came home I had not the Privley to see him
Untill that he was Killed for he was killed the
Day that he Arrived at Philadelphia 9 months
All the 11 Days after your Departure I was delivered
With a Dead child which I believe was through
trouble concerning you I got quite well over it
Thank God for his Mercies & I am doing as well as
Won in My desolate Situation Dear William all
I want in this world to Make me happy to be
Blesed with your Presence once more I should
Be More Unhappy if it was not for My Mother

For She has bien a every thing to me that a Mother
could be & I believe had she Ben your own Mother
She could not Regret your absence more than she
has done, Joseph Warner William Windall &
John Fored, and Likewise enough Lang goin in Love
to you enough Lang is marryed if you cannot Return
when this Reaches you miss no Opportunity of writing
except you brace something Pertiulary

I Conclude with My Love and Respect Likewise
My Mothers & I Remain tile Death your
Affectionate wife

Mary Ann Watson

January the 8th 1812

Sir I Wm Watson, an American, now take this
opportunity of Acquainting you of my
being Cast a way on the Saull
west Cost of Jutland in an english
man of ware the name of which is the
St. George And fished out of the
half Schooner Capt. Jno Goff
And I am sorry to inform you
that I have Lost every article of
wewables my self and protection
thanks be to God are Safe.

Sir I am desires to no
if it is posabee for me to Get Cleir
without Going to England pleas to
Send me an answer and what is best
to bee done for I am Resolved never
to return to Serve in a man of war
I have wrote 4 Letters to Wm Limma
without any answer I am Sir
Married in the State of Dillewear
the No of the protection is 7777

I am Sir your obliged
umble Servant Wm Watson

Boren Jyland Ringkiobing Amt Frands Sinder
Notsum Vogn.

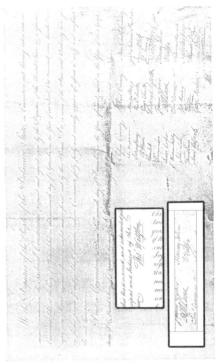

Four pictures.

Upper left: *George Washington, Allen McLane and the Continental Army crossing The Delaware River on Christmas Night 1776.*

Upper right: *The Wilmington ship Nancy in the port of Charlotte Amalie on the Danish West Indian Island of St. Thomas in the autumn of 1776, when the news about the Declaration of Independence reached the port and officer Thomas Mendenhall from Wilmington as the first, hoist the American Flag, The Stars and Stripes, in a foreign port.*

Lower left: *The Delaware Ratification of the American Constitution. Delaware was the first State to enter the Union. Two of the signers were The 1811 Wilmington Port collector Colonel Allen McLane, signing for Kent County, where he lived in Duck Creek Cross Road (Smyrna) on the day of signing, December 7, 1787 and Colonel Thomas Wattson from New Ark, Pen Cader Hundred, New Castle County.*

Lower right: *Flag ship HMS St George with damaged masts and rudder and HMS Defence in Danish waters somehow between November 16 and Christmas Night 1811.*

List of References

In the following *List of References*, a *"%"* indicates that a document probably once existed, but searching the archives, the document has not been found.

Archive documents

State Archives, Delaware.

%   Certificates of marriage

0   Thomas P. Doherty Genealogical research notes from various Delaware archives. Mostly related to Delaware Watson and Warner's genealogy. Notes are made in cooperation with the author in the period 1997-2001. To be published by Thomas P. Doherty himself.

Historical Society of Delaware

1   *"Revolutionary Patriots of Delaware, 1775-1783, Genealogical and historical information on the men and women of Delaware who served the American cause during the war against Great Britain, 1775-1783,"* Henry C. Peden, Jr., M.A., Family Line Publications, Westminster, Maryland, 1996.

2   *William Hemphill's papers.* Box 26. Folder 9.

Landsarkivet for Nørrejylland

3   Protokol, *"Skodborg-Vandfuld Herreds justitsprotokol, 1802-1816,"* (nr. B 77 B-9). Landsarkivet i Viborg.
72) (*) Protokol, *"Ulfborg-Hind Herreds politiprotokol, 1808 -1816,"* (nr. B 80 B-67). LNV.

4   Protokol, *"Ulfborg-Hind Herreds strandingsdokumenter 1806-1812,"* læg nr. 156 (nr. B80A-88).

5   *Letter by the American, **William Watson**, born in Delaware, to the North American Consul Master Saabye in Copenhagen.*

6   Generalkommandoen for Nørrejylland, Justitsprotokol 23/1 1811 18/5
            1813 No. 2, 38-d2.

National Archives II, College Park, Maryland, United States of America

7   State Department Records 1789-1824

            Consular Despatches, Great Britain, Denmark and Netherlands,
            Records of Service, Diplomatic posts, London, Copenhagen,
            Amsterdam, and Rotterdam. Diplomatic instructions to the Posts
            1803-1815.

8   Record Group 59,

            Entry 930. Folder 14.
            Inventory. No. 15. *List of Impressed Seamen. From Captain Carter in
            Liverpool. The list is holding* **Amos Stevens**.

9   Folder 4.

10   Folder 6, Volume 499, *"Consular Posts, London, England." Register
            of Impressed Seamen, October 25, 1811 - September 30, 1812.*
            **'St. George William Watson with Protection certificate No. 7777."
            Feb. 27 1807. In transit by the Department of State -The St.
            George wrecked on the coast of Denmark in Jan. 7 1812. All her
            crew lost July 20, 1812. D.R.'**

            (Dispatches by The American Consul in Copenhagen Mr. Rudolph
            Saabye and his successor, John M. Forbes and Mr. Irving who was
            special Minister to Denmark from Feb. 22, 1811 to June 30, 1812 -
            The date when the USA declared war against England. A gap exists in
            these records after June 30, 1812 to Jan. 1827. During these 15 years,
            no American Minister was appointed to Denmark. Duties were
            covered by G.W. Campbell, Minister to Russia and Christopher
            Hughes; Jr., charge d'affairs to the Netherlands. Mr. Saabye
            communicated mainly on the subject of the 140 American ships seized
            by Danish and French privateers including issues surrounding
            individuals from those ships. Most of Mr. Saabye's communication,
            however, dealt with seamen' s requests for assignment to duty in more
            tropical climate. Many of the despatches in the files include enclosures
            of Danish Foreign office notes, or notes and letters from Americans in
            Denmark. 'From this I conclude, *that* **William Watson**'s *letter,
            although not found, would definitely have been the sort of*

communication which would be reported." These findings, makes it likely, that **William Watson** has returned to the USA **before** the War of 1812).

11   Series 928, *"Letters Received Regarding Impressed Seamen, 1794-1815',*

12   Box 10, *Letter from* **Mary Ann Watson** *of Wilmington, Del. U.S. America. To* **William Watson***, Mariner, Onboard his Britannic Majesty's Ship St George on the 28ᵗʰ of June 1811 perforce.*

13   American Consulate in London, A complete leather-bound index covering 1798-1888. A-Z. 943 pages.

14   Mr. Irving's log of claims in London under the Treaty of 1794, many executes in the period 1800-1806. The logs discuss the claims by ship-owners and masters due to losses of ships, cargoes and seamen. There is no mention of the **Ino**.

National Archives, Washington DC

15   %Port of New York Marine Archives
Shipping clearance logs for New York and Philadelphia, 1798-1808.
(Licenses and proofs of ownership for the period of 1803-1809 were checked for both large and small vessels, with negative results regarding the **Ino**)
% Protection certificates Indexes, Protection certificate abstracts and Protection certificates Philadelphia. 1797-1875.
(searches are made for John Brown, Amos Stevens and William Watson).
% Applications for release of impressed seamen. 1804-1817.
(unbound letters from wives, mothers, friends of impressed and captured seamen requesting assistance from the US government.
Clergymen or schoolmasters wrote in case the family couldn't write)

%State Department-Foreign Ministry Transport board correspondence 1804-1815 re impressed seamen and prisoners of war
%Seamen Protection certificates 1796-1815

Pentagon Library

%   Search for protection certificates.

National Maritime Museum, London.

16   *"Tekniske og historiske data om HMS St. George og HMS Defence,* samt Adm. AGC/Pt," NMML.

Public Record Office, Kew

17   ADM. 51/2216, 'Captain's Log, HMS Cressy," PROK.

Public Record Office, London

18   Fanshave letter, 1812.

19   ADM 1/1431. *Correspondence on the loss of HMS St George, HMS Defence and HMS Hero.*

20   ADM 1/5424. *Proceedings of Court Martial held onboard HMS Raisonable in Sheerness on April 27th and 28th of April 1812. Inquiry of the English survivors of the stranding of HMS St. George and HMS Defence on the west coast of Denmark.*

21   ADM 7/64 *Convoy list to Lloyds.*

22   ADM 12/154-31

23   ADM 12/154-31.1.

24   ADM FO 22/62.

25   ADM FO 22/ 63.

26   *Altona Mercury*, Jan. 9, 1812. p44

27   ADM 7/95.

28   ADM 7/795.

29   HMS Ariel 51/2128.

30   HMS Bellette's Master's log Adm. 52/4425.

31   HMS Bellette log ADM 51/2158.

32   HMS Bruiser ADM 51/2032.

33   HMS Cressy 51/2216.

34   HMS Comus ADM.

35   HMS Cressy log ADM 51/2976.

36   HMS Defence log ADM 37-248.

37   HMS Defence log ADM 37/249.
        Listing all 5 impressed seamen from the Boston schooner.

38   HMS Defence Muster Book ADM 37/1479

39   HMS Defence Log ADM 37/2066.

40   HMS Defence Log ADM 37/2067.

41   HMS Defence Log ADM 37/2207.

42   HMS Defence Log ADM 37/2210.

43   HMS Defence Log ADM 37/2729.

44   HMS Defence Log ADM 37/2751.
        The last existing muster book from HMS Defence now located in the
        Public Record Office in London. All papers from the wreck of the
        HMS Defence disappeared in the waves south of the village of
        Fjaltring on the west coast of Jutland, Denmark.

45   HMS Defence Log ADM 51/1651.

46   HMS Defence ADM 55441.

47   HMS Defence Log ADM 51/1826.

48   HMS Defence Log ADM 51/2259.

49   HMS Dictator ADM 51/2293.

50   HMS Dilligence ADM 51/2257.

51   HMS Dreadnought ADM 51/2290.

52   HMS Egeria ADM 51/2318-53602.

53   HMS Gordon ADM 51/2441.

54   HMS Helder ADM 51/2310 53602.

55   HMS Orion ADM 51/2614-53477.

56   HMS Mercurious ADM 51/2564.

57   HMS Rose ADM 51/2762.

58   HMS Royal William log ADM 103/521.

59   HMS Prince William ADM 51/475 53745.

60   HMS Salvador Del Mundo Log ADM 8/99.

61   HMS Sheldrake ADM 51/2837.

62   HMS St George Log ADM 51/2216.

63   HMS St George Log ADM 37/2843. *The last existing Muster Book holding the crew onboard the St. George filed in the Public Record office before the loss of the ship. Other older and damaged muster books that* were *found spread out on the beach, where St. George* was *stranded near the village of Fjand on the west coast o*f *Jutland, Denmark, is located in the National Archive in Copenhagen.*

64   HMS St. George log ADM 51/2345.

65   HMS Victory ADM 51/2934.

66   HMS Vigo ADM 51/2949.

67   HMS Woodlark ADM 51/2976.

68   HMS Egeria's log Adm. 52/4474.

69   HMS Hercules log Adm. 51/1684, 1805-1806.

70   HMS Hercules Muster book Adm. 36/ 16365.

71   List of St. George's defekter med tilhørende meldinger fra
Admiral Saumarez før strandingen , ADM 1/13, PROL.

72   HMS Princess ADM Log 37/2404.

73   HMS Victory's log Adm. 52/3878. PROL.

74   HMS Vigo's log Adm. 52/4650. PROL.

74-1   HMS Censor 1811.

74-2   HMS Pyramus 1811.

Rigsarkivet (National Archive), Copenhagen.

75   Admiralitetet, Indkomne sager 1812, nr 1-205, ADM 952.

76   Admiralitetet, Indkomne sager 1812, ADM 954.

77   Admiralitetet, ADM 953, 'Indkomne sager 1812, nr. 206 -440," RK.

78   **Archiv for Søvæsen**, 1829, Bd. 3.
Departementet for udenlandske anliggender, Amerikas
Forenede Stater, 302, 1806-1842.

79   nr. 155 >

80   lb. nr. 2914

81   **Det Danske Militære Institut**, 290.4, 200K, pakke 12+13, Forsvarets
Arkiver.

82   **Det Holsteinske Militære Institut**, 1804-12, Pakke 1, Forsvarets
Arkiver.

83   **Det Kongelige Landkadetkorps**. 1789-1813. Pakke A49.

84   Ansøgninger om kadet og frikorporalpladser 1810-1813.

85   1810-1817 A34. Fra andre afdelinger og lignende.

86   1713-1812. G1. Stambog med register.

87   1812-13 U20. Eksamenslister.

88   1716-1814. Ø 33.

89-0   **Forsvarets Arkiver**, 600A 1807-15, Nr. 534.

89   **Generalitets og Kommisariatskollegiets 1. Departement**, Indkomne
        Justitssager 1811, **Forsvarets Arkiver**.

90   **Generalitets og Kommisariatskollegiets 1. Departement**, Indkomne
        Justitssager 1812, **Forsvarets Arkiver**.

91   **Generaladjudantstabens Bureau**, Protokol Nr 1, 1812, nr 1-1299,
        Forsvarets Arkiver, 91C.

92   **Generaladjudantstabens Bureau**, Protokol Nr 1, 1812, nr 1300-ud,
        91C, **Forsvarets Arkiver**.

93   **Generaladjudantstabens Bureau**, Protokol IIA, 1812, nr 1001-1400,
        91C, **Forsvaret Arkiver**.

94   **Generaladjudantstabens Bureau**, Protokol IIA, 1812, nr 1001-1400,
        91C, **Forsvarets Arkiver**.

95   **Generaladjudantstabens Bureau,** Protokol IIB, 1812, 91C,
        Forsvaret Arkiver.

96   **Generalkommandoen for Nørrejylland**, Justitsprotokol 23.01.1811-
        18.05.1813 nr. 2, **Forsvarets Arkiver**.

97   **Generalstabens 1. Afdeling**, kopibog, 1812, nr 1, 1-2144, **Forsvaret
        Arkiver.**
        Ad. N. 16/1812 Liste over nogle gjorte engelske krigsfanger.
        (Listen fra Tellequist 28. januar 1812 i Randers over de overlevende
        englændere og amerikanere fra bl.a. St George of Defence. **William
        Watson, John Brown og Amos Stevens** er på listen.
        *"Amerikanerne er efter allerhøjeste tilladelse fritaget for at udleveres
        til de engelske"*).

98   **Generalstabens 1. Afdeling**, kopibog, 1812, nr. 1, 2145-3067,
        Forsvaret Arkiver.

99-0 **Generalstabens 2. Afdeling**, kopibog, 1812, nr 2, 1-1227, **Forsvaret Arkiver.**

99 **Generalstabens 2. Afdeling**, kopibog, 1812, nr 2, 1228-2144, **Forsvaret Arkiver.**

100 Journal over rejsende i Korsør 1813-14, **Forsvarets Arkiver** (Amos Stevens and John Brown listed).

101 **Kancelliet Rev. Dept**. Sager vedrørende kontrollen med rejsende ved færgestederne iflg. Kane Cork 20. oktober 1812.
15c. III. 08.10.1812-14.06.1814. Middelfart-Snoghøj.

102 **Kommissionen for Københavns forsyning m. brændsel** .

103 Krigsfanger. Indkomne skrivelser. **Forsvarets Arkiver. Justitsarkivet. Generalauditøren** 1809-14 pakke 1.

104 48b) Krigsfanger -Indkomne skrivelser. **Forsvarets Arkiver. Justitsarkivet. Generalauditøren** 1809-14-pakke 2.

105 Krigsfanger. Indkomne skrivelser. **Forsvaret Arkiver. Justitsarkivet Generalauditøren** 1809-14pakke3.

106 Liste over Admiral Saumarez meldinger angående St. George efter strandingen Adm. 1/14.

107 *"Papirer fra de engelske orlogsskibe Defence og St. George (SK 1004-1008),"* **Søkrigskancelliet**, RK

108 58a) 1004

109 d23,

110 d28,

111 d30,

112 d38aa,

113 d38,

114 d73,

115   d83,

116   d83a,

117   d84,

118   d85,

119   d86,

120   d89,

121   d94,

122   d95,

123   d96,

124   d97,

125   d103,

126   d108,

127   d120,

128   d121,

129   d127,

130   d127ff-3,

131   1005

132   1006

132-1   Meddelelser fra Krigsarkiverne, 1888, De Engelske overfald.

The New York Historical Society,

133   Allan McLane Biography, handwritten, no no.

Books.

134   "*A History of the Original Settlements on the Delaware River, from its discovery by Hudson to the colonization under William Penn. To which is added an account of the ecclesiastical affairs of the Swedish settlers, and a history of Wilmington. From its first settlement to the present time,*" Benjamin Ferris, Middle Atlantic States Historical Publications Series No. 17. , 1846. Library of Congress Catalog Card No. 72-184091.

135   p68-69,

136   p91,

137   "*Af Holstebros Saga,*" J. Aldal, Holstebro, 1933, 33 sider.

138   "*Bidrag til Ringkøbing Bys Historie. Udtog og Bearbejdelser af Ringkøbing Raad-stue arkiv,*" Kay L. Brand & J. I. Bøgner, 1942, s. 275.

139   "*Building the Wooden Fighting Ship.*" Dodds & Moore, London, 1984, 128 pp.

140   "*Colonial Delaware. A history,*" John A. Munroe, KTO Press, 1978, ISBN 0-527-18711-9.

141   p16,

142   p249,

143   "*Danmarks Kapervæsen. 1807-14,*" Kay Larsen, 1915, 205 s.

144   "*Danmarks søfart og søhandel fra de ældste tider til vore dage,*" H. C. Beering Liisberg, Bind 1-2, 1919.

145   "*Danske og norske krigsfanger i England 1807-1814,*" Carl Roosing, Prisonen, 1953, pp 233.

146   p33

147   "*Delaware Genealogical Research Guide,*" Thomas P. Doherty, 2nd Edition, 52pp, 1997, ISBN 1-887061-07-X.

148 *"Delaware, Two Hundred Years Ago, 1780-1800*," Harold B. Hancock, 1987, Middle Atlantic Press Inc., Wilmington, Delaware.

149 p10,

150 p36,

151 p173,

152 *"Den Danske Historie'.*

153 p260

154 *"Den Svenskä Historien 1611-54', Bind 4, Jan Cornell & Sten Carlsson och Jerker Rosén, Stockholm, 1967, Bonnier.*

p103,

155 p139,

156 p180-182,

157 p186,

158 *"En dansk Søemands, af han selv skrevne, Hændelser på sine søetoure fra 1798 til 1830*," N. M. Nielsen, 1831, 84 sider.

159 *"Englandskrigene 1801-14*," L. Lindberg, København, 244 pp.

160 *"English literature and the Great War with France."* A. D. Harvey, 1981, London, 162 pp.

161 *"Forgotten Heroes of Delaware*," Emerson Wilson, Cambridge, Mass., Deltos Publishing Compagny, 1969,

162 p32

163 p188

164 *From the declaration of war by France in February 1793 to the accession of George IV in January 1820."* The Naval Historie of Great Britain, New Edition, Bind 5. London .1886.

165   *"Fra heden til havet,"* A. Jeppesen, København, 1975, 218 pp.

166   'Fighting Sail.'"

167   p16

168   *"Her skete det, 2. Nørrejylland,"* Palle Lauring, Det Schønbergske Forlag, 1968.

169   *"Historisk-topografisk Efterretninger om Skodborg-Vandfuld Herreder,"* O. Nielsen, 1994, 568 sider.

170   *"History of the State of Delaware."* Henry C. Conrad, Vol. I-III, Wilmington, Delaware, 1908. Wickersham Company, Printers and Binders, Lancaster, Pa.

171   p453

172   p521

173   *"Holstebros Historie gennem Tiderne,"* J. Aldal, 1274-1939. Holstebro, 1939.

173-1   *"Klitfolk," Tage Heft, 1942, s. 116-118.*

174   *"Kommandør Charles Dudley Pater. Et historisk vidne,"* Palle Uhd Jepsen, Hardsyssels Årbog, 1987.

175   *Kongelig dansk Hof og Stats-Calender* fra Aarene 1811 og 1812. 2 bind. Nr. 2 og Nr. 3. RK.

176   'Letters of Samuel Dalton of Salem', The Essex Institute Historical Collections, Vol. 68, Oct. 1932, p. 321-329.

177   *"Livet ombord på fregatten Jylland,"* Bernt Kure, Høst og Søn, 1996. A1.

178   *"Mine Hændelser i og uden for det Engelske Fangenskab i sidste krig,"* Johan Christian Federspiel, Roskilde, 1841, 146 sider.

179   *"Narratives of Shipswrecks of the Royal Navy between 1793 and 1849."* W. O. S. Giley, 1851, London 336 pp.

180 *"Navies of the Napoleonic Era."* O. von Pivka. Devon .1980. 27 pp.

181 *"Nye strandingshistorier."* L. Mylius-Erichsen, Nordisk Forlag, 1905.

182 *'Prologue to War England and the United States 1805 1812.'* Bradford Perkins. University of California Press, Berkeley and Los Angleles, 1963.

183 p8-9,

184 p28,

185 p93,

186 p126,

187 p167,

188 p171,

189 p172,

190 p232,

191 p233,

192 p234,

193 p271,

194 p272,

195 p292

196 *"Reminiscences of Wilmington, in Familiar Village Tales, ancient and new."* Elizabeth Montgomery, Middle Atlantic States Historical Publications Series No. 4, 1851. Library of Congress. Catalog Card No. 79-186090. ISBN 0-8046-8604-1.

197 p176,

198 p177-180,

199 *"Skibbruddet på Vest-kysten af Jylland den 24. December 1811. Et* *historisk Maleri.*," S. Møller, Aalborg, 1812. 19 pp.

200   "*St. George og Defence,*" Palle Uhd Jepsen, Fiskeri- og Søfartsmuseet, Esbjerg, 1995.

201   p51-53,

202   P58,

203   p62,

204   p64,

205   p83,

206   "*Søkrigen i de dansk norske farvande 1807-1814. Fra tabet af flåden til freden i Kiel.*," C. F. Wandel, 1915, 501 pp.

207   "*The Ship. The Century before steam 1700-1820,*" A. McGowan. London, 1980, 60 pp.

208   "*The War of The American Independence, Military Attitudes, Policies and Practice, 1763-1789,*" Don Higginbotham, New York, The Macmillian Company, 1971, 509 pp.

209   p137,

210   p152-153,

211   "*The Wooden World An anatomy of the Gregorian Navy.*" N.A.M. Rogers, FontanaPress, 1986.

212   p39

213   p54

214   "*Under krigen 1807-1814,*" Constantius Flood, 1892, Kristiania, 280 pp.

215   Bog, "*Vort Folks Historie gennem Tiderne, skrevet af danske Historikere.*" Schultz Danmarkshistorie. 1942. Bind 4.

216   "*Øen Holmsland og dens Klit,*" Evald Tang Kristensen, Viborg, 1891. 64 sider.

217   'Forgotten Heroes of Delaware.' Emerson Wilson, Deltas Publishing Company, Cambridge, Mass., 1969.

218   "Wilmington, Delaware, Three Centuries Under Four Flags, 1609-1937." Anna T. Lincoln, Rutland, Vermont, The Tuttle Publishing Company Inc., 1937.

219   p23,

220   p26,

221   p37,

222   p90,

223   p272,

224   p411,

Dictionaries and Encyclopedias.

225   *Dansk-engelsk samt engelsk-dansk Marine-Lexicon*, indeholdende benævnelser på alt, hvad der vedkommer Søevæsenet, samt kommando-ord og talemåder, der bruges til søs, Carl Leopold Harboe, 1838, Bind 1-2.

226   *Dansk-engelsk Søleksikon*, L. H. de Saint-Simon, 1808. 176 s.

227   *Dansk Marine-Ordbog*, Carl Leopold Harboe. 1839, 504 s.

Newspapers.

Aalborg, Denmark.

228   'Julestranding ved Fjaltring," *Aalborg Stiftstidendes Julenummer*, 24/12 1950.

Copenhagen, Denmark.

229   *Dagen* , 31. dec. 1811. København.

Holstebro, Denmark.

230   *Holstebro Avis*. 1911. 23. dec.

Lemvig, Denmark.

231   'Den store strandingstragedie ved Fjand Julen 1811," J. Gr. Pinholt, *Lemvig Folkeblad* ,1/10 1940 s. 1-2 .

Ringkøbing, Denmark.

232   *Ringkøbing Amts Dagblad*. 1904, 3. aug. og 27 aug. og 1937, 30. sept. og 30. okt.

233   *"Vestkystens store juledrama der kostede 1300 mand livet*," 24/12 1961.

Philadelphia, USA.

The Pensylvania Gazette.

Wilmington, USA.

234   *American Watchman,*

235   30.06.1810

236   04.11.1809

237   *Mirror of the Times and General Advertiser,*

238   05.03.1799

239	28.12.1799
240	06.09.1800
241	15.08.1801
242	27.08.1802
243	15.03.1803
244	*The Wilmington Mercury (To the patrons of the Delaware Gazette)*
245	11.10.1798
246	14.10.1798

Deeds.

Wilmington,

247 C2-p.1. Pen Cader Hundred, New Castle County, Delaware **Thomas Watson** Thomas Cooch deed.

248 G2-101 / 1787 p.58, New Castle Hundred, New Castle County, Delaware. John Watson Grantor/ Major Thos. Watson Grantee.
(The signature, from May 22, 1792, made by Major **Thos. Watson** from Pen Cader Hundred in New Castle County Delaware, in the above-mentioned deed, is the same signature that can be found on the Resolution of December 7, 1787 signed in Dover, Delaware.
A facsimile of this resolution, that makes Delaware the first State in the Union can be found in 'History of the State of Delaware' by Henry Clay Conrad, Vol. I, page 154, published by the author in Wilmington, Delaware, 1898. Thos. Watson sign for New Castle County, where he lives and Allen McLane signs for Kent County, because he lives in Duck Creek Cross Road, with his wife and one-year-old son.)

249 **Notes,**

250 '*Captain Luke Watson and his descendants.*' Charles W Petit Notes, Wilmington, Delaware, Dec. 15, 1941.

250-1 Authors own notes and counting based on the last existing muster books of HMS St George and HMS Defence (**44,63**) from august 1811 and the other muster books from earlier that year.

Periodicals, papers.

251 *"A history from the earliest times to the present."* William Laird Clowes. The Royal Navy, Vol. 5. 1900. London.

252 'Bidrag til en beretning om de to engelske linieskibe St. George og Defence's forlis på den jyske vestkyst den 24. December 1811," 54, *Hardsyssels Aarbog*, 5. bind, 1961. , Arne V. Fransen

253 *"Danmark i Nødsaarene 1801-1814,"* 1940, 99 s. ,Studenterforeningens danske Bibliotek

254 *Dansk Fiskeritidende. 1911, 1937, 1938, 1942,1950 og 1951.*

255 *Danske Statstidende. 1811 og 1812.*

256 'De nærer sig af vrag" , *Foreningen Danmarks Folkeminders Skrifter, Bind 87, 1995.* Christian Tarbensen Christensen.

257 'De store engelske krigsskibes stranding 1811', *Hardsyssels Aarbog*, 5. bind, 1911. P. Storgaard Pedersen

258 *"Det Nørrejydske Redningsvæsen ,"* C. P. Eisenreich, 1972, 368 pp.

259 *"Dødmandsbjerget',* Husvennen, 1897, nr. 48, s. 383, J. Gr. Pinholt.

260 'Efterretninger om strandinger." (indsendt af Læge H. Torbøl, Nr. Nebel). Fra Ribe Amts udgave af *Historiske Samfund for Ribe Amt.* 1923-27. Bind 6, s. 494-511.

261 'En engelsk Krigsfanges Oplevelser i Jylland i Vinteren 1809," *Samlinger til Jydsk Historie og Topografi*, Louis Bobé, 190-08, 3 rk., bind 3, s. 369-417.

262 'Falkenberg strandejer af Ryssenstens nordre forstrand ," *Hardsyssels Årbog*, 1995, Anders V. Langer.

263 'Fortællinger og sagn om Sønde r Nissum Sogn." , *Samlinger til Jydsk*

Historie og Topografi. 1868-69. Bind 2, s.291-322, A. Sørensen

264   Viborg Samler. 1812.

265   'Hvorfor strandede Sct. George og Defence på Vestkysten ?"
       Tidsskrift for Redningsvæsen, 1/5 1972, nr. 5 , 39 årg., P.E.
       Christensen.

266   '*Impressments of American seamen*', Studies in History, Economics
       and Public Law, edited by the Faculty of Political Science of
       Columbia, Volume CXVIII, No. 1, whole number 262. Zimmerman.

267   p12,

268   p18,

269   p46,

270   p54,

271   p64,

272   p62,

273   p69,

274   p140,

275   p142,

276   p150,

277   p152,

278   p157,

279   p176,

280   "*Impressments and the American merchant marine 1782 - 1812 An
       American view*," George Selement?

281   "*Merchants, Millers and Ocean Ships, The Components of an Early
       American Industrial Town*." Peter C. Welsh, Delaware History?

282   p41

283   p51

284   *"Nogle episoder fra krigen 1807-1814,"* C. Klitgaard, 1906-08, Samlinger til Jydsk Historie og Topografi, 3 rk. Bd. 5 , s. 176-188.

285   *"Oksbys gamle kirke og kirkegaarde før 1891,"* J. Olsen, Ribe Amts Årbog 3, s. 118-131, 1905.

286   Samlinger til Jydsk Historie og Topografi. Bind 2, s. 312-313, lærer Sørensen i Sdr. Nissum.

287   *"Strandinger"* s. 312 313, Samlinger til jysk historie og topografi, 1 rk. 2. bind, 1903.

288   *"The Melancholy Fate of the Baltic Ships in 1811,"* A. N. Ryan, Mariners Mirror, Vol. 50, 1964,p. 123-133.

289   *"The Naval Chronicle."* Vol. 27 & Vol. 28 1812. London. 04.09.1812

290   *"The Sammarez Papers,"* A. N. Ryan (Editor), The Navy Records Society, London, 1968.

291   *"Wilmington's Maritime Commerce, 1775-1807."* Sara Guertler Farris, Delaware History?

292   p39

293   p44

294   p51

Weekly magazines.

Denmark.

295   'Da havet tog 1391", *Hjemmet*.19??.

296   Jydske efterretninger, *1812*.

297   *"Sømandsliv anno 1811,"* Ulla Pors Nielsen, UD og SE, nr. 6, juni
          1987.

Maps

Historical Society of Delaware

298   'Birds Eye View Of The City of Wilmington, DEL'. *Drawn, Lith &*
          Print. By E. Sache & Co. Baltimore. Published by Julius Krause, No.
          500 Shipley St. Wilmington, DEL. (1864-65).

The Royal Library of Copenhagen

299   'L'Amerique Septentrionale'. *Par G. De L'Isle Geographe. A Paris.*
          Printed in Denmark by Ballermann & Sons A/S.

World Wide Web.

300   'What ship is That?" by Joseph C. Mosier, The Hampton Roads Naval
          Museum, England 2002, http://www.cronab.demon.co.uk/belt.htm